Gunship

John M. Davis

The Complete Series

Editing: Daniél Lecoq

Dear reader,

Well, the ride is over. Gunship, which began as a standalone book in 2011, has now come full-circle and draws to a close several books later.

So much of my life is invested into this collection. The characters of the Gunship series have seen me through some of the toughest times in my life, as well as some of the best. Long after this series comes to rest, the characters will consume my thoughts. I am so thankful for being a part of their story.

As with every collection, there are many more people to thank.

First and foremost – God almighty. Without his grace, nothing is possible. My wife Cassey, who finally convinced me to follow my lifelong dream of writing. My children, McKenzie and Dawson. You two are not only my reason for living, but you also teach me so much each day. I truly love you both.

I also need to thank a host of others for their help in making Gunship the series that it is. Amanda Elizabeth and Tony Jones Photography. You guys gifted me the first cover, and it continues to bring interested readers in. I could not have found a better Sarah Blaine. Scott McGregor, you are the epitome of Adam Michaels. Not only does the Glimmeria cover rock, but you cooked a mean chicken breast following that shoot.

Daniél, Gene and Robert. You guys each helped out when I needed it. From proofing to beta reading, Gunship is better because of you. My good friend James, who heads up SVP. Thank you. I've come a long way since uploading the first manuscript at your crib. So has the series. Thanks for everything, including Vladris. My brother Daniel, who did amazing work on the original Gunship cover.

Last, but certainly not least, the readers. You each make this happen! Your support of this series has meant so much to me. Thank you, truly. We've taken this trip together.

In closing, thank you. From the bottom of my heart. My dream continues because you care enough to support it. For that, I am truly grateful.

John M. Davis

Gunship

Strangest weather. Adam thought as the high winds
continued to push across the barren, almost lifeless
ground outside. The border planets always seemed to
have the toughest climate, no matter the season.

When you were on the fringe of charted space, you could
be sure of a few things. Rough weather, rougher living
and the roughest damn drinking establishments known to
mankind. Those were the facts.

"Another hand, or should we just count you out
Michaels?" the dealer asked, a thick beard of black
covering most of his experienced face as he continued
shuffling the deck of cards, only slightly moving his
thumbs as the cards crisply fell into place.

"Let's get something straight right here and now. You
don't ever count Captain Adam Michaels out." he said as
he raised his glass for a long drink of the roughest ale he'd
ever fallen victim to.

"The pay in for this round is seventy credits." The
dealer said as he surveyed the table, giving his best effort
in an attempt to block out the dozens of scoundrels in the
background drinking ale and most likely telling lies.

"I'm out." Captain Michaels said quietly as he stood up
and walked away from the table, doing his best to ignore
the taunts and insults directed his way as if to keep some
of his dignity.

"Watching the news huh?" he said as he sat down on a
raggedy wooden stool beside Dalton at the bar.

Wearing a long, brown duster and a stubbly dirt colored
beard hiding the scars of his past scuffles, Dalton had
been a part of Adam's crew for nearly five years. Old
military friends, fighting in the Glimmerian War had
brought them close together, each earning the trust and
respect of the other.

"Hell no," Dalton replied with a slyly grinned face.

Adam laughed as he motioned the bartender over to

them, ordering a tall glass of water as covertly as possible in order to maintain a decent reputation among this night's patrons.

"All I'm hearing is some pencil necked jackass talking about impending civil war between the colonies. You think I give a damn about politics?" Dalton asked.

Obviously having already consumed his weight in alcohol, or even more if it was a good night, he continued puffing on a withered cigar that sat limply in the corner of his mouth.

"Tastes like watered down piss if you ask me, or even weaker than that," Dalton said loudly, with his full intention of the words hitting the bartender's ears. "Not that I would know what watered down piss tastes like, or any piss for that matter," he quickly added as he turned to convince Michaels of the fact. "Of course, if I have, I wouldn't know about it." Dalton added, drawing a strange look from the Captain.

Adam had drifted away from the conversation a bit, the loud events of the bar in full swing becoming nothing more than white noise as he noticed a man enter the front door of Paulie's Bar. Not the run of the mill scum that usually frequented the place, this man carried himself with a certain swagger, there was a military feel about him.

He looked the part well enough too, with the dark green cargo pants, solid black t-shirt and shaved head which had a look of shimmering marble to it.

Michaels had needed another crew member for some time now, a hired gun if nothing else. He and Dalton could both handle themselves well in a firefight, but an extra set of arms slinging shells would always come in handy in his line of work. He was a cargo transporter. Not the kind you contact through a government office, more like the type that considered a checklist of felonies to be an honest day's work. The black market kind. Transporting things that needed to be moved, all while skirting the law and dealing with only the worst of the worst. That was his job, and he did it well.

"Be back in a couple of minutes." he said to Dalton as he stood up from the sad excuse for a bar, which was nothing more than aged wooden boards poorly assembled by hand.

Adam made his way toward the stranger sitting at one of the corner tables as the smell of must, smoke and public perspiration hit him in the face like the heel of the heaviest of boots.

"Mind if I sit?" Michaels asked as the stranger glanced up at him for a moment, quickly going back to eating his plate of bread without so much as a word. "Every single time I come here, the bread seems to get worse," Adam said as the man continued to eat without missing a beat. "Got work here or just passing through?" Adam added, hoping for some kind of response.

"You Legion?" the stranger said, looking up from his plate with stern intentions.

"Legion? No. Hell no," Michaels quickly replied. "Far from it friend. Legion patrols and my ship might be on a first name basis, but it's for all the wrong reasons." he added.

"In that case, no I don't have work yet. Not sure about the just passing through part, I'll get back to you on that one." the stranger replied.

"I see. I'm former military myself, if you don't mind me asking, where did you serve your time?" Adam asked.

"Gali Special Forces." the stranger replied.

"Fresh out I take it?" Adam asked.

"It's complicated." the stranger replied.

"It usually is. Interested in a job?" Michaels quickly asked, almost expecting the answer to be an even quicker no.

"Who's asking?" the stranger calmly answered.

"Captain Adam Michaels. Rather not get into the details of the type of work we do, at least not until we make it official. For now, I guess you could consider the type of work we do to be, well, off the grid." Michaels replied.

"Off the grid is where I live." the stranger said, as he continued to eat without pause.

"I see..and you would be?" the Captain asked.

"Roman Raines," the stranger responded without hesitation.

Finishing his meal, Roman pushed the empty plate to the side, its thick green glass dragging across the table's coarse wooden surface as he looked at the Captain. "What kind of job?" he asked.

"Well, we do pretty much anything that needs to be done. From medical supplies to weapons, we transport anything that pays well enough, under the radar of course." Michaels replied cautiously.

Roman gave no reply, just an ice cold stare as a welcome for Adam to continue laying out the details.

"Truth is, sometimes what we take people aren't willing to let go of. Other times, when we deliver the goods, people start second guessing the whole payment process and, well, gunfights tend to ensue. Would be your job to help protect me, my crew and our ship. In return, you get ten percent of the take and free room and board. I decide to let you go, you go. You decide to leave, you are free to do so." Michaels explained in a stern tone of his own."Sounds fair enough. I'll think it over." Roman replied in a humble tone, his desolate blue eyes focused on the Captain.

"Well enough then, I'll look forward to it. You can find me at the bar next to the drunk in the brown coat, the one yelling about the alcohol." Michaels said as he stared in the direction of the bar, watching Dalton bitch the bartender out over the house brew as only a drunkard could do.

Slowly standing to his feet, Adam took a deep breath as he began heading back toward the bar, his thick leather boots striking hard against the creaking wooden floorboards as he switched himself into babysitting mode.

"What'd he say?" Dalton asked, wiping a bit of ale from his lips with the sleeve of his duster.

"He's thinking it over." Michaels replied as he sat back down and motioned for a glass of whatever it was they were passing off as the house special here at Paulie's.

"Well, that's damn thoughtful of him," Dalton said with a sarcastic look on his face as he yelled to the bartender. "Hey! Do you have anything stronger than this shit?" he yelled, the chubby man decked out in what looked to be borderline rags for clothes quickly nodded yes and motioned that he would be over in a few moments.

"Well, let's hope he decides soon, otherwise this trip has been a disaster. Jones fucking us on a deal we came through with, it's been raining since we landed, and who only knows what this shit is that I'm drinking." Dalton said under his breath as he turned the glass up, never flinching as every drop of it punished his throat on the way down.

The night continued on its normal course of action in an establishment such as Paulie's. Stories being conjured and told by those who consumed the most drink. Poker games filled with lies, heavy smoke and even heavier drinking. Pickup line after pickup line used on one of the very few women brave enough to set foot inside the run down dwelling. Not even several hours of drinking what could have doubled as Gunship fuel had Dalton the least bit sideways, although Captain Michaels kept telling himself when it came time to stand up and walk away, he would be hard pressed to.

Yep, everything seemed normal on this rainy night, that is until Michaels caught glimpse of a group of Legion guards passing a nearby window; moments from entering the bar.

"Ah shit." Michaels said in a low and discouraged voice.

"What is it?" Dalton said, turning to the door as it flew open.

The Legion soldiers were unmistakable, wearing the dense red outfits that were finely stitched and trimmed in black leather. Solid black riot style helmets with the standard tinted face shields.

"Ah shit." Dalton said moments later, agreeing with the Captain's previous assessment.

He slowly began to reach for his short barrel shotgun, which looked antique. But the gun, which was covered in a dingy haze, had gotten him out of more than one close encounter.

Michaels quickly grabbed his arm and gave a slight nod. "Not yet, too many of them. Chances are they aren't even here for us." he said as the four guardsmen quickly approached them with battle rifles aimed and ready.

"Captain Adam Michaels!" one of them shouted in a loud and administrative voice.

"Really? Is it too much to ask for one lucky break now and then? Just ONE?" Michaels said under his breath, almost as if he were talking to some higher power.

Anyone who had known Adam long enough; knew all too well the fact that he had the worst luck of anyone in the Skyla System, or possibly even all of charted space. Women, authorities, games of chance, it didn't matter. He was the unluckiest man alive, and he felt abandoned, if not shunned by the Gods because of it.

"You are under arrest and subject to prosecution for possession of illegal materials per item seventy-one of the Legion Articles." one of the officers pronounced aloud as two more of them disarmed both Michaels and Dalton.

The fourth guard yelled "Back, otherwise you will be getting the same!" as Roman approached the conflict.

"That's kind of the idea," he replied as he looked into the direction of Captain Michaels. "Twenty percent sounds about right, don't you think?" Roman asked Michaels as the men remained under gunpoint.

"What do I think? I think they should be arresting you for attempted robbery. Hell, I would rather rot in a Legion prison cell for the next decade of my life. Twenty percent?" Michaels asked in disbelief.

"Have it your way friend." Roman said as he turned to start walking out of the bar.

"On the other hand, fifteen percent sounds about right." Michaels replied.

Roman turned back to face them for a moment, his blank stare was an obvious sign of mental calculations at work, not to mention the thought of Adam negotiating a deal while being arrested.

"I can do fifteen." he said as he walked toward the Legion guards and their drunken prisoners.

"STAND DOWN!" one of the soldiers yelled as a last warning; not even remotely phasing Roman.

In what seemed like the most basic of motions, Roman thrust his arm under one of the Legion guards rifle hand, sending a shot bursting into the air. In that same moment, he buried a hard fist into the ribcage of the defenseless man of the law, immediately grabbing the vacated rifle from the air and aiming down the iron sights with precision. Surprised, the remaining three Legion troops fumbled with their rifles for a moment before laying them on the ground and reaching skyward.

"Well, you can damn sure pick 'em, I'll give you that much." Dalton said to Adam as he collected their weapons from one of the hostage soldiers. "Yea, I would have to agree," Michaels said, looking at Roman with amazement.

"Best be getting out of here, but before we do." Michaels said calmly as he returned to the card table, pulling an empty cloth sack from one of the large pockets of his faded brown coat; quickly filling it as he raked the card games winnings of every man into it.

"Like I said folks, don't ever count Captain Adam Michaels out." he said as he grinned widely, obviously proud of robbing the men at gunpoint.

As Dalton grabbed an almost full bottle of whiskey and raced toward the door, keeping his piece pointed in the direction of the Legion soldiers, Adam glanced back at Roman for a moment.

"You got the job." he said as he dashed out of the door.

It wasn't the first time Roman had disarmed four men at once, although to his knowledge, it was the first time he had done so and then followed it up with chasing two heavily intoxicated fugitives down one of the busiest streets on the small mining planet of Antillia.

He began to wonder if he had made the right choice, trying his best to figure out what fifteen percent actually meant in terms of money. At this point, it didn't matter. He couldn't stay here, he was wanted by the Gali government for unspeakable crimes; as well as the Legion because of the incident only moments ago. So at least for the moment he was part of the Gunship crew.

"Kelly, get ready to get us the hell out of here!" Dalton yelled into a com unit as he sprinted down the filthy streets of the impoverished town, both Adam and Roman right behind as the rain poured down; a staggering stench of cheap whiskey all over Dalton like a thrift store blanket.

"Copy that. Anything I should know about?" a female voice responded.

"The Usual. Just have us ready to lift when we get there, gonna have a whole lot of the wrong kind of company on our asses." Dalton replied.

"Not again." Kelly responded in a puzzled voice.

Within minutes, they could see the ship. It was easy to spot to the naked eye, strikingly antique; with the only difference being antique gave the impression of value. The Gunship that Adam had poured so much of his heart and soul into, had more of a junkyard feel to it. Different shades of gray on its exterior gave away the fact that it had been pieced together from other ships.

"I may just hang out here and take my chances." Roman said jokingly, earning an immediate response from the Captain.

"It doesn't look like much, but it's pulled me through a hell of a lot of scrapes."

As they approached the faded blue metal grating of the ship's ramp, a thin Asian man with long brown hair and a white tank top that was littered with grease stains slowly walked down, holding Roman at the end of a single barrel shotgun.

"Who's the trailer?" he asked.

"Relax Kato, he's with us." Adam said as he waved everyone inside.

"May want to put the toy away tan man, before someone gets hurt." Roman replied with heavy sarcasm as he walked right by Kato unwaveringly.

"Don't judge a book by its cover I guess," Roman said as he looked around once aboard. "I'm impressed." he added, his eyes skimming the cargo area of the ship.

Several wooden crates were stacked nearby, as well as a couple of very large bins made of reinforced sheet metal. The outside of the ship may have looked like a train wreck on its best day, but Roman immediately recognized the interior to be that of a Gunship.

Once a very popular model, the Glimmerian forces leaned on them heavily during their loss to the Legion in the first Glimmerian War. Once the war had come to an end, they were considered obsolete and quickly phased out in favor of more high tech vessels. The more advanced things became on a ship, the more likely they were to fall apart when you needed them the most, which is why Adam preferred the older model ship. It was solid, built to take a pounding and so basic that it reminded the Captain of himself; his core values simple, yet unwavering.

Kato followed the men inside aggressively hitting a red button by the door, followed by a hard turn of a switch to seal it airtight before they took off for orbit.

"Punch it Kelly, I'm on my way up," Michaels said as he pulled the com unit from his pocket and headed up a narrow steel ladder that would eventually lead him to the bridge of the ship. "Dalton, put Roman in a room and give him the grand tour. I'll catch up with everyone shortly." the Captain added as he disappeared up the ladder.

"You're gonna love the armory." Dalton said proudly as he motioned Roman to walk with him.

Kato stayed in the cargo bay, shotgun over his shoulder as he held onto a stainless steel handle bolted to the wall until they broke orbit from this sad excuse of a planet, the vibrations of liftoff jolting throughout the ship.

Shortly after the Gunship had fully entered the system, Michaels met with Roman on the observation deck of the ship. It was nothing more than a small balcony with two large windows made from hardened glass looking out across the stars, but it was considered to be the perfect place to talk business amongst the crew.

For the next hour or so, the Captain heard all about Roman's past; or so he thought.

Everything from his many years of service with the Gali special forces, to the recent events during the past couple of years that had him moving planet to planet, doing his best to elude the Legion while making a living for himself.

"Sounds like it'd make a good book." Adam said jokingly, trying to make the newest member of his crew feel a little more comfortable.

"I suppose it would." Roman replied with a slight grin.

Adam went on to do his best in explaining each member of his crew's story to the newly acquired gun. How he had fought alongside Dalton during the Glimmerian war less than a decade ago, and how he was still the weapon obsessed alcoholic which he had become famous for then.

He explained how Kelly came to them fresh out of flight school, having graduated in the top of her class, she had decided that she would rather work for herself. It presented her a much better chance to see the star system, even the planets on the fringe of uncharted space. It was that, or start making a living taking orders from some suit and tie who would have been signing her paychecks if she would have accepted a job flying a standard commercial transport ship, and that just wouldn't be her style.

Kato had been introduced to Michaels during a two week stint in the prison system of Anon. They had formed a bond that only terrible food and forced manual labor can provide, which led to Michaels helping Kato escape a short time after the Captain himself had been released. Since then, Kato had served as the ship's mechanic as well as an extra gun when needed.

At last, there was Luck. The rest of the crew referred to him as Adam's pet, but the Captain saw him as much more than that. Sure, he was a reminder of the best hand of poker that Michaels had ever played, winning the android in a high stakes game back on Montague.

Still, Adam had grown fond of of him and thought of Luck as being as much a part of this crew as anyone else. Luck had his purpose on the ship, he was a decent mechanic and also knew enough about flying to get the ship to its destination under emergency circumstances.

Still, everyone knew that he was more of a trophy than anything else, giving Adam the opportunity to bring up his rendition of that game whenever he saw fit. Which, painfully for the crew; was quite often.

Long after the conversation was over and Roman had made his way to the crew quarters for the night, the Captain remained sitting in the same chair made of solid stainless steel, finding himself drifting off a bit, thinking of everything important in the here and now.

The ship's maintenance, his crew's safety and value to the overall scheme of things. He even wondered, as he had done from time to time, what kind of life he would be living if he were settled down on a decent planet somewhere; living a normal life.

At times, he found himself missing the feeling of

settling down with a wife and children, even though it wasn't a feeling that he had been fortunate enough to experience. The thoughts that raced through his head all too often seemed to end up with the same conclusion time and time again. He loved what he was doing, from the near fatal gunfights to the deep space travel. Especially the deep space travel.

It's hard to explain what space travel is like until you've actually been there. The near frigid temperatures of the ship's interior that you are forced into getting used to. The constant silence of a vast nothingness as you learn to block out the sound of the ship's engines, all while surviving on freeze dried rations and what few supplies you were able to load before leaving the last settled world.

It sounded horrible, that is until you learned to appreciate the beauty of the stars slowly passing you by; almost as if memories were being revived in slow motion.

Most people will say it all looks the same, but the moment you begin to appreciate the simple things, suddenly you realize how beautifully different every trip becomes. As Adam sat on the observation deck, he had almost as many thoughts racing through his head as stars spread out in front of him.

It didn't matter though, all of the problems within the system, the challenges his crew faced every single day and the friends he had lost during the Glimmerian war; all of that was simply put on hold every time his ship became interlocked with the stars. It was the one place that nothing else mattered.

"Into the steel I see." Roman said as Dalton continued meticulously cleaning nearly a dozen weapons.

Everything from the basic combat pistol to the punishing double barrel shotgun, it was all right here, laid out on a coarse brown blanket in front of them.

"Into the steel, hard liquor and the steel that produces the hard liquor," Dalton said jokingly. "I'm also infamous with the ladies, you might have heard?" he added.

"Nope." Roman replied with a sarcastically fluctuation of his eyes.

"What about you? I'm sure you've had your hands on plenty of steel yourself in Gali?" Dalton asked.

"As well as liquor and women," Roman replied as both men laughed quietly. "Yea, I've been trained with quite a bit of everything, still prefer the tactical blade," Roman said, pulling a combat knife from a black leather band that wrapped around his leg. "Never jams up on you and it's just as accurate." he added, throwing the blade end over end throughout the room with blazing speed, hitting the wooden post of Dalton's makeshift gun rack, the bulk of the blade burying deep within its unfortunate wooden fibers.

"Nice throw, but too much damn unnecessary work for me." Dalton replied, quickly shouldering a short barrel shotgun and cutting two shots loose, hitting both over and under the blade; chopping the piece of post down to the thick steel floor.

"Nice accuracy." Roman said.

"You should see me when I'm sober." Dalton replied.

A few moments after he had laid the shotgun back in line with the other weaponry, Kato burst into the room, a semi-automatic rifle in his arms and at the ready, responding to the gunfire.

"You know, I normally consider it a rule to kill anyone who draws down on me twice." Roman said calmly as he looked into the barrel of Kato's rifle.

"Is that a fact?" Kato asked, tightening his grip on the weapon as he continued a deadlocking stare with Roman.

"Calm down jackass, I fired the shots; not him." Dalton said, making his way to Kato.

"I don't care who fired the shots, I'm thinking more about him just threatening to kill me." Kato replied.

"Think you're fast enough, then I'm game." Roman said, bringing a tense urgency to the room.

"RELAX! Nobody's killing anyone," Adam said as he

entered the room. "Put the piece away Kato," Michaels added. "NOW!" he yelled, finally convincing Kato to slowly lower his weapon.

"You muthafu... " Roman began to yell, charging into the direction of Kato as the Captain drew his revolver with blistering speed, holding Roman at gunpoint.

"This ends right now. You both understand?" he asked with neither man responding.

"It either ends or I'll personally airlock the both of you and hire two more guns when we land on Tameca," Adam added. Seconds after Kato had walked away, Roman held his hands up and backed off slowly. "Good, after seeing what you did to those damn Legion soldiers, I'd have to hire two men to replace you. And I don't want to spend that kind of money." Michaels said in an attempt to lighten the mood of the room, quickly holstering his revolver and walking away.

"See why I drink?" Dalton said, turning up a shot glass full of spirits before catching his breath and tossing a spare glass to Roman.

"I'm starting to paint the picture." Roman replied, pouring himself some of the light red bubbly.

"You know, you may want to be a little more friendly when it comes to Roman, he may end up saving your life one day." Adam said, catching up to Kato.

"That will be the day." Kato replied, turning to enter the confined engine room as the Captain stood for a moment; watching him disappear into the steam filled cave made of faded gray steel.

"System checks out fine." Luck said, his upper body under the control panel of the pilot's gauges.

"Alright, everything looks good up here as well, switching over to self pilot." Kelly replied, clicking several buttons as she slowly stood from the plush leather seat to see the Captain board the small bridge area.

"How's the grid?" Michaels asked.

"We didn't pick up anything on our way out other than

a little com traffic, looks like a clean getaway." Kelly replied.

"Good. That's good." the Captain replied, taking a seat in one of the two chairs that were stationed behind the pilot.

"We got into a little bit of local trouble with the Legion back there, shouldn't exactly be combing the system looking for us," Adam added. "I need you to plot a new course out for us, we need to make a stop in Tameca before hitting the outer plains." Michaels said as both Kelly and Luck looked on.

"Yes sir Captain. We got a job in Tameca?" Kelly replied curiously.

"Not sure just yet, maybe; will be a big payday for all of us if things work out," Adam replied, the thought of the Hunters cemented into his mind throughout the entire conversation. "I'll pull everybody together when we get there, go over all of the details. Try to bring us to the edge of Tameca City somewhere, without drawing a lot of attention. Good job back there." the Captain replied with a nod as he left the bridge to head to his rack for a few hours of much needed slumber.

The hazy gray rain began hammering the Gunship the moment it made its approach into Tameca's atmosphere. It had been a very short flight, having left one of its farthest moons before flying into one of the larger planets in the system. A semi-sweet sight to the Captain as he awaken to see the distant city skyline from a small circular window near his bunk. He was glad to be landing, still he couldn't help but think cautiously of the hidden dangers that always came attached to such a setting. A gigantic planet, which was predominately covered with water, held one of the most highly populated cities throughout the system. Tameca City, known for its massive number of ports; it was a smuggler's paradise.

Sure, there was a Legion presence here, however the run of docking ports was so immense that they simply couldn't check them all, relying on the help from its citizens. The same citizens who feared the most ruthless clan of criminals on Tameca, or any of its moons for that matter. The Hunters.

An almost vampiric group of criminals, they were feared, even by the Legion soldiers themselves; which served almost as a free pass to conduct underhanded business and wreak havoc abroad. It was the cannibalistic nature of the Hunters, combined with the stark white skin tone that caused many people to label them as vampires. Human enough, they bled and occasionally were even killed.

Still, the fact that they moved with exceptional speed and were so proficient with hand to hand combat only added to their legend. It was the Hunters who had brought the Gunship to Tameca, though the rest of his crew remained unaware of the fact.

Adam didn't like the idea of dealing with clientele such as the Hunters; but they had been looking for someone to move goods and were offering a lot of credits to anyone who was brave enough, or stupid enough, to accept the job. A very risky job, one the Captain knew he had to take in order to make financial ends meet; although selling the idea to the crew wasn't going to be the easiest of tasks.

With the crew gathered in the loading bay area of the ship and the vessel snugly nestled between two large hills of high grass, or as smugglers like to call it, a rural landing pad, the Captain knew that it was now or never. He had to sell the idea of working for a group with a name that was more ruthless than the luck that he had been burdened with his entire life. They would be lucky to finish the interview, much less the job unscathed, and it would take every one of them to pull it off.

"The Hunters! Have you lost you're damn mind Adam?" Dalton yelled as the rest of the crew looked on, his loud voice echoing against the hollow walls of the nearly empty cargo bay.

"I don't care how much it pays! If I can't kill 'em, then I don't want to go into business with the bastards!" he added.

"Relax, will ya? We do the job, collect the money. That's it. It is that simple." Michaels replied.

"I'm with you Captain, the Hunters don't intimidate me." Kato added.

"Easy for you to say, sitting back here at the fort while my dick's out there on the chopping block!" Dalton replied angrily.

"Captain, what does he mean you can't kill them?" Kelly asked. Michaels frowned slightly, looking at the floor for a moment before looking in her direction. Before he could say anything, Roman calmly replied.

"They die. Not easily done, but possible. I've put a few in the grave myself."

Adam spun around to see Roman still sitting on an empty crate behind him, quickly asking "You can? You have?". Roman replied with a slow nod.

"Define a few?" Michaels asked. The look he received from the former Gali commando let him know that it was a good damn many, which Adam wasn't sure should put his mind at ease or throw a red flag.

"I've put an entire rifle clip into one of the beasts myself! It did little to slow it down; much less kill it!" Dalton said with disbelief, as the rest of the crew looked on.

"What do you mean beasts? Captain?" Kelly asked, glancing hard at Michaels.

"Go on Adam, tell her." Dalton said with heavy sarcasm, earning a long glance from the Captain. "Everybody just calm down for a minute. Relax. Feels good to be alive doesn't it?" Michaels said, trying unsuccessfully to lighten the spirit of the crew.

"Alright, they aren't human; at least not entirely Kelly." the Captain said, referring to the Gothic appearance of the Hunters. Their hair and skin void of pigment, solid black leather attire and above all things, their uncanny desire to feast on the flesh of human beings.

"Any person that eats another person has some damn issues," Dalton said with heartfelt emotion. "Unless she's hot and it aint' for keeps."

Even though they kept to themselves, almost like a secret society, they were infamous among the citizens of the star system. Almost demonic in nature; relying on sleek weaponry and a code of honor that rivaled even the Mafia families of the small planet of Benza, which were also notorious for their hardline methods of getting the job done.

"Doesn't matter. By the time you and Luck get back with the supplies and the ship checks out flight ready, we should be back from our meeting with the Hunters and then it's business as usual." Michaels said, trying to calm the crew down before turning to get a list of needed supplies from Kato.

As Adam turned to the exit of the ship, he could see Dalton and Roman gearing up for the much anticipated meeting; both men looking more than ready. Roman was equipped with nothing more than a large combat knife and a military grade pistol, each strapped to a separate leg with thick leather bands.

Dalton, on the other hand, was going heavy. And for him that spoke volumes. He had an arm sized buoy knife strapped tightly to one of his legs, with two older Knocker pistols strapped to the other, earning their unique nickname from the ability to either cut a man in half at point blank range; or bash in the unlucky victim's skull quite easily with the brass shielding at the bottom of the weapon's handle. All of this, however, was overshadowed by his black flack jacket which held several grenades as well as two short barrel shotguns. Both guns over his shoulders and crossed behind his head.

"A little much don't you think?" Michaels said as he looked on in disbelief. "That's what she said." Dalton replied, laughing for a moment as he hesitated; finally taking the flack jacket off and tossing it onto a nearby table.

"Alright, but that's it. The knife stays. The sons of bitches 'aint eating me," he replied. "Hold the fort down now, ya' hear?" Dalton asked Kato sarcastically as the three men headed for the exit ramp.

"Kelly, you and Luck grab everything we need as far as supplies go and stay in contact with Kato back here on the ship. Steer clear of any Legion eyes on the street, we don't need that on top of what's already on our plate. Kato, we'll be in touch." said the Captain, as he glanced back long enough to see Luck and Kelly prepping the Rover.

It was nothing more than a large, mechanical vehicle used for carrying cargo, but he sure wished it were him riding inside of it at the moment. They both looked very comfortable to him, meanwhile he started out of the cargo bay door with the others, immediately hammered by a cuttingly cold rainfall.

Dalton glanced back for a second, the water falling around them like fireflies as he glanced in Adam's direction, his jacket already thoroughly soaked.

"If we end up marching in this shit only to die, I'm gonna be seriously pissed off." he said as Roman started laughing quietly.

Even Captain Michaels chuckled for a moment. Dalton was right, nearly a mile walk in front of them in some of the worst rainfall he'd ever seen.

They had walked nearly two hundred yards when the rover passed by, throwing water their way almost as if to mock them. Michaels tried to block out Dalton's cursing and focus on the city that sat on the horizon, but as usual it was easier said than done. He had been here a few times before, but could never quite get past the size of it. To his estimation, millions of people had come from every corner of the system to call Tameca City home. A lot of good citizens lived here, raised families and worked hard everyday to earn their place.

That said, a city of this magnitude was easy to get lost in; which had a certain luster to it from a criminal's point of view. Although Adam wouldn't admit it, everyone he had ties with in the city was on the wrong side of the legal system. It seemed like everywhere he went in Tameca, he found trouble. Sometimes he had a hand in it. Well, usually he had a hand in it. Still, he tried to convince himself that he had been incorrectly branded because of the few times when he was truly in the wrong place at the wrong time.

If ever there was a wrong place inside of Tameca City, it was Dusk Tavern. That was one place that never had a right time, full of the scum of the star system from open until close, at which time the more prominent criminals conducted business.

It was bad enough to be going to Dusk Tavern in the first place, but to march like this; cold liquid piercing their body from head to toe the entire trip? He couldn't think of a single reason that anyone would put themselves through such a drenching march only to wind up at the worst possible destination imaginable.

"At least they got good drink at the Dusk." Dalton said to the group as he grinned from ear to ear.

Michaels just shook his head for a moment before glancing up into the sky, wondering if there truly was a higher power that made a full time job out of torturing him.

After walking for what seemed like an eternity in clothes that were clinging to their skin from the rain, they had arrived at the edge of the city. The bright lights and hustle of thousands of bodies were a welcome sight to anyone who had just been on a trip through the system, though the Captain had a knack for attracting the wrong type of attention here.

It only took a few moments of holding up a fistful of

credits before a transport shuttle came to a screeching halt; adding a few more dings to the already wretched yellow paint job. It was like a roll of the dice whenever you used a city shuttle in Tameca City.

Sometimes you would land an android at the controls, and they weren't exactly famous for their conversational skills; providing a very serene trip to your destination. Other times, you were presented with a former convict or drunken lowlife who would give you the entire laundry list of rumors throughout the city in five blocks or less.

After a couple of minutes of convincing the driver; who Dalton swore did jail time with him several years back on the small moon planet of Jocom, that they truly did want to go to the Dusk Tavern He put down his small flask of booze and began the trip.

"Everyone is talking about the impending civil war between the planets," the driver said as he passed the first intersection on his way to the bad side of town; traffic so thick it was almost unbearable. "The council should be voting on it one way or another this week, but everyone in Tameca knows that it's just a tactic to stall for time while they raise a large enough army. We will be fighting alongside the Colonial army, or at least that's what every newspaper here has been saying." he added.

The Captain, Dalton and Roman all tried to look and sound interested, though the only person with interest in the war to come was the whiskey laden driver.

"So, what business do you guys have at the Dusk?" the driver asked.

"No business of yours." Roman sharply replied, earning him a glance from Michaels.

"What my friend means is, we are meeting some old friends there. The kind of friends who wouldn't really like to be the subject of conversation." Adam replied in a much friendlier tone than Roman had just finished with.

"Understandable." the driver said politely to the Captain as he gave the Roman a look filled with ill intention.

"I simply meant that it's a rough place. Wasn't sure why anybody would go there willingly is all." the driver said in a calm but probing voice as Dalton broke his stare from the window to answer.

"They got damn good liquor there. Some of the finest I've ever drank, and I've been around." The driver looked puzzled for a moment before answering with deep sarcasm.

"Yes, I bet you have."

"What the hell is that supposed..." Dalton began to ask, turning his entire body to the driver in the process. But before he could finish, he was cut off by Michaels.

"Can we stop with the drinking already! Don't you think about anything else?" he asked in a puzzled voice.

Dalton was obviously in a deep, concentrated thought for a few moments.

"Well yea. Guns. Women. You know, the essentials." he responded as Roman broke out into a loud laugh for several seconds.

The remainder of the ride lasted only a few minutes and was funeral quiet, the shuttle arriving at the Dusk as the driver looked around with paranoia; engine running loudly as the clanging of steel rods could be heard from its engine compartment.

As Michaels handed the driver a small fist full of credits and thanked him, both Dalton and Roman were already waiting outside, almost as if the drink would run dry if they waited a moment longer.

"Well, the place hasn't changed a bit." Adam said, referring to the borderline condemned look of the Dusk.

Wooden boards made up its exterior, the faded red color of the wood washed away with time giving the place a fragile look. The roof of course was still the same shiny aluminum material that had been the topic of discussion for citizens throughout the neighborhood.

It had been long rumored that the aluminum was put

into place to block the overhead scans from the city's security choppers, not that the security force was brave enough to enter the Dusk either way. It was a welcome sight to all three men as they cautiously approached the reinforced steel door that was guarded by two of the largest men any of them had ever seen.

Both wearing solid black shirts, cargo pants and boots, they fit the profile of higher end mercenaries. Armed with light machine guns, they were the type of security that if you weren't on the list; you weren't getting into anything short of a casket. That is, unless you had a fist full of credits.

As the three men approached a waist tall podium style computer, Adam placed his hand on the tinted glass top; trying his best to look casual as every fingerprint was thoroughly scanned. After a few moments, the tinted glass illuminated bright green, as the security detail slowly opened the door.

"Welcome Captain, they're expecting you." one of the mercenaries said.

The men slowly entered, taking extra time to survey the surroundings. It was nothing more that a small wooden bar that was polished to a very fine grain, along with a handful of stools and several thick wooden tables near the entrance. They were also quick to notice a door behind the bar at the rear. Walking into its direction, Dalton would get in position to cover it just in case things went sour; or at least Adam thought.

"Well, here's the liquor." Dalton proclaimed proudly, completely disregarding the rear door while cradling a bottle of molasses black bourbon, smiling as if he had just become a father for the first time.

So this is what the Dusk looks like after hours. Roman thought as he glanced around the room.

Very dimly lit, there were only a few white track lights on the ceiling and a handful of red lights, giving a subdued crimson glow at the foot of the bar. It was empty for the moment, however that didn't stop Dalton from helping himself to a shot glass, standing behind the counter preparing his drink as if he were working for tips before joining the others at a small wooden table nearest to the center of the room. Michaels kept his eyes locked on the rear door, meanwhile Roman kept watch on the only other door in the place, the entrance.

"Damn good bourbon, I'll say that much. Of course, I've never really had bad bourbon. Odd, don't ya' think?" Dalton asked his two comrades in a scratchy voice as he turned his glass up for a second hard shot.

"I don't like waiting around like this." Roman said softly, a statement which Captain Michaels was quick to agree with.

"So what do you think they are needing moved so damn badly?" Dalton asked.

"I don't know, but it looks like we are about to find out." Michaels replied as two figures appeared from the door directly behind the bar.

As they slowly approached, it quickly became obvious that they were in fact Hunters. One of them much larger than the other, they both were darkly dressed in all solid black leather, even down to the thick laced boots.

"Captain Adam Michaels?" the smaller of the two asked in a curious voice. "My name is Anwick. There was never any mention of escorts coming with you to the meeting." he said, visibly upset by the intrusion of both Dalton and Roman.

He motioned toward them slightly with one of his hands, prompting the larger of the two Hunters to approach the men. At least a foot taller than anyone else in the room, his arms were swollen from use; muscles rippling throughout the large limbs.

The same moment that the large Hunter firmly reached for their weapons in an attempt to disarm the unwanted strangers, Roman spun around and onto his feet; grabbing the Hunter's wrist with one hand and using the other to slam its head straight through the table, throwing wooden shards throughout the room. Anwick stood to his feet swiftly.

"What is the meaning of this?" he shouted at Michaels as he began to aid his friend.

Almost instantly, Anwick found himself looking at the bad end of two shotgun barrels, both in the grasp of a slightly tipsy Dalton. "You realize that at my signal, I could have this room full of soldiers who would kill and dismember you inside of thirty seconds!" Anwick stated firmly, glancing hard at Adam.

"Think so?" Roman asked calmly, applying pressure to the arm of the larger of the two Hunters, earning a painful screech.

"Relax! Everyone just relax," Adam said loudly as he remained seated. "You honestly didn't expect me to just walk in here alone did you? We both know what kind of reputation your kind has, and I would hope that you would consider me to be a bit smarter than that. You and I are here to do business, so let's do it." Michaels added as he motioned toward the chair that Anwick had left only moments ago.

As Anwick sat down slowly, he immediately glanced at Roman, who still had a commanding hold on his much larger opponent.

"Roman, let him go." Michaels said.

Responding with a slight nod, he pushed the Hunter several feet back, releasing his arm with the same motion.

"Lexion! Enough!" Anwick yelled as the larger Hunter began to walk directly toward Roman a second time.

An awkward moment of silence fell across the entire room as it quickly became evident to the Captain that should the Hunters have their way, Roman was unlikely to walk out of the Dusk alive.

"Anwick, I apologize. My crew is very protective when it comes to me as well as the cargo we transport. I hope you view this as an advantage when considering us for the job." Michaels said in an attempt to settle the dispute.

Anwick gazed through Roman for a few more seconds before breaking his stare and looking directly at Adam

"Very well. We have business to discuss," Anwick replied. "It is because you come so highly recommended that we are meeting here today," Anwick said, referring to all of the friends Michaels had made in the past that were connected to the wrong side of the Legion. "Simply put, we have a package that we need to you take and deliver in exactly one week to Gastonia. You will earn fifteen thousand today and another thirty thousand at the time of delivery." Anwick added, stating the terms with great clarity, his long and brittle white hair moving slightly as he spoke.

Michaels remained quiet for a few moments, finally giving his answer to the business proposal. "It's going to cost you twenty five thousand up front and another twenty five thousand upon delivery."

Anwick took several long, heavy breaths before replying slowly. "I do not negotiate Captain Michaels. I offer the terms, you take them. That's how I conduct business."

Adam glanced over in the direction of Dalton, trying to figure out how many shots that had made for him already. "I'm not negotiating. We both know it must be a complicated delivery, otherwise you would have done it yourself. A complicated job pays what its worth in risk. Otherwise, I'm not the right man for the job. That's how I do business." Michaels replied.

Anwick stood straight to his feet, prompting Adam to do the same a few moments later. "Very well," Anwick answered as both men stood only inches from one another. "I'll pay what you ask, however let me tell you this. You have one week. ONE. If you are even a second behind schedule on delivery, you should pray to the Gods that the authorities find you before we do. Otherwise death will be the least of your concerns."

Anwick gave a slight hand motion, prompting Lexion to

walk to the door behind the bar, giving three hard thumps on it with his bone crushing fist. Seconds later, the door opened as four more men dressed similar to the ones outside of the Dusk entered, however, the difference became quickly obvious to Michaels and his crew.

They were escorting a female prisoner, her hands in tight rope bonding and her head looking toward the floor. The Captain wasn't sure the reason, but as well dressed as she was, he suspected someone in a powerful position would be trying everything they could to get her back.

"What's with the girl?" Michaels asked, dreading he already knew the answer.

"You mean the package," Anwick said smiling, the dim light bouncing off of his shard like teeth. "One week." he added, holding a single finger up closely in front of Adam's face before walking through the door and exiting the room.

One of the armed men dropped a black leather bag to the ground at Adam's feet; several Legion credits spilling out of the bag a moment after hitting the floor. He looked at the men for a moment, eventually reaching down and grabbing the bag.

Lexion held the door open, the polluted air of the city sending a glimmer of light from the sunset as well as a push of civilized air into the Dusk.

"May we meet again." Lexion said smiling.

Roman quickly rose to his feet and replied "I'll look forward to it." as he quietly tapped his fingers across the handle of his combat knife.

Dalton secured the half-empty bottle of bourbon into one of the cargo pockets of his pants, finishing off the rest of the shot glass in one fast motion; alcohol burning a familiar path all the way down to the pit of his stomach.

"My compliments to the chef." he said as he handed the empty shot glass to the nearest mercenary.

As they began to leave, Lexion yelled loudly, prompting one of the well armed soldiers for hire to lead a young boy dressed in tattered blue clothing into the room at gunpoint.

"Wait, they have a child in there!" the woman yelled loudly, her soft and soothing voice of sincerity catching Adam's immediate attention.

"Not our fight," Dalton said calmly to Michaels. "We are talking about Hunters here Adam. Two of them to be exact, not to mention a pile of tin soldiers." he added as he nervously awaited a response from his Captain.

"Please! They are going to kill him!" she shouted desperately with tears flooding her vivid blue eyes, obviously concerned for the boy's life. "Please!" she said once more, grabbing Michaels by the arm; their eyes locking together as they shared a moment of fate.

Adam felt the urge to do the right thing beginning to overtake his better judgment, glancing at Dalton for a moment almost in apologetic fashion.

"Ahh shit!" Dalton was able to get out softly before the stinging feeling of worth that came attached to helping someone in need hit Michaels as he had turned back into the direction of the door. Kicking it solidly, the reinforced obstacle quickly flew open, smacking abruptly against the wall behind it and gaining the attention of Lexion as well as the four heavily armed men.

Adam's pistol threw two shots from the chamber almost instantly, the first hitting one of the armed men in the forehead and dropping him like a stone. The second shot pierced the chest of another soldier, throwing him against the wall before hitting the floor with an unforgiving thud; a trail of blood painting the wall bright red above him.

Michaels knew well enough to seek cover before attempting a third shot, diving behind a table in the corner of the room just in time as dozens of slugs began to chew at the wooden barricade that separated them. As the two soldiers began walking slowly in the direction of the Captain, escorting themselves with a blanket of lead from their automatic weapons, they were both knocked to the ground forcefully by shells from the shotgun Dalton held in his right hand.

An expert of his surroundings, he immediately dropped the empty weapon and spun around into the direction of the front door, putting a two handed grip on his other peacemaker. Anticipating the guards out front rushing them, he blindly fired two shots into the direction of the entrance. The first shell hit the frame of the door, sending up a wooden cloud of splinters, while the second shot found a target on one of the soldiers who fell to the ground in pain for a few moments before checking out of this life. Dropping his second empty weapon, he took shelter beside of the door, drawing both of his pistols at once; the dim light of the Dusk's interior shimmering across the brass inlays.

Michaels had made it to the boy and began to free his hands of the tightly bound rope when Lexion threw a backhand into his direction, sending the Captain several feet across the room. Smashing into the stockpile of intoxicating beverages, Adam fell limply onto the floor behind the bar under a storm of broken glass.

"Son of a bitch." Dalton said of the wasted liquor as he continued to exchange gunfire with the remaining soldier outside.

As Lexion followed the path of destruction which led to the Captain, Anwick once again entered the room, taken back for a moment by the devastation, he quickly focused his anger on Adam; who remained limp on the floor behind the bar. Anwick's hands clamored for revenge as both Hunters approached the Captain.

"Hey, bitches," Roman yelled across the room, successfully gaining their undivided attention. "Get some." he added, daring the walking beasts to a fight.

Anwick quickly made his way into the direction of the marked man, Lexion following suit and releasing the grip he had on the front of Michaels' shirt allowing him to fall back to the ground. Roman pulled his combat pistol long enough to throw it across the room, sliding roughly on the aged floor as he confidently drew his tactical blade and squeezed his hands for a moment; several of his knuckles busting back to life.

The boy was able to free himself in the following moments, running to the safety of stunningly beautiful lady as she stood behind Dalton. Firing several shots from the two pistols, he finally clipped the soldier outside on the shoulder, putting him down and rendering him defenseless.

"Kato, I'm activating the beacon. Come get us now!" Dalton said out of breath as he pushed a sequence of buttons on the com unit, throwing it out into the street; the small globe on the front beginning to emit a soft white glow. "Now we hold tight and pray that our ride gets here before they finish us off." Dalton said to the woman and child, putting them behind a small table near the door and checking the magazines of his pistols; the unmistakable odor of hooch on his breath.

When Captain Michaels began to get his bearings in order, he realized nothing on him was broken and began to slowly crawl in the direction of where his pistol had hit the floor; pieces of glass crunching softly under his bare palms. He didn't see his sidearm right away, instead he caught sight of a large piece of mirror laying in the floor at the corner of the bar. He was confident that he had never seen a fight like the one that was reflecting back to him through the reciprocating glass. Glimpses of Roman's body moving with perfect coordination as he carved flesh with both blade and boot.

He landed several fast punches into the face of Lexion, momentarily stunning him while his kick found its home in the chest of Anwick, staggering him back a few feet. More surprised than hurt, Anwick quickly unleashed a flurry of lightning fast punches and elbows onto Roman, most of them finding their mark as they sent Adam's newest crew member to one of his knees.

Furious, Lexion wasted no time putting a choke hold on Roman in an attempt to snap his neck and be done with the pesky former Gali commando. His grip hold of Roman's neck was released as a shot from the Captain's pistol embedded into his shoulder, causing Lexion to snarl his razor teeth for a moment; eventually casting a stare in Michaels' direction. That is how his life would end. Roman thrust his combat steel into the face of Lexion, following the stab with a swift elbow that broke the blade from its handle as Lexion fell to the ground, blood spilling from the edges of the eternally lodged instrument.

Shocked at the death of one of his best and feeling the sudden sense of morality, Anwick quickly began to exit at the rear of the bar, the room now flooding with soldiers armed to the hilt. Roman had reached the point of no return, rage flowing through his veins as if it were the very blood in his body. He let go of an unrelenting assault with his hands, grabbing the first soldier by the neck and using his free hand to pummel the man with the bottom of his fist. He then grabbed a second soldier with a choke hold that eerily resembled that of the now departed Lexion, this time more effective however as he snapped the man's neck in several places; dropping his lifeless body to the ground.

He was a killer, a damn good one at that. But even someone of his life ending skill was outnumbered as at least a dozen more armed men filled the room in response to the distress call of the soldier who had pleaded for help earlier during his firefight with Dalton. Michaels had made it to his feet and nearly reached Roman when they both realized the circumstances and were ready to accept defeat. As both men began to put their hands into the sky, Roman heard an unfamiliar sound, one that Adam knew all too well. The deep, throaty sound of the Mauler. It was a name the crew had decided on for the largest flash shotgun any of them had ever seen. Kato stood in the doorway holding the mauler, which gained its technical name not from a flash of light, but the flash drum under the barrel which held thirty rounds and required only an instant to reload.

The room began to thin out quickly as every burst that fired from the chamber of the massive gun seemed to add a larger variety of body parts to the wall. Kato had barely used half of the drum's capacity when the room was clear, other than a few enduring screams and realizations of lives coming to an end. Michaels and Roman helped one another out of the Dusk as Kato walked behind them, Mauler perfectly positioned to slay anything with a heartbeat that followed the crew outside.

"Damn I love that gun." Dalton said from the cozy confines of the Gunship, which was parked in the middle of the street and attracting a lot of local attention.

"Get us the hell out of here!" Michaels said in a weak voice as they passed Kelly on their way up the ramp.

The roar of the Gunship's engines combined with what seemed like an endless cloud of dust as the vessel began to liftoff. Several soldiers accompanied Anwick to the front of the establishment, firing streams of metal piercing shots into the direction of the ship. Only moments later, following a loud burst of air meeting motion, the ship was gone. The soldiers began to check the dead and wounded as Anwick stood there for several minutes, his eyes still locked onto the sky.

"All Clear." Dalton proclaimed as he made his way down the ladder from the gunner's roost and back onto the bridge of the ship.

"We need to talk." Adam said to to the woman as she continued to harbor the boy they had saved not even an hour ago from the clutches of the closest thing to the devil that he had ever known. She nodded and began to stand up, her long champagne colored hair giving the shimmering illusion of velvet perfection as she made her way toward the Captain and the door of the ship's bridge.

"Hey big man. First time in space?" Roman asked as he

took a seat beside the boy, who was obviously afraid of the situation he had been cast into.

"Yes. Yes sir." the boy answered with much reserve.

"You can relax, you are safe and among friends here." Roman replied, before asking the child his name.

"Troy." the boy responded a couple of seconds later, sounding much less timid than before.

"Care to explain to me what in the hell just happened back there?" Michaels asked in a puzzled and desperate tone. Before she could answer his question, he interjected with a bit of sarcasm. "Feel free to start with who you are and what the Hunters want with you so badly?"

It was a legitimate question from where he stood. Adam had a lot of things racing through his mind at the moment. How Roman had handled himself so well against an opponent who appeared far more capable, how many drinks Dalton had actually consumed back at the Dusk and still been accurate with a weapon or how one of the most beautiful women he had ever laid eyes on, stood in front of him about to answer a question that would most likely affect the remainder of of his life.

"My name is Sarah Blaine," she answered in a soft voice, something Adam hadn't heard a lot of in his line of work."My father is the Admiral of the newly formed Colonial Army; they want to use me as leverage against him, at least that would be my guess." Sarah added, waiting on a response from Michaels.

He didn't reply, a combination of letting her finish her story and the angelic sound of her voice were to blame. After several tense moments of silence, she began telling Adam how the Hunters had been working with Legion troops for some time now, how her security detail was ambushed back on Tameca and over a dozen soldiers had given their lives to try and protect her.

"The boy?" Michaels asked, almost dreading the answer, and praying that it didn't complicate things any further.

"I have no idea. I had never laid eyes on him before they

drug him into that room." Sarah replied, watching the stress overtake the Captain as he stood there speechless.

"You mean to tell me that my crew just put their lives on the line against the Hunters for a kid that you don't even know?" he asked furiously.

"Relax Captain, the boy is still alive because of you and your crew's heroic efforts." she replied, standing closely to Adam as they both began to feel a nervous interest in one another.

Adam wanted so badly to be furious with Sarah, to lash out at her with anger. Instead, he found himself thinking of how perfect she was in every aspect. "For what it's worth, you did the right thing back there." Sarah said with a soft and thankful voice.

He looked at her for a moment, his eyes communicating a tale of great sorrow to come. "Fantastic. Carve it on my headstone, because once the Hunters catch up to me I'm a dead man." he finally replied as he walked away, making his course back onto the bridge.

"Kelly, Luck, set course for deep space. We need to get as far away from the system as possible for a bit; avoid any Legion or Hunter tracking ships that may be looking for us." Michaels said as he sat down in an empty chair, physically exhausted and mentally broken down from the day's events.

"Yes sir Captain." Kelly replied as she and Luck both pressed several buttons on the control panel illuminated in front of them.

"Thanks for saving our asses back there." Dalton said as Kato continued checking the navigational system with a small, hand held data machine.

"Just doing my job." Kato replied, maintaining his attention on the work in front of him.

"You do your job well." Roman added as he stood in the doorway of the engine room, Troy right at his side.

"Thank you." he added, giving a long stare of appreciation to the man he had gotten off on the wrong foot with.

"You're welcome." Kato replied, glancing up for a moment acknowledging the sincere thank you.

As Sarah walked across the steel catwalk above the cargo area, she stopped for a moment to watch Roman and Troy. The highly trained former soldier was walking the young boy through a set of moves with a combat knife. It was a basic set of motions, still it was impressive to see a child handling a blade built for men of combat as well as he was. Lunging forward quickly, then swiping the blade swiftly as he brought it back in to a neutral position. She hadn't known any of these people for long, but she was glad to see Troy finding someone to begin looking up to. At least the time he spent with Roman was time he wasn't thinking about home, if he even had one.

"Could be worse, he could be learning Dalton's craft." Adam said as he approached Sarah, who was still standing there, admiring the young boy's courage.

Eventually she broke her stare and glanced at the Captain for a moment, joining him in placing attention on Dalton. The hardened space cowboy was laying on the deck below them drinking from a large green jar. Its contents were unknown, but from the way he was cradling the thick glass container, it was something of significant importance to him. He glanced up at the catwalk with a huge grin on his brushy face.

"Nice view huh?" he said, implying he was well worth the effort.

"So, if you don't mind my asking, what's the plan? I would very much like to see my father again." Sarah asked.

The Captain tightened his grip on the guard rail of pale blue steel, continuing his stare below for a few moments. "Well, we are painted into a corner at the moment," he replied, while finally looking into Sarah's direction. "We can't go back to the Skyla System, at least not for a while. Sure to be plenty of hunting parties out there looking for us at this very moment. On the other hand, the supplies aren't going to last forever; eventually we're going to have to make our move." he added.

"We are on the verge of war, a war of a scale that we have never seen I'm afraid," Sarah said. "I fear that not so long from now, the entire system will be engulfed in death and destruction. At some point Adam, you will have to decide which side you're on." she added.

"Doesn't matter. I've got a sheet of outstanding warrants as long as your leg, and now I have the Legion as well as the Hunters out for my blood. I'll have you back with your father soon enough, you have my word. In the meantime, we need to fall off of the map so I can figure out our next move."

"Well, whatever you decide, I'm confident that it will be the right move." Sarah said in a thankful tone as she began to walk away, reaching the other side of the catwalk before Adam finally responded.

"Sarah," he said as she turned to face him, her comforting smile causing the Captain to fall silent for a second. "I know we may not look like much, but I won't let any harm come to you or the boy, I promise." Michaels added in an attempt to reassure her of safety from the Hunters.

"I know that Captain." Sarah replied, smiling brightly as she she gave an appreciative nod and slowly turned to walk away.

Adam stood there for a couple of minutes after she was gone, trying to convince himself that Sarah wasn't someone he should be falling for. They were from two different worlds, both literally and socially. Still, he began to feel his heart drifting away from logic as he heard Dalton's voice yell from below.

"She's a keeper Capt'n." Adam glanced down for a moment, giving a sarcastic look, even though he couldn't agree more.

"No sir Captain, I checked three times. The readouts aren't normal." Kato said of the navigational information he had recently pulled.

"Meaning?" Adam replied, eagerly awaiting a positive answer.

"Not sure. It's not time to panic; just thought I would bring it to your attention." Kato answered.

"Look into it." Michaels said, giving Kato a quiet slap on the shoulder as an unofficial thank you.
"This area looks good." Adam said as he leaned between Luck and Kelly, pointing out a small spot on the pilot's grid.

The bright neon green lights and numbers of the panel illuminating an otherwise dark bridge. "Sir that area is uncharted." Luck responded after glancing down at the grid for a split second.

"Uncharted is what we need right now." Adam replied as Kelly began punching the coordinates onto a touch screen beside her.

"Should take us a better part of twenty six hours to get there Captain." she said as she double checked the numbers before finalizing them into the ship's navigational system.

"I can do twenty six hours. Set course, I'll let everyone else know." Michaels said as he began to leave the bridge while Kelly pressed a sequence of keys that pushed the ship's thrusters even harder; nearly doubling the torque.

Michaels motioned for Roman as Dalton continued, slightly intoxicated, to show Troy how to aim down the sights of an unloaded combat pistol.

"Hitting an uncharted area in a few days. Gonna sit tight there for while, wait until this thing blows over. Hate to keep the kid off world that long; no choice though, we go back now and we won't last an hour." Adam said in a low voice.

"No hurry. His entire family was executed by the Hunters for aiding the Colonials with supplies. Poor kid, I feel bad for him." Roman responded sympathetically.

Adam felt deep sorrow for Troy; glad he had made the decision to rescue the boy from the clutches of the Hunters, while knowing exactly what it felt like to grow up alone.

"Well, just try and keep him as busy as possible, he seems to cling to you and our resident drunk." the Captain replied. Roman agreed as he turned to join Dalton and Troy in learning to do something he had known how to do for decades, handle a sidearm. Of course, hearing the instructional advice from a man with slurred speech was like learning all over again.

"Give us a couple of weeks Captain, this boy gonna be dropping Hunters left and right!" Dalton yelled as Troy smiled wide.

Michaels could only try and imagine the grief Troy must be feeling, having those monsters slaughter his entire family, but at least he was safe now. No matter how feared the Hunters were across the system, he knew that his crew would fight to the death for its two newest passengers.

Usually during deep space travel, Adam would sleep very little and spent most of his time admiring the stars and enjoying true freedom. Not this night however. He had been beaten, nearly killed by gunfire, quite possibly met the woman of his dreams and taken on the responsibility of a child with no home to return to. There would be a lot of sleep in the Captain's future on this night, and he wasted no time; hitting his bunk and escaping into a dreamworld of infinite possibilities only minutes later.

Opening his eyes, Adam was first struck by the absolute silence of the ship's thrusters. A person is taken back by the loud roar and torque of things during their first few trips into the blackness of deep space. Adam had been through it hundreds of times however, and he had grown used to both of them. It was the lack of noise and vibration throughout the ship that raised sudden alarm with the Captain. Jumping to his feet, he grabbed his trusted gray revolver from a solid steel bedside table and used his free hand to rub his eyes for a moment, trying his best to wake up and be clear headed as he expected the worst. Slowly making his way down the narrow corridor, his right hand gripping the sidearm as he checked all of the crew's rooms, every one of them coming up empty.

Had the Hunters somehow found them? Legion soldiers maybe? Many scenarios played out in his mind as he continued his slow but determined walk, trying his best not to make any sound in doing so. As his feet hit the catwalk, he slowed his pace down considerably; knowing full well that its grated steel flooring was notoriously loud to begin with. Glancing over the rail as he slowly made his way to the center, he spotted his entire crew down the iron sights of his combat sidearm.

"Raise it by two credits." Dalton said as he threw a handful of poker chips into a pile.

Adam's initial reaction was that of relief, his crew was safe and sound. As that feeling began to fade, he began to wonder why they hadn't invited him to play in a game that he considered himself to be such an expert in. The Captain walked down the metal steps in a much louder fashion, immediately gaining the attention of the entire crew.

"You would start a card game without me?" Michaels said as he approached the table.

"Hell, you been asleep for nearly two days." Dalton replied, a primitive looking cigar that looked as though it had been hand rolled by a blind man hanging from the corner of his mouth. Adam shockingly gazed at his green and brown military style titanium watch, astounded that he had slept for such an extended period of time.

"We're sitting in uncharted space Captain, thought it best to kill the main engines, save fuel and not gain any unwanted attention." Kelly said, waiting for the Captain's approval.

"Good job," Adam said as he pulled up an empty chair, sitting beside Troy to help him play his hand with the best chance of winning. "Where's Luck?" Michaels asked, doubting anyone even noticed that he wasn't present.

"On the bridge running more schematics on the ship's vitals." Kato replied as he laid his spread on the table, smiling and raking the winnings in his direction.

Under normal conditions, Adam would remain focused on the hand of cards in front of him, however these weren't normal conditions. They were on the run, sitting in uncharted space and Sarah Blaine sat across the table from him, her beauty almost impossible to put into words. She had a look of such magnificent innocence, every feature of her face glowing with undeniable passion. He tried to keep it at nothing more than a passive glance in her direction every few minutes, until one of his glances had been answered by one of her own. How could he have let it happen? He dared not glance back for several minutes, going out of his way to ignore her while showing Troy the finer points of becoming a world class card shark in only a matter of minutes.

Finally gaining enough courage, he quickly joked with the crew and threw a glance her way; only to find that she had already been watching his every move. Sarah smiled softly as she continued to stare at him, causing him to begin playing nervously. He couldn't understand what was happening. Since when did he ever get nervous around women? In his line of work he met plenty of them, a lot of them tougher than the average girl; most of them could handle a weapon as well as any man and could hang drink for drink with Dalton himself.

Nobody like Sarah however, not even close. She was stunningly beautiful, very well spoken and above all, political. Political? His idea of politics involved small arms fire or even a good old fashioned bare-fisted brawl. They had nothing in common aside from being here at the same moment, the same spot together; something he knew deep down would be long forgotten by Sarah the moment she arrived safely back home. Still, the heart wants what the heart wants, and his was becoming increasingly dependent on seeing her as much as humanly possible.

Maybe he was reading too much into her smile addressed to him, he had to be. A love story between two worlds as different as their own is destined to fail.

"I think Troy has the hang of it," Michaels said as the boy played the winning hand and collected the pot with a smile that was larger than Dalton's tolerance for alcohol. "I'm going to go check on Luck, you guys enjoy the rest of the game." Adam added, being much more polite than usual.

As he stood up to make his way to the bridge, he glanced at Sarah once more, earning another inviting smile as he nodded his head slightly before walking away; trying to concentrate on not walking nervously as every single step landed abruptly onto the cold steel flooring.

Before the Captain could make it to the bridge, all hell started to break loose. The last thing you want to see during flight as a passenger, much less a Captain is pitch black. Several seconds of darkness stretched throughout the ship as Michaels reached around and found one of the corridor walls to hold onto. There was a flutter of light throughout the ship for a couple of seconds before going back to complete emptiness. The emergency lights, which were nothing more than small red bulbs mounted into the ceiling throughout the ship powered on, coinciding with a very primitive sounding siren that echoed through the entire vessel. Providing very little light, the red glow produced just enough for the Captain to begin sprinting in the direction of the bridge.

"What the hell is going on?" Adam shouted as he entered the bridge. Luck, sitting in one of the two pilot chairs spun around to face him.

"My guess is we took gunfire when leaving Tameca, must have hit our navigational system. Even worse, it wasn't until we went dark that I tried to fire everything back up. One of the thrusters is not functional and the life support system is substantially strained." Luck replied, emotionless as only an android could be in this situation.

"Can it be fixed?" the Captain asked frantically, taking a seat in one of the vacant leather chairs.

"No time sir. With limited life support and only temporary use of our second thruster, we are going to have to land somewhere close and soon. Going to be a hard landing at that." Luck replied.

Adam buried his face for several long moments in the palm of his right hand before standing to his feet.

"Find a suitable planet, I'm on my way to break the fantastic news to the crew." Adam replied as he walked quickly out of the door leading to still dimly illuminated hallway. *Fucking deep space.* he thought as Luck began taking scans of nearby planets.

"So, secure as many of your personal belongings as possible in your rooms and meet back in the armory. It's the safest spot on the ship, and from my understanding the landing won't be pleasant." Adam said as the crew looked on, dazed and facing reality.

"Are, are we going to be OK Captain?" a scared Troy asked, having already been through a lifetime of trauma in the past few days.

Caught completely off guard by the young boy, Michaels grew very quiet, unsure of how he should answer. Sarah bent over, placing her hand on the Troy's shoulder.

"You just stay right beside Roman, everything will work out just fine." she said in a very calming voice, glancing at Adam for a moment. He returned a nod of thank you as he quickly made his way back to the bridge with Kelly.

"He's right Captain, we either land to make repairs or we run out of air to breathe." Kelly said after looking over the calculations Luck had made.

"Fine. Let's do this." Adam said as he looked at a map of recent scans of nearby planets.

"This looks to be the spot sir, all of the planet's vital check out and there's a decent chance we could survive the landing." Luck added to the discussion, pointing to a spot on one of the black and white scans.

"Expecting trouble?" Sarah said as Dalton filled a field bag full of weapons to sit right beside a slightly smaller wooden crate that he had stocked with his finest drink.

"I like to stay prepared for anything." he replied with a slight grin.

As they made their way to the armory, the rest of the crew had already strapped in. Thick nylon harnesses were bolted to the wall, surrounding the weapons cache in the middle of the room. Kato held his restraints, nervous, but doing his best to hide it from the rest of the crew. Roman appeared to be expecting a lot less trouble, with only a combat blade strapped to his right thigh; he looked as though he was on the verge of falling asleep, Troy strapped in snugly right beside him. As Sarah strapped herself in with help from Dalton, he turned a small flask up and finished its contents before slinging it onto the floor and climbing into position.

"Well. It's go time." he said with confidence, almost as if he had done this dozens of times.

Two spots left. Sarah thought as she imagined the Captain would pilot the ship down to the surface. *What a brave man. A man's man.* she imagined as the red glow of the emergency lights did little to brighten the armory.

"Luck is going to pilot the ship down." Michaels said as he and Kelly entered the room and began strapping in. Smiling slightly in Sarah's direction, completely unaware of the faith she had placed in his courage just moments before.

Anyone who has has been fortunate enough to survive a ship to surface crash can attest to the same thing. The fall. Feeling absolutely helpless as gravity pulls you down faster than any human being should ever go, having nothing more to cling to than a safety harness bolted to the steel plated wall as you pray for forgiveness and intervention.

Objects began to fall throughout the armory as the Gunship dove into a deep descent that slowly led to a nosedive into the unknown, uncharted confines of the planet that the Captain had picked under pressure. It was the first time in a long while that Adam was afraid of dying.

Sure, the Hunters could have easily killed him back on Tameca. Still, he had a weapon in hand and at least some control of the situation. Falling from the sky at breakneck speeds tended to make him feel just a bit more helpless. Although he feared for his own life, he feared for his crew and the condition of his ship just as deeply.

Glancing around the room, everyone's individual feelings became crystal clear as their faces revealed all. Sarah cried softly, trying to comfort Troy while doing so. Kato stood solid, grasping very tightly to his safety straps, fingers red from the pressure of his clinched fists. Roman showed no fear, holding his crossed arms securely against his chest while his eyes remained closed. Dalton mumbled under his breath, leading the Captain to question if he was praying or cursing. Either way, he held a field supply bag full of weapons and a wooden crate of drink firmly against the wall with his large black boots.

The ship jolted roughly, causing a massive pull of gravity to one side of the vessel, nearly pulling the crew out of their confines and sending the wooden crate of alcohol smashing against the weapons cache in the center of the armory; shattering its contents.

"Oh no," Dalton yelled angrily as the crew looked on for several moments, waiting to see if he was brave enough to free himself in an attempt to salvage anything he could from the crate. The overhead lights fluttered for a moment before coming back on permanently, making visible what looked like a stream of ale and other toxic refreshments running out of the armory and falling to waste over the side of the catwalk. "Oh hell no!" Dalton added, overwhelmed with discouragement before clinching tightly as the ship dipped into a sudden spinning dive.

Adam heard the ship's thrusters trying to engage, which let him know they were inside the planet's atmosphere and it was almost over, for better or for worse. He could tell because of his extensive time aboard the vessel that the sound he heard was only one of the two thrusters, meaning the other was still malfunctioning.

He could only hope that Luck put the ship down in a spot that would do the least damage possible. If any of the crew survived, they needed enough of the ship left to attempt a repair job, otherwise it could be a very long time before they would leave this rock. If ever.

The entire crew could hear a loud alarm throughout the ship, those among them who had military training knew that it was a proximity alert, the time had come. Adam glanced at his crew one last time before settling his eyes onto Sarah Blaine.

He hoped that some higher power had not purposely placed the woman of his dreams into his life, only to end it a couple of days later. *I'm sorry for any wrong I've done. Please, just give me a second chance to make things right, a chance to do something positive for a change.* Adam thought.

A big part of him wanted to yell to her loudly that he had started to feel himself falling in love with her, no matter how forbidden it was in the eyes of society. What did he have to lose? Adam had convinced himself that if it truly was the last thing he would ever do, he needed to tell her. But there was no time.

The impact immediately caused the Gunship to go completely dark, sounds of metal tearing from its hinges all around them. Several of the bolts had torn from his harness upon impact, still enough of them remained intact to hold Michaels in place, he had hoped that the rest of his crew had been so lucky. A couple of minutes after the initial impact, Adam realized that he had survived. Good chance his back had been bruised from beating against the thick plated wall, but he was alive. Sparks flew as the main light above them shorted in and out, the live current hitting exposed wires that now hung above their heads.

"Everyone OK?" Michaels asked with true concern, although most of his focus was in Sarah's direction.

The Captain feared the worst as not a single person responded. Maybe he hadn't spoken loud enough for his voice to overpower the sounds of electric showers and hemorrhaging pipes.

"IS EVERYONE OK?" Adam repeated loudly, strong enough to be heard several rooms over.

"Hell no I'm not! You saw the crate shatter to pieces, all my scratch gone in a matter of seconds!" Dalton replied, prompting laughter and relief from the rest of the crew, putting the Captain's worries to ease.

As the crew slowly found its way through the complete darkness to the cargo hold doors, Michaels and Kelly made their way through the mangled corridors which were littered with scattered debris, heading for the bridge to congratulate Luck on a job well done.

The first one out was Dalton, solid black riot style shotgun in front of him, he slowly made his way down the ramp, which was slightly bent into an angle. Dalton, of course, still steaming over his forced alcoholism intervention.

While it wasn't worth a plummet to the surface at blazing speeds in the face of impending death, the scenery wasn't hard on the eyes in the least. Vibrant green grass swaying with a slow wind as they sat in a huge field surrounded by small hills and a distant tree line. It looked almost like a destination for someone in search of a getaway, rather than a spot picked at the last minute for a crash landing.

Dalton stepped from the ramp onto the welcoming soil, which gave way under his boots, moist from a recent rain as he began panning his weapon around slowly. The next person down was Roman, walking a bit more calmly with a tight grip on a large combat rifle, he immediately made way to the rear of the ship to try and assess the damage. Seeing a large trench dug behind the ship, dragging out for several hundred feet from the recent impact of the crash.

Sarah and Troy, obviously shaken up quite a bit, stepped onto the ground and remained close behind Dalton as he continued to thoroughly evaluate the landscape. Kato exited the ship slowly, holding a small pistol by his side and walking slowly toward the group as the Captain was right behind him.

Adam's first thought was of the sun hammering its rays down onto the ship, the slight wind blowing just enough to keep the otherwise intense heat at bay. They could have landed in much worse conditions, leaving him not only thankful for their new lease on life, but a second chance to tell Sarah exactly what was on his heart. All of it would have to wait for the time, however, as he faced the daunting task of giving the shell shocked crew even more bad news; walking down the ramp with a heaviness of heart to face his crew.

"Luck?" Kato asked as Michaels approached them solemnly.

Answering with only a regretful head shake, it quickly hit everyone that the android pilot, the hero who had saved them from a certain death, had himself perished in the crash. Moments later Kelly walked down the ramp, crying just a bit; not really knowing how to react to the demise of a synthetic human being.

"Now what?" Dalton asked as he strategically placed a large cigar in his mouth, nearly the length of a human hand as he sealed the deal with what could have passed as a miniature torch.

Giving him a scowl, Kelly walked to the rear of the ship with Roman, Dalton looked into the direction of Michaels with a puzzled look on his face before shrugging it off.

"Good question." Adam replied a couple of minutes later, looking at the nearby surroundings in the vicinity of the heavily damaged ship.

He honestly didn't know what move to make his next. Even if they could somehow find a way off of this rock, they were wanted by pretty much anything in the Skyla System that was attached to a heartbeat. The Legion wanted them locked up, especially after the assault that Roman had played such a vital role in. If they were lucky enough to avoid the legitimate authorities, the important people of the underground world surely wanted their heads on platters, and Adam was pretty sure there was a decent sized bounty attesting to the fact; meaning they would eventually have to deal with contract killers and mercenaries along the way. None of it mattered right now though, because from the looks of it, the ship was in no condition to fly; even if they somehow managed to repair it.

"I'll put Luck to rest, he may have been artificial but he deserves at least that much for saving everyone's life. You get with Roman, gear up heavy and scout the area, Kato and Kelly can look the ship over and assess the damage, see how long we are going to be stuck here." Michaels said, finally giving Dalton a definitive answer.

"What about Sarah and the boy?" Dalton asked as he started checking the weapons he had with him.

"They'll stay close to the ship, should be safest for them that way." Adam replied as he began to head inside to collect the body of someone very important to him.

No matter how ridiculous it sounded, Luck had become what the Captain considered to be part of the family, he would truly be missed.

Dalton and Roman were geared up and ready to move, waiting for the sunset to begin before heading out to survey the area. It was Roman's suggestion to travel at night, it would be a bit harder to move around, but the shroud of darkness would provide additional cover for the two man team in the event that there was life on the planet. Even worse, if they had been tracked by Hunters, they would need every advantage possible in order to try and even the playing field a bit.

Dalton was going heavy of course, with a large assault rifle, standard combat pistol and one of the oldest pump shotguns that Roman had ever seen. The majority of the gun was comprised of a faded blue steel, showing signs of significant use throughout the years. Mounted to a thick wooden stock that was marred with scars of abuse and age; it reminded Roman of something seen in a museum. Of course, he could respect the fact that Dalton knew his iron, so he had no doubt that it would follow through with the task of keeping the peace when called into question.

Although no bottle or flask was visible, Roman suspected Dalton had one somewhere in those faded brown pants of his. Most of his stash had just been disposed of in the most unthinkable of ways, so it was very possible that he simply had began to ration what remained of the alcohol.

As for Roman, he carried a standard issue combat pistol as well as a rugged military grade knife. Most of his gear consisted of rations, binoculars, a chart machine used for surveying and graphing a map of the area and a large com unit that could reach the ship from several clicks away. Michaels had insisted that they stay in contact, just in case they had indeed been followed. It was very unlikely, however, as the Captain made his living by walking with caution and today was certainly no different.

The two men headed out, wading through the tall grass as Dalton took intensely deep puffs from a cigar, the red embers of the burning end glowing in the darkened surroundings as Dalton glanced back to smile at everyone for a moment as if a parade had been assembled in his honor. Roman had left Troy with a snub nosed pistol and the very important task of protecting the crew. The weapon wasn't hot of course, Roman had removed all of the ammunition from it long before turning it over to the boy, still it gave the young man something positive to focus on and that's how Roman had gotten himself through the toughest of times.

As Michaels finished covering the grave of his high stakes poker winning turned close friend, Sarah and Troy approached him slowly, trying not to disturb him during a tough time in his life.

"I'm sorry about your friend." Sarah said apologetically as they sat on a decent sized rock near the Captain.

"Thanks. Truth is, I cheated my ass off the night I won him you know?" Adam replied, trying to lighten the spirits of the boy, while impressing the girl that he had so quickly fallen for.

They continued to talk for a while, Michaels showing Troy his method of holding a pistol as Dalton and Roman disappeared from sight, beginning to hit rocky terrain littered with thick brush and small patches of lush trees.

The two men moved quietly as they made their way to a high peak not far from the crash site, the only noise was an occasional curse word ejected from the lips of a painfully sober Dalton. Obviously high ground would save them a long road ahead if they saw anything of interest. Dalton sat down out of breath on a fallen tree trunk as Roman glared through the his set of binoculars, panning carefully as not to miss any details as the digital readouts of the eyepiece showed distance and altitude.

"Anything interesting?" Dalton asked, as he complained through body movements of the short walk they had already taken in, obvious after effects of his motivated smoking habit.

"Nothing," Roman replied as he attached the set of

lenses to the sketch unit, allowing it to print out the land they had already covered. "Not a damn thing." he added.

As the men continued on, down the slope and toward the next decent sized tree line, a slight rain began to fall that quickly turned into an unrelenting downpour.

"Damn, should have just let them arrest us back at Paulie's and been done with it." Dalton said as both me started laughing out loud, cold rain hitting them briskly in the face as they pushed forward.

Finally, they found a thick enough section of trees to shield them from a good bit of the rain, still it had taken its toll on the men; clothes soaked and the feel of filth all over them. Dalton kept his stash of cigars tightly wrapped in a thick brown cloth and tucked away in his supply sack along with God knows what else.

Taking shelter under a huge overhanging slate rock, they decided it was time to make camp for a bit and start back at first light. Dalton offered to take watch first, looking above and quickly painting the stars across what sky could be seen through the thick clouds overhead. Roman had heard enough complaining as it was, however, and didn't want to add legitimacy to it; taking first watch so Dalton could get himself a little shut eye.

Quickly taking up the offer, Dalton climbed into the stained green sleeping bag and rolled onto his side, shutting his eyes and within seconds drifting off into a dreamworld that was sure to include alcohol, women and an endless supply of guns and ammunition. Meanwhile, Roman sat solidly with his back against the rock and a battle rifle casually in the elbow sections of his arms, resting himself while indeed ready for anything.

"Captain." Kato said as he approached Michaels, who himself was pulling watch back at the crash site. Sitting at the top of the damaged cargo ramp, Adam was armed only with a solid black military issue pistol and a miniature set of binoculars, keeping watch on the tall grass around them while most of the crew slept.

"What is it?" Michaels asked quietly as Kato walked over, standing next to the Captain's position.

"One of the thrusters is completely gone, from the looks of it, we took gunfire on the way out of Tameca." Kato said regretfully.

"Fixable?" the Captain asked with glaring hope.

"It gets worse sir," Kato replied, pausing before sharing the bad news with the man in charge. "The gunfire hit our main fuel line as well, been leaking it out since we took off, good thing we landed when we did, otherwise we'd be stuck in orbit with no fuel to speak of." he added.

"So we look for some kind of fuel source, patch it enough to get into orbit and then send a distress signal. On the run or not, sounds like our only option at this point." Michaels answered, prepared for the worst.

"It gets worse." Kato said apologetically as the Captain shook his head for a moment, replying "How much worse can it possibly get?"

"Even if we found a fuel source, which is unlikely at best, four of the seven battery rods were damaged beyond repair. We got enough juice for systems check, possibly heat or emergency lighting if we needed it, but nowhere near enough to launch into orbit," Kato added as Michaels continued to shake his head. "Truth is Adam, we look to be here for a very long while." Kato said as he slowly turned and walked off to make his way back into the Gunship, trying his best not to wake the rest of the crew in the process.

Michaels continued to sit on watch, skimming the area with his eyes in the darkness and cursing the moment that Dalton's stash had crashed into a flood of waste. He could damn sure use a drink himself right about now. Stuck on an uncharted planet, next to no chance of them fixing the ship well enough to get off of the ground and being marked men throughout the entire Skyla System. Adam was definitely in the mood for some hard drink, something to to alleviate his mind of problems, if only temporarily.

Roman had settled in and slept for nearly two hours, when Dalton once again dozed off while pulling his shift of watch. It was almost daybreak, the idea was to get a few extra winks in before they were up and at it again, a full day's walk in front of them. Normally, he was a deep sleeper, nobody had ever come close to accusing him otherwise.

It was the sound of a small branch being pushed into the ground softly that did the trick, Dalton immediately spinning around with his shotgun, eyes wide open and looking into a thin, dark complected man who was obviously scared and appeared to be unarmed. Throwing his hands into the air, they had almost extended fully by the time Roman was on his feet and quickly approaching Dalton.

"Enough. Can't you see he's scared shitless?" Roman said of the trembling man as he pushed the barrel of Dalton's shotgun to the ground, making sure it didn't accidentally discharge into the direction of the native stranger.

"We mean you no harm stranger. My friend and I, we are having some difficulties with our ship; just looking for anything or anyone to possibly help us get back into space." Roman said as the stranger continued to look at the barrel of Dalton's so called peacemaker.

Roman grabbed the weapon from Dalton's clutches and threw it onto the ground, holding his hands up slightly to show the strange local that they truly meant him no harm.

"The name's Roman, this is my friend Dalton." After several moments of silence, the stranger finally spoke.

"My name is Aira." he said, his language broken at best as he remained very skeptical of the two men's intentions.

"Alright Aira. No way you could survive out here dressed like that," Roman said, referring to his thin white shirt that had been poorly stitched and makeshift pants of sack cloth. "Means you must have a camp nearby, can you take us there?" Roman added in a friendly tone.

"My village is not that far from here. Yes, I can take you there." Aira replied a bit more calmly.

"We would appreciate that." Roman answered as Dalton had picked his shotgun up and was wiping the dirt from its stock.

"Actually, I would appreciate not having such a fine weapon thrown to the damn ground like a piece of trash," Dalton added as he wiped the dirt from its well worn handle and holstered his weapon once again under his thick leather belt. "Besides, from the looks of him, I doubt they will be of any use." he added.

"Maybe not, but even the most primitive of races stockpile what they consider to the be the best of drink." Roman said convincingly.

"Lead the way friend." Dalton replied, speaking to Aira as if they were long time friends.

The two men quickly disposed of what had been a campsite through the night and began following Aira to the place he considered home.

As Captain Michaels started to awaken, he was hit with the overwhelming smell of a cooked meal. Easy to distinguish when you become used to eating rations from airtight silver packages three times a day. He wasn't sure what was being cooked at the moment, but it smelled like heaven and that was easily good enough for him. Standing to his feet, he took a moment to try and work a few kinks out of his body from the past several hours spent sleeping on the very unforgiving ground, and then glanced over in Kato's direction.

"What's going on? What am I smelling?" he asked, knowing Kato would have the answers having taken over watch in the middle of the night.

"Sarah's cooking. Found some rations that she said would taste a bit better cooked over a flame, so she's been working on it for the past hour now." Kato replied as Michaels walked into his direction, trying his best to fan the wrinkles out of his clothes by hand.

"Sure in the hell smells a bit better." Adam said, both men chuckling for a moment before he glanced around the corner of the ship to see Sarah doing her best to prepare a decent meal for the crew.

As the crew ate the thinly sliced and perfectly cooked meat, Adam continued to make strong eye contact with Sarah, the woman who had in may ways given him new reason to continue living.

"Captain, it's Roman." Kato said, handing Adam a portable com unit with one hand while holding a fork full of the tender meat in the other.

"This is Michaels, go ahead." the Captain said; trying his best to cover up the joy of the current meal in his voice.

"We have made contact with some natives here, several hours from your position. Will be speaking with more of them shortly, how are things on your end?" Roman voice asked through the crackle of the com speaker.

"Well, we are making it alright. No home cooked meals, but we'll manage," Adam replied, prompting the entire crew to laugh out loud. "Any chance the natives have replacement parts or fuel to trade?" Adam asked.

"Doubtful, the scouts are using sharpened sticks as weapons." Roman replied.

"Outstanding," Michaels replied in a sarcastic tone, taking a few moments to glance around at the rest of the crew. "Find out everything you can. Kato and Kelly have been working with the Rover, it's a little beat up but we should be able to use it if need be. At least until the fuel runs dry." Adam added as he laid the com unit down on a nearby piece of scrap metal.

"Will do." Roman replied as the steady crackling of the com went to silence.

As Aira led Roman and Dalton into the front of the

camp, several of the villagers ran indoors, watching the group pass by as they made their way to one of the larger huts. Made of scrap wood, bales of grass and mud, it didn't like a place that anyone should even consider living in.

"Who knows, The Dusk looks like shit too but they had great liquor." Dalton said grinning as Roman just responded with a slight shaking of his head.

Meeting someone in charge was never a pleasant experience, that is unless you were the one with the weapons, in which case it couldn't be matched. As Roman and Dalton entered the hut with Aira, they were face to face with an older gentleman, he wore many different necklaces made of shiny rocks and beads which gave them the indication of him being a very important man among the tribe.

"Welcome friends, I am Ceria," the older man said warmly, welcoming them to sit down on mounds of grass that had been formed to serve as chairs. "Please forgive my people, they are no doubt afraid to see strange faces among them." he added, as he too sat with Roman and Dalton.

"Where are all of the men?" Roman asked directly.

"And alcohol. Where is the drink?" Dalton asked, stringing his question onto the rear of Roman's.

"Of course," Ceria said as he began pouring a green liquid into rough looking cups that were no more that hollowed out stones. "The men are gone, most of them at least." Ceria said as he handed Dalton a cup of the local favorite.

"Out in hunting parties? I saw only women and children as we walked through the village." Roman responded, wanting to know every detail that he possibly could.

"No hunting parties," Ceria said, lowering his head in silence. After a few moments, he looked at the men and explained a ship coming every thirty moons or so, a handful of well armed creatures taking the men aboard, never to be heard from again.

"That is what my scout had first mistaken you for, but your friend's gun didn't look anything like that of the beast men." Aria added to the conversation.

"What the hell is wrong with the way my gun looks?" Dalton asked as he began turning his cup up and stopping abruptly. "This is some strong shit! What do you mean beast men?" he added, gasping for air as a side effect of the hardened home brew.

"They never say anything, they only force men onto the ship, knowing well that we have no means of protection against them. Those who have tried to fight back have been slaughtered on the spot," Ceria replied. "They walk as men do, but they are not men. Nearly two feet taller than any of us; brown tinted skin stretched across them as that of an onion, dark hair growing from them in thickets." Ceria added with remorse, thinking of all of the men who had departed against their will.

"This ship, how large is it? Are there any markings on it that may identify the creatures." Roman asked sternly.

"Twice the size of this very hut maybe." Ceria answered, as he drew a marking into the dirt floor of the hut, a large teardrop shape with a smaller shape inside of it.

"Don't like anything I've ever ran across." Dalton said, sipping his drink like a baby from its bottle.

"Husks." Roman replied in a grave tone.

"Husks? No worse than the Hunters that are no doubt combing the star system for us at this very moment." Dalton replied.

"Much worse. When Hunters have nightmares, they are usually dreaming of Husks. I've only ran into two of them in this lifetime, during my years with the Gali military." Roman replied, his eyes locked on Ceria.

"Well, you're here with us. You obviously killed both of the sons of bitches, so the crew should be able to handle three or four." Dalton said as he sat his cup down, not daring to ask for a refill of the strongest drink he had ever consumed.

"I ran," Roman replied, gaining an immediate look of disbelief from Dalton. "I put five slugs of a pistol directly into the chest of one, it only brought him to a knee. No way in hell I could have dusted two of them," Roman added, before switching his attention toward Ceria. "They usually have a handler with them, a human?" he asked.

"Yes, that is correct. Usually two of the beast men and a human bearing a rifle." Ceria replied.

"The difference between Hunters and Husks, other than the obvious mismatch, is that Hunters kill because they enjoy watching humans die. Husks do everything for the money. Mercenaries you could say, the handler is usually nothing more than the highest bidder at the time. My guess is they are pulling men from this village for off world slave trade." Roman said as Dalton remained sitting with a puzzled look on his face.

"You ran?" Dalton asked in disbelief.

"It's the one and only time I've ever ran from a fight. Believe me, I've regretted it every day since then." Roman replied as he stood to his feet and approached the door of the hut.

"Care for more?" Ceria asked of Dalton, ready to refill his cup. "No, I'm good." Dalton replied, wondering if he had ever muttered those words before.

As the next few minutes passed, Roman explained through the com system to Captain Michaels about the Husk and it was decided that Adam, Sarah and Troy would load the rover with weapons and supplies and meet up with the others, leaving Kelly and Kato to get the ship in the best condition possible. The villagers weren't expecting a visit from the beast menace for at least another ten days, giving Adam plenty of time to come up with something, anything that got them off of this piece of rock and back into the star system.

"If we could just send a hail through the com to my father, he wouldn't hesitate to send a rescue ship to our position." Sarah said as they traveled to the village, the bumpy terrain of the road that was no more than a path beaten by feet, throwing them back and forth inside of the industrial grade cockpit.

"The Gunship's com is barely functional, short range for the moment but no way is it capable of reaching off world. Besides, even if we could, as soon as the hail went out everyone with an open com would pick it up. Hunters, Legion, Mercenaries, hell even some of the higher end card clubs."

"What about the com unit of the ship that has the village so afraid?" Sarah asked.

"Doubtful. We'd have to somehow overpower the Husk to use their ship," Michaels replied, glancing in her direction for a moment as Troy seemed nothing short of amazed by all of the controls inside of the rover. "Not that I would ever back down from a fight, I just don't see the logic in starting one that we have no chance of winning." he added in an attempt to save face in front of the one woman that made his heart thump dramatically faster.

"We take them out, hijack their ship and use its com to hail Sarah's father, see if he could lend us assistance." Captain Michaels said as he sat inside one of the huts, huddled in the floor beside Dalton, Roman, Sarah and Ceria.

"I thought that wouldn't work?" Sarah asked, blindsided by Adam's change of plans.

"Yea. You know I love a fight Captain, but if they are anything close to what Roman says, we'd be in for one hell of a thrashing." Dalton added as he regretfully sipped on more of the local drink.

"It's the only option we have, I've put my head around it a hundred times during the trip from the cash site. Take out the Husk or die on this planet, and personally I'd rather die fighting." Adam responded confidently.

"Even if we did manage to take down the Husk crew,

wouldn't a hail bring the authorities right down on us? Not to mention the Hunters, or hell for that matter more Husk?" Dalton asked.

"Yea, it would. We'd have to pray that Sarah's father got to us first, and be prepared to hold like hell if he didn't." Adam replied, looking in Sarah's direction long enough to see a her smile, every inch of her face glowing with radiance as she realized the Captain had placed his faith in her.

"Sarah, you'd have to be damn sure that your father sends enough of an escort to get us out of here safely, good chance they would hit some stiff enemies on the way back off planet." Adam said very seriously.

"Trust me, the Legion may have us outnumbered in the ranks, but knowing my father, he'll come with more than enough soldiers to get us back safely." Sarah replied with confidence.

"Husk wouldn't expect to find anyone here other than the usual villagers, the advantage of surprise would definitely be in our favor," Roman added to the conversation. "Not to mention, I've got a score to settle with 'em, it's personal for me." he added.

"Well, we got plenty of weapons, the element of surprise and about nine or ten days to prepare for a fight. That should even the odds just a bit." Michaels added, making the plan official.

"Well, I still don't like it, but if there's going to be a fight then you can damn sure count me in." Dalton added, already in a fight against the cup of local drink that he had been so eager to get his hands on.

As everyone started to exit the hut, Sarah stopped Adam, holding him behind long enough to ensure they would be the last people to leave.

"Captain, why the change of heart?" she asked cautiously.

As he stood there, possible reasons raced through mind. What should he tell her? What had truly changed his mind about meeting certain death head on? Was it his growing love for her, had it clouded his judgment? Finally, breaking several seconds of silence he decided to answer her from deep within his heart.

"It would be easy to lay low, but the truth is I've been doing just that for too long now, taking the easiest roads along the way. These people can't fight them off, hell I don't even know if we can fight them off, but if it's my time to go then I'd at least like to die for something I think is right, and for those I love," he said, staring right into her eyes as the words landed on both her heavy heart and confused mind. "I guess I'm choosing my side." he added, earning a huge smile from her radiant face.

"I'm not afraid of dying, I'm afraid of living past this. Getting back to the system, only to have to sit and watch you walk out of my life. Having to see you walk away for good, that's what I'm afraid of." Michaels said, waiting on some kind of response from Sarah, one that would never come as she emotionally turned and walked outside to rejoin the crew and villagers without so much as a word.

Although he wasn't ashamed of his feelings for her, Adam waited several minutes before walking outside himself, trying to give her plenty of time to leave the immediate area. He wasn't sure how she had taken his confession and didn't want to make things any worse than they possibly were at the moment. How could he have been so stupid!

He had overplayed his hand? Much like he had a habit of doing in a game of cards, except this was far more important to him than any game of chance. This was life, his life, and a life that he couldn't bear to even think of living without Sarah.

Once outside, the Captain was met by Dalton and Roman as they began pointing out the best spots for an ambush and putting together the intricate details of the plan. Adam heard their words, but every one spoken fell on deaf ears as his mind was preoccupied with his love for

Sarah as he continued glancing over his shoulder; trying his best to locate his one true love and wondering how she had taken his earlier comments.

That evening as the sunset began to take form, everyone in the village would gather to eat a large meal, although basic, it appealed greatly to a crew that had eaten only rations for the last several days. Of course, some of them had been fortunate enough to enjoy Sarah's fine cooking, though they had been sworn to secrecy by the Captain as if the incident had never taken place. They had a solid plan when it came to fighting the Husk, which seemed strange to Adam. They could organize an assault on one of the deadliest species known to man, yet he couldn't explain his heart to Sarah without falling to pieces.

He only hoped that she would join them for dinner, it would give him some kind of idea as to the extent of damage his words had done to her. He couldn't control his feelings, his heart wanted what his heart wanted; but deep down he knew that a relationship between them could never survive.

He was nothing more than a smuggler who had no real future to speak of, even if Sarah felt the same way about him society would never allow them to be together. Her father, one of the top military figures for the newly formed Colonial Army would never allow his daughter to fall into the arms of a man with such a history of criminal activity.

As they sat and enjoyed dinner with the rest of the village, Adam remained focused on the empty chair that should have been filled by Sarah's overwhelming beauty. The biggest benefit of the crew spending time with the people of the village was to Troy, making friends with many of the natives who were not much younger than himself, giving Troy a sense of childhood for the moment without the worries or stress that came along with being alone.

Roman continued to spend time with the young man, however most of the crew had noticed a different side of Adam's newest hired gun, almost a sense of urgency on his part as if to think that he would surely fall to the Husk.

After dinner and a formal thank you to the villagers who had prepared it, Adam casually left the group, doing everything he could to find Sarah. If he was lucky enough to speak with her, honestly, he had no idea what he even planned to say. Apologize for the way he felt, maybe, although it was nothing that he had planned or could have avoided. On the other hand, maybe he would just reinforce his feelings to her as well as apologize for the inconvenient position that she had been unwillingly thrust into. One way or another, he had to do something. His heart and mind were too clouded to possibly stave off an assault by the Husk, he had to make things right.

There she was. As he entered one of the smaller huts, Sarah sat at a small table, the room barely lit by the flicker of a makeshift candle. Obviously deep in thought, Adam apologized for the intrusion and began to leave as Sarah stood to her feet, approaching him slowly; her warm hand soothing his tense shoulder with its touch.

They kissed deeply, with true passion and undeniable love. Even though it would surely have major repercussions if they were lucky enough to make it back to the system, at least for the moment Adam felt completely at peace. He tried his best to collect himself before responding to a few seconds in time that had truly changed his life forever.

"I know in my heart that when we return to charted space, the standards of society will eventually pull you back out of my life. All I ask for is this moment, to finally know true love, no matter how short it may last." he managed to say, forcing every word out as his heart continued to tremble.

"Shhhh." Sarah said softly as she held a couple of her

fingers to his lips. "Neither of us have any idea what the future holds. All we can control is right now, and right now I want to be with you. My heart has been with you since the moment our eyes first met." she added as he pushed her fingers away, grabbed her into the clutches of his arms and kissed her as if his heart must be connected to hers in order to survive.

The rest of of the night, they held one another tightly, their souls embracing one another as the rest of the crew and village celebrated what everyone had hoped would be the eventual downfall of the reign of terror that the Husk had forced upon them.

The next morning saw most everyone sleeping in late, after effects of the previous night's festivities. Adam was already awake, having been up for some time, he sat comfortably inside the Rover; watching the thick moisture fall from the sky, the water droplets bursting onto the windshield of the cargo craft as he sipped from a small cup of makeshift coffee.

Most of his morning had been spent in deep thought, what a new life with Sarah at his side would mean for everyone in the unlikely event that his plan actually worked for a change. There had also been a few Dalton sightings throughout the night, staggering around drinking from a large glass bottle, relieving his bladder under the night sky and even one instance where both events took place simultaneously.

The calm feeling throughout the village came crashing down quickly as a loud noise popped nearby in the air, causing the Captain to spill what remained of his coffee; startling him and no doubt pulling everyone else from a deep and restful sleep.

Adam immediately recognized the sound as he jumped from the confines of the Rover and raced to the bulk of the village in the pouring gray rain, looking straight into the sky, confirming the arrival of the Husk.

"Shit! How long?" Adam yelled into the direction of

Ceria as Roman and Dalton feverishly placed loaded weapons onto themselves as they tried to awaken.

"They will land in a field not far past the tree line. Five minutes, maybe less before they are here." Ceria replied sleepily as Adam double checked his pistol, ensuring that it was full of ammunition and combat ready.

"Sarah, stay inside! Keep Troy with you, if things don't go well, stay out of sight until they are gone and rejoin Kelly and Kato at the crash site." Adam said loudly, glancing through the shower of water into a nearby hut. Without responding, she began to cry fluidly as she grabbed Troy into her arms, holding him tightly in the corner of the primitive dwelling. "Sarah!" Adam said once more in a stern tone, making sure she understood her responsibility in case the worst were to happen.

"Yes." she managed to mutter, crying heavily which prompted Troy to become upset, sharing a few tears of his own.

"I will do everything I can to keep you both safe. Everything." Adam said convincingly as he stared into her eyes for a few moments; their hearts sharing a moment of passion through nothing more than a glance of love, before once again being overtaken by the stinging drops of rain. The plan had been cut short, no time for them to bring the mauler to assist them. It was simply a matter of Adam, Roman and Dalton facing two of the Husk monsters and possibly a human handler. Not very good odds for them by any means, but when a man has nothing left to fight for but the beating heart inside of his chest, it makes for a dangerous man indeed. Michaels was gladly prepared to die if it meant keeping Sarah safe.

Dalton remained prone at the far end of the village, only his head and arms were outside of the camouflage surroundings of the forest that surrounded them, his hands gripped a large caliber sniper rifle and his right eye pressed against the scope of the weapon. Roman had disappeared from sight, they weren't sure what he was doing for the moment, but everyone knew that when the killing began he would be in the middle of it, one way or the other. The Captain had nothing more than the long barrel revolver currently at his side and two shotguns tucked into the back of his worn brown pants, giving him a second option if needed. He was surgical with the revolver and knew that if he were accurate enough with the weapon, he would give Sarah and Troy a chance of survival as he positioned himself across from them and watching over the love of his life as if he were a guardian angel.

"If we don't kill these bastards, good chance they will be pissed enough to murder everyone in the village." Dalton said through his com unit, broadcasting his thoughts to both Adam and Roman.

"Then we kill these bastards." Adam replied, tightening his grip on the butt of his pistol and waiting patiently for the beasts to appear on the horizon. Minutes that seemed like days passed; waiting for the inevitable as nerves started to overtake logic.

"We got a problem." Dalton said. Michaels started to ask, when he saw the three figures approaching the village through the curtain of rain.

"Three of them." Adam said frantically under his breath, spotting a three Husk group with no handler. The Captain heard more chatter over the com, although he couldn't make the words out; his body numb from the circumstances almost as if he were in a dream.

"Captain!" Dalton's voice finally rang out, forcing Adam back to reality and out of the helpless daze that he had succumb to. "Do we proceed with the plan?" Dalton added, waiting for a response from the man in charge.

"We have no choice." Adam forced painfully from his lungs, knowing almost with certainty that they had no chance of winning, the appearance of the walking beasts reassuring that with every step closer toward the village. The sheer size of them had Adam stunned, he had never seen such a build on anything living. Add the proficiency with weaponry and the faster than average movements of the relentless killers, he saw no way of winning the battle ahead.

As Dalton regained his composure, he began placing the scope of his rifle onto the head of one of the Husk. Waiting for an official OK from Adam, he continued to follow the beast with the telescopic lens of the high caliber weapon. "Say when Captain." Dalton said, anxious to begin the blood letting as he noticed one of the villagers stepping out into the direct path of the Husk soldiers, his head covered with the hood of the sackcloth shirt which was quickly darkening with color at the end of the soaking rain.

"What the hell," Dalton mumbled to himself, wondering which of the locals had a death wish; the Husks merely slowing down, also in disbelief that anyone would dare stand against them. Taking his eye from the scope momentarily, he turned his head slightly to get a good angle on the com unit. "Adam, are you seeing this?" Dalton asked.

Before an answer could follow, Roman removed the sackcloth hood, standing in the hammering rain as if to taunt the three much larger opponents, a rugged combat blade in each hand as the wind blew ripples throughout his shirt.

Two of the three Husks began to slowly run towards him, each with a leg length machete tightly gripped by the superhuman strength of the nearly tree sized arms of the beasts.

As they were on him, Adam stepped from the doorway he had been well concealed inside of, holding his revolver forward and strategically firing all six rounds from the rolling chamber; hitting the same Husk with all of the piercing steel slugs, four in his upper chest and two punishing the neck of the beast. Obviously crippling the soldier with what would have killed six normal men, it fell to the ground screaming in pain as it bled openly onto the climate drenched ground.

The second Husk quickly shifted its attention into the direction of the Captain, who tossed the sidearm to the ground, reaching behind his back and pulling two short barrel shotguns from the back of his belt. Without thinking, his instinct pushed him to fire both weapons, one slug hitting the Husk in the chest and the second nearly missing, only grazing its arm slightly; sending a small cloud of skin and patched hair into the rain. Running through the pain of the recent chest wound, the beast leaped towards Captain Michaels in an attempt to kill him on impact.

Its jawbone and a majority of its chin were wiped clean from its face by a single shot of Dalton's long range killing machine. The bolt action gun spitting an empty shell from its top, and falling hollowly to the ground. Dalton quickly began trying to scope the third Husk up as it went into full sprint in the direction of the two downed warriors. He anxiously fired a round that normally would have hit, however the Husk moved much faster than a normal man as the shot missed, firing wide right of the creature which had reached the other members of the crew.

Striking Michaels with maddening rage, the beast sent the Captain flying onto the ground several feet away from him, sliding across the puddled ground. Adam immediately tried getting back to his feet only to fall back to the ground, simply dazed from the impact only moments ago. Roman thrust one of his blades into the direction of the Husk, who's raw strength knocked the combat steel from his hand, grabbing Roman with his free hand into a choking position.

"Fuck!" Dalton said loudly as he had another shell in the chamber, but couldn't get a decent shot in the scope because of the choke, which was slowly bleeding the life from Roman's limp body.

As he began to stop trying to fight back and had

accepted his demise, Roman dropped the other blade to the ground as his arms hung straight down by his sides, the Husk yelling loudly as he applied even more anger into the hold, trying to punish his victim brutally. Roman slid to the ground, falling face first into the mud as the monster suddenly let go of his grip of death. Spinning around, he threw his hand out and placed it around the fragile throat of Troy, who had escaped Sarah's clutches long enough to try and save his mentor by stabbing a blade into the back of the Husk.

As he squeezed firmly around the child's neck feeling small bones breaking as Troy grasped for air, a shot from Dalton's weapon zipped through the air and pierced the chest area of the beast, who immediately threw the young man who was fighting for his life to the ground. Adam stumbled to his feet, his first thought switched from killing the Husk to running to the aid of Troy, who was obviously in life or death condition. As the Husk looked down, realizing the shot had struck no vital organs, it yelled in rage as both of its friends lay dead on the crimson soaked ground beneath him.

During the enraged scream, several of its teeth were jolted from their sockets from a hard right hand thrown by Roman, who had lost his usual ice cold swagger and let emotion take control of his moves as he followed with several more punishing hands to the face of the beast. Not used to the defensive side of battle, the Husk could do very little to block the flurry of commanding fists flying in his direction. Letting a loud and tearful yell of his own out, Roman threw a punch that quickly turned into a cupped hand as it penetrated the throat of the monster, ripping several throat organs out in the process. The monster fell to its knees, slowly dying from the wounds as Roman kicked it in the chest firmly, pushing it onto its back in a large puddle of water. Roman fell to a knee, obviously in pain, slowly making his way back to his feet in an effort to check on Troy as did Dalton, who was sprinting to the child's location.

"Impressive. Stupid, but impressive." the crew heard from behind them as the Husks handler stood with a large automatic pistol pointed in the direction of the group.

Three sharp shots later, he lay face down in the rain, Sarah Blaine standing behind him holding an assault rifle that had been kept in the Rover.

"No sir, that's impressive." Adam said, giving a long look of thanks to the woman who had indeed saved his life at this very moment.

"How bad off is he?" Sarah asked, sprinting over to check on the seriously injured youth.

Dalton looked up at her with the most serious look she had ever seen him carry. "It's bad." he replied, immediately looking back down to help aid in any way possible. The next few minutes played out as if they were but a faint memory that had been faded with time, Michaels rushing Sarah to the spacecraft of the Husk; boosting the signal as much as possible before sending a message to her father of their position and condition. It was a long shot that he would even receive the distress call, however there was no time to properly prep the ship and hit orbit. They had to hope and pray that the long range com unit would do it.

As they returned to the nearby village, Dalton and Roman had assisted some of the locals in making Troy the best possible recovering setting possible inside one of the huts, placing him on a soft stack of grass and trying everything to keep fluids in the young man.

"We have to go. Now. Otherwise, the boy isn't going to make it." Roman said in a grave tone, passing the Captain and his newly found love.

"Can't do it. Help is one the way and we have to be here when they arrive." Michaels replied as several feet of heavy rainfall distanced the men.

"I wasn't asking permission, I was letting you know

that I'm going to prep the ship for takeoff." Roman replied.

"That's not going to happen Roman, don't press the issue." Adam said, hoping the former special forces soldier would come to his senses.

"I won't let him die Adam, don't try and stop me." Roman said firmly, turning to walk in the direction of the vessel.

"ROMAN! We WILL wait on help to arrive, that is a direct order!" the Captain said, pulling his revolver and aiming it at the hardened warrior. Stopping in his tracks, Roman turned to face Adam; both men giving impenetrable stares.

"I'm through taking orders from you. What? You plan to shoot me?" Roman said, walking closer to Michaels until reaching the end of the revolver barrel.

"I don't want to, but I will and I think we both know it," Adam replied, pulling the hammer back on the weapon, setting it ready to fire with just the slightest pressure. "You are a member of this crew until we're back in the system. That said, you WILL obey my direct order." the Captain added, calling Roman's bluff.

"The boy dies, and I'll kill you and anyone else who tries to stop me." Roman finally replied, walking past both the Captain and Sarah who continued to stand there for several minutes, finally returning to Troy's side.

"He ain't fucking around Adam." Dalton said, staring out of the small hut window as Roman sat on a large stone directly in the path of the relentless rainfall, a strong grip on his combat sidearm.

"Neither am I," Adam replied, giving Dalton a look to reassure him of that fact. "I don't want anything to happen to Troy any more than he does, but I'll be damned if I put the rest of my crew in danger to fly back into the system for a single person." Adam added.

The next few days were a mixed bag as Troy continued

to fight for his mortality, Roman kept to himself, only leaving the confines of his hut to sit by the boy's side; Kelly and Kato made a list of everything they needed to get the Gunship back into the sky and the rest of the crew stayed right by the side of Troy the moment Roman left it.

The crew, they all were heroes to the people who lived in this village on what could be considered one of the more primitive planets in the star system, or even uncharted space for that matter. They all knew that eventually Adam and his crew would be leaving by sky, to visit other planets that were much more civilized than this one; still, they made every effort to show their thanks to the heroes of the Gunship.

Every night filled with immaculate dinners and only the best lodging available, which wasn't much, but it was a gesture of gratitude that the crew wouldn't soon forget.

"Quick Captain, come quick!" one of the village natives yelled as he burst into Adam's sleeping quarters, which was nothing more than a back area of one of the larger huts.

As he jumped to his feet, revolver swiftly in his right hand, he could see the native pointing to the sky. "Quick, come!" he restated as he rushed back outdoors. As Adam stepped outside, he immediately recognized the sound of the sonic booms caused by several ships hitting the planet's upper atmosphere.

Within seconds, the sky was littered with military jets flying overhead, no doubt doing scans of the ground below as Dalton broke a red flare across his upper thigh and threw it to the ground. The markings on the ships as they flew overhead were unmistakable. They were the Allied Colonial Forces, Sarah's father had arrived.

As the ships broke into formation and began doing defensive flyovers, several heavily armored space to surface choppers began a descent, followed by a solid chrome shuttle. The choppers landed with a compelling thump as dozens of tactical soldiers, much like that of

Roman's former employer, began doing security sweeps of the village and surrounding areas. As the shuttle touched down,

Sarah sprinted to reunite with her father, who had exited and was waiting with open arms. He was a tall, well dressed man who obviously had the respect of his men. His white hair and peppered beard were indications that he had plenty of experience, and to the crew's delight, he had indeed brought a lot of firepower with him.

Rather than introduce himself to her father, Adam quickly explained Troy's condition and need of medical treatment, prompting a team to attend to the young man. Seeing the severity of his wounds, they escorted Troy to a nearby chopper, who was carried in the arms of Roman Raines.

"We picked up a small Legion fleet of ships approaching as we hit orbit. No doubt locked onto your distress call as well, may be a bit of a bumpy ride out." Commander Blaine said quickly to the crew as he hurried Sarah to his private shuttle. The remaining members of the crew, including the Captain, hopped aboard one of the choppers.

"Thank you for the drink my friend, we will return one day soon enough." Dalton said as he boarded, arms full of the local tonic of choice, doing his best to wave for a moment before the chopper door came to a close.

They had only been airborne a couple of minutes when everyone heard the first explosion. Moments later, it was followed by several more thundering booms as dozens of ships began firing tracer rounds. Adam was in a position to see out of one of the small windows of the crew area, and was simply in awe of the firepower that he lay witness to. Legion ships, three capital ships from what he counted, escorted by several smaller cruiser style ships. He only counted one capital ship bearing the Colonial marking, although there were wave after wave of ship to ship fighters that had launched from it.

He had known for a while that the star system was on the verge of a Civil War, however he had no intentions of being caught in the middle. He quickly realized, however, with the throaty sound of the ship's pounding cannons; that he was indeed witnessing the first acts of this inevitable clashing of the system's two powers.

As their chopper began docking to the Colonial capital ship, the entire crew could see that it had taken a brutal beating in an effort to rescue them. The docking area looked more like a make shift hospital as dozens of wounded were being pulled from Spartan star fighters as dozens more were suiting up to launch and try to replace the fallen. Soon after their craft had successfully landed and the rest were accounted for, a sequence of loud beeps rang throughout the ship. None of Adam's crew knew Colonial code, although it obviously seemed to be some type of general retreat order for the fleet, who began landing in the docking bay by the dozens.

It was only a few minutes after the loud screeches of military code that the capital ship began doing a full burn, all four of the huge thrust engines firing as the huge space fortress had soon put a great deal of distance between the fight and themselves.

"Father, this is Captain Adam Michaels. Adam, my father, Trevor Blaine." Sarah said nervously as she entered the heavily guarded bridge area of the ship along side her new found love.

"Captain, welcome aboard the Colonial Star Five," Commander Blaine said, firmly shaking Adam's hand for a moment before hugging his daughter with great joy. "We were able to bring your ship up from the surface before jumping away, my engineers are working on it for you as we speak." Blaine added, bringing a smile to Adam's face.

"That's great news. Thank you very much, for the rescue as well as the hospitality." Adam replied, much politer than usual.

"I'm afraid I do have some bad news. Our scout teams have reported that Legion forces have combed the uncharted planet. There is a good possibility that the native camp you were holding up in has been wiped out." Blaine said, reading from a paper report he held in his hands at the moment.

Michaels was taken back by the news, almost putting him in tears. "I don't understand that. They were of no threat to anyone. They had nothing to do with any kind of war, they were just innocent people; good people trying to survive." Michaels replied dramatically.

"I understand your frustration Captain. It's that very same reasoning that led to my taking a position with the Colonial Army. I will not fight under a flag who's military slaughters innocent human beings. The sole purpose of the Colonial Alliance is to put an end to the tyranny and death that the Legion uses to maintain its power," Blaine replied. "I must attend to repairs throughout the ship Captain, I apologize. However I would like to talk to you about this in much greater detail a bit later?" the commander asked.

"Of course. Again, thank you." Adam replied, ending the tense conversation with a quick handshake.

"What in the fuck is that?" Dalton said to Kelly as he lowered a shiny metal cup from his mouth in awe.

Neither of them had ever seen anything like it before. Standing nearly seven and a half feet tall, it was a soldier of some type, pure titanium exoskeleton with mechanical features intertwined with human bone underneath; its solid steel skull moving from side to side as the soldier patrolled that area.

"First time seeing a Goliath unit huh?" one of the Colonial engineers said, raising his head from the thruster of the Gunship that was undergoing repairs by himself as well as Kato. "They're a spectacle, no doubt about it. If you look closely at its right arm, you'll see that it's nothing more than a mini gun built around a titanium rod, damn things can fire up to five hundred armor piercing rounds per minute. That's enough to take down a small aircraft or a whole lot of anything on foot." the engineer added before turning back to continue working on repairs.

"Yea, a shit load." Dalton said in amazement as he took another long drink of his brew, unsuccessfully offering a sip to Kelly.

Roman sat in Troy's room patiently waiting for a miracle to happen.

He never really considered himself to be a religious person, although he had to wonder why any God would allow such a young child to lay here like this. Troy should be out doing things that normal children do, like playing games of chance or pulling pranks on one another. Yet here he was, no family, no home and very little chance of surviving. Maybe he felt guilty, the boy having help save his life only to find himself fighting for his own.

Maybe it was the need to be there for a young man who was doomed to the same kind of childhood he had thrown on him. Being homeless with no family and no means of survival was the biggest reason he had joined the Gali Army to begin with, or at least what he had claimed to be the Gali Army. When a person is faced with insurmountable odds like that, one of two things happens. Either you succumb to the odds that have been stacked against you, or you say fuck the odds and learn to take what you need. That was his attitude, and that's what made him such a dangerous person. Roman quickly stood to his feet as Troy's doctor entered the room.

"The plan is a simple one," Commander Blaine said as he looked throughout the crowd, which included Adam, Sarah and Dalton among many high ranking military officers and several dozen of the best soldiers that the Colonies had to offer. "A small team inserts near the heavily fortified compound currently being used as a staging area for the Legion, uses timed explosives to take out its major surface to air defense systems. We then hit them in force, crippling their ability to defend themselves, much less continue killing innocent civilians." he added, getting nods of encouragement from most of the room as well as a few loud chants of Colonial patriotism.

"Captain Adam Michaels will lead the first team, which will be comprised of highly trained Spec Ops soldiers as well as a handful of Husk loyalist warriors." the commander said, immediately taking the breath of his daughter Sarah.

"You can't!" she said in a low but frantic voice, having fallen in love with a man that would be walking into a hornet's nest of murderers.

"Someone has to show these bastards that they aren't the highest on the food chain, not anymore." Adam responded proudly.

"That someone would be me," Roman said as he entered the room, turning the head of everyone as he did so. "I'll go in his place." Roman added, approaching the commander.

"I appreciate the offer friend, however, this mission is for only the highest qualified of soldi, ." Commander Blaine had said, trying to reply as two of his personal escort soldiers approached Roman, holding him at the gunpoint of their battle rifles.

Pausing for a moment, clearly thinking of his next move, Roman struck one of the soldiers in the neck area, grabbing the rifle from his clutches as he fell to the ground. Before the second soldier had time to respond, Roman pulled two vital pins from the gun, disassembling it into three large pieces and using the stock that was no longer attached to the weapon, slicing the soldier across the face and rendering him defenseless.

Several more soldiers rushed into the room, weapons drawn and ready to kill if it meant protecting the commander.

"I'm the most qualified son of a bitch in this room. All I

know is killing, and I'm particularly fond of killing Hunters, which also makes me the most dangerous," Roman said, throwing the cluster of loose combat rifle parts onto the ground; showing Blaine that he had no intentions of harming him. "You just give me a weapon and tell everyone else to follow close behind and pick up as many of the body parts as they can; I'll kill every one of the bastards myself, and the weapon is optional." Roman added, having gotten the news that Troy would eventually recover to full health and feeling in the mood for revenge.

"I can see you are indeed qualified. Captain?" the commander said, asking permission before allowing Roman to go in his stead as armed soldiers continued to hold Roman at gunpoint.

Looking at Sarah for several tense moments, Adam once again focused his attention on the commander. "I owe this man a great deal. My life, an apology," Adam said, turning to Roman with an apologetic glance. "If it's his wish to go in my place, then all I ask is he kill as many Hunters as possible." Michaels added, smiling at the natural born killer.

Indeed, the plan was a solid one. From the personnel who would infiltrate the stronghold, to the weapons and tactics that would be used once they arrived and now the addition of Roman, whose hatred for Hunters nearly matched his skill in combat. A solid plan indeed. It would have to be, the Legion and its Hunter faithful were no pushovers. One of the more feared races in the charted star system, now with the backing of the Legion army as well as the news that Commander Blaine was about to unveil, the Hunters were even more of a solid opponent.

"We have confirmed through spies within the Legion Army that the Hunters have genetically developed a new breed of killer," Blaine said as the room quickly became deathly silent. "A super soldier if you will, matching many of the dimensions of our own Goliath units, the Hunters are calling this unit the Fang." The commander added as he pressed a couple of buttons on the podium that stood in front of him, displaying a series of photos onto the wall behind him with vivid detail.

"We are not exactly sure how many Fangs exist, only that they are currently being used as more of a tank, in terms of being accompanied by a small squad of Hunters. We believe there are not many of them yet, which is why it is imperative that we strike them now, before they have a chance to manufacture any more." Blaine added as he waited for a response from anyone in the crowd of gathered military brass and trained warriors.

"Hell, they don't look that tough to me!" Dalton proclaimed loudly, as the rest of the room grew loud in support of his statement. He had effectively bolstered the moral of the entire room, sadly, he would remember almost none of it as a side effect of his current drinking binge.

Helping both fallen soldiers to their feet, Roman glanced into the commander's direction with a look as serious as death itself. "Just give me a weapon, point me in the right direction and watch what happens." he said, slowly leaving the room to check on Troy before the upcoming battle of savages was to take place.

"He's recovering much faster than we anticipated. In due time the boy will be in perfect health." one of the Colonial doctors told Roman as they both stood outside of the ship's enormous infirmary, glancing through a reinforced window made of thick and frothy glass.

He had to recover quickly, it was a sign of his toughness. He would need plenty of that in the years to come, as life beat him down he would have to be tough enough to withstand the punishment and keep going. That was the way of things, the true mark of a warrior.

As Roman entered the room to see the young boy, he was amazed at how far he had come in the healing process, several of his neck vertebrae crushed, yet he sat up in his bed unassisted.

"Did I do good Roman?" Troy asked, wondering if his knife thrust into the Husk had met his teacher's approval. It was the first time in many years that Roman found himself fighting back tears. Eyes watering as he tried to dissipate his extreme anger against the Husk and his overwhelming feeling of joy, knowing Troy would survive something that he should have never even been involved with.

"Yes, you did good. Without your help, I wouldn't have made it. You saved all of us." Roman replied as he pulled up a chair beside the young man's bed.

He could see the happiness on Troy's face as he began to think of himself as an important part of the crew.

"Listen, I have to leave in a few hours to take care of some business. Some other people need that same kind of help. While I'm gone, I need you to look after the crew, can you do that?" Roman said, handing the boy a brand new combat knife he had collected from the ship's armory.

Seeing Troy's face light up, smiling from ear to ear as he eagerly snatched the blade; nearly was more than Roman could handle emotionally. To watch a young child go through losing his parents, nearly dying at the hands of some piece of shit mercenary and then be so enthusiastic about something as small as a blade. Roman held back, choosing instead to funnel his emotion into ending as many lives of the bastards who force children like Troy down this road, bastards like the Hunters.

Death, imprisonment, torture; none of these things concerned Roman any longer. He had become a monster, one that was hellbent on making the star system a better place to live, one slaying at a time.

After Troy had fallen asleep, Roman waited a few minutes to make sure the boy was comfortable before leaving the infirmary, passing Captain Michaels as made his way into the main hall of the ship.

"Troy alright?" Adam asked. Roman nodded his head, letting the Captain know that he was fine.

"Dunno if it was the alcohol talking or he has revenge on his mind, either way I just wanted you to know that Dalton pitched a fit on me, demanding to go with you and the rest of the first strike team." Michaels said. A few moments of silence passed, obviously due largely to the Captain having pulled a gun on Roman not so long ago.

"He's a hell of a shot, I'm sure there will be a few more Hunters laying dead if he's with us." Roman finally replied confidently.

"Listen," Michaels said, stopping Roman in his tracks. "You get in, plant the explosives and survive long enough for us to get there. You got my word, I'll get you back here in one piece."

Standing silent for a few seconds, the former Gali warrior finally looked up at Adam with his fiery but determined eyes. "Just look after Troy while I'm gone." Roman responded.

"You got it." Michaels answered as he watched Roman walk to the end of the narrow wide hallway before turning to make his way back to the armory.

It was a position that he had been in many times over. Roman sat in the back of a Chopper, waiting patiently as the rest of the crew for the operation slowly climbed aboard. Dalton eventually made his way onto the skiff, strangely enough appearing as sober as Roman had ever seen him.

"Stay calm. About to be something come through here that you don't want to see. Just remember that we are all on the same team." Dalton said softly, as the words had just finished escaping his lips when two heavily armored Husk soldiers boarded.

"Just stay calm man." Dalton added, holding his hand near the chest of his friend as he saw the fury of hell in his eyes.

"Sorry about the young boy." the first of the two Husk said, stopping in front of Roman and speaking with true sincerity.

Sitting calmly, or at least it appeared, Roman remained silent until the Husk gave up hope for a response and made his way past the men in the direction of an empty seat. Seizing the moment, Roman lunged towards the Husk, pushing him to the ground while holding a combat blade to his throat.

The second Husk tried to intervene, only to have his face come inches from the deathly hollow barrel of Dalton's pump action shotgun.

"No offense friend, but if you take another step towards 'em, not even you are fast enough to escape the shell in this chamber." Dalton said, wondering if the Husk was indeed fast enough.

"You ever so much as speak of the boy again, I'll make sure it's the last words that fall from your mouth." Roman said, daring the monster to call his bluff.

"ENOUGH!" one of the Colonial soldiers said, walking back from the cockpit area into the passenger section of the chopper. Pulling his sidearm out and pointing it daringly at both Roman and the Husk.

"This ends now. I'm Lieutenant Avery, I'm in charge of this operation and I swear to whatever God it is that you believe in, if this doesn't end here and now, I will personally shoot the both of you and dump you out of the side of the Chopper. Now, let him up." the Lieutenant said in a commanding voice, his body decked out in the Colonial blue and gray coloring.

Roman slowly let the Husk up, easing the edge of his blade from the monster's throat.

"Wanna be careful with that blade, next time you might not be lucky enough to have him save your ass." the Husk said with a smile as he slowly pushed himself to his feet.

"I make my own luck." Roman said confidently as he once again took his seat beside Dalton, who removed his shotgun as the second Husk was quick to be seated. As he started to follow Roman to where he sat, the Husk reached for his long blade, which was attached to the long of his leg.

"Steiner," the Lieutenant said loudly, sliding the top of his pistol back into the ready position. "Sit your fucking ass down, or make no mistake, they will be scrubbing your brain fragments from the inside of this ship before we launch."

"Now look who's getting lucky." Roman said sarcastically as Steiner slowly made his way to be seated, upset that a fight would not ensue between the two, at least not at the moment.

"You think they're gonna try and kill us the first chance they get?" Dalton asked his friend.

"You think it matters if they do?" Roman replied, letting Dalton know that he planned to kill anyone who stood in his way of reaping revenge for Troy's trauma.

"Either one of them makes a move on the other, shoot 'em." the Lieutenant said to another one of the operation's soldiers, this one wearing solid blue with heavy gray leather markings, signifying the equivalent of Colonial Special Forces.

As the skiff began to lift off, turning before exiting the launch area of the Capital Ship; Captain Michaels and Sarah were among the crowd that had gathered to watch the departure."Well, I had Roman figured out wrong, looks like. I thought for sure he'd try and kill a damn Husk," Adam said quietly to Sarah, laughing under his breath as the blast of the chopper hitting launch speed quickly drowned out any noise thereafter. "Yep, I'm proud of him for behaving so civilized." Adam added.

Though a small exterior window inside the infirmary, Troy watched as the skiff went into full burnout, disappearing seconds after it had launched from the huge military carrier. He wondered what Roman and his group of soldiers might encounter, wished that he was along with them for the ride and most of all, hoped that man he quickly began to look up to would make it back safely.

"Bumpy ride, damn you would think with all of this

money they are throwing around they would have designed a more comfortable seat." Dalton said aloud as he glanced around at the other soldiers in the passenger area, the strong glimmer of red light filling the cabin.

"Built for durability, not comfort." one of the soldiers responded, his solid blue helmet and visor giving away the fact that he was the only sniper among the group. If that wasn't obvious enough, he held a single barrel weapon that stood nearly three feet high, the butt of the weapon resting on the floor of the chopper.

"Damn fine piece you got there." Dalton replied, using the line that he had reserved solely for weapons and women.

"Thanks. Thermal EM scope let's me fire from nearly two clicks out and cut a man in half." the sniper replied, obviously good at his trade.

"I prefer to kill them up close myself." Steiner added, joining the conversation unexpectedly; staring directly at Roman the entire length of the comment. A long pause between the elite fighters, Dalton finally nodded his approval on the fighting tactics of the Husk.

"Makes two of us. Give me a shotgun any day." Dalton responded, if nothing else, to try an built a rapport with Steiner before turning his back on him once the fighting started.

"I have to admit Commander Blaine, I'm impressed." Captain Michaels said "I didn't expect to see this many soldiers." as he looked over a short metal guardrail from above, watching thousands of Colonial soldiers begin to mobilize.

"The fate of most of these men, if not all of them, rest on the shoulders of the men aboard that chopper," Blaine said. "If they don't get rid of the surface to air defenses, most of these men will be killed long before they reach the planet's surface." he added.

Adam didn't doubt for one second the ability of either

Roman or Dalton, rather, he worried about what they were flying into. So little was known of this new strain of Hunter, and he had a hunch that no matter how tough the Fang proved to be, neither man would even consider backing down.

"Adam, I've seen your warrant file," the commander said. Although Michaels didn't reply in words, his expression was one of shame. "The truth is I looked them over thoroughly, and to be honest, I didn't see a single charge listed that I feel I should be worried about. I think maybe your heart is in the right place and you've just been tangled up with the wrong kind of crowd." Blaine added, having no idea how true those words rang to Adam's ears.

"I've also read your military file, you fought in the Glimmerian Wars." the commander said.

"That was a long time ago." Adam replied.

"Once a soldier, always a soldier. At least that's my belief." Blaine replied.

"What I'm getting at Adam, is I believe you would be a good fit here in the Colonial Army. You have the right kind of experience, a heart for the innocent and the love of my daughter." he added.

Completely surprised by the statement, Adam soon realized that their love for one another could no longer be kept a secret, no matter how hard they had tried.

"A clean start. That's what I'm offering you Adam. A chance to wipe your criminal record clean and become a part of the solution instead of the problem, you and the rest of your crew as well." Blaine said. Deep in thought over the possibility of starting fresh, the Captain finally looked at the commander long enough to reply.

"I'll think it over and speak with my crew." Commander Blaine nodded his approval.

"Of course Adam, of course." the commander replied as he walked down the metal steps nearby to meet with the troops below in an attempt to keep moral up.

"Two minutes to touchdown," Lieutenant Avery yelled to the soldiers in the passenger area of the chopper. "Strike team goes first, Sweeper team goes second and sniper is with me, understood?" the Lieutenant added, trying his best to talk loud enough to be heard through the roar of the ship's engines on decent.

The soldiers all nodded in compliance as the chopper began a solid nose dive, the overhead light changing to yellow as the entire cabin grew bright enough to see the look on everyone's faces. Dalton counted a total of ten souls aboard, including himself and the Lieutenant.

"I know it's a bad time, but which team are we again?" Dalton asked Roman in a calm voice. Gaining an immediate stare from his friend, who was glassy eyed with adrenaline.

"Just follow me and shoot any son of a bitch who shoots at you." Roman replied calmly.

The chopper spun around, doing nearly a two hundred degree turn as it abruptly hit the ground, the cabin light switching from yellow to green.

"Go, go!" Lieutenant Avery yelled as the first four soldiers jumped off, all wearing Colonial Special Ops clothing; the standard issue dark blue with brown leather trim covering them from the neck to boot line. As they exited the craft, panning around the darkness with heartbeat sensors attached to their battle rifles, the second group of four hit the ground.

Roman, Dalton, Steiner and his Husk ally all four began searching the immediate area around the chopper, before finally grouping up with the first team. The last off were the sniper and the Lieutenant. Sprinting for the highest ground in the area, the sniper took position on top of a grassy hill, the wavy green blades at least two foot tall. He quickly pulled a thermal blanket over everything but his head and arms, the metal interior of the blanket setup to deflect any type of heat signatures that his body may give off, while the exterior of the blanket was a green camouflage that was designed to blend in with any surrounding. As he quickly set up his long range rifle, snapping it into a portable tripod; he zoomed the scope around to pick up any hostiles who may have seen the ship's approach.

"I got nothing in the scope, you're all clear." the sniper said as the Lieutenant waved the ship off, taking only seconds before it had disappeared into the night sky.

"Form up," Avery said into his com unit, as the remaining eight men bent to a knee close together, waiting on their commanding officer. "Strike team, move ahead and take out any patrols on the perimeter of the compound. Sweeper team on me." the Lieutenant said as the four Colonial Spec Ops soldiers instantly began a defensive sprint into the direction of the compound, which sat in the distance about a quarter of a mile.

"Sweeper team, we wait for them to clear the perimeter, then we move up and plant the explosives. Should be a couple of three hundred inch rail guns and a control box near the rear of the largest dwelling that controls the surface to air missiles. We need to take out all three in order to give the Colonial Army a clean landing. Understood?" Avery said as everyone agreed and waited for a signal from the strike team ahead.

The signal never came. "Eyes, got anything in the scope?" the Lieutenant asked.

"Negative, I got nothing." the sniper replied.

"Something is wrong. They've been gone way too long." Roman said quietly in the direction of Avery.

"Strike team, come in," the Lieutenant said into the com unit, waiting an extended period of time for a response that never came. "Fuck," Lieutenant Avery yelled in a low voice as he contemplated his options. "Eyes, we are moving up. Keep your fucking eye on that scope, any marks show up, don't hesitate to fire at will!" Avery said as he looked around at the four men.

"Fire your weapons only as a last resort. Now move out." the Lieutenant said as they began slowly making their way to the compound, taking extra precaution with every step.

The two Husk soldiers were in lead of the group, with Roman and Dalton following loosely behind them and Avery right on their footsteps. Stopping at the security fencing, the group saw a hole that had been made only minutes ago by the Spec Ops team.

"Slowly." the Lieutenant said as he motioned for the soldiers to continue through the break in the fencing. The first two Husk made their way through and threw their backs to the wall to cover the entrance of the other three men. Once everyone was inside, the first rail gun was in sight, only feet away from their current position out in the open. Waiting several minutes to ensure that they had not been detected, Avery finally gave the go ahead to the group; the explosives had to be planted.

As the first Husk slowly emerged from the corner into the open, he was immediately hit with a high caliber round from a rifle in the distance, the shell piercing his neck, sending him flailing to the ground. The shot hadn't killed him, but left him defenseless on the ground, reeling in pain as he bit down on his arm to prevent making noise that would give the group's position away. Two more suppressed shots followed, one striking his chest and the other piercing the back of his skull and killing him the very moment. A third shot was fired, this time from behind the group. "Got him, that last shot gave me his position." the Colonial sniper said after eliminating he Legion's sniper.

"Scanning the area, looks all clear but there is a damn good chance that he wasn't working alone." the sniper said as Steiner sprinted to plant the satchel of explosives, glancing only for a moment at his friend who lay in a pool of his own blood. With the charges in place, Steiner grabbed the body of his fallen clansman as he returned to the group, trying to remain out of sight.

"Surface to air missiles are the most likely to cause trouble for the Colonial Fleet, so they need to go first," Lieutenant Avery said, checking a map scan of the Hunter compound. According to the map, the STA Control Room should be in this building." he added, pointing to a small building on the computerized blueprint.

"Eyes open, Steiner take point, move out." the Lieutenant said quietly, putting the map away and once again firming his grip on the combat pistol.

As the approached the marked building, Avery checked his watch before informing the rest of the group that the Colonial force would be striking in less than twenty-two hours. "Still plenty of time, go in quietly and don't get sloppy. Now move!" the Lieutenant said quietly as Steiner pushed the large red door, which was made of reinforced red steel, opening it slowly with a small creaking sound.

The room was pitch dark, as Steiner moved inside slowly, his large shotgun in front and at the ready. Following closely behind, Roman and Dalton moved inside of the military target, Roman with a standard issue rifle while Dalton insisted on using his not so standard pump shotgun.

Suddenly, the interior lights came on, giving the soldiers an immediate picture of the building's interior, which was flooded with Legion soldiers who had all four of the strike team members kneeling at gunpoint.

"You're late." one of the ranking Legion officers said calmly as Lieutenant Avery pointed his pistol directly at the skull of Roman.

"I'm late because your damn sniper pinned us down." Avery replied sternly.

"Anwick requested you hold these three until he arrives." Avery said with a more relaxed tone as the Legion officer nodded.

"You should know, I make it a point to kill anybody who pulls a gun on me twice." Roman said calmly, his hands behind his head.

"I'll make a note of it." Avery replied, motioning a group of the Legion soldiers to lead Steiner, Roman and Dalton to a holding cell.

As they were leaving the large storage area, they were unfortunate witnesses to Legion soldiers firing a single into the head of each of the strike team members, killing them on the spot.

As they arrived to the holding area, the Colonial sniper lay in the corner of the room, badly beaten and unable to stand.

"Get inside you Colonial pieces of shit!" one of the Legion soldiers said, pushing Steiner into the cell with the backside of his rifle.

"Looks like I don't want to kill you so badly after all." Steiner said to Roman as Dalton tried helping the sniper to his feet.

"We got to warn the Fleet, they, there is an entire regiment of Legion soldiers here, Commander Blaine is walking right into a trap." the sniper managed to say as he continued to fight for a deep breath.

"First thing's first. We gotta get out of this holding cell." Roman said with purpose as he extended his hand to the much larger, former foe Steiner.

After the two combat juggernauts shook hands, which sent a shiver up the spine of Dalton, who imagined the possibilities of both men fighting together; they began pacing the cell and looking for anything that may aid in their escape.

"So, you're thinking my father's offer over seriously then?" Sarah asked as Michaels read through a stack of papers in his room aboard the Colonial Star Five.

"Of course, just the idea of starting over scares the hell out of me." Michaels replied, continuing to glance at unclassified military reports as he tried to get himself up to speed on the war between the Colonial and Legion armies.

"Well, you know, starting over with me at your side might not be such a bad thing." Sarah said convincingly as she slowly walked over to him, putting her arms around his neck passionately.

"Wait." Adam said, jumping to his feet.

"Wait? I thought that's what you wanted? What we both wanted?" Sarah said, very confused by the Captain's sudden change of heart.

"No, wait." Michaels said, holding a single piece of paper in his hand, then grabbing several more as he read them thoroughly.

"Who was in charge of your security detail back on Tameca?" Michaels asked impatiently.

"Um, Lieutenant Avery, I think, why?" she asked curiously.

Adam bolted out of his room without explanation, several papers tightly in his grasp as he sprinted through the halls of the huge ship on his way to the commander's quarters. Everyone he passed taking a second to watch his movements, wondering about his sense of urgency.

"Commander, Adam Michaels here to see you sir?" a Colonial soldier said softly, as he held the door of Blaine's cabin open.

"By all means, send him in." the commander said politely as he sat in a very lush leather chair behind a huge wooden desk that looked as sturdy as the ship it rested on.

"Adam, I take it that you have thought on my offer?" Commander Blaine said hopefully.

Throwing a small stack of documents onto the desk, Adam tried for a few seconds to catch his breath. "It's a trap." the Captain finally managed to squeeze from his lungs.

"Excuse me?" Blaine said, standing out of the chair in search of an answer.

"Lieutenant Avery is working with the Legion. Right

here in the documents are at least a dozen cases where his group came under assault from either Legion or Hunter forces, every single time he was the only one to survive. The Hunters do not leave survivors, trust me on that one." Michaels said confidently.

"Adam, that's outrageous. Avery is one of my most trusted officers." Blaine replied skeptically.

"Commander, your daughter's security detail back on Tameca, Avery survived that assault as well. Believe me, I met the monsters behind that, we damn near didn't make it out of there ourselves." Adam said in an attempt to force the commander to see reason.

"He's right father, Lieutenant Avery was acting strange that entire day. Our group was hit by four Hunters as well as a full squad of Legion soldiers. When I was taken into custody, I thought for sure that we would surely die, the rest of my detail already lay slain." Sarah said, arriving at her father's quarters and nodding in the direction of Captain Michaels to let him know that he had her support.

Commander Blaine stood silent for several very long moments, trying to connect the dots inside his mind.

"Commander, two of my crew are with the strike team. All I ask is the use of a ship; give me a chance to rescue them if I'm right about this." Michaels said.

"If you're wrong?" Blaine asked quietly.

"If I'm wrong, then I will apologize to Avery myself. You told me that my heart was in the right place, well my heart tells me that our men are in trouble." Michaels responded.

"Alright. I'll give you a chopper and a four man strike team, on one condition," the commander said as he slid a small blue box across the fine wood grain of the desk into the direction of Adam. As Michaels slowly opened the box, he was nearly taken over with emotion as he saw the insignia medallion of a Colonial Lieutenant. "The only way any of the soldiers on this ship will execute an order from you, is if you are a commanding officer. Besides, I know I can trust you with my daughter's life." Blaine said firmly.

"Sarah's life?" Adam asked, confused.

"That's right. You don't honestly think I plan on letting the man I'm in love with go it alone do you?" Sarah relied.

"But I don't thin... " Adam began to respond as he was quickly cut off by Commander Blaine.

"Don't worry Lieutenant, she's plenty capable. Who do you think trained many of the Special Ops soldiers aboard this ship?" Adam gave a long, blank stare in her direction.

"I know, I know. Us girls and our secrets." Sarah said as she smiled wide.

"You have a go Lieutenant." Commander Blaine said as Michaels was still in shock over the events of the past several minutes.

"Yes sir." Adam finally replied, turning to leave the commander's quarters.

"So we wait for Anwick to arrive, more than likely escorted by a couple more Hunters, and then we overpower them as soon as the cell door opens? Seriously? That's the plan?" Dalton asked in a joking manner.

"Do you see any other way out?" Roman replied, confirming the plan he had helped Steiner design.

"Look, I'm one for a fight, don't get me wrong. Hell, I'm even one for fighting against the odds; but damn, we are talking about a small group of heavily armed HUNTERS HERE," Dalton replied loudly. "We are talking suicide and everyone in here knows it!" he added.

"They will kill us regardless. We were only spared so the Hunters could slay us with their own hands." Steiner replied.

"So let's think of something that doesn't involve everyone in this fucking jail cell dying!" Dalton responded animatedly.

"All systems are checking out fine." Kelly said as she

flipped several switches at the helm of the reconstructed Gunship. It still had plenty of wrench time ahead, but the craft was starting to slowly look like a spaceship as a small crew had joined Kato in working on it around the clock.

"Getting good readings on life support, navigational and cabin pressure." she added, yelling the information out of a small hole in the side of the bridge that was being reinforced with plated steel.

The mechanical crew continued working with engineers as several Spartan model fighter ships also were receiving repairs in the same area of the Colonial vessel. Kato had paused for a few moments, watching the welding torches piecing the small ship to ship fighters back together; wondering what it must be like to fly something that was incredibly fast. The speed was offset by the disadvantage of having only a dual gun mounted to each wing that was capable of firing quick bursts of tracer rounds. It sounded good in theory, however, against a larger ship the tracers were only potent when the Spartans attacked in great numbers.

"I'm heading down ahead of the fleet." Adam said. Kato pulled himself the rest of the way out of the confines of one of the ship's thrusters long enough to see Adam decked out in the Colonial blue and gray, complete with his Lieutenant insignia pinned to the collar of his tightly pressed shirt.

"I like what you guys have done with the ship. Good job. I'll be back soon enough." Michaels said, nodding his approval before walking further down the maintenance deck.

"What was that all about?" Kelly asked, glaring through the temporary hole of the Bridge.

"I dunno. Did he shave or something?" Kato replied, clueless as to Adam's life altering decision to join the fleet. Grease smeared across his face as he held a massive chrome wrench in his right hand, once again pushing the creeper he rested on back under the work at hand.

Adam stood there for several tense moments, looking at the four man team of soldiers that had been assigned to him. Already seated aboard the Colonial chopper, they were ready to launch at the order of the newly pinned Lieutenant.

"Alright, listen up. "I'm sure you all have ready the mission brief and I'm confident that you know what you are doing. Simply put, we get in, get our soldiers and get out. Safely. All weapons stay suppressed unless ordered otherwise. If the intelligence on Lieutenant Avery is incorrect, we will then fall under his command and assist the first team with operations until the Colonial Fleet arrives. Any questions?" Lieutenant Michaels asked as the soldiers simply nodded firmly in compliance before looking into the direction of the loading door on the craft.

Sarah had joined the group, wearing an elegant red colored dress, she had accented her already perfect face with vibrant makeup and had her hair arranged as if she were about to attend a social dinner. Adam stood there speechless, wondering how many more tricks the woman of his dreams had up her sleeve.

"What? A girl's gotta look good." Sarah said comically as she finished boarding the chopper, hoisting a large black combat rifle in her right arm.

"Yes, you do." Adam replied as he sat down in one of the rough black leather seats near the cockpit area, nothing short of speechless.

"We've been cleared by the bridge sir. On your order." the pilot said in a disciplined tone as Lieutenant Michaels gave the go ahead, looking one last time at the safe confines of Colonial Star Five. With his order, the chopper slowly pulled from the thick steel flooring of the shipping bay, turning slowly as several of the crew aboard the capital ship looked on. Seconds later, the small craft executed a full burn, disappearing from sight and showing up on the Star Five's radar system.

"I'm telling you, it'll work," Dalton said loudly to the others, referring to his plan to stage a fight and try to lure one of the less prominent Legion guards to the cell. "I saw Adam do it once in the public jail on Star City." he added.

"A little difference between a local jail on a space station and a heavily fortified compound led by Hunters." Steiner replied grimly.

"It's the best plan so far." the Colonial sniper said, speaking up for the first time since being reunited with the group.

"Thank you," Dalton replied sincerely. "What's your name again chief?" Dalton asked. "Corporal Lassiter." the sniper replied, obviously still reeling from the injuries he had suffered during his interrogation time.

"See, I figure we stage a fight. Hell, Roman and the Husk population aren't exactly on the best of terms anyway. The guards come in to shake down the cell, we turn on 'em and get the fuck out of here." Dalton said, as if he were throwing a sales pitch for a new home, even closing things with his own variation of a realtor's smile.

"Sounds like a solid enough plan." Lieutenant Avery said as he approached the cell. Roman cut his eyes at Dalton for a moment, as if to mentally slap him across the face, before turning his attention back to Avery. "Now, let me tell you a really solid plan. The Colonial Fleet arrives, we purposely hold back our rail guns and surface to air missiles, convincing them that you idiots were successful. Then, once they are far enough in, we launch everything we have from the far side of the planet. They will be outnumbered at least three times over, crushing the backbone of the Colonial Army with one fail swoop."

The men stood there for a moment before Roman finally approached the front of the cell; thick steel bars the only thing separating him from Avery.

"So how much do they offer a gutless piece of shit like you to turn on his own kind?" Roman asked. Laughing for a moment, Avery returned the stone glare of Roman.

"Enough. Ask your friend Lassiter back there, they made us both the same offer, he was just too proud to take it." Avery replied.

Roman glanced back at the sniper for a moment, nodding his appreciation.

"He'll live to see the end of this war. You won't." Roman replied, walking away from the front of the cell.

"So sure are you about that? I plan to kill you myself when the Hunters arrive." Avery said confidently.

"Yea, I haven't heard that line before." Roman replied, sitting down beside Lassiter in the corner of the cell.

"Soon." Avery replied, walking away to regroup with his security detail of two Legion soldiers.

Kato slid out from his workspace for a moment, wiping his face of excess grease and obviously in deep thought. He quickly grabbed a piece of scrap paper from his workbench and began writing several items down in a concentrated manner.

"What are you doing?" Kelly asked as she peeked through one of the cockpit windows.

"Hopefully, modifications." Kato replied, immediately flagging down a deck hand to see if the listed supplies were available.

"Less than one minute out! Check your gear!" Lieutenant Michaels said loudly as the crew area of the chopper clicked over from red to yellow. The soldiers began checking their battle rifles and combat pistols, all of which had been previously double checked. The sun had started to break just a bit as the chopper hit ground, the cabin light turning green as everyone dashed out of the passenger door, their solid black boots crunching onto the brittle ground beneath. The chopper had to land farther out, obviously, because of the daylight that was upcoming; leaving the team with a good hike in front of them.

"Last chance?" Adam asked as Sarah just looked at him sarcastically for a moment before climbing down to ground level.

Everyone remained low as the chopper turned sharply, rising from the ground before hitting a full burnout. Shortly after they had made it to a small tree line nearby, two Legion jets flew past as a very high rate of speed. "Daggers. Moving fast, looks like the chopper didn't make it out of here off of radar." Sarah said regretfully. They listened quietly as chatter came across the Colonial com units of two fighter planes intercepting the chopper, soon after, the chatter was cut silent.

"Get in the supply kit and get the reflector blanket out, sure to be scanning the area soon." Sarah said.

Sure enough, only minutes later the Dagger ships passed over their area several times, scanning the ground for heat signatures. The crew lay quietly under the reflective blanket, as its exterior digitally changed to adapt to the terrain, camouflaging them from anything overhead as they kept eyes open for anything or anyone on foot. Nearly an hour after the Daggers had executed their last flyover, Lieutenant Michaels deemed it safe to move as the squad made their way to the compound.

"Well, I guess we're back to plan B huh?" Dalton asked as the rest of the prisoners sat quietly.

"First person through that cell door is dead by my hands, and I pray that it's Avery." Roman said softly, meaning every word of it.

"They will come at us heavy, knowing what we might be capable of," Steiner said. "Best chance would be to play it down until we are all out of the cell and under gunpoint. More room to move around." he added.

"For what it's worth, there's nobody I'd rather be busting out of captivity and more than likely dying with," Dalton replied, trying to lighten the mood of the men, who had the gloom of a death sentence hanging over their heads. "Of course, I'd like to be doing it with a bottle of whiskey in my hand, but beggars can't be choosers." he added, prompting the men to laugh for a moment.

Commander Blaine stood on an overhead catwalk as he watched regiments of men get into formation before boarding troop carriers. They would have to fly down under heavy Spartan escort, having no ship to ship weapons of their own. As impressive as the Goliath units were, there were still far too few of them to launch as an entire regiment, instead they were packaging two of them per troop ship in order to assist the ground forces. Little was known about the new strain of genetically enhanced Hunter, but he couldn't imagine anything strong enough to take down a Goliath unit, not even a Fang.

Everyone among the Colonial Fleet was prepared to fight and even die if needed be, still the commander placed most of his respect on the Spartan pilots. Having been one himself before moving up through the ranks, he understood that the survival rate for them were the lowest, seeing the most action in a battle such as the one that was to come. Dog fighting Daggers, escorting the ground force to a safe landing and avoiding rail gun fire; these were only a few of the responsibilities that had been cast upon the Spartan pilots. He was damn proud to have them in the Colonial fleet.

At first glance, the size of the Colonial attack force looked tremendous. However, it paled in comparison to the troops the Legion had at its disposal, which is why Commander Blaine could only hope that they were successful in catching the superior enemy off guard. Otherwise, it was inevitable that the Colonial Army would face a crushing defeat.

Avery waited outside in a slight rain, accompanied by two Legion troops as a small shuttle began descent, making its approach to the landing pad. The strange exterior, which had a ribbed texture and several pointed overhangs, let them know right away that it was indeed a Hunter vessel. At it touched down on the saturated gray pavement, dust blew out from the bottom of the ship loudly, forcing the men to look away momentarily. Soon after, a metal ramp began to lower, offering a glimpse inside; illuminated buttons blinking against the wall in several different color sequences.

A very heavily armed Hunter was the first down the ramp, surveying the immediate area for any possible threats. Seconds later, Anwick followed the armed Hunter down the ramp, followed by two more of the larger killers, all four dressed in black leather from head to toe, Anwick wearing a white medallion while the three soldiers were blanketed in a much heavier armor.

"Lieutenant Avery I presume?" Anwick asked, moving close to him, his skin pigmented with lifelessness as he teeth appeared filed to a point.

"That is correct." Avery replied formally.

"Job well done. I would much like to see the prisoners at once, especially the one called Roman." Anwick replied.

"Then it will be arranged at once." Avery replied, extending his arm as to welcome the Hunters into the compound.

"Two Hunter Carriers will land here for a short period, deploying troops as well as a handful of Fangs, at which time the Carriers will group with your Legion ships and prepare for an air assault." Anwick said as the group walked down a well lit hallway of solid white walls and ceiling.

"Indeed," Avery responded. "The force that we have assembled should be more than enough to shred the Colonial Fleet within minutes." he added.

"Good. Very good." Anwick replied.

The lights in and around the cell switched from dim to full bright as the prisoners jumped to their feet, Lassiter much slower, pulling himself up through the pain of his injuries.

"Roman Raines," Anwick said proudly as he approached the cell. "Much has changed since my friend Lexion lay dead by your hands." he added.

"If you are referring to my ability to kill Hunters, actually, not much has changed." Roman said insultingly.

"Yes. I was not aware of your past until your crew slipped from my grasp on Tameca. The deeper I dug into your files, the more impressed I became. So, do you mind if I ask you exactly how many of my kind you killed during your time with the Gali Special Forces?" Anwick asked, knowing Roman had never officially been a Gali soldier.

"I stopped counting after the first hundred or so." Roman replied, gaining instant stares from the other prisoners.

"Hundred? You said a couple?" Dalton added in amazement.

"You see, it seems that your crew has been carrying a cold blooded killer for some time now. Isn't that right Roman?" Anwick replied, looking heavily at the hardened soldier.

"In fact, the only reason he is with you is because he is being hunted by his own government," Anwick said as Roman looked up at him brashly. "Seems he turned on his own kind, killed a handful of Gali Special Ops soldiers in the process. As much as I want to kill you with my own hands, even I couldn't turn down the bounty they have placed on your head. I wonder what your precious Captain Michaels would say to this?" he added.

"I'd say ten percent sounds about right, don't you think Roman?" Michaels said from behind the group, standing beside Sarah and two of the Colonial soldiers, the remaining two on the opposite side of the group.

"I'd rather rot in this Legion prison cell, ten percent is chump change," Roman replied smiling as Anwick and his group stood in shock. "On the other hand, fifteen sounds about right." Roman added as Dalton grinned widely, his beard nearly falling from his face in the process.

"I can do fifteen," Michaels replied, looking over to Anwick, Avery and the escort soldiers. "Now open the door."

"Captain Michaels. You must know that there is no place you can hide that will be safe?" Anwick asked.

"Lieutenant Michaels, actually, and I'm done running." Adam said, pulling a long black lever on the stock of his rifle; arming it to fire. "Now. Open the damn door." he added.

As the group stood there waiting for Anwick's reply, Adam fired a shot, hitting one of the Legion soldiers in the head and deadening him on the spot. Pulling the pin back again, Avery stepped to the front, yelling, "Open the damn door!"

As Roman and Dalton exited the cell, Steiner followed close behind, helping Lassiter. As Michaels began to hand the men sidearms, Sarah walked toward the group, bluntly slapping Avery across the cheek of his face.

"That's for handing me over to them!" she yelled as Anwick, the three escort Hunters and a Legion soldier looked on.

"You bitch! I should have killed you myself and been done with it!" Avery managed to yell before having nearly an entire side of his face blown off by Roman's combat pistol.

"That's me keeping a promise." the Gali warrior remarked as they bolted the cell door shut, getting into position to move out.

"Ya'll hang tight now." Dalton said tauntingly.

"This isn't over Adam, I promise you that." Anwick said calmly with his face pressed against the bars of the cell.

"If not, this puts you down two to nothing." Michaels smiled, infuriating the Hunter, who began shrieking loudly.

"Damn glad to see you guys." Dalton said, getting a slight pat on his shoulder and nod from Lieutenant Michaels.

Commander Blaine stood in the command center of the Colonial Star Five, which was rendezvousing with three more of the Colonial Stars before launching the assault against the Legion. It was nothing more than a staging ground, ships falling into formation, giving the operation the best chance for success while limiting damage as much as possible. Surrounded by neon green grids on all of the walls and a huge grid which was mounted to the floor in the center of the room, crewmen used special graphing markers to update the grids with the position of the ships, while Colonial chatter broadcast throughout the room on several com units.

Even Blaine, who was the ranking officer on Colonial Star Five, didn't know what each panel in the room was used for. All he knew is that they were individually manned by members of his crew, who monitored everything from communication between Spartan pilots to damage control and assessment of the ship. There was no window in the Command Room that overlooked the stars; instead, he had to rely on the information of the grids to be correct. As he watched, a crew member listened to the chatter over his headset for a moment, before aligning the three ships on the central grid that represented the Colonial Star Ships.

"Everyone is in position commander, awaiting your go." the crewman said as Blaine took one last look around the Command Center, taking in the sights of a ship untouched, the looks on every soul's face as they awaited his command to officially send them into war with the Legion army.

"I wanted to take a moment to personally thank each and every one of you for your service to the Allied Colonies. To say that it is an honor to serve with you would be an understatement. Even as we get set to embark on an act of war that will forever change the complexion of this star system, I want you all to hold to the belief that we are doing so in the most innocent of fashions. To preserve our freedom and the freedom of those citizens who cannot defend themselves. Good luck and God speed," the commander said proudly through a hand held com unit, his message ringing throughout every ship, every headset and every Spartan pilot's helmet. "You have a go." he calmly said to the crew member as he mounted his com unit back onto the wall.

"So where's our ride?" Dalton asked.

"There is no ride, at least not yet. We find a place and dig down until the Colonial force arrives." Adam answered.

"Nice, but there will be thousands of people shooting, and that's only here on the ground. How the hell do they expect to find us?" Dalton replied, looking at Adam dumbfounded. Rather than replying, Lieutenant Michaels simply grabbed the medallion signifying his rank and flipped it over, exposing a tracking beacon.

"Oh, well, I guess that will work, but I would have done it differently." Dalton replied in an attempt to save face.

"We need to make it to the outer perimeter of the compound, much better chance of hanging out unnoticed." Adam said to the group as he strategically scouted the horizon.

Several rifles shots rang out as two of the Colonial soldiers fell to the ground abruptly. The rest of the group dove for cover, finding refuge behind a stack of metal shipping crates nearby. A small squad of Legion troops had noticed the intruders, sounding a screeching alarm that rang throughout the compound, prompting several sets of soldiers to follow in the pursuit of the Colonial group.

"Well, there's our dick flapping in the wind," Dalton said, pulling one of the seriously injured soldiers to cover, his body dragging roughly across the solid dirt surface. "Well, not all of us." he added after a punishing stare from Sarah. It was a solid spot of cover, but it wouldn't last long with the large number of enemies closing in on them, the metal shipping crates taking a pounding from the relentless gunfire.

"Well, looks like this may be it." Lassiter said.

"Just hold as long as we possibly can." Lieutenant Michaels replied as Roman and Steiner both grabbed rifles to join up with Dalton while Sarah helped tend to the fallen troops.

Pressing a makeshift bandage down firmly onto one of the gunshot wounds of a Colonial solider, Sarah stopped suddenly as she heard a thunderous scream nearby.

"What... the fuck...was that?" Dalton asked cautiously, joining the other men in staring at one of the Fang soldiers. Hulking tall, it was at least ten feet in height and the largest creature any of them had ever seen walking on two legs. A huge fang extending from the bottom of its mouth on each side, at least as wide as a human hand, solid white hair thickly braided and falling down the upper portion of its back. Heavily armored with a thick chest plate of black plate mail, it quickly became apparent to the Colonial soldiers that the weapons they were firing were having little to no effect as it continued a full sprint toward them unhindered.

The commanding officer of the group simply stood in amazement, having never seen anything like a Fang before.

"Adam! We need to move, NOW!" Sarah yelled, bringing him back into reality for a moment.

He nodded, frantically checking his surroundings in hopes of finding a way out of the impending slaughter of his team. He needed a miracle of some kind, they were surrounded and pinned down in a spot that provided no exit.

The bloodcurdling screams of the beast grew louder, before suddenly being silenced by the overpowering booms of hundreds, if not thousands of ships hitting the planet's atmosphere at full burn. The Colonial fleet had arrived with not a second to spare, the attack force descending onto the Legion fortress quickly and without retaliation. Adam noticed the Legion troops, who had been moving in on their position, had began scrambling to nearby buildings to prepare for the inevitable battle at hand. He prayed that the Fang who was bearing down on them would follow suit.

No such luck. Michaels quickly checked, only to see the monster continuing his rush towards them. Trying his best to hold back his emotion; wanting only to begin firing his rifle into the sky and curse the Gods who had returned the favor his entire life, he simply threw the rifle to the ground in favor of his two revolver style pistols. Adam closed his eyes, tightly gripping the wooden handles of the weapons as he knew the Fang would be on them in only moments.

"Adam get them out of here, now." Roman replied, as he stood there holding a combat pistol and hand length blade.

Steiner quickly joined the other hero, unsheathing his machete and pulling a shotgun to the ready with his free hand. Adam realized at that moment, Roman was prepared to die in a much different fashion than the one he had lived it, as a hero.

"GO!" Roman yelled as the Fang was close enough to hear the warrior's command. Adam pointed into the direction of the nearest building he could find as Sarah, Dalton and the remaining Colonial soldiers who were able, helped the wounded quickly to the building's position.

Lieutenant Michaels slowed his run down long enough to turn and look back at his friend, who alongside Steiner, was fighting valiantly in the face of death.

Having been shot several times, at least two rounds hitting it from point blank range directly in the face, the Fang fiercely struck Roman in the area of his neck and face; dropping the former Gali warrior. Before Steiner could intervene with a swing of his machete, the Fang fired two shots from a Hunter rifle, both finding their mark into the chest of Roman who lay limp in a quickly formed pool of his own blood.

Time seemed to stop. Adam considered going back for his friends and trying to help them take out the Fang. He also knew in his heart that Roman was either dead or committed to the act of dying. He glanced the other way, seeing Sarah waving him to her in slow motion, Dalton yelling to him with no sound reaching his ears. This was truly a moment that would stick with him for the rest of his life. He had to make a decision between what he knew was the right and running to the woman that he loved. He was tired of running.

As he loosened the grip on the handles of his pistols only slightly, Adam turned his attention back to the Fang, who was fighting fiercely with Steiner as Roman continued to lay lifeless in the same spot; blood soaking into the surrounding ground. It was time to fight back or die trying. Adam started a path in the direction of the fight when he was thrown several feet, before hitting the unforgiving dirt with tremendous force by a nearby blast. Explosions rang out around him as the Spartans had made it to near ground level, firing their weapons onto the compound in unison.

It took only moments for Michaels to recognize the desperation of Sarah's voice, yelling loudly enough to get his attention; his ears still ringing from the deafening explosion. He slowly stumbled toward them, shell shocked and heavily disoriented.

"What were you thinking?" Sarah yelled as she and Dalton helped the Lieutenant into the door of the small building. He didn't reply, instead, looking back to his friends only to see nothing but empty ground.

The thunderous booms of the explosions began to multiply as Legion forces sprang the trap, sending hundreds of air defense missiles into the sky followed by squadrons of Strikewings burning at full speed. Tracer rounds finished lighting the breaking dawn sky as hundreds of Colonial ships engaged the Legion attack planes in dog fighting tactics. Meanwhile, the Colonial Stars moved into position, firing their multiple ship to ship cannons at the approaching Legion Capital ships and Hunter Carriers.

"Have you located Lieutenant Michaels' tracking beacon?" Commander Blaine said, standing firmly at the central grid inside of the Command Center.

"Yes sir, he's indoors and the area is too hot for extraction. Will have to wait for the area to secure or they will have to come to us." one of his crew replied, charting several positions on a nearby wall mounted grid.

"Very well. Concentrate guns onto Legion ships, they will be much more populated than the Carriers." Blaine instructed as his crew members acknowledged the order and began relaying the instructions to the ship's weapons room.

"Our Spartans are taking a pounding up there." Lassiter said as the strike team continued to look outside.

"The entire Fleet is taking a pounding," Sarah replied. She was right, the Colonial Fleet was heavily outnumbered and taking great losses across the board. "Listen," Sarah said, quieting the rest of the crew. "Mini-guns!" she added as a Colonial sweeper team moved into sight, escorted by two of the very capable Goliath units.

The heavily armored soldiers of steel slowly made their way through a small portion of the compound, mowing Legion forces down in their wake. The lead continued to pour out of their automatic weapons, chewing into the flesh of the outmatched foes in red and black leather as the Colonial forces had almost reached Lieutenant Michaels and his team; when a group of two Hunters escorted a single Fang into the area. Aiming down the sights of one of his pistols, Adam's arm was quickly pushed away by the swift hand of Sarah.

"We are no match, not without Roman and Steiner. Gunfire would only give our position away." she said, pleading with Adam as he looked back at his team for a moment.

Lassiter, as well as two of the Colonial soldiers were wounded, one of them life threatening. She was right, they would be of very little help to the Colonial force outside, all they could do is remain sheltered and wait for the skirmish to end, hoping the Goliaths could end the life of the Fang.

However, hope was soon cut short. As the half dozen Colonial soldiers exchanged fire with the two Hunters, the Goliath units began to circle the Fang. The small-arms fire of the others tapered off quite a bit, which was an indication that everyone was watching the battle between the Goliaths and Fang ensue. It was the first of its kind, and a very good bookmark as to which side had the advantage throughout the star system.

For several minutes, the Goliaths maintained a combination of gunfire and punishing punches by way of their solid titanium arms. As it seemed the mechanical menaces were gaining the upper hand of the fight, one of the Goliath units made the mistake of overreaching during a wide angled punch, the Fang thrusting up to tear the mechanical arm from the shoulder of the super soldier. As the Goliath staggered several feet back, the Fang then pummeled the unit to the grown using its closed fists, turning its attention to the second Goliath. Falling back, the remaining Goliath began to lay down cover fire as the Colonial soldiers retreated.

It had quickly become obvious to Adam and his crew that the Colonials would fall in defeat at the end of this battle. Their only hope now was to find a way back to the Colonial Star Five before time ran out. The courtyard of the compound was littered with fallen Legion soldiers, ship wreckage from the thick sky above, Colonial men and women who had died for a cause they believed in and even the occasional Hunter.

They covertly moved from position to position, careful

not to alert any of the units in the open that were engaged in the mass bloodshed. The plan was to move back to the rear of the compound, leaving the same way they had arrived and hope that Colonial ships spotted their beacon before Legion forces caught up to them. It wasn't the greatest of plans, but Adam had thrown it together under fire and it was all they had to go with.

"Lieutenant Michaels." Commander Blaine's voice announced through Adam's ear mounted com unit.

"Go ahead!" Michaels replied, shocked to hear the Blaine's voice in the midst of he loud fighting around him.

"We have picked you up on the grid. If there is any chance you can move two clicks to the Southeast, there is a large Colonial unit dug in there to assist you." Blaine replied.

"Southeast. Move out now!" Michaels yelled to his group, responding to the commander's request. "Yes sir."

"Is Sarah alright?" Blaine asked cautiously, the few seconds of silence seeming like eternity.

"Yes sir. I have three wounded, four confirmed dead and two missing, presumed dead." Adam replied gravely.

"Understood Lieutenant. Get your people Southeast." Commander Blaine replied as the Colonial Star Five shook fiercely, several missiles hitting the large starship at once.

"Report!" Blaine yelled as the ship's interior lights continued their fluctuation.

"Structural damage to the starboard section of the ship, shields have absorbed substantial damage but are holding." one of his crew members said lifelessly.

"Take us down close to the surface. All cannons redirect fire to surface, make my daughter a safe path to walk through." Commander Blaine said before slowly taking a wall mounted com unit into his hand.

"This is the commander. I am issuing a general order to abandon ship. All remaining Spartans are cleared to launch, remaining soldiers are instructed to rally on the surface and support existing units. It has been my honor to serve as your commander." Blaine said as he slowly returned the com unit to its cradle as the ship was hit with several more breaking explosions.

The Legion and Hunter ships knew the Colonial Star Five was in serious trouble and had begun concentrating their fire onto the dying masterpiece, which was starting to tear apart at the welded seams. Dozens of Spartan ships launched simultaneously in an effort to protect the sinking ship, most of which were nothing more than small explosions shortly after launching directly into the concentrated gunfire from the Legion ships.

"Lieutenant, take care of Sarah. That's an order." Commander Blaine said across the com unit as the Colonial Star Five exploded, causing a rippling wave of fire throughout the sky.

"FATHER!" Sarah screamed as she began weeping uncontrollably, quickly grabbed by Adam as he stood speechless.

"Lieutenant Michaels, this is Spartan Nine One." Adam heard in an unfamiliar voice through his com.

"Go ahead." Michaels said, trying to hold himself together as Sarah continuing to cry loudly in the background.

"We have your position and are ready to assist you to the rally point." the pilot said as eight Spartans flew overhead at incredible speeds.

"Copy." Adam said softly, numb from everything he had lost in only a few short hours.

As the group looked ahead, they could see a flashing blue light, which every Colonial soldier would immediately recognize as a signal for friendly ground.

The group began to move as quickly as possible, Adam carrying Sarah as Dalton escorted them by shotgun. Lassiter was slowly moving unassisted, while the remaining Colonial soldiers were responsible for moving the wounded to safety. As they had almost reached the

Colonial camp, empty brass shells rained from overhead as the Spartans passed, firing their tracer rounds and killing nearly a dozen nearby Legion soldiers. Moments later the Spartans were heavily engaged by a squadron of Strikewings, however they had been successful in getting Michaels and the crew to safety.

Met by several Colonial troops, the wounded were immediately taken by medics who were decked out in solid blue with white trim.

"Lieutenant Michaels, you're needed in Outpost Command one of the soldiers said, pointing to a large blue tent which was surrounded by sandbags and three large rail guns pointed into the sky. Sarah accompanied Adam as the rest of the crew got a quick look over by one of the field medics.

"I'm fine, other than being in serious need of a damn drink," Dalton said loudly, wiping a blanket of dirt from his face. "And a hell of a lot of therapy." he added.

"Sarah, I'm sorry about your father." one of the officers said sincerely, placing his hand on her arm for a few moments. Although she had obviously been crying heavily, she did her best to put on a front of strength in front of the soldiers inside of the tent. She had to. They looked at hear as a beacon of strength. They had all lost during this short lived war, she had to press on, at least publicly.

"Lieutenant Michaels. We've lost the Colonial Star Five, seven of our larger cruise ships and the Colonial Star Three is in danger of being lost to us as well. We have sent a relay back to Colonial Command for reinforcements, it was swiftly denied." the officer said.

"Denied!" Sarah yelled as Adam try to hold her back while keeping her calm.

"Yes ma'am. There is a second battle happening this very moment on Tameca. Command relayed back to us that Tameca City is currently controlled by Legion forces, while Colonial forces are mounting to attempt a takeover of the city." he replied.

"What's the plan?" Michaels asked.

"Well Lieutenant, two Colonial Stars have been dispatched to help us evacuate everyone from the surface. The plan is holding onto as much rock as we possibly can until they arrive." the officer replied.

"Evacuate! We have lost so many men here, for nothing?" Sarah asked animately.

"There is no hope of winning this battle, we were outmatched minutes after hitting the atmosphere. Command wants us to group up with the remaining forces on Glimmeria, become the last line of defense in case Tameca City is a loss." the officer added as mortar explosion burst in the background.

Glimmeria. Now there was a word Adam hadn't heard in quite some time, but was far too familiar with. Having fought alongside Dalton in Glimmeria several years back, he was one of the few lucky ones to survive. It was primarily a wasteland, steep canyons of rock and scorching sands marked with the occasional small city. From what Adam had heard over the past few years, the larger of the cities had rebuilt after the grinding war, however the outskirts of the planet remained in ruin, controlled by smaller organized crime families.

When the war ended, he had promised himself to never return. Too many of his good friends had fallen, most of them right in front of his very eyes. Now, he was hoping to last long enough for a rescue, only to set a course straight for a planet that had haunted his dreams many nights over. As terrified as a reunion to the soil that had taken part of his soul, strategically it made sense. The Glimmerian government, as well as every crime family with Glimmerian ties he had done business with, had two things in common.

They were among the toughest people he had ever known, and they had a mutual hatred for the Legion.

Sure, their army was miniscule compared to the Legion's forces, but traveling across the system to fight on Glimmeria would put them at a huge disadvantage by stretching them thin and placing a huge strain on their resources. It would give the Colonial army, at least what was left of it, more than enough time to regroup, recruit new planets to their cause and prepare for an assault by the Legion.

"Well, then let's hold our ground. What do we have to work with?" Michaels asked.

"Sarah's father sent us everything he had on Colonial Star Five. He could of turned and ran, but I think he was more concerned with getting his daughter off of this rock safely." the officer replied, bringing Sarah to a emotional state.

"Colonial Star Three is sending us a bulk of its ground force before leaving the battle, should be here and ready within the hour. Looking at about forty battle ready soldiers, a dozen or so Goliath units and by the looks of it; just a handful of Spartans." the officer replied.

The meeting was cut short as the rail guns outside of the tent began thrusting pounding shots of lead into the air, Strikewing units flying overhead firing tracers into the encampment.

"Good bet if they didn't know we were here, they do now!" Lieutenant Michaels yelled to the officer as the sound of the gunfire pierced their ears loudly.

"Sir! Small group approaching on foot!" one of the privates yelled through the entrance to the tent, prompting the officers to flood outside to direct their squads.

"Hold this damn ground!" Adam yelled loudly, walking outside to regroup with Dalton, who had taken position beside Lassiter.

"Do you think they made it off of the Colonial Star Five before it...?" Sarah asked before being cut short by Adam.

"I wouldn't worry, I'm sure they did."

It was a lie of course, Michaels himself had been worried about Kelly, Kato and Troy from the moment he saw the ship go thermal in the explosion. It was a justified lie though, knowing Sarah was still hurting from the death of her father.

"Holy shit," Dalton yelled ecstatically. "It's Roman and Steiner!" he added.

"Give them cover fire!" Adam yelled, seeing the two friends being closely pursued by a small group of Hunters.

As the they continued to sprint for the Colonial encampment, Dalton stood up, waving his friends to their direction. Four Goliath units were quickly dispatched to intercept the Hunter party, and intercept they did; the titanium peace keepers sprinted past Roman and Steiner as their mini guns began unleashing a flurry of grave digging lead.

The Colonial soldiers counted five Hunters, who outnumbered the Goliaths, but were solidly outmatched from the start. Within the span of one minute, all but one of the Hunters lay dead, the fifth fleeing back the way he came only to regroup with a much larger Legion group of attackers. Obeying orders, the Goliaths began sprinting back, two of them not lucky enough to make it, taking a beating from the Legion gunfire until they finally could function no more.

Jumping over the sandbag barrier, Roman quickly fell face down, letting the man made shield absorb several shots that were fully intended to end his life. Steiner dove over just seconds behind, not as lucky as he took a piercing shot into his left biceps muscle and taking a good portion of it when it exited. In obvious pain, he remained on the ground for a few seconds as two of the Colonial field medics began numbing the pain while bandaging it the best they could.

Dirt began flying as bullets zipped through the Colonial outpost, soldiers diving for cover any place they could find refuge.

"The more of these bastards I kill, the better I feel about myself and life in general." Dalton said to Lasstier as they both fired long range rifles at the approaching group.

"Pretty accurate with that rifle, huh?" Dalton asked as Lassiter glanced down at the sniper insignia sewn onto his Colonial uniform.

"Yea, yea. Well I still say fightin' up close is the best way to handle things." Dalton added snidely.

For hours, the Colonial forces and Legion troops exchanged gunfire from only a short distance; the occasional flyover of aircraft, usually Legion Strikewings spraying stinging clouds of ammunition to the ground below. Roman had joined the fight, gaining a combat rifle from a fallen soldier and using it with precision. Steiner on the other hand, rested near the back of the encampment, a long barrel shotgun in his better arm as the few officers that remained met with Adam.

"We're being cut to pieces!" Lieutenant Michaels told a couple of the officers loud enough to overpower the sound of gunshots, who were quick to agree as huge chunks of rocks and debris flew around them while mortar shells hit throughout the camp.

"We have to fall back." Adam said as a rare Spartan squadron flew overhead.

"There's no place to fall back to. A couple hundred feet behind this camp, nothing but cliffs. Seemed like a strategic advantage at the time, no way of being flanked by a ground assault." one of the few remaining officers replied, immediately thrusting Adam into deep thought.

Sure, he was Lieutenant Michaels of the Colonial Fleet, but underneath all of that he was still the same guy who specialized in getting himself out of a pinch.

As he glanced around the Colonial controlled soil, he realized that over half of them were wounded, many who were doomed to perish before day's end. The Legion continued pounding them with fire, although it had slacked up just a bit; which was a good indication that they were organizing a mass assault to overrun the Colonial outpost. Adam saw no way out except for surrender. He knew a lot of the men wouldn't simply lay down arms knowing the Legion and Hunters intended to kill them regardless. Still, the blood wouldn't be on Adam's hands. Rather than leave it in the hands of the remaining officers, he decided to take it upon himself to tell the soldiers on the front line himself.

As he walked into the direction of Roman, Dalton and Lassiter who would be the first to hear it, three squadrons of Spartans flew past at dazzling speeds. Quickly after, several more squadrons flew past, causing everyone in a Colonial uniform to turn away from the Legion force and stare into the sky behind them. Two of the huge Colonial vessels had entered the fight, pounding the Legion's forces with their cannons without regard.

"Lieutenant Michaels, this is Commander Douglas of the Colonial Star One Seven, prepare your men for immediate extraction." a voice rang out inside of Adam's com unit.

Finally. Finally the Gods above had given him a break, and he wasted no time replying to the commander emotionally. One of the Colonial Stars moved in directly over the Legion compound, as it began firing relentlessly, causing multiple explosions throughout. Shortly after, two Hunter Carrier ships had come to the aid of the Legion; engaging the Colonial Star as the three ships returned earthquake equivalent shots onto each other.

The Colonial troops who had fought so bravely to hold their ground, had little time to celebrate as choppers began landing to pick them up literally moments after Michaels had received the message. The Colonial wounded were the first off of the surface, as Michaels opted to stay with his team until the final pickup to provide cover for the other soldiers evacuation.

"Sarah. Please." Adam asked, praying that she would be on one of the first choppers up and out of harm's way.

Instead, she refused a reply, grabbing her combat rifle and joining Roman, Dalton and Lassiter on the line. Even Steiner scoured the ground, eventually finding a long range weapon of his own and slowly joining the group in providing cover.

"We'll be on the next one up! Tell them to save a place for us!" Lieutenant Michaels said loudly to one of the officers as the chopper's thrust engines nearly consumed the conversation. "Will do Lieutenant! Good luck!" the officer replied as he motioned the rest of the survivors onto the skiff, leaving a handful of the Goliath units behind to assist the group of heroes.

As the chopper left ground, a huge explosion brightened the sky as if it were a sun on the brink of extinction. The Hunter Carriers had eliminated one of the Colonial Stars and every soul aboard it. Adam and his crew simply stood in amazement as thousands of lives came to an end at the hand of those who had murdered so many before.

With the explosion of the Colonial Star, the Legion ground force that had massed began an all out charge to the crew's location in an effort to eliminate any survivors. Lieutenant Michaels countered the assault the only way possible, unleashing the remaining Goliath units directly into the charging enemies. They stood no chance of course, but they would at least thin them out a bit and maybe buy enough time for the next evacuation chopper to land. As they cut loose the mini gun fire, dozens of Legion soldiers fell instantly, many others joining only seconds behind. Returning fire, and aided by a small group of Fangs; within minutes the Goliaths were nothing more than metal to be recycled long after the battle had come to an end.

"Just hold them! Hold them long enough for..." Adam began to yell to his crew before the second Colonial Star started backing away as well, no match for the Hunter Carriers.

Contacting them by com was of no use, the chatter

through his ear piece was condemning evidence that they were being left to die. A full retreat ordered by the commander, as those lucky enough to have gotten off this rock would be headed to Glimmeria to fight another day, while Adam and his crew remained.

He could see it in all of their eyes. The look of defeat, the submission to the inevitable. Sure, they had weapons and would take several of the bastards with them, but in the end there was no way out. Adam threw his combat rifle to the ground and pulled the two revolvers into position. He could think of worse deaths than fighting beside the woman you love, friends who would die for you and above all, freedom. They simply took a few moments, glancing at one another; nodding their appreciation and respect without saying so much as a single word.

"Let's take as many of the sumbitches to the grave with us as we can." Dalton said, readying his favorite toy, the snub nosed shotgun.

"It's been my honor everyone." Michaels said with respect as they heard a Strikewing approaching, coming in at blazing speeds from the sound of it.

He was wrong, it wasn't pushing high speeds, and it wasn't a Strikewing, it was his ship, the Gunship! He smiled as wide as he ever had before, his eyes full of tears as the titanium skiff lifted up beside them from the cliff below. Even Roman caught himself tearing up a bit as Troy looked out of the passenger window of the cockpit, sitting beside Kelly as Kato manned a large mini gun that had been mounted to the outside of the crew area. It was vastly smaller ship than the day of its crash landing, still Adam had never seen a more beautiful sight in all of his life.

The mini gun began to ring out, the tearing flesh of Legion soldiers falling from the bone as they screamed in morbid agony. The first in was Sarah Blaine, who immediately turned to begin firing her combat weapon into the direction of the attacking force. Next, Lassiter climbed in before going prone and using his long range rifle to end a few lives of his own. Adam stood there firing one round at a time, dropping a few Legion faithful before Roman could interject.

"It's your ship Adam, GO!" he yelled, his chest covered with bloody bandages proving the capable handy work of the Colonial medics. Michaels hesitated for a moment before sprinting to the Gunship to reunite with everyone.

As Roman and Steiner began to make a run for it, Roman's leg buckled as a bullet passed through, sending him to a knee. Stopping to help him to his feet, Steiner was immediately overtaken by a Fang, jumping on top of him as it tried to rip meat from his skeletal frame. It took four shots from Roman's rifle to get the attention of the beast, who pounced from Steiner to Roman, slicing its claws across his already wounded stomach, as Roman did his best to try and fight back. The gunfire from the ship was enough to hold the Legion guards at bay, but it wasn't possible to get a clean shot on the hulking beast without risking friendly fire.

"Fuck this!" Kato said, grabbing the Mauler that he had become so comfortable with over the years and jumping down to assist the members of his crew, while Dalton quickly took his place on the minigun. He sprinted to the fight as the Fang thrust his claws into Roman a second time, tearing vital organs and opening a river of blood onto the ground. With Roman defenseless, Steiner swung his machete with every ounce of power in his body, nearly severing the head of the Fang, which combined with several shots from the Mauler, was enough to send the monster to the ground screaming in pain. Steiner quickly hoisted Roman onto his shoulder and sprinted as best he could to the Gunship, Kato clearing a path behind them with the Mauler.

Reaching the ship, Steiner lifted his fallen friend carefully into the arms of Lieutenant Michaels, who was covered in blood within seconds of the transaction, laying

Roman onto the floor of the ship as he frantically tried to stop the bleeding. Steiner looked back as he boarded long enough to see Kato fall to his death, several gunshot wounds leading him to it. A small group of Hunters sealed the deal as they sent nearly a dozen more shells from a pistol into the chest of the fallen hero, who lay dead with Mauler in hand.

In shock from the events, Kelly trembled in the pilot's seat, thinking of nothing but the death of Kato and the imminent demise of Roman Raines.

"KELLY, GO!" Adam yelled with no result. "Damn, we gotta go now!" Dalton yelled inside the ship as gunfire ricocheted around him; prompting Sarah to quickly make her way to the pilot's chair, tossing Kelly, who was obviously in shock onto the floor.

Sarah quickly assumed control of the ship's flight stick, bringing the vessel to a full burn as Dalton shut the exterior door and helped Adam tend to the dying warrior.

"We've got to catch up to that Colonial Star, otherwise he isn't going to make it!" Adam yelled desperately, trying to stop the internal bleeding of the former Gali commando.

"He isn't going to make it either way Adam, it would take a miracle." Dalton said solemnly as the Gunship blazed a trail of neon colored fumes across the sky, hitting orbit as it chased its only hope for a miracle to Glimmeria.

Gunship II: Glimmeria

The wind blew steadily through the lush leaves that gave such a buxom appearance to the thick trees behind as Roman stood there, facing the pastel shimmer of the river before him. It was almost a surreal sight, the sky above filled with cotton white clouds moving slowly as he knelt to rub his hand in the dirt of the riverbed, small rocks slipping through his fingers and falling from his battle hardened grasp.

It had been such a long time since the warrior's eyes had last seen serenity such as was laid out before him at this very moment. Every second that he stood hypnotized by the perfected body of water, he made use of his senses, pulling every small detail into reality. Everything from the birds singing in their melodic language overhead to the sound of the small waves crashing against the front of his boots on the shore. Everything seemed so perfect.

His attention was immediately broken by movement to his left, a nearing boat full of passengers who stood grouped together on the front deck as it slowly made its way to the edge of the river. Roman's first reaction was to reach for his combat blade, he was a warrior well trained, and any soldier who had seen what his eyes had witnessed through decades of gruesome killing and tasteless wars would be quick to draw a weapon from suspicion. He realized quickly, however, that he was unarmed.

Unusual for the former Gali commando, but that feeling soon dissipated as Roman began to recognize the faces on the boat that was docking with the river bank in front of him. Some were fallen warriors who had passed away beside him during one of many conflicts through the years, while others were familiar faces of family and close friends long deceased.

What kind of madness was this? A multitude of things began to run rampant through his mind as he cautiously watched a man step off of the boat, his boots digging firmly into the water drenched sand as he slowly walked directly for Roman. Dressed in official blue, gold buttons holding the jacket closed, the man fit the part of someone who seemed in be in charge of a ferry such as this. As he approached Roman, the commando began calculating self defense tactics in his mind, just in case. He had never laid eyes on the stranger before and wasn't about to let his training go to waste. But there was no time.

"They are waiting for you Roman." the calculated man said in a somber voice, obviously referring to the faces aboard the ferry.

Having decided he had seen enough, Roman began to slowly back away before turning to quicken his pace into the direction of a heavily wooded area nearby.

"IT'S YOUR TIME!" the ferryboat operator yelled in a demonic voice, grabbing Roman by the upper portion of his arm in an attempt to force him onto the vessel of souls.

"FUCK YOU!" Roman yelled, pushing the man down onto the ground and quickly turning to run for the thick trees that were only feet away.

The perfect world of vibrantly painted surroundings soon blended with bright white lights as Roman tried to make sense of things, the birds quickly becoming sounds of advanced medical equipment as he lay on an operating table under nearly a dozen doctors and nurses, the flood of overpowering white lights blinding the man who had cheated death.

"I've got a pulse!" one of the doctors yelled loudly, as several machines remained attached to the hardened warrior, giving a readout of every vital sign in his body, both the human and the mechanical side.

Roman let loose a loud shriek of pain that was terrifying for everyone close by, a damn stern reminder of this being the first lifesaving surgical attempt using Goliath parts on a living human being.

Several hours passed as Adam, Sarah, Dalton and Steiner waited patiently for some official word on their friend. Kelly and Lassiter had offered to watch over Troy, who was still recovering a bit from his injuries at the hands of the savage Husk and was trying his best to adjust to the desert planet of Glimmeria.

"Lieutenant Michaels," a doctor dressed in solid white said as he entered the waiting room, Adam immediately jumping to his feet, a standard issue Colonial combat pistol having replaced his trusted revolver in the holster on his side. "Your friend should eventually make a full recovery," the doctor said, bringing immediate celebration among the crew who sat behind Adam. "We lost him for a couple of minutes, but he came back to us on his own. It's unlike anything that I or any of my colleagues have ever seen. He is one tough man. It will take some time for him to get used to the idea of being half mechanical, however I hope he eventually understands that without the Goliath parts, he wouldn't be alive." the doctor added.

"Thank you." Adam said, shaking the doctor's hand before turning to his crew.

"This calls for a damn celebration!" Dalton said, hinting to everyone that he needed a drink.

Glimmeria may have been a desolate place for the most part, but the Colonial forces had sat down in and around Kamira, which was the planet's largest city. Dalton translated that into having drinking locations nearby, and now that he knew Roman was going to pull through, it was all about keeping his self-proclaimed reputation intact.

"I'm going to stay here, sit with Roman and try to get Troy settled in with a local family." Adam said.

The Colonials had recently started to place homeless children with families on Glimmeria, which was a much better fate than they would have had if taken in by Legion forces, which would have amounted to nothing short of forced slavery. After the crushing defeat at the hands of the Legion in Tameca City, there were plenty of children without homes, and even on a large planet such as Glimmeria, placing the children would be a daunting task at best.

"I'm game." Steiner said, volunteering to go with Dalton and rage a bit at any of the drinking establishments nearby.

"Just keep your asses out of trouble, understand?" Adam asked as Sarah slowly placed her arm around his lower back in order to hold him with affection.

"Yes sir!" Dalton said sarcastically as the idea of playing hide and go seek with full bottles of whiskey danced in his head.

Having caught one of the Colonial Star ships in a narrow escape was the biggest factor in saving Roman's life. As impressive as it all was, it paled in comparison to the sight of things when Dalton and Steiner left the Colonial hospital and made their way onto the sun scorched streets of Glimmeria's largest city.

Kamira looked almost as if it were one huge military base now, the outskirts of the city protected by huge underground Mack guns, which were nearly two-hundred yards in diameter and could fire bursts of lead from the surface into space, essentially punching holes through the largest of ships.

They were protected by Razor turrets, nothing more than a clever term for huge steel towers, each manned by two soldiers that fired a twenty-inch rail gun into the direction of anything that approached the city unwelcome on foot.

The new Goliath Model Two soldiers patrolled the city streets, having replaced the original units with much thicker armor plating as well as the addition of carrying surface to air missiles. Last but not least, the Colonial Marines. They weren't as feared as the larger Goliath units or weaponry, but in force, they were still the backbone of the Colonial war effort.

This was literally the last place that the Colonial forces had to go, and they had thrown all of their eggs into a single basket in order to assure the safety of Glimmeria's citizens.

With everyone in Adam's crew having officially joined the Colonial ranks, they all had sworn the allegiance and wore the uniform. Of course, that didn't stop Dalton from covering his with the brown duster that he had become so used to wearing.

As much as the rest of the crew dreaded the mere sight of that raggedy ass leather duster that had followed his back so long that it was starting to fall apart at the seams, it was his security blanket, especially when preparing to hammer back as many drinks as he possibly could.

"Where's the closest pub?" Steiner asked as they stood in the street, the torturing rays of Glimmeria's sun reddening them every single moment of it.

Two Swordfish fighter jets quickly blew by overhead, drowning out Dalton's response. They were the design of the Glimmarian military, the extra-long nose of the ship as well as the unique ability to hug the ground within a few feet during flight making them virtually undetectable on radar.

"I dunno, but when we find one, if we see two Swordfish parked out front, somebody's taking an ass whipping." Dalton said loudly, upset over the intrusion as Steiner mockingly laughed.

"I think we can all agree that the ones fighting for control of the Skyla System are not the ones who should be in power." Anwick said as he sat at a large wooden table that was polished to a gleaming shine.

His teeth filed to a razor sharp point, the dead white pupils of his eyes fixated themselves on his business partner. Two of his toughest escort Hunters sat with him, stark white hair also flowing from their scalps as they remained stone faced and heavily armed. Across the table, three well dressed members of the Benzan Mafia sat, finely pressed suits and ties accented by sunglasses of solid silver.

"The weak do not concern us. Our only wish is to be left alone, so that we may continue to live in true freedom." the man sitting in the middle of the Mafia members replied, his lenses reflecting back nothing more than the look of the Hunters to Anwick.

"True freedom always comes with a price. Always," Anwick replied calmly. "It's time to weed out the weak and useless from our midst, and that begins with Adam Michaels," Anwick added, throwing down several sheets of paper that included Adam's photo. "Prove your capability to me by getting rid of him and in return, I will ensure that the Legion leaves your kind well enough alone once they have crushed the Colonials." Anwick said, eagerly awaiting a response from Cyrus.

Yelling a handful of words loudly in Benzan, a large man entered the room, very well dressed in a gray pinstripe suit with a face that was without emotion, as if it were cut from marble slate.

"I will leave the choice to Draco. Should he choose to enter into an arrangement with you, it will remain between the two of you. I have no desire to kill by way of contract, nor do I wish to be directly involved. That said, should he choose to decline, then we are done here." Cyrus replied.

"I'm sure if the money is right, Draco won't mind doing the dirty work. Am I correct Benzan?" Anwick asked, throwing a sackful of Legion credits onto the table, easily ten thousand or more. Walking over to pick up one of the photos of Adam, Draco smiled widely.

"Consider him a dead man. Officially. We fought together in the first Glimmerian war. I know how he thinks, how he moves." Draco replied in a deep tone of voice, leaving little doubt of his ability to end lives.

"Very well then. I look forward to hearing from you my brother," Anwick said, standing to his feet while smiling wide, the low light of the room reflecting from the large razor's edge of his teeth.

"Now if you will excuse me, I must meet with the Legion regarding our next major assault." Anwick added as Cyrus slowly stood and extended his arm as the two men in charge sealed the deal with a firm handshake, which was a legally binding contract in the world of terrorism.

"Anyone ever tell you that you are magnificent with children?" Lassiter asked as Kelly answered his question with only a glowing smile. They had spent the last several hours helping Troy get what few belongings he had together, which amounted to nothing more than the few clothes he had gotten since arriving and a combat blade given to him by the Gali warrior.

"Kelly. Will I ever have a chance to say goodbye to Roman?" the young boy asked, his question taking her by complete surprise.

"No need for a goodbye. As soon as he is done

recovering, I'm sure he will visit. The family you have been placed with is right here in Kamira, so you will be seeing plenty of all of us." she replied, bringing a brilliant smile to Troy's face.

"You need a hand getting Troy to his new home?" Lassiter asked, a bit nervous, but trying to hide it behind the mask of calmness that he wore to disguise his feelings for her.

"I can handle it," Kelly replied, pausing for a moment. "When I get back though, maybe you'd be interesting in going into the city together? I haven't had a decent sit down meal in a long time." she asked, her shoulder length blonde hair keeping his undivided attention.

"I would love to, as long as it doesn't include Dalton and an open bar." he replied, laughing a bit to calm the mood in the room, their unexplored love having grown every single moment since arriving on Glimmeria.

"Alright, I'll see you soon then." Kelly replied smiling happily as Troy gave Lassiter a hug before grabbing his bag and heading for the front door of the small apartment.

"Not soon enough." Lassiter said to Kelly with a smile before turning to Troy, bending down so they could speak at eye level.

"Don't worry, I'll personally make sure Roman comes to visit soon, alright?" Lassiter said as Troy grinned ear to ear, shaking his head in approval.

It was a huge bar, one of the largest Dalton had found himself at in many years. He had long considered himself not only an avid connoisseur of the full spectrum of alcoholic drinks, but a critic of drinking establishments both large and small. Sitting on a wooden stool beside Steiner, he was amazed at the number of tables, nearly a hundred of them, full of people playing cards, drinking and exchanging exaggerated truths.

"I'll say one thing, these umbrellas are damn classy."

Dalton stated, referring to the wooden umbrella in his latest mixed drink.

"Agreed, but some of us are more about quantity and less about quality." Steiner replied loudly, trying to talk over the background noise as he held an unmarked brew in each hand.

"I'm about both, I just call a spade a spade. And these umbrellas are all class, right down to the neon pink." Dalton replied, turning up his drink and downing in one lengthy swig what would have taken most men an hour to nurse into their bloodstreams.

Maybe it was the alcohol casting illusions in front of his eyes as it had done so many times before, but Dalton had convinced himself that a brunette sitting at a nearby table, the kind that became more attractive as the drinks became more available, had been throwing stares into his direction.

Never mind the fact that she sat at a table with another female and two men wearing the Colonial uniform, or that it wasn't true love. In Dalton's mind a casual glance from the end of an alcoholic beverage was true enough.

"Sit tight buddy, and watch the master work." Dalton told Steiner as he slowly got up from his stool, patting his much larger Husk friend on the back for a brief moment before attempting to walk into the woman's direction.

His lack of speed was a direct effect of the workload he had recently placed into his bloodstream, still he managed to stagger with swagger as he eventually made it to his destination.

Preparing for the show, Steiner turned to watch the events unfold, a frothy glass of house brew in his oversize hand. Quickly, he realized how he and Dalton viewed the world through different lenses. How the young lady looked very happy with the group she sat with, not to mention the fact that she was far from being even decently attractive.

"Excuse me miss. Care to join me for some fine wine

and casual sex?" Dalton asked blatantly, causing an immediate look of disgust to fall across the woman's face as he reeked of anything but fine. "What? You don't like wine?" Dalton added, confused at being shot down on one of his best pickup lines.

It had worked so many times before, granted most of them were not that easy on the eyes, in fact they were slumming it at best according to his standards. Still, at his age, getting turned down using his best line made him begin to question if he still had charm.

Both Colonial soldiers stood to their feet abruptly, one of them calling Dalton a string of words that would scar a child's ears for life, prompting Steiner to stand to his feet as well, the over abundance of muscular tone that was all too common with the Husk race was ever intimidating.

"Sit down big man, I got this," Dalton said loudly, turning to Steiner as he motioned him to sit and let things unfold without his intervention. "While you're at it, order me another drink. One with the pretty umbrellas." he added.

As Dalton began to turn back, the Colonial soldier who had cursed him only moments ago, struck him across the face with a hooking punch, knocking him onto a nearby table and slinging several drinks onto the floor beneath it.

"You son of a bi.." Dalton began to reply, before the second Colonial soldier kicked him in the ribs solidly, knocking the air from the drunken warrior's lungs.

Dalton tried to yell for help from Steiner, extending his hand in a begging fashion as he fought to catch his breath. Steiner remained calm, drinking slowly from his glass as he watched the master at work. Scooped up and thrown several feet, Dalton landed on one of the nearby tables, clearing everything from the top as it followed him to the floor, crashing all around him like a glass filled grenade.

Slowly standing to his feet, he finally responded with a thrashing punch of his own to the face of one of the attackers, followed by a punishing kick to the stomach of the other.

At least that was his intention, but with things blurred extensively because of the night's binge drinking and beating, he wasn't convinced he had even hit the right two men. Standing there for a moment, trying to get his bearings straight, he randomly sucker punched one of the customers who had been sitting at the now flattened table.

First on the scene, two Glimmerian warrant officers raced through the door of the large bar, quickly flattened by a sweeping elbow from Steiner, who had watched his friend endure enough. Dalton staggered behind the bar, looking deviously at the coward bartender for a moment as he began pouring a large glass of whiskey, the tall glass nearly emptying the entire bottle before it topped off.

"And I want a fuckin' umbrella." Dalton slurred loudly, pulling one of the neon umbrellas from another patron's drink and placing it in his glass of whiskey.

Moments later, he and Steiner were standing at the end of Colonial rifles held by warrant officers of their own military.

"Well, I guess we're cut off." Dalton remarked softly as both men were escorted out in hand restraints to be processed at a local holding facility.

Adam and Sarah sat in illustrious surroundings as they ate one of the finest dinners he had ever seen, the type of establishment that was usually reserved for those in high political position and the absolute wealthy. Tonight was different however, tonight was the turning point in his life, the defining moment of his soul. With nearly eighty people eating in the large ballroom of red velvet and stained wood finish, Adam stood to his feet for a moment, drawing Sarah's immediate attention as he softly placed his thick red linen napkin onto the table before taking a place beside her on one of his knees.

"Sarah," Adam said with truth and integrity of the heart. Her eyes exploded with emotion, filled with both tears and emotional connection as she stared at Adam, hanging on his every word. "The moment I met you, I became a different person. What you've taught me is that I have always been this person deep down, I have lived my life, destined to get to this very moment. You bring out all of the best in me, without you I would be a broken man, both heart and soul. I am asking you from the bottom of this thing inside my chest that beats uncontrollably when you are near if you would do me the honor of being my wife?" Adam asked as the entire ballroom full of citizens looked on.

"Yes, of course!" Sarah replied without hesitation.

Everyone started clapping quietly as Adam rose to his feet slowly and embraced Sarah into his arms, kissing her as deeply as the concentration of stars that filled the night sky. After several minutes of affection, the waiter slowly walked over to give Adam the news of his friends checking into lockup. Not the first time Adam had bailed Dalton out of jail, but to have to put such a magical evening on hold to do it should be a felony within itself.

"It's alright Adam, let's go get our boys out of lockup and spend the rest of the night planning the first day of the rest of our lives together." Sarah said softly.

He nodded, although he planned on giving both Dalton and Steiner a damn good ass chewing when and if he could actually talk the Colonials into releasing them. As they began leaving the confines of the lavish restaurant, everyone once again clapped softly to let them know they had been touched to be a part of such a magical moment.

"What the hell is your problem?" Dalton asked Steiner as both men stood in a small holding cell, Dalton pacing a path in front of the door while Steiner stood in a rear corner.

"Just watching the master at work." Steiner replied with heavy sarcasm. Before Dalton could answer with a small piece of his self proclaimed infinite wisdom, they both recognized footsteps approaching.

"You have a visitor." a well dressed and lightly armed Colonial soldier said to Dalton.

"About damn time, hell Adam's usually here to pick me up long before now." Dalton said with relief as Steiner slowly approached the front of the cell. Rather than seeing his longtime friend walking up to the cell, the young woman from the bar cautiously approached.

"The master son. Don't forget it." Dalton said softly as if to pour salt into the wounded pride of Steiner before pausing to grab his brown coat and fluff it a bit.

Several hours had passed, which were filled with lies, bedroom eyes and the aftermath of barroom lust between Dalton and the young woman. Never asking her name, it was his belief that a woman's name just complicated things unnecessarily, especially through the steel bars of lockup.

It was a bittersweet feeling for Kelly. Troy had been lucky enough to find a stable home on Glimmeria with a family that would love and care for him deeply. Still, like the rest of the Gunship crew, she had grown to love and care for him deeply as well. He would be safer here however, there was a raging war that would soon enough reignite only a few miles away.

She was quickly reminded of that as she stepped outside of the housing unit onto the crowded urban street as a full squadron of Swordfish jets flew overhead. She couldn't wait to catch a transport and get back to the arms of Lassiter, having come to feel a comfort and peace around him that she had never known, a feeling that only true love can bring.

She never made it back. Standing respectfully as only a Colonial soldier could, she felt a sharp piercing band of lead cut through her chest. Her first reaction was to draw her sidearm, *maybe the Legion invasion had began?* As she slowly turned, her sidearm shaking roughly while her body fought to remain alive, a second shot hit her chest only inches below the first, the muzzle flash of Draco's sniper rifle alerting her to his position in a second story window. Moments later she died, falling soundly onto the streets below.

Draco tossed a large golden coin out of the window, landing near her lifeless body. A Glimmerian coin that had been out of mint since the day they had lost the first war to the Legion, his calling card to Adam Michaels.

Several hours later Adam and Sarah were the first to join the Colonial investigators at the scene of the shooting. Visibly shaken by the body of someone who he had looked at as a little sister, someone he felt compelled to look after, Adam trembled uncontrollably as Sarah held his hand and tried to convince him that there was nothing he could have done to help her. *It wasn't his fault. Or was it?*

Adam spotted the golden coin laying near her body, immediately recognizing it and deciding there was a huge problem. The coins were only issued to a limited number of Glimmerians nearly a decade ago, a special group, the group he fought beside. His unit. He quickly realized that Kelly had died because of him, as would everyone else around him unless he could somehow find a way to protect them, like he should have been there to protect her.

"Kelly," Lassiter screamed as he sprinted across the street and fell on his knees trying to revive the lifeless body of his lover. "Get off of me!" he added as Adam grabbed him, both arms clinched around Lassiter as he drug him away from her body unwillingly.

"She's gone." Adam said softly as Lassiter cried uncontrollably.

The Colonial jailer escorted Adam down the corridor, the striking of their boots against the stone tiled floor making their presence immediately known.

"About fucking time. You forget about us or something?" Dalton asked arrogantly as the cell door opened.

Without a word, Adam simply turned and grabbed Dalton firmly by the front of his brown coat, picking him up a few inches from the ground and holding him against the cold brick wall. Exchanging nothing more than deep stares, it quickly became obvious to Dalton that his friend was a different person than he was only hours before.

"Get your fucking hands off of me!" Dalton yelled as Adam dropped him and loosened his grip. Steiner quickly intervened, easily holding Dalton at bay as Michaels looked onto both of them for several moments with the eyes of a man hellbent on revenge.

A few painstaking days had passed before Adam found himself standing under the large canopy surrounded by friends as a Colonial priest spoke words before committing Kelly's body to the ground. The only sounds that kept the entire funeral from seeming like a dream were the shots from Colonial rifles as the twelve soldiers fired them into the air in unison. Adam watched Lassiter deal with the loss of someone he couldn't manage to live without, he felt for the young man as he tried to imagine losing Sarah Blaine the same way. The thought of it was unbearable.

After the service and departure of a majority of those in attendance, Adam gathered his crew.

"We have a problem. The person who shot Kelly, left this." Michaels said, holding the gold coin up as the sunlight shimmered across it.

"Bullshit, ain't no way Adam. Those coins were specific to our platoon back in the first war. I should know, I dropped hundreds of them at every bar on this fuckin' rock," Dalton replied.

Adam answered only with a dedicated stare. "I'd say we do got a problem then, a big fucking problem." Dalton added, feeling Adam's sense of urgency.

"Whoever did this is coming for Dalton or myself, maybe both of us. The marksmanship and weapon they used to kill Kelly lets me know that none of you are safe. From this moment forward, nobody goes anywhere alone. Nobody." Adam added to the conversation.

"Steiner. You and Lassiter will stay with Dalton at all times. Pack plenty of firepower and stay indoors as much as possible. If they used a sniper rifle the first time, chances are they plan on striking again from a distance," Michaels said. "Roman, you will be with Sarah and I. Lassiter, I realize this is a very tough time, but I have to ask you to stay focused. Until we catch the person who did this, none of us are safe." Adam added.

Lassiter agreed with a nod, still visibly shaken.

"I know what Kelly meant to you, she was like a sister to me. I will go through the rest of my life blaming myself for not being able to protect her from this, but you have to shake it off for now. Put it on a shelf, the only way we can help her now is by catching the son of a bitch who did this. Understand?" Adam said.

"Yea, I understand." Lassiter responded after a long pause.

As the group split up and walked toward two different Colonial transports, Adam turned to face the others.

"Dalton, keep your ass out of trouble." Dalton stopped walking for a moment.

"Who me? Sure thing, scout's honor." he replied with a smile before once again joining his group.

"Dalton used to be a scout?" Sarah asked surprised.

"No, he didn't. That's what worries me." Adam replied, drawing a bit of laughter from Roman.

"Based on the information our spies have given us, the

Colonial base is heavily defended. Our forces will take heavy losses on their way to the surface." a Legion advisor said as Flag Officer Andrews stood for a few silent moments watching his forces staging on a wall mounted grid, his crimson red officer's uniform lined with thick black to match his shoes.

"We will send the invasion in two waves. Send the mercenaries and newly trained soldiers down in the first wave, let them take the blunt of it. Send the officers, battle tested soldiers and heavy equipment down with the second wave. Have them set up a forward base of operations so we can begin to funnel supplies and reinforcements to the front lines." Andrews replied.

"Yes sir. And what of the Hunters?" the advisor asked.

"Have them wait in orbit with Legion High Command. If the Colonials attempt an early retreat, the Hunters should be able to finish them off easily. If the Colonials dig in, we'll have the Hunters drop down to the surface to reinforce our lines." Flag Officer Andrews replied.

"Yes sir!" the advisor responded, immediately ordering his communications officer to relay the message throughout the fleet.

Andrews stood there for several minutes, admiring the view from the other side of the thick plated glass of the ship's bridge. Dozens of Legion capital ships and cruisers along with three Hunter carriers, all working together as squadrons of Legion fighter jets flew past, running drills in preparation of the upcoming battle.

"Sir. We've picked up a large fleet broadcasting Legion code in outer orbit of the planet!" one of the grid operators yelled as Commander Edwards walked swiftly toward his station.

"Set our condition to one, recall all Colonial soldiers and make them fully aware that this is not a drill," Edwards replied. "They are staging from the looks of it, we still have some time. Order all Mack stations fully loaded and

Swordfish and Spartans fueled and standing by. Bring every Goliath unit that we have online." he added.

"Yes sir!" the grid operator announced loudly, punching the orders into a computer that would mirror them to every outpost on Glimmeria.

"Better not be a fucking drill because this is the first time I've ever left a pitcher of beer sitting," Dalton said angrily as Steiner and Lassiter both had their thoughts on the impending battle rather than Dalton's lust for man drink. "And another thing, they need to find a way around this sweltering fucking heat, I'm already sick of it." Dalton added sharply as the group quickly left the Colonial bar along with everyone else, the exterior neon sign easily overpowered by the strength of sunlight as they began their walk back to the Command Center.

Having almost made it back, the men continued their slow march as they absorbed Dalton's constant barrage of bitching and moaning. Steiner had intended to let him know that his ranting was beginning to resemble that of a married woman, when the right thigh of the massive Husk warrior was struck with a shotgun blast, immediately putting him down to the ground yelling in agony.

Draco walked from an alley nearby, firing the second shotgun blast of the double barrel in the direction of Lassiter, barely grazing his back with the hot lead spray as he dropped the emptied weapon and calmly pulled two pistols. Lassiter found refuge behind a parked transport, drawing his combat sidearm and looking several feet down the road, watching a suddenly sober Dalton pull Steiner to the rear of another one of the transports which lined the sides of the city's streets.

"Adam! Where the fuck are you! We got the shooter a couple of blocks from HQ, we're pinned down and taking fire!" Dalton yelled into his com, throwing it to the ground as he stood to fire a blast from his own short barrel shotgun before dropping back down quickly behind cover.

Dalton's blast was returned with three ringing pistol shots, shattering the window above the head of the roughly bearded man smothered in his favorite brown coat as he sat with his back firmly against the thin steel of the makeshift barricade. As Draco approached the transport, he slowly rounded the front end, Dalton and Steiner easily in his sights. Before he could finish the task, however, his ribs felt the penetrating plunge of a shot from Lassiter's combat pistol.

The Colonial sniper had recovered enough to go on the offensive just in time to save the life of his friends.

Dalton aimed his shotgun in the direction of the assassin, but it was quickly brushed to the side as the shot made its way deep into the transport, the steel pellets scattering in a circular design as they embedded themselves into the thin steel and aluminum. Draco used his second arm to throw a hooking punch into the face of Dalton who crumpled at the bottom of the transport and laid motionless as Lassiter had began closing in on the Benzan contract killer.

Steiner, still reeling from his flesh wound, realized that if the assassin was to be caught or killed, he was the only one capable of doing so.

Dalton was incapacitated, while such an experienced killer would have made short work of a Colonial sniper. Grabbing Draco in a tightly clinched hold, the Husk used all of his strength to tighten the grip even further trying to snap the bones of the assassin. Draco finally was able to loosen himself just enough to swing his right elbow around and bury it into the face of Steiner, who was stunned but still on his feet. A hard right kick from the assassin changed that, sending Steiner to his back with a thud as Draco spun quickly, doing a back fist with his clinched knuckles wrapped in black leather glove, knocked the pistol from Lassiter's hand.

Forcefully pushing Lasstier to the ground, the much more qualified Draco jumped onto him, his arms pursuing the neck of the Colonial sniper in an attempt to snap it and be done with the pesky commoner. It was his own neck, however, that felt a sudden stiffness as Dalton wrapped both of his arms around it, burying his elbows deep into the shoulders of Draco. After several moments of struggle between the two, Draco clinched the back of Dalton's brown jacket and using most of the strength he had left, launched Dalton over his shoulder through the air as the wiley soldier of fortune crashed into one of the nearby parked vehicles, knocking him virtually unconscious.

As with any assassin, Draco had grown tired of the hands on fighting and picked up Lassier's pistol, which was the closest weapon to him, laying just a few feet away.

He hesitated for a moment, unsure of who to kill first, deciding finally to send Dalton to the afterlife as he aimed down the crisp iron sights at the man he had once fought beside. Meat tore from his shoulder first, followed by skin and muscle from his ribs as

Adam had arrived just in time to fire two shots from his pistol, both hurting the assassin a great deal. Draco quickly made it to his feet just in time to be blinded by several reeling punches and a solid elbow, all thrown into the Benzan's face by Roman Raines.

Draco tried to fight back, throwing several punches with deep intention that would have seriously wounded a normal man, but Roman was no normal man, the farthest thing from it would be the best assessment.

Blocking the punches with the thick aluminum on the backside of one of his partially mechanical arms, the other was thrown to the body of Draco, the sound of ribs breaking under pressure echoed loudly as Roman threw Draco face first into one of the transports, putting him out of commission.

"Enough," Adam said, doing everything he could to pull Roman off of the Benzan assassin. "We need to find out why." he added, Roman stepping away as Sarah continued to tend to Lassiter, Dalton and Steiner.

Flag Officer Andrews watched from a tall glass balcony as thousands of Legion soldiers had gathered in formation under him, awaiting his final words before boarding their drop ships which would be descending in only minutes to the surface of Glimmeria to begin the largest battle ever recorded. The ships were solidly constructed with steel plating thick enough to deflect the paltry shots of small arms fire, however they could hardly withstand the pounding of the surface based Mack cannons.

Every Legion soldier knew this, understood the significant chance that once they entered the drop ships, they could be entering nothing more than a death sentence. Still they stood loyal as their Flag Officer placed his hands tightly around the bannister and prepared to speak.

"It is my belief that only the strong should lead. Survive. Take a moment to look around, look into the eyes of those which you fight beside on this very day. You are the strong, and because of this you will survive. The Colonials have tried to separate themselves from the rest of the Skyla System, and in doing so have made a mockery of our very way of life. Today, it is our turn. The Colonials will either submit to our way of life, or they will perish to the will of the strong. May the gods be with all of you!" Flag Officer Andrews said boldly as every soldier began to cheer before chanting the Legion name.

Shortly after, each soldier began boarding their ships with great reserve as Andrews returned to the bridge which would serve as the control center of the Legion High Command for the upcoming battle.

Draco sat on a wooden stool, his hands bound with thick rope and his face bloodied like a scene from a horror film. He knew he was still alive, yet it all seemed surreal, almost as if he were placed snugly into a dream. Steel plated walls surrounding him, the serene silence of emptiness penetrated the air throughout the room as he sat there with no idea of what was to come next. Thick steel began to grind as the door slowly opened, Adam Michaels entering the room and pulling up a wooden chair to sit within arm's reach of the man who had taken the life of Kelly and nearly several others.

"Funny. Nearly ten years ago, you, I, Dalton and a couple dozen other lucky souls made it off of this rock in one piece. We would have given our lives for each other back then, and when we left we were on good terms Draco, so my only question is why?" Adam asked. Draco continued to stare at the solid steel door without so much as a blink, no response and no acknowledgement of Adam's presence, well versed in the tactics of interrogation due to his extensive Benzan training.

"Draco, I am the carrot. I'm in here to try and get the answers I need and maybe let you live to see another day. The rest of my crew is waiting right outside that door, including the man who was deeply in love with the young girl you killed. They are the stick, and trust me, none of them have a problem with cutting the answers out of you and leaving you here to die. So again I ask y.." Adam said, cut off by Draco.

"I did it to save my family."

"Who?" Adam asked in a demanding tone.

"You're in way over your head here Adam. If you plan to kill me, do it and get it over with. If I say anything, my family is dead, and I promise you I'm not going to let that happen." Draco replied.

"About three years ago, I was in a bad spot Adam. I needed money...a lot of money. I met a few people and before I knew it I was in with the Benzan Mafia. Yea, I know what you must think of me. I kill people, usually in cold blood and I do it for a paycheck." Draco said, turning to look into the eyes of his former brother in arms.

"Adam, you have to believe me when I tell you I didn't have a choice. Usually the people I kill, hell they all deserve it. I do society a favor by erasing some of the worst people you can imagine. This was different. Yea, it paid a lot of money and I know she was innocent Adam, but my family? What was I supposed to do," Draco added as Adam turned away. "WHAT WAS I SUPPOSED TO DO?" Draco shouted.

"So the Benzan Mafia is responsible for the death of one of my crew?" Adam asked bluntly.

"No. In fact, they wanted no part of it. They just allowed me the meeting, that's it." Draco replied.

"I need you to arrange a meeting, put me in the same room as the head of the Benzan Mafia." Adam said boldly.

"You know I can't do that! Adam, I'm low level with the family, I can't just call 'em up and start demanding that kind of shit!" Draco replied.

"I'll do it," Michaels said bluntly. "Who do I need to contact and how do I go about it?" Adam asked as Draco directed his attention on the other side of the room, reluctant to answer the question. "WHO GODDAMNIT!" Adam yelled, pulling his sidearm and pressing it onto the forehead of Draco.

"This is Commander James Edwards, the superior ranking officer of Colonial Command. Earlier today, our grid systems picked up a large Legion presence entering the orbit of this planet, leading us to only one conclusion, war is imminent. We have solid defenses set up on the planet's surface, the most capable soldiers in the Skyla System, but above all else we have reason. While the Legion looks to impose its will on a free people, we fight for the reason of freedom," he said, pausing briefly as everyone near a com unit on Glimmeria's surface continued to stop whatever they were doing to listen to the breaking news.

"A society in which innocent people may live in peace

rather than be slaughtered because of a political agenda. I ask that you all fight with reason, vigilance and the memory of those fallen Colonials who have allowed our freedom up until now. Good luck and God speed." Commander Edwards announced throughout every Colonial radio and com unit on Glimmeria.

Turmoil set in as Glimmeria's citizens faced the facts, a war with the Legion was at their doorstep, one that would forever change the face of their planet and those who inhabited it. Most of them were quick to evacuate indoors, trying their best to safeguard their families.

Groups of the mechanical masterwork Goliaths accompanied squads of Colonial soldiers who were armed to the teeth, requesting the citizens stay inside of their homes as Colonial Spartan fighters and Glimmerian Swordfish screamed overhead, their thrusters at full burn and ready for the upcoming fight. The Mack stations were already online, however there became a sense of urgency with the staff as they hustled to run full diagnostics and double check the ammunition storage for the surface to space cannons. They were the primary line of defense for the Colonials and the backbone of their strategic war effort.

Meanwhile, Commander Edwards strengthened the security forces inside of the Colonial Command Center. The large, atrium style room, which was made of plated steel and shatter proof glass, was designed to survive a nuclear strike. Therefore, all of the high ranking officials collapsed into the room with equipment enough to run the entire Colonial war effort behind the closed doors of what everyone had began to refer to as the "vault".

"Where are Lieutenant Michaels and Roman Raines?" Commander Edwards demanded to know as Dalton, Steiner and Lassiter stood front and center.

"I'm sorry sir, who?" Dalton reluctantly answered.

"Do not play with me at a time like this Dalton!" Edwards shouted, smelling the hint of soured lager on his breath.

"Sir. They left to meet with the Benzan Mafia in reference to Kelly's kille..." Lassiter finally admitted, interrupted by the commander.

"THEY DID WHAT? AT A TIME LIKE THIS!" Commander Edwards added in hysterical disbelief. Steiner and Lassiter both sunk their heads toward the floor as Dalton began to recite his soldier identification number as if being interrogated by the enemy.

"ENOUGH!" the commander shouted, bringing his face within inches of Dalton's own, the sight of his stubbled brown beard furthering the blurred vision of a furious commander.

"I should have your ass thrown in the brig for such blatant insubordination," Commander Edwards yelled as Dalton stared back planning his exit strategy, just in case. "However, with Lieutenant Michaels off doing business that is completely unauthorized, you are next in line in the chain of command Sergeant. I have no choice other than to put you in charge of the security detail of this building." Commander Edwards said.

"I'm sorry?" Dalton asked.

"I have to put you in charge. You can't follow orders worth a damn, but if the Legion makes it this far, I have no doubt in my mind of your ability to give them hell to protect the lives of everyone here." the commander answered.

"In charge? You mean like, as in giving orders of my own?" Dalton asked.

"Yes, in charge. Unless you are too drunk to do so?" Edwards asked.

Dalton stood motionless for a moment, cursing his chewing gum for failing to mask the stench of the morning's alcoholic adventure.

"No sir, I'm ready and capable." Dalton finally replied, stretching his eyes for a moment in an attempt to pull himself from an intoxicated daze.

"Good. You three hit the ammunition reserve down the street, grab plenty of small arms weaponry as well as the nearest Colonial squad, and then double-time your asses back. Set the squad up strategically and you three collapse inside and protect the vault as a last defensive resort. Sarah Blaine will remain inside of the vault with us, it will be a huge boost to everyone's moral hearing her voice through the com system," Commander Edwards ordered, turning to enter and seal the vault.

"Oh, and if you see Lieutenant Michaels before I do, send him directly to me. Understood?" Edwards asked.

"Aye Captain." Dalton answered.

"It's COMMANDER!" Edwards shouted. "Huh?" Dalton confusingly asked.

"JUST GO!" Commander Edwards yelled before turning to seal the vault.

"I wonder what's crawled up his ass?" Dalton mumbled as the three men turned to walk down the narrow hallway and onto the street.

"Now what?" Adam asked as he stood with Roman and Draco, the assassin's hands tied snugly with thick rope.

"Now we wait." Draco replied.

"Just to be clear, even though he's given me his word that we will not be harmed, if he does try anything, your ass will be the first one dusted." Michaels said of Draco.

"Relax. The Benzans are always good to their word, especially Cyrus. Of all of the Benzans I have met, he considers a man's word to be as important as the soul in his chest." Draco replied as they remained standing beside three of the mangiest horses Roman had ever seen.

"Looks like you guys have a friend coming." Draco said sarcastically.

"Fuck." Michaels replied, catching a glimpse of a Glimmerian lawman approaching them on horseback.

"Good afternoon." Adam said charmingly, unsuccessfully trying to change the scowl on the Sheriff's face as the dust settled around the hooves of the solid brown steed.

"Adam Michaels, Sheriff Barker. I have a warrant to bring you in to the Colonials." Adam hung his head for a moment before looking back at the lawman, who was still mounted on his horse, a large rifle laying across his inner elbows.

"Can't do it, at least not at the moment. I'm out here on business, when I'm done you can take me wherever you like." Adam replied. Sheriff Barker pulled the rifle up, aiming directly at Adam.

"I'm not in the business of making suggestions, a warrant hits my desk and I go out and fetch 'em. That's how it works." Barker said, his rifle's aim still true to Adam's upper body. Putting his hands in front of him to try and keep the peace, Adam replied. "May want to put the gun away, my friend doesn't take kindly to having them pointed in his direction." Barker adjusted the gun barrel slightly to aim it at Roman.

"Can your friend dodge bullets?" the Sheriff asked.

"Well actually." Michaels replied, knowing damn good and well that if Roman was pissed off, Barker would have been dead already.

The Sheriff started to reply, but was quickly drown out by the thrusters of a ship breaking orbit, falling quickly from the sky and hastily approaching to land near them. They all watched as the elongated blade design of the ship's front gave away the fact that it was Benzan, huge clouds of dust rising from the ground as the ship rocked back and forth slightly, finally touching ground.

"Sheriff, you need to leave now. Please." Michaels pleaded, not knowing what the reaction of the Benzans would be.

As the shuttle door began to open, the Sheriff glanced in its direction for a split second, which was all the time Roman needed. Pulling his combat blade and throwing it end over end with blazing speed and unparalleled accuracy, the knife digging into the flesh of Sheriff Barker's shooting hand and throwing him from the horse.

"Just stay down until the ship leaves, otherwise they may kill you." Roman said to the Sheriff as he walked over to him, grabbing his rifle and tossing it far enough away from him to be irrelevant.

Sheriff Barker remained on the ground, doing his best to stop the bleeding as he held the wound moments after Roman recovered his blade with a tug. Obviously enduring a tremendous amount of pain, the Sheriff did his best to remain silent as two Benzans exited the shuttle.

The first was a tall, slender man with dirty blonde hair braided down his back. He wore a pair of reflective silver sunglasses, a white long sleeve shirt with buttons and carried a solid black pump shotgun. He was everything the men had pictured a member of such a notorious crime family looking like. The second Benzan out, not so much.

Brunette hair with a slight but lustrous curl, she moved with perfect symmetry, deep blue eyes, a white v-neck shirt and gray cargo pants, she had a small machine gun pistol hanging from a black leather strap that draped over her shoulder. Unlike anything Adam or Roman expected, she was simply too damn beautiful to be in this line of work. Not society's definition of beautiful, which amounted to makeup, empty talk and a glamor filled wardrobe. She was a pure beautiful. The kind of woman who could make men do almost anything with a simple request. Of course, if that didn't work, she still had the machine gun pistol as leverage.

"The agreement was three passengers, not four." the tall Benzan man said as the attractive female kept a finger on the trigger of the rapid fire pistol, its barrel pointed to the ground.

"Relax Oz, the one laying down is a Sheriff who decided to show his damn face only minutes ago." Draco replied. With a slight nod of Oz, the female began to walk toward the lawman with intentions of ending his life.

"No! Please, he is of no harm. Simply came to serve a warrant on me is all." Adam said, stepping in front of the Sheriff in an attempt to plead for the man's life. It would be the very first time Adam and the young lady of such immaculate beauty locked stares.

"It's alright Sasha, leave him be." Oz said, standing by the ramp of the ship as he waited for everyone but Barker to board.

"Weapons." Sasha said as she began collecting everyone's killing devices on their way up the steel ramp which was outlined with glowing red bulbs. Taking it upon herself, she quickly reached out and grabbed the combat blade of Roman, attempting to pull it from its casing which was strapped around his leg. Meeting her grasp with one of his own, he gripped her wrist strongly as a warning.

"Careful." Sasha warned, breaking his hold on her and removing the blade as Adam nodded slightly to keep Roman calm.

He was calm enough, in fact he was impressed. A woman who knew her weaponry, could hold her own with words and had a undeniable beauty throughout her entire body. Not the textbook definition, Roman never had a need for that type of woman, they were much too weak for his taste.

Sure, she could have easily worn the clothes of a princess and blended well with the title. However, he thought she had a more gritty perfection about her, she could handle herself well in a fight, this much Roman knew the moment she walked from the ship for the first time. She was the first woman in a very long time who had gained his respect.

"If they so much as move the wrong way, shoot them." Oz said to Sasha as the two men began to buckle their flight harnesses.

"Get this fucking rope off of me." Draco said demandingly as Sasha quickly used Roman's blade to do so, sliding the steel between his wrists and the thick rope, which fell into pieces like a child's toy as she gave a simple upward thrust of the knife. Both Adam and Roman sat there, amazed at a woman who knew her steel well.

At the moment his bonds were no more, Draco's hand lunged to Sasha's leg, pulling her combat sidearm made of solid black steel and pointing it at the two men. As swiftly as he aimed the weapon, the barrel of Oz's shotgun touched the back of his neck, his tiny hairs standing to attention as the circular design of the barrel commanded respect.

"No harm is to come to them while they are under safe harbor from Cyrus." Oz said, holding the shotgun at point blank range.

"You would shoot me and watch them go free?" Draco asked loudly, surprised by the thought. Oz simply answered his question by pushing on Draco's neck with the shotgun, the unforgiving steel digging into his skin and quickly convincing him to lower Sasha's sidearm.

"It won't be forgotten my brother." Draco said sarcastically as Sasha forcefully grabbed her pistol, placing it back into her leg holster.

"The memories of a man who gets himself caught on a simple hit are of no concern to me." Oz replied with a touch of sarcasm himself as he strapped into the pilot's seat.

Only minutes later, Sheriff Barker stood to his feet, his injured hand wrapped as he collected his rifle and watched the Benzan shuttle once again hit Glimmeria's upper atmosphere.

Although Adam was preoccupied with hoping he and Roman would live to see another sunrise, at the same time he found himself intrigued with Sasha's intoxicating beauty and skills with a weapon. Moments after hitting the thin layer of the planet's atmosphere, his attention was quickly drawn to a small window of the shuttle as they entered space. Legion ships as thick as the sand on

Glimmeria's surface bunching together for the invasion to come, as he and Roman both sat silently in awe of the force they would soon be fighting against. Within seconds they both knew that the Colonials were outnumbered at least three to one, and there was no doubt that the invasion was being carefully planned before execution.

Adam suddenly found himself wanting to be back on the planet's surface, helping his friends prepare for a fight which would surely lead to the death of them all. Meeting with the Benzans to find the person who initiated Kelly's death was deeply important to him, however, she was gone and nothing would ever bring her back. But he still had a chance to inform his friends of the fight to come, maybe talk them out of a battle in which they had no chance of winning and in doing so, save their lives.

"Hey, check it out." Lassiter said to both Dalton and Steiner as they began the short journey on foot to the ammunition storage building as ordered, the Husk still moving rather slowly as the soreness of his bandaged right thigh had started to catch up to him.

"What is it Private Lassiter, I'm a busy man." Dalton replied, flexing his newly assigned command.

"Private?" Lassiter replied, amazed at Dalton's newly found dedication to the uniform, not to mention his ability to use the term outside of the bedroom.

"Didn't see this coming." Steiner said laughing as Dalton returned the comment with a stern look before noticing what Lassiter had seen only moments ago.

Glimmeria's citizens had began crowding the streets, cheering the many soldiers who were preparing for the upcoming battle against the Legion. Many of them clapped loudly, while a few of the women had thrown flowers as a sign of respect. In only a few hours they would no doubt be instructed to remain in their homes, preparing as if a disaster was inevitable while forced to huddle around small radios and listen to the progress of the war. Still they welcomed it with open arms, realizing that these soldiers represented a free tomorrow for each and every one of them.

It was a very emotional moment for all three of the men, leveled by the sight of so many people who were counting on their help to remain free, rather than slaves who would spend the remainder of their days under horrible conditions while doing the Legion's manual labor. Both Lassiter and Steiner secretly wondered if Dalton's stare of concentration was one of gratitude or lust, as he continued glancing for several moments at the flower bearing women with saliva ridden lips as they slowly continued their course to collect ammunition.

"Looks like this is the place," Dalton said, several armored skiffs exiting through a huge set of steel bay doors which carried the painted insignia of the Colonials. "Automatic rifles, grenades and as much damn ammunition as we can carry, got it?" Dalton ordered, flashing his Colonial badge to an officer behind a thick steel desk as Lassiter and Steiner both began to join dozens of other Colonials in rummaging through huge wooden crates full of precision weaponry.

"What the hell is this," Lassiter asked as he began to laugh, Steiner looking for a moment before shrugging without an answer. "Looks like it belongs in a museum." he added, tossing the gun back into the direction of the storage bin.

The beat up wood grain stock of the single shot rifle, instead found its way to the palm of Dalton's hand as he snatched it from the air just moments before it would have been discarded.

"This, greenhorn, is a Glimmerian Thumper." Dalton said insultingly as he stroked the weapon with vain intention.

"And they wonder why the first Glimmerian War was lost." Lassiter replied with heavy sarcasm of his own.

"Don't look like much at first glance..." Dalton said as he was interrupted.

"Actually, I glanced at it three times, and it still looks like a raggedy piece of shit." Steiner said, bursting into laughter as Lassiter quickly joined him.

"Laugh it up." Dalton replied, sliding the thin metal chamber cover open for a second to make sure it was loaded, before sliding it shut forcefully and aiming it to a corner of the warehouse, a quickly created smirk on his face as he fired the weapon.

Everyone's attention was instantly abducted by the loud pop of the shell jolting from the gun's chamber and slamming into the thick stone corner, rock shrapnel flying several feet as the round exploded with force.

Still holding his shit eating grin, he turned to the other Colonial soldiers, who had stopped collecting gear to stand and watch. "Say something," Dalton dared of them as he turned back to his friends. "I don't give a damn what uniform a man is wearing, one of these exploding rounds hits him and it'll ruin his weekend." he added, smiling so widely that his whiskey scarred teeth made a rare appearance.

"Report!" Commander Edwards demanded as he leaned over to view the large monitor of one of the many Colonial workstations that was tucked snugly inside of the vault as its alarm rang loudly.

"Sir," a lower ranking officer said, standing to his feet to face the commander. "Our grids show the Legion staging area has reached the fringe area of our Mack Cannons." he added.

"Good. You have my permission to make them pay for their first mistake of the day. Start pounding the son of a bitches out of the sky." Commander Edwards said sharply, ordering the first shot of the battle as he glanced around the room for a moment to admire such a group of loyal Colonials.

Only a few moments later, everyone on Glimmeria's surface heard the first shot fire. The large, pounding hollow burst of one of the Mack cannons illuminated the sunset filled sky for a moment, sending dedicated lead screaming into outer orbit. Everyone on the street stopped to watch as the city's fallout siren began blaring with painstaking volume, a mask of silence falling onto the city as everyone began to get indoors as quickly as possible. It had begun.

Three more thumping blasts fired in unison, this time panic and screaming overtook the city as everyone both Glimmerian and Colonial began to quicken the pace of whatever they were doing, sprinting for either safety or the nearest military outpost.

"Ahh shit," Dalton said in a dedicated tone of voice, upset that they had not had the adequate time required to fetch a full array of weaponry. "Grab the whole damn crate, we 'aint got time for bullshittn'." he added, Lassiter and Steiner looking at each other and both quickly coming to the solid conclusion that Dalton had been the only one bullshitting.

Steiner easily pulled his end of the huge crate from the floor, his hulking arms barely straining as he hoisted his half to waist level, strength in full supply.

Meanwhile, Lassiter struggled with the other end, repositioning himself several times and trying to find the easiest spot to grab hold of. Finally managing to pull his end off of the floor a bit, doing everything he could to keep it raised at the height of his knees and punishing his back in the process while the rest of his body shook slightly from the immense weight.

"Let's go private, cowboy the fuck up." Dalton ordered, walking quickly outside carrying nothing more than the badly scarred Thumper and leaving the men to follow slowly. Lassiter doing his absolute best to convince himself not to drop the crate of weapons and begin pistol whipping the arrogant man in command.

A few transports zoomed by them before Dalton saw an opportunity present itself, walking in front of the large flatbed truck and holding his newfound rifle in the face of its driver.

"Need this vehicle, official Colonial business." he said brashly.

"But...but I'm not Colonial." the Glimmerian stated, obviously shaken. Rather than give a reply, Dalton simply pulled the ready pin back on the weapon which led to the driver jumping out of the transport as if his clothes were on fire.

"Aight' boys, throw it in the back," Dalton ordered, Lassiter barely able to continue walking, much less throw it anywhere with the additional weight of the crate pulling his frame within a foot of the ground. "Hey, where the hell do you think you're going?" Dalton asked, pointing the gun back at the Glimmerian driver and then flicking the barrel in the direction of his struggling Colonial mate.

Outraged at the idea of not only having his transport stolen red handed, but having to help the thieves load their belongings was unheard of in the man's opinion. Of course, opinions don't mean a damn thing when you have a long barrel rifle pointed in your face.

Moments later the man helped Lassiter with his side of the crate, finally lifting it onto the flat bed well enough to appease their ranking officer.

"Thanks bud." Dalton said with gratitude as the man simply told him to fuck off in native Glimmerian and walked away. "When this war is over, you're hitting the gym little man." Dalton said to Lassiter, which would almost have certainly started a fight if the Colonial sniper could have walked upright.

Driving the vehicle only a couple of traffic congested blocks, Dalton leaned out as he spotted a small Colonial assault team setting up a defensive barricade on the corner.

"Hey you. Take this group to the Colonial Command Center on orders from Commander Edwards, get inside and await further instruction." Dalton said loudly, trying to vocally overpower the blasts from the Mack stations which had now become nonstop.

"Yes sir!" the squad leader yelled, sprinting for the command center, his eight man squad tucked in closely behind him.

"Get the lead out, it's about to be on!" Dalton added.

"Double time it!" an impatient Dalton yelled to Steiner and a nearly crippled Lassiter as they had resorted to dragging the crate from the parked vehicle's location into the command center. Opting to pull a small flask from his brown coat and consume a great deal of the contents, Dalton gritted his teeth from the burn before looking into the sky to see the beauty of distant death. The Mack shots streaming as well as the thruster burns of hundreds of Colonial and Glimmerian fighter ships lit up the early night sky as if it were one big fireworks exhibition.

"Sir, early reports indicate several direct hits on medium size Legion ships in orbit. Still no indication of return fire." one of the Colonial officers stated as Commander Edwards stood with Sarah Blaine, dozens of high ranking officers checked data from all of the monitors throughout the room.

"There won't be any return fire. We are hitting troop ships, they intend to take heavy losses in exchange for getting Legion boots on the surface." Sarah said.

"She's right. Contact all Colonial outposts within the city, tell them to be prepared to cut off the power grid and have every rail gun they have go to standby." Commander Edwards ordered as the officer began to relay the message to every military building in the city.

"I'm not getting a great feeling about this." Roman said as he sat with Adam at a huge table made of solid glass inside of a heavily wood trimmed room on board the Benzan base ship. It was a smaller, cruiser size ship, but they had seen plenty of effective cannons on its exterior when the shuttle was boarding. They both had little doubt that the Benzan ship, although a small one, could hold its own against any Colonial or Legion base ship if needed be.

"Relax. If they would have wanted to kill us, they could have done it as soon as we boarded the shuttle." Michaels replied as the security coded door quickly opened.

"Adam Michaels I presume," Cyrus said, entering the room with Oz closely by his side. "I must admit, I'm surprised that you would have the testicular fortitude to ask for a meeting with someone in charge of a family that has such, well, questionable notoriety," Cyrus said curiously. "My question is why?" he added, sitting down at the table in front of both men while Oz remained standing.

"Your assassin killed a young lady that was a member of my crew. Not only that, but she was like a sister to me." Adam replied.

"Yes, Draco informed us of the kill, for the record, I am sorry for your loss. She was collateral damage from what I understand." Cyrus replied.

"Under normal circumstances, I would have buried your knuckle dragger in the desert and been done with it, but these are not normal circumstances." Adam replied.

"No. No, indeed they are not. You are a guest on my ship, at my mercy and alive right now only because I have allowed it to be so." Cyrus replied, letting Adam know that he was in control of the meeting.

"I understand, and I respect the fact that you are a man of your word. My quarrel is not with you, or anyone aboard this ship. Just the person who ordered my execution and in turn led to Kelly being assassinated." Michaels replied.

"I see." Cyrus said.

"I want to know who it was, so I can cut out the middle man and either end his life or my own in trying to do so." Adam replied.

Cyrus stood to his feet quickly, momentarily startling both Adam and Roman as they remained seated.

"Adam Michaels, walk with me for a few minutes," Cyrus asked as Roman looked at his friend as if to talk him out of it. "I am a man of my word, do not worry," Cyrus replied. Adam slowly stood to his feet, skeptical of the Benzan's intentions but seeing no other choice. "Hold him here until I get back." Cyrus said as Oz nodded, his gun remaining in the direction of Roman Raines.

"I like you Adam Michaels, it seems as though your heart is in the right place, and on top of that you have zeal," Cyrus said as they exited the room, slowly walking side by side. "It's because of this that I am about to share some privileged information with you, information that only a handful aboard this ship themselves know." Cyrus said as he stopped to look over the edge of a very long catwalk of glass which was positioned directly in front of a huge shatterproof window looking out into space. "I can give you this information, along with the name of your killer, but before I do, you must agree to remain on this ship until the battle on Glimmeria's surface has begun." Cyrus said, turning to look at Adam as he awaited a reply.

"What? My friends are down there this very minute preparing to be invaded. They are counting on me to join them." Adam replied.

"Join them in what, Death?" Cyrus responded. "Take a look at the armada that the Legion is staging outside Adam. You and I both know that the Colonials have absolutely no chance of victory here. Your friends will be wiped out inside of a week." he added.

"Maybe, but they are the closest thing to a family that I have," Adam replied, gaining the full attention of Cyrus with those very words. "You have to try and understand, I would rather risk my life to try and save them than to live and watch them die from a distance." he added.

"Interesting." Cyrus said, turning back to the thick

shatterproof glass which separated them from the stars.
"Alright Adam Michaels. You agree to remain on this ship
until the Legion launches their forces. In return, I will
personally send you with a crew of my best down in a
shuttle to rescue those you speak so highly of. You have
my word." Cyrus added.

Adam stood there for several moments, trying his best
to think the decision through clearly before turning to the
head of the Benzan family. "Deal."

"The man you seek is not a man at all, he's a Hunter
named Anwick." Cyrus said before pausing.

"FUCK," Adam shouted, putting his fist against his
forehead slowly as his knuckles began to turn red from
the squeezing of his clinched fist. "I had that son of a bitch
in the sights of my gun and let him go. Kelly would still be
here," he added as his eyes began to tear a bit with both
sadness and anger. "He's fucking dead!" Adam yelled,
throwing his fist down as rage began to consume him.

"Indeed. At least he will be if our upcoming meeting
ends poorly. It was recently decided among the Benzan
family that we will sever all ties with the Hunter tribes. It
was an agreement that we were forced into, and it's one
that my people simply have had enough of. We are not the
murdering mafia that we have been labeled, and any kind
of arrangement with the Hunters only strengthens that
stereotype of our people. I have asked Anwick to meet
with me so I can deliver the news face to face," Cyrus
said, pausing to look through the large window that held
back deep space. "There is a good chance it will not end
well for one of us. It was bound to happen eventually
though, the two toughest kids in the school yard fighting,"
Cyrus replied. "Which is why I need you to remain on this
ship." he added.

"But I want to kill Anwick with my own..." Adam said,
Cyrus immediately cutting him off.

"Have no fear, he may hunt men, but the men aboard
this ship he wants no part of. He will be dead within

minutes by my own hands if the discussions end as poorly as I believe they will, I can assure you of that." Anwick replied.

Adam looked out across the sharp contrast of the stars as he simply replied with a nod of approval and wishing he could go back in time long enough to take care of Anwick when he had the chance.

"You know Adam, the way you speak of your friends as family, it begins to remind me of myself at a younger age," Cyrus said calmly, Michaels giving him full attention. "I think when all of this is over, you and I should have another talk." he added.

The city streets were littered with Colonial choke points, its military establishing sandbag bunkers on almost every corner which usually protected a large rail gun. Sweeper teams of two Goliaths and four Colonial soldiers patrolled the streets to soon be used as backup firepower against the Legion as both Swordfish and Spartans flew overhead in attack patterns, waiting for the first sign of contact. And the Mack cannons continued to fire. The thumps of life ending lead being launched into the air sounded almost harmonic, their neon blaze trailing behind them momentarily illuminating the sky with every shot.

"Set up a perimeter here and do not fall back unless I give the order." Dalton said, ordering the squad of Colonial soldiers to position themselves in the front lobby of the command center.

"Yes sir!" the squad leader quickly replied, motioning his men to take cover with all eyes on the front door as Dalton, Steiner and Lassiter continued to the center of the building to position themselves outside of the vault.

"We're in place." Dalton yelled loudly, his voice penetrating the thick glass of the vault, Commander Edwards nodding his appreciation as he turned to face Sarah Blaine, her mind obviously on other things.

"I wouldn't worry, I'm sure Adam is alive and well." Edwards remarked.

"I just can't understand him willingly going to the Benzan Mafia, they are not a group to be pushed." she replied.

"Based on what little time I have spent around your husband to be, neither is he." Edwards replied.

"I just wish he would contact us, only long enough to let us know that he's alright." Sarah added.

"I'm sure he will soon enough, however, I think the bigger issue is when he returns." Commander Edwards said regretfully as Sarah turned to face him, dreading the words she knew would follow next.

"Sarah, you know that once he has met with the Benzan people, he will be considered a fugitive himself and no longer a part of the Colonial effort." Commander Edwards said.

"I realize that's usually the case, but with everything he has done for us, I thought that maybe..." she replied, Edwards cutting her off sharply.

"No Sarah. He cannot be an exception to the rule, you know that. If your own father were here this very day he would tell you the same. You are going to have to put your personal feelings aside if and when he returns. I don't expect we will go as far as to incarcerate him, but I do expect you to stay clear so that I can enforce Colonial law when I dismiss him from duty." Commander Edwards said.

"I understand." Sarah replied.

"I will allow him to stay here on Glimmeria, ensuring that you two may still be married and have a life together." Edwards added.

"Sir!" one of the Colonial officers yelled across the vault as the grid began picking up contacts. Walking quickly to the station, it soon became evident to everyone inside of the glass chamber that the Legion had launched its invasion.

"Darken the city and sound the alarms, now we meet them face to face." Edwards ordered as every officer who sat at a computer began relaying the message as well as monitor all of the movement from both sides of the battle.

"My god, there are so many of them," Sarah said softly as her eyes locked onto one of the Colonial grid monitors, watching waves of dozens of drop ships begin hitting Glimmeria's atmosphere. "All squadrons, this is Sarah Blaine. Multiple incoming contacts, cargo unknown, you are authorized to go weapons free. Repeat, weapons free." she said into her headset sending the orders to all Colonial fighters in the air.

Moments later, the entire city fell under a shroud of darkness, its electricity cut by Colonial Command, which was using the strategy of forcing the Legion to attempt to land blindly while masking any potential casualties on the ground. Several minutes later, dozens of large blue flares were vaulted hundreds of feet into the air, casting enough light onto the Legion's ships to present them as targets to the Colonial aircraft and rail guns, which had began to stream bursts of piercing metal into the air.

"Sir, early reports indicate at least a dozen Legion cruisers, each dropping dozens of Spider Pods from the sky." one of the Colonial officers said.

The commander had encountered the Spider Pods only once before, nothing more than a small round ship that carried a dozen soldiers and once landed, transformed into a mobile rail gun that would escort its cargo.

"Tell our air units to continue to fire on the small targets, and have the Mack stations redirect their fire from the cruisers to the small targets as well." Commander Edwards ordered, knowing the cruisers had no intention of landing.

The Mack cannons began angling their shots, ripping each Spider Pod it hit into thousands of pieces, the light armor no match for a weapon designed to destroy the largest of ships. Their pounding bursts of lead, combined with the array of rail guns and attack fighters had eliminated nearly half of the small, troop filled ships when the first one landed on Glimmerian soil, marking the first time a Legion military ship had touched the planet's surface since the original Glimmerian war nearly a decade before.

Distant explosions continued to ring out as both Adam and Roman watched Glimmeria through a small glass window inside of their sleeping quarters. "We've got to get back down there and help them." Roman said with desperation as Adam continued to watch the planet, which looked like it had fallen victim to a large thunderstorm, fully engulfed in brilliant flashes and explosions.

"Not much we could do to help, only two of us Roman," Adam replied. "Besides, they should be able to hold them off long enough for us to get down there with the Benzans." he added.

"Do you think we can trust Cyrus?" Roman asked, also considering the possibility that the Benzan leader was simply holding them there until Anwick arrived in order to be turned over to the Hunters for reward.

"I think so, at least that's what gut tells me." Adam replied, both men startled suddenly by a light knock at the door of the sleeping quarters.

Roman slowly walked to the small steel door, spinning the large circular handle to unbolt the door to be opened. Sasha stood there trembling, an emotional wreck as she looked at both men with her eyes fluid with tears before falling into the arms of Adam.

"What's wrong?" he asked, glancing at Roman curiously. It took Sasha a few moments to collect herself, the woman who had broadcast such a hard appearance when they first met had become nothing short of hysterical.

"They plan to kill him." she managed to finally push from her lungs as she sobbed uncontrollably. Adam continued to look puzzled as Roman spoke up to ask.

"Kill who?" Sasha began to pull herself away from Adam just a bit in an attempt to stand on her own as he found himself not wanting her to leave his grasp, which scared the hell out of him.

"Cyrus. I overheard Draco in his room speaking with the Hunters through a secure com link, he plans to kill Cyrus when the meeting takes place and then turn you both over to Anwick." Sasha said a bit more calmly as if to try and suddenly mask her emotions.

"Why are you bringing this to us? Shouldn't you be having this conversation with Cyrus?" Adam asked.

"I tried, but he is in a meeting with Oz and to be honest, I don't know how far this goes. I'm not sure who I can trust with this information, other than Cyrus himself and both of you." she replied.

"What makes you believe you can trust us?" Roman asked suspectedly.

"When you first contacted our ship, Cyrus had me run a complete background check on both of you. Adam, you showed up on the sheet twenty seven times for various offenses," she said as Michaels smiled wide, proud of his criminal achievements.

"It was you however, Roman, who threw us for a curve. You showed up but once, almost as if you had never existed. The Gali Special Forces had a condition one on you. Such a high priority to them combined with the fact that the Hunters want you dead so badly could only mean one thing. Greyspine. We know what you've done." she said tactfully.

"Greyspine? What the hell is she talking about Roman?" Adam asked, never having heard of the small moon planet before.

"No time for that now Adam. Can you get us any weapons?" Roman asked of the girl, eager to avoid talking about his past.

"Small ones. Two pistols would be about all, otherwise

they would pick up on them quickly." Sasha responded.

"Pistol works for me." Adam replied confidently.

"I'll pass on the pistol if you can just get me that blade back." Roman said speaking of his tactical knife.

"I'll take care of them both at once. Cyrus has already arranged for the Hunters to dock a shuttle within the hour, so if I get the chance to speak with Cyrus in private..." Sasha said before being cut short.

"No. Let us handle this. We just need those weapons and to be put close to the initial meeting, if that's possible?" Roman asked.

"I'll make sure you are close." she replied as she turned to Adam. "Thank you." she said softly, having regained her composure as she quickly left their quarters to retrieve the two weapons.

"What's this about Greyspine?" Adam asked as Roman had sealed the door back tightly with a firm turn of the handle.

"It was a long time ago Adam. Besides, the real question is what is this shit about soon to be married, but falling for Sasha?" Roman replied with a question of his own, desperate to avoid the subject for as long as possible.

"What are you talking about?" Adam asked, although he knew Roman spoke the truth. He never was very good at masking his feelings for others.

"You know what I'm talking about. The air in here got thick real quick from the tension you and Sasha were sending back and forth," Roman replied. "Right now though, we both need to concentrate on getting off of this damn ship alive. The rest will work itself out in the end." he added.

"Redirect all Mack and ship to ship fire onto the larger Legion vessels on their way in." Commander Edwards ordered.

"But sir, in doing so we will allow thousands of Legion boots to hit our soil." a Colonial petty officer replied.

"Let them land, but we WILL control the skies of Glimmeria. Now execute my order!" Edwards replied bluntly.

"Right away sir!" the petty officer replied, quickly making his way to a nearby com station to relay his commander's wishes.

After taking nearly a minute to readjust the trajectory of the huge subterranean guns, their gleaming shots began tearing into the flag ships of the Legion which had all began to descend behind a cloud of smaller ships filled with grunts. The first few minutes saw a handful of the very large spacecraft ripped to shreds, the rocketing lead punching holes through their most vital areas as they soon became nothing more than large masses of fire free falling to the planet's surface.

The Legion tried countering the shots with the deck guns built onto the ships, however they were of little to no effect as the overpowering torque of the Mack shots continued reaming not only their most decorated officers, but much needed supplies as well.

"The Colonials are completely ignoring the smaller craft! Our command ships are being cut into pieces! Call the Hunters from orbit and get their asses down onto the surface!" one of the Legion Captains commanded, screaming the order across the bridge of the ship as pounding shots steadily hit its reinforced exterior.

"Yes sir!" a seated crew member replied, attempting to make contact with the Hunter vessels in orbit as his own ship's power began to flutter from the substantial damage of the Colonial shots it had absorbed.

"Tell them to wait," Anwick replied through the com system aboard his private shuttle as it made its way to the docking area of the Benzan warship. "Do not follow them into battle without a direct order from me. Do you understand?" the vampiric monster added.

"Yes my lord." his second in command responded with

absolute obedience.

"Thank you Garrison, I can always count on you my friend. This will not take long. Tell them to stand on their own two feet for a change." Anwick said, smiling of the insult and also the excitement of learning that Adam Michaels was being held by the Benzans.

"Believe me my friends, I have no intentions of turning you over to them. Anwick will arrive and try to force my hand, at which time I will gladly discontinue the treaty he has seemed so willing to force upon us." Cyrus said to Adam as he stood with Roman, their hands in front of them locked in thick chains.
"The restraints are necessary only that Anwick would not suspect anything as he boards our ship." he added. Adam nodded to agree, a small pistol tucked snugly under his belt and hidden by a lightweight brown jacket. He glanced at Roman, wondering where his friend had hidden the tactical blade delivered to him by Sasha as well as to ensure he was ready to fight, which he was indeed.

Only two of the Legion's flagships survived the Mack onslaught which was accompanied by both Spartan and Swordfish gunfire. Though intact, both were seriously damaged on their way to landing several miles from Glimmeria's capital city, immediately setting up a forward operating base for the massive group of soldiers on foot who had hit Colonial soil less than an hour before.

"Any word on the estimated time of the Hunters arrival?" the highest ranking surviving Legion officer, Sky Admiral Cook asked.

"They refuse to engage without Anwick, who is tied up in a meeting at the moment." one of the deck officers replied.

"MEETING," Sky Admiral Cook yelled loudly as he

looked around the badly beaten bridge area of his ship, loose wires sparking as they hung from overhead like snakes from a vine.

"Have all units fall back and establish a perimeter with the forward operating base. The last thing we need is to be scattered throughout the wastelands of Glimmeria to be picked apart!" he added.

"Yes sir, right away." the deck officer replied firmly, sending Cook's orders out through the ship's on-board com.

"Commander, they have set up a few clicks from here." Sarah said, pointing to a map in the vault that was made of thick glass and colored marker.

"No doubt trying to regroup," Commander Edwards said as he approached Sarah steadily. "Have our birds run patterns over that entire area and give them orders to fire on anything that moves. In the meantime, order a large ground assault team to assemble, we need to hit them before they have a chance to dig in too deeply." he added.

"Right away sir." Sarah replied, speaking clearly into her headset so all of the Colonial soldiers would understand his orders without question.

When Anwick began to exit the Hunter shuttle slowly and board the Benzan warship, an exuberant smile painted to his face as his narrow eyes of emptiness locked onto both Adam and Roman.

"Cyrus, I must admit that you have done the job well. I did not expect to see both men standing before me so soon, their hands wrapped in chains." Anwick said as two very large and heavily armed Hunters followed him down, their semi-automatic rifles looking as though they could have easily punched a hole through the most battle tested of metals.

"It was nothing of my doing. In fact, they came to me." Cyrus replied, as Adam wondered how many more of the Vampiric monsters waited on the shuttle of pointed steel which gave the illusion of fangs.

"Is that so?" Anwick said, puzzled but excited nonetheless.

"It is, as is the fact that I have no intentions of turning them over to you," Cyrus said, his words freezing the Hunter in his tracks as he slowly turned his white complexion of death to the Benzan leader. "Furthermore, this treaty of peace that seems to exist between our two people is no more. We want no part of this political war and refuse to be included in the same sentence as those who mercilessly slay men for pleasure." Cyrus added.

"You should consider your last words wisely Cyrus, as you are no longer the leading member of the Benzan Mafia. I have promised that position to Draco in exchange for his unwaivering loyalty."

Anwick said with gleaming confidence as he glanced in the direction of Draco. Pulling his long barrel shotgun up to the face of Cyrus, Draco slowly cocked the hammer of the weapon and solidified his position as the new leader.

"Tell your people to throw their guns to the floor and I might spare your life." Anwick said as both Sasha and Oz had began lifting their guns into the direction of Draco and the Hunters.

"Draco? I pray that you understand the consequences of your actions." Cyrus said as he turned to plead with a man he had placed full trust in.

"Shut the fuck up old man! Better do as he says and have 'em drop their pieces before all of you die here standing." Draco yelled, breaking the heart of Cyrus in the process. "Do as he says." Cyrus said as he nodded uneasily to the remaining Benzans.

"I'm surprised that you have made it this far Adam." Anwick said bluntly as he began to approach both of the prisoners.

"No choice. Had to find out how deep this treason went." Adam replied as within but a single moment's breath, he pulled the small pistol and cemented a hole into the forehead of Draco with unmatched speed. Having taken the entire group by surprise, Adam quickly adjusted his aim, which was still hindered by chains and fired a second shot at the Hunters' head man.

The uncanny ability to move with urgency was the only thing that saved Anwick's life, a shot which would have penetrated his heart instead passing quickly in and out of the flesh of his shoulder as he turned away. Both of Anwick's escorts turned their weapons in Adam's direction, the first firing wide as Roman clinched his hands together and thrust them upward, knocking the rifle from the grip of the beast.

As the second escort soldier tried redirecting his aim into the direction of Roman Raines, the blade which had been snuggly tucked into the length of his boot was now in hand, the serrated edge cleaving into the chest of the soldier. Both Sasha and Oz scrambled for a moment to regain hands on their weapons as Cyrus just stood silent, deeply impressed with Adam's pistol skills, Roman's ferocity and above all, the fact that they had went to battle for him. It was in the waiting moment of that very breath that his heart decided both men had earned his respect, which is something the cold body of Draco lacked.

With Anwick fleeing to his shuttle and both escort soldiers locked into a crimson filled fight to the death with Roman, two final Hunters emerged from the Hunter craft in reaction to the gunfire. One was immediately cut to his grave by the punishing shots of both Sasha's machine gun pistol and Adam's weapon. His one final shot before reload desperately seeking the back of Anwick, but instead striking the back of his leg, crippling the beast momentarily as the remaining escort soldier dragged him onto the shuttle.

Roman had given his best effort, but a mortal man wrapped in chains, no matter how skilled he may have been, was simply no match for two of the toughest soldiers that the Hunter clan had to offer.

His blade knocked from his hand, the only thing that had kept him in the fight and alive up to this point was his mechanical side, which had began to surrender as well. One of the Hunters dove at him with numbing rage, its teeth fully exposed in an attempt to kill the human menace once and for all. Never making it to him, the Hunter's face and shoulder region became nothing more than a cloud of soiled fluid at the end of the shotgun held by Oz. The second close enough to attempt the same, was faster than a reload by Oz, but not by Adam. He had reloaded his pistol with more speed than any of the Benzans present had ever witnessed, aiming and firing all six shots directly at the beast.

Riddled with holes and screaming in life ending agony, the Hunter was short work for Roman after he reclaimed his tactical knife, making it slow as he carved an apology out of the dying beast. The Hunter's shuttle quickly disengaged, pulling from the deck in a last ditch effort to return to its base ship. Everyone with a weapon fired into the air, but it was Sasha's gunfire that hit the fuel tanks which burst open and began to bleed a trail of fire and smoke. Anwick had made it back into open space, but with no hope of returning to his ship, they simply began a steep dive into the atmosphere of Glimmeria.

Adam walked with purpose toward the Benzan shuttle which had brought him here.

"Adam. What are you doing?" Sasha asked.

"I think it's time the Hunters became the hunted," Adam replied as he made it to the entrance of the craft. "That son of a bitch will not live to see tomorrow's sunrise, I promise you that." he added as he turned and disappeared into the shuttle.

Adam had begun pressing the necessary sequence of buttons when he turned to see Oz carrying Roman on board as Sasha followed closely behind. "We're going with you, it's the least we can do." Sasha said softly as she shut the hatch of the shuttle and sat down to strap in for the decent.

"Sir! Picking up a warship with Benzan identification firing on the Hunter ships in orbit!" Sarah exclaimed loudly, knowing in her heart that Adam Michaels had played a role in the unfolding events.

"The Benzans are still wanted fugitives, stay focused on the battle here on the ground." Commander Edwards replied as Sarah patiently watched her com screen hoping the Benzan warship survived the fight.

"Continue firing all main batteries onto the Hunter Carriers. Those blood sucking bastards have just started a fight they can't win." Cyrus said from the elegance of the Benzan ship's bridge. Taken by surprise, the Hunter ships fell victim to several devastating shots before turning their own weapons into the direction of the Benzan Warship.

Several minutes passed as they exchanged knockout punches of lead, the surviving Hunters abandoning their sinking Carriers by the dozens in small escape pods, all dropping hastily into the atmosphere of Glimmeria on their way to the surface.

"Commander, all three Hunter ships have dropped from our grid system but the Benzans remain." Sarah said with relief filled joy.

"Alert the Mack stations, have them fire on the Benzan vessel until it is destroyed." Commander Edwards replied sharply.

"But Adam?" Sarah asked with desperation, turning to face her commanding officer.

"Adam isn't up there. We are picking up his Colonial beacon several clicks away from here," he replied. Sarah sat motionless, unsure if that was good or bad news as she feared for the man she loved so dearly. "Don't worry Sarah, I'm assembling a strike team to reach the beacon as soon as possible. In the meantime, have the Mack stations fire on the Benzans, as well as anyone else who shows up in orbit that isn't an official ally." Commander

Edwards said.

"Yes sir." Sarah replied, slowly turning to direct his orders to the large weapons stations.

"What the fuck are ya'll cheering about?" Dalton yelled to the Colonial soldiers in and around Colonial Command who were celebrating the demise of the Hunter Carriers. "They still outnumber us three to one, get your guns out of the air and point them at Legion troops and shoot!" he added, his voice ringing through the mortar shocked streets of the city.

"Dalton, Steiner," Commander Edwards said, making a rare appearance outside of Colonial Command. "Get your asses over here, double time!" he added, surrounded by a dozen of the finest trained soldiers stationed on Glimmeria.

"Picked up Adam's beacon a few clicks from here," Commander Edwards said, pointing to a spot on a small map as shots rang out around them, the violence moving closer to their position by the minute. "I'm putting Lassiter in charge of things here, you two take this Colonial strike team to them, see if Adam is still alive. If he is, you bring him back here in one piece, got it?" Edwards asked. Dalton nodded as clouds of broken concrete mixed with sand began falling around them, Legion troops making their way to the end of the street and meeting stiff Colonial defenses in the process.

"Aight, listen up! We are gonna backtrack, walk around the gunfire instead of straight into it." Dalton said loudly as a much larger Steiner stood beside him, the Colonial soldiers listening to his every word.

"Sir, we are being pushed back!" one of the Colonial grunts yelled in Lassiter's direction as a small group of Legion faithful had broken the Colonial lines.

"Hold the line at all costs!" Lassiter responded frantically.

"Ahh hell." Dalton said as though he was being hindered, turning to face the Legion threat as he fired six devastating rounds from the Thumper in succession, all but leveling the entire city corner that the Legion troops had occupied just moments before.

"Keep these fuck stains in line!" Dalton yelled in the direction of Lassiter, winking at him as he ordered his strike team to deploy in a flanking move that would lead them to the edge of the city and eventually in the direction of Adam's beacon. Lassiter simply gave a glassy eyed look, not from the combat around them or even the wake of death caused by the Glimmerian Thumper, but the term Dalton had just thrown his way. To his estimation it was a new low, even for Dalton.

"Adam are you alright?" Sasha asked, her portrait perfect face merely inches from his as he tried to regain his senses.

The rough landing had thrown him from his seat and against a thick steel plate near the deck of the small ship's interior. He wanted to respond to her, but before he could, his attention was pulled from her angelic face to the rear of the shuttle as Roman and Oz both fired their weapons out of the ship's only exit.

"Yea, I'm alright." he responded slowly. Sasha crouched over him, her lips but inches from his as she smiled softly.

"Better get up then, I would hate to think your reputation was going to be affected." she said softly as her eyes locked with his almost as if they were destined to.

A few seconds later Sasha slowly stood up, her aerodynamic curves no longer straddling him as he was slow to his feet as well. Rather than speak of the fireworks exploding inside every limb of his body which would he feared would eventually force him to deal with conflicting feelings, he instead turned to the two men at the shuttle entrance. "What's going on?"

"We got clipped by rifle fire as we made our approach, had to bring the shuttle in hot. Before we knew it, Hunters were falling out of the sky all around us." Oz replied, shouting his response before turning back to fire his shotgun out of the door. Roman steadily dispersed rounds from a battle rifle, but it was obvious through his body movements that the shots were having little effect.

Adam turned to Sasha, taken back for a moment by the look of true infatuation as he slowly took her rapid fire pistol and turned it onto the windshield of the shuttle, spending nearly an entire clip of shells as the thick glass began to crack. He turned to hand her the weapon back, their eyes locking onto one another once again as he found it unnervingly tough to stop himself from continuing the kiss which had played out in his mind only moments ago.

Turning back swiftly, Adam began thrusting his foot forward, the thick sole of his boot cracking the glass in multiple places with each strike.

Finally the entire windshield was knocked from the shuttle, Adam extending his hand to the soft grip of Sasha as he helped her up and out of the newly constructed crawl space. Adam was right behind her, crawling out onto the scorching sand as they motioned for both Roman and Oz. Oz sprinted across the small confines of the shuttle, quickly pulling himself out of the wreckage to join the others. Roman was a bit slower, firing all of the ammunition from the rifle before dropping it and pulling himself through as well.

They counted six Hunters scattered in the immediate area, even more falling slowly from the sky as the attached parachutes drifted the escape pods to the surface in a motion that resembled that of a tumbling feather. Other than the small town which lay over the horizon, there was literally no cover as the group of four sprinted for the cluster of wooden structures, rifle shots from the distant Hunters clipping the sand behind their heels all the while.

"Cyrus, we are dead in the water until we are able to repair the ship's engines." one of the Benzan members said grimly.

"Have someone get right," Cyrus replied, his words cut

short by a massive explosion on the starboard side of the ship. "Report!" Cyrus shouted, the remaining Benzans running to both what little working equipment that remained as well as the large glass window of the warship.

"The Colonials are firing on us!" one of the men yelled animately as he looked through the thickened glass to see a glowing shot from the surface based Mack cannons scream by them.

It was a damn tough ship, solid from the treated steel exterior to its heart and very soul. Still, Cyrus knew that it had already taken a beating and would soon succumb to the staggering shots of the Colonials.

"Give the order to abandon ship. Take any weapons and gear you have time to collect and regroup on Tirious." Cyrus said somberly, knowing full well that he didn't intend to make the trip with them to the small snow filled moon.

"And you sir?" one of the Benzans asked as the rest scrambled to escape skiffs, the warship's alarm sounding loudly.

"You know the Benzan way. A commanding officer always goes down with the ship, not that I would have it any other way." Cyrus replied as he placed his hands on the cold steel of the guard rail that surrounded the bridge.

He thought of every single battle that the ship had pulled him through, every deep space run that he himself had made while aboard.

"As my final order, make sure our people on the ground know the rendezvous point. Adam and his friend saved my life without question, so I wish for them both to be invited into the Benzan family. Now go Helon, carry out my orders and present yourself proudly as a Benzan." Cyrus added. Helon nodded, accepting the job of personally delivering the final command of Cyrus.

Helon turned to one of the remaining shuttles, his closely shaved hair of blonde highlights quickly grabbing another one of the scrambling Benzans, this one much taller with very dark skin and stark white dreadlocks as the two men boarded the craft, glancing a final time at Cyrus with a look of complete gratitude.

As the escape shuttles all bust into flight on their way to Tirious, a single ship broke from the pattern, diving steeply as it hit the atmosphere of Glimmeria to find Adam, Roman and the remaining two Benzans. Cyrus slowly turned his head, looking around the empty Benzan warship without regret as two shots from the surface cannons hit, ripping the large craft into several pieces, all of which burst into explosion only moments later.

Several intense minutes of fighting filled everyone's ears with explosions, ringing lead as it zipped through the air and screams of agony as both Colonial and Legion troops died for their factions. Eventually, the shelling died down and Colonial troops outside of the Command Center relayed the message of hope.

"Legion forces are falling back." Commander Edwards walked within inches of the thick glass which separated Lassiter and himself, picking up a mobile com to speak directly with with the loyal soldier in command.

"Good job. Have your scouts move forward, clear the area and then advance fire teams along with Goliaths." the commander said.

"Yes sir." Lassiter responded, turning to direct the men to carry out the orders with haste.

"Alright, pony up," Dalton said, flexing his thin veil of command. "Lieutenant Michaels is several clicks from here and needs our help. Instead of marching the entire group into a damn Legion ambush, I'm gonna need a scout to get ahead of us and find a clear path." he added as a Colonial sniper stood up holding a large bolt-action rifle in his hand.

The huge scope on the weapon immediately caught Dalton's attention, almost in a romantic sense, as he began to daydream of holding such a fine piece.

"You'll do." he said as Steiner tossed him a long barrel shotgun, then picking up a standard issue combat rifle for himself.

"Damn you Michaels!" Anwick yelled loudly as he remained strapped into the wreckage of his shuttle, his escort soldier having died on impact, its head bloodied from the instrument console. Anwick slowly began to crawl from the wreckage as he was met by a small group of Hunters, his eyes fixating on the sky above as dozens more of the escape pods drifted to the surface in a poetic manner.

"Are you alright my lord?" one of the larger Hunters asked, all of them wearing heavy black leather clothing and armed to the teeth.

"I will survive. Regroup with the others and on my command we will sweep through the surrounding area and slaughter anything with a heartbeat." Anwick replied, holding his shoulder which he believed had become dislocated during the crash, his two gunshot wounds nothing more than an afterthought.

"Yes my lord!" the Hunter replied soundly as the group turned to organize the survivors. "God damn you Adam Michaels. God damn you!" Anwick said under his breath as his eyes sliced into the town ahead.

"Sarah, we got a problem. The numbers you gave me fall about three miles behind Legion lines. Even if we were lucky enough to get to them, there is no way in hell we could get them back. And if we picked up the ships, it's a good bet the Legion did too." Dalton said into his com unit, the entire strike team laying low on the top of a sand dune which overlooked the coming road.

"I'm organizing a large tactical team, just do your best to get to them and dig in until we can get the team to you." Sarah replied with desperation.

"Will do," Dalton replied, placing the com unit back on

his belt. "Well fuck. Isn't this some shit? Just a small strike team out here, dicks flappin' in the wind with who knows how many Legion troops ahead." Dalton said loudly to the Colonial team.

"A lot. Looks like they are staging a large ground assault up ahead." the Colonial scout said as he kept his eye firmly pressed to the scope of his weapon. Dalton slowly climbed to the scout's position on the sand dune, glancing through a small set of binoculars.

"Looks like we are going around. These sumbitches are setting up a permanent base!" Dalton said as Steiner remained under a brown tarp, his eyes locked onto the horizon making sure the Legion had not found them. Minutes later, the group slowly made their way through the sandy cliffs of the area, keeping a safe distance from the Legion base as they worked their way around to get to Adam's location.

Shards of seasoned wood flew through the stagnant air of the room as Roman was the first person to walk inside of the abandoned building, kicking the door open as a thick coating of dust lay on top of the tables that once served a purpose for the townsfolk. As he slowly swept his gun from side to side to assure the building was safe, Adam entered followed by Sasha and finally Oz, who spent a couple of minutes trying to secure the door back that Roman had nearly jolted from its hinges.

"This is as good of a place as any, the Hunters are sure to be on top of us soon and I really hope Anwick is still alive, because I want to kill that son of a bitch." Adam said firmly as Oz began to make his way up a narrow ladder to the loft of the building, the creaking floorboards covered with ample dirt.

"I'll keep my eyes on the door," Roman said as he rested behind a stack of wooden crates at the entrance. "If they come through, we'll be right here to back you up." Adam said as he and Sasha found a small stack of their own at the rear of the room, glancing up for a moment to see Oz in position at the only second story window that overlooked the rear of the building.

"Our scouts report that Legion troops have fallen back and are forming a forward operating base." Lassiter said through his hand held com as sporadic gunfire continued in the distance.

"Copy that. We are going to continuously air strike their position until we are able to mount a ground offensive. Your orders are to further solidify the defenses outside of the Colonial Command Center, understood?" Commander Edwards asked from the comfort of the vault.

"Yes sir, copy that." Lassiter replied.

"Gonna air strike the shit out of them! In the meantime, pull your forces up and dig in solid. We are the last line of defense until further notice!" Lassiter shouted to his troops through a thick succession of explosions. The heavily equipped Goliath units remained back in close vicinity of the command center, along with the mounted rail guns and a handful of Colonial troops as the bulk of the grunts moved forward a couple of city blocks.

Oz made a low sound as he held a clinched fist in the direction of the others, Roman immediately placing his back against the wall at the foot of the door with a blade in one hand and a combat pistol in the other. Holding up the number four and moving his hand in a circling motion, the others knew quickly that a group of four were patrolling the area.

"Hunters?" Adam asked quietly as he looked to the high loft area. His question was simply answered with a nod. They were Hunters indeed.

Adam buried his face into one of his hands for a mere second before lifting it and firming the grip on his standard issue rifle. Sasha watched him for a few moments to make sure he was alright, before also turning her attention as well as her rapid fire pistol into the direction of the building's entrance.

Roman extended his arm slowly to the others, hand flat to let them know that someone was about to enter the door which was shut but not latched because of the blunt force trauma that his boot had been guilty of. The creaking of wood could easily be heard through the blanket of silence in the room as the door began to open slowly, the light of Glimmeria's moon saturating the otherwise pitch black surroundings of their hideout.

Tightening his grip on the blade's handle, Roman counted steps in his head to try and determine how many were gaining entrance, ready to blood let on as many as need be. "Roman, wait." Adam shouted in a whispered voice as everyone watched a dog enter cautiously. The amber colored animal looked half starved and was mange covered, but came right to Michaels as he knelt and extended his hand, quickly grabbing a piece of stringy meat jerky from a supply bag.

"You are just full of surprises aren't you?" Sasha asked, impressed with Adam's good hearted nature as she smiled softly. He was true to Sarah Blaine, in his heart he knew that to be a fact. Still, he found it was becoming increasingly tough to deflect the overpowering beauty and compassionate nature of Sasha.

As Roman slowly began creaking the door back to a closed position, it was thrust open abruptly by a large Hunter clad in thick black armor, knocking the Colonial sworn warrior to the floor. Sasha was the quickest to respond to the surprise guest, her pistol ringing out over a dozen shots that bit into both the armor and flesh of the beast. As it fell to the ground in tremendous pain, a second quickly followed behind, met with equal haste by the tip of Roman's blade as it plunged into the demon's ribcage.

Yelling with angered pain, the Hunter grabbed Roman tightly with both hands as the mechanized warrior began throwing a barrage of tightly placed elbows into the head of the beast. Although it didn't break the Hunter's hold, it did loosen it enough for Roman to see two more sprinting behind the monster right outside of the building.

The grip was let go when the demon dropped Roman to grab the back of its skull, a rifle shot finely placed by Adam which had plunged into the thin bone wall and struck its brain.

The first Hunter began to rise slowly as the second fell quickly to its death. Oz fired a loud and throaty round from his shotgun which nearly cut the beast's torso in two, dismembering the instantly dead creature as it tumbled back. Without his blade, Roman dashed outside to face the last two on his own, a brave but reckless idea for someone who at his best could only match one of the demons in battle.

"Roman!" Adam yelled loudly as he began to dash out to the aid of his friend, very quickly grabbed by the hand of Sasha.\

"Adam. There are too many of them! He gave us the opportunity to flee, we must go now!" she said loudly, Oz opening the window for them to climb out of as their only exit.

Adam turned to her before quickly spinning back to the direction of the front door. Several shots rang out, a few of them were from Roman's pistol while a majority were not. A good indication that their friend lay dead outside on the still hot sands of Glimmeria.

Before any of them had a chance to respond, the flimsy front door once again flew open, this time slamming against the wall behind it as two Benzans stood in the doorway, the first surveying the room with his rifle drawn as the second, dark skinned warrior drug Roman's bloodied body indoors.

"Helon, Zavious!" Sasha shouted loudly as she sprinted to them, relieved to see friendly faces.

"Appreciate you saving my friend out there." Adam said appreciatively as he knelt to check on Roman Raines.

"Wasn't a problem, we only had to slay one of them.

Your friend had already killed the other." Zavious replied. Roman slowly stood to his feet unassisted and nodded his gratitude.

"I'm fine Adam, a little blood never hurt anybody." Roman said, wiping his face clean of it with a dirty rag from the building's floor.

"Best be hauling ass out of here, I'm sure everyone in town heard the gunshots." Oz said, quickly stepping down the ladder to greet his old friends.

"I agree, but before we do, I have to carry out a final order from Cyrus." Helon said.

"Cyrus. How is he?" Sasha asked impatiently. The shaking of Helon's head was all the answer she needed, the leader of their family was dead.

"Adam Michaels," Helon said with intention as he pulled two Benzan amulets from his light grey jacket of silk and pinstripe. "Cyrus wanted to extend an invitation to the both of you, wanted you to become official Benzans as reward for saving his life." he added. Adam glanced at Roman for a few tense moments before turning back to Helon.

"I...I don't know. Of course I want to, it's just, it's just I am supposed to be married soon to one of the highest ranking Colonial officers." he replied.

"Yea. You are full of surprises." Sasha said, obviously hurt by the news of Adam's previous engagement as she walked outside quickly.

"At least think it over?" Helon asked. "When this is over and we are safe, I'll give you an answer." Adam replied.

"Good enough. And for the record, your Colonials shot down our ship and directly led to the death of Cyrus." Helon replied, tossing the amulets to the two men before turning to meet with Sasha outside as Adam stood in disbelief.

"Fucking politicians." Roman replied as the rest of the group slowly made their way outside as well, heavier now by one pitiful sight of a mutt.

"This fucking sand gets down in your boots and really pisses ya' off." Dalton said in a bitchy tone, slowly making his way to the top of a large sand dune to lay beside the Colonial sniper who had his rifle and scope mounted into a tripod.

"The good news is Lieutenant Michaels' beacon seems to be coming from that small town in the distance." the sniper said as Dalton squinted his eyes before staring it down through his small set of military goggles.

"The bad news?" he asked, almost dreading the answer.

"Pan your eyes over about fifteen degrees to the right." the sniper responded. Dalton slowly moved the binoculars with his eyes firmly pressed against them, stopping and squinting deeply before looking once more.

"Well I'll be goddamn." he said in frustration as he put his lenses down and contemplated the group's next move.

"That's not the only group of Hunters, I spotted several more throughout the town. Looks like they beat us here and are looking for Adam as well." the sniper said.

"I don't believe this shit." Dalton said in a coarse but whining voice. "Man I hadn't had a hot shower in three days. Aint' had a fucking drink in so long that I'm an ace from putting my tongue in rehab. I Got a promotion through the ranks of a military that hadn't even cut me the first paycheck yet and now here I am, balls deep in the sand out here trying to rescue a couple of friends who are surrounded by a buncha' flesh eating bastards who want me dead." he added, trying in his mind to count the days since his last drink.

"Alright," Dalton said as he began back down the dune, pausing to turn to the sniper. "Keep your ass locked in this spot. Guess me and the boys are going down there. Need you up here relaying the Hunter's movements and ready to bust a cap." Dalton added, sliding down the dune slowly before the sniper could even respond.

"What's the situation?" Steiner asked.

"This damn sand is the situation." Dalton replied, dumping his boot out while holding his foot off of the ground slightly, his eyes teared with frustration.

"You alright?" Steiner asked.

"We are out here in this shit getting ready to walk into a hornet's nest of Hunters, and Commander Edwards is back at the fort with his ass on plush!" Dalton replied, forcing his thick brown leather boot back on in a single motion.

"Hunters? How many?" Steiner asked. After looking in the direction of the six Colonial soldiers close by, all of them wearing the look of a rookie in combat, Dalton turned back to Steiner. "Does it really matter how many?" he replied.

"Listen up," Dalton said, walking to the group slowly, swagger filling his officer's strut with Steiner by his side. "Any of you rooks seen combat other than boot camp?" he asked. Two soldiers raised their hands as the other four stood there awaiting his orders.

"Well then, you two are with us," Dalton said. "You two as well." he added pointing to the largest of the two remaining. "If nothing else, these big sumbitches might slow the Hunters down long enough." Dalton said to Steiner as he quietly laughed.

"Soldier, you stay here and cover the sniper's six. Anything comes up here, you do your best to dust its jimmy off. Got it?" Dalton asked.

"Ye...Yes sir!" the new recruit answered, fumbling with his weapon as he crawled to the sniper's position.

"What about me sir?" the last remaining soldier asked impatiently. "Can you run fast?" Dalton asked.

"I...I guess so, why sir?" the soldier asked.

"When we get down there, I want you to break off from the group and scavenge for ammunition and alcohol." Dalton replied.

"Alcohol sir?" the soldier asked.

"Yea, for the love of God, especially alcohol soldier. Peel

them damn eyelids back and find what you can. Grab it, and elbow to asshole your way back to the group. Got it?" Dalton responded.

"Yes sir." the soldier replied, confused more than just a little bit.

"Do you think now is really the time to be worrying about whiskey?" Steiner asked as the men began slowly wondering into the direction of the town under the cover of night.

"Perfect time. He looks like could outrun me, and besides, we get into it with the Hunters, you really think that scrawny sumbitch is gonna make a difference?" Dalton replied.

"Hadn't thought of it like that." Steiner replied, a wide grin plastered onto his face.

"Of course not, that's why they left me in charge." Dalton responded proudly.

"Alright, best ease our way out slowly and hope we don't hit any Hunter patrols." Adam said to the group as they slowly moved a few feet from the building in which they had been hiding, using any form of cover they could.

"Shh." Roman said quietly as he clinched a fist to the others, moments later gunshots began to ring out as if they were in the center of an independence parade.

"Back inside, quick!" Adam yelled as the entire group sprinted for the entrance once more. "Are they fighting one another?" Sasha asked Adam.

"Not sure." he replied, the door cracked as he watched and listened closely.

"Eat it you whiskey hoarding bastard!" Dalton yelled loudly.

"Or, maybe I am," Adam said. "They are with us, actually," he added, grinning to the group with embarrassment. "Let me see your light." Adam asked of Helon, who quickly handed him a small flashlight. Adam held it in the crack of the door for a few moments, blinking it repeatedly to gain Dalton's attention, eventually successful, though the mangy looking dog with Adam had caught on much faster.

"Open it!" Adam said firmly as Zavious pulled the door open instantly, the rest of the group with weapons drawn as Dalton, Steiner the Colonial sniper and the fleet footed scrawny solider quickly rushed in, bottles clanging inside of a sack that was draped across the shoulder of the weakling greenhorn.

"It's good to see a friendly face." Adam said as he smiled.

"We'll you are about to see a lot more faces, although I don't suspect they are gonna be looking too friendly." Dalton replied as he tried to refill his lungs with the warm Glimmerian air.

"I thought I told you to keep your ass up on the dune?" he asked of the sniper, still struggling with exhausted lungs.

"We were flanked sir, no way I could have held them off on my own." the sniper replied.

"Sir?" Adam asked as the Benzans looked on, trying to make what they could of both Dalton and the oversize Husk warrior standing at his side.

"Yea, they put him in charge." Steiner said sarcastically with his heavy Husk accent.

"Seriously?" Adam asked amazed.

"Hell yea seriously, they trust me to make the smart calls out here." Dalton replied.

"Yea, like sending your boy into a saloon full of Hunters for whiskey." Steiner added.

"How the hell did I know them certifiably dead son of a bitches would be packed in there drinking the town dry?" Dalton angrily asked.

"Alright," Sasha interjected. "We need to worry about how we are supposed to get out of town without getting killed." she added.

"We ain't leaving." Dalton replied.

"We're not?" Adam asked, still amazed that Dalton had been placed in charge of actual human lives.

"Nope. Sarah said to hold up here. Said they are forming a large ground team to come in and get us," Dalton replied as he bent down with fresh air in his lungs. "Where did ya'll pick up this cute pup at?" he asked as everyone in the room looked at him, wondering if he had overlooked the chronic mange of the abused dog. Then it began to make sense to a few of them, viewing both Dalton and the dog as both being a little bit on the trashy side.

"Poor sumbitch looks like he 'aint ate or drank in weeks. Private, what were you able to grab before they started shooting?" Dalton asked as the Benzans began picking their spots inside of the building, digging in for any fighting to come.

"Not much sir, I didn't have time to..." the Colonial private replied, Dalton snatching a bottle of whiskey from the sack and cutting his explanation off in the process.

"Double brown whiskey. This shit is so strong it would cure the blind, good job private." Dalton said, the young soldier standing a bit taller and proudly answering. "Yes sir!"

"Be a damn good name for you mutt, Whiskey it is." Dalton said as he poured a large amount onto the floor, the dog lapping it up before it had time to spread.

"Unbelievable." Sasha said, pausing when she heard Dalton bless the animal with the name Whiskey.

"Wait until he has a few drinks in him. May want to keep that gun close by your side." Adam replied, chuckling a bit.

The layout was simple. Dalton, Whiskey and the Colonial sniper were in the loft. Meanwhile, Helon, Zavious and Oz covered one side of the room, the three of them behind what looked to be an old wooden sales desk. Adam, Sasha and the scrawny Colonial soldier remained at the rear of the room behind empty crates while Roman and Steiner covered the door.

"I'd hate to be the unlucky one who barges in first." Sasha said, referring to the giant like size of Steiner, who held a short barrel shotgun, and the blade skills of the partly mechanical Roman Raines.

"Yea, or the first half dozen even. Those two can fight like no other two I have ever seen." Adam replied softly.

"So. Not to pry or anything, but this Sarah that Dalton spoke of..." Sasha asked as Michaels nodded before she could complete her sentence.

"Yea, that's her. When we met I was on the run, no real direction in my life. She pulled me into this war I guess, but I couldn't have walked away from her. Love her too much, I guess it was a package deal." he replied.

"Well I hope this isn't over the line or anything, but I just think she is a really lucky woman. I just never understood how you could love someone and try to change them at the same time," Sasha said. "Of course, that's probably just an issue with me. One of the many issues." she added, laughing softly. Adam thought deeply about what she had just said. Sarah had changed him, be it for better or worse. Once upon a time he had no direction, lived by the seat of his pants and enjoyed true freedom. And here he was. Trapped inside of a war he truly wanted no part of, decked out in an officer's uniform and under the heel and command of a politician somewhere. All because of his love for Sarah. When, to his knowledge, she hadn't changed anything for him. "No, you make a good point. And thanks for the compliment." he finally replied as he returned her smile.

"Can I ask you a question Adam?" Sasha asked in a heartfelt tone.

"Sure you can." he responded.

"What do you really think will become of myself and my people if and when we do make it back? Do you think the same Colonials who blew our warship out of orbit will let us just walk away when this is over, free and clear?"

Sasha asked.

"Sure I do," Adam responded, although he hadn't even thought about it up until that moment and knew in his heart that she was probably right. "I give you my word right now, that no matter what I choose to do when this is over, you will walk away free and clear." he said.

"Can you really make such a commitment though Lieutenant?" Sasha asked.

"I'm not making that commitment as a Lieutenant, I am making it as Adam Michaels, and my word is good." he replied.

"Thank you. I believe you." she responded with a smile. "The world paints our people to be criminals, but I assure you, we are not." she quietly added.

Adam sat quietly, filled with inner emotion as his grief of the loss of Kelly battled the emotional distress he saw on Sasha's face. He had always been a great judge of character, and he knew in his heart that her words were saturated in nothing but the truth.

"Sasha, you have my word. When we make it back, you will walk out of there a free woman." Adam finally replied as he stood to his feet.

Once the mightiest city on Glimmeria, the Colonial spectacle of a military base looked more like an urban wasteland. Only seconds separated explosions throughout the city as rockets, grenades and anti-aircraft artillery had been going since the Legion had landed on solid ground. Their far superior numbers on the ground had managed to take out all but one of the Mack stations, the last one heavily fortified by the Colonials who still feared assisting armies coming to the aid of their counterparts. What seemed like such a great accomplishment for the Colonials as the Legion base ships in orbit were strategically destroyed by Benzan gunfire, quickly became only a side note. The Legion had already sent its entire force, intending to dig in and fight a war of attrition. The base ships were nothing more than empty warehouses in the sky operated by the smallest of skeleton crews when they exploded. That said, a majority of the Legion's supplies had been destroyed with them, meaning victory would have to come swift if it were to come at all.

"Sir, Colonial Command remains under heavy guard, and we have the streets locked down tight." Lassiter reported to Edwards as the Colonial leaders scrambled to update their war maps, communications coming in from all corners of the city.

"Good. We have reason to believe that the Legion is staging a very large assault force with plans to hit this area. We are trying to pull back the pockets of soldiers throughout the city and organize a defensive perimeter," Commander Edwards replied. "Get your men resupplied and do your best to assign soldiers to new platoons as they make their way to Command." Edwards added.

"Yes sir!" Lassiter replied swiftly as he left the vault and returned to the streets outside.

"Any word on Adam and his crew?" Commander Edwards asked, slowly approaching Sarah Blaine, who had been organizing all of the communications for the Colonials.

"No sir. I'm sure they are alright, probably just inside of Valencia and unable to send out a transmit without having their position compromised." Sarah answered, trying to convince herself as she spoke the words.

"I see." the Commander replied.

"Sarah, I want to make sure that you are alright with what has to be done when they do make it back," he added. "Leaving Glimmeria without authorization, conspiring with wanted criminals and direct insubordination." the Commander added as Sarah sat in her chair, numb to the fact that if her soon to be husband could beat the odds and make it back alive, she would have to stand by and watch him be discharged while his crew was arrested.

"Yes sir. I know it has to be done." she reluctantly replied.

"Good Sarah. You are the ideal soldier, putting your Colonial duty above personal feelings. Your father would be so proud of you. We have already been contacted by the Gali government about Roman, seems he is very high on their list of wanted fugitives. Turning him over to them would go a long way toward helping our cause." Edwards remarked as he placed his hand on her shoulder for a moment before walking to the rest of the stations in the Vault for updates.

"Yep, she's locked down tighter than a tick's ass." Dalton remarked as he looked through the town streets, the morning sun illuminating the scope of the sniper rifle.

"Nice." Sasha remarked, already disgusted with Dalton's demeanor.

"He's right, their defenses are solid." the Colonial sniper added. Adam took the lenses and looked for himself, noticing the pockets of heavily armed Hunters patrolling the streets.

"I have an idea." Adam said, grabbing Steiner's field pack full of supplies and sifting through until he found a blue flare.

"Sure you can make the shot?" the Colonial sniper said after having his rifle commandeered by Dalton, who laid prone with his eye pressed to the scope.

"Don't worry son, at this distance I could split the hair on a tick's a..." Dalton responded before being interrupted.

"What is it with you and your fixation on the ass end of a tick?" Sasha demanded to know.

"Adam, unless you got a stout drink to offer or my first paycheck in hand, I don't gotta put up with this shit!" Dalton responded angrily.

"Just shoot the damn flare Dalton, everybody else be ready to get down to the back of the stables if they take the bait." Adam said as Dalton fired the weapon, its muzzle flash hidden within the silencing tube that was attached to the barrel.

Within a second, blue smoke began filling the landscape on the opposite side of Valencia. Only moments later, several Hunters began yelling loudly as they braced for a Colonial assault. The few Fang units among them made their way to the far end of the main street, the barbarically large creatures facing the smoke and ready to let their menacing teeth slaughter any approaching Colonials.

A majority of the Hunters dashed to the smoke, weapons at the ready, which was cue enough for Adam and his crew to sprint to the back of the large, wooden stables. A much larger and more strategically placed building, it had already been cleared by the Hunters which made the probability of them checking it again slim to none.

Roman sunk his blade into the thick wood only feet from the ground, pulling the steel slowly across in a straight line, his bulging arms forcefully splitting wood slowly as he followed it with a solid kick that broke open a crawl space about three feet high. One by one they crawled on their stomachs across the desert floor and into the long abandoned building, the last in was Adam, who did the best job he could of putting the fallen boards back into place to appear untouched.

"Dalton, you're with our sniper up in the loft. Keep eyes on everything and let us know of any movement. Roman, you and Steiner set up near the stable doors. Good chance when they figure out the smoke was a decoy, they'll do a half-ass sweep of the town. They come in here, take care of 'em quick." Adam said as everyone took position throughout the large interior and Dalton bitched under his breath about loss of command. Michaels and Sasha dug in behind a stack of musty hay near the newly made entrance at the rear of the building.

"Plan is, we'll hang here to back up Roman and Steiner if need be, try to get our com system linked up in the meantime." Adam said as he pulled the long range com system from a small suitcase in Steiner's field pack, which was a small metal square with several knobs, and hooked it to a table top satellite dish, which he sat on the empty crate in an effort to pull signal in.

The Hunter force inside of Valencia prepared to do a sweep of the town, just as Adam had predicted, when two Swordfish screamed overhead, dropping hundreds of rounds onto the town while taking return fire from assault rifles. It quickly took the attention off of them and onto the skies as the soon to be sweep was halted. "Well, that was a lucky break." Sasha said.

"It wasn't luck. My guess is the Colonials were doing a quick flyby to scout the town so they could put together the right group of soldiers to come get us." Adam replied.

"What's coming across the com unit?" Dalton asked softly, laying on the loft with his head hung over the side smiling, the mange ridden whiskey laying at his side.

"We can't send anything, it'll give our position away." Adam said. "But from the sound of things, we're getting beat up on the ground." he added. "What about Colonial Command?" Dalton asked, thinking of the post he held until being sent to save Adam's neck.

"It's still there, but from what I can make out there is a large Legion force trying to take the ground, sounds like that entire area has become the front." Adam replied.

The sniper whistled quietly, getting Dalton's instant attention. Moments later, Dalton turned back to everyone on the bottom floor of the stable and began giving hand motions to let them know what was outside of the door.

"Two Hunters coming." Sasha relayed to Adam, who had put a rifle to his shoulder and the sights on the door. "Armed with standard rifles." she added as she continued to watch the loft. "And I have no idea what that means?" she said, confused of the signal. Adam broke his attention from the door momentarily to glance at Dalton, who was turning his hand upside down next to his mouth.

"That means that they have liquor." Adam said, turning back to the door as Sasha stood there nothing short of speechless.

Both Hunters pushed the stable doors open slowly, the wood creaking as light from the desert heat permeated the entire building and illuminated thousands of dust particles that had yet to settle. Their thunderous laughter was cut short as Roman moved with exceptional speed, the titanium plating on his elbow crushing the lower jaw of one of the demons. Before either man had a chance to respond, Steiner grabbed the second man and wasted no time snapping his neck under the pressure of his sheer strength as Roman dug the serrated edge of his blade into the intestines of the first.

As if the stables were engulfed in flames, Dalton scaled the wooden ladder and reached the ground with unmatched haste. It took only moments of searching the bodies before he found a small bottle of rock whiskey.

"Fucking cheap ass bastards. Could have at least had something decent on 'em." Dalton said in disgust as Roman and Steiner dragged the bodies out of sight and quickly closed the front door. "Oh well, with the day I've had, it'll do." he added, climbing the ladder much slower than he had descended, almost as if he had become an instant cripple.

"Adam." Roman said, tossing back a small radio he had found on one of the bodies.

"Some crew you have here." Sasha commented.

"I know what you must be thinking, but they're loyal and get the job done when it's on the line," Adam replied. "Also, I'm sorry for ever misjudging you." he added.

"I'm not sure what you mean?" Sasha replied curiously. "When we arranged to meet with the Benzans, honestly, I did think you were criminals. It's all I had ever heard, ya know? I had always been told that the Benzans were cold-blooded killers, so I guess I had just started to believe it myself." he answered.

Sasha sat there for a minute, full of emotion and empty on words. Thinking back to her family being slaughtered only a few years back when she was a teen, and how Cyrus had taken her in, trained her and most importantly, been like a father to her. "Don't worry Adam, I understand." Sasha finally replied.

"No Sasha, I don't think you do," Adam said as she smiled slightly.

"What you said back there made a lot of sense to me. We are more like one another than you will ever know." he added.

"I used to fight the system too. I can remember the deep space runs, just looking across the stars and truly feeling freedom." Adam said.

"I know that feeling. Almost like you are witnessing something magical about the stars that you weren't intended to." Sasha replied.

"Exactly." Adam responded. "Does she share your sense of freedom?" Sasha asked.

"No, unfortunately not. I guess the time comes in everyone's life when they have to make the decision though, who they want to be and what they want to live for. I chose love." Adam replied.

"You guys want some of this to take the edge off?" Dalton said, his head falling in front of them as he hung down from the loft with the rock whiskey bottle in his hand.

"No thanks." Adam replied as he began to remember what life was like only a year ago. His original crew that included Kato and Luck, both victims of the war that Adam had drug them into.

"Sure, why not." Sasha replied, surprising both Adam and Dalton as she turned the bottle up and took a healthy swig.

"Alright, alright...save a little for me, damn." Dalton said nearly prying the bottle from her hands in order to salvage what he could.

Adam hadn't truly seen the kind of smile that Dalton currently had on his face since before they had gotten drug into this damn war. Their lives had consisted of card games, saloon brawls, black market jobs and a type of family atmosphere aboard the Gunship that was hard to explain, unless you were a Benzan.

Whether it was the effects of whiskey or the traumatic events of the day, she spent the next hour explaining to Adam what Benzan life was like. He found himself relating it to the life he used to live when he was free. Before he was Lieutenant Michaels, he was Captain of the Gunship. It didn't have a Colonial logo painted on the side of its thick plated steel, in fact it didn't have anything more than a film of rust coating. He started to realize that even though he was indeed in love with Sarah Blaine, his life had been changed so dramatically for the worse.

As night began to fall on the town of Valencia, Adam started to do something he had not done in a while. Search his soul. Maybe convince himself that he knew the definition of true happiness, and if by some miracle they made it off of Glimmeria alive, what changes he would have to make in order to become truly happy again. When it came to love, he had followed his heart. However, when it came to being a free and happy man, he realized that he had done everything but follow his heart.

Sure, his heart belonged to Sarah, it had since they very first moment he had laid eyes on her. Still, he thought a lot about Sasha as he lay there during the night. Not just because she had a pure beauty about her, but because he envied the life that she had chosen to live. Missing it very much. Living for the moment was the only real definition of happiness in his opinion, and Sasha lay there doing just that, sleeping like an angel and taking life one day at a time.

Suddenly, explosions rang out all around them as the Hunter controlled town had come under siege by Colonial forces. Dalton and Roman had already been wide awake, pulling watch as everyone else quickly jumped to their feet and tried to assess the situation. Realizing it was the Colonials by the sound of their weapons, Adam immediately got on the com unit and sent a communication to let them know they were hold up in the stables. Moments later, the group could hear the explosions backing off of their area a bit, the Colonial cannons redirecting their fire in order to avoid hitting them.

"I got another idea." Adam said, pulling Roman and Steiner to the side. A few minutes later, Adam and Sasha had taken guard at the door as both Roman and Steiner had put on the uniforms they had removed from the dead Hunters.

"This looks ridiculous!" the hulking Steiner said, his pants legs a good foot higher than the tops of his boots and so tight you could make out the patterns of Husk hair underneath.

"A couple more drinks and you might be looking mighty fine to me," Dalton said jokingly as everyone took a moment to giggle about the underhanded joke. "Or not." Dalton added in a serious tone as Steiner sent him a blood curdling scowl.

"The quicker we can get out there and kill some of these damn flesh eaters, the sooner the Colonials can come fetch us." Adam said.

"Shouldn't take us too long." Roman replied as he and his horribly outfitted comrade equipped themselves with Hunter rifles and waited at the door for an all clear from the loft before cracking it open and sprinting across the street.

"You two keep your eyes wide up there, any Hunters get after them, you do anything you can to clear a path." Adam said shouting up to the loft as the roar of explosions in the distance intensified.

"You got it Adam." Dalton replied, pulling the slide loader of the sniper rifle back and putting his eye to the scope.

"Hey that's my gun!" the Colonial sniper contested loudly. "Steiner is a big sumbitch...you 'aint. I'll listen to him, but your ass I'll whip." Dalton replied snidely, taking no chances in defending his two friends.

It had only been a handful of minutes when Dalton spotted a small group of Goliath soldiers at the edge of town making minced meat out of the heavily out gunned Hunter soldiers. Several tense moments later as the three mechanical masterpieces began to enter Valiance, a whole squadron of Colonial soldiers behind them, two Fangs entered the street from a Hunter choke point. They were much more intimidating than even the model two Goliath. Sure, the alloy steel and chain guns helped the mechanical backbone of the Colonial army mow through normal foes, but the Fang units were anything but.

Several feet taller than even Steiner, they looked more like a monster than a man, the face of of demon with two arm sized fangs hanging from their top jawbone.

They spent a moment exchanging gunfire before realizing that tactic was useless, both the Goliaths and Fangs had thick enough plating, whether alloy or skin, to deflect any small arms ammunition. Instead, they began to pick up the pace as they geared up for a fist to fist showdown with one another. Passing a large metal dumpster, one of the Fangs was stunned as Roman quickly stood up and swung the stock of his rifle, smashing it to bits across the face of the biological killing machine. The second Fang stopped suddenly, turning into Roman's direction, when the three Colonial Goliaths began letting a blanket of lead unleash onto it, if nothing else to blind and confuse it. Immediately, Steiner jumped onto the face and shoulders of the much more powerful foe, doing his best to hold on long enough to put the barrel of his weapon into the neck area of the oversize flesh eating monster.

He emptied his entire clip as the Hunters' prized unit

began to die slowly of internal bleeding, standing in the same spot as it screeched in agony. Meanwhile, Roman and the second Fang were engulfed in an all out brawl of clashing steel and determined flesh when Roman saw his friend fall.

A Hunter sniper hit Steiner in the back with a high caliber weapon as he stood there to place a full clip into his battle rifle. Right away, Roman sensed the severity of the wound as meat and vital tissue sprung from Steiner's chest, the round making its way completely through the hulking beast as he fell to both knees. A couple more shots followed closely after, knocking Steiner face first into the sands of Glimmeria, dead.

Fury took control of Roman as he seized the second Fang and began tearing flesh from any seam of its skeletal frame that he could possibly put his hands on. Two of the Colonial Goliath units had fallen at the end of a hailstorm of Hunter gunfire when Roman found himself beside the remaining Goliath and a small group of Colonial soldiers who had thrown down arms in surrender. There were simply too many Hunters.

Adam had seen the loyal Husk fall dead in the street and made his way up to the loft with extreme haste, grabbing an emotional Dalton and pulling the rifle from his hands before he could get a true shot.

"Dalton, there are too many!" Adam said sternly.

"I don't give a shit anymore Adam! I've had enough of watching my fucking friends die." Dalton shouted back as he made his way down from the loft to the front door of the stable.

"Step back. I don't want to shoot you, but if you leave now you will sign the death warrant of every one of us." Sasha said as she aimed her silencer equipped machine gun pistol at the man who had nearly reached the end.

"Bitch, you better move. None of us would even be in this position if your kind could stop killing for five fucking minutes. Now get out of my way, otherwise you 'aint gonna like how this ends." Dalton said angrily.

Sasha pulled the load clasp back, assuring him that the weapon was ready to discharge at the slightest bit of pressure.

"Dalton! You need to calm down before you do something you will regret for the rest of your life." Adam said, grabbing the left arm of his pissed off friend.

"Nope. I aint' gonna regret this Adam." he said as he planted his fist firmly into the face of Michaels, knocking him back into the thick wooden wall.

"Down on your knees, hands behind your head soldier!" Sasha demanded of Dalton as the Colonial sniper continued watching the Hunters round up any survivors outside, which included a badly outnumbered Roman Raines.

"No Sasha. If he wants a damn fight, he's gonna get one." Adam said boldly as he stood back to his feet and threw the large, Colonial issued pistol to the ground.

"Sounds good to me, I'm tired of watching you march my friends to the grave over a war that some whore dragged you int..." Dalton replied as Adam landed a left jab and a harrowing right hook onto the man, stumbling him back as he remained standing.

Obviously reeling just a bit, Dalton placed his hand across his beard for a minute, surprised if nothing else that Adam struck him back.

"Well, you got balls after all." Dalton managed to spit out before Adam landed three more punches, followed by a crisp right elbow which he had angled skyward, knocking his belligerent friend onto his back. Adam immediately got on top of him and placed his forearm across the throat of Dalton, choking the life from his body.

"Yes, I know that Luck, Kato, Kelly and now Steiner have died because of decisions I'VE made. I have to live with it every fucking day, and I'll be damned if another one of my crew's names is going to be on that list. So either you help me free Roman, or you carry your ass back

to Colonial Command and wait for me to bring him back,"
Adam said with grave calm before letting go of his choke
hold and picking his pistol up, pointing it directly at the
face of a broken down Dalton. "Now what's it gonna be?"
Adam asked.

"Just give me a fucking gun and let's find a way outta
here already." Dalton said somberly as if to admit defeat.

"You aren't seriously gonna give this guy a gun are
you?" the Colonial sniper said, shocked at the notion.

"This isn't the first time we've had a physical
disagreement, I'm just glad I won this round," Adam said,
smiling a bit as he extended his hand to help Dalton to his
feet. "We go way back. If I step out of line, he puts me
back in it, and vice versa." Adam added.

"That elbow got me, you dirty fightin' fuck." Dalton
replied, using the arm of Michaels to help himself up.

"You sure you're not Benzan? You act so much like
everyone that I know, I'm not even homesick anymore."
Sasha said to Adam.

"Our rescue party got their asses kicked, and as thin as
the Colonial forces are spread, I seriously doubt they will
be sending another," Adam said to the group. "Means we
are gonna have to go it on our own." he added.

"The Hunters took the survivors into a building up the
street, probably not more than two hundred yards from
here. Roman was with the group they took." the Colonial
sniper said.

"I've never known Hunters to take prisoners?" Sasha
said in a puzzled tone of voice.

"They don't. Plan on getting as much information as
they can from them and putting a bullet in their head
would be my guess, which means we gotta work fast."
Adam replied. They would have the perfect opportunity
soon, as the sun had started to set, painting faded blue
and shimmering light red across the sky. The town would
soon be engulfed with complete darkness.

"Sir, reports are indicating that our lines are being pushed back." a Colonial officer said as he stood before Commander Edwards.

"Give a general order to fall back here to Colonial Command. If the Legion tries to take this complex, they will pay dearly in lives." Edwards replied.

"Yes sir!" the officer replied as he turned to execute the order. "What is the status of Adam's rescue?" the commander asked as he turned to a very distraught Sarah Blaine. With her eyes full of tears, she simply nodded no.

"Once our remaining forces fall back and we regroup, I will try to put together a second tactical team to go get them, don't worry." Edwards replied to calm her before walking to the other stations inside of the Vault.

"This is a general order of retreat. Repeat, fall back. Remaining Colonial forces are instructed to fall back to Colonial Command and await further orders." Sarah said calmly into her com unit, holding the tears back long enough to broadcast with a hope filled voice.

"In the event that the Legion would begin taking control of this complex, we have strategically placed nuclear warheads on every level of the building. Our engineers have been able to bring Colonial Star Twenty Two to flight ready status. Most of the weapons and defense systems aboard are not functional as of yet, however as a last resort, it will evacuate us and the small group of Colonial soldiers off of Glimmeria to the small moon of Thisia, where we have been assured safe harbor by the Thisian government." Commander Edwards reluctantly announced to everyone inside of the Vault.

"What of the rest of the Colonials?" one of the officers asked, bringing a harsh expression to the commander's face.

"There is simply very limited room on the Colonial Star. The remainder of our forces will be left here to stave off the Legion until we can come back for them." Edwards replied. He expected to have to explain the plan in great detail to the most important members of the Colonial government. However, the conversation was cut short as the soldiers outside of the Vault under the command of Lassiter, began firing their weapons in the direction of the building's main entrance. The Legion had made it to their front door and all hell had broken loose.

"Lassiter! You must hold them until the Colonial Star arrives to evacuate us!" Commander Edwards proclaimed through the com unit in the Vault as they eyed one another through the shatterproof glass.

"Will do sir. Highly recommend pulling any available air units to the area to assist." Lassiter replied, his voice nearly impossible to make out over the com unit as gunshots rang out all around him.

"Negative. Remaining air units are escorting Colonial Star in behind command, you must hold the Legion troops back at all costs." Edwards pleaded.

"Understood sir," Lassiter replied into the com unit before throwing it to the ground. "Dig in and earn your independence!" he yelled loudly to the troops that barricaded the halls of the building, mostly flesh with a few mechanical Goliaths assisting.

"Sarah. Begin the process of packing up all vital equipment and Colonial documentation. You, remain with Sarah at all times from this point forward." Edwards demanded of one of the Vault's very few and heavily experienced soldiers. As Sarah began to explain to Commander Edwards that an armed escort wasn't necessary, she saw several Colonial soldiers gunned down on the other side of the glass as they were in the thickest of firefights, which prompted her to stay quiet and do as he asked.

Roman sat in a small room with six Colonial soldiers, all tied to chairs with thick rope and waiting to join the last two soldiers who were taken out for questioning, along with the remaining Goliath, to the land of the dead. As the door opened up slowly, the same Hunter who had come for the others stood in deep thought, trying to decide who they would torture for information next as two very large and well armed guards stood on the inside of the door. He was dressed in battle tested black leather armor from head to toe with a slight trimming of silver, much of it saturated with dried blood and a dusting of sand.

"Him." he said, pointing to Roman as the two Vampiric guards walked slowly in the direction of the doomed soldier. "Make it quick, I grow tired of dealing with these pathetic humans." he added as Roman suddenly noticed a strange look about his face. As his eyes drifted down from the Hunter's face to his large torso, he could see the tip of a large blade sticking out of his stomach, a waterfall of blood crashing onto the floor. Dalton stood behind him, the Hunter's body falling to the ground shortly after as Dalton reclaimed the arm length machete in Roman like fashion, throwing it end over end at one of the two remaining demons, and in non-Roman like fashion, hitting the Hunter with the handle of the knife.

"Oh shit." Dalton said, stunned as the knife hit the floor making a small clanking sound. Before the flesh eating guards could get the drop on him however, Sasha stepped in and fired her palm sized machine gun pistol, droplets of red mortality finding a home on the wall behind them, quickly bringing a stinging demise to one of the Hunter guards.

The remaining demon quickly aimed his rifle in Sasha's direction, firing a shot that ricocheted off of the floor, a chair smashing into the side of its head and busting into dozens of splintered pieces. Roman had not only thrown the object in which he had been tied to only moments ago, but had lunged on top of the reeling Hunter, using the thick rope which bound his hands to choke much of the life from the wounded beast.

After collecting the large blade, Dalton caught sight of

two more of the heavily armed beasts as they dashed into the small dwelling. Once again, he threw it end over end in the direction of the door with the same results as it clanged against the wall and fell pitifully to the ground.

"Fuck it." Dalton said, swiftly pulling his pistol and pecking away much of the flesh of the first demon inside, the screaming Hunter falling against the wall and clutching its face with his claw ridden hands. The second Hunter in was immediately dismissed by a group of shots from one of the Hunter rifles which Roman now held.

"Dead or alive, bring them to me!" Anwick yelled, his pale white skin flush with pink tint as revenge overtook him. Several more Hunters, nearly a dozen, quickly ran out of the saloon up the street, cautiously panning their large rifles around as they tried to assess the recent screams. The horrified townsfolk continued glancing from their windows, most having never seen a Hunter in their lifetime, much less watching one fall.

"Cut their bonds and let's get the fuck out of here!" Dalton yelled in Roman's direction, having given up hope on ever obtaining any type of skill with a blade. It only took seconds for the former Gali commando to slice his thick bonds, as well as those of the Colonial prisoners as they collected what weapons lay on the floor and hastily proceeded outside.

"There!" one of the Hunters exclaimed, pointing to the group of escaping Colonials as they fled the building and hopefully captivity. The Hunters, however, were much quicker than normal men, steadily closing the gap between the fleeing prisoners and those who wished them dead. Anwick remained back at the edge of town as he watched his minions of murder pursue a group of people who he wanted to watch die, slowly and painfully. He had killed thousands of men, women and children during his time, but could not remember a single one that he wanted to perish more than Adam Michaels.

He would never get that chance. As he watched his men

fade into the far reaches of the distance, Adam Michaels stepped from the shadows of the building which marked the beginning of town.

"Reap it you son of a bitch!" he said as he stepped from behind two wooden barrels, pointing his standard issue Colonial combat pistol into point blank range of Anwick and firing all six shots in succession. Anwick's inhuman speed was enough to dodge a majority of the shots, although two of them hit him deep in the chest, greatly reducing the flesh demon.

Having expended his ammunition, Adam struck Anwick across the face with the heel of the pistol before throwing it to the ground. The two wounds, coupled with gunshots suffered earlier had reduced Anwick to nothing more than a normal person. Adam threw several punches into the face of the kneeling Hunter, who eventually threw a drastic backhand of his own, putting Adam onto his back.

"I will snap your neck and watch you die a slow death!" Anwick screamed, standing to his feet only to be met by Adam's lust for the revenge of his fallen friends. A devastating uppercut, followed by a thrashing right elbow to the face of Anwick send the monster back to the ground abruptly.

Adam's quest for retribution was cut short however, as he approached Anwick heavy footed and was quickly grabbed by the throat, the Hunter's spiny white fingers wrapping around quickly and their accompanying claws digging in. With maddening rage setting in, Anwick used the grip to pick Adam up off of the ground a couple of feet and hurl him into the wooden fence in front of the nearby building, smashing several feet of it into pieces.

"You have cost me time, extreme amounts of stress and many faithful lives," Anwick yelled loudly, starting to approach Adam before stopping abruptly. "And now here you are," Anwick said, looking at Adam as he lay on splintered wood and scorching sand, broken by the injuries newly gained. "The worst part of it is if your loyalties would have remained with me, I have no doubt that we could have worked well together. As hard as it was for me to end you, says a lot about the high level of smuggler you must have been." Anwick added.

"You have no idea." Adam said, his face bloodied as he sat there prepared to die.

"Nor will I." Anwick replied. "Does such an outstanding smuggler have any last words?" he added, slowly approaching Adam for the kill.

"Yea. I sure could use some Whiskey right about now." Adam replied, Anwick stopping for a moment to laugh at the beaten man.

"I am afraid the saloon is much to far to fill that request." Anwick answered.

"No. I said I sure could use some WHISKEY right about now." Adam replied, placing a great deal of emphasis on the word Whiskey as the eye sore of a mutt sprung from one of the barrels and barked wildly.

"What the?" Anwick said in a low voice, surprised by the invasion as he turned to the sound of Whiskey's barking. Adam quickly pulled a compact pistol from behind his back, having been tucked away behind his belt throughout the entire fight. Moments later, Anwick lay dead, his blood drenching the sand as Adam continued holding the pistol which smoked from all six shots fired.

The Colonial force had nearly been caught, when they stopped suddenly and spun to begin firing on the group of Hunters. In unison, sand covered tarps flew into the air as Helon, Zavious and Oz stood entrenched in them, firing heavy weaponry at the suddenly matched foes.

The Hunters were outnumbered by a group filled with equally tactful killers, several who were pissed off to say the least. The next few minutes were engulfed in a firefight from the worst imaginable hell as lead, blades, blood and cursing all flew freely into the air and onto the sands of that small patch of Glimmerian soil. Adam and Whiskey had sprinted to help his friends after confirming the death of Aniwick, arriving when the fight had freshly come to a close.

One of the Colonial soldiers was alive, but in bad shape, the rest, including the sniper, lay slain on the sand. Helon and Oz had both fallen, each with grimacing claw marks all over them and multiple gunshots to the chest. Sasha was nearly unscathed, but was grieving loudly at the death of the two Benzans as Zavious lived, effectively making him the highest ranking member of the Benzan family. Roman stood tall, covered in blood, most of which belonged to the fallen Hunters as he did his best to survey the damage around him. Dalton lay with the dead Hunters, his shirt ripped to pieces from both claw and blade as he had tried unsuccessfully to fend off two of the near immortals himself.

It wasn't until Whiskey went to him, licking his face and leaving tongue trails of cleanliness that Dalton started slowly moving his head around, at first not understanding if he were dead or alive. A few more times of raw tongue dragging unkempt whiskers was all it took to remind him that he was still alive, and in need of a damn drink.

"Please tell me that's all of the bastards. If not, shoot my ass now and leave my belongings to Whiskey." he said, painfully pulling himself to a sitting position as the surviving chuckled a bit.

"That's all of them. The remaining Hunters and Fangs left a short time ago to aid the Legion's siege on Colonial Command." Adam said.

"And Anwick?" Roman asked.

"He won't be waking up to the tongue of a mangy dog. I dusted that son of a bitch like crops." Adam replied proudly.

"He ain't mangy. He's just like me, in need of a damn good woman and a damn good drink." Dalton added, Whiskey sitting down right beside him and looking at the rest of the group as if to second the notion.

"They're inside the building!" one of the soldiers yelled, relaying the message to Lassiter.

"Hold your ground!" he replied, sending what Goliath units that remained up closer to the fight. Legion troops by the dozen had breached the entrance to the building and set up a makeshift barrier using large sandbags as even more troops piled in. The plan was to bring in the heavy Shock Troops next, however they were met with swift gunfire on the outside by several units of Colonial soldiers who had returned to command as instructed.

That's when everyone outside first saw it. The gigantic shadow cast by the last operational Colonial Star as it made its approach, carefully planning its landing behind the complex. It was met with streaming Legion gunfire, however the small arms weaponry had no more effect on the huge Colonial ship as would rain or direct sunlight. Its hardened plated steel exterior was made for deep space travel and could withstand multiple nuclear strikes, combat rifles couldn't begin to dream of doing any type of significant damage, not even in unison.

"Sir, Colonial Star Twenty Two is on approach." one of the officers announced as a majority of the staff continued helping Sarah prep the equipment and supplies. This was literally the last remaining group of political and military command for the Colonial government, and if they fell here in the battle of Glimmeria, the Legion would win the war and once again rule the Skyla System unopposed.

"Have them land and load the supplies and equipment, however we have not lost the battle yet. I will remain here with Sarah as long as there is hope of winning, just have the Colonial Star prepared to launch if needed. Instruct all remaining Swordfish and Spartans to do defensive flyovers until ordered otherwise." Commander Edwards said.

"Yes sir!" the officer responded, quickly turning to carry out the order.

Lassiter's men continued the full on gunfight with the few Legion soldiers who had breached the entrance, eventually taking a majority of them out while suffering heavy losses themselves in the process. Four remaining Legion soldiers who realized they were cut off from the central attacking force and surrounded by Colonials, threw their weapons down onto the ground and placed their hands behind their necks in surrender. They were swiftly taken into custody by a returning group of Colonial soldiers who entered the Command Center to rejoin their ranks.

"Take them to the holding cell on level two." Lassiter said loudly as his few remaining soldiers checked the wounded before re-securing the entrance of the building.

"What's the situation out there?" he asked.

"Sir. The streets are torn up pretty bad. Pockets of Colonials held up throughout the city, most of it controlled by Legion forces who are getting one hell of a fight from Glimmerian locals." one of the Colonial soldiers answered, his face blackened by the fog of war.

"Do they have air?" Lassiter asked.

"No sir, the only air we have seen has been our own, and they were few and far between. What they do have is a lot of Shock Troops and Spiders on the ground." the officer answered as Lassiter forwarded the strategical information into the Vault via com unit.

"How many troops do we have outside of the building?" Commander Edwards asked as he stood on the other side of the thick protective glass.

"Hard to say sir. I'd estimate two dozen who are battle ready. A lot of injured and dying alongside them." he responded.

"Legion troops?" the commander asked. "A lot sir. Hundreds. We were able to get here because we hit them out of the blue and they fell back before they realized we were so few. No way we could hold off an all out assault." the soldier replied.

"Lassiter, post every Goliath you have left at the entrance and bring your men into the Vault. Bring as much ammunition as you can carry, I'm ordering a full evacuation." Commander Edwards said.

"Yes sir." Lassiter said hesitantly, thinking of the faithful Colonial soldiers who were holding their ground throughout the city, waiting for reinforcements that would never come.

"Command One, this is Spartan One-Five-One, your area of evacuation is clear. You have an all green." the voice of a pilot passing overhead announced through the com unit in the Vault. Commander Edwards stood beside Sarah Blaine, each one pressing a sequence of keys on the wall which opened a door from the Vault to the area outside the rear of the building, their entire field of vision engulfed by the sight of the massive Colonial Star. As Commander Edwards and the remainder of the soldiers and personnel exited the building to board the base ship, Sarah turned to the Vault door which led to the internal portion of the building, entering her key code and unsealing the door to allow Lassiter's team access to the ship.

It was only a matter of minutes before the Colonial Command Center would be overrun with Legion forces, the remaining Goliaths would buy them a few more minutes, but they had once again fallen in crushing defeat.

"What about Adam?" Lassiter asked as he carried satchels full of ammunition. "All we can do is wait for him in high orbit. The entire city is overrun, and it will only be a matter of days before the Legion has more ships here. Our window of escape is closing, but we'll give him every last second of it." Sarah said, obviously upset at the possibility of her soon to be husband's capture.

"Colonial Command, this is Sky Commander Tess Weston of the United Gali Army. Please identify the coordinates of your friendlies so that we may assist you."

a female voice rang out across the Vault's com.

"What?" Commander Edwards said under his breath as he turned back to the com system. Visible from outdoors, a huge armada of warships and troop filled landers bearing the seal of Gali had arrived, beginning to darken the sky with such heavy numbers. Without the equipment hooked up and operational, there was no way for Colonial Command to know that Roman's home planet of Gali had indeed sided with the Colonials in the struggle of the Skyla System and had sent the bulk of its armed forces.

"Commander Weston, this is Commander Edwards of Colonial Command. I will instruct all remaining forces to engage their rescue beacons, everything else is fair game. Thank you." he said frantically.

"You're welcome." her voice answered as the roar of the landing shuttles full of Gali troops could be heard throughout Colonial Command. The warships were moved low to the ground, their cannons pounding pockets of Legion troops and occasionally even Hunters as it took only hours for Legion forces to issue a formal order of surrender. It was only one battle, the war was far from over. But at least now the Legion knew it no longer had control of the entire system. Gali, Glimmeria and several other planets who would soon join the Colonial side of the war had taken control of nearly a third of the Skyla System, which would give the people of those planets hope of freedom for their children.

"Adam continued to try and reach Colonial Command with the portable com unit, his message finally picked up with heavy static by one of the several operators who was collecting and dispatching information to their troops across Glimmeria.

"Sarah!" the operator yelled quickly. She had been talking with Commander Edwards as well as a handful of Gali top military, but all of that ceased to matter when she realized it was a message from her soon to be husband, and that he was safe.

"It's still not safe enough Sarah. Groups of Legion holdouts planet wide. I'm sending a group of Colonial Spec-Ops to bring them home." Commander Edwards said, Sarah disappointed but quickly agreeing to speed up the process of bringing them back safely.

"While they take care of it, you and I need to talk." he added, Sarah looking at him suspiciously as he pulled her off into a corner for privacy.

"Is it nearby?" Adam asked anxiously, everyone else waiting for Dalton's verdict, a map of the surrounding area in hand as they were all cramped inside of a sand crawler and heading for the extraction point. It was nothing more than a utility vehicle the town had used for repairs, and after seeing what the group had done to the bloodthirsty Hunters, they gladly gave it away with no strings attached.

"Well fuck me raw." Dalton finally proclaimed with disgust, balling the map up and tossing it onto the floor of the Sand Tracker as Whiskey rode shotgun.

"Want to dumb it down for us maybe?" Sasha asked sarcastically.

"We gotta turn this molasses moving bitch around and head the fuck back, the extraction point, I shit you not, is right outside of Valencia. The other side of Valencia. That dumb enough for you?" Dalton replied snidely before cursing Colonial Command under his breath.

"You have got to be kidding?" Adam said, beside himself in disbelief.

"Do I look like a stand up comedian to you?" Dalton replied as the Sand Tracker slowly began turning to follow its own tracks back into town.

"This is ridiculous, if any of the Hunters return we all know they will pick us up the minute we show back up." Zavious said.

"No shit, we might as well hang streamers on this bitch and radio them ahead of time, maybe they can organize a homecoming parade in our honor." Dalton replied as everyone inside of the overcrowded antique of a vehicle broke out into laughter for the next few moments.

A little over an hour later, the Sand Tracker had come to a complete stop, everyone huddled outside around the small crumpled map in front of them as the vehicles headlights provided enough illumination for them to see it in an otherwise completely dark environment.

"Alright, the plan is simple enough. We move everyone to the far side of town on foot with as much ammunition as we can carry, lay low in the hills and wait it out.

"What about Legion patrols? We got no cover out here." Dalton asked.

"All we can do is hope. "I can handle first watch," Sasha said, holding her suppressed pistol machine gun up. "Besides, I'm well rested." she added.

"Not by yourself you're not." Adam replied. "I'll cover first watch with you. The group loaded back up, moving cautiously to an area that was perfect for digging in and holding on until the Colonials could save the day.

"I can't believe we are going to rescue them, and then watch everyone but the man I love be imprisoned by the very government that they have sworn to protect. I mean Dalton and Steiner are there on our orders!" Sarah yelled.

"It is out of my hands I'm afraid. I will make it a priority to assure them all a fair trial as well as a very lenient sentence, but when the Colonial Parliament hears of their conspiring with the Benzans, well you have been with us long enough to know the answer to that." Commander Edwards replied.

"They will want them executed!" Sarah said loudly.

"I'm afraid you are right. Your father was a lifelong friend of mine, it is that I hold your family in such high regard that I will personally see to it that their lives are spared, Dalton, Steiner and Roman at least. The Benzans will receive no special treatment." Edwards replied.

"Nor would I expect them to." she replied, considering

them to be cold blooded killers.

"Sarah, I think it would be best if you were the one who orders them into custody. They will listen to your reasoning before that of an old man in an officer's uniform." Edwards added.

Sarah looked across the sand of Glimmeria with such mixed emotion. Her entire life had been dedicated to the thought of a star system without corruption. Her father had raised her to value law and righteousness above all things, but was that supposed to include compassion and love? She knew in her heart that the right thing to do would be to rescue the man she loved and bring the rest of them to justice. But she loved Adam, and she knew that in doing so, she may lose him forever. She loved him more than any man that had ever been a part of her life, short of her own father. "I'll take care of it for you." she finally replied, knowing that her struggling heart was no excuse for making the wrong decision.

"Thank you Sarah. I specifically plotted the extraction point close to Valencia to give them all the best chance of survival. For your sake, I want them alive and well when we arrive." Commander Edwards said before slowly taking his leave to return to the bridge of the ship.

"The son of a bitch wants us dead, I know he does!" Dalton commented loudly as he and Roman remained awake, the other survivors sleeping solidly.

"Who wants us dead?" Roman asked.

"Commander Edwards, that's who; the cocksucker," Dalton replied. "He sent us all out here while holding Sarah and Lassiter there. She's like a daughter to him and Lassiter is his idea of a perfect soldier. The rest of us he could give two shits about, knowing good and well we were out gunned. Then has us backtrack to the same place we almost died only hours ago." he added as everything remained silent.

"Ya hearing me man?" Dalton asked as Roman nodded to let him know he felt the same way.

"My loyalty is to Adam to the end. As much as I like Sarah, I'm starting to realize that since the day we met her, bodies have been dropping faster than panties in my presence." Dalton added as the two men laughed quietly, Whiskey sticking his head up for a moment almost as if he was fluent with lingerie.

"Sounds like your friends are still awake." Sasha said, sitting next to Adam as they both watched the sand filled horizon.

"Yea, I doubt Roman does a lot of sleeping as of late. With his newly fitted mechanical parts, I'm not even sure he needs to sleep anymore. And Dalton, well he rarely gets a good night's sleep unless there's an empty bottle of whiskey close by. I'm sure watching Steiner fall isn't helping much either." Adam answered as he and Sasha both remained silent for a moment.

"So, we got a few hours. Catch me up on the Benzan lifestyle. Seems like pretty much everything that I've been told of them was untrue." Adam said.

"I'm afraid I am not the kind of girl who likes talking a lot about herself." Sasha replied. That was a first for Adam, who gave her a huge but faux smile as he couldn't make the connection between a woman and selflessness. Finally, deciding to break what had become a very awkward silence between the two, he spoke up. "Well, I guess in that case I can ask Dalton to come out and entertain us."

"Where would you like me to begin?" Sasha asked, bringing a laugh to both of them quickly.

"Yea, he has that effect on people. He's really not as bad as he comes across when you get to know him. He's loyal and a damn good friend." Adam replied.

"I understand." Sasha answered.

"What I still can't figure out, is how you and the crew ended up fighting a politician's war?" she asked, changing the mood of the conversation to one of seriousness.

"Good question," Adam answered. "It wasn't long ago

that I was just like you. I thought I had everything figured out. Then, of course, I met Sarah, and it wasn't long after that everything got clouded I guess. Most of the people that the Colonials are trying to protect are honestly good people. I figured it was time to change who I was and start doing something positive." he added.

"If you don't mind my saying so, I don't believe you have changed. This person you seem to think you once were, that's the only person I have seen since you arrived on my ship. You seem to have things figured out to me, loyalty and friendship above all else." Sasha said, a very long silence falling after her last word as Adam began wondering if she was right. Had he really changed at all?

"So, what about you," Michaels asked. "I'm still curious as to how you ended up with the Benzans and what day to day life is like?" he added.

"It's a pretty simple story I'm afraid. If the person chooses to wear the amulet, they are from that point forward recognized across all Benzan families as one of their own, taken in and taught the lifestyle." she added.

"And what lifestyle would that be?" Adam asked.

"Everything from how to handle a weapon and defend yourself when there is no weapon, to helping the poor and defending the otherwise defenseless," Sasha replied. "In my case, a close friend of the family who was more like an uncle to me, decided after my family was slain that my only hope for survival would be with the Benzans." she added.

"I'm sorry to hear about your family," Adam replied somberly, looking at the ground for a few moments. "So Cyrus took you in?" Adam added.

"They all took me in as their own. Cyrus was like a father to me, but there are many other families, just as they are many other clans of Hunters," she replied. "Adam, you should consider the offer to become one of us. I know it will complicate things for a bit, but personally, I would really love the opportunity to spend every day with you." Sasha added, taking Adam by complete surprise.

"Well, I am certainly flattered by the offer. It's only fair to tell you though, when we return, my place is by Sarah's side until death. We had planned a wedding until the Legion arrived." Adam replied.

"Very well, all I can do is extend the offer, but it is your choice as to where life will take you." Sasha replied.

For the next few hours, Adam told Sasha the stories of the first Glimmerian War, his long career as a criminal smuggler and of course, the friends who had fallen that she would never have the opportunity to meet. Sasha continued telling Adam of the Benzan lifestyle as well as of the friends she had made, and sadly lost along the way. They laughed together, showed concern and even let go of some emotional feelings, venting to one another in a strict matter of trust. Personal accounts that only good friends could possibly accomplish through the bonding of a friendship.

"Adam! Picking up all kinds of Colonial traffic over the com unit." Dalton yelled loudly, running out to Michaels and Sasha as the rest of the group slowly followed.

"Gear up, they're coming." Adam said to the group after listening to the chatter for a couple of minutes. A small group of Legion faithful, not even a click away from their position, began firing tracer rounds into the sky. It was a tearful sight for nearly everyone when they saw the tracer rounds begin to be answered by Colonial rail gun fire, which could only mean one thing, their rescue chopper had arrived!

Within the span of thirty seconds, the rail guns had not only taken out the machine gun nest on top of a large sand dune, but a majority of ground around the Legion troops as the fast moving lead continued chewing into the sand and its underlying layer of clay. The survivors began flocking to the chopper in a single group, the com units continuing to broadcasting a message of the arrival of Gali forces, but this time around it was Sarah's voice.

Adam grabbed the com unit with both hands shaking, pressing the communication button and pausing for a moment to think his words carefully.

"I've waited a long time to hear that voice." Adam said eagerly into the transmitter, nervously awaiting a response.

"Adam! Where are you, is everyone safe?" she asked. "We are on our way home...Steiner didn't make it." Adam replied, his lips shaking from the emotion of hearing Sarah's voice again and the loss of his loyal crew member.

A long silence followed before Sarah replied with a heavy heart. "We see you on our grid now and will be eagerly awaiting your return."

The transmitter was flooded with com chatter as Glimmeria was now overflowing with military help from several planets who had followed Gali's lead. As the shuttle continued its path to the landlocked Colonial Star, Adam took one last look outside of the windshield, promising himself yet again that he would never return to Glimmeria as long as he lived.

"None of us would have made it out of there alive if it wasn't for everyone's hard work. Thank you." Adam said, nodding his appreciation to Roman, Dalton, Sasha and the rest of the exhausted survivors, including Whiskey.

"He grows on ya' don't he." Dalton said as everyone laughed and looked forward to the idea of living to fight another day.

Glimmeria had been lost to the Legion, a crushing defeat under the heels of the far superior force that was assembled by worlds filled with people in search of freedom, though much of its largest cities lay as nothing more than a pile of rubble.

What few soldiers remained would join the Colonial Parliament in devising a new strategy based around the newly gained support. Right now none of that mattered to any of them, especially not to Adam, who waited patiently as the shuttle docked onto the floor of the launch bay. He would finally see his future wife's face once more, which is something he had started to doubt would ever be afforded him again by the gods.

As the shuttle door opened to allow the crew's exit onto the interior of the Colonial Star, they were met by a squad of soldiers aiming combat rifles in their direction.

"Adam Michaels, step aside. Your crew is being placed under arrest for abandonment of military post as well as aiding known fugitives." an older gentleman with a lengthy white beard proclaimed.

"Well, it looks like Sarah has let herself go all to hell." Dalton said, sarcastically comparing her to the old man. The soldiers glanced at the sad excuse for a dog in Whiskey before they began placing hand restraints on the Zavious, Sasha and Dalton, while Roman resisted the attempt.

"Try putting those on me, see what happens."

With a bit of convincing on Adam's part, Roman soon placed a set of restraints on himself, all while continuing to dare the soldiers to lay hands on him.

"Don't worry, I'm sure it won't take long to clear up this misunderstanding. Where is Sarah Blaine?" Adam asked the older gentleman.

"I'm right here Adam." she said, stepping out of the shadows of an unlit room nearby.

"Adam, I'm sorry. I'm under direct direct orders from Commander Edwards himself to take them into custody." she said, her heart pleading with his own.

"Sarah this is my crew. My family." Adam replied somberly, still in disbelief of everything that was happening.

"I have to admit Adam, she doesn't seem like your type." Sasha said, drawing a scowl from Sarah as she tried to figure out the relationship between the Benzan beauty and her husband to be.

"You realize they haven't built a prison cell yet that can hold us, right?" Dalton asked Sarah, his question completely disregarded.

"We'll see." the Master of Arms finally responded as the group started to move slowly into the direction of the prison block.

"I have arranged for the Gunship to be fueled and waiting in hangar bay two when we get there." Sarah said to Adam as the group continued its slow pace to lockup.

Taking several minutes, they passed groups of Colonial soldiers who stopped to watch, never questioning her actions because of their deep rooted respect for Sarah and what she had given for the cause of freedom, while at the same time dumbfounded by seeing the crew arrested.

Just as promised, when they arrived, the Gunship sat in one of the launching bays, its reflective chrome exterior immediately catching the eye of a crew who had given up hope of ever seeing it again.

"It's fueled and supplied, just as you ordered my lady." one of the Colonial deck hands said proudly.

"Thank you." Sarah replied before turning to Adam. "We need to get out of here for a couple of days, just you and I. Sort through all of this." she said.

"Not without my crew Sarah, you know that." Adam replied as everyone stopped to watch the heated discussion.

"Commander Edwards pulled a lot of strings to keep you a free man Adam, your friends chose their own paths." Sarah replied.

"Free? Leaving here in a ship without my crew isn't freedom?" Adam replied angrily.

"This war is over for you and your crew, if you stay, the Colonial Parliament will see to your release from the military and not even I can stand in the way of that." she replied.

"Sarah, let's just go. The battle is over, your father is gone. Let's all just go right now, start a new life beyond all of this." Adam said, pleading with his lover.

"I wanted to go alone, just the two of us and have this

conversation. But if you insist on doing it in front of everyone else, fine." she replied as her eyes watered with emotion. "We can't start a life together Adam, I'm sorry. My place is here with the Colonials, with a military that longer wants you involved." she added.

"So this is it? Just like that we are finished?" Adam asked. "Maybe not forever, who knows, when the war ends you..." Sarah replied as Michaels interjected.

"No Sarah. You once told me to make a choice, now I'm asking you to do the same. Either you leave with me and we do things the way we need to, or you stay behind and choose your war and grudge against the Legion over the love we have for each other. Period." Adam said sternly. "Adam, I have to stay, you know that." Sarah said emotionally. "I thought what we had together was so much stronger than all of this, at least until now. Now I don't know what to think Sarah." Michaels said, trying his best to hide the pain consuming his every extremity.

As the group looked on, Adam turned back to look at Lassiter. "You with us, or staying behind to fight this pointless war to the end?" he asked, almost already knowing the answer.

"Adam, you are a true friend to me, but my place is by Sarah's side fighting for freedom. Kelly would want it that way." Lassiter replied.

Michaels simply answered with a head shake of pity before turning to the ship's ramp and suddenly stopping in his tracks. He glanced back at Sasha for several tense moments, remembering the promise he had made her not so long ago.

"I can't let you do this Sarah. I made her a promise." Adam replied, turning his attention to his former lover.

"Adam, it's going to be hard enough watching you leave like this, you know I have to keep them here." Sarah replied as she turned to Lassiter to give him the go ahead.

Lassiter readied his combat rifle, as he walked toward the prisoners with the full intention of ushering them forward.

"Belay that order Lassiter! Don't do this Sarah, don't push me into something that we will both live to regret for the rest of our lives." Adam said pleadingly.

"I'm sorry Adam." Sarah replied uninterested.

"Then so am I." Adam replied, pulling his pistol and aiming it directly at Sarah Blaine.

"What the hell are you doing Adam?" Sarah asked, shocked that the man she had come so close to marrying would go so far as to threaten her life.

"You leave me no choice." Adam replied, holding the weapon surgically steady.

Lassiter turned his rifle, aiming it directly at Adam, moments later feeling cold steel held by Roman Raines, who was a master of escaping loose bonds and blade smuggling.

"Think you're quicker with a combat blade than I am with this trigger?" Lassiter said jokingly, almost to mock the warrior.

"Wanna find out?" Roman replied, digging the edge into Lassiter's neck just enough to draw a trace amount of blood.

"Adam, there's no going back from this." Sarah said sternly, realizing that he was fully prepared to die trying to keep his promise.

"We outnumber you two to one!" a Colonial soldier said loudly, all of them taking aim on Adam and his crew.

"After watching you get your asses kicked twice by the Legion, I'd say that puts the odds in our favor." Dalton replied as he laughed, now holding two short barrel shotguns that he had recollected from one of the soldiers, his hands still tied with chains as Whiskey sat close to his feet.

"What's the logic Adam," Sarah asked. "You have nowhere else to go, we gave you the last chance you'll ever have at a decent life?" she added.

He seemed to mentally check out for a few moments,

thinking long and hard about his decision to come because of his strong belief in staying true to his word. He looked at his crew, then directly at Zavious.

"Extend the offer to Dalton and you have yourself a deal." Adam said.

"Done." Zavious replied with truth in his voice. Adam pulled the medallion from his pocket and placed it around his neck with a single free hand, his pistol never faltering.

"Is this what it has come to Adam? You are planning to live a life committed to a family of murderers and thieves? The trash of society." Sarah asked.

"Did this redheaded whore just call me trash?" Sasha asked Dalton, ready to throw fists with Sarah.

"I believe she did, and I believe Whiskey needs an official Benzan invitation as well." Dalton replied, glancing to Zavious who nodded simply to keep the peace.

"Relax Sasha, she's not worth the effort," Adam replied, holding Sasha back with his free hand, while looking straight through the woman he had once thought to be so perfect. "Of course, it would have been nice if I would have known this the day we met." he added.

"Go ahead then. Adam, you do realize that once you lift off, I will order our allies to blow the Gunship into nothing more than wreckage inside of a minute?" Sarah asked, the look on his face was a dead giveaway that he hadn't considered that angle yet.

She was right, even if he somehow managed to get away, the sky was so thick with Gali warships that they wouldn't have a chance in hell of getting out of Glimmeria's orbit.

"Give me your guns." Roman said, taking the shotguns from Dalton's grasp, putting them on both Sarah and Lassiter at point blank range.

"You can't be serious?" Sarah asked, surprised.

"Dead serious you bitch. Adam may be in love with you, but after hearing you call Sasha's people trash, I got no problem putting both you and your wet nurse on ice."

Roman replied of Lassiter.

"Our people trash, actually...now." Adam added, Whiskey barking loudly.

"You've seen my poker face before, if you think I'm bluffing, try me." he added.

"Roman, I'm not gonna leave you behind!" Adam said loudly. "What are they going to do? Imprison me? Kill me? I'm already fucking dead Adam, look at me," Roman yelled, referring to his synthetic laced body. "What in the hell else can they do to me that hasn't already been done?" Roman asked, not expecting an answer. "Get everyone else the hell out of here, I'll give you the time you need for a clean getaway." Roman added.

"Adam looked into Roman's eyes for a moment with appreciation. "I will be back for you my friend, and I'm saving a medallion for when the day comes." Adam said as he nodded one final time.

"If you come back Adam, my love for you will not play favoritism again. I will see you imprisoned." Sarah said.

"Hadn't heard that line before," Adam replied, not even glancing in her direction. "Soon my friend." Adam said to Roman as he turned to enter the Gunship.

"This isn't over!" Sarah yelled, as he turned to face her one last time.

"Yea. It truly is." Adam replied, holding Sasha's hand as they followed Dalton and Zavious up the ramp and into the Gunship, Whiskey stopping momentarily as he pulled a mangy leg up and let urine fly onto the deck of the Colonial Star.

"Damn I love that dog." Dalton said smiling as he slowly sealed the ship's door air tight.

Moments later, he and Dalton made the preparations to lift off, the shiny vessel leaving the Colonial Star in full burn.

"You've started a war you can't win Roman." Sarah said as the heat from the Gunship's thrusters whipped across their skin.

"Says the bitch who's tucking tail and hiding behind everyone else and their army on her last remaining ship." Roman replied stone faced.

Several minutes later, one of the deck officers on the bridge of the Colonial Star turned from his grid screen.

"Sir, we just picked up an unidentified craft heading away from us and moving fast!" Commander Edwards quickly walked to his station to see for himself, the Gunship almost out of striking distance.

"Set gun coordinates and get the firing solution, quickly!" he said as he turned to face the entrance to the ship's bridge.

"Belay that order private." Roman said, holding Sarah, Lassiter and several other Colonials at gunpoint as they entered the bridge.

"This is outrageous!" Edwards said, motioning for the crew's security force to take control of the situation. They stopped abruptly as one of the shotguns swayed into the direction of Commander Edwards, the other remaining firmly on Sarah.

When it had become clear to him that his own security detail would not be able to intervene until Roman decided he was damn good and ready to let them, Edwards ordered his soldiers to drop their weapons slowly to the ground and place their hands behind their heads.

The Gunship had gotten away, broken orbit and disappeared into the drop cloth of stars which illuminated the skies of every planet in the system.

"Officer Lassiter, escort Roman to the prison level." Sarah said seconds after he decided Adam was long gone and threw down his weapons.

"If he even begins to attempt escape, kill him." she added.

"Yes my lady!" Lassiter agreed with unwaivering loyalty, Commander Edwards doing his best to regain the look of someone with authority.

"Mr. Raines, I hope you do realize that our willingness to hand you over to the Gali government was a key factor in them coming to our aid." Commander Edwards said as Roman turned to face him, his hands wrapped in chain and realizing that he would now have to pay for his role in Greyspine.

"That's right Roman, you will be on a Gali warship within the hour. May god have mercy on you." Commander Edwards added as Roman was led away by Lassiter and the small group of Colonial soldiers.

Adam hurt deeply, trying his best not to show it as they set course for Tirious. He knew that with the companionship of Sasha and a new home among the Benzan family, that with time his heart would heal into something that was once again capable of love. Watching Dalton comb the thick and tangled hair of Whiskey down into a smooth shine, Adam knew that even the worst looking of situations could turn out fantastic in the end. And above all else, he began contemplating an escape plan for Roman as the feeling of freedom began to set in, true freedom. Plenty of time for reflections of the past to run through his mind.

Gunship III: Reflections

"I'm surprised you would have the balls to show your face again." Walter Jones said with sarcasm.

The small time crime boss stood in a less than fine suit, two armed men at his side. They weren't killers, that much was obvious by the deer in headlights look upon their faces. They anxiously held Dalton at gunpoint using rifles, and that always had a way of rubbing him wrong.

"Aw now, no need to be so rude about it. How about you get these boys to lay down arms so we can have ourselves some honest dealings?" Dalton asked casually.

Walter Jones laughed, knowing Dalton and crew were smugglers and that was about as far from honest as it could get. Not to mention he owed Dalton James and his friend Adam Michaels money from a job previously completed.

"Now why in the hell would I do that?" Walter asked.

A split second later, one of his armed men fell to the ground in screaming pain; victim of a sniper's shot from the far distant.

"Well sir, cause you 'aint got a choice for starters. I got a sniper up above with you all scoped at this very moment. That's the biggest reason I got the balls to show my handsome face again," Dalton said, smiling wide. "Now where's the money?" he asked.

Walter Jones had planned to screw him a second time of course, but didn't want to risk the possibility of his own demise in the process. Throwing a sackful of credits to Dalton's feet, Walter scowled heavily. "It's all there."

"You may think I'm somewhat of a stickler, but after you gave Adam and me a sackful of blank paper on the last go round, I think I might be counting it this time." Dalton said, bending down to unzip the bag.

It was filled with credits alright, and he was due two thousand for the job recently completed. "Looks like about two thousand." Dalton said as his fingers quickly fanned through the money.

"I told you it was all there." Walter replied. "Yea, but see," Dalton said walking a bit closer as he pulled a tightly rolled cigar from the pocket of his good as new brown coat, blazing up the tobacco stick and adding heavy smoke to the mix. "You still owe me three thousand for a job already done. And I can't figure out the exact number without an adding machine, but I'm thinking you need to be handing over the rest of it if you wanna walk out of here alive." Dalton replied.

"Are you insane? You know I don't have three thousand more credits on me," Walter Jones said loudly. "I'd be a fool to carry that kind of money." he added.

"Yes sir, I'd be inclined to agree," Dalton replied, stroking rough fingers through the course patch of his beard. "Well, how about you boys empty your pockets into the bag, including your watches and such. Then we'll just call it even." Dalton demanded, kicking the sackful of credits a bit as it moved closer to them in the lifeless dirt.

"Are you kidding," Walter asked snidely. "Why don't you get on the ground and take the man's gold tooth too for God's sake?" he added loudly as his gun struck man still lay on the ground, a blanket of pain and agony doing little to quiet his screeching.

Several minutes later Dalton stood there with a smile painted to his face and a loaded bag in his hand. "God damn you Dalton James, you'll pay for this!" Walter yelled, his man now one tooth shy and rolling on the ground in pure oral pain.

Never one to pass up a suggestion to make money, Dalton had pulled a pocket knife from his brown coat; using its small set of pliers to jerk the golden tooth from the man's skull. It would only fetch thirty or so more credits, but that was money owed to him by Walter Jones and he wasn't about to leave it laying. Of course the man would have to do without tough meat in his diet for the next few days, but that was of no concern to Dalton.

"Well boys, it's been a blast. I guess this is it until next time." Dalton said in his usual wise ass tone, turning to walk away from the deal gone sour.

"Dalton, if you ever show your face here again I swear I'll cut that damn smile from your skull," Walter yelled. "You tell Adam Michaels I said the same!" he added.

"That 'aint gonna happen." Dalton replied, his cigar burned down to nothing more than a saliva ridden stub.

Shortly after, Dalton boarded the ship, walking up the steel grating of the ramp as he was greeted by Whiskey. His pooch had been with him for a while now, a loyal friend who even sported his own custom made brown leather coat. It wasn't as thick as the one Dalton wore on his back of course, but the couturier had thrown it in for free. Together they looked almost like twins, the fur on Whiskey's face just a tad thicker of course.

"Where's the Capt'n?" Dalton asked, petting Whiskey for a moment before standing with the bag of credits, jewelry and that single loose tooth.

"Right here." Cambria said, slowly moving down the spiral stairs that led from the cargo hold to the crew's quarters. She was perfect in every sense of the word, her lush curves tightly wrapped in form fitting cargo pants and tight t-shirt that did wonders in showing off her upper body. The upper body that interested men, of course. Her skin had a glow of white satin about it, which only brought more attention to her vibrant blue hair.

She was from the Drifts, a series of smaller planets on the fringes of charted space. Some of the planets lacked modern technology, while others simply shunned it altogether. Everyone from the Drifts had a unique look about them, and hers just happened to be a look of insatiable sex and electric innocence.

Cambria Sims was still fairly new to smuggling, which was the biggest reason she laid down the kind of money she did for Dalton; which amounted to nothing more than drinking money. He had experience, was wise to the way things worked in this type of life and when things went wrong he was plenty capable of taking care of things with his own two hands.

"Damn you are a welcome sight for sore eyes." Dalton said, watching such a beautiful woman head into his direction.

Kneeling down to retrieve the bag full of credits while looking up at him with a smile, her pouty lips only inches away from the most vital area of Dalton's body, the part wrapped in a zipper; Cambria smiled slightly.

"I still say we should take this to the next level. I could make an honest woman out of you." Dalton said as Cambria slowly stood to her feet, purposely keeping herself only inches from his body so their lips could be nearly touching when finished.

"Maybe one day cowboy. For now though, good job on today's catch." she replied softly as though she was ready to kiss him, instead turning to head back to the crew's quarters.

"One day you are gonna be courtin' me exclusive. You watch and see baby, I'm gonna break you down." Dalton said, grinning ear to ear as Cambria walked away slowly, her ass moving with only the slightest of bounces; a perfect testament to her capable curves. Rather than answer, she turned slightly and smiled at the experienced smuggler.

"Now Whiskey, there goes a real damn woman. I know my away around the bedroom as good as any man, but my gut tells me she'd be able to show me a thing or two," Dalton said under his breath with his trusted pooch by his side. "I'd almost give up drinking for fifteen minutes with..." Dalton added, interrupted by the shuttle pulling from the planet's surface.

He quickly made his way to the ship's entrance, spinning the wheel which served as a handle, the metal door sliding shut as he bolted it into place with three locks.

"Goddamn steam engine, I still hadn't got used to it." Dalton said with ill intent.

Cambria was Captain of the Outer Heaven. It could house only a small crew but was proudly made in the Drifts, needing nothing more than constant steam to operate. It had its advantages and disadvantages of course, but made almost no sound which was ideal for smuggling. It was a deep space capable ship, though it looked more like an airship or elongated balloon. A mixture of solid steel and thickened glass, the Outer Heaven was a marvel of Victorian technology.

"Good shootin," Dalton said as he turned to nod his appreciation to Skulls. His God given name wasn't Skulls of course, it was Trevor Lagrange. But he had a very odd hobby. He enjoyed collecting skin, bones, teeth and even the occasional shrunken head. A hobby that quickly led to his nickname. "This is for you pal." Dalton said, pulling the still bloody golden tooth from his pocket and flicking it to the strange man.

Skulls was a very tall human, nearly seven feet. He was far from large though, a majority of his frame nothing more than pale white skin and sturdy bones. He wore black leather from his boots to collar, though it was very loose hanging. A black top hat sat firmly on his head as the stringy haired man simply nodded his appreciation.

His Salvation model sniper rifle hung by a nylon strap down the middle of his back. The Salvation rifle was a much older model and being bolt action made it less popular because of the accuracy needed to make a kill. Skulls loved the weapon because he was accurate. Damn accurate. Anytime he pressed his eye to the telescopic lens mounted onto the rifle, death would surely ensue.

"Best head up and get your cut." Dalton said, turning to make his way up the spiral stairs. They were narrow, made of all steel and noisy as hell; having taken a verbal lashing by Dalton more than once during the routine hangover.

Cambria stood near the crew's table with Tank as they emptied the contents of Dalton's bag, credits piling high. Tank also answered to his real name, Greg Shelling, but Tank fit more appropriately. The dark skinned man was huge, at least six and a half feet tall with a muscular frame to go along with it. He stood there in a sleeveless white t-shirt, green pants and boots of black leather. His usual attire, day in and day out.

"I'm keeping this watch if that's cool?" Tank asked.

"Be my guest, too much flash for me anyhow." Dalton replied as Tank held up a watch of rock solid silver.

"Here's your cut, plus a bonus for job well done." Cambria said, laying a stack of credits out in front of

Dalton, accompanied by a wind resistant lighter that had been salvaged from the pocket of Walter Jones himself.

"May want to quit giving me gifts like this, people are gonna start talking." Dalton replied, winking at the flirtatious Cambria Sims.

"I'll leave Trevor's cut on the table." Cambria said.

"'Aight. Me and Whiskey are beat, I'm dragging my sorry ass to my rack. Room for two if you change your mind." Dalton said, looking heavily at Cambria with a smile.

"Never know, tonight might be the night." she replied with a smile. Of course in the back of his mind he knew it wasn't going to happen, but flirting with a girl who was so perfectly sculpted with genetics seemed to make the trips through space more manageable.

Whiskey was the first one in, immediately jumping onto the foot of the military style bunk.

Dalton sat down several moments later, handing Whiskey a long string of jerky before leaning over to take his boots off. "I'm getting too old for this shit." he said under his breath, unlacing his boots a bit before forcing them off. Leaning over to a night table, Dalton picked up a photo taken with Adam Michaels during their first war on Glimmeria.

Dalton was decked out in an old brown duster with shotgun in hand, his arm wrapped around the man who had been like a little brother to him. He smiled a bit, remembering the day it was taken and the great night of drinking that followed. "I miss you old buddy." Dalton said in a low voice, finally placing the photo back onto the bedside table as he turned the lamp out and tucked in for bed.

Nine months earlier.

"Next." the prison cook said solemnly as a single line of the most incarcerated men in the Skyla System waited patiently.

Roman stood there, gazing out of the small window behind the buffet line that wasn't suited for an animal to enjoy, much less a human being. The stars looked as beautiful as ever, even if only from a window that was less than ten inches wide.

"Prisoner Raines," a heavily armed guard shouted loudly, using the wooden stock of his shotgun to push Roman forward forcefully. "He said next!" the guard added as Roman turned to face him for only a moment.

There was a time when pushing Roman Raines in such a way would have been considered suicide, however this was no such time. His hands and feet were both tightly bound in heavy chain as deep scarring was visible all across his body; a place that once was home to nearly indestructible Goliath shielding. Less than a month after he had been aboard, the warden thought it best that Roman's metal exterior be removed with surgery in order to better protect his guards.

It was a procedure that had been given only a slight chance of success, and if Roman would have died on the operating table then life aboard the prison ship would have continued without him. And die he did, for nearly two minutes he had escaped this life of caged horror only to be brought back with electrified paddles. The next few months were spent under heavy guard in the infirmary, his gaping wounds healing slowly on their own without the assistance of pain killing treatment. He wished that he would have been left dead, rather than being brought back to this nightmare of bad food and torture.

"Still looking for your friends I see," Zane said, almost in a joking fashion as the badly scarred body and fully bearded face of Roman Raines slowly sat down in front of him in the prison mess hall. "It's been nine months now. They 'aint comin'." Zane added.

"You let me worry about that." Roman said with stern intent, his eyes reflecting a hollow rage.

"All I'm saying is we need to start working on our own exit strategy. Just in case." Zane replied. He was a large man, there was no doubt about that. A bit over seven feet tall, the former soldier had a rock like complexion across his face with a roughly shaven head which left a thick patch of brown hair in mowhawk fashion. Roman took a few moments to let Zane's words set in as he glanced around.

A single file line of once mighty warriors now left humbled, begging for a spoonful of slop as though they were less than human. Then there was the window. That damn window. Every single meal since Roman had been locked up he glanced out of that ten inch window into the cluster of thick stars hoping to see the Gunship arriving to save the day. Adam Michaels had given him his word that he would return, and Roman knew Adam was a man of his word. That said, the possibility that Adam had tried and failed started to become the only good explanation.

"You're right. We need to get to work on something of our own. I'd rather die trying to get the fuck off of this ship than live like this." Roman said, glancing up at the gun rack.

It was the name of the cage that overlooked the prisoner's mess area and standing inside was a prison guard with a high caliber rifle and the authority to shoot to kill.

"It's about time my brother. It's about time." Zane replied, smiling slightly before once again becoming stone faced as a patrolling guard walked by their table.

It was Corporal Raykes, a guard that Roman knew all too well.

"What the fuck are you staring at?" Raykes asked, walking by the table slowly.

Rather than respond, Roman continued his stare, eyes cutting through the man who hid behind the authority of a badge. "That will be one motherfucker I'll enjoy killing. Just hope I get the chance." Roman said in a low voice as

Raykes had moved down a few tables.

"Not your favorite huh?" Zane asked.

Roman remembered his arrival to the prison ship. How Raykes had spit in his face and dared him to retaliate. How he had heard the faint laughter of Raykes during his forced surgery, steel being pulled from flesh without remorse.

"Son of a bitches like that put on a good front, but when it's killing time they cower down. I'll either kill the bastard or bring him to the point that he wishes for death." Roman replied as the guards began ordering them to stand and return to their cells.

"They are waiting for you my lady," Lieutenant Lassiter said calmly as he approached Sarah Blaine. "Sarah. Are you alright?" he asked as she burst into tears.

"I can't do this anymore," she said crying heavily. "I can't go on without Adam next to me. It's killing me inside." she added.

"My lady, everyone is outside waiting for you to deliver your acceptance speech." Lassiter said with panic.

"Tell them to find someone else. How can I possibly lead the Colonial Army if I can't even sleep at night? I miss him!" Sarah replied as she continued to cry heavily.

Once lovers on the verge of marriage, Sarah had chosen her Colonial duty over the man she loved. Truly loved. He was a man of virtue and truth, something she hadn't seen a lot of in the military. She had regretted her decision only minutes after watching him fly away, their storybook love shattered because of a mistake that had haunted her every since.

"Sarah. Just go out there and tell these people what they need to hear. Let it come from your heart. As soon as you are finished we will get to work on finding Adam." Lassiter replied.

"Really?" Sarah asked, calming just a bit.

"Yes my lady, I will personally see to it. Now please,

take a moment and then lead these people to the freedom they so desperately need." Lassister replied. Sarah simply responded with a nod of gratitude as she began to wipe away the aftermath of tears and poised herself to deliver a speech.

Several moments after Lassiter had left, Sarah reached into a drawer on her thick wooden desk. She took several pills, chasing them with a glass of pure water as her eyes fixated onto a photo of Adam Michaels which had remained on her desk. She had no intentions of taking her own life, but rather medicating herself to the point of making life bearable. A habit that had become increasingly dangerous, but made her numb to the pain.

Sarah sat for a moment, overwhelmed by the loss of her true love as the medication began to mask the hurt inside of her. She had all but stopped crying, looking out of a small window behind her desk. Hundreds of Colonial brass were outside waiting, each of them sure that Sarah Blaine was excited about taking over the military side of their government.

Of course she would show them the mask of happiness, though she was slowly dying inside. After convincing herself to push through this technicality of taking command; looking forward only to the possibility of once again seeing the man who held both her heart and soul captive, Sarah left to deliver her speech.

"What's on your mind?" Dalton asked, a look of whiskey laden concern on his face. His smile was covered in the usual scruff, unkempt hairs flaring wildly.

"Just thinking that maybe it's time to move on. Starting to give up the idea of somehow finding a way to work things out with Sarah." Adam replied as he took a drink from the frothy mug of ale before looking around the lodge. It was one large room built of shaven tree trunks and mortar. The perfect combination for a dwelling that was torch lit and heated by two gigantic fireplaces. It was filled with Benzans, all of which had come in to escape the unrelenting snowfall while grabbing some brew.

While they were highly trained killers, the Benzan Mafia did its best to stay out of sight and out of mind. The small moon of Tirious provided perfect cover for them, a refuge of thick trees and constant snowfall. Bitter conditions that kept even the toughest law officers far away. In fact, aside from the Benzan settlement there was no other life on Tirious. Giving them a huge area to train, live and feel the embrace of true freedom.

"About damn time, we should have been trying to rescue Roman a week after we left." Dalton replied, lighting a hand rolled cigar and biting the end off, spitting it onto the floor.

"I couldn't agree more," Adam replied. "What were we supposed to do though? It's pretty obvious that the Benzans have their own pecking order and we are at the very bottom of it." Adam added.

"They are a strange group, I'll give you that much. But the 'sumbitches treat Whiskey like he's royalty so I can live with strange." Dalton said before taking a lung jarring puff from his cigar and turning up a bottle of rough scotch.

"Yea, Whiskey is a hit. That much is a fact." Adam replied, turning to look at their four legged pet for a moment. The once mangy dog was doing a lot better now, his thick fur gleaming as he was outfitted with a small leather saddle which held several bottles of rock whiskey.

He would move from table to table, a Benzan calling for him and then trading a nice leg of meat or savory cut of bread for some of the hard alcohol. He was considered to be the one waiter that everyone loved and tipped with perfectly cooked beef.

"Little 'sumbitch eats better than I do." Dalton said with near envy.

"If you want I can saddle you up and let you move from table to table." Adam said, smiling wide.

"I hear ya. Hell, a few more stiff drinks and I might just take you up on that." Dalton replied as he noticed Adam deep in thought.

"My advice is just to forget about Sarah. I mean, hell, you have any idea how many women I've bed down and left sleeping? The number is staggering." Dalton said.

"Yes, sadly I do, we've been running together for many years. And I wasn't bedding Sarah down. Well I was, but it was because I love her." Adam replied.

Nearly a decade. That's the amount of time since Adam and Dalton first met, fighting side by side against the Legion. Although the first Glimmerian War was lost, they bonded well under fire and had been smuggling together every since. Brothers in every sense of the word outside of birth. Just as Dalton had a passion for booze, Adam had a passion for women.

He was no Romeo, though he could have easily been. Adam was a man too true to his values for that kind of lifestyle, instead having the habit of throwing his heart out there far too often. He was quick to fall in love.

Sarah was different though, and Adam knew it the moment they first locked eyes. He saw through her high profile, lavish clothes and impeccable vocabulary. He saw the true Sarah Blaine, the goodhearted woman beneath that had so long needed someone to see the true her. She had fallen for him because of that very reason. Although he was on the wrong side of things when they met, running from the law and God only knows what else, he looked at her the way she had only wished everyone saw her. They had fallen so madly, deeply in love.

"Love. Now there's a four letter word for you right there," Dalton said, sharply swigging several ounces of scotch. "Love is an unnecessary emotion. It's for the weak minded. Do you have any idea how many women have gotten the boot because they fell in love with ole' Dalton James?" he asked, drinking a second helping of the not so smooth scotch.

"I'm thinking none?" Adam replied with humor, holding his hand up as if a contestant on some sad excuse for a game show.

"Shit son, you must not know me well. There have been plenty," Dalton replied brashly, puffing deeply on his ill constructed cigar. "But I live by the creed." he added.

"The creed?" Adam asked, scared by the notion of his friend standing for anything.

"The creed. You can give a woman your liquor but you don't ever give her your heart. Ever. That's where you messed up with Sarah." Dalton replied.

"I didn't give her anything, she took it," Adam responded. "That's what love is. You meet someone and they unexpectedly change your life. I loved her, hell I still love her with everything I have." he added with conviction.

"I agree, this scotch is easy to fall in love with." Dalton said, drawing a strange look from Adam. Less than a second later Sasha approached their table. Her perfectly rounded hips and fur sheathed breasts were the immediate attention magnets of several men in the room, including Adam.

"What are you guys deep in discussion about over here?" Sasha asked, smiling a bit as she sat down with the two men; her slightly curled brunette hair bouncing a bit.

"I was just telling Adam that he needs to love. Find a good looking woman like yourself and give her his heart." Dalton said flirtatiously as he grinned wide.

"Your friend is right Adam, you should consider his advice." Sasha replied. Adam continued to stare at Dalton with a ghostly look unbelief, wanting so badly to reach across the table and smack the hell out of his so called friend.

"I mean, take Sasha for instance. She is the definition of what a woman should look like. Plus she's impressive with a weapon and mighty good to you. Better scoop her up and make her an honest woman before someone else does." Dalton said.

"Thank you," Sasha said with true gratitude before turning to Dalton and noticing scotch born lust painted all over his face.

"Well then." she said, turning back to Adam who was still burning a hole through Dalton with a wide eyed stare.

"Hey." Sasha said, waiving her hands a bit to gain his attention. Adam turned to her, and though Dalton had said what he did out of lust, he was right. Sasha was woman perfected. She was not only beautiful, but treated Adam with such a level of respect. Plus the thought of her and Dalton ending up together was almost unbearable.

"Well I need a couple more stiff drinks," Dalton said, rising to his feet slowly. "How about you Sasha, need a couple of stiff ones?" Dalton asked, smiling wide as Adam immediately cast a warning stare to his friend.

"No thanks, I'm fine." Sasha said to Dalton as she slowly pulled her chair closer to Adam, her backside gracefully becoming one with the wooden seating beneath her.

"I'd be inclined to agree." Dalton replied.

"Barkeep is liable to send you packing if you ask for any more drinks. Says he has never seen someone down so much in a single sitting." Sasha added with a smile.

"Is that so?" Dalton asked, turning his attention to the clean shaven bartender. "Well in that case I'm gonna go order a few more just to piss him off," he added with a smile of his own, the large cigar saturated with both ash and saliva as Dalton chewed it slightly. "Ya'll be good." he added, starting for the bar and turning for a moment, hidden behind Sasha's back as he did his best to mimic the two of them making love. Adam tried hard not to smile back, knowing it would give his friend's plot away.

"So." Sasha said, her face glowing behind a perfect smile.

"So." Adam replied playfully.

"We haven't really talked about us since arriving."
Sasha said.

"Us?" Adam asked.

"Yea, as in you and I together in more than just a
friendship fashion." Sasha replied, still glowing but with a
look of seriousness in her eyes.

"I'm not trying to avoid the whole conversation. It's just
that I don't know if I'm ready to be in another
relationship. It's only been..." Adam replied before being
cut off.

"It's been nine months. Nine months Adam. At some
point you have to let Sarah go," Sasha said. "She's gone.
You have a different life now and chances are you will
never even see her again." Sasha added, trying to talk
some sense into Adam's reasoning.

"Hey Adam, come check this shit out!" Dalton yelled
from the bar, both of his hands holding large mugs fulled
with ale.

"I'll be back in a minute." Adam said, eager to join
Dalton and dodge the current conversation at any cost.

"Oh you have got to be kidding me." Sasha said under
her breath as she glanced at the bar to find out why
Dalton had stolen Adam.

"Still a looker, even if she did try to lock me up." Dalton
said as Adam sat beside him and noticed Sarah Blaine on
the large television behind the bar. Dalton had started to
explain that she was being promoted to Colonial
Commander, but his words were simply mumbled as
Adam blocked everything else out and focused his
attention onto the woman he had so passionately loved.
The more she spoke, the more Adam was reminded of his
strong love for her to this very day. Even if it was a one
sided feeling, it was a feeling that he couldn't control and
his heart pushed his hands to begin trembling slightly.

Adam broke his attention from the television for a
moment to casually glance across his shoulder at Sasha.
His intentions were to see if he felt the same when

looking at her, but his eyes were met with her own as she stared at him with discouragement. Adam of course smiled and tried to act as though his very pulse wasn't directly connected to Sarah's speech, however his head quickly turned back to watch it.

Everything about her was as beautiful as he had remembered. Her hair sparkled with red purity and her eyes told the truth about the beauty of her very soul. It was a forbidden love now, but for Adam it was a love that he continued to find himself lost in.

"I'm telling you man, between you and me, she was a catch." Dalton said in a hushed voice.

"A catch," Adam replied sharply. "You think I don't know that man? I would do anything to go back to life with her, even if it did mean the Hunters on our asses," Adam added, looking back at the television for a moment. "Besides, what happened to not ever falling in love?" Adam asked.

"Yea, well yea," Dalton replied, firming up on the bar stool a bit. "I'm just saying if someone was stupid enough to fall in love, which we both know they shouldn't, it should happen with a woman like that." he added.

"Yea, tell me something I don't know." Adam said, once again turning to the television and watching Sarah Blaine's every movement.

Her features were so perfect, her movements soft and her intentions true.

"Sasha." Dalton said a bit under his breath.

"No, I said tell me something I..." Adam said, cutting his words short as Sasha took a seat right beside him. Adam glanced over at his sorry excuse of a wingman for a moment, nodding his head as if to ask Dalton to leave them be.

"Well, I best be going to check on Whiskey." Dalton said standing up and tipping his head slightly to the Benzan beauty, only to moments later mock a session of intimacy behind her back. Again Adam gazed at him, stone faced and tight lipped, turning his attention to Sasha.

She sat there, smiling back although it was obvious that she was truly worlds away in thought.

"Listen. I don't want you to think I'm avoiding the conversation that we both know needs to happen. It's just that I feel something very strong for you and it scares the hell out of me." Adam said.

"You do? So just to clarify, this feeling isn't one sided?" Sasha asked.

"Of course not," Adam said, smiling. "For God's sake I pulled a gun on my wife to be just to get you to safety." he added.

It was the truth. Adam did in fact have feelings for Sasha. Strong feelings. But they were cloudy at best, and he was doing everything he could to figure them out; in need of more time to do so.

"So where do we go from here Adam Michaels?" Sasha asked.

"That's the big question," he replied. "I just need some time to think things over and clear my head. Ya know? Spend time getting to know you without bullets flying at me." he added, bringing instant giggles to Sasha's face.

"You truly are amazing Adam. Take all of the time you need then and just know that as a Benzan I can't guarantee it will be done without bullets flying at you." she replied, causing Adam to ease up and laugh a bit.

"Things will work out for us in the end. Right now I just want to live free and do it with you in my life." Adam said, smiling at her as he held her hand a bit.

Was he starting to fall for Sasha? The thought had entered his mind more than once. He knew without a doubt that she truly was in love with him and he didn't have to become someone else to earn it. But what about Sarah Blaine? He simply couldn't ignore the feeling he had been instantly overcome with as he watched her on television only moments before. He couldn't breathe, it felt as though he would die if he couldn't hold her in his arms once again and that wasn't fair to Sasha. She deserved the best man he could be, and that wouldn't be something he could offer until his heart was completely free.

"Well, looks like we're needed." Dalton said, regretful that he would have to leave perfectly good drink behind and turning up his mug to finish as much as possible before approaching their table once again.

Adam turned to see Kraid enter the building, he was the man in charge and it showed. Every single Benzan falling silent as he entered under the guard of two heavily armed warriors, not that he needed it. His legend of ending lives was one of great lore, the very broadsword sheathed to his back had sent a hundred or more Hunters back to the hell that they had been spawned from. He casually glanced across at Sasha, nodding slightly as his curly black hair shifted with ease. As he turned to exit back into the unforgiving peace of the falling snow, he pointed to a table near the entrance and motioned them along as well. Both men stood up slowly, their posture firm as fur covered their otherwise striped dress suits of black silk.

"Time to put together a rescue plan." Adam said under his breath as they all stood to their feet slowly before following Kraid.

"About fucking time." Dalton replied with the smell of must tainted whiskey on his breath as both men waited for Sasha to lead the way.

"Let's go meet the man." she said with a calm resolve as the three walked out into the serene blanket of white. They had been among the Benzans nearly nine months now, and although Adam and Dalton had both caught sight of Kraid in the past, neither man had actually spoken to him.

Dalton stopped for a moment, slapping his leg and giving a curl of the lip with a whistle quickly following. Seconds later the clanging of bottles could be heard as

Whiskey sprinted out into the snow, running just a bit to the side as the weight of empty bottles in the saddle pushed onto him.

"Poor 'sumbitch done got vertigo from carrying all this alcohol," Dalton said jokingly as he laughed alone and knelt down to pet his most loyal of friends. "Oh hell no, is this mustard?" he added, rubbing his fingers harshly across the mutt's back to remove a small mustard stain. "Oh hell fucking no." Dalton added, glancing gratingly back into the door of the lodge and secretly wishing he knew the identity of the condiment perpetrator.

"Come forth!" Victoria shouted as she sat in the large throne chair sculpted of rock and gold.

The Hunter Queen had been awakened following the killing of so many of her species at the hands of the Benzan Mafia. Garrison, the highest ranking of the surviving Hunters from the second battle of Glimmeria approached nervously, kneeling as low as his trembling body would allow.

"RISE! Tell me of your failures!" Victoria shouted, standing quickly to walk down and face the unfortunate survivor.

"My...my queen," the Hunter said shakily. "The Benzans ambushed our ships and hunted us on the surface..." he added before his words were cut short.

"You survive to tell of this story while Anwick lays on a stone slab in the next room," Victoria said angrily. "We are the most feared race in the Skyla System. Do you know why that is?" she asked with focus.

"No my lady." the Hunter replied out of necessity.

"Because we always get retribution against those who have betrayed us. Always. You and the other survivors have betrayed me by not fighting to the death to save the life of Anwick." Victoria said before turning to walk back to her throne chair and once again be seated.

"Take him!" Victoria commanded as two Hunter Elites

walked into the throne room. They were a rare sight, even for the fearless members of the Hunter race. The elites were more like knights, outfitted with thick black armor and the pupil free eyes of a demon.

They were a rare sight because there were so few of them, only the finest mortal warriors earning the right to immortality. It didn't take many. One Hunter Elite had the abilities of an entire room full of his standard kin, and they were heartless. Much more heartless. They would slaughter an entire room full of their own kind in order to kill someone who posed a threat to their queen. It was their sole purpose to protect the queen, a job they did well. And at this very moment they followed a direct order from the one who commanded them, dragging the doomed Hunter into a room filled with the rest of what few survivors had returned from Glimmeria.

"Please my queen, I beg of you!" Garrison yelled as he tried unsuccessfully to escape the grasp of an elite before resorting to grasping for what little texture the stone wall provided. His large Vampiric fingernails dug into the wall, but the sheer strength of the elites continued forward; splintering the doomed Hunter's nails as one of the elites pulled a longsword of grey and black. As the door of thick rock and worthy steel shut tightly, screams of her own race began to filter throughout the throne room, a slaughter of cowards the source.

Not so long from now, his flesh along with the flesh of others slain would become feast for the queen and her most loyal. Tissue tasted the same once applied to the burning of flame, no matter human or otherwise. Cindered meat was the preferred dish of Hunters, and if their hunger grew enough, the source of meat was of no concern. They had their fair share of enslaved humans for the very reason of food, though the occasional failures of a Hunter would bring the queen to the point of no mercy. They indeed feasted on their own kind.

After only a couple of minutes the screams halted, the

sound of razor edged blades chopping flesh were all that remained. The door opened once more, creaking heavily as the two Hunter Elites emerged to bow before their queen; covered in both blood and loyalty.

"Rise my warriors. It is retribution against the Benzans that I now seek. Gather our most battle tested soldiers and see to it personally that not a single Benzan heartbeat sees another sunrise." Victoria said confidently.

"Yes my queen." one of the elites responded, his voice deep and mighty as if he were a God of battle.

Both knights stood firmly and walked away, blood dripping from their armor and forming the path taken on the harsh stone floor of the Hunter fortress.

As the large monsters of flesh walked slowly through the halls of the Hunter compound, the elites soon slowed their pace as they approached a large metal door. It was thick steel, both gothic designs and Hunter text forged into the face of it. As the door made a low grinding noise against the rock mounting, both elites approached their military leader. Vladris. He was one of the few Hunters to claim stake on a hell hound, a dog born again into the ranks of the undead.

They mutated a bit differently during the turning process, of course, and their skin became thick. Almost leather-like with rising patched across their backs. It gave the look of thorns for eyes that knew no better. The hell hound slowly turned as the Hunters approached, recognizing them a bit while showing his teeth in protection of his master. Its teeth were thick, although needle-like and nearly alive with hunger. Its eyes subtly glowing of crimson red as it made a strange noise of warning. Hell hounds were not to be trifled with. An ability to end lives with ease behind their shard filled smile and eyes of fury.

Thousands would be the best estimate when it came to lives ended by the blade of Vladris, the same blade that was tightly strapped to his back as he looked across the bannister of the balcony. Built into the side of a stone mountain, the Hunters had fortified their base to protect and serve their queen. Though they never slept, each Hunter had a period of downtime in which it would rejuvenate itself.

Vladris had been turned by Hunter Elites many years ago, giving such a valiant fight in protecting his King. He had been a Ronical Knight, at least throughout his human life and up until the Hunters felt the need to turn him into an undead warrior. The Ronical Kingdom fell shortly after, succumbing to the rule of Hunters. However, the fact that Vladris in human form had slain two of the mighty Hunter Elites earned him a bridge to immortality when he finally was killed in battle. The hand of a surviving elite turning him in only minutes. His former kingdom was one of nearly endless rainfall, and the sight of it brought a calm to his soul. At least what remained of it, as Vladris looked across the bannister and into the thick jungle as rain poured heavily, leaving with it a serene melody.

"Our queen has commanded us to assemble a group of warriors. One that will prove the demise of the Benzans." one of the elites said as Vladris continued to stand, his hands wrapped around the steel bannister as he looked into the heavy downpour.

For him it was soothing, and many nights he would spend his downtime simply gazing into the rainfall and enjoying the gift of immortality.

"Then it shall be so," Vladris replied, slowly turning to face the others, reaching down for a moment to calm his hound. "Handpick our finest and outfit them with the basic tools of slaying. I will personally see to it that our queen's wishes are carried out." he added in a rough but dedicated voice as both elites nodded and turned to execute his order.

While they were all elite knights for the queen, the rest knew Vladris was by far the strongest. A few even suspected the queen had secretly feared him, something Vladris had also picked up on. His loyalty ran deep, but the fact that he was unstoppable led to a bit of envy by the queen. The Hunter race followed Victoria out of fear, but on the battlefield they followed Vladris out of respect.

"You shall soon feast on an endless buffet of man flesh." Vladris said, his muscular build kneeling to show affection to the most loyal of pets.

The hell hound, which stood nearly three feet high, seemed soothed by the voice of his master, turning his head slightly as if to show off his pale white hide.

"The speech was great my lady. Exactly what our people needed to hear." Lieutenant Lassiter said calmly as Sarah sat in a chair of velvety red plush.

"Thank you. I'm not sure how I got through it, Adam is the only thing on my mind," Sarah replied. "I should be focused on the upcoming confrontation with the Legion, but I just can't. I feel so helpless." she added, turning her head a bit to avoid tears.

"About Adam my lady, I have a plan," Lassiter said as he approached Sarah to sit in a chair beside her. "We have solid information on the Benzan's favorite hideout." Lassiter said as Sarah looked at him with unconvinced eyes.

"They are not a group to be negotiated with, so the hard part will be trying to convince the Benzans to allow us to speak with him," Lassiter added. "I will assemble a strike team, and then plead with Adam to at least return here to meet with you," Lassiter said.

"I have known Adam for some time now. I feel confident he will at least meet with you Sarah, as long as I promise him he's not walking into a trap." Lassiter added.

"No. I will plead my own heart, it's the only way he will listen. I'm coming with you." Sarah said.

"Sarah, listen. We are to begin a major assault on the Legion in less than one day, not to mention the Benzans are not to be taken lightly. There is no guarantee that I will even walk out of there unscathed, the last thing our people need right now is to have its leader in harm's way. I would advise you to stay here and..." Lassiter replied, sharply cut off.

"I'm coming Lieutenant Lassiter, that's an order. I ruined a good thing with Adam. It's my fault and now I have to try and make things right and hope he can forgive me. Just make sure the crew we take with us is loyal and capable. I will not let fear of the Benzan people stop me from seeing the man I love again. I'll make sure our war effort is in strong enough hands." Sarah said.

"At once." Lassiter replied, turning to leave the room and assemble the best he could. He still wasn't sold on the idea of Sarah coming, but he was the ideal soldier.

She had given him a direct order and he wasn't the kind to disobey them. All he could do now is place as much of a safety net around her as he could, and give his life for her if needed be. Especially with his growing feelings for her, though they remained hidden. Sarah continued to stand there, looking across the stars through a huge window of reinforced glass and Colonial writing.

She wondered if Adam ever thought about their near marriage, or if he even bothered himself with thoughts of her. These past nine months had seemed like decades to her. Things were different now, and that was something that scared the hell out of her.

Tameca City was once considered one of the best locations to live and prosper. Of course that was before war had torn throughout the Skyla System and pushed the reeling Legion into Tameca City seeking refuge. They were all but beaten, having lost the second war of Glimmeria, but more importantly the support of several planets following the loss. Planets who had shifted to the Colonial side, and now what remained of the Legion consisted of worn down troops, mercenaries and forced volunteers from planets once controlled by the ailing military.

"They will be on us within days! Our own scouts have confirmed it!" Lieutenant Rommel shouted across the crude steel table as three more Legion officers remained seated.

"It takes only one victory, one show of force to turn the tables in any fight." a highly decorated officer replied calmly as he remained sitting.

"My Lord, there can be no victory here! We must issue a formal order of surrender!" Lieutenant Rommel answered, shouting his reply furiously.

Lord Riven stood to his feet slowly, as the highest remaining officer left among Legion forces, he embraced the fight to come and expected no less from those who served beneath him. Standing to his feet, dark red uniform of cotton stitch and black trim; a look of disappointment pasted onto his face as he held a Legion sidearm out and blistered a shot into the forehead of Lieutenant Rommel. Standing for a moment, Lord Riven casually wiped spotted blood from his officer's jacket as the lifeless shell of a body that had been Rommel abruptly fell to the floor.

"Sometimes, it's simply a matter of rebroadcasting fear into those who look upon us," Lord Riven said, slowly sitting back down and laying the glock style pistol onto the cold steel table in front of him. "There will indeed be victory here, and I will not tolerate anything less. Are you with me?" Riven asked sternly as both remaining men looked on.

"Yes my Lord, to the end!" one of the men said loudly, reaffirming his position in the regime.

"We'll see." Lord Riven replied, standing slowly to walk out of the room and deliver his next order.

It would be an order that would change the complexion of the war forever. Every epic tale of war had to include a good guy and a bad guy, it was a story as old as time.

Lord Riven didn't just accept the role of bad guy, he embraced it. In order to be bad, truly bad, one had to be feared.

Fear was earned through acts of violence so savage that onlookers dared not question. Only fear would turn the tide of this war now, and Lord Riven was the perfect man for the job. As he slowly picked up a com unit that would relay his orders throughout every Legion post on Tameca, he smiled a bit. Almost as if pleasure would be forthcoming.

"I will be away briefly as the rescue mission begins." Sarah said as a filled room of both Colonial brass and high ranking soldiers listened.

"Rescue mission?" one of the soldiers sitting near the front of the room asked. Sarah looked across to the man who would be handling the Colonial side of the upcoming battle, General Ortega.

"Yes," she replied, turning to answer the soldier directly. "We received word only minutes ago that Legion forces in Tameca City have started opening fire on civilians. Women, children," Sarah said, taken back by the freshly received report. "Anyone who is refusing to join their war effort is being executed on the spot," she added. "General Ortega will lead our troops into battle, and it appears that we will be doing a bulk of fighting on foot. The Legion appears to have little to no air support left, which means more casualties on our end as well. We will have to meet them on their turf." Sarah said.

"I have asked General Ortega to begin the strike sooner than expected in order to save as many civilian lives as we possibly can. However, your lives will be on the line as well, so I thought it only appropriate to ask all of you face to face." Sarah added. One of the Colonial Spec Ops soldiers near the back of the room stood to his feet, looking around for a moment before refocusing his attention onto Sarah Blaine.

"We'll go. And when we arrive, the Legion will fall." the soldier stated proudly as the room began to cheer.

"Good. That means you are all out of gear, get your asses in check and double time it to the launch bay!" General Ortega shouted as the room of cheers turned to a full eruption of motivated yelling.

As the group of soldiers began to file out of the room with courage and conviction, they immediately halted and joined the crowded lobby who stood quietly, stunned by the video footage being broadcast across the mounted video monitors on the adjacent wall. News coverage sending both still images and video feeds out of Tameca City, which was mostly engulfed in flames as explosions rocked throughout the city at random. Legion firing squads lining up and gunning down helpless civilians as they attempted to flee their homes. Sarah began to tear as did many of the Colonial soldiers, still images of bodies piled several feet high being shown, filled with both women and children who were still cindering from a fiery death.

They watched as Lord Riven gave an interview to the news team, bragging of the Legion's hold on Tameca as he promised to continue the killing while daring the Colonials to intervene. General Ortega looked onto the gutless murderer as he continued his interview for the news crew, smiling as though he were proud of killing so many innocent.

"The Colonials would be wise to stay clear of Tameca or any other Legion controlled ground." Lord Riven stated in a threatening manner as the Colonial soldiers stood silent, watching in horror.

"Let's go goddammit, these people need us!" General Ortega shouted, doing his best to break the shocking quiet of his best soldiers while showing them such threats did nothing to intimidate him. And they didn't, in fact General Ortega now thought of the upcoming battle as personal and would have gladly fought it for free.

Other planets were sure to send help as well, but most were days out even by full burn. The Colonials were the closest force, stationed in Glimmeria and stocked with enough firepower to possibly put an end to the massacre at hand.

"General Ortega, I am more than willing to come..." Sarah said as the stocky man turned for a moment to cut her short, scars across his face from past battle experience.

"Thank you for the offer my lady, but that is not necessary. I will not stand for war crimes such as these and give you my solemn promise that when the black of our boots hit Temecan soil, the only massacre will be against those who have committed such butchering. You just work on bringing Adam back to us." he said, smiling a bit before turning steadfast and following his soldiers to the three Colonial Star battleships which would be under heavy escort by several well armed ships filled with battle hungry troops.

The city of Rockheed began to tremble as though a minor earthquake had set in, moments later the large outlines of Colonial ships both massive and commanding respect made their way into the pale green sky of Glimmeria.

Citizens stopped to witness such a fantastic force of freedom seekers heading for war, and leaving behind just enough soldiers to hold the fort down. Ninety percent of Colonial forces were propelling into the sky, their ships in full burn and plotting course for Tameca City, and as the fully equipped soldiers glanced out of the windows lining each ship, the onlooking citizens quickly vanished and were replaced by scattered stars as they hit deep space in full burn.

"So Adam, Sasha tells me that rescuing this prisoner Roman Raines is a priority for you?" Kraid asked as he sat calmly in his thick leather chair, a long desk of polished wood separating them.

"That's right. He stayed behind and gave us an out, otherwise we'd all be locked up." Adam replied.

"You've been with us now, what six months?" Kraid asked. "Nine months actually." Adam replied.

"You could say six though because I've been drunk for at least three of 'em." Dalton added as both Adam and Sasha turned to stare a hole through him as Whiskey barked loudly to testify to the truth of it.

It was the moment Adam began to turn his attention back to Kraid that he first noticed it. A photo behind the desk on a small bookcase, Kraid holding Sasha with sheer love on the faces of both. They were ex-lovers, and that complicated things even more for an already overwhelmed heart that slowly beat inside the chest of such an honest man.

"It's very important we get our friend back," Adam said to Kraid, before slowly turning to Sasha. "He's always been honest with me and that means everything." he added, letting Sasha know right away that he had become wise to her past relationship with Kraid.

After listening to Adam and staring at Dalton for a moment, wondering what kind of first impression to make, Kraid reached into a door on his desk and pulled out a handgun of gold. Fully functional, it was an semi-automatic pistol although a bit larger than the standard. The bright light from the snowy day outside gleamed into the room and refracted off of the gold plating of the piece as Kraid laid it onto the desk, pushing it into Adam's direction.

"Every ship's Captain carries one of these, about time you did the same." Kraid said with a slight smile, glancing at Sasha for a moment himself.

It was Sasha who had ended things between them after life became too complicated. Kraid had never gotten over her smile, the touch of her hand. He still held very strong feelings for her even though he dared not show it. As he and Sasha exchanged glances, Adam felt that there was a bunch of history between them, history that couldn't have blindsided him at a worse time.

"The intel I have on the Gali ship is that it is maximum security, which is why I'm sending two of my very best along with you," Kraid said as the two men from the lodge slowly entered. "Captain Michaels, meet Primal and Stage." Kraid added.

It was easy to see where Primal got his nickname. He looked more beast than man as both Adam and Dalton stared at him to determine if he was actually human or another race entirely. Indeed human, he was badly scarred with bushy brown hair on both his scalp and face. A very tall and stocky man, Dalton found himself instantly becoming more attractive standing beside Primal.

Stage seemed to be the opposite. Well dressed with a finely trimmed pinstripe beard of black that perfectly meshed with his crop cut hair. He wore a set of reflective sunglasses and carried a very large pistol on his side that the Benzans referred to as a hammer. It was the most common firearm among their people, its deep and throaty firing sound resembling the strike of a hammer. "If your friend is still aboard that ship, we'll get him." Stage said with calculation.

Adam sat there in deep thought, he didn't like the idea of two men who he knew nothing about coming along for the ride. Especially having just pieced together a past relationship between Kraid and Sasha. He wanted to believe if it came down to it, they would put their lives on the line to save his, but he just wasn't convinced. In fact, he wasn't even sure he knew Sasha at this point.

It's not the the fact that she had a past, everyone has a history. It was that he had to find out about it by surprise when he had already started to favor her. This whole rescue plan was starting to worry Adam, but it was his only option at this point, and Roman had been locked up far too long. Adam owed his own freedom to the man and the least he could do was return the favor.

"I appreciate the help." Adam said, standing slowly to his feet and extending his hand. Kraid, who wanted to hate Adam so badly for capturing the affections of Sasha, extended his arm to shake hands. It nearly killed him, shaking hands with a man who would be walking back outside with the woman he loved so much. But she had made it clear that her love life wouldn't include Kraid, leaving him helpless to do anything more.

"I'll have my men fuel a ship for you." Kraid said, smiling a bit. *Is this son of a bitch planning on killing me?* Adam thought as he nodded while broadcasting a fake smile. He didn't want any trouble, but just like his life up until now, doing the right thing always seemed to surround him with it.

Both Roman and Zane stood there with a small group of prisoners, watching the new arrivals slowly exit the Gali shuttle which brought them in once a week. While the rest of the group meticulously watched fresh meat exit onto the steel deck of the prison grinder, wondering who they could intimidate and control; Roman and Zane continued to look the shuttle over.

"It's a Zion 400. Gonna take at least three men to pilot it out of here, and no less." Roman said as he studied the ship from its rounded silver nose to the dual thrusters which were mounted onto the rear.

"Going to have to try it with two, I don't know anyone else we can trust enough to include." Zane said under his breath.

"I do." Roman replied with confidence as he watched a large man exit the shuttle under heavy guard. Slightly larger than Roman, the man's physique looked as though it had been etched with the sharpest of knives as his closely cropped black hair seemed as confident as his strut.

"Yea, and who's that?" Zane asked with interest.

"My brother." Roman added as he continued to stare at a man whom he had close ties with. Quinton.

"So that's when they caught me," Quinton said as he sat at the steel table, its legs bolted to the floor of the recreational area as both Roman and Zane listened. "I had an entire shipment of weapons, warrants for my arrest on a dozen or so planets and the blood of a Hunter on my hands." Quinton added.

"A Hunter? Can't honestly say I have ever met someone who has fought one and lived to tell about it." Zane replied.

"Really," Quinton asked, turning to look Roman in the eyes. "I take it he doesn't know?" Quinton said.

"Know what?" Zane asked as Roman began to reflect on a past that he had so long tried to leave behind.

"I'd say you have met someone that has fought a Hunter and lived to tell about it," Quinton said with a bit of laughter. "Roman here has killed hundreds of the bastards, including one of their queens." he added.

"Bullshit." Zane said sharply.

"No, it's true. I can't believe you've been locked up with him for this long and it hasn't come up yet," Quinton replied, gaining a stern look from Roman. "Ah hell, I'd say it's alright to talk about it now. You've been caught. We both have. Might as well lay it all out there for him." Quinton added.

After a few moments of looking at Quinton, Roman turned to Zane, ready to reveal at least part of his past.

"Several years back, my unit was dispatched to work security for the signing of a treaty," Roman said reluctantly. "Seemed like just another security detail, I figured I would be back out drinking a few hours after the politicians did their thing," he added as his eyes began to tear just slightly. "When I was eight I watched both of my parents get murdered in cold blood. Goddamn Hunters cut them down in the middle of the street like they were garbage. I tried to fight them off but I wasn't anything more than a boney ass runt." Roman added before taking a long pause.

"When I walked in to secure the conference room for the treaty signing and found out my own government was signing a treaty with the Hunters, I lost it," he added. "I waited for their queen to arrive, and even with a large security detail of her own I struck. I buried a blade flush into that bitch's skull and twisted it hard enough to know for a fact she wasn't walking back out of there." Roman added.

"I remember hearing about that. The shit was all over the news. The Greyspine Massacre." Zane said.

"Yea. When I struck Queen Lethra, I guess the Hunters thought it was a coordinated assassination and all hell broke loose in that fucking room. We were the absolute best our government had to offer," Roman said, pausing for a moment to glance at Quinton. "But they had their elites and eventually I realized there was no winning the fight, it became a matter of survival. Two of my own damn men held me at gunpoint when I tried to take a shuttle. Those are the only two men I have ever killed that I regret day and night." Roman replied.

"No wonder the Gali paid such a high price to lock your ass up." Zane said.

"They have been tracking me down every since, trying to bury me under a prison. The Hunters have been tracking me to cut me into small pieces and I knew deep down that eventually one of them would catch up to me. Can't run forever." Roman said.

"Don't have to run anymore little brother, I got your back." Quinton said.

"After my parents were struck down for nothing more than sport by the Hunters, Quinton and his family took me in. Raised me the best they could," Roman said. "I've dedicated my life from that point on considering them my family and trying to kill as many of the Hunters as I fucking can." Roman added.

"So we can trust him as our third man?" Zane asked, already knowing the answer.

"You can trust him with your life, Quinton hasn't ever let me down." Roman replied.

"And I'm not about to start now." Quinton added, turning to Zane as a prison guard slowly walked behind them. "Good. Very good." Zane said in a low voice.

Normally dressed for only the most glamorous of events, Sarah was outfitted in a snug fitting pair of blue military pants and a long sleeve shirt which was stitched from thermal material.

"And you trust everyone coming along?" Sarah asked with hope filled intent.

"Yes my lady, they are absolutely your most loyal followers." Lassiter said as they boarded through the small entrance which was reinforced with thick bolts and blast shielding.

Sarah stopped, glancing across the crew area of the cabin into the faces of the men in which she placed her life into the hands of. There were three of the very large Husk race, barbaric as well as beast like, they bore a heavy resemblance to the mythical minotaurs of old. Two Goliath V2 soldiers were seated at the rear of the shuttle, both programed to use their robotic frames and small mini-guns to defend Sarah at all costs. Finally, Lassiter had hand picked three Colonial soldiers. Human, as well as the most able and trusted he knew. Each had lost so much throughout the war and looked to Sarah with the utmost respect for leading them into the direction of freedom.

"Umm, Lassiter. Maybe we should discuss the group you have selected." Sarah said, unconvinced of this being a group she could trust. One of the large Husk warriors stood to his feet, his near eight foot frame only inches from touching the ceiling of the shuttle. Walking into the direction of Sarah, the thick hair which covered his bulging arms gave them a grizzly appearance as he stood before her. Kneeling down to the floor, the Husk stared low with loyalty.

"My lady, it is truly an honor to be standing before you this very moment. Please know that I will use every fiber of my being to defend you to my very own death." Sarah looked taken back by such loyalty coming from the heart of a warrior who could easily have broken her into pieces.

"Never mind, they'll do." Sarah said calmly as she took a seat with Lassiter near the front of the shuttle.

"Tigon Twelve to tower. Requesting permission to launch." the shuttle's pilot said into his helmet mounted com unit.

"Affirmative Tigon twelve, safe voyage." a voice replied loudly over the console mounted speakers which surrounded the pilot. "Only the brass know you are onboard, I told everyone else that I was taking out a strike team to bring in a Colonial fugitive," Lassiter said. "I figured the less people in the loop, the better." he added.

"Good thinking." Sarah said, continuing to stare out of the window and hoping with every piece of her soul that Adam Michaels would forgive her.

As the shuttle pulled slowly from the deck of the ship and made its way into the void black of space, Sarah continued looking through the small window positioned near her seat. How could the survival of my heart depend on a single man when all of this exists? Sarah thought as she imagined so many planets around them filled with a variety of people. She started to think about the times shared with Adam.

How, only minutes after meeting, Adam had risked his life for hers and that of a young boy; going toe to toe with the Hunters in the process. In fact, he had went to bat for her so many times, only to have it thrown back into his face when she asked him to leave.

"Are you alright my lady?" Lassiter asked quietly, the shuttle traveling quickly through the curtain of twilight.

"Yes," Sarah replied, her stare into space never faltering. "Just thinking about everything Adam did for me. I was such a fool." she added with truth.

"Adam is a smart man when it comes to the character of a person. I know you are sincere, and I'm sure he'll see it too." Lassiter said.

"I truly hope so," Sarah replied, turning to Lassiter with trembling eyes. "I miss him so much." she added.

"Attention," Kraid yelled, instantly silencing the crowd of Benzans who had been drinking and socializing in the lodge. "I have just been informed by some very credible sources that the Hunters are assembling soldiers to invade us. They would come to our lands in an effort to spill our blood," Kraid added, many loud shouts following his words from Benzans who were ready for a fight. "I say let them come! For they will not find trembling women and children here, they will not find the usual intimidated cowards they face; only battle tested slayers of the undead!" Kraid yelled holding his broadsword high into the air, its handle wrapped in leather bonding as the entire room filled with nearly two hundred warriors shouted uncontrollably. The noise pierced not only the smoke filled lodge, but the valley behind the Benzan settlement, crisping the leaves and snow with echos of madness.

The loud shouting of insanity fueled by rage continued, as did the billowy grey stacks of smoke which climbed from their fires and into the heavens. And the snow continued to fall relentlessly. This was their home, their fields of killing and though the Hunters were damn formidable in combat, the Benzans welcomed the challenge with open arms.

From the time a Benzan child learned to walk, they

began training. For years they would learn hand to hand combat, everything from breaking bones to the finer points of strangulation. When they reached their teenage years, only the best of Benzan women continued training with men. Wielding anything from a long blade to a compact firearm, they were taught everything about killing. How each of their more notorious foes were slain easily and how the Benzan code demanded of them that no fight should ever be avoided. While the lesser Benzan women began learning survival tactics, the men and stronger women simply learned how to slay without regard.

They knew all too well that the Hunters were damn hard to kill, almost monster-like in their way of reaving humans. They did not care. When it came to battle, no man, human or otherwise, would ever witness a Benzan back down. Ever. They would fight to the death for the most simple of reasons, and when it came to defending their homes and protecting their families, they would slay any man or beast who stood in front of them.

"I say come God damn you! Come!" Kraid yelled loudly, once again holding his sword into the air, its pale blue complexion in need of salty warm blood.

The sword had been with the Benzan people for centuries, passed down from leader to leader as a token of authority. It had slain so many. As the gigantic arms of Kraid held the blade high into the infusion of smoke and snow, the Benzans yelled wildly. Waiting for the arrival of the immortals so they could be immortal no longer.

"Adam," Sasha said, quickly following him out of the lodge and into the heavy fall of cloud born snow. "Adam wait, we need to talk about this." she added, stopping him in his tracks.

"No Sasha, we don't." he said, turning slowly to face her with the serenity of nature flooding around them.

"I'm sorry Adam, I didn't think it would matter. It was a long time ago." Sasha said, visibly upset.

"It doesn't. The fact that he obviously still has feelings for you combined with the fact that I was starting to fall for you myself. That matters." Adam replied sharply.

"What are you saying?" Sasha asked, moving in a bit closer as the snow fell poetically around them.

"I don't know Sasha, every single time my life begins to make sense it gets turned upside down. I never thought I would say this, but I need calm. I need something solid that I can count on for the rest of my life. Lately I haven't been able to find that." Adam replied.

"I can be that Adam Michaels." Sasha said softly, gently putting her arms around him and kissing his lips slowly as luster filled flakes fell from the sky around them.

"My Lord, do you wish us to stay and fight?" Stage asked nearly in a yell to be heard over the chants of a war to come.

Kraid had seen the kiss between Adam and Sasha, his stare fixated onto them through a small window in the lodge was crushing to say the least.

"No. I promised Adam we would help free his friend and I am a man of my word. Go, and when you return you can help us count the slaughtered beasts," Kraid said confidently. The group of Benzans yelled with hellbent fury as Dalton found himself yelling if for no other reason than to give himself an excuse to raise a little hell without recourse, Whiskey even joining along with vicious barking. "And when the job is complete, Adam and his friends are not to return. Am I clear?" Kraid asked in a whisper.

"Yes my Lord. Crystal." Stage replied.

The Hunters sat in war equipped shuttles inside the face of a large mountain as gripping rainfall moistened the surrounding area. Five shuttles, each holding nearly twenty of the most battle tested Hunters, along with two of the elite variety. While they would all carry the standard Hunter designed rifle, which was a semi-automatic weapon capable of punching holes through the thickest of men, they were on a different mission. One fueled on revenge and retribution, and for those very reasons it was their intention to cut their foes into pieces. Slicing flesh from bone with perfectly edged swords which they each carried, harnessed onto their backs and nearly alive with the hunger for blood.

As the five shuttles slowly began to pull from the rocky terrain, many of the undead warriors gazed through the small windows into a curtain of rain and wondered if it would be the last time their eyes would see the gothic beauty of the queen's cavern. A series of several large doors cut into the face of a mountain with outlines of tribal style writing surrounding them. As feared as the Hunters were, they knew well the ferocity of Benzans in battle. In fact, the Benzans were famous for it. That said, Hunters still considered themselves at the top of the food chain and this was a perfect example of an unstoppable force clashing with an immovable object. Many of each species would perish in the battle to come, if not all of them, which made the presence of Hunter Elites among them bring comfort.

Legend tells of the rise of Hunter Elites. A time when scattered nations of vampiric beasts clashed with one another, the elites were born to defend their queen. They were the epitome of horror, easily slaying the most dominant foes in battle, and that was reason enough for the Hunters heading to the upcoming slaughter between nations to feel a bit more confident as they set course for the well known location of the Benzan hideout.

"The plan is pretty damn simple," Zane said as both Roman and Quinton looked on. "When the next transport shuttle arrives in a week to deliver new prisoners, we take the ship." he added.

"How the hell do you plan on doing that? We were under heavy guard the entire time, at least six riot ready soldiers aboard the shuttle." Quinton said.

"Our ship only places two guards in the landing bay. We take them out and meet the shuttle as normal. Wait for the guards aboard to exit with the prisoners and then use the element of surprise to our advantage," Zane replied. "Third person waits up on the steel catwalk near the entrance of the landing bay. They'll be responsible for keeping everyone on this orbiting hell out of the landing bay until the other two take the shuttle and are ready to make an exit." he added.

"Who's responsible for what?" Roman asked with concentration. "Look, I trust you, but I'm not stupid enough to hang out up on the catwalk. I got no intentions of you two taking the shuttle and leaving my ass high and dry." Zane said.

"I'll take the catwalk," Quinton said. "I will only have been here for a week anyway, so there would be a good chance one of the guards aboard the shuttle would recognize me." he added.

"Then it's settled." Zane said.

"One thing," Roman responded, looking abruptly into the dead gaze of Zane. "We will not leave without Quinton." he added.

"Agreed my friend." Zane said with a touch of nervousness in his tone.

"Only question now is how to get to the landing bay?" Quinton asked.

"You will ask to be treated in the infirmary," Zane responded, his stare directly on Quinton. "Roman and I will stage a fight. We have to make sure it's severe enough to get thrown into the hole, and we have to time it just right. Otherwise we will miss the chance to jump that shuttle," he added. "When we pass in the hall under guard, they will force you to face the wall," Zane said to Quinton. "The very moment we pass by, Roman and I will both spring on the guards and do our best to overtake them. As we do, you will turn and help us. Grab as many loose weapons as you can, going to need them in order to hold that catwalk." Zane added.

"I like it, it's a good plan." Quinton replied as Roman continued his stare on Zane, wondering if he could be trusted. Not that it would matter. He was easily willing to kill Zane if need be in order to make sure he and his terrorist brother Quinton left safely.

Primal pressed a sequence of several buttons in front of them as Stage turned from the cockpit area of the shuttle to face the rest of the group.

"Gonna be about a six hour flight to Arch City. Try and get some rest." Stage said loudly as the ship's thrusters began to do a slow burn as the shuttle remained grounded in the knee deep snow. He turned to face the instrument panel and assist Primal as both men pressed several buttons and logged their course.

"Arch City?" Adam asked, bending over into Sasha's direction slightly while doing so.

"One of Gali's larger cities. Plan is to overtake the crew of the shuttle that transports prisoners to the ship that houses Roman. Land as though it's a normal drop off, then grab him and get out of there before the guards aboard realize what is going on." Sasha replied.

"Arch City, random moon, I don't really give a damn. Anywhere but here. I'm freezing my ass off." Dalton said loudly as his lower jawbone trembled. He sat in the rear of the shuttle huddled into a chair with his thin brown coat pulled around him as though it were a straightjacket; Whiskey sitting pitifully by his side.

"You know, if you would just have replaced that raggedy ass brown piece of cloth with an actual climate jacket when they offered, you'd be nice and toasty right about now." Adam said smiling, his thick green coat with fur lined hood a perfect escape from the cold conditions.

"Fuck you buddy, the brown coat stays!" Dalton said with pride filled anger.

"Mmm...toasty." Adam replied in mocking fashion,

unzipping his thick coat a bit as if to purposely let cold air in.

"Everybody wants to be a comedian all of the sudden." Dalton said bitterly as he took a quick shot of rock whiskey from a small metal flask, petting Whiskey who gazed at the rest of the crew with the saddest of looks in his eyes.

Although Adam continued to chuckle a bit, deep down he knew the humor was a mere cover for the strangling emotions inside of him. His heart, his very soul missed Sarah Blaine so badly. The same heart and soul that knew deep down Sarah was gone, and had started to fall for Sasha. As the Benzan shuttle slowly began to lift from the ground and climb into the heavens, Adam's eyes remained locked onto the cloud of snow that the thrusters had formed below them. He wondered if Sarah ever bothered her own thoughts with him, or had she moved on, making Adam nothing more than a disposable afterthought?

Space travel had a way of forcing you to think about things that otherwise stayed buried deep inside. It was for this very reason that Adam dreaded their upcoming journey to Arch City, though it was long overdue. Roman had stayed behind so that Adam, Sasha and Dalton could escape. Adam Michaels was a man of his word, and now it was time to make good on a promise to free his good friend. Adam tried to focus his attention to that, although the memory of Sarah remained in the shadows of his every waking moment.

"What's on your mind?" Sasha asked nearly an hour after their shuttle hit orbit.

"Nothing much," Adam replied, breaking from his concentrated thought for a moment. "Just thinking about everything, it's been a crazy year for me." he added.

"Believe it or not, I understand. There was a point in time in my own life when I had given up on the idea of true happiness." Sasha said.

"Really? What happened?" Adam asked.

"You came along." Sasha replied. Though it would have sounded like the perfect line coming from a smooth talker, Adam knew she was sincere. He could see it all over her face.

"Does he always do that?" Sasha asked, breaking the awkward silence between them.

"Always do what? Snore?" Adam asked, turning to Dalton.

"No, I've heard people snore before. That's not what he's doing. In fact, I'm not sure what he's doing." Sasha replied as they watched the scruff painted Dalton sleep at the rear of the shuttle. It was a mixture of snoring and mumbling, a bit of laughing thrown in as well.

"Wondering what he's dreaming about?" Adam asked.

"Oh my God!" Sasha said loudly, but in a whispered voice as Dalton reached down to adjust his man tool while still sleeping, grabbing his crotch area roughly.

"Congrats." Adam said, patting Sasha on the back softly.

"Congrats for what?" she replied.

"You are pretty much the only attractive woman he has seen for some time, so my guess is he's dreaming about you." Adam replied.

"Oh my God!" Sasha said again as Dalton mumbled in his sleep and readjusted his crotch a second time.

"Wait. So you're saying I'm attractive?" Sasha asked with a smile on her face.

"I'm sure you know the answer to that. Must have hundreds of guys telling you that you're attractive each day." Adam replied.

"I'm not worry about hundreds of other guys, just Adam Michaels," Sasha said playfully. "What do you think?" she asked.

"Well ma'am, I think you are very attractive," Adam said. "In fact, I can't see a single feature on you that I would even think of changing." he added.

"Oh really?" Sasha replied.

"Yes really," Adam said. "In fact, I would lay you down right now and make passionate love to you if Dalton wasn't awake and smiling at us." Adam whispered into her ear. Sasha, who longed for Adam's touch, quickly turned to see Dalton sitting upright and smiling back at her.

"Oh my God!" she said as Adam began to laugh.

"Well a damn fine hello to you too." Dalton said snidely.

They were heading for Arch City, and that was a good thing. It meant they were heading away from the Hunters who were arriving to their own destination with a single purpose.

Eliminate the Benzan race once and for all. As the five Hunter shuttles broke from deep space and into low orbit, the Vampiric beasts prepared themselves, double checking both weapon loadouts and armor fittings. Normally, the Hunters feared no man. However, the battle to come was different. Meeting the Benzans on their own home soil meant fighting a race of men who would defend their families with barbaric passion.

Their assurance of victory was the accompanying Hunter Elite soldiers. The knights in solid black armor calmly sat at the rear of each spacecraft, almost as if the flight itself were the only burden to them. In just a very short time they would be involved in a small scale battle of flesh shedding and soul reaping. Still they sat there. So calm that they almost looked lethargic. But when the dying began, every Hunter knew the elites would in fact move and cleave with unnatural speed.

They had expected to hold the element of surprise, however, as the Hunters descended from the clouds they began to make out figures in the thick of the falling snow. The Benzans were waiting, poised by the heat of large bonfires as they waited in a spread open field that was flat and ripe for the planting of severed limbs.

"Land there," Vladris said to his shuttle's pilot, pointing to a large area less than a half mile from the Benzan's current position. "We will meet them on their own fields and soak them with the blood of cowards." the elite added, his strangely deep, almost demonic voice enough to rattle any normal man.

"Yes Vladris, at once." the pilot replied as the convoy of Hunter shuttles diverted its path into the direction of its new destination.

"Prepare yourselves, for tonight we feast of the blood of beasts!" Kraid yelled as nearly two hundred Benzans began to shout loudly, every single on of them well armed. With the blistering cold of snow consuming most of their vision, the Benzans remained near the bonfires for warmth and in close quarter as they awaited their adversaries.

As they looked through the thick snowfall at one another, it was a very sobering moment for most. Many would fall in the battle soon to be, and every man knew it to be the truth deep down. Though they believed they were more skilled with both gun and blade, the Hunters were not to be taken lightly. Many of the men had wives, children even. Kraid had sent them into the deep terrain of the mountains, their chosen fall back spot in the event of a battle so dangerous. Nearly forty wives and children under the escort of only five Benzan warriors, it was simply all Kraid could spare. The women possessed every needed survival skill and the five warriors sent as escort were his absolute finest. While it pained him to not include the five skilled warriors in the battle to come, he knew the others would fight harder knowing their families were well protected. Kraid was a reaver of both man and demon, having sent more Hunters to the grave than any other Benzan still breathing. Even so, his heart thumped with both adrenaline and nerves, knowing damn good and well the vampiric bastards would sent their best, and that was sure to include elites.

The first sign of the fight to come was the glimpse of what appeared to be two hell hounds that could be seen through the curtain of white snow. Moments later, the Benzans realized the Hunters were in full charge as they rapidly approached, swords drawn and eyes locked in.

"They come!" one of the Benzans yelled frantically as they all prepared for the stinging of steel, cold and yells of death. The exceptional speed of the Hunters allowed them to match the hell hounds in full sprint, stride for stride.

"Wait. Wait," Kraid yelled to calm his men, assuring they remained close together. "We must fight as one group. Do not let them intimidate you, for today they face the most skilled killers in the Skyla System!" Kraid added, pulling his broadsword, its edge gleaming a bit from the reflection of the diamond like snow that consumed them.

The thunder of feet and yells of barbaric and demonic fashion seemed to quiet for a moment, at least in the mind of Kraid who held his broadsword as he drew his gold plated pistol, firing a single shot which hit a Hunter directly between the eyes; his horned helmet had been split in two as blood poured from the skull of the filthy beast, quickly saturating the spongy white snow that would soon become a crimson river.

Using his free hand, the Benzan leader immediately thrust his sword down, striking one of the hell hounds at the top of its skull and driving the instantly dead beast into the frozen tundra. The second hell hound stopped in mid stride, realizing the Benzans were not the usual buffet of ease.

"Fight!" Kraid yelled as within a single instant, the field was filled with hundreds of Benzans and nearly a hundred Hunters, blades exchanging viciousness as the screams and gunshots could be heard for miles in the otherwise calm of falling snow.

"You alright?" Lassiter asked as Tigon Twelve

continued its full burn, the twin thrusters providing a trailing path of flame.

"I wouldn't wish this on anyone," Sarah said, sitting in her seat and looking out across the landscape of stars. "The worst part of feeling this way is knowing that I did it to myself. I just want to go back and leave with him, do things right." she added.

"You can't go back," Lassiter said, slowly taking a seat beside her. "So many times I think the same way, wishing I could go back to the day Kelly was murdered, go with her and perhaps prevent it all from happening. Deep down I know it wouldn't matter. It was her time to go." Lassiter said.

"Strangely, this isn't helping much." Sarah said, laughing a bit. "Oh, I'm not saying anything has happened to Adam. My gut tells me otherwise. If there is anything we know about him, it's that he's a survivor. I'm sure he's fine." Lassier replied.

"I hope so," Sarah replied in a much more serious tone. "If anything has happened to him...anything." she added, turning to look out of the window of the shuttle once more. "I wouldn't be able to live with myself." Sarah added. Lassiter was at a loss for words, instead placing his hand on Sarah's shoulder for a moment before standing to his feet and checking on the Colonial soldiers who had made the trip with them.

They were a grit filled bunch to say the least. The much larger Husk sitting to the front of the group, outfitted in thick armor plating they remained solemn.

"Everyone alright?" Lassiter asked as he made his way slowly by each seat to the rear of the shuttle. The Husk simply answered with slight nods, quickly returning their attention to the windows which overlooked the stars.

"Hoping the Benzans are reasonable so we may return to the fight quickly." one of the Colonial outfitted soldiers remarked.

"I understand, but the Legion will fall in due time. As

for the Benzans, I wouldn't expect too much reasoning from them." Lassiter replied softly, Sarah overhearing his words.

"And if you're right sir? If the Benzans are not willing to allow us an audience with Adam?" the soldier replied.

"We're not going for the opportunity to speak with him. We're going to get him. Sarah has suffered enough, and we will either be allowed to speak with Adam or we will use force to complete the mission." Lassiter said, leaning in a bit toward his men. "When we arrive, you men will remain with Sarah while the Husk and Goliath units accompany me. I will state our demands and be reasonable in doing so. If they are unwilling, we will use force until they become willing." Lassiter added, turning to Sarah who was staring out of the window.

I care too much for her to see her suffer like this. Lassiter thought as he watched Sarah for several long moments. His heart still longed for the soothing touch of Kelly, and having held her lifeless body in his arms had been devastating.

Through his own suffering, Sarah had been there. She saw to it that his heart healed enough to move forward. Now it was time to return the favor. She was a good woman, amazing actually. Everyone made mistakes, Lassiter knew that. It was Sarah's open admission of guilt for letting Adam walk away that made Lassiter understand how amazing she truly was.

Several times Lassiter had avoided her because he felt something more, feelings he shouldn't have. They scared the hell out of him, and rather than put Sarah through even more, he wanted to remain her friend. At least for now. Sarah turned to see her best friend watching her as she smiled softly back to him for caring.

"Face the wall prisoner Raines!" one of the two prison guards said sternly as Roman slowly stood and faced the wall of his cell.

He was the only resident, his former cellmate having been put into protective lockup following their one sided melee. Roman was new to the prison life, at least aboard this ship, and his cellmate saw that as an opportunity to prey on the former terrorist. Simple plans of taking Roman's share of food, but stupid plans nonetheless. His cellmate quickly discovered that Roman Raines is intimidated by no man, nearly crippling him before the guards could rush in and stop the carnage. Roman was slapped an even tougher sentence after beating two of the rescuing guards profusely as well, prompting them to treat him with extreme caution from that day forward.

It was also the first day Zane began to notice him, his effectiveness during the scuffle was exactly what was needed to put together a decent plan of escape. While every prisoner respected Zane and answered to him in some fashion, none could be trusted enough to maim and possibly even kill interfering guards when the time came. Zane saw it in Roman's eyes the day of the melee, and knew from that moment forward that not only was he capable of killing if needed, but there was a good possibility he had done so in his past.

"You move an inch and I'll paint this fucking wall with your brain matter!" one of the guards said loudly, holding a riot style shotgun directly to the back of Roman's skull.

Meanwhile, two more guards tossed his cell, throwing what little possessions were inside onto the steel deck of the ship and kicking them out of the eight foot by six foot space. The cell was down to nothing more than the steel sleeping rack which was tightly bolted to the wall. They were given no mattress, and there was no toilet to speak of. They were led down the hall at gunpoint for five minutes every day to the latrine, and that was their one and only time to dispose of human waste outside of their cell floor.

"Still hadn't figured out what you guys look for?" Roman said laughingly, his face nearly touching the wall as the guards continued their toss of the cell.

"What the fuck do you think we're looking for? Weapons and contraband." the guard holding him at gunpoint replied.

"Come on, you've read my rap sheet, do you think I need a weapon?" Roman said. "You can read, right?" he added. "Shut up!" the guard yelled.

"Yea, I can read. Got to be honest, for such a high profile catch you sure don't look like much to me!" the guard added loudly as his friends finished tossing the cell, laughing at the guard's remark.

"Don't let the bad shave and dirty clothes fool you. If I wanted you guys dead you'd be dead already," Roman replied with a grin. "Don't worry though. I like you. You remind me of someone I once knew." he added before feeling the barrel of a weapon pressing hard against his neck.

"I told you to shut up." the guard replied sternly, reminding Roman of the pecking order while opening a small flask of rock whiskey with his free hand and sneaking a small swig. Roman continued to face the wall, although the smell of the rock whiskey soon brought a smile to his face. It was almost like being back home with the Gunship crew.

"Alright move!" the guard said firmly, holding his gun on Roman as the three guards led him down the hall slowly, making their way into the mess hall to join a handful of previously escorted prisoners.

It had been one of the most violent battles in recent history for both races as body upon body fell lifelessly to the blood drenched ground, a crimson river making its way through the deep drifts of snow as if to become a permanent fixture. The Benzans had all but fallen, only a handful remaining and retreating back into the direction of the lodge, trying to move defensively while avoiding the tripping hazard of dead flesh. Two dozen Hunters remained, including three of the mighty elites. Their accompanying hell hound feasted on severed flesh, still warm as the snow fell while the remaining Hunters collected themselves. The rest had fallen in battle as a result of the Benzan's concentration of force onto them, taking heavy losses from the standard Hunters in doing so.

Kraid, who now stood covered in a mixture of blood, both freshly wet and dried, ordered the remaining warriors to seal the doors of the lodge if only to give them a moment to breathe.

The Benzans had been defeated, over confidence their achilles heel as they each prepared to die with honor while taking as many of the cannibalistic Hunters down with them as possible. Rather than rush in to slaughter the remaining five Benzans, the Hunters backed away a bit, giving Vladris a moment. The mighty Hunter Elite stood tall, red plasma dripping heavily from his blade as he ran his fingers across the bitter cold steel, placing them into his mouth to taste the spoils of victory.

Bending down onto a knee, Vladris ran his hand calmly across the back of his hell hound, which had taken the lives of a couple of Benzans on its own. He slowly rolled his neck, the sound of moving tendons and small bones popping as he prepared for the final showdown.

"My brothers. If we fall today, know that your families are safely hidden in the mountains and that you died as heroes." Kraid said, doing his best to catch a deep breath as the chilled air worked against him. The remaining Benzans were covered in shades of blood and exhausted from swinging iron to flesh, yet they dug deep for the final fight to come. Thousands of wooden splinters filled the air of the room as the Hunters finally burst the lodge door open by force, knocking one side from its hinges.

Holding his mythical sword of silver and severed flesh out in front of him, Vladris pointed it into the direction of Kraid, blood oozing down the blade and dripping steadily onto the grain finish of the wooden floor. Though he realized he was going to die, win or lose, Kraid stepped forward with his broadsword tightly clasped into one hand and his gold plated pistol gripped and positioned near his side. They exchanged a deep stare, the fluid red pupils of Vladris locking with the determined brown eyes of Kraid. Though they fought under different banners, they were both warriors and each knew that one of them would fall today. They were prepared to go with honor and this was their way of once and for all proving which bloodline was the more dominant.

Vladris thrust his hulking sword down with thunderous power, Kraid barely quick enough to evade the attack as a foot or more of the sword buried into the thick wooden slats beneath them. Kraid immediately swung his sword with a sweeping motion in an attempt to decapitate the Hunter Elite. Vladris ducked with intent, swiftly pulling himself back upright; grasping the gun hand of Kraid and squeezing until the Benzan dropped the golden piece. Powerfully uprooting his sword, Vladris arched it into a swing which ricocheted off of the Benzan's broadsword.

Staggered for a moment, Kraid quickly thrust his sword forward, clipping the solid black armor of Vladris as thick leather and trace amounts of blood dispersed onto the polished wooden wall behind him.

Glancing at his minor wound for a moment, Vladris was overcome with a beast like rage as he refocused his attention onto Kraid. Inhumanly fast and without warning, Vladris struck the Benzan across the face with a thunderous backhand, sending him reeling. The staggered Benzan leader was merely able to lift his sword just in time to block the downswing of the Hunter Elite's sword, though it did him little good. The trunk of Kraid's sword clanged as the powerful swing knocked it from his hand, the elite's blade biting deeply into the flesh of his shoulder. It was at that moment the remaining Benzans knew defeat was at hand and quickly lashed out at the Hunters with swords arcing wildly. Moments later, each

Benzan had fallen lifelessly to the floor leaving only Kraid.

"Do you intend to turn him my Lord?" one of the Hunters asked as Vladris stared at his beaten opponent for several long and silent minutes. Kraid would either be sent into the afterlife for eternity or he would join the ranks with the Hunters. A choice that was now in the hands of Vladris. Hunter Elites possessed the unique ability to turn their defeated foes into Hunters, but reserved the privilege to only a select few.

"Our work here is done then my Lord?" one of the Hunters asked of Vladris as the elite soldier skimmed the area through a large window of the lodge. The sight of butchered bodies lay on the ground around them, slowly becoming hidden by the ongoing fall of heavy snow mixed with the pasty grey smoke of the bonfire. Several Benzan buildings stood in the distance, catching the elite's attention. "No. Check the rest of the buildings for any survivors. Anything that may speak of stray cowards away from the nest." Vladris commanded.

"At once!" the Hunter replied with obedience before turning to lead a small group of the undead warriors into the direction of the buildings as Vladris slowly stepped back outside, focusing his attention into the sky and its blanketing flakes of snow that fell directly down.

"My Lord, the Colonials are approaching Tameca." one of the Legion soldiers said loudly as he entered Lord Riven's quarters. It was a reinforced room, snugly fit into an underground bunker and equipped with everything needed to operate in the worst of conditions.

"As expected," Riven said. "Wait for them to hit atmosphere and fire all of our ballistics at them." he added.

"All of them my Lord? Every missile?" the soldier asked.

"Yes." Lord Riven said sharply, turning his eyes to the questioning soldier.

"Right away my Lord!" the soldier replied loudly with obedience, turning to execute Riven's order.

Tameca City was once a proud place, flourishing with opportunity and the citizens who lived there in chase of it. As the soldier exited the bunker to execute Lord Riven's order, the sight of present day Tameca City was gut wrenching. A majority of it on fire, intentionally set by Legion forces as both retaliation against those who opposed Legion rule and a warning to anyone who may approach to give aid. Many of the same citizens who once shared laughter and memories on its streets, now lay dead on the very same paths of asphalt, bodies piled high as they burned without mercy.

It had become a large scale holocaust, what little remained of the city now part of a Legion controlled warzone. They had been bested during the battle for Glimmeria, losing a majority of their high end weaponry in the process. What remained was a stockpile of surface to air missiles, armored assault vehicles, plenty of small arms weaponry and soldiers who had been intimidated into seeing the war to its end. They had no help coming, no reinforcements. Just a severely outnumbered force that was entrenched into the city and slaying at will.

"Alright. You've been trained for this and have the superior firepower and numbers. These civilians are being murdered because they want a Colonial government, so as Colonial soldiers it's our job to protect our soon to be people at all costs." General Ortega said, scanning the launch bay of a Colonial Star, which was filled with thousands of battle ready troops. "Most of our convoy is staying in orbit around Tameca, cutting off all escape routes for the Legion in hopes of the war ending here. It's our job to end it, and by God we will end it!" he added, thrusting the crowd of warriors into a loud cheer. Moments after, the synchronized cheering turned to panic as the Colonial Star began getting pummeled by an array of Legion fired missiles.

It was a tough ship, built with the very purpose of taking blunt force trauma for extended periods of time. Hundreds of potent warheads gleamed into the sky however, most of them hitting the ship's hull and rocking the already battle weary frame and engulfing it into a curtain of flame.

When the general order to abandon ship rang out across the com system of the ship, soldiers began sprinting frantically throughout the halls, trying to make their way into the launch bay where General Ortega had already set up an evacuation detail. "We stay until the ship loses power!" Ortega shouted, explosions ringing in all corners of the flying fortress.

"Make sure everyone is armed to the teeth and well supplied, when the power fails we have to go, at that point it's only a matter of time." General Ortega added loudly, the troops near him handing both weapons and survival packs to the evacuating personnel.

"Mayday, Mayday, this is the Colonial Star Thirty-Seven. We are going down, repeat we are going down. Ship is evacuating to the surface of Tameca. Repeat, ship is...ohh God, ohh God!" the ship's pilot could be heard yelling up until the second that the Colonial Star was no more, the tomb of steel and circuitry exploding, leaving behind only faint screams and fiery particles of debris as the night sky of Tameca illuminated as though an eclipse were taking form.

"We barely made it sir." one of the Colonial soldiers said frantically as General Ortega looked through the plated glass window of the military shuttle, watching the ripples of destruction where the Colonial Star had been only moments before. Listening to the unorganized chatter being broadcast over the shuttle's com, Ortega finally punched in a security code before picking up the com.

"This is General Ortega. We have lost our ride but not our resolve. Sky Command, please organize a rally point on Tameca's surface based on my location beacon, we will regroup and complete the mission as planned." he said calmly into the hand held com before placing it firmly back onto the communication board near the shuttle's pilot. "One way or the other this battle will prove the end of the Legion's reign of terror." he added, speaking the words to the armed soldiers of his shuttle.

Minutes later, their military issued shuttle began hitting waves of turbulence, a direct effect of the fighting that was taking place below them. The ship's diamond shaped legs slowly bit into the hard crust that covered Tamera's ground, frozen dirt which was typical of the coldest season of the year. A massive Legion force was pushing to their direction, a well organized attempt to end the Colonial force before it could regroup.

"Laze their positions!" General Ortega shouted as he exited the shuttle steadfast. One of the Colonial snipers quickly shouldered a large device, similar to a weapon, but with no firepower of its own. "Keep it locked in!" Ortega ordered loudly as he contacted the remaining Colonial Star ships with a mobile com. There is a vast quietness of space that is nearly indescribable, the luminous littering of stars everywhere as pure silence engulfs them. This very silence was broken abruptly as ten thunderous booms broke out, all high potent missile strikes firing from the launch tubes of an orbiting Colonial Star and directed to the location of the laze.

The Colonial outpost, while under a heavy bombardment of Legion fire, had already started to take in Tameca's citizens. Refugees on their own planet, all of them shell-shocked and grieving for those lost as they staggered into the grasp of armed Colonial soldiers. There was a cluster of zinging sounds, followed by rocking explosions throughout the Legion camp nearby. The Colonial warheads struck earth with such velocity, such authority, that only craters remained that filled with ash and flesh. "General, do we attack?" one of the soldiers asked as the silence of missile strikes no longer floated through the sky. "Just wait, hold the line and wait until I give the order." General Ortega demanded.

"Yes sir." the soldier responded. Less than a full minute after the missile strikes, one of the remaining Colonial Star ships hovered down slowly from orbit, moving over what remained of the Legion encampment as its deck cannons began chewing into anything that moved. Dispatching dozens of the Glimmerian designed Swordfish fighters, the Colonial Star began a slow ascent back into the heavens and the quiet space which orbited above.

"Now you may go." General Ortega said proudly, a majority of his soldiers running to the sad remains of the large Legion camp as they shouted loudly with pride. "Lieutenant!" Ortega shouted. "Yes sir!" the man replied with discipline. "Continue finding our new citizens food and make them as comfortable as possible. I'm taking a strike team in." Ortega commanded. "Yes sir!" the Lieutenant said loudly, saluting for a moment before turning to continue organizing relief to the citizens lucky enough to have made it to them.

"Be landing in less than ten minutes, time to wake up." Stage said loudly as Dalton slowly left his dreamworld of fast guns and even faster women and began to get his bearings in order. Primal and Stage were both at the controls of the shuttle, gliding it to the planet's surface for the rescue plan ahead. Meanwhile Adam and Sasha sat closely together on a cushioned bench seat a few feet away. Dalton's first thought was that of Sasha's perfect body as he tried his best to convince himself that she hadn't followed him back from the world of dreams. He realized Adam was no longer wearing a climate jacket about the same time he glanced down to see himself snugly underneath it.

"Man, get this fuckin' shit off of me!" Dalton said, throwing the Benzan jacket several feet as both Adam and Sasha began to laugh loudly.

"Aww, but you looked so cute laying there huddled up underneath it." Sasha said as Dalton stared her down will ill intent.

"I 'aint going for cute. I'm going for casual." Dalton replied sternly, proudly pulling his faded brown coat together in the middle as if it were a tuxedo. Several small rips littered the jacket, which reeked of cigar smoke, whiskey and God only knows what else; accented by a few stains of dirt and lipstick. Still, Dalton smiled with pride. It was his resume of sorts, a visual reference to his experienced past.

"There it is." Primal said as everyone took a moment to look out of the shuttle's windshield. The entire planet of Gali looked as if it were swampland, thick green brush covering nearly every portion of it. Arch City, however, was a different story entirely. It wasn't the largest city Adam or Dalton had ever seen, but it was large enough. Two huge silver arches cascaded over the city, while several thousand buildings were positioned below, a few skyscrapers and the rest mid sized buildings or less.

"How are the watering holes here?" Dalton asked, his tongue growing weak of alcohol starvation. "They got anything you want here. Drink, women and weapons. You name it, they got it. As long as you got the credits to pay for it that is." Primal replied, turning for a moment as he answered.

"Shit boys, Dalton James hadn't ever had to pay for a woman. I pride myself on that." he proudly replied as Whiskey was quick to second the notion with a loud bark.

"Must be the coat." Sasha replied as Adam broke out into an uncontrollable laugh.

"I hear 'ya. I'm surprised you 'aint sittin' back here with a real man now that you know what one looks like." Dalton replied

"You tell her brother." Primal said, chuckling just a bit. "Alright already, we need to get focused on getting Roman out of lockup." Adam said.

"Agreed," Stage said. "We're going to have to be on top of our game to pull this rescue off." he added.

"Oh, I'll be on my game alright. Hell, Whiskey and me are both liable to walk out of the nearest bar with a nice piece of strange. Shit I'll be on top of something for sure." Dalton said, licking his lips a bit as Whiskey began barking loudly.

"I think I'm going to be sick." Sasha said in a low voice as she watched Dalton practice his best pickup lines on Whiskey at the rear of the shuttle while it docked onto the landing port of the city.

While the Legion was fiercely outnumbered, they had dug themselves in deep, pockets of soldiers doing what would have been a valiant job if not for the worst of reasons. Equally as resilient, Colonial soldiers fought back. Holding their ground while slowly gaining more. Surviving citizens began to pour in, staggered and starving as the Colonials soon found their outposts overwhelmed. Not with attacking soldiers clad in red and black trim, but common folk, mostly women and children clad in dehydration and the blood stains of their loved ones.

"Keep them away from windows and potential entry points." Lieutenant Scott said, holding a large metal door open as citizens poured in, many falling from gunfire close by as Legion troops ended as many lives as possible.

When the senseless murdering first began, over half of the Legion ranks surrendered, their core values not involving the slaughter of unarmed people. However, those who remained were with skill and without soul, gunning down even toddlers as if they were armed soldiers.

"Seal the door and get me a link to the sky!" Lieutenant Scott yelled, doing his best to get the survivors into the large rooms of the vacant factory.

"Here you go sir." one of the Colonial soldiers said, handing Scott a wired com unit. "This is Bravo Forty Two Blue, repeat, this is Bravo Forty Two Blue. Requesting evacuation of Tamecan citizens as well as reinforcements on ground. Repeat..." Lieutenant Scott said, his plea abruptly cut short.

"Negative Bravo Forty Two Blue. Be advised we are under fire from hostile forces. I say again, the Republic of Theron has joined the battle and its army has engaged us in war. Advise hold ground and make due until Colonial allies arrive." a voice responded, cracking heavily due to the distance between coms.

"Estimated time of arrival?" Lieutenant Scott asked, his hopes of a swift victory crushed.

"Reinforcements are approximately two days out. I say again, two days out." the voice replied, distinct sounds of pounding cannons in the background. "Copy." Scott replied.

"Actual, this is Bravo Forty Two Blue. Did you copy the last?" Scott asked, his battle ripened hand holding the com only inches away from the smooth shave of his face.

"Copy that. Do your best to secure our location. I'm ordering several platoons back to your area to assist." General Ortega replied.

"Copy that sir, Bravo Forty Two Blue out." Lieutenant Scott replied, handing the com back to the soldiers with him, which were less than fifty and new to the acts of war.

"Listen up," Lieutenant Scott said loudly, gaining the attention of each soldier. "It is imperative that we fortify our location until help arrives. I want four men at each entrance and heavily armed. As the refugees come to us, two soldiers exit to assist while the other two cover. Every remaining soldier, including myself, will set up a staggered perimeter in the hallways. Protect the rooms of refugees at all costs. Understood?" he asked loudly.

"Yes sir!" they replied, checking their ammunition levels. "Sergeant Ramon, assign the soldiers to their posts." Scott ordered. "Yes sir." the Sergeant replied.

The Republic of Theron. Bastards. Lieutenant Scott thought as Colonial troops ran around him to secure the building as quickly as possible. Nobody saw it coming, although they should have. The Republic of Theron has been murdering its own citizens for decades now, so why would the Tamecan people be any different. Hindsight is twenty-twenty they say, but the fact that Theron was a major trading partner with the Legion, equipped its army with Legion weaponry and had so much to lose if their trading partners fell made sense. Someone missed the signs and because of the oversight, Colonial ships and Theron cruisers were engulfed in one hell of a fight as they drifted in orbit.

Two Colonial Star ships remained, their escort cruisers having been sent down to Tameca filled with troops and supplies. Both ships had taken a hell of a beating, but remained intact as they orbited side by side and were exchanging cannon shots with six Theron cruisers. The Theron ships were much smaller than the mighty Colonial Stars, but were designed by Legion engineers and bred for one purpose. War. They were heavily armed with deck cannons, motorized chain guns and only the thickest of steel plating.

Still, the Colonial battleships held their own. Much like two larger and more capable animals defending themselves against a pack of hungry wolves, they continued exchanging shots of bone shaking lead. One of them began to falter, its hull damaged beyond repair and quickly splitting, eventually leading to the order of abandon ship. The Colonials were swarmed, and though they had done significant damage themselves, it was endgame. The soon to be demolished Colonial Star redirected its fire strictly to the surface of Tameca, striking all known Legion locations as its crew abandoned ship in route for the surface.

Meanwhile, the only Colonial Star still intact pulled out

of the fighting, setting course for deep space in wait for reinforcements that would arrive from all over the Skyla System. The Theron cruisers didn't attempt chase, knowing full well the injured Colonial ship could still deal extraordinary amounts of damage. The truth was, as the chatter hit the waves of Colonial coms on the surface of Tameca, its soldiers shared one feeling. They were alone. There was no guarantee that help was on the way, and if indeed it was, there was no exact time table for its arrival. They simply had to dig in and do their best not only to survive, but protect the citizens of this once great planet while doing so.

"My Lord," a Hunter said as he approached Vladris, who remained standing in the fields of gore and wrapped in his own blood covered armor of thick leather. "We went through the personal affections of their leader," the Hunter said. "It seems there are a few Benzans living abroad, as well as a shuttle with five passengers which left only hours ago." the Hunter added, handing the flight log to Vladris.

The demon in charge of the group of Hunters assigned to eliminating the Benzans stood there. Silent, the tribal markings on his smooth scalp visible as the wind blew roughly, hell hound by his side.

"The remaining elites will accompany me to Arch City, I will personally see to their executions myself. You are to return to our queen with the list of Benzans living throughout the Skyla System. Tell her of our great victory here and inform her that as soon as my task in Arch City is finished I will return to resupply and hunt the remaining." Vladris said with authority.

"Yes my Lord, at once." the Hunter replied, turning to quickly execute the wishes of the elite.

As the other two surviving elites joined Vladris in standing and looking into the falling snow which surrounded them, he finally pulled his attention away from the sky.

"Now it is certain that we are the most dominant race in this galaxy. Our brothers fought with bravery against mortal men who fought in fear, which is why their people lay slain on the ground today and we leave to tell of the battle," Vladris said in his deep and demonic tone. "Now we go to Arch City in order to finish our task." he added as the three elites walked to a nearby Hunter shuttle in order to begin their journey.

Quinton sat down at the cafeteria table next to Zane and Roman as all three men began to eat whatever it was scooped onto their tray. "Not gonna miss this food, that's for damn sure." Zane said as he dissected it with his plastic fork.

It was nothing more than mush formed by a large spoon and stood on its own once it hit the plate. The most common prison feast was algae, although that was a bit too luxurious for men of their standing. They usually got more along the lines of the algae leftovers mixed with thistle weed, which was the fancy name for the stringy weed that excavators removed to get to algae deposits.

"They treat us like fucking animals." Roman replied, eating his food without reserve which included a brown water. It was dubbed "meat juice" by the prisoners simply because it gained its brown color from softening good meat before the guards ate it.

"They've got their shots in on me since I've been here. Slapped me around a bit, spit on me and talked down to me. When the time comes, I plan on gutting as many of these low down bastards as I can." Roman added.

"I don't have much of a story to tell yet, but I do know that last week I was eating buttery Tamecan crab and now this is staring me in the face." Quinton said, pushing his plate to the side.

"Eat my brother, we're going to need every bit of strength we can get." Roman said, pushing the plate back in front of Quinton.

"You got a point." Quinton said as he slowly began to choke down each bite of the pathetic bliss of chow.

"So, when we do get out I guess your first order of business will be with your friends and their broken promise huh?" Zane asked. Roman sat there for a few moments, his body overtaken by the numb feeling as he thought about the Gunship crew who had been saved because of his staying behind.

"No. If Adam could have gotten me out of here he would have. It was my choice to stay behind, not his. I don't hold him at fault for this." Roman finally replied.

"Hell, for the right price I'll take care of him for you." Zane said jokingly. Quickly grasping the table's edge and slinging it to the floor, Roman grabbed Zane by the front of his shirt and began pummeling him in the face with a closed fist.

"If you ever threaten another friend of mine motherfucker I'll kill you!" Roman yelled as the prisoners began to shout in riot fashion.

The ship's alert siren sounded loudly as shuffling feet thundered their way into the cafeteria. Meanwhile the guard in the gun cage above fired a warning shot, a stern reminder to each prisoner that any man standing when the second shot rang out would be punching his ticket to the grave. Every prisoner, including Quinton, hit the floor with their hands behind their heads as Roman and Zane continued to go at one another.

"You're a dead man!" Zane yelled with maddened rage as he threw a hooking punch which found its mark on Roman's chin.

Rather than stagger and fall however, Roman turned his head back to Zane and landed a rising elbow under chin and into the throat of his adversary, causing Zane to flip over a nearby table.

By this time the ship's guards had arrived, six total were first on the scene. Closing in on Roman first, he quickly fed a back fist as he spun around, following it by a numbing elbow that nearly knocked the first guard out of his boots. Jumping onto the second guard that entered, Roman began beating the life out of the man clad in riot gear. Noticing the guard who stood in the gun cage taking aim on Roman, Quinton quickly reached for the first fallen guard's rifle, aiming with precision and hitting the chest of the cage guard which put him down abruptly.

As the other four guards rushed into the crowded eating hall, the remainder of the prisoners quickly stood and began to overpower the seriously outnumbered officers, besting them within a few seconds. Taking both the baton and rifle of the guard he had beaten to death, Roman quickly glanced at his brother before sprinting out of the room, Quinton following with rifle in hand.

"You're fucking dead Roman Raines, do you hear me," Zane yelled through the crowd. "Somebody climb up and take the gun cage. You three take a rifle and secure this room, the rest of you follow me. We're taking the ship." Zane announced while pointing his finger, the rest of the prisoners following out of his much earned respect.

It took the Gali prison guards several minutes to truly assess what was really unfolding. A full scale riot. When they finally came to terms with prisoners running loose, well armed and programmed to kill, they sealed off as many doors as possible. Solid steel blast doors closed, their latching mechanisms locking remotely as the guards still had control of the security station.

How long that control would last, however, remained to be seen. The security station was housed in a circular room, only accessible by a narrow catwalk, and currently it was filled with armed prisoners who were engaging the guards in a gunfight. During which, the large antenna used to communicate both throughout the ship as well as to approaching ships was destroyed. Deliberately, of course, the prisoners hoping they had done so before a distress signal could be sent.

As she heard the news come across the com, Sarah sat in her seat, stunned just as the rest of the shuttle's crew was. "Reports indicate several thousand Colonial soldiers perished in the explosion. General Ortega has formed an operating base on Tameca's surface and is asking any civilian nearby in need of rescue, to please relocate to the large set of warehouses near the Tameca City bridge. Again, all civilians and crash survivors are being asked to make their way to the industrial section of Tameca City, the Colonials have a secure forward operating base in the warehouse section of the district. More news as we receive it." the man's voice broadcast in a looped message across the Colonial com.

"Oh God, I should have stayed behind." Sarah said, her words filled with regret.

"Sarah, there is nothing you could have done to help. You may have even been on the ship when it exploded, or fallen into the hands of Legion soldiers. General Ortega is very capable, you need to focus on the idea of possibly seeing Adam again." Lassiter replied.

Sarah nodded, leaning back in the plush of her chair a bit and turning her attention to the window on her left, casting stares out onto the landscape of what would soon become Arch City.

"Don't concern yourself with the ongoing war Sarah, just focus on Adam. I want to see you happy again." Lassier said, placing his hand on her own for a moment as she looked at him with appreciation.

"I just hope he hasn't completely forgotten me." she admitted, her stare never breaking from the window.

Lassiter quickly removed his hand from Sarah's, careful not to show his growing feelings for her.

"That's very unlikely to ever happen my lady." he replied, at a loss as to what else he could possibly say or do to comfort her.

Sarah knew Adam wasn't likely to forget her anytime

soon, instead, she feared he had possibly grown fond of Sasha's company. She couldn't blame Sasha for wanting to be with Adam if it were the case, but that didn't make it any easier for her to think about. The fact that he was an amazing man was one thing. The fact that she may have lost the affections of such an amazing man forever was something else altogether, and the mere thought of it made her feel helpless.

Meanwhile, the quiet continued at the rear of the shuttle, although everyone checked their weapons for readiness. Arriving at the hideout of Benzans unannounced was not wise for anyone, especially anyone bearing Colonial markings on the side of their ship. They had sought Benzans as criminals, jailed them and fired weapons on them at pretty much every opportunity. All of the soldiers aboard Tigon Twelve knew they wouldn't arrive to open arms, and killing would quite possibly ensue. They had to be prepared for anything.

"Sir, our allies have arrived and driven the Colonial armada from our skies," a Legion soldier said, walking quietly into the room that Lord Riven had declared his. "However, reports indicate they have help from both Gali and Sion coming." the Legion soldier said somberly as Lord Riven stood in his chambers, staring at a battle map posted on the thick walls of the fallout shelter.

"Good. We must welcome our allies to the fight and coordinate a strike against the Colonials who were left behind to die like the worthless cowards that they are," Lord Riven replied. "We must do this quickly and then ready ourselves for the arrival of more invading armies. In time, enough slaying of heroes will serve as warning to anyone else that dares invade." he added.

"Yes sir. I will ask the Theron armada to land at once." the soldier replied with respect.

"Thank you my loyal friend." Lord Riven replied.

The bunker protecting Riven was still in good shape,

repelling the attack from a dying Colonial Star less than an hour before. Other Legion strong points had not been so lucky, many of them laying in shambles, still smoking from the display of desperate measures by Colonial forces. Only a few hundred Legion soldiers remained, at least functional soldiers. Acting on Riven's orders, they began to execute their own, doing away with the injured by way of bullet rather than care for them. It was a sickening display of barbarism, but one Lord Riven felt was necessary in order to continue at full speed.

As the Theron armada began to land its warships, flooding thousands of fresh bodies to the fight, Admiral Sweed remained on his ship under heavy escort as he awaited a meeting with Lord Riven. His warriors, with skin of deep tan and eyes of greyish tint, were human in every other sense of the word. A heart beat inside of their chest, and they walked upright on two legs with two arms holding weaponry. Still, the eerie sight of their gaze and complexion was not a welcome sight for most. Lord Riven and his Legion faithful were the exception, greeting their longtime allies as if they were brothers.

"My lady, we are only a few minutes out." the Colonial pilot said said as Tigon Twelve began to descend from the stars into the thick snow clouds of the Benzan's last known hideout.

"Would be best if you stay aboard until we meet the Benzans face to face in order to be sure of peaceful talks," Lassister said. "Sarah, I insist." he added, cutting her off before she could even respond.

Sarah simply agreed with a nod of the head as the Colonial soldiers and Husk all double checked their weapons and inspected every inch of body armor.

"Sir, something's not right!" the shuttle's captain shouted back into the passenger area as the loud thrusters of the ship nearly overwhelmed his words.

Sarah's heart began to plunge as she saw huge stacks of

smoke rising from what remained of the hideout, most of the buildings burned to the ground with only the lodge remaining. Moments later, mountains of slain bodies became visible to the crew. The crisp from cold corpses left laying in the snow, immediately bringing Sarah to tears. Her sudden burst of emotion became a heavy cry as the shuttle touched down onto the blanket of while, Husks exiting first with large rifles at the ready.

Even for the Husk, the sight was grim. Severed limbs, mortal wounds of gunshot entry points and burning flesh stood visible to them, a small river of blood flowing through the snow beyond their ship a bit. The Hunters had been here, that much was evident by their fallen warriors laying in the deepening drifts of snow. The surviving vampires had taken their time before leaving, that much was also evident by the gruesome cutting and maiming of the already fallen Benzans. They had taken their time with them, filleting the flesh from bone whenever possible. After looking around the immediate area thoroughly, the Husk warriors motioned the rest of the Colonials outside.

The remainder of the crew exited slowly, Sarah under the protection and escort of the Goliath V2 units.

"You men search the lodge, find any records or information that may lead to Adam." Lassiter said.

"Yes sir!" the Colonial soldiers replied, quickly turning to execute his order. Meanwhile the Husk soldiers searched the dead, at least what was left of them, in hopes of some indication of Adam's whereabouts.

"Don't worry Sarah, if Adam is here we will find him." Lassiter said, attempting to comfort the hysterical woman who was deeply in love.

"The battle is still fresh, not more than a day ago." one of the Husk announced, walking toward Sarah and Lassiter. "No Hunter ships remain, which would lead us to believe that they walked away when the battle was over." he added.

"I can't live without him Eric...I just can't." Sarah said to Lieutenant Lassiter as the small Colonial crew continued searching for clues of both battle, and the whereabouts of Adam Michaels.

"I understand Sarah, believe me, not a day goes by that I wonder what a life with Kelly would be like." Lassiter replied.

Rather than respond, Sarah stood silently in shock, the heavy snowfall bringing large flakes quietly to the ground. Lassiter took her with his free arm, holding her close to comfort her while his remaining hand gripped a black combat pistol. As the frozen water constructed with such beauty fell onto her, covering her hair and shoulders a bit, Sarah prayed. She simply couldn't survive without the one man who would have loved her unconditionally. Thinking of him made her breathe heavily, thinking of his demise made her not want to breathe at all.

Her life had been mounted onto the wrong beliefs for so long now, she wanted to change, wanted so badly to be truly happy. And that simply wasn't possible without Adam. So she prayed as hard as she could ever remember praying.

"Sir," one of the Colonial soldiers yelled, sprinting over to Lassiter's location. "It looks like a Benzan shuttle was logged as leaving shortly before the battle. Heading for Arch City." the soldier added. Lassiter turned to face Sarah, who was sobbing uncontrollably.

"My lady, Arch City is where the Gali prison transports are based. Could very well be Adam attempting to rescue Roman." Lassiter said, loosening his grip of her, though he didn't want to.

Stopping in mid sob out of shock, Sarah continued to look at Lassiter as she began to wonder if it was a possibility. If maybe God had answered her prayers in only a matter of seconds.

Was there a single moment waiting, a moment that she would be held by Adam Michaels once more? Sarah would have gladly traded the remainder of her life for one such moment.

"If we are going, we need to go now," one of the Husk said, holding up a gothic style medallion. "Hunter Elites fought in this battle, meaning they were here to wipe the Benzans out. Good bet they know about Adam's shuttle and are tracking it as well." he added.

"Hunter Elites?" one of the Coloniel soldiers asked.

"Yes," the Husk warrior replied. "Not something we want to run into. Trust me. And if we do, best be damn good and prepared for one hell of a fight. A fight like you've never seen before." the Husk replied.

He went on to explain the superior skills of a Hunter Elite, how they were born to end lives, direct offspring of the queen as well as only the most tenacious fighters turned undead.

"It has to be Adam's shuttle, he's nowhere to be found here." a second Husk said.

"My lady, we need to go now if there is any chance of saving him," Lassiter said. Sarah agreed with a shaking of her head as Lassiter began to recall everyone back to the ship. "Don't worry Sarah, we have enough muscle here to take out a Hunter group, elites or otherwise." Lassiter said as they boarded, although the Husk soldiers knew better.

"Well, that went well." Quinton said as both he and Roman took a moment to rest behind a large system of piping.

"I can do complicated as long as we get the fuck off of this ship." Roman replied.

"Good. From the sound of things it's going to be real complicated," Quinton said as heavy gunfire was being exchanged throughout the ship. "Think he is really capable of taking the ship?" Quinton asked.

"Not sure and don't care. As long as we can take the landing bay when the time comes, he can have the ship and all of the bad memories that go along with it." Roman replied.

"How are you on ammo brother?" Quinton asked.

"About three fourths full." Roman replied after glancing down at the neon green charge count on the rifle's side.

"A little under halfway for me." Quinton said.

"As long as we do things smart and conserve what we can we should be fine," Roman replied, tucking the officer's baton into the back of his prison issued pants. "We'll lay low and let Zane fight it out with the guards. All we need to do is worry about whoever is left standing when the transport ship arrives." Roman added.

After nearly an hour of gunfire being exchanged, the armed prisoners finally took the Security room, allowing them to unseal the ship's locked down hatches and move around at will. The Gali prison guards were highly trained, most of them former commandos themselves. However, they were outnumbered, if not overwhelmed by the volume of prisoners on the overpopulated ship. Before they were given warning, a third or more of the ship had already been lost to them.

For hours the sound of heavy gunfire throughout the ship continued, Gali trained guards fighting the massive riot of former Gali soldiers turned prisoner. Both Quinton and Roman waited patiently as they remained out of sight, positioned behind a large set of steam filled pipes. For the first time in many years Roman began thinking about his past, something he usually avoided. Looking down to his scarred body, he remembered the Goliath parts that had been forcefully removed and events that led him to having them in the first place.

He thought about everything, even the lies both he and Quinton had told Zane. Glancing at Zane for a moment, he nodded his appreciation. They were indeed like brothers, but for very different reasons than those Zane had been given. Greyspine. Yea, Roman had been there, and he had indeed killed the Queen of Hunters on that very day. But he was not a Gali commando, not even a soldier in the least. He wasn't even supposed to be there. He was a terrorist, at least he had been for the majority of his life. His family had been murdered at the hands of Hunters, that much was true. Quinton and family had taken him in, though the family was a terrorist group named Black Cell.

Watching his family cut down in cold blood had done something to Roman. Opened his eyes, if nothing else, to the reality of how the world worked. The strong survived. And he had promised himself he would survive at any cost while slaying as many Hunters as he possibly could. After Black Cell fell to the Hunters, Roman and a handful of its members went on the run.

Killing the Hunter Queen, Black Cell had been dressed as though they were Gali soldiers. Rather than watching his government sign a treaty of peace with the murdering bastards who had slain his family, he watched the Hunters blame Gali. They called it a setup, and soon that led to war. The war between Gali and the Hunter tribes lasted nearly two years with neither side declaring victory. The Hunters had been killed to the point of near extinction, while Gali fell from a major power throughout the Skyla System to merely an afterthought. Their ranks had depleted to crisis levels.

They never signed a treaty of peace. Instead, there was a unspoken understanding between the Gali and Hunter tribes. They kept their distance. Live and let live. So many had died on both sides, all because of Black Cell. If they were found in Hunter occupied space, the members of the former terrorist group were painfully executed. As they were rounded up in Gali occupied space, they weren't given the pleasure of death, instead sent to live out a life unfit for a dog aboard this prison ship of horrors. As Roman looked himself from toe to hand slowly, he knew it in his heart. He would never stop killing. Hunters and sympathisers of Hunters. They were and would always be his targets.

Meeting Adam and his crew, Roman's agenda had first been to kill the crew and take the ship. Planning to find as many members of Black Cell as he possibly could and continue the fight. What he quickly discovered, however, was the feeling of family aboard the Gunship. He began to like Adam and crew, feeling accepted among them. They treated him with respect, he felt as though they were what his brothers and sisters would have been like if not slain by the Hunters.

Soon Roman's motives changed and he just wanted to remain with the Gunship crew, hoping to outrun his past forever. As he stared across to Quinton, Roman began to wonder who he was. Was he still the terrorist linked to Black Cell, the killer who had sworn his life to ending the Hunter race? Or had his time with Adam and crew changed him? He knew that in not so many days he would be faced with the very decision, and he wasn't sure where his heart would lead him.

"There you are, we have been wondering where you took off to." Adam said as he slowly approached Sasha. She had made her way back to the shuttle, sitting on its steel ramp and watching the night life of Arch City unfold.

"I'm fine. Just spend so much time in space anymore that when I get a chance to sit and watch the world in motion, I like to take it." Sasha replied.

"Mind if I sit with you?" Adam asked, his curious affections for her growing stronger by the minute.

"As long as you don't pull out any of those horrible pickup lines." she replied, both of them laughing as they thought of Dalton's poorly choreographed one liners, many of which had already been used tonight.

Though he had seen no payoff on the empty compliments as of the moment, Dalton began to see a trend. His furry friend Whiskey attracted women, a lot of them, which made him man's best friend indeed.

"Listen," Sasha said, continuing to stare across the highway to the hotel where they would all spend the night, though Dalton's would more than likely be spent in the lobby bar. "I hope I haven't put any pressure on you. It wasn't my intention at all." Sasha said softly, turning to Adam as they continued to sit on the shuttle's ramp, their arms wrapped around peaking knees in front of them.

"You haven't," Adam said, pulling his left arm up and placing it around the shoulders of Sasha to pull her close. "Besides, I'm the great Captain Adam Michaels. I am wired to deal with pressure." he said mockingly as they both laughed softly.

"Yea, you are quite the living legend." Sasha replied, smacking him on the arm playfully. Moments later, they had engulfed one another with a shared kiss, a deep linking of lips which drown in life altering passion.

The kiss was fantastic, and they both silently agreed on the fact. Looking into each others' eyes afterward and sharing a moment that no amount of time could ever take away.

"So, I'm not completely over her. Just so you know." Adam said, continuing to hold Sasha with his left arm as they turned their attention back to the hotel.

Finally he felt comfortable enough to admit his lingering feelings for Sarah Blaine.

"I know. I'm alright with that as long as what we do have is something real." Sasha replied.

"It's real," Adam said. "Just wanted to be up front about my feelings is all. Us smugglers and our damn passion for telling the truth." he added as Sasha turned to look at him with sarcasm.

"What about Kraid, are you over him?" Adam asked.

"Um, yea. Only about five years ago." Sasha replied, huffing a bit.

"Relax, I was just asking." Adam replied in his own defense.

"In the spirit of honesty though, I don't think he's over me." Sasha said.

"In the spirit of honesty," Adam agreed, both of them giggling once more. "Means he either plans to kill me or sent his boys to make sure I stay away from you." Adam said.

"Why do you say that?" Sasha asked.

"Call it a smuggler's intuition. That and the fact that they are heading this way." Adam replied, Sasha quickly turning to see both Primal and Stage making their way across the busy street.

"Damn." Sasha said out of frustration.

"It's alright. That kiss will be lasting me several hours yet." Adam replied, smiling as he turned to his sparking love interest.

"We were able to knock down the transmission tower. Looks like we control the mess hall, security room, cell blocks one through seven and about a third of the administrative wing. The man still controls the rest." one of the prisoners said as he stood holding a riot style shotgun.

"Concentrate as much manpower as you can on the administrative wing. We take that, we take the ship's armory." Zane replied. He was certainly in command, several loyal friends at his side as they worked on a strategy to take the remainder of the ship.

"We outnumber them by a long shot, but they're well trained," Zane said as the group looked on. "We need to take the armory and keep the landing bay. If we lose the landing bay then we lose our ticket off of this ship." he added.

"What about Roman?" one of the prisoners asked.

"You let me worry about Roman Raines. You just keep that landing bay secure and we'll leave his ass here high and dry to sort it all out after the fact, and that's only if I don't find him first," Zane replied as he shouldered a shotgun and motioned two of his loyal friends to accompany him. "Time to go hunting boys. Time to go hunting." he added.

"Look, all I'm saying is that I should be getting paid fifteen percent from you, combat pay from the Colonials and 'aint seen a damn dime of nothing," Dalton said as he sat with Adam at the long bar of wood and silver polish. "Which is why drinks should be on you." he added.

"I'd be glad to pay for drinks if you didn't bang 'em down like you had one day left to live. Not to mention you've bought every woman in here a drink, and most of them more than one." Adam said, a wide smile on his face.

"I may only have a day left, hell, with some of the shit you drag us into it's anybody's guess." Dalton replied.

"Tell you what. I'll pay up if you get rid of that raggedy brown coat once and for all." Adam said, stoking the already emotionally intoxicated Dalton James.

"Fuck you and the horse you rode in on buddy," Dalton said loudly, drawing unwanted attention from several of the patrons. "The brown coat stays!" he added.

"Here," Sasha said, slapping enough credits onto the bar to pay for Dalton's venture. "Now shut up and quick bringing stares our way, we're here to pull off a heist for God's sake." she added sternly.

"What about Whiskey?" Dalton demanded to know, his trusted pooch to be treated like royalty now that he understood a woman's attraction to such a cute dog.

"Sure, order any drink you want." Sasha quickly responded, staring at Adam for a moment in disbelief.

"I meant the dog." Dalton said loudly, his demands ignored. "Damn she's got an ass on her." he mumbled, watching the Benzan beauty walk away, her heart shaped backside bouncing inside form fitting pants.

One of the bar's video feeds switched to the news coming out of Tameca, causing the entire crew to once again join Dalton at the bar in silence as they watched on.

It was one of those sobering moments in life, an event takes place and you know that it will remain written in history forever. You never forget where you are when the news arrives, and for everyone here, they remember the bartender turning the volume up loud enough for everyone to hear clearly.

The hardest hitting of the video segment was a montage of photos showing the level of savagery in which civilians were being murdered. It was the news of a downed Colonial Star, however, that hit Adam hardest as he tried to catch his breath; feeling as though he had been kicked directly in the stomach. He waited, hanging his hopes on every word of the news journalist as he awaited the fate of Sarah Blaine. Instead, they didn't mention her name a single time. She is the elected Colonial leader for God's sake! Adam thought, stunned of no news on the woman his heart still hurt for.

"Bet them 'sumbitches are getting' paid," Dalton said loudly, several patrons of the bar, including his own crew, turning to look in disbelief. "That's right folks, my name is Dalton James and I work for a deadbeat employer." he added, bringing chuckling in the rear of the gathered group.

"Dalton, people are dying." Sasha said snidely.

"People are always dying. That's politics for you. That's why, unlike pretty women and whiskey, I just can't do 'em," he replied, changing his facial expression a bit. "I mean whiskey as in the drink." he added.

Sasha, who began to reflect on her own family being murdered as she watched the events unfold on the video feed, grew angry and wanted to lash out at the drunken man.

"Hey, just let it go," Adam said, grabbing her softly and immediately noticing the hurt in her eyes. "Want to walk outside for a few minutes, just the two of us?" Adam asked, turning to gaze at Stage and Primal as if to dare them to join.

Rather than respond, Sasha got up slowly to accompany him and stared through Dalton with anger as she walked away.

"Guess she's a voter." Dalton remarked as Primal began to explain the fate of her family.

"What's going on?" Adam asked with sincerity as both he and Sasha walked away from the hotel a bit, approaching a metal bench located nearby as the hustle and bustle of citizens continued walking around them.

"I don't know. Seeing those video feeds just made me think about my family I guess. It's tough to walk through the day as though nothing is bothering me." Sasha replied.

Her words struck home with Adam, who found himself pushing through each day as though it were an uphill battle as well, wanting to hold Sarah Blaine one last time.

"Try to focus on the positive things. We're together, we're out in space enjoying a freedom which many will never know. The past can't be changed, no matter how hard we wish it," Adam said. "What you need to understand is, my heart still isn't completely free. Soon, there will come a time when it is and when that happens I'll be knocking down your door begging for a chance to be with you. Hell, any sane guy would. You're beautiful, intelligent and I gotta admit you have a knack with handguns." he added, bringing a brilliantly sweet smile to her face as he placed a finger on her cheek to wipe away the most visible tear.

"And Dalton..." Adam began to say.

"Ohh GOD, Dalton James." Sasha replied with exhausted patience. "I know. Believe me, I know. Please understand though, he's a good friend and I would do anything for him. Just like I would you." Adam replied, slowly placing his arm around Sasha to hug her a bit in the chilled night.

"Adam Michaels, you are a good man." Sasha said, enjoying the moment as she sat there, held by a man who had her heart and genuinely cared for her.

"Yea, well there are at least a dozen outstanding warrants that say otherwise." Adam replied, both of them starting to laugh quietly as a light rain began to fall.

First as nothing more than a mist, the water quickly became heavier. Rather than run for the hotel, Adam pulled his climate jacket up, placing it above both of their heads as Sasha's face remained pinned to his chest.

As the thick cold of rain fell, Adam protected Sasha with his jacket, using his other arm to hold her tightly as they kissed. Their bodies, even souls, connected at that very moment. Lips passionately feeling each other out as Adam's hand moved up, his fingers quickly flowing through her satin black hair. The rain fell so hard that it was almost impossible to see ahead. Almost. Unfortunately for them both, Stage saw the blossoming love unfolding as he stood at the front entrance of the hotel, watching his leader's love falling for another.

"They're hitting us with everything they have sir." Lieutenant Scott said loudly, the pounding of lead hitting weakening concrete. He stood in one of the building's interior hallways with several Colonial soldiers, including General Ortega.

"I don't care how much they hit us with Lieutenant, these civilians are to be protected at all costs. Is that understood." Ortega asked.

"Yes sir. I only fear that soon we will have no walls protecting them." Lieutenant Scott said.

"Then we will throw our own bodies in front of bullets to protect them until help arrives. Is that understood?" General Ortega said sternly.

"Yes sir, of course." Scott replied.

Outside the warehouse, dozens of armored Theron vehicles continued their barrage of gunfire onto the crumbling outer walls. Grey slate turning to rubble and sliding down, both Theron and Legion soldiers by the hundreds waiting a safe distance back, ready to enter and kill everyone when the time was right.

As General Ortega entered one of the larger rooms on the hall, his two posted Colonial soldiers moved aside to allow his entrance. Nearly fifty refugees, most of them women and children, sat in the floor.

They had been battered by the stench of war, most of them bloodied and holding their children's ears as the building rocked from intense gunfire.

"Excuse me. Sir. Can you please talk to my son, explain to him we will be alright." a woman said, slowly approaching Ortega.

She wore what once was a very upscale business outfit, dress pants and button up shirt; covered in the fog of war of course. Dirt and blood was all over the woman who was obviously someone of importance, at least before Tameca City had been destroyed. The general skimmed the room and saw it on all of their faces, even in the eyes of his posted soldiers. They saw no hope. They needed reassurance that victory was still possible.

General Ortega approached the young boy as the entire room fell silent, eyes fixed onto the fearless leader of the Colonial effort.

"Have you ever seen a Husk son?" General Ortega asked, kneeling down to the young boy of no more than six years of age.

"No sir." the boy replied timidly.

"Husk are some of the most battle-tested warriors the Skyla System has to offer. They are strong, savage and much more capable than the cowards who are outside right now firing their weapons at us," Ortega said, standing a bit so he may address the rest of the people in the room as well. "All we have to do is hold out. Gali has sent a large force of soldiers to help all of us, and with them, thousands of Husk will also arrive. All we need to do is hold on until they get here," General Ortega said. "And son, I promise you this," he added, bending over once more to place his right hand onto the shoulder of the young boy. "My soldiers will hold this factory and keep you safe until that time comes." General Ortega said, bringing a huge smile to the face of the young man and reassurance to the rest of the refugees who looked on.

The fire that burned to help these people strengthened inside of the posted Colonial soldiers as well, their demeanor once again becoming that of an unstoppable force.

Roman held his hand out, silently warning his Black Cell brother of footsteps approaching. Quinton was a bit larger than Roman, though both were built sturdily. Quinton gripped the stock of his rifle tight as Roman held both firearm and riot stick, the blunt weapon down at his side as they listened. There were three Gali guards approaching, all slowly and as quietly as possible, weapons in front of them and at the ready.

Roman glanced back to his brother for a moment, his back firmly against the steel of an interior wall just inside the doorway. Outside, the guards approached with caution in the narrow confines of the hallway. Roman held up three fingers, passing the information along to Quinton. Next, he held a clinched fist to let his brother know a fight was unavoidable and without pause he swung the clinched fist around, hitting the guard in front and jarring several teeth loose from the man's skull.

Immediately pulling the helpless guard back to his feet, Roman used the flesh of his unconscious victim to absorb several gunshots sent his way by the remaining two lawmen. Roman then threw the dead flesh to the flooring below, jumping onto the second guard with no remorse. They had beaten him, spit through the bars of his holding cell on many occasions and now that the tables were turned, Roman saw no reason to be gentle. The last guard quickly took aim at the former Black Cell terrorist, but was nearly cut in half with a string of shots fired from the weapon shouldered by Quinton.

Knowing well that more would come to the shots, be they guards of prisoners in hunt of the two men, Quinton did his best to pull Roman from the second guard. It took a few moments, Roman resisting as he continued to punch heavily on the guard he had already beaten to death and beyond.

"We have to go now! Won't be long before we hear the shuffling of feet. Zane's or more of the man's." Quinton said, finally able to pull Roman from the beaten guard.

Roman stood on his own, spitting onto the lifeless body as Quinton let go of his bear hugging grip. "They got what was coming to them my brother, now we gotta move! Got to get to that landing bay and find a place to hold up." Quinton added.

"Yea they got what was coming to 'em, and I got a lot more to give." Roman said abruptly, having found the hate he harbored against the people who had treated him less than human. Checking the guards for weapons, they found a Gali prison radio that would come in handy for the rest of their escape. Quinton placed it into the back of his pants, the two men quickly leaving the scene and heading into the direction of the landing bay.

"Hit me." Dalton said, a stringy brown cigar hanging from his lips. He was the only man in the hotel bar enjoying a cigar that had the undeniable look of poverty.

Everyone else dressed with class and smoked only the finest of rolled pleasure. Not Dalton. Never the type to care about anyone's impression of him, he smiled wide, a bottle of rock whiskey and shot glass in front of of him.

"He wins again!" the dealer exclaimed as the small crowd that had gathered at the card table cheered on. Dalton was on a winning streak, and though two beautiful woman had found their way to him primarily because of the credits he had laying on the table, Dalton was convinced his charm was the hook.

Rock whiskey was by far the cheapest alcohol in the entire Skyla System, aside from home brew of course. In fact, the only reason the hotel kept it in stock was for the occasional homeless citizen that collected enough money to enjoy a drink of the stagnant brew. For Dalton, it didn't matter. He could be rolling in money and never forget the rough patches he'd been through. For nearly eleven days during the first war of Glimmeria, he and Adam survived on nothing but rust water and vermin. Left behind by their own soldiers, abandoned and given up for dead. What the rest of the hotel lobby didn't understand was compared to rust water, rock whiskey was fine wine. Dalton understood this, and was a survivor because of it.

"Does he know what inconspicuous even means?" Stage asked, puzzled with the thought of Dalton drawing so much attention his way before such an illegal heist.

"I don't think his mind is on the heist." Sasha replied as they all watched Dalton slide a free hand down onto the ass of each of the two women.

Both had bleach blonde hair to go with the look of well used, to say the least. Well used was an afrodisiac to Dalton, however. To him a woman who had been around was a woman worth chasing. She knew the score, understood the game and was less likely to fall in love with the brown coat booty chaser.

His four legged friend of thick fur was present as well, gaining just as much attention from the women who rubbed on him as though he were their own. Yep, Dalton was hot. Winning hands and hearts, even if the hearts chased his money.

"Come on, we gotta get going." Primal said, tapping Dalton on the shoulder.

"I'll be up in a few." Dalton replied, a handful of cards in his left hand, while his right maintained a firm grip on the heart shaped ass of one of the women.

"I said now." Primal demanded sternly, hushing the crowd. Dalton gained a strange look on his face, one that normally wasn't attached to cheap women and equally as cheap whiskey.

"Be right back." he said, kissing one of the woman deeply and petting Whiskey slightly.

"What the fuck did you just say," Dalton yelled, standing to his feet swiftly and pushing Primal back several feet in the same motion. "Don't nobody tell me what the fuck to do primate." Dalton added loudly, enraging Primal, who dashed at him with ill intent.

A drunk is pretty easy to take out, but unfortunately for Primal, Dalton could hold rock whiskey like a camel of sort. Easily evading his charge, Dalton pushed Primal as he passed, using the Benzan's own momentum to send him crashing into the table and smashing the fine wooden grain into shards on the floor.

"I was knocking boots when you was wearing diapers you big hairy 'sumbitch." Dalton said loudly, jumping on top of Primal and throwing fists into his direction. The Benzan blocked most of the punches, which turned to slaps, letting Primal know he'd been bested.

"Enough!" Stage said, starting for the men and his weapon.

"It's a fair fight," Adam said, pulling his sidearm with surgical haste and holding it on Stage who turned back to look at him with bitterness. "Let them decide when it's enough." Adam added.

"You dare pull a gun on me?" Stage asked.

"I've dared to do a lot of things, and you are pretty low down on that list friend." Adam replied.

"Sasha." Stage said, waiting for the Benzan beauty to intervene.

"It is a fair fight Stage." she replied, making the man furious. "First you betray Kraid for this common thief, and now you insult me!" Stage said, pissed to the highest point that fury could take him.

Sasha pulled her automatic pistol out, pointing it at Stage for a moment as she leaned in to kiss Adam deeply.

"Kraid doesn't own me and neither do you." Sasha replied, letting the man know right away that she was her own woman.

"You will be dealt with in due time," Stage said to her, glancing at Adam and Dalton for a moment. "And you two, you're both dead men!" he added.

"Now there's a line that's been used more than my damn pickup lines," Dalton said, turning to Sasha as if to convince her that his pickup lines were still semi-fresh. "Plus, if you two clowns really are the best Kraid has to offer then you might want to consider another line of work. Something like ranch work or waiting tables. Hell, apply here, they may hire you on. Cause you sure in the hell 'aint no killers." Dalton said, letting Primal back to his feet slowly. Dalton grabbed a fistful of credits from the pile of rubble near the spot that used to be home to a table, pulling one of the women close to him.

A mixture of kissing and talking to the woman as he groped her heavily, Dalton told her to split the remainder of the credits with the other woman. Their company tonight had been well worth the money, which was several thousand credits. Both women hugged Whiskey, a perfect nightcap to their ass kissing of the man with the winning hand. Meanwhile, Primal walked away slowly, his stare never breaking from Dalton while doing so.

"I guess this means the rescue is off." Stage said sarcastically.

"Nope. Just means you two outlaw wannabees are finding your own ride home," Dalton replied. "Now go on, get!" he added, shooing them away like unwanted strays. Stage looked at him strangely, quickly realizing the shuttle they had actually arrived in was now Adam's property.

"Best if you both hit the road." Adam said, at gunpoint of course. Sasha wasn't crazy about the idea of turning her back on the two Benzans, but now that she knew what Kraid thought of her; she wasn't crazy about returning to the Benzans either. She had just needed someone to love her, since her parents were executed it had been the Benzans. Now, she had started to look to Adam for that sense of love, and she trusted him with everything inside of her.

"Simple. We just hang out by the shuttle, when they come out we dust 'em." Stage said as the two men furiously walked across the busy street.

"And Sasha?" Primal asked.

"No harm is to come to her. She's just confused, that's all. Kraid will straighten her out." Stage replied.

"Find the ship." Vladris said as the other two Hunter Elites carried heavy rifles in hand.

"There. The numbers match those of the Benzan shuttle." one of the elites said, the pointed claw of his thick white hand showing the way.

Vladris led the group, a long blade sheathed to his back as his leg held a pistol and his massive hands clinched the stock of a rifle. A few citizens stared hard. Some had never seen men with such a look, while others knew all too well they were Hunters and were taken by surprise as the demonic clan of murderers rarely appeared in such a public place. Vladris and his two accompanying Hunter Elites slowly approached the Benzan shuttle, the moon reflecting lightly from the shaven head of Vladris. Meanwhile, his accompanying elites looked equally as savage, their braided locks of shimmer white and teeth of luminous death only two of many features that led the citizens nearby to steer clear. The normal Hunter simply had a lifeless look in its eye, the pupil void of any pigment. Hunter Elites, however, had a slight red color which seemed to glow a bit. Much like the embers of a freshly discarded fire.

It wasn't clear which group of warriors first caught glance of the other, but to every citizen unlucky enough to be in the area, it was damn clear that lead began to fly without remorse. Stage hit one of the Hunter Elites with two solid shots, both slamming into the trunk of his chest, knocking the undead beast back a bit. Primal was too close for gunfire, his first reaction instead was to begin swinging fists at the demon closest to him. Quickly bested however, Primal fell to his back, sliding quickly out of the way to once again gain footing. The hair covered Benzan drew a long blade from a sheath on his right thigh, his full intention to attack. Quickly however, he found himself on the defense; the large blade barely able to withstand a downward strike from the sword of a Hunter Elite.

"What is it?" Adam asked as Sasha looked through the drapes of the hotel room following the distinct sounds of gunshots.

"Oh God, it's Stage and Primal." she replied in shock, Adam joining her at the window seconds later.

He had never encountered a Hunter Elite before, but was pretty damn sure that's what stood on the ground below. Three of them to be exact.

"Dalton, pack our shit right now." Adam said.

"Just a second, let me finish this..." Dalton replied, cut short as he and Whiskey lay on one of the large beds.

"Now," Adam yelled sternly. "We got Hunters down below and they 'aint the garden variety!" he added.

Spilling what remained of his tall whiskey glass, Dalton jumped to his feet with haste, quickly sitting to try and put his boots and coat back on with frantic pace.

"I'm sick and tired of this fucking bullshit," Dalton muttered, pulling his brown coat on quickly, though it wrapped his body a bit crooked. "Going from winning card games, surrounded by fine looking strange and endless streams of whiskey to running from these dead 'sumbitches. It's always these dead 'sumbitches. I told you not to take the fucking job in the first place. Told you not to do business with Anwick. I told you. Didn't I tell you?" Dalton mumbled loudly as he continued to fight his feet into the thick leather of his worn boots.

"Shh." Adam said quietly.

"Well I did..." Dalton began to reply.

"Shh," both Adam and Sasha insisted. "They're gone." Adam said quietly, glancing out of the room's window for a moment. About the time he finished uttering the words, a solid knock came at the door.

"Shit." Dalton motioned with his lips, no actual sound escaping. Sasha motioned Dalton to answer the knock, stalling them long enough for Adam to open the window that led down by fire escape.

Dalton looked back at her puzzled, having no idea who was even at the door. Sasha motioned him once more as the knocking grew heavier.

"Um, if this is about child support you got the wrong room." Dalton said cheerfully, drawing a strange glare from both Adam and Sasha. Seconds later, the shots of Hunter rifles blew gaping holes through the solid wooden barrier on hinges. As the door swung open, smacking roughly against the wall behind it, Dalton held his shotgun out and discharged two shots. Blind as to what his target even was, but following the creed of a smuggler. He who gets shot at shoots back.

Vladris and his two battle hardened knights of undead walked in, the first elite hit with both shotgun blasts at close range, putting him down onto the ground in pain. The same elite had been struck with two shots from Stage's weapon only moments before, and the four combined wounds had seriously injured the knight of immortality. Dalton was too close to the Hunters and too far away from the window to jump out, opting instead to stand on the other side of the bed. Out of desperation, Dalton began throwing liquor glasses, pillows, magazines and anything else his hands could grab into the direction of the two standing Hunters.

Whiskey pinned his ears back, letting loose a growl proving he was ready to make the ultimate sacrifice for his proud human owner as he caught sight of the Hunter's accompanying hell hound. As the second Hunter Elite stood there, staring at the pathetic halfway house for fleas, he was struck with several shots from Adam's pistol.

"Dalton, bring your ass!" Adam yelled, moving as Sasha then peeked in, firing her automatic pistol into the direction of Vladris.

The Hunter Elites had no choice but to stay hidden behind a wall as the bullets chewed into the wood while a drunk and his dog made their escape. The hell hound growled loudly, its voice a mixture of undead anger and warning.

"Told you not to take that fucking job," Dalton muttered under his breath a bit as his body shook with adrenaline; Adam and Sasha sliding down the large corner rail of the fire escape. "Don't let him hit the ground!" Dalton demanded, dropping his four legged friend as though he were a fur covered feather into the waiting arms of Adam Michaels.

He was safely caught, though the velocity of his fall knocked Adam to the pavement. Dalton slid down right behind, knowing well enough that Hunters would not be far behind.

The three smugglers turned fugitives ran hard, a brown dog at their side throughout as Hunter Elites trailed them on foot by less than two hundred yards. Dalton stopped abruptly.

"Go to the shuttle and get that bitch ready, just don't leave me!" he yelled, Adam pausing slightly before turning to resume his getaway.

Sasha was in first, hitting the necessary switches to fire up the engines by the time Adam ran up the steel ramp, his boots striking loudly on the grated steel.

"Hey boys." Dalton yelled, the Hunters slowing their run to a walk. "Go. Get the fuck out of here!" Primal yelled under his breath, doing his best to hide below a small ship docked near the Benzan shuttle.

"Got one hiding under here." Dalton said, smiling a bit and pointing to Primal before turning to haul ass and join Adam and Sasha.

"You bastard!" Primal yelled loudly, Whiskey barking at the Benzan for a moment before leaving to catch up to Dalton.

"Go!" Dalton shouted, he and Whiskey both sprinting up the shuttle's ramp and diving into the passenger area. One of the Hunter Elites had given chase, his arms clinching the edge of the passenger area as the shuttle began to lift off.

"Told you. Told you not to take that fucking job Adam!" Dalton said angrily, forcefully kicking the elite flush in the face several times and eventually causing him to release his grip, dropping back to the ground. Dalton fell back onto the deck of the shuttle for a moment, door still open as he gave a sigh of both frustration and relief.

"Dalton, close the door so we can break atmosphere!" Adam said loudly.

"Wait. I'm trying to decide between shutting the door or jumping out my damn self and putting an end to this shit." Dalton replied with sarcasm, finally moving his body over enough to kick the large button which drew the ship's door closed. Primal watched their shuttle ascend into the clouds, glancing for a moment at Stage who lay dead on the ground, his vision filled shortly after with that of the near grin upon a hell hound's face. His screams lasted only seconds as the immortal pet's teeth shaved through the flesh of a life short lived.

Tigon Twelve was a solid Colonial shuttle, but its current crew had pushed it to the limit as the silver ship ate fuel without remorse during its full burn.

"Not long before we get to Arch City my lady," Lassiter said loudly as the loyal soldiers all patiently waited with weapons at the ready. "When we get there, you are to remain onboard with the Goliaths. Is that clear?" he added.

It seemed strange, Lassiter giving orders to the leader of the Colonials. However, he was concerned for Sarah's safety and she was aware of the fact, though she had no clue of his mounting feelings for her.

"Just find Adam before they do." Sarah replied.

"Don't worry my lady, if he's there we'll find him." Lassiter responded as he sat directly in front of the mighty Husk warriors who were prepared to fight to the death for Sarah Blaine.

Arch City was located on the small but highly populated planet of Gali, known for its upscale living conditions, high priced fashion and modern technology. None of that appealed to Sarah Blaine, instead she only prayed that Adam Michaels was here and that he was safe. Of course, she wanted so badly for him to forgive her. Possibly give her a second chance at the storybook romance they once shared, but her love for him was the unconditional kind. Even if he refused to speak to her again, she just wanted him safe, wanted him happy.

Sarah had always been taught that she was in control of her own life, her own destiny. Which is why this was so hard to deal with. She couldn't control her heart's longing for Adam Michaels, it simply wasn't an emotion that could be turned on and off with the push of a button. In fact, nothing about the events which were about to unfold gave her any control. She was helpless. Was Adam alright? Would he forgive her and possibly give her another chance? It was all taking a huge toll on her emotionally, and none of it was to be controlled or decided by her. Instead, she could only pray for his safety and plead for his forgiveness.

"Sir. You better let us take the lead on this. If the Hunters have an elite in their ranks it may take all of us to bring him down." one of the Husk said with reserve as the human Colonial soldiers looked at one another. It was a staggering thought, anything taking all of the mighty Husk warriors to kill.

"Well enough, but I will be right behind you with my Colonial team. The Hunters do not intimidate me." Lassiter replied proudly.

"Ever see a Hunter Elite?" the Husk asked.

"Not up close, why?" Lassiter asked. The Husk remained silent as they began checking their weaponry for several tense moments.

"Just let us take the lead. They are not to be taken lightly." the Husk finally replied.

"We are hitting the upper atmosphere now sir, should be on top of Arch City within minutes." the Colonial pilot said as he turned to Lieutenant Lassiter for a moment.

"Circle the city low and try to locate the Benzan shuttle. We'll have eyes on the ground looking for any signs of Hunters." Lassiter replied.

"Yes sir." the pilot responded, turning to bring Tigon Twelve down low and begin looking for the shuttle's identification number and description.

Zane slowly walked down the corridor of narrow steel and aged plating as gunshots rang out in the distance. "Just keep your eyes peeled open and if we find them leave Roman for me." he said in a low voice which was answered by silent nods as all three men held riot style shotguns out in front of them.

Hearing footsteps, the men stopped and crouched to a knee in wait of what enemies might be ahead. Moments later, two Gali prison guards turned the corner, each with a repeater gun in hand. The Gali repeater was a semi-automatic rifle that fired hollow point shells, though the stock of the weapon was short. Best suited for close quarter combat, the well trained guards preferred them in the event of a prison uprising or riot.

Zane and his men stood up, quickly firing bursts from their shotguns as one prison guard immediately fell to his death. The remaining was hit in the leg, falling as he returned fire. The shots fired from his repeater easily cut through both flesh and bone, dropping one of Zane's men and chewing into the plated steel wall behind him. The injured guard tried to crawl back around the corner, blind firing his repeater while doing so. Seconds later Zane stood over him, smiling slightly before burying a shotgun blast into the guard's face at point blank range.

"Grab their weapons and let's head back. We go much farther and we are liable to run into a nest of the bastards." Zane said as they collected the weapons and key cards from the fallen guards, both Roman and Quinton watching from the rafters nearby.

Their plan was to climb down from the steel beams which held the ship intact shortly after Zane and his remaining henchman had turned back, however additional Gali prison guards arrived before they were able to put the plan into action. Checking their dead, they soon gave chase themselves, a total of eight soldiers carrying the deadly repeater rifles.

"What now?" Quinton asked quietly as both men waited a few minutes before slowly climbing down onto the steel deck of the ship.

"Now we work on making our way to the landing bay." Roman said steadfast as he checked both corners of the short and narrow hallway.

"Gonna be hell taking it, Zane is likely to be expecting us to try." Quinton remarked.

"Zane's got it all figured out. Except for the fact that my hands have killed more men than his eyes have seen. He has no idea what I'm capable of when I'm pissed off." Roman replied.

"And let me guess my brother, you're pissed off right about now?" Quinton asked. His question was simply answered with a stare that he had only seen Roman give a few times before. Indeed...he was pissed off.

"They left nothing behind." one of the Hunter Elites said as Vladris helped him search through everything. The third elite had suffered several gunshots and was sitting in the floor near the bed of the room, grimacing with pain.

"I know where they are heading. At least I will." Vladris said, holding the receiver of a tracking module in his hand, the glow of pulsing red running through it. "I just want to know who were are dealing with," Vladris added, turning to his wounded brother who sat in the floor. "Will you make it?" he asked. "In time. The gunshots were dead on but I will heal." the Hunter Elite replied, doing his best to stop the bleeding of a nearly foot wide hole that gaped into his chest.

The elite knights possessed the ability to heal quickly, tissue regeneration only one of many Hunter traits. They were damn hard to kill, and the elite sitting in the floor with a grin of pain had four gunshots attesting to the fact.

Their voices were easily heard by the approaching Colonial strike team, which walked with light steps into the direction of the room. Its door stood wide open, bloody footsteps leading them from the carved bodies of both Stage and Primal to their current location. The Husk gently pulled the blades from their backs, slowly bringing them to a ready and hoping not to alarm the Hunter Elites. They had no such luck. Vladris heard the silent but distinguishable sound of steel sliding against leather as the Husk unsheathed their blades.

"At arms!" Vladris yelled, though one of his elites was in no condition to fight. Both Vladris and his battle ready soldier pulled their blades with just enough time to meet the Husk on even terms, steel clanging against steel as every one of the warriors fought for survival.

Hunter Elites were the top of the food chain. That said, Husk were damn worthy opponents and in numbers they were slayers of Hunters, no matter the breed. The elite who continued battling previous gunshot wounds slowly made his way to the same fire escape Adam's group had used to flee less than an hour before. A Hunter Elite fleeing was practically unheard of, but catching the sight of a full strike team led by Goliaths in the hallway, the demons knew there was no victory to be had.

"Get him to the shuttle!" Vladris yelled. "We will track them from the air!" he added loudly, motioning his able elite to pull the injured out of the window and onto the fire escape.

Meanwhile, Vladris held his Vampiric fashioned blade above his head at a slant, daring the three Husk who circled him to make a move. They knew the dangers of fighting an elite, even with three to one odds the Husk were over-matched. The equivalent of three finely trained attack dogs circling a Lion. What they didn't know, however, was that they stood before the top Hunter Elite. A fact they would soon learn the hard way.

The first Husk dashed in, his blade thrusting in front of him. A solid move against most, but not Vladris, who easily slipped past and cleaved his own blade into the shoulder of the beast. The Husk painfully screamed as the small bones of the shoulder area and attached tendons snapped unmercifully. Vladris quickly pulled his warm, salty steel from the Husk flesh, swinging it around and plunging it into the stomach of a second Husk. The beast like warrior immediately dropped his blade, a look of death slowly pasting into his eyes. Only Samuel remained, and he had promised to give his life for Sarah Blaine if need be. He was ready to do just that, though it wouldn't be on this day. Goliaths stormed the room, letting loose a wave of death worthy lead into the direction of a fleeing Vladris.

Sarah entered with the remainder of the strike team. She wanted to desperately search for Adam, but her first concern was that of a dying warrior. The Husk who had been cut from shoulder to chest sat in the floor, slowly bleeding out as his life flashed before him. Sarah knelt with him, doing her best to comfort the dying beast, an act that only grew stronger the loyalty of the remaining Husk. Never before had he seen such compassion for his kind by a human being.

Normally the Husk fought beside humans who paid them well and discarded them from thought afterward. Yet Sarah's face told a different story. She cared for the dying Husk as though they were her own children. She was a leader worth dying for, the Colonial cause a noble one and that was reason enough to convince his people to follow her.

"Rest easy my brother, this is an honorable death. Your attacker will soon join you by my own hands." the remaining Husk said.

"Thank you my lady, I will sit with him. You find the one you love." the Husk said with great respect.

"Is he?" Sarah asked.

"No, he's not here. They were though." Lassiter replied.

"How do you know?" Sarah asked with hesitation. Lassiter held up a half empty bottle of rock whiskey, the preferred drink of Dalton James.

Sarah began to laugh a bit, relieved at least that they were alive and well.

"How will we find them now?" she asked, looking to Lassiter for some kind of comforting answer.

"I overheard one of the Hunters say they would track them using a location device. The same kind of location device I had our men plant on the Hunter's shuttle before we entered the hotel." Lassiter replied with a grin, holding a small receiver with a luminous blue glow.

Sarah breathed a bit easier, knowing eventually she may once again lay eyes on Adam Michaels and simply nodding to Lassiter for his quick thinking.

"The bad news is when we do catch up to them, we will be seeing more of the killers who caused such quick death of two Husk warriors. I just hope we have enough firepower to fight them off again." Lassiter said.

"You let me worry about that." the remaining Husk said, approaching them with the blood of his own race on his hands and a look of revenge in his eyes.

As Lassiter and the Colonial soldiers cleared the hotel room, Samuel helped Sarah to the safety of the doorway.

"My lady, I am sorry that we failed you." the Husk warrior said regretfully. Rather than reply, Sarah simply broke down into tears.

"Sarah are you alright?" Lassiter asked as he hurried back to the room's entrance to find the source of her sadness.

"These warriors died for me. Died because of my love for Adam, I can't live with that. People are dying because of my mistakes!" Sarah said regretfully as she sobbed loudly.

"My lady, the Husk and Hunters live to slay one another. If these warriors would not have fallen here, eventually they would have fallen to Hunters somewhere. We are bred for this, to die in battle is the greatest of honors." Samuel said.

"At least we know Adam made it out alright," Lassiter said. Seeing the thought bring comfort to her as she smiled a bit, Lassiter walked closer. "We know they had to leave in a hurry too, not like Dalton to leave good liquor behind," he said as Sarah began to laugh with emotional relief. "Don't worry, we'll find them soon enough. At least you know Adam's still alive." Lassiter added. In Sarah's heart she already knew he was alright.

This was Adam's world, he made a living escaping with his life. He was a smuggler, and a damn good one at that. Her fear would be his unwillingness to even listen to her pleas as she laid her heart out in front of him. She had to be able to convince him of her true sincerity, otherwise Sarah would have to live out the remainder of her life without him. She wasn't sure that was even possible.

"It's gonna be tough," Quinton said as both he and

Roman stood in the shadows of piping near the prison ship's landing bay. "I'm counting fourteen of 'em, including Zane," Quinton added. "All abundantly armed and waiting for us to try and take the landing bay." he added.

"In other words it's a fair fight." Roman replied.

"Yea, something like that my brother." Quinton replied, smiling a bit as he turned to his fellow terrorist. Before they could put any type of plan into effect, the ship began to shift abruptly.

"What the fuck?" Quinton asked with shock. "Looks like Zane's men have taken the control room," Roman replied. "So what's the plan now?" Quinton asked.

"Same plan. When that prison transport docks, we gotta be sure that we have control of the landing bay. Otherwise we are going to be stuck on this floating jail a lot longer than expected." Roman replied.

The two men moved a bit farther back into the shadows as a six man group of Gali prison guards rushed by and immediately opened fire into the direction of Zane and his men. Heavily outgunned, the six guards soon began to fall back, not that it would matter. More of Zane's men flanked their position and cut them to shreds with a hail of gunfire within only minutes. Knowing well enough that there was no chance of winning the fight in front of them, Roman and Quinton both remained in the shadows. The sight of dead prison guards being looted reflected back to the cutting pupils of Roman Raines, who did his best to memorize the face of every murdering bastard before him. Eventually their time would come, and when it did Roman would do his best to make sure he was a part of it.

"This shit 'aint gonna work Adam." Dalton said sarcastically as he stood there, dressed in a stolen guard's uniform. It was a snug fit, but manageable. His concern was the fact that they had decked Whiskey out in a guard's shirt as well.

"Relax." Adam said as he and Sasha both wore the same uniforms.

"Relax?" Dalton said in a stunned tone. "How the fuck are we supposed to explain a dog wearing a prison guard's shirt? Hell, the badge on the front is dragging the ground!" Dalton said loudly.

"Just tell them it's a K-9 unit or something to that effect." Sasha said, turning to Adam as they both began laughing.

"I 'aint telling 'em shit. If it looks like they 'aint buyin' it then I'm gonna start shooting." Dalton replied angrily.

"Trust me. They are going to smell whiskey on your breath long before they catch a glimpse of the four legged variety." Adam added as Sasha burst into full blown laughter.

"Damn smart ass." Dalton replied, covering his mouth and nose for a moment before blowing to test Adam's theory.

"Relax, the hardest part will be passing as a prison transport shuttle with Benzan markings all over the outside of our ship," Sasha said as she began the landing sequence. "I'm shocked they haven't hailed us by now, the landing bay is sitting wide open. May not buy any of this." she added.

"They don't have to buy anything for long, we don't have a single prisoner. Just land, look official when you exit and then start letting lead fly. Hopefully catchin' their asses off guard will be enough." Dalton replied as Sasha guided the ship onto the path of flashing red lights which lay on the prison ship's deck.

Roman's attention was immediately taken by the sight of the transport shuttle to the left as it began entering the ship's landing bay.

"When it touches down, wait for the guards to exit the shuttle and then we make a run for it. Kill anything with a heartbeat, but do not stop running." Roman said.

"Got it." Quinton replied.

"Wait for them to exit and then spring the trap." Zane said as he stood with two of his men who were decked out in Gali prison guard outfits, while almost two dozen armed prisoners waited patiently inside of the room which controlled the landing bay doors.

"Here we go." Adam said as the shuttle touched down and a mixture of grey steam and smoke blew underneath its frame. Sasha followed Adam out of the shuttle door, walking slowly down the ramp as they skimmed the landing bay with an observant eye.

"How many did you bring us today?" Zane asked as he approached.

"Actually we come bearing room for one more." Adam said quickly, pulling his gold plated pistol of Benzan craftsmanship and firing the first shot with such speed that Zane and his men still had no idea what was happening.

His shot surgically pierced the shoulder of the man to the left of Zane, rendering him defenseless as lead passed through the backside of the wound. As Zane and his remaining follower pulled their weapons to the ready, Sasha instantly cut Zane's other loyal friend down, her machine gun pistol tearing both cloth and meat as the man fell down in gripping pain. Outnumbered, Zane caught a glimpse of both Roman and Quinton sprinting for the ship from the corner of his anger ridden eye.

"Now!" he yelled as armed prisoners flooded from the landing bay control room in all directions.

Looking up to the shuttle entrance, Adam quickly extended his free hand, catching a fully loaded shotgun which had been tossed by Dalton. Nodding his gratitude, Adam turned and began firing shot after shot into the crowd of armed prisoners. Meanwhile, Dalton remained crouched at the entrance of the shuttle with a Benzan bolt action sniper rifle in hand.

"Take that ya' little bastard." Dalton mumbled as he fired a steadfast shot which instantly dropped one of the armed men. Whiskey remained near the shuttle's cockpit, waiting until the gunshots ceased and it was clear to leave.

Roman was a reaver of men. It didn't matter their weapon set or skill, he was simply unmatched when it came to blood letting and moments like these only added to his mounting legend. The combined movements of his Gali rifle and guard's baton allowed him to easily make a path through those who remained standing. Quinton did most of his work by way of rifle, zipping hot lead into the wall of guilty flesh before him.

It wasn't long before Zane's ranks had thinned and the thought of mortality began to set in. Dalton and Whiskey both exited the ship slowly as they joined their group during the last seconds of the gunfight.

"No, that's Roman!" Adam yelled as Sasha pulled her pistol up and into the face of the former terrorist, not recognizing the man who had endured months of hell.

"Apologies my friend." Sasha said, slowly lifting the pistol away from Roman Raines, while continuing to use caution around the warrior's Black Cell brother.

"I told you I'd be back." Adam said proudly, answering the look of gratitude cast by Roman. Through all of the turmoil, Zane managed to gather himself from the floor, sprinting quickly out of the landing bay as his heavy feet clanged against the grated steel deck of the hallway.

Roman thought long and hard about everything he had endured on the Gali prison ship. The food, the guard induced beatings, the inhumane living conditions and the fact that he had started to lose hope. He had truly started to believe that Adam and the Gunship crew had left him for dead.

None of that mattered now as Roman stood there, continuing to stare at the Captain of the most loyal group he'd ever been a part of.

"You're a man of your word." Roman finally said, extending his arm to shake the hand of Adam Michaels.

"I told you I would be back." Adam said again, proud of the fact that he was able to pull it off.

"Didn't say you would have Hunters right behind you though." Roman replied as everyone turned to see a Hunter distinct shuttle entering the landing bay.

"Ahh fuck," Dalton yelled, smacking his leg frantically and whistling until Whiskey began to run back to their position. "Get them little legs running!" Dalton added, crouching for a moment to coax Whiskey into moving quickly.

"Shit! Must have placed a beacon on our ship back at Arch City." Adam said with disgust.

"We better move now." Roman said sternly, motioning the group to follow him down the narrow hallway and into what would be no less than a hornet's nest of guards and rioting prisoners exchanging gunfire.

"See you lost a little weight and picked up a new friend." Dalton said jokingly as the entire group jogged slowly into a storage room. Filled with large wooden crates, it would be the perfect place to dig in and make a last stand if it came to that.

"This is my brother Quinton. As far as the weight, well I'm sure you all have noticed my lack of chrome." Roman said calmly, though his mind had already drifted back to the prison doctor barbarically pulling the meshed steel from his flesh.

"Your brother? You mean there are two of you?" Dalton asked, stunned by Roman's statement.

"Many more than just two." Quinton said, a bright smile painted onto his face.

"I hate to break up the honeymoon here, but it would be wise to knock off the small talk and find cover. We don't know how many Hunters we are dealing with." Sasha said, the thought of Hunter Elites still fresh in her memory.

"She's right. Not to mention the entire prison ship is in a full scale riot. Guards are scattered and the prisoners are armed and on the hunt for us both," Roman replied. "I'll take the front with Quinton." Roman said as both of the Black Cell members positioned themselves crouching behind a desk at the entrance to the room. Sasha waited quietly, hoping in her heart that Adam would position himself with her.

It would give them the perfect chance to be alone, and even under such stressful circumstances her heart felt so many different emotions for the true to his word smuggler. Their kiss in the rain still haunted her every waking moment, she wanted to live in that kiss forever.

"Dalton, you and Whiskey hide behind something. If we are going to die, I want to do it with my crew." Adam said, quickly joining Sasha as they took up residence in the corner behind a forklift type vehicle.

As Vladris stepped off of his shuttle slowly, gothic black boots striking the ground, the void pupils of his eyes skimmed the perimeter of the room. Quickly joined by his hell hound, who's ears skimmed the area for sound. Their keen senses instantly heard multiple gunshots being exchanged throughout the ship, but a prison riot was of no concern to him. Seeing out the execution of the last remaining Benzans were his only priority. Having left Arch City to regroup with more of the undead murderers, he turned to motion the rest of the group. Two additional Hunter Elites slowly exited the craft, followed by three of the less dangerous Hunter strain.

"Stay here and hold the landing bay until we return." Vladris commanded of the three Hunters as he turned and walked into the narrow hallway under escort of two more Hunter Elites.

Soon the three ultra killers had disappeared from sight, taking with them only precision pistols and articulate swords of destruction.

Nearing the storage room, the Hunter Elites were taken off guard by a group of equally surprised prisoners. Heavily armed, the startled prisoners began to open fire without regard, clouds of bullets floating through the narrow confines of the hallway. In a normal scenario, six heavily armed men might stand a chance against a single Hunter Elite. But this was far from a normal scenario.

Three elites in close quarters led to a speedy slaying of the six prisoners, their flesh gouged to the bone and spines severed from the body. The screams and pleas of the prisoners being mutilated could easily be heard by Adam's group, which was positioned nearby in the storage room. They tried to remain focused, though both Adam and Dalton were horribly reminded of so many friends lost during the first Glimmerian War.

The screams of a dying man who is unready to go sound the same, no matter the killer or pleading man. The screams always sound the same. And that was a sound that both men had witnessed so many times first hand, a sound that made the skin of both men crawl. *Told him not to that that fuckin' job.* Dalton thought as they nervously waited.

With their jet black armor coated with the crimson splatter of blood and boots drenched in it, the Hunter Elites kept moving forward, stopping to glance in each room. Roman Raines was prepared to die to get his friends to safety as he clinched a combat blade in one hand and riot style shotgun in the other. They had came back for Roman and shown a type of loyalty that he had never known, and he wasn't about to let them die in front of him. He glanced at his Black Cell brother for a moment, turning to nod his appreciation one last time to Adam before moving his attention to the door. Vladris and his two skilled slayers stopped for a moment, looking into the room with malicious intent before taking fire from the end of the hallway. A three man group of prison guards held a riot shield and fired piercing rounds from an automatic sniper rifle. Hitting one of the elites with multiple shots, the monster fell to the deck in agonizing pain. Sprinting to their position quickly, Vladris and the other elite made short work of the guards, butchering the men into afterlife.

"It's important to me that these people make it to safety my brother," Roman said with a grave tone as Quinton looked at him solidly. "They are good people. They don't know about our cause, but they are like family to me as well." Roman added as Quinton nodded slowly.

Roman stood quickly, motioning the group to the door as the Hunters turned to exit the hallway.

"We gotta go now and pray they didn't leave many behind to guard the shuttles." Roman said.

"I'll take point, Quinton will watch the flank." he added. The group quickly ran out of the storage room and backtracked into the direction of the ship's landing bay.

"Well, there goes that idea." Dalton said as the group sprinted into the landing bay, quickly gaining the attention of the three Hunters left behind. As the Hunters contacted Vladris and his group by radio, Roman dropped his pistol to the ground, reaffirming his grip on the combat blade.

Hunters considered themselves to be at the top of the food chain, and when they were challenged by blade wielding cattle, they were quick to answer the challenge. The Hunters quickly drew their swords, impressions of both skulls and demons engraved into the pewter handles of the weapons.

"We got this." Roman said with thirst on his breath. Quinton was quick to join as Dalton tossed him a well built Glimmerian combat blade.

Adam and the remainder of the group stepped back to watch the fight begin, ready to move to the shuttle quickly in the rare case of victory. They could have easily opened fire onto the Hunters, but there was a code of honor among all warriors in the Skyla System, no matter the flag.

"Be ready to bury some Hunter ass just in case." Adam said as the group quickly readied their weapons.

"All this shit and I still gotta buy my own damn drinks." Dalton said jokingly, though Adam knew him well enough to understand Dalton was trying his best to disguise fear. There was a good chance that every single one of them would die right here, the map of their lives drawn to a conclusion in this very landing bay.

"I've killed a Hunter Queen, you grunts aren't shit to me." Roman said insultingly, bringing anger to the faces of the immortal soldiers of death.

They were some of the best warriors ancient civilizations had produced, and now there was a feeling among everyone here. The best warriors of days gone by facing the most skilled warriors still mortal. While Adam and his crew were stunned at the former Black Cell member's statement, Adam was the only one to think it through. That's why he had been running. That's what led them to meet for the first time, and why the Hunters wanted him dead so badly. Sasha was the first to notice what the rest of the group quickly caught sight of. Three Hunter Elites. Walking into the landing bay, one seemed to be reeling from gunshot wounds slightly. Vladris looked at the group, especially the Benzans as he paced back and forth, dragging the tip of his blade across the floor. They would wait until the current fight was finished before blood letting, but wanted the group to see the sword which would end their lives.

"You're up next and you motherfuckers aren't walking out of here alive." Roman said bluntly, pointing his blade into the direction of Vladris, who quickly shifted his attention to the Black Cell terrorist.

"Your terrorist group has caused much grief for our people. Acts that you will soon be apologizing for by the edge of our blades." one of the Hunters said.

Terrorist group? Adam thought as he watched Roman's movements, perfectly choreographed with those of Quinton.

He wondered how much he actually knew about Roman

Raines. What kind of criminal had he been harboring aboard his ship since day one? It didn't matter, Roman had only been a good person since that day. That's what counted in his book. Especially since all of their lives depended on the skill of Roman and Quinton at this very moment.

The first Hunter made its move, lunging at the men with life ending intent. His sword was quickly parried away by the boot of Quinton, who threw a bone rattling elbow into the jaw of the beast. As he began to lunge to the wounded Hunter, Roman surprised all by spinning and burying his blade into the face of another Hunter, catching the beast off guard and ending its life in the same motion. Firmly planting his boot onto the chest of the lifeless Hunter, Roman pushed its carcass from his blade, bringing fragments of cartilage and bone with it.

Shrieking from anger, Vladris began to pace with purpose, his eyes focused onto the mortal man who had made such short work of the perfect species. While the injured Hunter staggered to gain his senses back, the untouched Hunter dashed for Roman with its blade extended. Side stepping the monster, Roman mockingly kicked it in the back, using its own momentum to push it to the ground. He glanced at Vladris for a moment before turning to slash the reeling Hunter who had made an attempt to attack him from behind.

Slashing the stomach of the Hunter, Roman quickly gave a second slash that filleted the beast from waist to shoulder and then arched a stab which plunged into its back. The dying Hunter screamed before Quinton kicked it directly in the face, jarring several teeth loose from the dead Hunter's mouth. As if Vladris wasn't enraged enough, Roman spit onto the body of the dead Hunter to insult their race.

Screaming with fury, Vladris unbuckled his armor piece by piece, throwing it to the ground with conviction. His pale white skin was fully exposed, throwing every bit of armor from the waist up onto the ship's deck. He wanted to end the life of Roman Raines, and do it without the aid of armor. Stiffening his body up for a moment, Vladris displayed muscle tone matching his skill with a blade. Both in plentiful supply.

Roman and Quinton circled the remaining Hunter slowly, swagger filled steps from both men who waited for the perfect opportunity to strike. It was a feign from Roman that grabbed the Hunter's attention, but the blade of Quinton that ended the Hunter's life. Roman playing decoy just long enough for his Black Cell brother to thrust the shimmering blade deep into the spinal area of the Hunter, twisting the steel bluntly before pulling it upward and spilling the intestines of the creature. The two brothers had made short work of three Hunters and now stood covered in blood as well as anticipation. Vladris was obviously calling the shots, as well as very important to his people; which made him a marked target to the Black cell brothers. "He's mine." Vladris said commandingly as his curved fingernail directed his finger into Roman's direction.

Adam's entire group remained speechless after watching the two brothers make such short work of three Hunters. Finding no suitable words to describe what his eyes had just witnessed, Adam simply gave a look of awe as Quinton made his way over to stand with the group. It was well known that dogs had a dislike for the Hunter race, a fact that had come to fruition because of the Hunter Elite's uncanny ability to turn both humans and animals into undead themselves. Whiskey hid behind the ramp of the crew's shuttle, watching the battle unfold in vivid black and white detail. Meanwhile, Roman and Vladris walked a slow circle, neither warrior removing eyes from the other.

Vladris wielded a longsword, an advantage that Roman had quickly countered by wielding a second combat blade. The shimmering silver blade his brother had used only moments ago, now sitting in Roman's second hand. The idea of Roman fighting with a combat blade was testament enough, but when he held two blades the Gunship's crew could only try and imagine the possible destruction which could soon follow.

"When I cut the soul from your body, I will show your organs to your friends as they too lay dying." Vladris said calmly, dragging the tip of his sword a bit as both men continued to circle.

"Got it all wrong fang man. When this is over, my friends and I will be leaving on that shuttle, and you will know that your sense of immortality was false, that you were nothing more than a mortal masquerading as an elite warrior." Roman said, stopping to face the elite.

Just like the instant of sunlight filling a landscape, Roman dove at Vladris with both blades extended. Stabbing at the Hunter, Roman continued to thrust the blades down as he landed beside the elite. Using his massive forearm to block the forearms of Roman, Vladris used his sword bearing arm to lay both fist and iron across the face of the Black Cell warrior, knocking him onto his back several feet away.

Though quick to his feet, the nagging sensation of pain shooting throughout his face remained. His sight blurred by throbbing red as trace amounts of blood mixed with sweat and fell helplessly into the whites of his eyes. Such a punishing measure of blunt force trauma usually rendered his foes helpless, and Vladris was impressed with the zeal of Roman Raines, even if he was a man marked for death. Quinton started to intervene, but Adam quickly grabbed him, shedding light on the fact that two move Hunter Elites stood at the ready, their rifles drawn.

"Come on Roman, dust that 'sumbitch!" Dalton yelled, knowing deep down that in hand to hand combat Roman was the best shot they had at walking out alive. His motivation was quickly prolonged by the barking of Whiskey, who remained hidden near their shuttle.

Roman began to reflect on everything in his life up to this very moment. His family murdered at the hands of the Hunters, Black Cell being wiped out by the blood sucking bastards and how he felt alone in the Skyla System. Alone, other than Adam and the crew of the Gunship, a group that took him in and treated him like part of the family. He would be damned if he let them fall dead here at the hands of three Hunter Elites.

As Vladris jumped in for the kill, his blade struck metal, bouncing off of the grated deck of the ship as Roman spun quickly and split the ribs of the Hunter Elite wide open. His blade easily filleted the dead flesh of the mighty elite, shocking the immortal if nothing else. He was only wounded, still Vladris was more taken back by the thought of a normal man giving such fight to a Hunter Elite. He had not been given a wound of this magnitude in several decades, if not longer.

Vladris staggered a bit, sword hanging down by his feet in one hand while the other covered the newly carved flesh wound. "He always did prefer the blade!" Dalton said, the idea of him possibly living to see another day exciting him. Wasting no time, Roman dashed in with incredible speed. Though not incredible enough. Vladris instantly used the hand covering his wound to grab the neck of Roman Raines and pull him into the air, looking into the eyes of such a dedicated warrior as he searched his soul. Seconds later, Vladris plunged his massive sword into the chest of Roman, lifting him into the air a bit higher by the length of his blade as he shook the life from the departed warrior.

Roman Raines was dead. After cheating the afterlife so many times before, Roman was finally ended. He lay there on the blade of Vladris, blood gushing down to its handle as Roman glanced at Adam a final time as if to apologize.

"NO!" Quinton yelled, running to the aid of his dying brother in arms before being hit with the unforgiving fire of a Hunter rifle. The bullet made a clean pass through the shoulder of Quinton, who lay on the floor suffering from both flesh wound and grief of the soul. Adam was fast to pull his pistol coated in gold and fire six shots, providing enough cover until he could grab Quinton and drag him behind the control booth of the landing bay.

Sasha opened fire, letting a swarm of angry lead loose with intention to kill. The Hunter Elites were faster than both normal man and normal Hunter however, dodging the gunfire long enough to seek cover of their own.

"Hold them back while I turn him!" Vladris said, laying Roman's lifeless body onto the deck in front of him and pressing his hand firmly to the dead warrior's chest.

Several minutes passed as both groups continued to exchange gunfire, when finally Roman's body began to show signs of the transformation. Opening his eyes slowly, the most noticeable trait was the milky white pupil of his eyes, a clear sign that the Hunter Elite's venom had done its job.

Roman had become one of the undead monsters that he had spent a lifetime hunting down. He was now the enemy, a fact that Adam and his crew had yet to discover. As fanged teeth began to slowly push their course into Roman's mouth, his previous wounds reversed; healing themselves in only a matter of moments.

Adam was the first to notice, quickly joined by the others. A Colonial marked shuttle making its approach into the landing bay. They were outgunned and not long removed from a painful death at the hands of Hunter Elites. Still, Adam's world seemed to stop as the Colonial shuttle slowly touched down onto the deck, steel connecting with steel. Standing there without breath or words, the grip of Adam's revolver loosened as he held the pistol at waist level by his side. His eyes had not caught sight of Sarah Blaine, but his heart already knew. His own death was no longer of any concern to him, just seeing her one last time.

Bullets continued to zip strategically through the air as Dalton and Sasha remained focused, exchanging gunfire with the Hunters. The Colonial strike team was first to exit the ship, closely followed by Lassiter. Sarah Blaine walked slowly down the ramp under the heavy escort of two Goliath soldiers and her loyal Husk warrior Samuel. Her own eyes immediately locking onto those of Adam Michaels. Sasha slowed her own gunfire, glancing deep into the heart of Adam as Dalton's shotgun continued spending large shells, its shooter cursing in the process.

Sarah nervously ordered her own Goliath escorts to the fight in an attempt to save Adam and what remained of his crew. The mechanical warriors quickly sprinted across the long deck of the landing bay, passing the Colonial strike team just before arriving to the fight. A fight began to ensue of epic proportions, the Hunter Elites holding their own against such an incredible force.

When Roman rose to his feet, it wasn't obvious to most that he was a Hunter. Or that it was even Roman Raines. So many bodies were slaying, firing weapons and yelling that the confusion distracted almost everyone from the fact. Almost everyone.

"Roman's a goddamn Hunter!" Dalton yelled loudly, nearly stretching the beard from his face in the process.

Whiskey began to bark without pause, Dalton holding him back with a free hand by his collar while blindly firing his shotgun with the other.

Adam and Sarah continued a stare of fate. An unspoken communication of sorrow, apology and above all, forgiveness. The stare was finally broken by Adam as Dalton's words rang true. Adam turned abruptly, looking over his shoulder as Dalton sprinted past. Already having thrown his weapon to the ground, he was now carrying Whiskey with both arms and running as fast as he had since boot camp more than a decade earlier.

"Roman's a 'mutha fuckin' Hunter!" Dalton added wildly

as he ran past.

Adam caught sight of him. Roman stood there at the side of Vladris, the warrior's skin already beginning to turn chalk white. While his eyes milked over to merely void of any color, Roman could still see unhindered. His first sight being that of his brother in arms laying dead on the deck of the ship. His heart continued to feel. And his hatred remained. His hatred for the Hunter race. He reflected back to a time when he was a young child, the Hunters slaying his family as he stood helpless. As he watched Dalton sprint away, Adam and Sasha preparing for their own deaths and the Hunters pushing to them, Roman remembered two important things. His new family was still alive and at the mercy of Hunters. And he was no longer a helpless young boy.

Roman turned to glance at Vladris momentarily, quickly following with a witching backhand that put the leader of the Hunter group to his back. Adam had drawn his pistol, but didn't fire. Instead his body fell into shock as he held his hand out, leading Sasha to quit firing her weapon as well. The remaining Hunter Elites and Goliath units both turned their attention to the newly born super killer. Roman's freshly clawed handed swiped with intent, gouging the throat of an elite, ripping with it vital organs for survival as the Hunter fell face down. One of the Goliath units had aim on him, its rules of engagement clear. Leave no Hunter standing. However its mechanical arm was violently jerked from place, sparking wires flashing as the swinging arm now held by Roman planted flush into the face of another Hunter Elite. As the elite stumbled back, his head was aggressively pulled to its side, snapping the neck of the so called immortal.

Roman's flesh was hit several times by the stout slugs of the remaining Goliath's chain gun, only hurting enough to enrage the newly turned monster. Roman jumped onto the mechanical work of art, butchering him quickly by ripping away the parts needed for operation. Both Adam and Sasha stood silent, not knowing where their friend's heart was at by this point. They were both prepared to shoot if need be, though it would have little effect.

"Roman's a goddamn hunter!" Dalton screamed, finally making his way to Sarah, Lassiter and her large Husk protector.

Samuel had drawn his sword, standing in front of Sarah Blaine in case his destiny ended here.

"Did you hear me? I said Roman's a..." Dalton yelled almost like a screaming child before turning to see the wake of destruction in the near distance.

Vladris stood to his feet, his hell hound having backed off a bit and watching from the shadows. He had taken the time to turn Roman Raines, given the man a gift of immortality and now he would have to end the man only recently turned. Vladris drew his sword slowly, walking in a circle as Roman turned to face him. Both had been great warriors in days gone by, in a previous life led by mortal standards. Both had life ending skills now that were unmatched by anyone, alive or otherwise. It was unheard of for a Hunter to turn on his own kind by free will. And though Vladris was shocked at the mortal will of Roman Raines, he knew only one Hunter Elite could walk away from what would be a barbaric display of slaying in the moments to come.

"Go my brother. It is not your day to die," Roman said in a low but stern voice. "Tell your queen I will be coming for her soon enough." he added.

"You do not dictate my fate or that of our queen." Vladris replied, his sword still at the ready.

"Search your soul, it will tell you otherwise. Your queen is weak, I have seen it. She relies on the true warriors to do her work. Go back and tell her I am coming. There will be a place for you in the future." Roman replied, acknowledging that Vladris had given him the gift of life.

Vladris knew Roman's words were true. He had known for a while that his queen had grown arrogant, weak even. As his mind stuck to the fact, he soon found himself more concerned about dealing with a substandard queen than slaying Roman Raines.

"Our day will come soon enough," Vladris said, pointing his sword directly at Roman before backing away slowly. "Scucca...come!" Vladris added, motioning the hell hound to him.

Instead, Scucca slowly approached Roman Raines, sitting down at his feet and making public his new owner. Scowling at his recently lost pet, Vladris glanced back to Roman. "Soon." he said, his stare never faltering. Moments later Vladris turned to slowly jog away, into the shadows which led to the heart of the riot.

Adam and Sasha both stood there silently, trying to make sense of Roman having become one of the immortal Hunters; not to mention Sarah's arrival. "So are you still Roman enough that..." Adam had started to ask as Roman turned to them both.

"Don't worry. I'm not going to kill you." They both breathed a bit easier, approaching him with a great deal of caution.

"Good. Didn't much feel like getting killed. At least not today," Adam said with a grin, his words never phasing Roman. "With just a little time I'm sure the Colonials can fix this. Have you back to normal." Adam added. Roman turned directly to him, the newly born Hunter Elite only feet away from both Adam and Sasha.

"I'm not going back. This is the end of our journey together." Roman said. "There has to be something we can do to help you." Adam replied.

"I don't want to be helped. I am what the Hunters fear now, and I will bring their race to its knees. Don't try and stop me, it's taking everything I have this very moment to suppress the Hunter inside of me." Roman said abruptly, his voice altered a bit with demonic dialect.

"I'm not trying to stop you Roman. You're my friend, hell you're like family to me. I just want what's best for you. That's all." Adam replied.

"Then leave me be. You once told me I was free to leave, and now I am. Adam, it's taking everything I have left inside of me to not continue killing here. The Hunter side of me is strong. It's not safe to be around me now." Roman replied, a man torn between immortal and mortal in his eyes as they began to tear slightly.

The biggest battle to come for him would be the battle within.

Adam understood. His friend wasn't leaving because of a lack of friendship, he was leaving because of his deep respect for the crew. It was for their own good.

"Well then, It's been an honor." Adam finally said calmly, extending his arm. Roman fought it.

The inner urge to kill for the sport of it, an urge forced onto him by the Hunter DNA. His soul was still strong, at least strong enough to extend his own arm and shake hands with the Captain of the Gunship.

"Goodbye old friend." Adam said as Dalton yelled loudly, clapping his friendship and gratitude.

"Until we meet again." Roman replied, quickly breaking his grip and turning into the direction of the Hunter shuttle that Vladris had arrived in, hell hound following closely behind.

As Adam watched Roman pull the Hunter shuttle from the ship's deck and slowly exit into the backdrop of stars, it suddenly hit him. Sarah Blaine was waiting. Adam quickly spun around, his eyes locked onto the stare of Sarah as she stood by the Colonial vessel. Dalton cautiously began making his way back to Adam and Sasha, this time forcing Whiskey to follow on foot. After several deep moments of exchanging apologies through their stare, Adam turned slowly to Sasha.

"Go Adam." Sasha said with regret.

"But I don't know what I'm supposed..." Adam replied, unsure of which woman held his future in their hands.

"The look between you both just answered every

question I had. I love you Adam Michaels, and I want you to be happy no matter what. So go, please." Sasha replied.

Adam wanted to plead with her, maybe ask for time to think things through. Deep down he knew that his time was up. He had to choose between his love for Sarah Blaine or his possible future with Sasha Riley.

Sarah stood there, her beautiful red hair swaying slightly as tears filled her eyes. She had prayed for a second chance with Adam, her one mistake having forced her into nearly a year of regret.

"Just tell me what we had was real Adam? That's enough for me." Sasha said. A lie of course, she loved Adam from the pit of her soul. But she wanted him to be truly happy and had seen a look between Adam and Sarah that was undeniable.

"More real than you will ever know." Adam replied, nodding as he slowly turned to begin walking to the woman who had waited so long for the return of his embrace.

Sarah began crying a bit from happiness, her hands shaking as she prepared to once again hold the man of her dreams. Meanwhile, Sasha started to cry just slightly, her Benzan toughness standing in the way of her true feelings.

Adam had walked nearly mid-way when he stopped for a moment, realizing that these last fifty or so feet would lead to the rest of his life. Everything he was, everything he would ever be was tied into this very decision. It was in that single moment that he felt it. He thought about a life without Sasha Riley and his breath evaporated, body numb from the thoughts of leaving her behind. He had felt this way about Sarah Blaine as well, but not anymore. As he looked into Sarah's eyes, he knew she would be best loved through the memories they had shared.

"I'm sorry." Adam said in a very faint voice as he stared at Sarah for a moment, turning back to Sasha and moving with a touch of haste.

"I forgot one thing," Adam said as he walked close to Sasha. "I can't live without you," he added, holding a hand out as he waited for her own. Sasha immediately burst into heavy tears as her heart tried to make sense of things. "My life changed the moment we kissed in the rain. I care for Sarah, and I always will. But I love you. I've loved you every since the moment we first kissed, and I can't go back from that. I just can't." Adam added, grabbing Sasha tenderly into his arms.

"I'm not the leader of a mighty military force Adam. Honestly, I don't even know where my life will go from this point forward." Sasha said, her body trembling as Adam continued to hold her with a comforting calm.

"I don't care. I just want us to go there together." Adam replied.

Sarah Blaine stood there, devastated. Her life had just been ripped from her from only fifty yards away.

"Get her onto the shuttle. Fire up and wait for me." Lassiter said commandingly, the Colonial Husk nodding and slowly helping Sara Blaine up the ship's ramp.

"Roman's a fucking Hunter." Dalton said as he approached Adam and Sasha locked into an embrace.

"Yea, I'm well aware." Adam replied, both he and his lover giggling a bit.

"I told you not to take that job Adam. I told you." Dalton added as the two lovers laughed a bit harder, locked into a poetic glance of destiny.

"Enjoying yourself?" Lassiter asked with a wise tone as he approached Adam.

"Roman's a fucking Hunter," Dalton replied, Lassiter answering with a stone carved gaze. "Well he is." Dalton added, walking away a bit to allow Lassiter time to speak.

"No hard feelings here Eric." Adam replied, finally pulling his arms from holding Sasha in order to face Lassiter.

"Sarah is back there right now crying her very soul out because of you." Lassiter replied harshly.

"No sir, she's crying because of the mistakes in our past. I care about Sarah a lot, but I can't live in the past. I have to move on." Adam replied.

"Yes. You do. All of you need to move on." Lassiter said.

"Now what the fuck is that supposed to mean?" Dalton asked with ill manners.

"It means you all better move on, far away from Glimmeria and as far away from Sarah as you can possibly get. I won't watch her go through this kind of pain for someone hardly worth the effort twice." Lassiter replied.

"Well now," Adam said, stepping within inches of Lassiter's face in order to look him dead in the eyes. "May want to word things with a bit more caution. We aren't in your usual Colonial comfort zone at the moment." Adam added. The Colonial shuttle fired its engines, loud torque nearly overwhelming the shouting conversation taking place.

"No, you're not in Colonial space at the moment. But if you ever venture into it again, I won't put you in prison. That would bring too much pain to Sarah. I'll just have you executed without her ever knowing. Are we clear?" Lassiter said loudly.

"Are you threatening..." Adam said, his question sharply cut off by Lassiter drawing a pistol and pointing it into their direction.

"Crystal clear," Adam replied, motioning Sasha, Dalton and Whiskey to turn and head for the Benzan shuttle. "Oh and just so we are clear, it's a two way street," Adam said, turning to face Lassiter one last time. "If I were you, I'd make sure this was the last time you ventured outside of your Colonial comfort zone." he added, turning to accompany his friends to the shuttle.

It would be the last time Sarah Blaine would see Adam Michaels through human eyes, watching him enter the Benzan shuttle doors through a window on her own ship.

Her Husk protector lay dead as Vladris approached her slowly, his hand extended with clawed fingers gripped her chin.

"You have fought the Legion valiantly, an effort that is worthy of immortality." Vladris said, his voice both calm and demonic.

Sarah cried softly, her mortal life about to come to an end as Adam's ship began to pull from the deck; losing both her love and mortal life in the very same instant.

Moments later as Lassiter watched the Benzan shuttle leave distant site, he turned to the Colonial ship, only to watch it pull swiftly from the deck. He wanted to yell at the top of his lungs, wanted his ride to hold long enough for him to get aboard. However the shuttle quickly left, a trail of orange fumes scattering behind by way of full burning thrusters. Seconds later he fell to his death, multiple rifle shots plunging into his thin frame as guards had once again taken control of the prison ship.

***

Roman's shuttle slowly fell from the clouds on the planet Cres Nine, along with a heavy rain as the Hunter designed shuttle quickly approached for landing. It was a well known gangster hideout, one that Roman had deep ties with. And it was on the moon planet that Roman would begin building his new family. The Roman Empire. A family that would become large enough to stand against the Hunters and their queen, at least if Roman had his way. The newly born Hunter Elite smiled a bit as his shuttle slowly approached through a curtain of rain, his dagger-like teeth showing crisply as Roman extended his arm down to pet his loyal hell hound.

As the Benzan shuttle pulled down for its landing on the small mining planet of Antillia, Dalton looked from a window, secretly hoping their faces weren't recognized for events that took place nearly a year before. They had met

Roman, beaten several officers of the law and robbed a table full of patrons at gunpoint. Whiskey sat beside Dalton, his head of tangled fur laying on the man's lap as Dalton continued his train of thought.

Normally he was excited when landing here, even if only to refuel. Paulie's was here, and piss poor drink aside, they at least had a stockpile of it available.

This time was different though. Dalton's mind wasn't on the alcohol. He watched Sasha sit on the lap of Adam Michaels, their overwhelming love for one another very obvious. Dalton was sick and tired of the Hunters. He was tired of running, tired of the Colonial war effort and had started to wonder if there was a Sasha out there waiting for him. How would he ever know if he was constantly on the run from a nation of undead. And now Roman was a fucking Hunter too.

"Guess now is as good as any time to tell you Adam. I plan on staying here when you two pull out." Dalton said with a serious tone, one he rarely used. Sasha turned first, quickly standing to her feet and offering to take the controls so Adam could talk to his friend.

"What are you talking about?" Adam asked quickly as he walked to the rear of the shuttle to sit with his friend. "I know the loss of so many friends has taken its toll." he added.

"That's what has me thinking," Dalton said with a touch of sorrow. "Running all the time, the war. It's not my fate man." he added.

"Come on man, this will pass. You and I are like brothers." Adam replied.

"We are brothers, in every sense of the word," Dalton said as he turned back to Adam. "Which is why I need you to understand, something else is out there waiting for me. I can feel it." he added. A moment of silence fell throughout the shuttle as both men dealt with the inevitable. Dalton was leaving Adam's crew to go his own way.

"I gotta find my Sasha. She's out there somewhere and between you and me I hope she has just as nice of an ass. She doesn't have a sister does she?" Dalton asked in a hushed tone as both men laughed a bit.

"I'm not ever going to find her running from the Hunters or fighting this damn war. Hell, I never wanted any of this. I did it because I think so much of you." Dalton added with much more seriousness attached to his words.

"I understand," Adam replied with a solid head shake. "At least let me buy this round of drinks at Paulie's as a thank you." Adam added.

"Damn straight. Hell, if I knew it took leaving to get my drinks paid for I woulda' done it a long time ago." Dalton replied with a wide grin. Adam just laughed a bit, putting his hand onto the shoulder of Dalton out of gratitude, petting Whiskey for a moment as he turned to make his way back to the pilot's area.

"I'm sorry." Sasha said gently as Adam sat down beside her, the shuttle on its final moment of landing.

"No need for that," Adam said, reaching over and holding her hand. "I make it a rule not to feel bad for the end of things, but rather happiness that I ever had a chance to experience them," he added. *"**Besides, this is hardly the end. Just the end of a single chapter in what is going to end up being a long story**."* Adam said, turning to face the love of his life.

Adam, Sasha and Dalton sat at their usual table in Paulie's bar the entire night. Talking about friends lost and experience gained. They laughed for the most part, though a little crying followed when talking about the life and death of Kelly, Steiner and Kato. Adam also found the time to tell the story of Luck one last time, which prompted Dalton to order another stout drink. The laughs continued as though they were family, Whiskey sitting directly at Dalton's side with the best display of loyalty imaginable.

It seemed blurred into a single night, though several nights later Dalton sat at the same table. Drinking and laughing by himself as Whiskey stood in the same spot by his feet.

"That guy? The homeless one at the rear of the bar?" Cambria asked of the bartender as they both stood there, staring at the broken man tightly tucked into his brown coat.

"That's the one. Knows more about smuggling than everyone else in here combined. Be a big help to you all." the bartender replied.

"Well he looks down on his luck. May be able to hire him at a fraction of the going rate." Cambria said.

"Down on his luck? This son of a bitch is buried under the casino." Tank replied.

"Guess if we plan on smuggling, this is what the future holds for us one day." Skulls added, his loose fitting leather clothing moving just a bit.

"The hell it does. Not me, I got too much game for that." Tank added as they all watched Dalton pour a bit of ale onto the floor for his loyal dog.

"Wish me luck." Cambria said, taking the rest of her liquor in a swift shot before slamming the small glass to the bar and standing to make her way to Dalton's table.

"Mind if I sit?" Cambria asked politely.

"Darlin' with hips like yours, you can do whatever the hell you want to." Dalton replied with a grin.

"Alrighty." Cambria said with a smile, slowly placing her perfectly sculpted body onto the small wooden chair. Barkeep says you are the man to talk to about hiring onto my crew. If I can buy you a drink and..." Cambria said confidently, cut off abruptly by Dalton.

"I'm in." he replied.

"You're huh?" Cambria said, taken back by his willingness to work a job he knew nothing about.

"I just hit on you and instead of the usual slap to the face, you smiled. After which you offered to buy me a drink. I'm in. Consider me hired." Dalton said.

Cambria smiled a bit, still trying to read the man wrapped in a lipstick stained coat of brown armor.

"Care to know what my crew plans to do? What your job entails?" Cambria asked.

"Don't matter much either way, I've done it all. And twice if it was fun the first go 'round." Dalton replied with a grin.

"Alright then. Order whatever you want and when you are done here, just head outside. I Captain the "Outer Heaven" and her crew," Cambria replied softly. "I'll tell the barkeep to put it on my tab." she added, standing slowly and noticing Dalton's eyes shift from her own to her perky breasts.

"Will do Captain," Dalton replied as she smiled a bit and turned to walk away. "Now there goes a real damn woman right there Whiskey. She let me flirt with her, looks good as hell and even bought the booze. This could be love." Dalton said in a low voice as he watched her ass bounce slightly, making her way back to be seated at the bar.

Whiskey barked loudly, gaining the attention of Dalton.

"Bullshit. I done laid claim to her, find your own." he added, looking into the sad eyes of his lust filled pooch.

"What'd he say?" Tank asked as Skulls looked on.

"He's in." Cambria replied, motioning for another shot of Paulie's finest.

"Nice. So he knows we plan to smuggle?" Tank asked.

"Nope." she replied.

"Well he at least knows we plan to work in The Drifts, right?" Tank asked.

"Nope." Cambria replied.

"Well what in the hell did you tell him?" Tank asked in disbelief. "Nothing, I just bought him a drink." Cambria said, glancing back at Dalton who seemed to be in a deep discussion with his loyal dog. She saw a playful charm about him, almost child-like. She also knew seconds after meeting him that when it was on the line he was the type that would get things done. Exactly what their crew needed. She turned her attention to the window behind the bar, watching the rain fall elegantly onto the ships outside, including her own. The adventure of the Outer Heaven was about to begin, and though she had no idea where smuggling would take them, she looked forward to every moment of it.

"So I don't understand why we are coming back here if I pulled a gun on two of Kraid's most trusted?" Adam asked as Sasha piloted the shuttle down onto the snowy surface of the Benzan home world.

"Benzans have disagreements all the time, you are still one of us and..." Sasha said, catching sight of bodies laying all over the ground and partially covered in snow.

Adam saw her grief instantly, taking over the controls as Sasha began to cry loudly. These were her people, and from the looks of it most had been slain by the Hunters. The shuttle touched down onto the crisp snow of a nearby field as Sasha hurried to the exit of the ship.

"Wait." Adam said, unable to stop her from making her way outside. He slowly exited to see Sasha standing there, crying as the snow fell from above. Hundreds of bodies lay slain on the ground; nothing short of a massacre.

Adam walked up behind Sasha slowly, placing his climate jacket onto her and wrapping both arms around her waist tightly.

"Let's resupply, refuel and get out of here. I'll take care of everything, you need to get back on the shuttle. No need to see this." Adam said.

As his words hit the cold of wide open air, Adam and Sasha both caught glance of someone opening the lodge door, prompting Sasha to begin running into its direction.

Adam had started to ask her to wait, but instead pulled his sidearm and sprinted behind her; knowing full well she wouldn't stop either way. It was a woman in the doorway of the lodge, a Benzan woman.

"It's Sasha and Adam!" the woman said loudly.

The Benzans inside, which included the women, children and five heavily armed escorts, lowered their weapons as Sasha and Adam entered slowly.

"What happened? Where is Kraid?" Sasha asked as Adam tried to catch his breath, not used to the cold planet's air. A few of the Benzan women began crying as one of the escorts shook his head, letting Sasha know Kraid had been slain by the Hunters. It took several moments to sink in. Her former lover and the leader of her people was dead. A vast majority of her people lay slain in the bloody fields of snow right outside and it was only a matter of time before the Hunters returned.

"We need to go. Now. The Hunters will send a return party to scout the planet, and if we are here they will end us." Sasha said, trying to appear calm.

"Go where? We have nowhere left to run." one of the soldiers replied, feeling bad for his slain brothers while a bit lucky that Kraid had selected him as one of the few to protect their women and children.

"There is something. I need the escorts to come with me, the rest of you pack any kind of supplies you can. Weapons, food and anything vital to survival," Sasha said, the survivors taking a moment before dispersing to collect any needed supplies. "Come." Sasha said as Adam and the five Benzan soldiers followed quickly behind.

Their shuttle had flown for less than ten minutes when Sasha descended it back onto the frozen tundra of their homeworld. "It's here. Something Kraid had been working on with a few of his closest," Sasha said. "In case of an emergency, and I think this qualifies." she added.

As they all exited the shuttle slowly, Sasha led them

into what looked like a large cavern. The first thing that stood out to everyone was the cavern had an open view to the snow filled sky above. Then, their attention quickly shifted to the reason Sasha had brought them here. A ship. A very large ship, which seemed to be outfitted with capable weapons. It was a pale shade of black, the words *North Star* painted onto the front.

"Kraid said it would hold a few hundred people if need be. Its navigational unit has information on another existing Benzan colony," Sasha said, turning to the group. "But it's a travel into uncharted space. A long trip from what little Kraid spoke of it." she added.

"Why have we not heard of this before?" one of the soldiers asked of the large ship.

"Because he planned to leave you, as well as most of the other Benzans behind in the event of emergency. It's the reason he and I parted ways," Sasha said, glancing at Adam for a moment. "I could not be with a man who thought so little of our people. Every single one of you is important to me, and you will be important to the Captain of the North Star. Adam Michaels." she added.

"Captain?" Adam asked, stunned.

"Yes. You are the only surviving Benzan that bears a golden weapon, signifying Captain. And if any of you take issue with the fact, let him speak now and remain behind to fight the Hunters on his own." Sasha said, turning to the soldiers.

"No. We have no issue with Adam as the ship's Captain." one of the soldiers said, all five showing a loyal face to the smuggler.

As the group of soldiers boarded the Benzan shuttle to return to the survivors, Adam and Sasha stayed behind to prep the ship; as well as make love in the most romantic fashion imaginable. Their souls became one for the next several hours aboard a ship that soon would embark on its quest to find other Benzans.

A perilous quest, but one that not only had to be taken

in order for their kind to survive, but one that both Adam and Sasha looked forward to. They would begin a life together without a war pulling them down or the thoughts of ex-lovers hindering them. Completely free to love and live their lives. Adam held Sasha softly in his arms as the Benzan shuttle arrived once more, full of survivors on its first of many trips to come; the lovers helping the surviving Benzan women and children aboard their new home. At least their new home for a long time to come. They would all escape the clutches of a war torn solar system...though they would soon fall into the clutches of yet another. One much more brutal.

"Speak to me of your failures! Who is this you dare bring before your queen?" Victoria shouted as Vladris and Sarah Blaine approached with purpose.

"Your successor." Vladris replied sharply, pulling his blade with speed and slashing upward; Victoria's severed head rolling onto the stone floor of the throne room. Victoria's two stationed guards rushed to her aid, seconds later joining her in the afterlife as the blade of Vladris bit sharply into the core of their flesh.

His unmatched skill with a blade would soon enough be put to the test by Roman Raines. However, there would be no test today. Vladris knew as well as every Hunter in the palace that he was the elite of all present.

"My queen," Vladris said, kneeling as Sarah Blaine slowly sat down in the throne chair, her skin having quickly flushed to little pigment as the Hunter venom was doing its job. She was as beautiful as ever, even if undead. "I will protect you with my life from this moment forward." Vladris added.

"Good. Rise warrior, we have work to do. Together." Sarah said, her voice having changed drastically from serene to unnerving.

As Vladris walked through the palace, he did so with

resolve. He knew that Sarah Blaine would be a strong queen. Someone finally worthy of his unwavering loyalty. Entering the living area of the Hunters, dozens of them catching sight of him, Vladris threw Victoria's severed head to their feet. "Let any of you who would stand against me do so now," Vladris said, drawing his still pulsating sword, a crimson fluid running down the edge of it. "We have a new queen. A much stronger queen. Either you agree to bow before her, or you stand against me and we settle the matter right now, in true Hunter fashion." he added, daring any of them who were brave enough.

Several minutes later he entered the throne room once more, nearly fifty Hunters behind him as they all knelt to their new queen. "The Hunters before you are the very strongest. We are loyal to you my queen. The others will follow without question." Vladris said.

"Rise warriors. For now we begin our rise to power." Sarah said calmly, bringing a grimacing smile to the face of Vladris and the rest of the elites, including Kraid.

The union of Legion and Theron forces had pushed General Ortega's soldiers to their breaking point. Tameca City was nothing more than smoldering wastelands as Lord Riven forced his army forward, his attempt to end the assault against their regime. He was nearly successful and knew it. He felt it in his bones as they had formed a massive group outside of the large warehouse that General Ortega had secured the wounded refugees. Lord Riven's feeling of victory instantly turned to nothing more than the black smoke that rose into a sky full of Gali war ships. Help had arrived for what few Colonial soldiers that remained. And the Gali had spared no expense, throwing every able bodied soldier into their effort as the sky quickly blackened out, ships blocking every speck of sunlight and landing with haste.

"Sir, help has arrived!" Lieutenant Scott yelled loudly,

prompting General Ortega to join the refugees as everyone looked through the dingy glass windows and places where windows once sat.

The Theron began pounding their weapons into the sky, though their best effort did little to slow the Gali as ships began landing, full of troops with hearts full of payback. They too had seen the horrific video feeds broadcast from Tameca and arrived bearing no offer of quarters. They were there to execute every single person involved with the Legion, Theron descent or otherwise.

As the young man who had listened to General Ortega stepped up to a small window of his own, he saw them. The huge Husk warriors exiting their shuttles by the hundreds, firing chain style machine guns as they cut through the Theron soldiers; exposing them for the cowards they were. General Ortega was given his first communication since being left on Tameca's surface. Paul Lassiter was dead and Sarah Blaine was missing. Effectively leaving Ortega in charge as the ranking Colonial officer.

"Sir, we have captured the Legion's leader." Lieutenant Scott said following several hours of widespread gunfire throughout Tameca city. Ortega nodded, though his thoughts remained with Adam Michaels. General Ortega knew in his heart that Adam had killed Lassiter and taken Sarah Blaine. Soon enough the search for Adam Michaels would begin. However, the battle at hand was his first priority. Ortega glanced around the room, looking into the faces of the refugees who had lost so much. Family, homes and lives. They had been crushed.

"Sir, where should we take him for processing?" Lieutenant Scott asked as two Colonial soldiers held Lord Riven in restraints. General Ortega looked into the eyes of the soulless man, the person directly responsible for such a massacre.

Colonial code would call for a trial by jury, a lengthy legal fight to convict a person who had been responsible for such war crimes. But Colonial code was of little concern to General Ortega, who would soon become commander. As everyone in the room looked on, General Ortega drew his sidearm and fired a single shot, hitting Riven between the eyes and removing a great portion of the back of his skull in the process. "The shallowest grave you can find." Ortega replied, his soldiers dragging the corpse outside. It was soon strung up for all to see, a reminder to everyone that justice had prevailed and Tameca was, and would always be, a world where free people lived.

And that's how the story of the original Gunship crew would end. At least a story of how their time spent together would end. For each of them it was just the beginning. Fate had placed them onto their own paths to destiny. Roman had become immortal, and his agenda now included ending as many Hunters as possible. Adam chose the love of Sasha, and together they would begin a journey of their own. One that would introduce them to something horrific and devastating. Sarah took her place as the rightful queen of the undead, soon to launch a full scale war against every mortal being in the Skyla System. And Dalton found another job. One that included a visually breathtaking Captain and free drinks. It would present him and his faithful pooch with plenty of opportunities to tell the stories of his life so far. Including his favorite, the one where Roman was a fucking Hunter.

Geartown

"Never cry over spilt milk. It could have been whiskey." - Dalton James

And there he sat. Dalton James. A veteran of several wars and several bars, both the drinking and incarceration type. He wore a heavy brown duster as testament, if nothing else, to his storied life up until this point.

He was a smuggler, and moving illegal merchandise through space while skirting the authorities had both an upside and a downside.

For the past decade he had worked for his good friend and former military comrade Adam Michaels.

After the first Glimmerian War they decided that no man in political position would ever force them to live out another day, choosing instead, to fetch a ship and begin the black market work of great risk and great reward.

Anything they could do to earn a living, they did it. Every cargo hold of illegal merchandise moved, led to connections on the wrong side of the law. And with each underhanded deal they pulled off, their reputation grew. By the time the older model Gunship, one that the Glimmerian government leaned heavily on during the first war, was fully staffed with crew; they had become notorious.

Such notoriety led to a job offer from the Hunter Clan, a sadistic group of Vampires who were both wanted and feared. Offering a huge payday, Captain Adam Michaels took the job, double-crossing the Hunters a short time later. He had fallen in love with his cargo, Sarah Blaine. And the direction his heart led him, also led the crew through violent times.

Eventually they went their separate ways. Various reasons, of course, but Dalton's reasoning was simple. He was sick of running from the undead. A near death experience has a way of making a man feel alive, even if it includes bullets flying into his direction. But so many near death experiences, sometimes on a daily basis, has a way of wearing down even the best of men.

Dalton had reached the point of wanting something more. A peaceful calm, if nothing else. And so he left the Gunship, and her crew, setting off onto his own path in search of his own destiny.

A destiny that was sure to include his running mate Whiskey. The four legged bucket of fleas was Dalton's best friend. Whiskey was a good ear to talk to, had a stomach for alcohol and even a way with the ladies. They wore matching brown coats, and together would take on the Skyla System, one shot of hard liquor at a time.

The former soldier turned smuggler quickly found himself hired by Cambria Sims, Captain of the Outer Heaven. She was brilliantly beautiful from head to toe, shocking blue hair and cream white complexion only further accenting her perfectly sculpted curves.

She had offered him a paycheck, even paid for both Dalton and Whiskey to get fitted for custom brown coats, rather than the bargain rack faux leather that currently covered their backs.

In exchange, Dalton would bring experience to a crew of

faces that was fresh to the black market world of smuggling. Though none of that mattered to him.

All that mattered was the fact that they would no longer be running from the undead. Dalton had made damn sure of it, or at least he had thought so up until the moment his eyes caught sight of a poster that plunged into his heart like a chilled dagger.

The Outer Heaven had landed in the Drifts. A very primitive, yet extremely elegant string of planets on the fringe of uncharted space. A mixture of Victorian influence and steam powered engineering, its citizens had shunned the modern lifestyle of computers and thrust engines for wind-born airships and a luxurious, yet simplistic, style of living.

Dalton had considered it a paid vacation of sorts, going to stay a while in a much calmer environment while throwing a few brews back. But all of that changed as he slowly read the header of a poster hanging on the wall of the airship transport terminal. Do not provoke the undead.

Afraid to ask, Dalton simply sat there. Stunned. As they waited for a transport from the terminal to Geartown, he continued to stare at the poster which had shattered everything he thought he knew about their upcoming trip.

The terminal was the one centralized location on the planet, and each Drift planet had one. Simply put, you landed your ship here and then boarded an airship. Hundreds of airships came through daily, each one stopping in even the most remote locations.

Some of the destinations were large cities, Victorian styled skyscrapers peaking to the heavens with their clockwork shaped tops and brass accented artwork. Others consisted of dusty towns populated by colorful characters who had a curiously playful charm about them.

"Is he OK?" Tank asked.

His God given name was Greg Shelling, but was soon handed the name Tank based on his unbelievable size. A bit taller than anyone currently sitting in the transport station, Tank was packed out in terms of muscular composition. His skin resembled a thin coat of dark paint as it stretched across his physique, barely able to contain the bulging muscles that were easily seen as he wore a solid green shirt with short sleeves.

Skulls simply shook his head.

Trevor Lagrange by birth, Skulls earned his name branding through the odd hobby he took so seriously. Collecting teeth, bones and severed fingers from the dead. Easy enough for him, because when the Salvation model sniper rifle that currently hung down by his side was in hand, people had a tendency of dying.

Skulls resembled an undertaker at first glance. That is until you got close enough to see the solider in him, the wrinkles on his face merely a map of battles seen and horrors lived; at which point you wished he were merely an undertaker.

His rifle was a very unpopular model, the bolt action considered outdated. But Skulls preferred the weapon because it had pinpoint accuracy when looking through the large telescopic lens mounted on top. It was a very elegant weapon in his mind, and a well respected rifle among snipers.

His stringy hair flowed from beneath a dark top hat, mushrooming out a bit in the back and falling wildly down between his shoulders. Loose-hanging black leather clothes covered the body of such a tall and thinly boned man. And for such a strange Human, vanity was important, regularly slicking his black pants with grease to create such an obvious luster.

"Dalton. Are you crying?" Cambria asked with shock.

Dalton didn't reply, though his eyes remained crisped with tears. He simply continued his stare onto the poster warning those entering the Drifts of the undead. Zombies you could call them, though citizens knew them as Drifters.

"It's alright. They aren't a common sight, more like cattle if nothing else. They are mindless and without intention." Cambria said in an attempt to calm Dalton a bit.

"They're undead," he replied, fighting back tears of rage as he bit into his lower lip. "I'm tired of the undead. So fucking tired of people that should be taking a dirt nap trying to put my ass six feet under." he grumbled.

Whiskey gave a long and deeply pitched whine. Even the charismatic dog had seen his share of immortals.

"Best bite your lip because our ride is here." Tank said with a bit of chuckling mixed in as he stood up and began watching a large airship swoop down to them.

It was the typical transport airship, nothing more than a large and elongated hot air balloon; cabin area below constructed of metal with luxurious wooden trim.

Dalton gave a look of ill intent as he also stood to his feet, his stomach turning into knots as he glanced one last time at the poster warning of Drifters.

Everything about the Drifts came across to him as being outdated. Even the very poster which currently had his attention, reminded him of an old military poster. Bold words at the top with a poorly colored sketch below.

Both Skulls and Cambria slowly stood, the Captain putting her arm around the experienced smuggler for a moment.

She was from the Drifts, and to her, Drifters were just a

common thing. A background detail, like snakes in a sand-filled desert or deer in woodlands. Even so, she tried to empathize with Dalton.

"We'll be fine. Trust me." she said with a poetic tone, her undefinable beauty helping to comfort Dalton.

As the airship slowly elevated back into the sky, heavier by a couple dozen passengers, Dalton found himself staring out of the thickened glass windows surrounding them and wondering exactly what he had signed up for.

He had known about the Drifts for most of his life, and honestly, up until now, hadn't cared about them one way or the other. In his mind, anyone who shunned technology deserved to live in huts made of dirt and grass. He had just thought them to be basic and written them off.

The impression he had gotten since arriving was different. Much different. Sure, they lived without the modern technology that the rest of the Skyla System coveted. But they did it in a very artistic way. Even the very balloon they traveled in now, was a helium filled canvas of linen. The fabric was almost a portrait of style, dark browns accented with gold flakes. And then it was pulled together and held into place by brass links of chain. As it wrapped around the balloon, the links locked together with a large brass medallion; a lion's head designed and pressed into the coin-style lock.

They were headed for Geartown and from what Dalton could gather, it was full of opportunities for a young smuggling crew. All kinds of people who had goods to move off world, and were willing to pay a smuggling fee in order to avoid having their goods so heavily taxed by local government.

With his frustration of the walking dead soon turning to anger, Dalton sat in the wooden booth-style seat and continued to look out across the clouds and thriving green pastures below. He quietly cursed the Drifts and their damn regulations on modernized weaponry.

Twenty seven. That's the number of capable weapons he had to leave back on the Outer Heaven. If a shotgun fired too wide of a spread, it was against regulations. A digital counter on the side of a battle rifle, against regulations. Needless to say his grenades had been left behind as well, adding to an already pissed off demeanor.

He carried only two weapons at the moment, which was as close to naked in front of clothed women as he had been in a very long time. At least in public. A Magnum style revolver that held six rounds inside of a rolling chamber and would damn near cut a man in half, as well as a large buoy blade strapped to his leg that would complete the cut if his revolver failed.

"I wouldn't sweat it. Hell, I hear they hunt Drifters down here like big game man. We may throw a few beers back and go on the hunt ourselves." Tank said in a low voice.

"I 'aint huntin' shit," Dalton said loudly, gaining the attention of every passenger aboard the airship. "Anything comes at me and can't recite the alphabet is getting shot up." he added, turning for a moment to glance across the isle.

"The fuck you lookin' at?" Dalton asked belligerently as an older man with literate glasses and a finely pressed suit looked on.

"Calm down Dalton, you're scaring people." Cambria said, quickly sitting beside him.

Dalton wanted so badly to mouth off in response, but after catching sight of her beautiful face he started to realize that his soul began to ameliorate every single time she was near. So calm down he did. For the next several hours Dalton was silent, staring out of the window by his seat as the airship coasted passionately through the clouds.

As they made their approach, Dalton's first reaction was one of curious suspicion. When he had first met Cambria Sims, she stood out. Her loudly colored hair and choice of clothing style was refreshing, but out of place. Looking across the streets of Geartown as the airship landed softly, Dalton realized that he and Whiskey would now be the ones out of place. Every citizen he caught sight of looked unique. Women with blue, watermelon green and even neon purple hair walking abroad. Outfitted in corsets and carrying small umbrellas that were stitched of glamor.

It 'aint even fucking raining. Dalton thought as he watched the women, all who seemed overwhelmingly attractive to him, twirling their parasols a bit as they walked in Victorian-style dresses. The men he caught sight of, appeared to be the opposite for the most part. Tophats, aviator style caps of leather and even a few gas style masks. Most wore either Victorian influenced shirts filled with ruffle or sharp suits, complete with a pinstriped vest.

He knew deep down he was about to step off of the airship and into a world he knew nothing about. Usually comfortable in his brown coat, this was the first time he began to feel that he would have to shell inside of it a bit; do his best just to try and fit in.

And he felt sorry for Whiskey as well, having to endure the same type of out of place awkwardness. That is until he glanced down at his flea-bitten friend only to discover Whiskey wearing a pair of oversized goggles. Tank and Skulls had placed them on the pooch, and the goggles seemed to have the perfect fit as Whiskey stared back at Dalton. Sad eyes now protected by clear lenses and rounded brass as he stood a bit more firmly, proud of both his brown coat and his Victorian specs.

"What the?" Dalton managed to mutter as everyone stood to their feet ready to exit the airship.

"It's showtime." Cambria said playfully as she cast a warm smile into Dalton's direction.

"You call it showtime, I prefer go time." he replied in a low voice, glancing down to make sure his revolver was still holstered before breathing deeply and following the crowd off of the airship.

Geartown wasn't nearly as large as Dalton had envisioned. It was in fact...a town, and a small one at that. The fact that so many people wanted goods smuggled off world held true. It's just that a majority of the citizens in and around Geartown favored the around part. Houses scattered throughout the croplands and wooded terrain that surrounded such a Victorian-style town. Still, Geartown had everything it needed; including a watering hole for those who preferred adult drinks.

"Trading Post?" Dalton asked.

"Yep. That's the name of Geartown's busiest building. Serves as a general store, mail dispatch, surplus shop and saloon." Cambria replied.

"I've never heard of a mail dispatch and saloon in the same building." Tank added as the group walked from the recently landed airship into the heart of Geartown.

They continued to skim the town with their eyes, each wrapping their thoughts around the same idea. If it weren't for the beauty, the damn near artistic perfection of the town around them, it would otherwise be a dusty town on the edge of nowhere. But the Victorian influence around them was obvious, as the gold flaked trim and brass accents of daily life in Geartown were simply marvelous to anyone who visited.

"At this point who gives a damn. She's buying and I'm drinking, don't really matter what sign is hanging from the front door." Dalton replied, a grin of long-overdue plastered onto his face.

"Well said." Skulls added, holding his bolt action rifle behind his neck.

Tank and Skulls broke from the group, heading into the direction of Geartown's finest, not to mention, only hotel; The Stage Inn. Meanwhile, Cambria, Dalton and a slightly promiscuous Whiskey made their way to the Trading Post. Dalton quick to notice that Whiskey was walking with a bit more strut.

Must be the goggles. Dalton thought as the three entered the large building of wooden shingles and thick brown logs.

Dalton just wanted to fit in, maybe slip into the building unnoticed and hang out until they found a job and got their asses back into the familiar territory of space.

However, as the three entered through a heavily creaking door, nearly forty people suddenly turned to see who had arrived. A shroud of unnerving quiet draped across the room as only small sounds of glasses connecting with wooden tables could be heard. Maybe it was Cambria's look of angelic sexuality. Possibly Dalton's rugged look of a poverty-stricken ranch hand. Of course, there was always a dog standing close, outfitted in a thick brown coat with large brass goggles to accent the look.

But the truth was it had nothing to do with any of the above. They had recognized Cambria Sims, and knew all too well her badly ended romance with Johnny Edmonds. The same Johnny Edmonds who currently sat at the bar looking into her tantalizing eyes, and the same Johnny Edmonds who had earned his nickname the hard way.

The Revolver. He was by all accounts the fastest gun in or around Geartown and everyone knew it to be the truth.

"Welcome back." Johnny said as he rose to his feet, clapping loudly in the process.

He had everyone's attention, except for Dalton, who quickly walked past him and sat down by the bar.

"Double shot of your strongest." Dalton said quietly to the barkeep as he too turned back to watch the former lovers speak.

"When you told me you were leaving Geartown to live out in the black, leaving to find a ship and crew," Johnny said as he stood close to Cambria, their eyes interlocked. "I had no idea you'd come limping back with a single buster and his homely looking bag of fleas."

"Let it go Johnny, we've been over for a long time now." Cambria said, noticing Dalton finishing the large shot of rum before standing to his feet.

She tried to motion Dalton to sit back down, but it was of no use.

"Yea Johnny. She went out and fetched her a real man. Aint' got no use for make believe cowboys anymore." Dalton said provokingly.

"Careful outlander. Best sit back down and put those lips on the rim of a glass before they get you killed." Johnny said as he continued to stare at Cambria.

"Only thing these lips are going to be on, boy, is that pretty little woman standing in front of you." Dalton said, earning a very strange look from Cambria in the process.

"Alright. You've had your chance, and now you gotta die." Johnny said as he turned slowly.

Dalton was the first to go for his revolver, barely raising it from his holster before Johnny's barrel was aiming down at him.

"Oh shit." Dalton said, stunned by the gunslinger's speed. He hadn't seen anyone that fast with a pistol. His good friend and former Captain Adam Michaels maybe, but even that was a stretch.

"Law says I'm within my right to cut you down right here where you stand." Johnny said as Dalton felt a sober panic flow through his rum tainted blood. "But I'm not going to, I like your demeanor outlander." Johnny added, pulling his pistol down, holstering it once more with blazing speed and slapping Dalton on the arm a bit.

"Damn straight you're not." Tank said, hoisting his large shotgun up into the direction of Johnny as he and Skulls entered the building.

Immediately, fourteen men stood to their feet, each pulling a sidearm and taking aim on Tank. Skulls was quick to pull his rifle as well, determined to take a few with him if need be. Reluctant to do so, Dalton finally pulled his revolver and held it to the face of Johnny.

"Everyone!" Cambria shouted. "Calm down! We just came in for a drink and a little down time for the evening." she added. "Johnny, call them off!" she said, her voice of soothing persuasion doing the trick.

"Do what she says boys." Johnny said, the large group of men slowly putting revolvers back into their side mounted holsters. Johnny then turned back to Dalton.

"I let you live because you are new here, won't be extending the courtesy twice."

Both Tank and Skulls kept their weapons raised as Johnny and his group slowly left.

"Gotta go anyway beautiful, taking a Drifter hunting party out tonight." Johnny said with a smile before turning to exit the large room.

"Well that was fun." Dalton said as he slowly sat back down and ordered another stout shot of rum.

"Point of interest," Tank said as he slowly sat down. "The next time someone has that many armed friends, it would be helpful to know BEFORE I draw down on him." he added with emotion.

"Sorry, it all happened so fast." Cambria said with apology.

"Don't sweat it baby, I still love you." Dalton added as he slammed the shotglass down and gritted his teeth from the burn.

"Speaking of which," Cambria said as she slapped Dalton across the top portion of his arm. "What is this about your lips being on me?" she asked.

"Did I say that? I never said that?" Dalton replied in an attempt to back out of his ill chosen words. "Stay out of it!" he added angrily as Whiskey barked loudly as if to turns state's evidence on him.

"Been a long time since we've seen anyone stand up to The Revolver." a woman with soft blonde hair said as she slowly approached Dalton, pink accents glimmering across her soothing flow of locks.

"Mind if I buy you a drink?" she asked, Dalton turning to his crew with a hard look before turning back to accept her offer.

"Well, um, I gotta go find some more ammunition anyway." Tank said, standing to his feet slowly.

"And I should look into finding us work." Cambria said, slowly standing to her feet as well. Her lushly curved bottom reason enough for Whiskey to stand quickly, though his most important part was already standing to attention, watching her every move through the thick of his goggles.

As they waited for Skulls to follow suit, the sniper sat there, skimming the interior of the building. Cambria cleared her throat slightly as a suggestive hint, one that never struck home with the skilled killer. Shortly after, his chair was kicked hard by Tank, who motioned him away with a tilt of the head.

Skulls looked at Dalton for a moment and shrugged before standing and following the group.

About fucking time ya squatter. Dalton thought, before turning to the blonde with a manufactured smile painted onto his face. "My name's Selina, and you are?" she asked playfully.

In most cases a name meant something, stood for beliefs or heritage. Not to Dalton. In his mind a name was merely words strung together and tied snugly around curves and parts capable of sexual loving. Like a wool blanket. And just like a wool blanket, when it got wet it got clingy.

"I'm Dalton. Dalton James." he said with a grin on one side of his face, though he had indeed contemplated using an alias.

As Cambria and group exited the Trading Post, once again the Geartown normal seemed anything but to both Tank and Skulls. Glancing through the busy street of such a small town, Skulls noticed a majority of the townfolk glancing back.

"What's that about?" Tank asked as he glanced up into the air, a tall wooden tower standing above the entrance to Geartown.

"Warning system of sorts," Cambria said after a quick glance, her explanation falling from such tender lips.

"If you hear the bell on that tower ring, means a Drifter is nearby. If you are unarmed they ask you to get indoors as a precaution while the sniper up there scopes and shoots." she added.

Skulls glanced at that moment, uninterested up until the word sniper was uttered. He was damn good with a scope and knew it. Rightfully so, he was thinking of the art of sniping most times and when another skilled shooter was nearby, Skulls found himself feeling almost competitive.

"Is he any good?" Skulls asked.

"Hasn't been a Drifter reach town before," Cambria said softly. "But I'd say you're a bit better with a rifle." she added to calm the artifact of death collector.

"And here I was trying to calm Dalton down. How bad are these Drifters?" Tank asked.

"They wander in close to town sometimes, but you were right to calm him. They are mindless and roam the badlands mostly." Cambria responded.

"Are you crying?" Selina asked as Dalton indeed teared up a bit, quickly blaming it on the house liquor through hand motions.

"It's just that Roman was a good friend and now he's a Hunter. One of the walking dead and it's a hard pill to swallow." Dalton finally replied.

Well this Roman sounds like a good enough guy. But the way you beat him in a blade fight and turned the Hunters away single-handed, that's amazing." Selina remarked.

"Thanks babe. It wasn't easy. All I had was a blade and a six-shot revolver, but eventually I sent about twenty of the bastards to the grave or running. Got bored with it all to tell you the truth, and that's when I found myself here." Dalton said, lying without reserve.

"In fact, I drew slow on Johnny on purpose. I wanted to see his hand to holster motion, so the next time we meet

I'll be well prepared." Dalton said, further piling onto the heap of cattle shit verbiage.

"That's amazing." Selina said as she wrapped both of her near glowing arms around the waist of the brown coat wearing weaver of lies.

And the day continued, falling slowing into the clutches of night as a fully starred sky draped above Geartown.

The Trading Post continued to see newcomers to its establishment as the daily airships and roar of a steam powered train brought more outlanders to Geartown. For such a small town, it was booming around the clock with brand new faces. Some in search of smuggling work, just as Cambria and her crew were. Others arriving for the thrill of the hunt, or even just to visit such a beautifully crafted society of simplistic living.

You could always pick the outlanders from a crowd as they stopped to see what the loud noise of the incoming train actually was. Geartown citizens had grown so used to the iron passenger train screeching into the heart of town that they continued with their routine without pause. For everyone else, the commanding sound of iron sliding recklessly on steel rails was piercing.

The train came complete with a shotgun toting soldier in the front compartment and a heavily armed rear platform. A gatling style mini-gun was mounted to the rear with four soldiers who stood heavily armed. The train, and others like it, made their way between Geartown and several other towns. Each separated by The Badlands.

The rolling hills of high grass and thick trees had earned its name for a reason. Drifters roamed, sometimes in groups of four or five through The Badlands, not to mention criminals. Gangs led by Johnny Edmonds and his type, and sometimes they felt the need to take a train by force; robbing its passengers, while stripping the steam engine of any valuable armor and weaponry.

The Royal Army, which was the military backbone of the Drifts, sometimes routed supplies through The Badlands as well. Of course they knew of outlaw activity in the area, but such an underfunded army was already stretched to its limit. And so the trains served as both a transportation system and armored supply vehicle.

A couple hours after arriving, Cambria and her group had returned to the Trading Post, sitting at the far side this time in order to afford Dalton some personal space.

"I'll never understand what he sees in women like that." Cambria said as she watched Dalton continue his conversation with Selina.

It was at that very moment that Dalton casually slid his hand down to Selina's ass, prompting Cambria to adopt a look of disgust across her face.

"Well, if you don't understand, I'd be glad to explain it to you in detail." Tank said as Skulls chuckled a bit while Whiskey barked.

Even the flea-induced warrior of a four-legged variety knew the game. And though Dalton was the one about to score, Whiskey knew that when he did, it put the smuggler into a great mood. Which meant a healthy leg of finely-cooked meat and possibly even some smooth hootch. A good complimentary prize to a long night spent swimming under cheap hotel linen.

"No, that's quite alright. Spare me the details." Cambria said with sarcasm.

Her look of sarcasm quickly vanished, turning ghostly white as everyone inside of the Trading Post heard it. The warning tower bell rang once. Quiet fell through the building as everyone listened closely, a single shot firing from the sniper's rifle inside of the tower.

"Tessa 112." Skulls said. "Accurate but weak, they should be using better." he added.

Normally the bell would toll once more, letting the people of Geartown know that the Drifter was down and they were safe. But not this time. The bell began to ring continuously as several shots rang out from both the sniper's rifle and a shotgun held by the tower's other stationed soldier.

Panic of the unknown quickly set in as everyone inside of the Trading Post stood up and began running to the door in search of answers. And answers they got, watching a group of Drifters climb the wooden tower while a larger and more coordinated group made its way into town.

Nearly two hundred of them total. Some of the citizens and outlanders began firing their weapons into the crowd of Drifters, while most simply fled as quickly as possible, sprinting for any building that was still located on the side of town the Drifters had yet to reach.

As the creaking of wood led to the large warning tower falling quickly to the ground below, Dalton grabbed Selina's arm.

"Stay here!" he said with compassion. "Everyone, stay here!" he yelled, catching the attention of his crew and a handful of citizens who were ready to flee.

"Close those goddamn doors! Now! Get 'em locked up and start piling anything in front of the windows you can!" Dalton yelled, knowing deep down if there was one place in town designed to keep people out, it was the Trading Post.

It didn't matter the planet, the town or the situation. Through his years of experience, Dalton had learned that society went out of its way to protect both money and hooch, putting them smack dab in the best location for survival.

"Hate the fucking undead." Dalton mumbled as he shoved a large table closer to the door.

"He's right," Cambria replied. "This is the one building in town with all of the valuables. Thicker walls, doors and very few points of entry." she added, talking loudly as screams accompanied gunshots outside.

"Nothing to worry about my rosy red ass!" Dalton added with anger, upset over another showdown with those who knew life after death.

As the majority of those few lucky citizens inside began pulling the furniture to the door, doing their absolute best to blockade the entrance, a heavy knocking came.

"Help me...please!" a man cried out, continuing to relentlessly beat his fist on the door.

"Go on! Get! Gonna bring them 'sumbitches over here in hordes!" Dalton responded with anger.

"Please, I have a child!" the man replied.

"Ah shit." Dalton mumbled as he opened the door just slightly, catching sight of the man holding an infant.

"Move this clutter out of the way!" Dalton yelled to those inside as he pulled his revolver to the ready.

Tank joined him at the door, shotgun in hand as they both waited for the citizens to once again move the heavy furniture. Dalton expected to see the undead as the door opened once again. He had studied the poster at the transport station, even heard the bell tower ringing.

But as the door opened to allow the man and his child a safe place to hide, Dalton's arm dropped down to his side; still holding the revolver in hand.

"Oh my God." he managed to push from his lungs as Whiskey stood at his feet, both of them witness to hundreds of Drifters killing citizens in the streets. Mutilating their bodies, climbing the exterior walls of buildings in order to reach windows and many of them pulled to the light that now shined outside through the open Trading Post door.

As a large pack began sprinting to the open door with unnatural speed, Dalton shakily pulled his revolver to the ready. Firing all six shots in succession, five Drifters fell to their deaths. Five headshots and one miss, not bad work in the pitch black of night while under the influence of alcohol.

Two Drifters remained as they continued their sprint of immortal fury. Dalton had nearly made it back inside when they were on him, infected teeth prepared to dig into his duster smothered flesh.

The first Drifter quickly became nothing more than dead flesh as Tank fired his shotgun, the Zombie's head dissipating into a fine red mist. The last remaining Drifter of the group lunged, though its entire body was nearly cut in half by a single shell fired by Skulls. The sniper had mounted his bolt-action Salvation rifle to a table at the far end of the Trading Post, using its front end tripod to balance the heavy weapon.

The gunshots had done away with the small pack, but gained the attention of every remaining Drifter; at least two hundred turning to sprint into the direction of the Trading Post as more of the undead arrived to Geartown. Yet Dalton stood for a moment, simply in shock at how many Zombies were closing in on them.

"Better," Dalton said, still holding his empty revolver. "Better be getting inside and putting as much between us and them as possible." he added calmly, shock having numbed his usual panic.

As Dalton staggered back inside, Tank quickly secured

the door and began helping the citizens pull the heaviest furniture back in an attempt to barricade themselves in. Dalton staggered to the bar, empty revolver in hand and hanging by his side.

"Are you alright?" Cambria asked.

Usually full of life and sarcasm, Dalton simply sat on a bar stool, grabbing a bottle of whiskey without even a hint of reply.

"Dalton. Are you alright?" Cambria asked again, a bit more firmly as she sat down beside him on a stool of her own.

"Just fine." he replied calmly.

Cambria looked down at Whiskey long enough for the pooch to respond with a concerned bark, wet whiskers flaring wildly.

"Dalton. I need you to be alright. We all do. You are the only one here with enough military experience to see us through this." Cambria said.

"We're going to die." Dalton replied in a calm voice, throwing back a shot of the hellacious brown hootch.

"Hey," Cambria said, moving a bit closer while lowering her voice. "I need you to be positive." she added.

"Oh I am," Dalton said as he took another shot. Screams of the dead began to blare throughout the Trading Post as dozens of Drifters beat and clawed the wooden door of the large building. "I'm positive we are going to die." Dalton added.

Cambria stood up slowly, taken back by the submissive attitude of such a seasoned warrior. Maybe it was meant for them to die, no hope of surviving to speak of. Still, she knew someone had to take charge of the situation. At least give everyone the faint possibility of hope.

"Talk to Dalton. See if you can get his head back into the game." Cambria said to Tank in a low voice as the dead continued their quest to find a way indoors.

Cambria then turned her attention to Skulls, who's eye remained pressed to the telescopic lens of his rifle's scope.

"Good job staying focused Trevor. Just keep your eye on that door, you are literally our last line of defense if something goes wrong." Cambria said softly.

Though Skulls acknowledged her statement, his eye remained on the scope. A few others stood near the door, their pistols at the ready. But even Skulls knew they would delay the Zombies, at best, if they somehow got inside.

"What are we supposed to do?" Selina asked loudly, her words frantic as the noisy dead continued their job of trying to rip through the wood. Cambria turned to answer her, though it was a question in the minds of all sixteen surviving citizens.

"I...I don't..." Cambria began to reply, sharply cut off by Dalton James.

"We need to collect as much damn firepower as we can find. Guns, ammunition and if it comes down to it we can even make a few Molotov Cocktails," he said, motioning to the large collection of man drink inside of the Trading Post. "Need to put a bulk of our firepower at the door. It's the only way they can funnel in, and it's a strategic choke point in our favor." Dalton added as Cambria began to smile a bit.

She found her own mind easing as Dalton's extensive military background began to show. He was a lot of things, but the soldier of many wars is who she needed right now. They all did. And as Whiskey rose to his feet, standing proudly beside his best friend, Dalton smiled a bit.

"But the cocktails are a last resort. Got it?" he asked as everyone near him nodded. "Waste not want not." Dalton said as he glanced to the alcohol, and quickly back at Cambria who was smiling wide.

"Also be a good idea if we can get a small group to the roof of the building. Be able to assess how many there are and see if we can find a way out for ourselves." Dalton said.

"The train," Cambria replied, gaining everyone's attention. "The airships will see the Drifters long before landing, and that's sure to turn them away. But the train is heavily armed and couldn't stop in time even if it wanted to. We just need to figure out a way to get on it when it comes through." she added.

"Is there a way to the roof?" Dalton demanded to know as he clinched the shirt of the bartender in the process.

"Yes...this way," the bartender replied, the chubby man then quickly leading them to a small area in the rear of the Trading Post. "Ain't many windows to speak of, but this ladder will take you all the way up to the roof." the scraggly looking man said as he led them to a narrow red ladder that was firmly bolted to the wall.

Cambria was the first one up, her perfected backside serving as a man lure of sorts. Both Tank and Dalton nearly began fighting for the chance to climb up right behind her, Tank finally backing off after reading into the scowl on Dalton's face. As the smuggler started up next, he heard Whiskey, who was whining in a begging fashion.

"Ah shit." Dalton said with frustration, wanting so badly to enjoy the view of Cambria as he climbed but not daring to leave his faithful pooch behind.

"Don't worry, I'll enjoy the view for you." Tank said with a chuckle as he mounted the ladder to climb.

"Are you guys coming?" Cambria asked, looking down

for a moment.

"Don't I wish." Tank replied under his breath as he climbed steadily.

"Damned smart ass." Dalton said with frustration. As they climbed what seemed to be at least two stories by way of ladder, Dalton clinched Whiskey tightly, all while listening to Tank's lightly spoken sexual innuendos.

Finally making it to the top, Cambria forced open a thick door of steel and anchor bolts. The thickness of the door was such that she couldn't force it completely open, Tank placing his arm around her to help the steel loose. Dalton scowled at Tank making a play on such a beautiful woman, then turning his scowl to the true guilty party. Whiskey glared back as if to apologize, wide eyes staring through the thickened lenses of his goggles.

As Dalton and Whiskey made it topside, the brown coat booty chaser slammed the door as if to break up a romance. Tank turned to grin as Cambria remained standing, her eyes locked onto the receiving end of a set of binoculars.

Dalton approached slowly while the screams of both undead and citizens who would soon join them rang out below, though they had calmed a bit. A very good indication that few living folks remained.

"Is Skulls on the door?" Cambria asked, her eyes still skimming the area below.

"Yep, she's locked down tighter than a tick's ass." Dalton said proudly. Cambria turned to look at him, a daze upon her face.

"That's pretty good." she said, smiling a bit.

"Thanks." Dalton replied, his thick beard doing little to cover the grin beneath it.

Finally getting his own hands on the binoculars, Dalton

began to skim the surrounding area. "Has to be a way out of this 'sumbitch," he mumbled as his eyes continued to focus. "What the..." he said under his breath, locking his sight onto a fixed position.

"What is it?" Tank asked, moving closer to the roof's ledge to stand beside Dalton and his trusty sidekick.

Dalton stood there, staring out onto the group as he tried to put two and two together. "The Revolver," Dalton replied in awe. "Johnny fucking Edmonds." he added, watching the gunslinger tear his way into town by way of pistol.

Suddenly, the thick steel door sprang open, Selina quickly pulling herself to the rooftop.

"Woman, what the hell are you doing up here?" Dalton asked sternly as Tank walked with him, both approaching the bar girl slowly.

"They're in." she replied frantically.

"Huh?" Tank asked.

"They're in!" Selina yelled to confirm their worst fears.

"What the fuck do you mean they're in?" Dalton asked with emotion. His question was immediately answered by the sound of a sniper's rifle firing below.

"Oh shit." Dalton finally said as Tank began helping others up onto the roof.

"Help them up!" Cambria yelled with panic as screams flooded beneath them, accompanied by seemingly non-stop gunshots.

The barkeep was up, as well as Selina and two other men who seemed dazed at best.

"Where's the kid?" Dalton asked with no answer following.

"Where the fuck is the kid?" he asked again, this time with a commanding voice as his arm grabbed the shirt of the barkeep.

"We couldn't get anyone else to safety. There are too many." the man replied in self-disgust as he tried catching his breath. They got in through the front door, pushed it open and before we knew what was going on, they had flooded the place and separated us in the process."

"Fucking undead." Dalton mumbled as he checked the rolling chamber of his capable revolver, reloading it as quickly as he could.

"Dalton, what the hell do you think you are doing?" Cambria asked.

"That kid is down there surrounded by a horde of these non-hygienic fucks." he replied as he headed to the steel trapdoor. "Might be other people down there trapped, we don't know."

"What about Skulls?" Tank asked.

"Skulls is a trained killer with a weapon! This kid 'aint got nobody but us. I'm a lot of things that most people would be ashamed of, but I ain't a coward." Dalton replied with truth as he readied himself to go downstairs. And at that very moment, Cambria Sims began to feel an emotion she hadn't felt in a very long time. Love.

"Don't lock this door until I'm back, you got me?" Dalton asked of Tank, answered with a nod of the head.

"Cambria, don't you let him..." Dalton added, turning to his Captain. Whiskey quickly let loose a firm bark to assure his best friend that if needed, he'd protect the door himself.

"Don't worry, I won't. You just go get that kid." she replied, a smile on her face that no crew member had ever seen before.

As Dalton began to quickly leave the rooftop on his way back down, the group watched him as though he were nothing short of a hero. Something this town needed at the very moment he had arrived, even if their hero cursed the gods on his way downstairs and left a blanket of Rum stench behind.

"Stay on this door, I'm going to try and get Johnny over here to help." Cambria said, moving quickly to the roof's ledge as the walking dead continued to terrorize the streets below.

"Doesn't he want us dead?" Tank asked.

"Well, that was before all of this. Besides, Johnny is easy to forgive. Just keep your eyes on that door." Cambria answered.

"Don't worry, it's locked down tighter than a tick's ass." Tank said with a smile.

"Not really that clever now that I've heard it again." Cambria said, turning to begin finding Johnny Edmonds once more.

"Well you thought it was funny when Dalton said it." Tank replied with childish envy.

"Yea. Yea I did, didn't I?" Cambria said under her breath.

As she gazed through her binoculars in an attempt to locate and coordinate with Johnny Edmonds, she continued to think about Dalton James. Of course he wasn't the kind of guy she could see herself ever falling for. But every single time she learned something new about the hardened smuggler, it led her to believe he was a completely different man on the inside. A kind, compassionate man with an exterior that was nothing more than a mask to the world.

Besides, he did have a damn cute dog. As Cambria broke her stare for a moment to glance down, the lustful eyes of Whiskey glared back at her through thickened goggles. Well, maybe not that cute. she thought as the brown coat sporting dog licked his tongue across his lips.

Dalton knelt slowly on the floor below the ladder, the tail end of his duster laying slightly on the wood grain. A Colonial soldier is trained to always assess the situation and then react. And as Dalton James remained knelt close to the floor, he first glanced up.

It was dark, but he saw a handful of stars above that let him know his friends were indeed keeping the door open for his return. As he glanced around the back of the Trading Post, he saw a few bodies, bloody trails and expended shells.

What stood out as bothersome to Dalton was the lack of noise. Only moments before, gunshots rang out in near parade fashion. Now things had become deathly quiet and that scared the hell out of the former soldier.

Pulling his large revolver to the ready, a trickle of light refracted from the chrome of the barrel as Dalton slowly made his way to the end of a hallway which led to several smaller storage rooms and eventually the main drinking area. It was the first time Dalton had dreaded entering a bar in, well, forever.

Glancing out of the doorway momentarily, Dalton began to enter the main room when he suddenly stopped dead in his tracks. A natural reaction to the sound of steel coming to a ready as a gun stood prepared to fire. He slowly turned to see Skulls kneeling in a small room to his right, large sniper rifle at the ready.

"It's me damnit!" Dalton said under his breath.

"Get down." Skulls replied.

Taking a moment to fully register, Dalton finally knelt

to the floor. A mere second later, dedicated lead burst from the rifle of Skulls, slicing through the air and into the formerly dead flesh of a Drifter who was approaching.

"We gotta move, now." Skulls said calmly as he pulled his rifle from the ready in order to exit to the roof.

"I came down for the kid, we gotta find..." Dalton replied, cutting himself short as he spotted both the man and accompanying child, sitting snugly behind Skulls.

"Good work," Dalton said. "I'll be right back, don't let them shut me out." he added.

Skulls nodded firmly as the quiet killer led the old man and child to the safe confines of the ladder.

"Where's Dalton?" Tank asked as he helped Skulls to the roof.

"Don't know. Didn't say." Skulls replied as he ushered the older man and confused child to the rest of the survivors.

"Didn't say?" Tank asked in disbelief.

"Well fuck that, we need to at least shut the door until we know something." he added, reaching for the trapdoor.

The well muscled warrior stopped short, small hairs standing tall all over his body as the sound of a pistol readying halted him.

"You would dare pull a gun on me?" Tank asked, furious that Skulls had the guts to hold a piece in his direction.

"You scrawny little bitch, I'll beat the fucking sense back into you." Tank added, walking slowly to Skulls.

"Tank! Enough!" Cambria yelled, demanding her crew member stop at once.

"He pulled a fucking gun on me!" Tank yelled in reply.

"He's waiting for Dalton. We all are!" Cambria shouted

back.

"We'd be doing the same for you if you would have had the guts to go yourself." she added.

Tank scowled for a moment at Skulls to let him know the issue wasn't over.

"They're here, they're safe," Tank yelled as he pointed to the older man and child. "My question is where the fuck is Dalton?" he added.

"Right here, why did you miss me?" Dalton replied as he slowly climbed the ladder, gunshots ringing out behind him.

"Tank wanted to leave you down there." Cambria said in disgust.

"Is that a fact?" Dalton asked as he stood to his feet. "Well sir, no liquor for you." he added as he pulled three of the tallest bottles of rum from his coat that any of them had ever seen.

"You risked our lives for liquor? You son of a bitch!" Tank yelled, storming into Dalton's direction.

The much larger man stopped abruptly, his face merely inches from the barrel of Dalton's revolver.

"Best think this through. You got the physique and clothes to fit the part, but I'm a true soldier boy. I'm not playing commando; I am one." Dalton said with wily sarcasm, though his words held nothing short of the truth.

"Damn. I'm falling in love with this guy more and more every minute." Johnny Edmonds said as he climbed up behind the experience-worn smuggler, a couple more bottles of whiskey in hand.

"Now Skulls, you can shut the door." Dalton said, his eyes still locked onto those of Tank.

"I won't forget this. Next time maybe I got your back, maybe I don't." Tank said as Skulls secured the lock that bolted the thickened trapdoor into place.

"I could give a damn young man, just remember that kind of respect is a two-way street." Dalton replied as Whiskey growled heavily.

"Young man. That's clever." Cambria said in a low voice, intrigued by the man known as Dalton James.

"What's it like out there beyond town?" Cambria asked as Johnny approached her.

"It's bad girl. Real bad." he replied, spitting a bit of tobacco drenched saliva onto the rooftop.

"What?" he asked as she stared at him in disgust.

"Over the ledge maybe?" Cambria replied.

"Oh uh, yea." Johnny said, spitting a second wad of saliva over into the crowd of undead below.

"Best we've come up with is getting to the train somehow." Cambria said as her eyes skimmed the horizon.

"That's a bad plan. Really bad plan." the gunslinger replied.

"Huh?" Cambria replied.

"Me and the boys," he said, taking a moment to pause. "We hit the train a few hours ago. Left it sitting out there beyond the hills. At least a six or seven mile walk." Johnny said.

"You robbed the train and left our only escape vehicle out in the middle of nowhere? Really?" Cambria asked furiously.

"Well hell, I didn't know these son of a bitches was gonna get coordinated today. Hell, we was thinking about the money." Johnny replied in his own defense.

"And the boys?" Dalton asked as he approached loudly.

"Some of 'em got dusted during the robbery, the rest are laying nearby. Dead fucks killed 'em on the way in." Johnny replied.

"You know I hated your guts until about thirty minutes ago, right?" Johnny asked as he turned to Dalton.

"Yea, I figured as much. You don't have much of a rack on you though darling, so I wasn't going to lose a lot of sleep over it tonight." Dalton replied with a grin.

Cambria watched the two men converse for a moment, all while deep in thought herself. Johnny was the typical cowboy, strong on the outside and empty on the inside. Even though Dalton appeared the same at first glance, Cambria now saw through all of that.

If nothing else, the broken man used his brown coat to cover the true man inside. He had a heart, and Cambria suspected it was a big one. Her suspicions were confirmed when Dalton gave himself away with a soft glance into her direction while conversing with Johnny.

"Cambria," Skulls said as the entire group has stopped to stare her way. "You alright?" he added.

"Yes, fine," she replied as she quickly broke from her daydream. "Just trying to think of a way out of here, that's all." she added.

"Aint' no way outta here." Dalton replied as a group of Drifters had begun beating on the steel door which separated them from the small group of survivors that had found refuge on the roof.

"And even if there was, where the hell would we go?" Johnny asked. "Me and the boys came back to Geartown because we figured it would be safer. The hills are crawling with the bastards." he added.

"Well we can't stay here, that fucking door 'aint gonna hold forever!" Tank yelled as he remained sitting.

"Relax, would ya?" Dalton said as he glanced at Tank sharply for a moment. "The door will hold, it's a choke point. Hundreds of the fuckers down there, but they gotta come up the ladder single file. And 'aint one of them gonna be strong enough to bust through," Dalton said calmly. "But eventually we do gotta find a way off this roof. Gonna be needing food and such." he added.

"And you're sure we can't get to the Cliffs?" Cambria asked of Johnny.

"Trust me, if it was doable I'd be there and not here." Johnny replied.

"Well we sure in the fuck can't stay here!" Tank yelled with frustration.

"Well hop on down there and clear the way for us big boy." Dalton replied, a slight grin on his face. Tank's attempt to get up and confront the smuggler was easily stalled by a warning growl on Whiskey's part.

"Alright, guys," Cambria said loudly, trying to overpower the loud beating on the steel trapdoor by the undead. "We need to work together. Figure out an exit strategy." she added in a more convincing tone.

"Well the hideout up at Mulden Cliffs, like you said, would be the perfect spot to hold up if we could make it. Got plenty of supplies and and weapons just waiting to be dusted off. It's well hidden and only one way in. Even if the fuckers followed us up, we'd be able to thin them out once they started funneling up the narrow pass to us." Johnny said as he remained deep in thought.

"Say they was pretty thick outside of town too?" Dalton asked.

"Thick as thieves," Johnny replied. "And coming from a

thief that's saying something. They are organized now though, don't make a peck of sense. Just yesterday they were brainless and random." he added.

"Best bet would be for us to sleep on it. Get some rest and then maybe sort things out come sunup." Cambria added.

"Skulls, you take the door and I'll watch the ledge. We'll pull first watch," Dalton said. "In a few hours we'll rotate out with Johnny and Tank. Go on down the line until sunup." he added.

"Sounds like a good plan." Cambria said as she looked for a place to rest.

The roof on its own was pretty large, to her estimation it was about thirty feet wide by thirty feet long. Aside from the steel trapdoor that stood between the survivors and flesh eating dead below, there were a handful of steel pipes along with a flat surface of concrete.

They had plenty of room. The problem seemed to be the lack of supplies. No type of shelter, little food and nothing to put between themselves and the cold concrete they would be resting on.

Shortly after, the group became quiet. It was the perfect opportunity to rest, though little sleep would be had. Dead flesh pounding roughly onto the thickened steel of the roof's trapdoor.

Quiet times were always the worst for Dalton. He was a man with a laundry list of life events, most of them not so great when it came to re-living them. And as he sat on the ledge of the Trading Post, with legs dangling and cigar ashes falling down onto the crowd of Drifters, he began to think about his old crew.

"Damn woman, you got a death wish or something?" Dalton said, quickly pulling his revolver to the ready as Selina approached softly.

"You are alive, right?" he asked as the barrel remained on her.

"What does this tell you?" she replied, wrapping her arms around his neck and kissing him deeply.

"Tells me this trip 'aint been a total loss." Dalton replied with a grin.

"May I sit?" Selina asked. Dalton simply pointed to the ledge beside him as Selina sat down gracefully.

"Do you think we'll be alright?" she asked in a somber tone.

"Hard to say," Dalton replied as he took a deep inhalation of Rum treated cigar. "I expect that if anyone makes it out of Geartown alive, it'll be us." he added.

"I hate that all of this happened, but I'm really glad you're here." Selina said as she looked deeply into the smuggler's wide eyes.

"I'm sorta' glad I'm here too," Dalton replied, drawing another lung debilitating puff. "Truth is, this has me feeling more alive than I have in a long time. Don't get me wrong, I could do without the crowd of undead. But otherwise, it's kinda peaceful out here in the Drifts."

"It can be," Selina said with a grin. "At least before all of this happened anyway." she added.

Dalton agreed with a nod, flicking his cigar stump onto the crowd of animated flesh below.

"Technology has a way of complicating things. Has a way of pulling people apart and taking the luster away from life's greatest moments." Selina said.

"That's deep," Dalton said, his eyes widening just a bit. "I get it though. "I've been a lot of places and seen a lot of unhappy people. Most of them were living on the cutting edge of technology." he added as he pulled a small flask from his coat.

"Crash landed once; well, more than once," Dalton said prior to taking a healthy swig of whatever his flask was readily offering. "The planet was off the map, nothing to speak of really. Just a village full of the most primative people you could ever meet. But they were good people...happy people." he added as Selina squeezed him a bit in hugging fashion.

"Really? What happened to them?" Selina asked, intrigued by his story.

"Oh they all died," he said, starting to take another swig as he realized the damage. "Not that we are gonna die or anything." he added quickly.

"Well this is a very encouraging conversation." Selina replied softly.

"Ah, don't fret it none babe, I'll come up with something." Dalton said.

"I hope so," Selina said with a concerned look. "Everyone is looking to you." she added as she slowly stood up to find a nice spot to rest for the night.

They were looking to him, especially Cambria at that very moment. Watching his every move. Wondering why such a good hearted man would hide away from the world beneath the shield of his brown coat. As she lay there, she continued to stare at him. The way he sat calmly on the ledge let her know of his experience in battle, but the way he gently placed his hand on the pup beside him let her know of his good spirit.

She was becoming confused under the worst possible conditions. But still she thought only of Dalton James as she slowly drifted into a world of dreams.

"All we can do is sleep it off," Dalton mumbled as he sat on the rooftop and prepared his duster in a way as to present the illusion of a fine mattress. "Nothing else we can do." he added as he lay down and rolled away from the group of survivors.

It would be hard for them to sleep. Damn near impossible, actually, as dead flesh continued pounding against the thick trapdoor of steel which separated them. Eventually, seemingly hours later, the beating subsided. Those on watch noticed a lack of interest by many of the Drifters, who began finding their way back out into the streets in search of less difficult victims.

The interior of the ship was different from anything he had ever seen before. That's what had first caught Dalton's attention. Gauges that looked alien, yet eerily of death.

As Dalton first sat up, his reaction was to check for Whiskey. But the faithful running mate was nowhere to be found. As was the same fate for his sidearm, in fact, as Dalton felt around for it his holster was no longer a part of the uniform. His eyes told a tale of unanswered questions as he glanced down to see himself clad in solid white. It seemed surreal.

Jumping swiftly to his feet, Dalton began to visually search the room. Solid steel walls, though not a single seam could be seen with his naked eyes. He wondered how such a ship could have even been constructed, seemingly flawless in every respect. There did appear to be a door, and as the wily smuggler began to approach it slowly in search of answers, three colored triangles illuminated the wall directly above it. All of them brilliant red and further adding to the mystery.

Moments later, the door opened quickly enough to startle Dalton back against the wall. His reasoning led him to only two possibilities. Either he had been drugged or the Drifters had indeed found him. Maybe his dream was merely a part of the conversion process, leaving the mortal world and joining a very feared nation of walking dead.

Normally, Dalton would have played out each scenario in his head, but his train of though was interrupted as two figures entered the room. Though visible, they both seemed a bit blurred, almost as if his eyes could not focus them. Both were clad in solid white, from boot to riot style helmet. Even the shielding of their helmets glimmered a satin white, while three red triangles formed a larger triangle as the only marking on their helmets.

Dalton felt the need to ask questions, and had started to approach them before stopping dead in his tracks. A tail of some sort was visible as the soldiers turned to the side in order to watch the door. It extended slightly from the rear of their helmets and seemed to penetrate the top of their spinal cords. Though the soldiers remained perfectly still, the brown tail wiggled a bit, its tissue both knobby and covered in scales.

It was unlike anything the smuggler had ever seen before, the sight truly scaring Dalton for the first time in many years. He felt a chill run through his skin, raising bumps all along his arms as his hands shook a bit, preparing to fight for life if needed be.

All of that changed with the entrance of a third. Solid white cloak, hood pulled up to protect both emotion and identity. Dalton's heart nearly stopped beating when it became evident what was about to occur. The hooded figure carried a glass cylinder in one arm; inside the cylinder a small creature. Its tail matched that of the ones draping from the helmets of the posted guards, though the rest of the creature was also visible.

It was almost flat, though it had six legs clad in scales of dark brown and the eery tail that appeared to form a large needle-like shape at its tip. The creature began striking toward Dalton, almost as if it were a venomous snake waiting to be loosened from its cage. As the cloaked figure slowly pulled the hood from its head, Dalton began to cry aloud.

"Help us." Adam Michaels said, a monster similar to the one encased in glass attached to his skull with tail running down into Dalton's former Captain's spine. Just as Sasha's overpowering screams could suddenly be heard, Adam threw the encased monster toward Dalton, its glass confines quickly disappearing as the freed monster lunged for him.

"Dalton!" Cambria said in a loud whisper, trying her best to force the smuggler to awaken.

He had started to come to a bit, though he remained, for the moment, between the world of dream and that which required oxygen for survival.

"Dalton, are you alright?" Cambria asked again, this time her words filled with concern.

"Yea," he replied, hand gripping his head a bit. "Splitting headache and," he added, seemingly holding back for a moment. "Really bad dream."

"It's alright, we all have them." she replied.

"Not like this one. God, it seemed so real." Dalton said.

Cambria gripped his shoulder for a moment, a gesture to let the smuggler know she was by his side.

"I woke you up because day is breaking," Cambria said in a soft voice. "Be a good idea to assess our situation."

"Off 'yer asses!" Dalton yelled loud enough to wake everyone who still slept. "It's time to put our heads together, find out what we got and what we don't got." he added, nodding his appreciation to the Captain of the Outer Heaven.

"It's official. What we got is eleven survivors, five

bottles of hooch, three bottles of water and two cans of pork and beans." Tank said with a touch of disgust.

"Twelve survivors." Dalton added as Whiskey barked loudly in order to be counted, his angle, simply put, to be considered for the pork and beans.

"We also have guns." Skulls said.

"Yep, that we do got. May just be our biggest asset at the moment," Dalton replied, turning to the remainder of the survivors. "I know my crew and Johnny are damn capable with a weapon," he said with pause. "Any of the rest of you a decent shot?"

The barkeep, older man who held a child in his arms and one of the younger men stepped back a bit. Experience with a weapon was surely not on their list of skills.

"No Dalton, I don't. I'm sorry." Selina said.

"It all good," he replied with a cowboy wink. The kind that was accompanied by fatigue, bad hair and whiskey laced breath. "What about you?" he asked of the remaining man.

The man had medium length hair, dirty blonde, though his clothes were anything but. The light-skinned man wore dress slacks and a pinstripe vest that rested over a white shirt.

"Yea," the man replied. "I served with the Legion during the first Glimmerian War. I put a right many Colonials into the grave, so I guess that qualifies."

Dalton bit his tongue as he thought back to the first Glimmerian War. He had been involved as well, on the Colonial side, and had watched dozens of his friends butchered in a losing effort. There was even a good chance that the man who stood in front of him fired a shot or two that may have ended the life of a friend.

But these were different times. Different circumstances. Once bitter enemies, they now stood together with a common goal. Survival.

"I fought there as well. Fought for the Colonials," Dalton replied as the air that surrounded the group seemingly got very thick. "And if we were in any other situation, the words you just spoke to me would have been paid for with teeth," Dalton added, looking the man from head to toe. "But the war is long over, and we need every gun we can get."

"Fair enough," the man replied, extending his hand. "The name's Christopher."

He was testing Dalton, and the brown coat smothered man of ill-repute was sure of it. Purposely crossing the line to see if Dalton meant his words. His gut told him to slug the son of a bitchn' redcoat, or better yet, shoot his ass and be done with it. But Dalton soon realized his gut hungered for food too, and the sooner they smoothed things over when it came to Glimmeria, the better.

"Dalton James." he finally replied, shaking hands with a man he would have been under orders to kill back on Glimmeria.

"We need to figure out if this is the spot we call home, or if we go looking for something else." Johnny said.

"This is the spot. It's a safe spot, otherwise they would have gotten through during the night." Cambria replied.

"Agreed," Dalton said. "So we need to form a small group. Go scavenge what we can and get back before nightfall."

"What are we supposed to do for food all day?" Selina asked.

"What we got goes to the kid," Dalton said with seriousness. "We can make it days without eating if need be, but won't have to. Just need to make it through one."

"Well who's going?" Tank asked.

"You and I got things to work out, so we're both in." Dalton said.

"Huh?" Cambria asked with amazement.

"One of the things you need to understand about smuggling is there will be arguments," Dalton replied. "Lots of arguments," he added. "Hell, my previous Captain and I used to fistfight when it came down to it."

"What the hell does this have to do with scavenging?" Tank asked.

"You need to learn that no matter what we got going on between the two of us, we always get each others backs." Dalton said.

"Yea right." Tank added, blowing the advice off.

"Which is why you aren't taking a weapon." Dalton said.

"The fuck I 'aint!" Tank replied with anger.

"You'll be carrying all of the luggage. You a big 'sumbitch, we'll be able to carry a lot more this way. And I'll be there to watch you back, just like Johnny will."

"You a crazy motherfucker! No way in hell that I'm going out there unarmed, especially with you and Johnny. I'll be dead within five minutes!" Tank said.

"No you won't, cause what you will learn really quick is the smuggler's creed." Dalton replied.

"Oh yea, what's that?" Tank asked, his words filled with both mystery and sarcasm.

"That no matter how bad you piss me off, I got your back." Dalton said, nodding his head to show everyone the truth of it.

"Or as I like to say, trust not, eat not." Johnny added.

"Skulls will stay behind," Dalton said. "Not that you're no good in combat my man. But in the event that we come hauling ass back with a crowd on us, you're the only one skilled enough to thin them out."

"I have no problem providing overwatch. It's what I do best." Skulls replied with a nod of approval.

"Ever have to use a slugger to bring peace back to the bar?" Dalton asked of the bartender.

"A bat? More times than you can count." the barkeep replied.

"Same principle," Dalton said as he un-sheethed his large blade and handed it to the man. "Drifter comes up, you swing for the hills. This blade will cut the sumbitch' in half."

"I'm coming too. Right?" Cambria asked, hoping to impose her authority.

"Not this time out. If things go to shit we need someone capable of putting together a rescue plan." Dalton replied.

"What am I supposed to do? Just hang out here?" she asked.

"Hand Christopher a piece and keep these people safe. Stay on that trapdoor and pray we make it back in one piece." Dalton said.

Several minutes later, the survivors had laid out everything they would need for the scavenging group's trip. Several empty sacks, a couple of throw sacks using thick shirts and a few bare-chested men.

"Dalton, I cannot believe you had the nerve to ask me for my shirt!" Cambria said, furious that he had used the excuse of Drifters as reasoning.

"Hey, just trying to do my part." Dalton said, chuckling as Johnny, even Tank, joined in the laughter a bit.

Skulls, Christopher, the barkeep, old man and another survivor all lent their shirts. It would allow the three man scavenging party a chance to scale down the rope, rather than attempt their way down a stairwell which led to sure Drifters.

They geared up, weapons in hand and belt, while Tank's firm grip held a dozen or so makeshift sacks.

"We'll drop down and hit the Eastern side of Geartown. Remember to keep sights on us." johnny said as a very pale-chested Skulls nodded.

And while Dalton embraced Selina one last time, harboring his body in the warmth of her own, even he noticed the dedicated stare of Cambria Sims. He had seen it many times, and knew that it was one of love unexplored.

He tested his theory, purposely walking past her without saying a single word.

"Dalton," Cambria said, approaching him slowly. "Please be careful."

"Will do," he said with a grin. "And when I get back, I think it's time we had a little talk."

"Talk. About what?" Cambria asked, her question answered with a simple glance.

Oh God! Cambria thought. How could he know? How could he possibly know my feelings? Are they that obvious? Did keeping them a secret even matter to her anymore? She had fallen so suddenly, so head over heels with a man who might be marching to his own death just to feed the survivors.

Knowing it could be their final moment together, she wanted to reach out and kiss the man so desperately. Plead with him, beg him if needed be, to stay and let someone else go in his place. But she knew why had had thrown himself in the situation. Because otherwise, the scavenging group wouldn't survive.

"Just take care of my damn dog and quit with the last moment together ever look." Dalton said with a smile.

Cambria wanted to curse his arrogance, maybe even curse herself for exposing such feelings. Instead she just smiled wide and nodded her head, doing her best to hold back tears that could have easily fallen if she would have let them.

The plan was a simple one. Repel down the rope made of less than expensive shirts, which they had knotted together to form a rope. Johnny would lead the group, his familiarity of the town was key.

Tank would follow next, his large size allowing him to carry the bulk of what they had found. Even though his job for the upcoming trip was technically that of a pack mule, it was also the most important. He would be the one who brought back needed supplies for an extended stay.

The flank of the three man group was Dalton, who carried his revolver in hand; three more handguns tucked into the leather belt around his waist. The pockets of his pants were shoved full with ammunition clips and spare bullets. He was responsible for protecting himself, as well the pack mule.

And so the three assigned to loot Geatown eased themselves over the side of the roof, one at a time, each praying the shirts held as well as they had hoped.

Skulls had spotted some Drifters roaming several blocks away, as well as a group directly in front of the Trading Post. And the sniper's hand motions let the group know where the Zombies were located, directing them almost like some sort of gothic GPS system.

"We gonna need a lot of food, tents, blankets and weapons if we can find em." Dalton whispered, just loud enough for the two men in front of him to hear.

Johnny acknowledged his words with a nod, holding their position at a standstill while peeking from the corner of a nearby building.

And though they had to remain hidden for nearly thirty minutes, eventually the three man scavenging group made their way, cautiously slow, out of the sight of Skulls and deeper into Geartown.

Cambria felt a chill come across her at the very moment they disappeared from sight. It wasn't the temperature of the low-passing winds, but rather one that made her, for whatever reason, truly believe that she would never see Dalton again.

And even though they were no longer visible in the bright rays of sun that fell down onto the Drifts, Cambria continued her stare for several minutes. Praying, if nothing else, that her gut feeling was wrong.

"Keep on your scope," she said, a bit of panic in her voice of deep concern. "Please."

"Don't worry, I believe they will be fine." Skulls replied.

Those who remained back on the Trading Post rooftop seemed to finally grasp the devastation. The previous night had been filled with screams, terror and non-stop fighting for their lives. They had been given no time to sincerely think about the events which had unfolded.

Bodies laying out in the streets surrounding their building. Most, if not all, mutilated and dead by horrific measures. There was no doubt that the very building beneath them was filled with more of the same.

Drifters walked among them. And they knew but one purpose. Killing. And as the survivors looked from their rooftop of safety, they saw the bodies, smoking buildings and walking dead throughout the streets.

"It will be alright." the barkeep said, trying his best to comfort Selina as she began to sob heavily.

"How could this happen?" she asked, her words falling between two outburst of tears.

"Let's just hope it's contained to the Drifts," Christopher said. "So we can find a skiff and get the fuck out of here."

Cambria didn't respond. As she turned to Christopher, she wanted to. So badly, she wanted to respond to the man she knew was less than half the man Dalton James was.

She didn't know the complete history of Glimmeria, but she did know of both wars there. She knew that Dalton had fought for the very side she would have, if it would have been her. The side that just wanted to be allowed to live. The side that fought, only as a last resort, to protect their families.

And as she watched Christopher, his every move giving clue to the character of the man, she knew he was a coward. He had more than likely killed several Colonial soldiers during the war. Soldiers, just like Dalton, who were forced into protecting everything they lived for. But he had done it from a distance, maybe with the odds heavily in his favor. At least that was Cambria's opinion, as she saw a man who only wished he could measure up to a Dalton James.

Whiskey had been quiet since the group of scavengers departed, choosing instead to take his place near the elderly man and child who sat far from the trapdoor. The faithful pooch watched over the pair as though he were a ill-bathed guardian angel. And, while his eyes skimmed the group, his head remained flat to the ground.

"What's your name old man?" Christopher asked.

"Carlos." the elderly man replied softly, doing his best to keep the babe in his arms calm.

"A little old for a baby aren't you?" Christopher asked.

"Are you watching the trapdoor or writing for a newspaper?" Cambria asked sharply.

"Just trying to get to know everyone," he said without even turning into her direction. "That's all."

"He's not mine," Carlos said. "I found him in the street about two blocks down. Didn't seem right to just leave a infant boy laying."

"What about you, what's your story?" Christopher asked of the other surviving man.

"Name's Kieth," the man replied. "I sell prospecting licenses," he added. "Or at least I used to."

"Wow, a licensing official. How exciting." Christopher said with sarcasm.

"True. Not all of us can be cold-blooded killers fighting under the Legion flag," Kieth replied. "If I was the killing kind, I would have killed your kind with a brown coat on my back."

"What the hell did you just say?" Christopher asked angrily.

"That's enough," Cambria added, stepping between the two men. "Been enough fighting down below, we don't need it up here too."

"Fair enough, but don't get too comfortable being in charge." Christopher said with a grin.

Tank held the large sack open as Johnny filled it with haste, pushing his arm onto the shelf and then raking the groceries inside.

"Seems like you are picking all of the heavy shit." Tank said.

"Getting all of the protein I can find. It will keep us a

bit fuller for a bit longer." Johnny replied.

"Shh." Dalton added, using one of his arms to calm them to silence as sever Drifters walked by the front door of the small general store.

"We need to speed this trip up, they seem to be getting thicker outside." Dalton said in a whisper.

"Alright," Johnny replied, his voice just as low pitched. "Tank, you grab as many more groceries as you can carry. I'll look around for anything we can use for an extended stay. Survival gear."

Tank simply nodded, still steaming a bit over being assigned the group's pack mule. He froze in place, however, as the ringing of a small bell attached to the front door rang out.

A single Drifter had entered the building, leaving the front door open in the process.

Johnny quickly made his way back, a single bag filled with loot and three brand new tents, still folded and sealed, draped across his shoulder.

Once the Drifter had gotten far enough inside, Dalton sprang from behind to grab the monster around its throat. It tried to bite, tried to fight back, but a quick plunge into the forehead, a knife blade held by Tank, changed the struggle as the Drifter fell limply to the floor.

"We got to move!" Dalton said, this time loudly as several Drifters passing by had spotted the killing of one of their own.

"Might as well use the front door, and don't stop running until we make it back!" Johnny yelled as the three men began sprinting. Tank, who had never been accused of lacking in the muscle department, hoisted four large sacks filled with groceries with ease.

His muscles flexed hard, proven by the sudden outline

around the bulging in his arms. Yet he was able to keep up with a pistol-wielding Dalton and Johnny as the three men stayed only a dozen or so feet in front of a large crowd of animated flesh.

Dalton opened fire, staying to the rear of the group as he executed nearly a half-dozen Zombies at close range.

"I found an old radio back there," Johnny said loudly as the group continued its brisk run. "It's an older, crank-type model, but it was brand new. Ran across a flare gun too."

"We need every bit of it, good thinking." Dalton replied.

"Should have enough food for weeks if we ration it right." Tank added, as the group slowed down, quickly finding every street blocked by a few Drifters.

"Johnny," Dalton said as the three men began to back up into one another. "What you got in your bag is damn important. You get it back there, ya' hear?"

"What are you rambling about?" Johnny asked.

"The street to our left runs right back into the Trading Post. I remember the street light," Dalton said. "You and I thin out the bastards blocking that direction, then you run for it. Tank and I will hold up the remaining."

"I 'aint going back without 'ya." Johnny said.

"Yea you are. You have them get a damn rope of some sort ready and waiting for us." Dalton replied.

"Don't have to worry about that, I found a rope back there as well. Two to be exact." Johnny replied.

"Well you get your ass up to that roof and have ropes waiting. We'll be a few steps behind, and coming with a whole lot of bastards on our heels." Dalton said.

"Make it back." Johnny said, patting Dalton on the shoulder for a moment before joining the brown coat wearing smuggler in clearing a path. As the last Drifter fell, Johny Edmonds sprinted away, bag of vital equipment over his shoulder.

"Alright brother, let's dust these 'sumbitches," Dalton said, pulling a second pistol out from his belt. "Just stay behind me." he added, shots ringing out a mere moment later.

Dropping eight Drifters with his first eight shots, Dalton dropped the empty piece and pulled another from his belt, letting more shots loose in the process.

And so continued the killing, the cleansing of life after death by one Dalton James, until his last revolver, a shiny Magnum, clicked empty.

One remained. A single Drifter remained, coming to the men, slowing only to make its way across the heaping pile of bodies which lay truly dead at the hands of Dalton James.

"Where are the others?" Cambria said frantically as the men helped Johnny over the ledge and onto the rooftop. "Johnny." she yelled.

"They're coming," he replied, heavily winded at best. "They stayed back a ways to cover my flank," he added. "Two ropes in my bag. Get 'em and tie them to the steel pipes up here. Be ready to throw them down in a hurry."

Cambria stood to her feet, in shock and praying, as the group quickly sifted through Johnny's bag to find the rope. Placing them around the piping system, and re-enforcing the knots to hold, they all patiently waited for sight of Tank and Dalton, as well as whatever horrors may be behind them.

"Only one of them," Dalton said as the Drifter approached, its teeth snarling gruesomely for fresh flesh. ""I'll draw him to me, and when I do, you stab that 'sumbitch right in the back of his skull."

As his words closed out the sentence, Tank fired a gunshot that flew by, striking the Drifter in its forehead and killing it stone cold dead.

As Dalton James turned to find out where the shot came from, he saw the barrel of a solid black pistol bearing down on him.

"Now let me tell you my version of the smuggler's creed," Tank said with a bit of a grin. "You really think I would come out here without a fucking gun on me? I'm a smuggler!" he yelled.

"Yea, I know you are man. Just calm down." Dalton replied.

"Don't tell me to calm down man," Tank said. "You don't know the half of it. I am calm," he added. "The minute I found out you and Christopher fought on different sides of the Glimmerian War, me and him sat down. Had ourselves a real long talk."

"What the fuck are you rambling on about?" Dalton asked, the sound of Drifters closing in on them becoming louder.

"You won't get away with this!" Cambria yelled as Christopher held her at gunpoint. Her own gun, the same one he had, only moments before, used to shoot Whiskey, now reflecting back to her.

"Shut up you bitch!" Christopher yelled, a second gun pointed into Johnny's direction. "I know you're fast with a pistol, but I already got the bead on you. And the sniper over there, just keep your damn eye to the scope. You turn around, just the slightest bit, and I'll end both of them." Christopher added.

"See Dalton," Tank said somberly. "This group of survivors needs to be led by the strong. And while Christopher is up there handling business, it's my job to dust your ass and leave you laying for the Drifters."

"You 'aint got it in you." Dalton replied, walking very slowly toward the gunman.

"Sure I do," Tank replied, pulling the slide lock back on his pistol. "And right about now, Christopher is killing that sack of fleas you travel with. And when I get back, plan on having my way with Cambria."

"I'll fucking kill you!" Dalton James yelled, Drifters closing in on them quickly.

"Only one problem with that statement. You'll be dead." Tank replied.

And with a single shot, the life of a smuggler officially ended.

Gunship V: Roman

And They were on him. Tu'nak knew well that the Hunters were closing in quickly. He knew not the number, nor the weapons in which they carried; he only knew of their intentions.

The Hunters were drinkers of mens' souls. Vampires by every definition. They wore Gothic black, carried the most elegant of weaponry, and, above all, thirsted for the salty sting of Human blood.

Tu'nak was Human enough, though his structure nearly spoke a different tale. A shade above seven feet in height, the warrior had packed muscle onto his gigantic frame throughout a lifetime. Such meaty flesh was considered a top catch by the Hunters, and that was all the more reason for them to track him down. Slay him and feast on the seasoned frame of the warrior.

Yet, they needed no more reasoning aside from the one

they carried. Their queen had ordered it. She had demanded Tu'nak, and the remaining warriors who rose against the Vampiric race be hunted down and slaughtered. A group of warriors who answered but to one.

Roman Raines.

Roman had been one of the mightiest warriors ever recorded into history by Human hand, spending an entire lifetime slaying the very Vampires who hunted him.

When he met demise, the flicker of a hero's journey coming to a close, the Hunters turned him. He would be a great addition to their cause, becoming one of their mightiest slayers.

However, the Hunters underestimated Roman Raines; or rather his hatred for their kind. Indeed, his body had transformed from a dying Human into a warrior of the afterlife. But his objectives remained true. Kill every last Vampire, cleansing Humanity of the bastards forever.

And so Tu'nak ran, swiftly and with the guarantee of safety if he were able to make it back. Because the fact was, it didn't matter how many Hunters were on him. Nor did it matter the weapons they carried with them. None would be near the strength in battle as Roman Raines was.

As the warrior's feet crunched the freshly-fallen snow with haste, his legs continuing a stride of panic; his lungs working hard against the air of frigidness as he finally made it back to their base of operations.

Nothing more than a large cabin surrounded by the foliage of trees, blankets of snow covering the round hills which also held the personal shuttle of Roman Raines.

"Were you followed?" Roman asked as Tu'nak quickly approached the steps which led to the cabin's entrance, lungs throbbing from such bone-stabbing cold.

Roman wore a coat of fur, one that reached the length of his body and was white with a peppering of black. A single blade hung by his side, one of rugged craftsmanship, but elegant nonetheless.

"Yes," Tu'nak replied, his chest throbbing with the pain of cold air forced in. "A scouting group."

"Get inside and inform the others. I will join you shortly." Roman replied, his voice ringing with a touch of demonic tongue as gray smoke floated up to the clouds, a single campfire to blame. His long hair of white and black nearly blended with the icy surroundings, as did his chalk-white skin.

And there he stood, sword in hand as he walked a small circle, slowly facing the thickly-wooded area near camp.

"You can show yourselves. I smell you. Take arms and fight with honor, our code requires it." Roman said loudly, the chill of his voice overpowering that of the air.

Without warning, a Hunter jumped into sight from the wooded area, the demon holding sword in hand, fully extended and determined to end the life of Roman Raines.

Instead, however, the soldier of immortality quickly became otherwise, the trunk of his body severed in half by a chopping swipe of Roman's blade.

The two bulks of flesh, both of them completely lifeless, fell to the snow before much of the gushing blood which followed, soaking the ground at the mighty slayers' feet.

"Go. Run back home with fear and tell your queen of the legend known as Roman Raines!" he yelled.

"We will speak to our queen of no such warrior," a Hunter replied loudly, a total of two making their way into the clearing. "My mouth is capable of no such lie."

"Then your lifeless body will speak of it for you." Roman said as the two demons began to circle him.

Swordplay was indeed important to the Hunters, looked upon as honorable warfare. But no training they could have completed, no mentor among them, could have prepared the two Vampires for the skill with blade which ran through Roman's veins every moment of every day.

With just the slightest of feigns, only enough to force one of the beasts into a parry, Roman quickly turned to plunge the bulk of his blade into the chest of the other, unsuspecting demon. Then, knowing well that his enemy was on the door of death, Roman jerked loose his sword, crushing it down onto his other opponent.

The Vampire, who was recovering from a parry proven unnecessary, only found time to raise his blade to deflect the downswing of such a warrior. And, in most cases, it was a fine move. However, he was fighting Roman Raines on this day.

The punishing power of the Vampiric slayer of Vampires continued his swing, forcing it through the defending steel and shattering the victim's sword; finding a home in the upper skull of his outmatched foe.

As Roman forced his blade back out single-handed, bringing with it large fragments of bone, he slowly sheathed it once more while watching the doomed Vampire's lifeless body fall to the ground.

"We must find another home. The attacks grow more common." Gore said as Roman's group of warriors approached at arms.

The Husk warrior, a race that looked both of Orc and demon descent, had long hair falling from a majority of his large frame. The brown locks that were so common among his race did little to cover such a specimen of muscle, though it was covered in scars. He had seen many battles, and survived to tell of the horrors that had accompanied them.

For his people hated the Hunters, and their only goal in life was to end as many Vampires as possible; making him a perfect fit for Roman's Empire.

"I agree," Roman replied. "The scouts they send pose little threat, but may one day be replaced with Hunter Elites."

Everyone stood silently at the notion. Hunter Elites

were the equivalent of Knights, though they were capable of acts unspeakable. Each had been a slayer of men while alive. So much, in fact, that they had been given the gift of immortality. Roman was one such Knight, or at least it had been planned so. He had been the first to ever resist their influence, and though he seemed unmatched in battle, he would now face the best warriors because of it.

The best warriors that centuries had spawned. Some kings, others but common men whose legend had grown in battle. Each Hunter Elite was, in his own right, the best warrior of his day. Once turned, they added the Vampiric traits to their own skill in battle. And towering above them all, Vladris.

No Hunter feared, their genetics would not allow such an emotion. But all Hunters, even Hunter Elites, knew of Vladris.

They knew of his legend, recognized him to be the greatest of their ranks and respected him because of it. And though he had seen many times of war, ending thousands of lives as both Human and Vampire, he now remained by the side of their queen; Sarah Blaine. Praying for the day that brought a battle which he and Roman Raines both knew was imminent. Their own.

"Where are we to flee? Draden asked.

The warrior was of Dragonborn descent. His people were clad in scales rather than skin, his a dark orange. Draden carried a long-blade on his side, and was capable with it. However, his gift was of a defensive nature. His exterior of Dragon hide made him nearly impossible to slay, all but the truest of swings merely deflected.

"I say we stay and fight the bastards!" Pica yelled.

The Human archer was small by definition, his frame only about five and a half feet in height. The longbow that he currently held was about the same. And together, they were mighty. It took nearly everything Pica had to force the bow into a ready position, but the arrow that flew from his weapon of choice had decimating power.

"I'm glad you feel that way my brother. I have no intentions of fleeing," Roman replied, turning his gaze to Draden in the process. "But we need to leave this cabin and strengthen our ranks before moving forward."

"Moving forward?" Gore asked.

"There will come a day not long from now that our fight is taken to the Hunters. To their very doorstep. Their queen will know of my legend," Roman replied. "Come Scucca!" he added, a Vampiric hound of hell joining his side as the group entered the cabin to work on a thorough strategy. Each warrior taking heed as Scucca could not be trusted, often times lunging after any and all, aside from Roman of course.

Sarah Blaine knew of Roman's legend. Not only had word of his slaying made it back to her, but there was a time when both were mortals. Friends even, that had traveled together on the same Gunship crew. A smuggling crew that encountered many dangers along the way, and one in which Roman had defied the odds to save their lives many times over.

Sarah knew of Roman's abilities well, and it was the reason behind Vladris remaining at her side. Not that she was afraid of death, not by any means. But because she wanted nothing more than to witness the fall of such a warrior, one that had promised to end her.

And though Sarah knew of Roman's legend, she had also started the process of reading the Hunter archives. And with each story she read, came a story of Vladris ending the legend of what Humanity had considered its best. Sarah believed in her heart that Vladris would surely end him.

"My queen," Vladris said, bending low to the floor of her throne room.

"Rise warrior, for only you are decorated in battle enough to speak to me on the same level." Sarah replied.

As Vladris slowly stood to his feet, his level of respect

for her grew. She had replaced a queen who earned nothing of the such from him. She had been a coward, a butcher of her own people. The very reasoning behind Vladris ending her by his own blade.

Sarah had done the opposite, giving her race hope while treating them all with a level of respect that none had ever known.

She wanted to end Humanity, at least the part of it that hunted Vampires, this much was true. But not for the same reasons as those who ruled the Vampire nation before her. She didn't want them slaughtered because of sport; she considered the Hunters to be the most dominant race.

And for that very reason, society would either live by their laws of die by their hands. The Hunters were to become the ruling government under her reign, or so she planned.

As Vladris stood there, a slick-shaven head that was home to several tribal tattoos, he gazed with respect. His pearl white pupils cutting into her with appreciation as a two-handed sword of reaving remained strapped to his back with leather bonding.

"Thank you my queen," he replied, his voice soft and polite by Vampiric standards. "I have received word that our scouts have been slain."

"As expected." Sarah replied.

Normally, during the conversion process, a Human grew worse in appearance. Not Sarah Blaine. She had grown exceptionally more beautiful, if that was even possible. It was almost as if she had been born to become a vampire, not fully blossoming until her conversion.

Both her lips and eyes nearly glowed a crimson red, the rest of her skin whitening in a way that brought with it purified beauty. She looked as though she had been hand-carved from ivory, and then accented with the perfect coloring in all of the important places.

"Should I form a group of elites?" Vladris asked.

"No," she said quickly, turning to nod her answer as well. "Roman will expect such a move and doing so will only bring the loss of mighty warriors to our ranks."

"Shall I track him down myself?" Vladris asked.

"No." Sarah replied, turning to look out of the large opening which served as a window.

The Hunters had built what was the equivalent of a castle, inside the confines of a hollowed mountain. For centuries, each queen had lived here, overlooking their homeworld of Ronica through the large opening in the side of their mountain.

"You do not believe I would prevail against him my queen?" Vladris asked.

"I believe nothing less than your victory against him," Sarah replied, quickly making her confidence in his abilities known. "We will need to defeat Roman Raines by out-thinking him. I have a plan, and it involves you doing something completely different."

"Thank you my queen. Speak it and it will be so." Vladris replied.

And so began the plan of Sarah Blaine, queen of Vampires; a plan that would surely bring an end to Roman Raines.

As Vladris stood in his own room hours later, built of stone block and vaulted ceilings, he remembered pieces of his mortal life. There was a large door which led to a balcony, and as Vladris walked onto the tiled floor of stone which overlooked a gushing river below the mountain, he remained deep in thought; a curtain of rain falling across their kingdom.

Ronica had always been such a beautiful planet. Its warfare being fought with steel, be it sword, arrow tips or axe. Its method of transportation one of horseback, and its climate filled with rain. At least ninety percent of its days filled with the hammering of rain, falling with intention from the heavens above to the soil which its people called home.

The Ronical Kingdom had been one of the last to fall under the rule of Vampires, staving off the sky-born demons time and time again.

Vladris had been one of the mightiest of Knights, slaying hundreds of Vampires over a period of time which spanned nearly a decade. And, as several Hunter Elites finally pinned him down in battle, Vladris remained true to his legend; slaying a few of them as well, before falling himself.

Shortly after, The Ronical Kingdom fell. Ronica's people had fought with such courage, such desire for life, that after the war had ended the Hunters allowed them to live. Under Vampire laws and rule, of course, but none were to be harmed without good cause.

Vladris had helped earn his people, to some degree, freedom. The Hunters even thought so highly of their champion that they defended the Humans on Ronica as well; placing their castle here and treating the Humans who remained as though they were better than simple cattle.

Every hard rain that lay before the eyes of Vladris reminded him of his mortal life on Ronica. Reminded him of the King he once served; the woman he once loved.

In fact, when fighting the Hunters many years ago, it was the thought of his true love which led to such feats on the battlefield. And, even to this very day, Vladris thought of Amelia when locked in battle. Her memory and loss of life fueled Vladris, tapping into an emotional rage with sword in hand that had brought him many victories.

Most across the Skyla System had thought the Hunters to be without emotion. None had ever seen tears flow from the eyes of such a mighty warrior, as they did this very moment. His pain a true love lost forever; forever his death sentence. For he was immortal, cursed to live the remainder of a life never-ending without the warmth of his lover.

And so the tears flowed heavily from the eyes of such a mighty soldier, a warrior who gripped the banister of the balcony and prayed for a time when someone could best him in battle, ending such a gripping emotional pain.

Roman and his group of warriors rode hard, their mounted horses pushing forward in the blind of snow. They concerned themselves not with thoughts of bandits, highwaymen or even Hunter groups. For they rode with Roman Raines, arguably the greatest Vampiric warrior in history. Arguably.

Between that title of legacy and Roman stood Vladris, and in his very soul, Roman knew the day of confrontation was drawing near. Soon the warriors would meet in battle, it was destiny. And though he knew not the outcome, Roman believed on that day Ronica would know with certainty who deserved the title of greatest.

"Soon the snow will turn to rain. Let us make camp for the night." Roman said as the riders began to slow, finally spotting a small patch of trees which would provide cover enough to burn a campfire.

Most notably, Pica was the first to welcome the mention of camp. Though he only carried a longbow, it was one of both exceptional quality and craftsmanship. It remained in such condition because of Pica's caring hands, conditioning the weapon regularly, just as he did on this very night by the light of a campfire.

Using a small piece of grit paper, the Human slowly brushed across the tough wood of the bow, doing away with any dings it may have recently acquired through use. Then, he brought the longbow back to a shine with a rag which he dipped into a small jar of oil. Clear, almost as if it were alcohol fit for drinking, Pica continued to care for every inch of his weapon.

"The way you stroke your weapon grows me to wonder of your intentions on this night." Gore said as the group burst into laughter.

"Worry not for me," Pica replied with a snarl. "But for that rust covered blade which rides your back as poorly as you ride your mount."

As the laughter of the group grew, even Roman was forced to break his concentration a bit. He regularly meditated, losing himself into thought and mind as Scucca, his hellhound, stood guard over him.

With a loud bark which chilled hot tempers, Scucca glanced at the group as if to warn them of their growing noise.

"This rusty blade has killed many warriors," Gore replied, though his eyes remained on Scucca. "A slew of them holding the very bow that you covet so greatly. The rust will fall from my blade when it finds a new home in bloody flesh, which may be that of a dog should Roman turn a blind eye." he added, staring as if to dare Scucca to move on him.

"And if the blade strike doesn't kill him, the gangrene of rust surely will!" Draden replied, causing the entire group to burst out loudly.

"I hear you my brother," Gore replied, turning his attention to the Dragonborn warrior turned campfire jester. "And many of the cowards wielding bows which my blade has slain had scaled-hides as you do."

Rather than reply, Draden scowled at Gore, defending his people with a stern look. Quickly after, however, the stern look turned to Scucca as well.

"That damn dog is the devil himself." Tunak said, the muscle-bound warrior also eying the guard dog of Roman Raines.

"Aye," Gore said. "And should the the devil snarl his lips to me one more time, he will lay testament to what my rusted blade can do."

"Save it my brother," Tunak said, gently sipping from a metal cup filled with coffee as the light of fire illuminated their faces. "Not so long from now we will be knee-deep in Vampires. Save what little life your blade has left for them."

And with that joking insult, the entire group began laughing once more, followed by Draden tossing Gore his oily rag.

"We'll see whose blade chews more flesh when the dying begins my friends." Gore lashed out, though moments later he began shining his blade and ridding the rust.

Roman heard the chatter of his group, and normally would have warned them to be more silenced. But he understood the situation. The Hunters knew they were coming, they must have.

Normally Roman and his group would have encountered several Vampire scouts during their ride. However, they had not encountered a single one. Nothing. Which led him to believe all of the blood-sucking bastards had been called back to the castle to lie in wait.

Strangely, since being turned to the ranks of the undead, Roman not only found the art of meditation relaxing, but felt as though it provided some sort of link to the mind of Vladris.

He knew not of the location of Vladris, or what thoughts crept into the warrior's mind; but rather a feeling of connection. Roman had often wondered if the same feeling was had by all Hunters, or just himself. He had promised himself that should he ever take a Vampire alive, he'd get the answer to his question. Unfortunately, no day had yet come. He simply enjoyed killing them too much.

Roman also wondered of Scucca. What had spawned such loyalty from the dog, at first sight no less. The Vampiric hound of hell had partnered itself with Roman from the very first encounter, and he was still unsure why. As badly as Roman Raines wanted to watch the Hunters' castle burn to the ground, he felt an overwhelming need to visit their archives first. He wanted to learn as much about the race which he was forced into, because, like it or not; he was indeed a Vampire.

The battle of Callian saw thousands fall, hundreds of thousands even. The Husk allied themselves with what remained of the Ronical Kingdom, brining their massive blades into battle.

And though the damned green-skinned Husk were born to slay us, still we pushed them back. Our elites were killing Husk Tribals, their warrior of warriors, at a ratio of three-to-one.

As our great army began to crush what few Husk which remained, an unknown warrior arrived with but twelve knights. And though our enemy's force remained below a hundred warriors, standing against thousands of our own, the warrior led them to victory.

Our own people are beginning to call them the twelve angels. They are whispering that the human warrior is a God among men. Could it be so? Could a God walk among them and protect such a beautiful kingdom?

Our queen has announced such talk is to be considered treason, and that anyone guilty will be led to the gallows. Still, secretive chatter continues among our own ranks.

As Sarah continued to read the Hunter archives, she grew to understand the power in battle which Vladris possessed. Having him nearby made her feel completely safe, as if the Gods did not have power to harm her. For such a warrior to have been turned, giving him the strength and speed of an immortal, Sarah truly believed it was the Hunters' destiny to rule civilization.

"We approach Marlock," Roman said, his chilled voice only adding to the vivid mist which escaped his lips on such a cold morning. Adding a bit more eeriness to the sight of a hound spawned of hell running beside them.

The snow had subsided, leaving behind drifts deep with powder and a cold that hurt to the bone. Roman had known of Marlock throughout his lifetime of hatred for the Hunters. And as legend had spoken of it, he had imagined a great city, its buildings filled with warriors who remained true to their fight against the Vampires. A great city marked by the hanging of red skulls from limbs of surrounding trees. A warning to any Hunters who might approach.

It soon became evident to Roman Raines that the legends spoke of a lie, at least in the description of Marlock. It was no city, not in the least. Merely a village of only a few dozen dwellings, each made of thick logs and cemented mud.

He hoped that the rest of the Marlock legend held true. It spoke of an army so mighty, so in love with the bloodlust of Vampires, that the Hunters could not remove them from their city. Or in this case, small village.

"Let us hope the warriors put up a better fight than the beauty of their home." Gore said loudly as the group slowed to a trot.

"Or that their women are easier on the eyes." Tunak added, prompting laughter from most.

"Silence," Roman demanded, turning to his group for a moment. "A warrior can never be judged by his surroundings. To do so is unwise. The mightiest I have ever had the honor of doing battle with, or against, came from such conditions," Roman added. "For these men know of no comfort, they know of no luxury. They only know of pain, which makes for a dangerous warrior indeed. A grizzly among men."

"A grizzly growls in my stomach," Pica said, his bow strung to the back of his thick coat. "Let's hope these dangerous warriors know of food." he added, the entire group beginning to laugh once more.

"Halt!" a man cried, walking from behind a nearby tree with crossbow in hand.

The stranger looked impoverished, as though he had not seen the basic Human comforts in many days. Still he stood there, his crossbow aimed directly into the direction of Roman Raines.

"What business do you have here?" the man asked, as nearly a dozen more men walked from surrounding trees, each carrying either a large sword or man-slaying axe.

"We slay Vampires, that is our business. Have we arrived among friends of the same purpose, or do the legends of such a city merely speak a lie." Roman responded, turning to face the crossbow wielding man.

"Liar! You are a Hunter yourself!" the man yelled.

"Indeed," Roman said calmly, turning his head a bit to view the remaining men as the snow steadily began to fall once more. "But I am of no threat to you. If it were the case, you and your friends would already lay in a pool of your own fluids."

The man continued to look at Roman, into the eyes of a warrior who knew of life after death, yet traveled with men.

"You know it to be the truth," Roman said. "We wish to eat, rest and then talk of an assault against the Hunters."

"You lie! To speak of such is to speak of suicide." one of the other men cried out, his grip holding a one-handed axe.

"To speak of suicide would be for another man to call me out as a liar." Roman warned.

As they continued to look Roman over, thick white hair braided down to the warrior's lower back, eyes nearly glowing as hot coals would, the man who held a crossbow nodded a bit.

"You are the one everyone speaks of. The demon which hunts demons, are you not?" the man asked.

"I am the demon who hunts Vladris. I seek to end his reign of terror, slaying with him the legend which follows. The rest of the dead Vampires laying in my wake have simply gotten in the way." Roman said sternly, moments later grinning a bit.

"Then yes, the tales of Marlock are true," the man said, returning the grin. "Take them in at once! They are heroes among us!"

And with that short, but fate-altering conversation, the warriors led Roman and his group into Marlock. Food they would have on this night, only the finest Marlock had to offer. For Roman's legend was growing across Roncia, having already reached the ears of such a secluded village and its warriors.

"Bring him!" Sarah yelled, her voice anything but demonic as the Vampire queen sat in a luxurious throne of jewels.

As Vladris entered her throne room, carrying with him a young man with bound hands, he tossed the baggage down abruptly.

"Enough! No harm is to come to this prisoner," Sarah said loudly, warning her finest Hunter. "If one of our own but splits a single hair on his head, you had better slay them in my stead."

"Yes my queen." Vladris replied, not quite understanding her fascination with the young man, but daring not question her.

"You will not be harmed. You have my word." Sarah replied with a smile.

And though the prisoner's face, which remained under the veil of a sackcloth bag, couldn't see the queen of Hunters; her voice sounded familiar to him. Almost soothing.

"And that's when Roman sprung from the trees and together, we slew nearly a dozen of the bastards!" Gore said loudly, slamming a steel mug to the table.

It was filled with a warmed brew. A drink similar to what humans considered ale, though it contained several herbal extracts as well. The people of Marlock considered it to have both healing and relaxation qualities; not to mention it would warm the bones of even the mightiest of warriors.

"Your numbers are far less than I had expected."

Roman said with seriousness as the entire group, nearly thirty strong, looked back at him.

"We were once very formidable, just as your legend speaks. But years of war against an enemy who outnumbers us so greatly has taken its toll." Anthony replied. He had been the first to confront Roman's group hours before, crossbow in hand and served as leader of their people.

"And this other group of warriors you speak of?" Roman asked.

"Indeed," Anthony replied. "They are out on a supply raid and are not expected to return for the duration of four more days."

"Four cold days." Pica said, causing a chuckling-stir throughout the group.

"We realized the Hunters hate cold. They will enter snowy fields to do battle as long as they understand it is temporary. So we dug in here," a large warrior replied. His hair was a bit short, and fiery red at first glance. His faced was marred with scars of war, his eyes further speaking of their woes. "They know we are here. Yet they have been unable to break us in a single battle...and unwilling to stay for more."

"This is my first in command, Bral," Anthony said. "One of the finest men you will ever meet, and even more so when it comes to combat."

"Then it is indeed an honor." Roman replied, nodding to such a highly of spoken warrior.

"I do not understand your travels with the Vampires' dog if you are indeed a slayer of the undead?" a man asked, speaking loudly as a two-handed sword lay snug to his back, strapped with leather bonding.

"Four!" Anthony said loudly, scolding his warrior.

"It is alright," Roman said, staring hard at the sword-strapped man. "I myself do not understand it. From what I have learned along the way, the hellhounds marry themselves to the strongest of warriors. Scucca was by the side of Vladris when we first met, yet he left with me."

"Then you truly are a greater warrior than Vladris? If it is true, we may very well turn the tides of war!" Four replied.

"Roman, I apologize. Four speaks out of turn." Anthony added.

"I understand his questions, and have one of my own. Why Four?" Roman asked.

"Because, no matter who we face on the battlefield, he fights as well as their four best warriors." Anthony replied.

"Interesting." Roman said.

"So our plan?" Bral asked, always the one for strategy when it came to battle.

"Spread the rumor of a great assault against the town of Bainson," Roman said. "The Hunters will deplete their ranks to seek such a battle and defend the town. Then, we strike their castle with our best men. It will be defended, but they should not be able to hold us. We will reach their queen long before the Hunters dispatched to Bainson return."

"It is a solid plan. There are many humans who worship Vampires in Bainson." Bral replied.

"First we must rest for the night and finish filling our bellies." Roman said.

"Agreed, my friend." Anthony replied, extending his hand to the Vampire which stalked his own kind. And with their handshake came a treaty of death to come.

Sarah's favorite place throughout the castle wasn't the room that held her throne, which had been the favorite of so many before her. Instead, she found herself drawn to the room of archives. She felt compelled to find out as much about the Hunters as possible.

And on this great day, the day of our Lord 4072, our army of undead faced its toughest. A small army on the planet of Ronica, led by their King and a warrior among their finest. A warrior which fights like no other our species has ever encountered. A warrior who has slain many of our kind, including four elite Knights dispatched by our very queen.

Perhaps we have underestimated the will of humankind. The resolve of such an outmatched opponent. They must know of their inevitable demise. They must see the death and destruction around them. Yet this warrior of light gives them hope. Strength. Whatever the cost, whatever measures must be taken, this warrior must be ended if Ronica is to fall under our rule.

Sarah continued to read through books which were inked by the hand of Vampires hundreds, possibly even thousands of years before her eyes skimmed the pages of the moment.

Today our species did the unthinkable. Retreat from battle. With our numbers strong and our greatest elite, Graddon, on the battlefield, swift victory was sure to follow.

Yet we were bested, Graddon falling gruesomely to this knight of light which wields a longsword. He is the one our own people have spoken of as an angel. Our queen has called him a glorified farmer, yet he has, by his own hands, killed hundreds of our kin. Members of our own species have even begun speaking of him as the devil, if not the angel he appears to be. The very devil! They say he is un-slayable, though speaking of a human in such a way is considered treason.

Sarah stopped abruptly.

"My queen." Vladris said.

"What is it my champion?" the pale white display of beauty replied, a corset snugly fit around curves of perfection.

"The prisoner is under watch and being treated kind, just as you instructed." Vladris replied.

"Thank you my champion," Sarah said with pause. "I will soon explain to you my reasoning, as well as our plan."

"You need not explain a thing to me, my queen." Vladris responded.

"A warrior of such valor deserves an explanation, even from his queen." Sarah said with both admiration and intrigue.

"Thank you my queen." he replied, nodding slightly before turning to leave the doorway.

Sarah wanted to know more. More about their race, and just as importantly, more about her champion warrior. Skimming through the pages of the Hunter Archives, she saw talk of a split in their ranks, the coming of a second queen and a war that would see the two Hunter factions fighting each other. Yet, none of it concerned her.

As she reached the next entry dedicated to the knight of light, her eyes began to focus with concentration.

Today our queen executed dozens of our own species. Each of them guilty for speaking of this knight of light, Vladris, in such a God-like fashion. He slew Graddon, our very best, and did so with such ease. Our next move was to trap his caravan away from the confines of such a beautiful castle, slay him by the roadside. Queen Vivian dispatched her three finest elites, a sure death sentence for any Human warrior. Yet, Vladris lives.

Our three elites fell in battle, along with a dozen Hunters as only two arrived back to speak of the battle. They brought with them a prisoner. A woman named Amelia. She seems to have the affections of Vladris, which our queen feels could be the achilles heel of such a mighty warrior.

Only time will tell of what is to become of her. But, as of this very moment, they are doing things to her. Unspeakable things. Many of our own warriors have reported her screams from behind the wooden doors in which she is being held.

Sarah stopped at that moment, having tried to imagine a warrior such as Vladris dealing with the loss of love.

She too had lost her true love in Adam Michaels, feeling condemned, even cursed, with immortality. Forever to think about a love never realized; to grieve for the one her heart longed for.

Vladris had dealt with this very pain for many years now. And it was a trait that made him even more honorable in her eyes. The strongest warrior among her people growing even stronger in the affections of his queen.

"Non-sense! There can be no such victory, and to speak of it is insanity!" the warrior cried out.

"Silence Ranthra, you speak out of turn!" Anthony replied loudly, trying to lull the large warrior.

He was outfitted in brown fur, beneath which, rested a hide of leather that was finely stitched. The hulking warrior's head shaved clean with a scar protruding from the top of his skull to the outer edges of his top lip.

"I speak the truth," Ranthra replied with emotion. "To march us onto the doorstep of the Hunters is a death sentence to all who would be foolish enough to follow you."

"Careful with your words Ranthra." Anthony said in a cautioning fashion.

"Your courage I do not question, for I have seen it many times over," Ranthra replied, turning to Roman. "It is the courage and abilities of this man. The man who claims himself better than Vladris."

"Not a believer?" Roman asked calmly.

"I have seen Vladris fight, even clashed my own sword against his. I have the very scar upon my face to show for it. Luckily, my life as well. Vladris cannot be beaten!" Ranthra exclaimed.

"Not by a warrior who walks the path of a coward." Roman replied.

"I walk no such path, and you are in no position to question that statement." Ranthra said, drawing his sword and placing its tip to the Hunter Elite's throat.

"Enough Ranthra!" Anthony yelled, standing to his feet.

"No, I want to see what this slayer of Vampires is truly capable of! Vladris went through my group of warriors, six of us in total! If he is as mighty as he speaks, let him prove it right here!"

"Only six?" Roman asked, a bit of sarcasm on his words as he remained sitting for a moment.

Then, without a hint of warning, Roman stood to his feet and spun with inhuman speed, smashing Ranthra's head through the table before them. With the powder of wood filling the air, Roman maintained his grip on the back of Ranthra's neck, pulling him back to his feet abruptly before tossing the bewildered warrior against a nearby wall.

As Ranthra slid to a sitting position, nearly unconscious, Roman met his next challenge head on. The Vampiric warrior clutched the throat of a second warrior who rushed, applying enough pressure for the man to drop his axe, at which time Roman kicked him square to the chest, knocking him back against the opposite wall.

A third warrior joined the fray, dagger extended fully in an attempt to end Roman's growing legend. Instead, his journey was cut short as Roman grabbed the warrior's wrist, his firm grip snapping the man's wrist as though it were but a dry twig. A backhand sent the reeling warrior to the floor with a thud, Roman having secured his dagger in the process.

Throwing it end over end with surgical precision, the dagger dug into the wall behind a fourth warrior, merely inches from the man's face.

It was a warning, and Roman made damn sure it was a warning well received as he all but dared the warrior to continue with the gaze of his eyes.

"Six warriors, six-hundred warriors. It does not matter. I will have my fight with Vladris before whatever God you pray to. Any man who thinks me unworthy of ending the demon of demons, let him speak now." Roman said, a harsh truth blanketing his words.

No man dared step forward, the Hunter Elite having bested many of them in a matter of seconds. At that moment each one of them believed Roman would be the warrior to end Vladris. Every one except for Ranthra, who had been the only warrior who could claim an exchange with both legends of battle. In his mind, the battle could go either way. He was unsure of the outcome, but damn sure that he was officially in on the plan to reunite Roman and Vladris in battle.

Vladris stood on the balcony which overlooked the bursting water of a river below. Many things raced through the mighty warrior's head as he continued his stare onto the horizon at distant. Rolling hills littered with trees, all seemingly so full of life.

"His name is Troy." Sarah said, slowly entering the quarters of Vladris.

"My queen." Vladris replied with a slight bow.

"In my travels with Roman Raines, my human travels, Troy was taken in by our crew," she said. "I am very fond of the boy, but my fondness is minascule compared to Roman's."

"You plan to use the prisoner as leverage?" Vladris asked.

"I plan to turn Roman to our cause. I intend to force his hand by making him choose between total submission to our will or the death of Troy, because I know he will not allow the boy to die." Sarah replied.

"But he is a Vampire now. His affections for the boy may not remain." Vladris said.

"They will remain, as does the hatred for our own species. He will be forced to choose to accept his place among us or the death of a young man he thinks of as a son. And he will choose the safety of Troy." Sarah responded.

"And if he does not?" Vladris asked.

"Then you will have your chance to prove the better warrior." Sarah replied.

Vladris longed for the battle. He knew that some of his own race had begun chattering of a demon who possibly could best him. Every chance Vladris had to solidify his own legend, was a chance he yearned for.

"Speak to me of Amelia." Sarah asked.

Vladris turned away from her, once again facing the balcony and view of the rolling hills curtained with rain. It was thought to be an insult to turn away from their queen, though he thought the outcome worse had his tears been discovered.

"My queen?" Vladris finally responded, masking his overwhelming emotion. The very mention of her name sending shock waves throughout his entire body.

"My champion, your show of affection for her is not a weakness. It is a strength," she said, approaching him easily. "Turn to face me. Tell me of your method in dealing with love lost, for I am cursed with the same fate."

"Killing," Vladris said bluntly as Sarah's fingers comforted the face of such an agonized soldier. "When I am on the battlefield, sinking blade to flesh and cleaving apologies from enemies, my mind is not concerned with Amelia."

"Tell me of her. It speaks of Amelia in the archives, but briefly. Tell me of the type of woman she was." Sarah said.

"She was perfect. I have never met a woman who brought me more happiness with her mere presence. Everything about her made me better, and I do apologize for my weakness with emotion my queen, but think not that I am weak on the battlefield." Vladris said.

"I know only the opposite. The archives speak in great detail of the warriors who have faced you, all of them falling swiftly." Sarah said as they stood only a few feet apart.

"It also speaks of greater days. A time when the

Hunters were a single society, led by both queen and king." Sarah said, the look of intentional seduction in her eyes.

"My queen?" Vladris said.

"Become our king. Rule at my side, and let us unify every Hunter to our cause. I am no Amelia, but I may provide a comfort from her constant memory, and you from the constant memory of my own love lost." Sarah said.

Vladris stood there. At first puzzled, though he soon began to realize the potential behind such a marriage. Maybe Sarah could help him forget, at least to a degree, his Amelia. Together they could rule without their own personal struggles, and do so in striking fashion.

"My mind must be clear when facing Roman Raines, be it in battle or brotherhood. Once he is either with us, or in an eternal grave, then I will gladly become your king." Vladris replied.

"Good," Sarah said, smiling as wide as her powder-white face would allow. "For these people already look to you as their king. And I look to you as my champion." she added, leaning in to kiss the warrior who would help elevate their species back into one of total dominance.

"I have not seen snowfall this thick in many years." Tunak said, several of the warriors sitting inside the cabin, watching the frigid moisture fall to the ground.

"It is a sign," Four said. "Roman was born to end the life of Vladris!"

"Perhaps," Ranthra said loudly, doing his best to overcome their loud chants. "Or perhaps Roman has severely underestimated his enemy."

No chanting followed the statement, only silence as everyone stopped to hear his reasoning.

"I mean no disrespect to Roman," he said, both Tunak and Gore acknowledging his honesty. "But I may claim to be the only warrior among us to have faced both men in battle, albeit shortly. Vladris moves unlike any man, or monster, that I have ever faced. No legend, besides his very own, tells a tale of such ability to slay." Ranthra said.

"You have yet to see Roman's true ability to slay. For I was with him when he had but a single blade; yet five Hunters still fell. Five!" Tunak shouted.

"I do not doubt your claim warrior," Ranthra said, easing the tense of their exchange. "But I ask you this. If Roman is a Vampire, it means he did indeed fall in battle. Who then? Who was the warrior to slay him?" Ranthra asked.

"Vladris." Roman replied, shutting the door abruptly, his body-length coat of fur covered with snow.

"Vladris?" Tunak asked, the entire group stunned with the information.

"Indeed," Roman calmly replied, his stare cutting into Ranthra. "A better question may be who introduced Vladris to his death?"

"I do not know for sure, and think no man does. You would have to dig deep into recorded history to find the answer you seek." Ranthra replied.

"Or dig my blade deep into his own flesh, for Vladris knows the answer. Vladris saw the face of his slayer, much like he will see my own face." Roman responded.

"I think it not important at the moment either way," Anthony said, following Roman inside and seeking a source of heat to defeat the chill of his bones. "This snow will hinder our travels greatly. We would be wise to remain here until the sky breaks for our long journey ahead."

"No," Roman said, his voice unwaivering. "I leave as scheduled. Any man who wishes to remain behind is free to do so," he added, the blaze red of his eyes brightening a bit. "But he who seeks to become legend will accompany me, for Vladris will fall by my sword. I swear of it."

And the group of warriors remained silent, each man contemplating his own destiny. Wondering what the outcome would be when the two legends finally collided. Anyone accompanying Roman would surely be slain if Roman fell, but if he was successful in bringing down the mighty Vladris? If indeed he possessed the skill to slay the demon of demons? Roman, as well as any warrior who stood with him, would forever be considered legend across Ronica. The dream of every true warrior.

"You would be wise to hold your tongue to Roman." Anthony said, walking quickly to catch up with Ranthra. A few warriors had left the cozy confines of the small lodge to seek good-burning wood for its fireplace.

"And you would be wise to remain here, as I intend to," Ranthra replied, turning to face their leader by committee. "I do not doubt the abilities of Roman in combat, as everyone suspects. But I do not doubt the abilities of Vladris either. The legends hold true, for I have seen it with my own eyes. To follow Roman into a battle with the demon of demons is to throw yourself on your own sword. All while saving yourself the journey of days by horseback. I'll not ride hard to a rematch of swords which saw Roman fall during the first battle."

"So your choice has already been made?" Anthony asked, bitter cold masking his voice with droplets of fog.

"My mind was made the moment I saw Vladris first swing on the battlefield. The Gods spared my life on that very day, and I will not spit in their face by marching into the same scenario again." Ranthra replied.

Anthony shook his head for a moment, silently, before turning to begin a walk toward his small home in Marlock.

"So now you think me a coward?" Ranthra asked.

"No my friend," Anthony replied, turning to face him once more. "I have seen your bravery in battle, time and time again. No, I begin to question the definition of courage at this moment, and when it becomes ignorance."

"Go my friend, for you have much to think about on this night." Ranthra replied.

"Are they treating you well?" Sarah asked, slowly entering the room in which Troy was being held.

Their castle was complete, right down to a full-size dungeon. Yet Troy had been placed in a room only yards away from Sarah's very own. One normally reserved for important guests among their kind.

"Yes." Troy replied, wanting to hate Sarah for being a Vampire, while also remembering the respect he held for her human memory.

"I have no intentions of harming you," Sarah said, walking closer to him. "Leave us." she added, turning to the two Hunters who had been assigned to Troy's door.

"I have no intentions of harming Roman either." she said.

"Roman? He's here?" Troy asked with enthusiasm.

"Not yet," Sarah replied. "But we expect to see him soon enough. I intend to ask him to remain here," she added. "And there is a place for you as well."

"Roman Raines will never join you! He despises your kind, as do I! Hunters killed my family in front of me, and you ask me to remain here to live among them?" Troy asked, his voice raising in the process.

It was the first time Sarah had seen the boy's temper. She remembered holding him as Hunters closed in, remembered calming his fears as Adam Michaels and the Gunship crew protected them both against certain death.

"I think with time Roman will come around." Sarah said with a smile, brilliant white teeth cresting across such an angelic face.

"I think you're full of shit!" Troy yelled, prompting the guards to come back into the room. "I think you will soon find out how mortal you truly are, at the tip of Roman's blade...you bitch!"

As the two Hunters approached, Troy decided it time to show his hard-earned skill. Kicking swiftly toward the floor, his foot caught one of the Hunters above its knee, instantly breaking the femur bone and sending the soldier to the ground in pain.

The second guard was met head on, Troy grabbing the monster's wrist. Of course, a young man barely eighteen years of age, he hadn't the ability to overpower the beast. Mythra. The art of stick-fighting, based around momentum-shifting. Troy had studied the art since losing his family, at first to occupy himself. However, he had quickly mastered the art and it displayed at this very moment.

Letting loose the Vampire's wrist at the perfect moment, Troy used the monster's own momentum, allowing it to slam onto the ground. And as the guard began to get back to its feet, Troy's swift kicks broke the beast's forearm in several places.

The same foot kicked the base of a nearby table, loosing a wooden leg which was quickly kicked into one of his free hands.

"Time for me to take my leave you Vampiric bitch!" Troy yelled, pointing the table leg into her face.

Shocked, Sarah simply walked back a bit. She had never seen Troy as anything other than a feeble child. Yet here he stood, two of her mighty warriors laying defenseless and her own safety in jepoardy.

Vladris slowly walked into the room, Troy's attention shifting to the large warrior.

"Back my queen, I will handle this."

And step back Sarah did, knowing well that she had underestimated Troy this entire time. She also began to wonder if Vladris facing Roman was wise. Had she become too comfy in her new role? Had she underestimated Roman Raines as well?

Troy's art of fighting allowed him to take advantage of larger opponents, and his mind knew that could prove disaster for Vladris, for he was a much larger warrior.

"Well come on." Troy said provokingly, continuing to hold the shattered wooden leg of a table in the Hunter's direction. He grew impatient, tired of waiting for Vladris to enter the fight with a mistake.

With the speed of the very rays of a sun, Vladris thrust his arm forward, wrapping Troy's attacking hand and squeezing until the wooden leg fell to the room's floor. The demon's freehand then plunged in, clawed fingers gripping Troy by the throat and forcing him to the wall, his feet leaving ground in the process.

"Vladris!" Sarah yelled, continuing to want no harm to come to the young man.

"I have left very few lives to walk away," Vladris said harshly, his large eyes brimming with both red and black pigment. "Know now that if it were not for a queen's command and a lover's wish, your lungs would plead for air as I ripped your head from the scrawny shoulders which held it."

And with that statement of caution, Vladris loosened his grip of tenacity, letting Troy stand on his own feet once more.

"Are you alright my queen?" Vladris asked.

"I am fine my champion." Sarah replied.

"What happened to you?" Troy demandingly asked as he began to breathe easier. "You used to hate the Hunters. I was there when your own father, the same father who fought against the Hunters, died in an explosion of flame!"

"Yes, that was unfortunate," Sarah replied. "But those were different times," she added. "Different times indeed."

Sarah turned to Vladris for a moment while her two Hunters slowly gathered themselves from the floor. This was her species now, and it was her job to protect them at all costs.

"Change of plans," Sarah said firmly. "If Roman denies his place by our side, Troy will indeed die. In front of the warrior."

"Understood." Vladris said with a grin.

"And double the security detail on Troy's door." she

added.

"At once." Vladris said.

The morning light of Marlock brought with it more snow, falling powdery-white onto the ground without reserve. Roman sat on a fine horse, a steed which had been outfitted with the toughest armor available, at least by such a secluded group.

Tunak and Gore quickly joined him, as did the rest of his group, slowly galloping their own steeds to his piece of ground.

"Draden, Pica. You are to remain here. Should I fall, these people need someone to continue the hunt." Roman replied.

"Roman," Pica said, his large bow once again strapped to the upper of his back. "We want to fight."

"A fact I both know and respect," Roman replied. "But you know the location of my ship. You will be able to care for my dog," he added, glancing down at Scucca. "You will succeed me should I fall." he added.

"We understand," Draden said, the brilliant-white light of snow refracting from his Dragon-scaled hide. "And we wish you luck warrior."

"I make my own luck." Roman replied, thinking back to a time when his human flesh leaned on the spoken line heavily.

"And what say you?" Tunak said loudly, his voice echoing toward the group of warriors led by Anthony. "Who is ready to accompany us to the fall of the mighty Vladris?"

Four climbed to his mount quickly, the peppered-gray horse then trotting to Roman's group.

"That is all? One warrior?" Tunak asked loudly.

"Relax my brother, it takes but one to slay Vladris and end his legend of lies." Roman said, nodding his respect to Four.

"Four is as capable as any that I have. He will serve you

well in battle, and I will personally see to the proper care of your hound and warriors." Anthony replied.

"Gratitude my friend," Roman said, demonic eyes skimming the group a final time. "I will return in one week's time with the head of a legend so easily spoken," he added. "If not, continue my legacy and bring their race to its knees."

"Either way, it will be done. You have my word." Draden replied.

And with that final exchange of words, Roman, Tunak, Gore and Four would turn to head away. Disappearing quickly into the thick of snowfall, well-supplied and well-intentioned.

"Sir, we have just received word of Roman Raines departing Marlock for us." a Hunter said, entering the lavish quarters of Vladris.

"Good. Let him come." Vladris replied.

"Should I double the guard?" the Hunter asked.

"You have made me aware, which is as good as doubling the guard. So no, it is not necessary."

"And the queen, sir? Should I attach a personal escort team with her?" the Hunter asked.

"I am her personal escort team!" Vladris yelled, approaching the intimidated warrior of death. "Do you not think me capable of slaying Roman Raines?" Vladris asked.

"Of course sir," the warrior replied. "There are those among our ranks that whisper of his ability in combat, but I am not one such warrior."

"Whispering is the work of a coward. Any warrior who believes in something so strongly, would proudly announce his belief. To whisper is to be weak." Vladris responded sharply.

"Yes sir." the Hunter said.

"You may go. Inform the others I will be speaking shortly." Vladris commanded.

"Yes sir." the Hunter warrior replied, turning to execute an order as the black leather of his boots struck loudly onto the stone-tiled floor

"Forgive them. They do not see you as I do, for they have not seen your history of battle." Sarah said, approaching her new love slowly.

"My queen." Vladris said, kneeling slightly in order to show his respect.

"Many among our ranks have heard of your legend, but have not seen it with their own eyes." Sarah said, wrapping her arms around the neck of the capable warrior.

"Their eyes will learn of it soon enough." Vladris said.

"I will offer him a place at our side, and I am a woman of my word. Please know that if he accepts it, he is not to be harmed." Sarah said.

"I would expect no less from you my queen. But I have seen into this warrior's eyes. He will not submit to our will, and you should expect no less from him." Vladris replied.

"Either way, he will be given a choice. And be it an end to his reign of terror against our race, or an end to the breath in his lungs, this will soon be behind us my champion." Sarah said.

"Yes my queen." Vladris replied.

"I have no idea? He has gone mad!" one of the Hunters who stood in a watch house on the castle wall said, speaking to another.

"Surely he knows of Roman's ability in battle? Surely he would rather be enjoying a fine meal this night?" the other guard remarked as they watched him. Their hero among heroes, sitting outside of the castle gates.

A single chair of banded leather and wood beneath him, and a single sword of massive-scale strapped onto his back. Vladris sat there, patiently awaiting the arrival of Roman Raines.

He understood, of course, that Roman's arrival was many hours, if not days away. And that the warrior traveled with others. Still, Vladris intended to do things in such a way that his legend would never again be questioned.

"Sir, is there anything you need?" a Hunter asked, walking through the gates slowly, daring not disturb the hero any more than necessary.

"Yes. Assemble our finest and bring them here, before me." Vladris demanded.

"Yes. At once." the Hunter replied.

Nearly an hour after Vladris had ordered it so, twenty of the finest soldiers the Vampires had to offer slowly made their way outside of the gates. Forming into a single group in front of their hero and awaiting his next command.

"Most of you have learned of my abilities in battle through words. Legends told, passed down through generations," Vladris said, standing to his feet slowly. "And I am aware that a few have even started to whisper of this man-demon. Roman Raines. Even going so far as to whisper of his ability to best me in combat." he added, cutting his words to approach the faces of each warrior.

"There is a reason that legend of my ability to end lives continues to be passed down. Reasoning that each of you will now know holds true with your very own eyes," Vladris said in a sharp voice. "And while the rest of you whisper in fear, I await the warrior who comes. I long for a fight with the man which so many of you fear. Because, when this man who rides to our gates to end my legend arrives, he will soon beg for grace moments before the very blade strapped to my back slays him. And each of you will then know who to fear. Who to make legend of. Now go, cowards, and do not disturb me further!" Vladris yelled as if to dare any of them to speak.

As the group of Vampiric warriors turned to once again

enter the castle, Vladris returned to his chair. Turning his back to their castle and facing the rolling hills of Ronica before him as the rain began to fall down.

"We make good time," Tunak yelled loudly as their horses drudged through the thick of mud, finally having left the clutches of snow-filled mountains. "It is unusual to see no patrols this close to their castle."

"They have cleared a path for us. Their hero believes in the ability to slay me. An ability which he does not possess, but makes for an easier ride indeed." Roman replied with confidence.

"We will be on them by nightfall." Four said.

"Then we will stop to make camp. I wish to face him in the light of day." Roman replied, bringing his horse to an abrupt halt.

"I agree. If we are to slay the demon of demons, the daylight will give us an advantage." Gore added.

"I wish to face him in the daylight, not for an advantage," Roman said sternly as his body dropped from horse to ground below. "I simply wish to slay him during a moment in which many eyes can see."

For the next few minutes, Roman and Tunak made camp with a small tent of white cloth, while Four and Gore collected any dry wood they could find. In such a rain-filled environment the task proved daunting, but eventually they had collected enough to produce heat throughout the night.

Vladris knew they were close. He had made the journey several times himself, and knew that they had to be just beyond the tree-line at horizon's end. It also warranted the assumption that Roman wanted his fight during the day, and that sat well with Vladris. He too wanted a thick of witnesses for their battle. And though he knew Sarah would attempt to bring Roman to their cause, the hero among Vampires had a feeling throughout his gut that it wasn't to be.

So Vladris remained in his chair, dedicating such a quiet night of rainfall and breeze to his thoughts. Though he had no intentions of falling in battle, he knew that if it were to be, he had lived a life worth speaking of. He had known of both lust and love. Known of greed and loss. He stared across the very hills which once worked with Ronical farmers to produce crops to feed their mighty army.

He remembered the king he served during his mortal life. An honorable man, one that was cut down by the Vampires shortly after Ronica began to fall.

He remembered, while still in the realm of a mortal, defeating the Hunter champion in battle. His own abilities besting those of the Vampiric legend. Vladris began to wonder if Roman Raines was one such man. Was it meant for Roman to cut Vladris down in battle, ending a life, and along with it the memories of a Ronica that once flourished?

But soon his thoughts began to turn to Amelia. His love for her had been one of such truthful purity. From the tip of his sword to the bones in his chest, he loved her. Everything he was or would ever be was tied into the woman who would never return.

And that very emotion, one of horrific loss that would forever remain, was the emotion which allowed him to fight like a lion. As if he were a hundred lions in battle. And as the chills of a loss never-ending began to consume him once more, he knew it to be the truth. Roman Raines could not best him.

And so he spent the remainder of the night thinking of his beloved Amelia, a life before the rule of Vampires and, of course, the rain. The soothing rain which hit the trees of a distant horizon, bringing with it a sound which calmed the warrior and allowed him to control his anger.

Vladris was not alone in thought on such a night of

pouring rain, however, as Roman also reflected back on his life up until this point.

His entire family slaughtered for sport at the hands of Hunters. His involvement in killing one of their queens and a life sworn to ending the bloodline of the race which he considered to be the cancer of man.

Roman did not fear death. A direct effect of having nothing to live for. His only purpose was to slay those who deserved death, and he did so well. By most accounts, Roman Raines was the deadliest warrior alive, but not all of them.

Many still spoke of Vladris, hero of the Vampires. If he were able to slay the demon of demons, it would not only send ripples of fear through the Vampiric race, but solidify his legend as the greatest warrior to ever live.

He believed he could do it, and planned to do it alone. Pulling a dagger from his waist, he planted it firmly into the ground of their campsite while the others slept. Then, pulling a necklace from beneath his robe, a key to his shuttle dangling from it, Roman placed it around the dagger's handle. And with that, the Vampire who hunted his own kind walked away from camp and into the direction of a castle not far away. Alone.

Vladris was first pulled back from his memories with Amelia as a bell began to toll throughout the castle, one the Hunters reserved for the unusual event of an army marching to their doorstep.

As Vladris stood to his feet, he wondered how fitting it seemed. Roman walking to their castle by himself and to the toll of a bell that signified an entire army. One warrior looking to capture the legacy of another, almost as if two complete armies were nearing battle. Though only two champions stood, less than a hundred yards apart.

As Hunters began to make their way to the castle's entrance, they soon partitioned off a bit to allow their

queen a quick passage to the two warriors who had
become locked in a stare.

"I have long awaited this very moment, even seen it in
my dreams." Roman said, squeezing his fists with
crushing power.

"I respect your courage warrior. Just as I have
respected each warrior before you, all of them dead by my
hands." Vladris replied.

"Enough!" Sarah yelled, approaching the two soldiers of
destiny with two soldiers of her own. Escort soldiers who
held Troy in chains.

"It's been a long time Roman Raines." Sarah said, her
demonic tone very soothing by Vampiric standards.

"Not long enough you crazy bitch." he replied.

"Still the feisty warrior. Such a trait will be of great
value to me when you bow your loyalties." Sarah
responded.

"A long time indeed, then, as you've forgotten that I bow
to no one." Roman said.

"Perhaps," she replied with a grin, motioning her escort
soldiers to remove a hood from Troy's head. "Or perhaps
you'd like to rethink your loyalty to me."

As Roman laid eyes on Troy, his first reaction was the
yearning to pummel those responsible to death. Troy had
been like a son to him, at least up until the point of
becoming infected with Vampiric DNA. He had purposely
avoided contact with the boy from that point forward,
hoping to protect Troy from the horrors which now
followed him.

However, Roman's rage soon turned to desperation,
feeling as though he had already been beaten in battle.

"He has no place in all of this. Free him." Roman
demanded.

"Well that depends on you," Sarah replied with a heavy
tone. "If you bow before me, before all of those which look
on at this very moment; in return I will allow the boy to
go free."

He would be bowing to a bloodline which had stolen everything from him. But if he refused, they would take the one thing he had left. Troy was as much like a son as any boy could have ever been; and worse, he was innocent of any crimes against the Hunters.

Roman approached the group slowly, taking his massive blade and burying nearly a foot of steel into the moist ground as he continued his walk.

"That's far enough." Vladris said, holding his own blade out in order to keep Roman and Sarah distanced.

"All I know is killing," Roman said, holding his hands up slightly as a gesture of good faith. "But Troy has a chance to live a life of value. Become something more than all of this," he added, staring directly into Sarah's eyes. "I need your word that he will be allowed to leave, never to be followed. Never to be brought into this again."

"You have it, as long as I have your loyalty." Sarah quickly replied, a smile beginning to brim across her face.

"And I need a moment to say farewell to the boy. Given our history, I'm sure you understand that I want to make peace with him?"

"Make it quick," Sarah replied. "Cut the boy loose." she added, turning to her personal escort soldiers, each of them clad in banded steel of black.

"Don't talk, just listen," Roman said as Troy approached him. "Take the set of footprints my boots have made and follow them as fast as you can run. Just beyond those trees, not even thirty minutes away, a group of warriors loyal to me have made camp. When you arrive, tell them I've sent you. Tell them I've left a dagger, necklace and dog for you. Have them wait until midday for me, and should I fail to return, they are to lead you to my shuttle."

"Roman, I don't want to leave you here. Maybe together..."

"No!" Roman replied fiercely. "I've always looked upon you as my own son. I can't protect those I've lost, but I can still protect you. Go." he said, holding his battle-hardened hand out for Troy.

As the two men locked hands for a moment, showing both respect and truth, Troy turned to begin a sprint for the trees which were only a few hundred yards away. Roman watched the young man run to safety, finally turning back to Sarah and her group.

"Alright Roman, I've delivered my end of the bargain. Now, bow before me and help us deliver our bloodline to a future of absolute dominance."

He had never before bowed. Not to the Gods above, nor to anyone with blood in their veins. And though it hurt as much, if not more, than a defeat on the battlefield, Roman lowered himself to the ground. His knee had never touched ground for the cause of obedience, yet his pants began to saturate just a bit from the rain-drenched soil.

"Good," Sarah said with a feeling of accomplishment. "Now rise warrior and join your brothers."

As he rose slowly, waiting for the perfect opportunity to strike, his eyes remained locked onto the queen of Vampires. And with the slightest flicker of his eyes, came a large knife which had been tucked into the back of his pants.

Sometimes it's unbelievable how a single moment changes the world around us. One second, frozen in time, that has the ability to alter who we are and how we believe.

As Roman turned his torso, ensuring every ounce of power went into the flight of the knife which left his hands, even the smallest muscles of his body popped to life under his pale skin.

Though he had bowed, the Hunters still had thought of him a bit cautiously, and that very caution saved Sarah's life. Though the blade struck home, it missed its mark as she slipped to her right. The knife which was meant for the base of her skull, instead drove into the meaty flesh of her shoulder. A wound that would not come close to slaying Sarah, though she screeched as if it would.

"Protect our queen!" Vladris yelled, turning to face Roman in what was now an inevitable showdown.

Roman had reclaimed his large blade, pulling the massive handle skyward, its gleaming edge covered with a bit of damp soil.

"Now you will know of the origin behind my legend." Vladris said, holding his sword out provokingly.

"A legend which dies today." Roman replied.

"We'll see." Vladris responded, quickly swooping his blade forward.

Roman was able to parry the shot easily, though he seemed a bit surprised by the sheer amount of force behind the bite of Vladris' steel.

Roman then lunged forward, his sword leading the way as he quickly turned the forward strike into a circular motion, chopping toward Vladris.

However, Vladris quickly stepped back to easily avoid it, stepping back a bit more.

"You disappoint me Roman Raines. You carry the traits of a Vampire, and still I could have beaten you in the days of my own mortality." Vladris said in mocking fashion.

The one thing Roman had learned through his years of fighting was the defining moment. A single breath in which your mind catches up to the body which follows your emotions. A moment when a warrior knows who's better, and as Roman's mind caught up to his extremities, he understood it to be true. Vladris was better.

He would never admit it, or even show evidence of it on his face. But as Roman's muscular frame fought with all of its might to deflect steady shots by Vladris, he began to grow tired. His hatred for Vampires had fueled his fight so far by rage. However, the rage had began to die out, losing ground to a body that longed for a deep breath and a moment's rest.

Vladris continued to strike with unrelenting fury, each angling of his blade similar to that of a serpent's strike. And though silver flashes of his blade were visible to everyone else, Vladris only saw one thing. The face of his love lost, Amelia.

His rage on the battlefield seemed to slow everything down around him, as it did each time he went to war. Literally a lion with sword in hand, the figure of a ghost nearby, her magnificent body shrouded within a satin-blue dress.

Roman quickly came to understand the warrior he fought against as tears began falling from the eyes of Vladris. Roman was good. Damn good. Yet Vladris struck as though he were a God, piercing shots sapping the life from Roman, not from wounds, but from the simple defense against them.

The trunk of Vladris' blade hit like a perfectly-forged hammer, taking with it the will of Roman Raines, as he began to understand. Vladris longed to die.

He had prayed that Roman was the warrior that growing legend spoke of. Perhaps, just maybe, the warrior who was destined to end him; and end his personal suffering in doing so.

He is not the one. Vladris, you must continue your journey among mortals. For our day will come.

Words which escaped the lips of Amelia's ghost, standing only feet away from the dying battle before his eyes.

"Yes my love." Vladris replied, speaking to a figure which only his eyes saw, leading Roman to think him mad. Not that it would matter as he lay on the ground, sword raised, with only the ability to deflect continuing shots.

Roman Raines had been bested. And while he lay there, sword lifted and shaking roughly from the trauma of steel exchanged, he considered throwing his weapon and allowing Vladris a chance to plunge bitter-cold steel into him. It would be the perfect punishment for the Vampiric warrior who had so easily defeated him. But it was not to be.

He was falling close to the end, evident to both Tunak and Four as they rode swiftly to the fight. Their horses covered the open ground at alarming speeds, rushing to aid Roman and his plans to slay Vladris.

"Riders approach!" a Hunter proclaimed loudly as a dozen or more archers pulled to take aim, the rest of their ranks quickly making way to ground level and, with any luck, the castle gates.

Both of the warriors who approached on horseback held shields high, arrows meant to end them instead biting into banded leather.

Vladris had placed himself outside of the castle's gates in order to prove his abilities, purposely keeping any help out of reach. Both Tunak and Four had depended on his confidence as the tool to slay him. And as they rode within feet of the Vampire Elite, both warriors quickly left mount in order to stand on the same sacred ground shared by Vladris and Roman.

Tunak came in, charging with full-rage as Four quickly hoisted Roman to one of the steeds. A quick slap to the animal sent it sprinting for the nearby wooded area.

The plan was, Four and Tunak would fight Vladris with the man advantage. Overpower the demon, or at least die trying.

However, their plan was swiftly cut short as, without the slightest of warning, Vladris thrust his sword forward with incredible speed. Its bite found a mark on the vitals of Tunak, digging into the warrior's chest and pulling his soul out as Vladris jerked his blade loose.

Four was a huge warrior, and his blade matched quite well. But even he saw no victory. Even if he somehow bested Vladris, dozens of Hunters had now made it to them.

"You have cost me the greatest moment of my finest victory. For that, your death will not come swiftly." Vladris said as he walked a small circle around Four, eventually plunging his sword into the ground.

Four had began to ask if Vladris intended a fight without blade. However, the Hunter Elite was quickly on him, grabbing wrist first, and then shoulder, on his way to the kill. And as Vladris sunk huge fangs into the face and upper-skull of Four, the warrior dropped his massive blade, body jerking uncontrollably from pain redefined.

"Run them down! Kill them...all of them!" Sarah yelled from her spot nearby as she tended wounds, demanding her champion seek justice.

Moments later, well over a dozen Hunter Elites thundered past the castle gates on steeds of nightmarish appearance, Vladris removing his sword from the damp ground and quickly grabbing the mount of an empty steed reserved for him.

"Go my champion, for this is your finest day. The Hunter Archives will long speak of your wrath against our enemies." Sarah said to herself, proudly watching Vladris and his finest chew up ground as their steeds rode hard into the forest.

"Help him from his mount, quickly!" Troy said as both he and Gore gently pulled Roman from the steed.

"Is Vladris defeated?" Gore asked, his Husk tone chilling to Troy's ears.

"Vladris cannot be defeated, this much I am sure of now. We must ride back at once. Inform the others that the Hunters are coming." Roman replied.

"But Four, Tunak?" Gore asked.

"I saw Tunak cut down with my own eyes. Four could not have made it out of there with his life." Roman said with regret.

"But he fights like..." Gore began to reply.

"Vladris stood before him! As did dozens of Hunters. He is not coming back, but the demons are. We must go now!" Roman yelled.

And with his words, Troy helped Roman back to his mount before joining Gore on their own steeds.

Moments later they were gone. Riding hard toward the city which Hunters could not take. Marlock. Or so the legends claimed. A claim that would soon be put to the test as Vladris and his group of soul-reavers were not far behind.

And as the rain slowly turned to snow, an ailing Roman, Troy and Gore raced toward Marlock as though their very lives depended on it, which they did.

Troy wondered what the future held for him against such an immortal army. How a life of simplicity had stood before him until the early morning hours in which Vladris had snatched him, literally getting thrown into a world of warfare.

Gore thought of the same thing, every ride to and from battle. Death. He concentrated on what needed to be done in order for him to end up on the right side of the very word of death. On this day, he wondered how he could possibly escape his soul departing a world of mortals, glancing down to a slightly-rusted blade hanging by his side. Quickly remembering the same warriors who mocked it, would give their own lives for him.

And as the snowfall began to intensify, large flakes flying into the face and peppered hair of Roman Raines, he thought of a second chance. His first attempt to slay Vladris had been a campaign of legacy building.

And though Roman was a warrior of almost supernatural abilities, that only afforded him the equivalent of a puncher's chance in the grandest fight of all-time.

He was outmatched and knew it. But perhaps, just perhaps, he would be stronger this time. Fighting for the fallen and those who could not fight for themselves, rather than his own legacy. For he too was a lion, and he was wounded and desperate. A hellhound sprinting by his side all the while.

"Someone approaches!" Bral yelled as the others came rushing.

"It's Roman, he has defeated Vladris!" Anthony said loudly.

"They do not have the glow of victory upon their faces, and ride as though death follows closely behind." Ranthra replied.

"Quickly, help Roman from his mount!" Gore yelled as both he and Troy joined the others on foot.

"What of Vladris? The others...Four?" Anthony asked.

"I faced Vladris sword to sword, yet he still lives," Roman said with pause. "I would not be alive now if not for Tunak and Four coming to my aid."

"And what of them?" Ranthra asked blatantly.

Roman answered his question with a stare, one of both remorse for the fallen and ill-intent toward Ranthra.

"Roman believes they are coming here to end us all, which means we need to dig in if we are to survive." Gore said.

"No," Roman replied, shaking his head with regret. "You are to take Troy to the ship as planned."

"But Roman, I..." Gore began.

"Troy is my son!" Roman replied, stopping to look at the young man once more. "If I am to face Vladris again, I cannot do so with the worry of Troy."

"But you said Vladris cannot be beaten." Troy replied, catching the attention of the entire group.

"He cannot. At least not by the hands of a single man. Together, however, we may be able to finally rid our world of the mightiest of demons." Roman replied.

"When will they come?" Draden asked, the Dragonborn warrior's eyes skimming the tree line.

"I'm not sure, but it will be soon," Roman replied. "And I cannot ask any of you to stay for this fight, not against such odds."

"We are with you to the end." Pica replied, pulling his freshly oiled bow to the ready.

"As am I," Ranthra said, glancing to the warrior in charge as he wielded a massive axe of razor-sharp iron. "There is strength in numbers, and I will defend my home."

"Indeed," Roman replied with a grin, nodding his respect to Ranthra. "Gore. A word."

"Yes?" Gore asked, approaching Roman so the two could talk without hinderance.

"I am asking you to take Troy because I believe we will fall. Perhaps we will be able to thin their ranks, or even slay Vladris. But I do feel as though my time has come."

"Then why stay behind? We can flee to my homeworld, regroup, and then arrive back in force?" Gore asked.

"Because I don't flee. If it were not for the longing of seeing Troy one last time, I would have stayed behind with Tunak and Gore to meet my own demise."

"I am not used to you speaking such words of defeat." Gore said.

"Nor am I," Roman replied somberly. "But I have seen into the eyes, the very soul of Vladris. He speaks with ghosts and fights as though he were already dead. He has nothing to live for, and because of that he fights as though he were a lion. I have a concern for Troy now. It has weakened me."

"I will take Troy to my homeworld, you need not worry for his safety. The Husk there, my own family, we will care for him as our own should you fall in battle. Only concern yourself with the fight that is coming and a moment of victory." Gore replied.

"Thank you my brother." Roman replied, shaking hands with his loyal friend before turning to Troy.

"Gore has promised to take you to safety. Await word of my battle, and always do by him as you would by me. Understand?" Roman asked.

"Yes," Troy said with tear-filled eyes, reaching into a long pocket on his leg. "This blade belongs to you. You gave it to me when I was but a child. Take it, and you bury it into that big-fanged son of a bitch. If you care anything for me, you'll do that."

"Take care...son. No matter what happens from this moment forward, you are destined to live a warrior's path. Always." Roman replied, looking at the young man for a moment before hugging him.

As Gore and Troy walked away, the young man turned to look upon Roman one last time.

"They killed my family, your family, our friends, and most of all, tried forcing both you and Sarah into a life of servitude. You make them pay, do you hear me? YOU MAKE THEM PAY!" Troy yelled, showing for the first time a warrior's rage in doing so.

Roman gave no reply verbally, though his heart had already committed itself to Troy's words. And as Roman watched his son ride off with Gore, headed to the location of a small ship that would pull them from Ronica and place them into the safety of Huven, the large Husk homeworld, he felt as if the Hunters had taken from him once more.

"We approach my lord, should I have our warriors pull back and scout the area?" one of the Hunter Elites asked, near-blizzard snow falling around them.

"No, ride harder. I grow sick of this cat and mouse game which holds my destiny in the balance. Ride hard and slay quickly!" Vladris demanded as the small, but well-experienced band of undead warriors stormed toward Roman, who stood by himself at the edge of village.

Turning from the entrance of a small building, Pica loosed an arrow that flew as quickly as it killed, hitting an elite in the forehead and fragmenting skull as the demon cried in misery.

"Run them down like cattle and slaughter them as such!" Vladris commanded, jumping down from his mount as the horse remained in full-gallop.

"Now, coward, we finish your journey to the world of

ghosts." Vladris said, his sword pointing at Roman Raines as warriors, both undead and living, fought in the background. Steel clashing against steel with a hellish-fury.

"One would ask which world you live in?" Roman replied, pulling his own blade to the ready. "I know why you fight; what makes you mighty in battle. For I fight for the same reason."

"All you know of me is what my legend speaks of. A legend which will grow volumes this very day as I sever your skull from its body." Vladris replied angrily, cleaving a blade strike down that narrowly missed its target.

"Perhaps. Or perhaps you fight for a slain family as I do. A woman maybe?" Roman said, noticing the look in the eyes of Vladris as he spoke the words. "So it is a woman."

Roman's words were cut short as Vladris came in with a soul-damning flurry of sword strikes, each barely blocked by Roman's own blade, and taking with them respect.

"We are no different Vladris. The Hunters have also taken from me loved ones. It's that very emotional rage which has allowed me to fight the Hunter DNA which runs through my veins." Roman said, surprising everyone as he then sunk his sword into the ground beside him. "Join us my brother."

Vladris watched with curiosity as Roman Raines stood unarmed, his hand extended to offer the demon of demons a chance to become brothers in arms.

He also watched the same figure appear, as it did every battle before. The ghost of Amelia walking among them, looking at her truest of champions.

"This warrior is one of truth. He fights for his loved ones, and protects those who cannot protect themselves. He is a very admirable man. Join him." Amelia's ghost whispered softly.

Vladris stood there, clashing steel becoming a slight background noise as the mighty warrior remained deep in thought. Both the past and the present weighed heavily as he contemplated the future.

"What does your gut tell you to do? Your lover?" Roman asked.

"My lover speaks of you as an admirable warrior. Thinks I should fight beside you in battle," Vladris replied as Roman began to smile a bit. "Unfortunately for the both of you, my heart has started to love another." he added.

Just as quickly as Roman realized Sarah Blaine had the affections of Vladris, he pulled the dagger Troy had gifted him and spun low to the ground, a move which allowed him to escape Vladris' blade while plunging the dagger's steel into the demon's chest.

Vladris staggered back, dropping his sword and trying to pull the small blade from his chest. The shock upon his face told the tale of a demon who had never been struck in battle before. At least not until the day he was turned to the ranks of the immortal.

"You've had your chance and now you must fall, an act which your own legend will speak of." Roman said, approaching the wounded lion slowly, carrying his sword with a stone-hardened grip.

And as Roman Raines hoisted his blade high, preparing to slay the mighty Vampire of legend, his senses alarmed him with pain. An arrow loosed from the bow of Pica digging through his thick armor and into flesh.

As Roman turned to speak of the misfire, Pica loosed another and another, both shots deliberately eating into the stomach of Roman Raines, who dropped his blade.

"Traitor!" Draden yelled, sprinting over bodies of the dead with a long blade in hand.

The Dragonborn warrior fell quickly, an arrow of cold steel biting into his face, loosed from Pica's bow only feet away.

And so the remaining warriors fell swiftly, leaving only Roman, who had fallen to a knee as life slowly left his body.

"As your soul departs, take with you this. You are by far
the toughest warrior I have ever faced," Vladris said,
finally ripping the dagger from his chest, then raising his
own blade. "The Hunter archives will speak of you as a
legend. This I promise to you my brother."

Roman nodded, accepting his ticket to the afterlife. He
was done, knowing a life of only misery and killing, except
for the brief period he spent with his friends, his family,
aboard the Gunship crew.

It would be the very faces of that crew, the very
personalities of those he had grown to love as family,
which he would remain in thought about during his
eternal rest.

And the life of Roman Raines would end with a single
strike, an arcing sword which severed his head from its
body; just as Vladris had promised.

At the close of battle, Vladris placed the head of Roman
Raines into a large bag of leather stitching, tightening the
knot of rope as he glared to his Hunter soldiers, a single
contact of eyes which would grow his legend as immortal.

"I have held my end of the bargain. Now I hope your
intentions to hold your end remain true?" Pica asked as
he approached Vladris and the remaining Hunters, bow in
hand.

"Indeed. You will soon be turned to the ranks of the
immortal to fight alongside us as a brother. You have
proven your loyalty."

"Take care warrior, and enjoy your reign of terror.
Because it ends soon at the hands of another." Amelia's
ghost said, her words blatantly ignored by Vladris as he
mounted his steed of hell once more.

"Now we return to our queen. There is a wedding to
take place; a wedding which will unify our people."
Vladris said with a stern voice, as if to dare any Hunter to
speak.

"I don't want to leave him behind." Troy said as Gore began firing up Roman's shuttle, pressing dozens of necessary buttons which illuminated red.

"Roman did not survive. Otherwise, he would have made it back by now. I'm sorry," Gore said with regret. "But you will be among friends on my homeworld, all of which hate the Hunters."

Troy began to respond, but as the shuttle slowly lifted from the moist ground, Roman's ghost became visible to the boy.

"Avenge me son."

As Troy saw those words loose from the lips of such an honorable man, be it from the afterlife, he understood his destiny. Continue building Roman's Empire, and eventually strike against those who have been responsible for so much loss.

"It's alright. Even now, I feel as though Roman is with us." Troy replied with a smile.

Scucca remained by the side of Troy since their first encounter, just as he had done with Roman Raines. A sight that was rare among hounds of hell. Much more so than the snarling of teeth currently directed toward Gore.

"As do I young warrior. As do I." Gore replied, casting a stare of dare to the hound before pulling the flight stick harshly as the shuttle went into full-burn and made orbit.

The trees were crisped with rain, as were the blades of grass which led to such a beautiful place. And though their castle was one of murder, torture and devine obedience for the undead, on this very morning it looked perfect.

Sarah Blaine was to wed Vladris, and bring the idea of unity and strength to their people. Hundreds of years had passed since the Hunters were ruled by both king and queen, times spoken of in the archives as the very best among their race.

But the wedding had grown well beyond a simple gesture to unite their people. They both had grown fond of the other in such a short period of time.

Sarah was a compassionate queen, a trait which Vladris respected greatly. She was also both beautiful and comforting to him, bringing with her a soothing calm.

Vladris had become Sarah's champion. She had joined those who truly believed he could not be bested in combat, bringing to her the feeling of safety. She felt at peace around him, which made her transition from human to Vampire much more bearable.

And as they locked eyes at the alter, hundreds of the best warriors the Hunters had looking on, Sarah grinned softly to her champion.

"And should any man or woman object to these two being locked in matrimony, let them speak now or forever hold..." the minister said, stopping short as he joined the rest of the crowd, turning to look to the rear of the chapel.

Quickly, both Sarah and Vladris turned as well, determined to end whoever had intruded on such a perfect ceremony.

However, as a man stood to his feet, hooded robe of brown and while; Sarah quickly felt faint. Adam Michaels. Sarah's first true love and former Gunship Captain, removed the hood and smiled.

It was almost as if relative time stopped, the chatter around them non-existent. The only thing that seemed real to her was his glowing smile, the chisel of his chin; and to him, her undeniable beauty.

And though Sarah Blaine was now queen of Vampires, her guards rushing to apprehend her first love, she knew it was only a matter of protocol. She had no intentions of harming him, but rather hearing him out. Why had he arrived, why now? And she wondered if his reasoning even mattered? Because, in the end, Sarah would have another chance to hear the strength of his voice. The ability to look upon him again, which is more than she could have ever dreamed of.

She cared not how he had managed to find his way into such a heavily protected castle, but rather the fact that her life of clarity had just become murky beyond explanation.

As Vladris tried to make sense of the man covered in brown satin, his attention quickly shifted to the ghost of Amelia, who stood at the rear of the chapel. She had never before appeared to him beyond the fields of battle.

But as her lips made out a single word, Vladris felt a chill run across all extremities.

Soon.

Legendary

PROLOGUE

This war has been emotionally draining to say the least. What first began as an infection among the mindless wanderers of the

Drifts, soon became the plague of our time.

We didn't realize the truth of things until it was too late. What we had thought mindless zombies, were actually hosts for a small crustacean-like species we've come to know by a single name.

Priests.

By the time our soldiers discovered their ability to control the body of a host by implanting itself into the upper-spine of its victim, we had lost several key battles against the new enemy.

Many heartbreaking losses have led to colonial worlds falling one by one, our new adversary overwhelming us on all fronts. It was the loss of Glimmeria, however, that sent a clear message to those of us in charge.

We are defeated.

Now I must do the unthinkable. Sign a bill that will save our race, while damning so many to their doom. I must announce our defeat to those who remain to listen, and focus not on those who will indeed perish by the stroke of my pen, but on those who will survive because of it.

-Colonial Commander Aaron Ortega.

Ronica

"Adam," Sarah said with gentleness, approaching the smuggler as he stood, watching the rolling hills before them and feeling as content as ever. "They're ready."

For seconds which seemed to bleed into eternity, Adam stood silent, pulling every crisp moment into his mind. The world of Ronica simply breathtaking.

"Have you ever just looked out onto the hills? Just to soak them into your memory?" he asked, remaining mesmerized.

"More times than you could ever know. Many nights I have stood on my balcony, listening to the calm of rainfall." she replied with a hushed tone.

There was a period of several moments, each filled with the vivid of color and rush of cool breeze. As if the smuggler had never slowed to enjoy such things.

"I guess it is starting to sink in," he said, adjusting his head a bit to watch a small flock of birds soar overhead. "This may be one of the last times I'm able to see such a view."

"Perhaps," she replied, studying the worry in his eyes. "They're waiting for you."

"Of course." Adam replied, slowly turning.

He did so, of course, as nearly a dozen colonial soldiers held guns onto the queen of vampires. Sarah. Though her personal escort was also nearby, their own weapons at the ready. Their conversation having taken place in the midst of so much nervous firepower.

"I want you to know that I've done all I can do as their queen," she said, the pair walking slowly into the direction of a large castle which the Hunters had called home for many years. "I've managed to get you an audience with the eldest of vampires, but they will not easily be swayed." Sarah added.

He dreaded it. A meeting with the race of vampires whose acts were usually unspeakable. The Hunters were vampires in every respect, blood sucking monsters that enjoy feasting on human flesh. Though they often seemed to keep to themselves, it wasn't unknown for an occasional member of the race to stray from Ronica to begin his or her own agenda elsewhere, resulting in bloodshed among the human population, which only furthered their stereotype as a horrible race.

"I know, thank you," Adam replied, speaking from the heart to a woman he once loved. "And I want you to know that I'm sorry for putting you into this position. Truly." he added.

"Just speak to them from the heart Adam, and fate will take care of the rest." Sarah replied, a warm smile upon the face of such a beautiful woman.

Though she'd become a vampire, Sarah's beauty had remained intact. Even more so, depending on who you asked. She had the same elegant curves and angelic voice as before, though her skin appeared much whiter.

She had once been widely considered the most compassionate person alive. Daughter of the acting commander of the colonies, she was a true advocate of humanity.

The wrong type of Hunter had strayed from Ronica and soon their paths met, dragging Adam into things during the process. Stumbling onto true love during the worst of circumstances. Their love for one another had simply been storybook, though several events tested them.

When he faced the decision of a lifetime, Adam walked away from the woman his heart loved so truly. Unknowingly handing her to the Hunters with his decision.

There were many regrets throughout his lifetime, but none of them greater. A bad call which spawned from pride and bitterness, leading to the death of a woman he truly loved. At least partial death.

He knew she was a vampire because of his inability to forgive. Still, he saw her just as beautifully as ever. Feeling butterflies while in her presence.

As Adam was led into the castle, a large security detail following behind, Sarah watched him walk away. Searching her own feelings for a man she once was prepared to marry.

She had loved him with everything not so long ago. From the pit of her stomach; her very soul. She loved the man who walked away once more – this time on business.

"Good luck Adam Michaels." she said with a dedicated, yet hushed, voice.

Aboard Colonial Star Triumph

"I am having trouble accepting this." Commander Ortega admitted, his emotions torn in half as he sat on a long couch of plush red, several advisers standing nearby.

"Sir, this decision is not on you." one of the advisers remarked.

"In fact, it is the only choice. We're left with no options." another adviser added.

"Sir, we have been crushed," a second adviser added. "Our mightiest of bases, Glimmeria, fell as though it were a dying leaf in the fall of year. It is in my opinion that nothing can be gained from our situation outside of the greater good."

"Yes," Ortega replied, standing to his feet. "I understand the logic. My heart bleeds for every person we leave behind. Truly, it does." he added with sincerity.

"Sir, if we had time to gather more ships, perhaps we could save them all. We simply do not have the time. The realization of defeat came too late."

"Doctor Arness," Ortega said, turning to the high-ranking adviser. "I wonder if you know what a burden this is, having to decide the fate of thousands by the stroke of a pen? I wonder if you feel for the same for these innocent people as I do?"

"Sir, I understand you convictions," the doctor said, though his primary role throughout the fleet was political. "But I also understand that we may not even have time to form the fleet, much less expand it. The horde cares not for our guilt or convictions. They simply come." Doctor

Arness said.

"Yes. I'm painfully aware," Ortega replied. "You have often been the voice of reason for me when my heart is worn too openly on my sleeve."

"Just doing my job sir," Doctor Arness commented. "Someone has to be here to keep things in perspective. Sadly, innocent children will have to die in order for us to survive. The fleet needs us."

With the delivery of his statement, the two marines stationed by the door of their private quarters exchanged glances. Obviously shaken by Arness' ease when it came to loss of innocent life, though they understood the chain of command.

"In just a few moments, you'll be broadcast to every monitor in the Skyla System. Everyone needs to hear strength in your voice and indecision in your heart. Even if it is not entirely there, our citizens need to hear it." one of his advisers said.

"Now more than ever, they need to hear it." Ortega replied, agreeing with the logic of his advisers.

"As soon as we deliver the speech, what remains of our government can begin the process of supplying for the journey to come." Doctor Arness said.

"We have enough ships to make this type of journey?" Ortega questioned, turning to the men.

"Yes sir," one of them responded. "Some of them are a bit older, but certainly capable of deep space travel. We can make any necessary repairs once we're on our way."

"Good," Ortega nodded. "Supplies?"

"That is our main concern at the moment," the adviser admitted. "Fuel, water, food and ammunition will all be in short supply. Especially after being sacked so many times by the Priests." he added, stitching truth into his statement.

"As will hope. I cannot leave people behind without a fighting chance," Ortega said. "I will not leave them here without at least a small chance of survival."

"Sir, we've selected the location for several reasons. It is the furthest away from the Priest's main force, but it is also one of the resource-richest planets of our system. Full of minerals to fuel a civilization and plenty of land to grow crops. Our survivors would have a good chance to rebuild, should they somehow find a way to turn the Priests away."

"I wonder if your confidence would be as firm if you were to be left behind?" Ortega asked.

"Sir?" the adviser replied, both men with a look of shock.

"That is the way of a politician, is it not? Save his own skin by sacrificing the skin of others?"

"Sir, I assure you. We've done the best job possible given our circumstances. For both sides involved." the adviser replied.

"Indeed," Ortega commented, seeming to take a moment to breathe and focus on the task at hand. "Let's just get it over with," he added, scooping up several papers and heading for the door to his quarters, surrounded by the bustling of suits and ties. "Let's doom nearly half of our race to certain death. For the sake of politics."

Drift Planet - Sandila

"Your card skills are as bad as your Priest-hunting skills!" a man proclaimed, erupting laughter throughout the small bar setting.

The boasting man was very much on the chubby side, an unshaven beard masking most of his face as he began reaching for the pot of gold. Or, in this case, three packs of fresh cigars and a near-full bottle of whiskey.

"Not so fast you cocksucker," Dalton replied sharply, slamming his own cards onto the table. "Three gems and two zips – now give me my damn winnings."

"That's impossible!" the large man claimed, grabbing Dalton by the wrist in an attempt to stop him from collecting his winnings.

"As will be your attempt to eat solid food with a wired-up jaw," Dalton warned. "Which it will be, if you don't unhand me. Friend."

"Let it be Daniel." one of the other players commented, the small table holding four players total.

"Well, alright then." the chubby man calmly replied, releasing his grip of the smuggler's wrist.

"Besides boys, hell, plenty enough to go around." Dalton said with a grin, hinting of pouring everyone a shot; a suggestion that immediately brought cheers throughout the sunlight-poor room.

As his shaky hand began to pour the first shot of whiskey, Dalton's attention followed everyone else to the only door of the sad dwelling. Embers of filth highlighting such a dank pub as rays of light poured in. Its walls held together with nails, while cracks of sunlight bled in through mismatched wooden boards.

Dalton had a good idea who was entering. She had a way of showing up each time he was preparing to embark into the land of no good, and it really would have pissed him off – if not for the fact that she was so incredibly easy on the eyes.

His captain, Cambria Sims.

Cambria slowly entered, her vivid blue hair standing out among the pack of thieves and self-admitted outlaws. And though she eased the door closed once more as if to enter the room unnoticed, the bar had become silent enough to hear the aging of wood. Nearly.

"Better hide the whiskey mate, your boss lady is here." one of the players taunted, chuckling a bit.

"Dalton James don't have to hide a damn thing." he commented proudly, though he casually corked the bottle of whiskey and eased it into the inner of his brown coat.

"Yea," another player mocked with laughter. "Sure he don't."

"She says jump and the man asks how high." the

chubby card game loser said.

"How about I jump across this table and pistol-whip the shit out of you? How about that?" Dalton asked with a scowl, lips cutting though a beard of brown.

"Relax boys, she is sitting up there with the monitor." one of the men commented, noticing Cambria sitting to the front of the building; her seat at the bar directly in front of the news monitor.

"Another round?" a man asked, having scooped up the deck of cards in an attempt to shuffle.

"Nope," Dalton said, though he wanted nothing more than to blister the men once more at a man's game. "Gotta go check in with my captain."

Though laughter ensued, the smuggler shrugged it off, locking eyes onto a man who had eased his way onto a stool beside Cambria.

So much for honor among thieves. Dalton thought, casting a hard glance to the man. "Cocksucker."

Pausing for a moment, Dalton turned his attention to the pub's door. Believing he'd heard a distant scream, though no others among them heard it. Either they were all too drunk to have heard the bone-chilling cry for help, or Dalton was drunk enough to imagine it.

Finally shrugging it off, he once again focused on his walk to the bar.

"Hey Cambria," Dalton said with a grin, one that was quickly returned by the young lady of impeccable beauty. "Hey guy with no chance of getting into Cambria's pants."

Both the blue-haired beauty and local patron developed strange looks across their faces, for different reasons, of course.

"I wasn't going to..." the man began to reply.

"Save your shit Mahone, I've known you long enough. Probably using the same damn lines as always on this young specimen of insatiable beauty."

It was the first time he'd openly hit on a woman while

warning off another man without at least a pause for breath. A fact that made the smuggler grin a bit.

"Dalton, really. He was just being nice. That's all." Cambria proclaimed.

Yea right, and I'm the fucking commander of the colonies. That silver-tongued son of a bitch is a bigger booty-chaser than I am, and that's saying something. Dalton thought.

"What takes up 12 docking spaces...six women pilots," Dalton spouted off, striking home with Cambria, who had heard the joke only moments before. "Or maybe he hit you with the old...What do you call a woman who can't make sandwiches?" Dalton asked, knowing he'd exposed the panty-snatcher. "Single."

"Well, I'll take my leave." Mahone stated, knowing he'd been given away by the man who would have been his wingman on any other occasion. This was different though. This was love. Though neither Dalton nor Cambria would admit it.

Dalton was careful to watch the man walk away too, as though he were a mighty dog protecting its master.

"Wow, I feel like an idiot." Cambria confessed.

"Don't," Dalton replied, though his eyes cautiously watched Mahone walk away. "Most of the skanks that come through here would have been in bed with him after the first line," he added, quickly realizing the damage of his own words. "Not to say you're a skank."

Cambria answered his confession with a laugh.

"Wow, and I thought his lines were bad."

A short moment of silence fell between them, making each a bit uncomfortable.

"I don't know, I just feel a need to watch out for you. That's all. Places like this, they're in my blood. I know what's going through most of these people's heads before they do. It's like I'm a psychic or something."

"A psychic with whiskey on his breath." Cambria replied.

Ah fuck! Dalton thought, though he broadcast a look of confusion.

"It's alright, this is a bar. I expect it. Besides, it kind of feels good knowing I can come into a place like this and be safe." Cambria admitted.

"Yea," Dalton said, his mind wandering to distant places as he thought of her statement. "I understand that."

"Can I ask you a question? A serious one?" Cambria asked.

"Technically you just did," Dalton replied with a smile. "Sure you can, you know that."

"How come you never let anyone close? I see through the whole comedic front you put up, I just don't understand why? Why can't you just be open about what's on your mind? In your heart?" Cambria asked.

It was a damn good question, and Dalton knew it. His silent reaction for several moments only confirmed it to her.

"Not sure really. I reckon I'm just afraid of losing people," he admitted, becoming as serious as Cambria had ever seen him before. "Each time I open up to someone, I lose 'em. One way or another, I lose 'em. Be it in a gunfight or to the undead," he added. "I hate the fucking undead."

"Fair enough." Cambria replied, accepting his answer at face value.

"Now let me ask you something." Dalton said.

"Shoot," Cambria replied with a grin. "Though not literally."

"How come we talk about anything and everything but the obvious? Each time we get close to talking about us, you shy away from it. I don't know what to think?" Dalton asked.

"Us?" she asked.

"Ah, never mind then. I suppose my idiot brain just conjured that up. Won't happen again." Dalton replied, standing to his feet, upset by her lack of feelings for him.

Cambria offered no reply, simply turning her head away from him. Though she did so in order to mask her emotions.

A part of her wanted to grab the smuggler and unload her own feelings onto him. Be with him. But her reservations prevented her from it, not seeing how a relationship with him would ever work out for the best.

Cambria had a way of over-thinking things, usually for the worse. She was confused, and the tears which began to swell in her eyes were proof of it, eventually beading softly down her cheeks a bit.

"Dalton, wait." she asked, turning to him.

"What?" he demanded to know. "What is it?"

"Commander Ortega is on the monitor." Cambria said, deflating all of Dalton's hopes for love with her reply.

The smuggler offered no reply, instead walking to the bar as he joined dozens of others, all preparing themselves for a rare speech by the commander.

"First off, I would like to confirm the rumors of Glimmeria falling. They are unfortunate, but true. Our army has fought valiantly in the face of this plague of man, but we are steadily losing ground.

My fair people, this is not a decision that has come easily for me. Though I fear it is our very last option and the window of opportunity is quickly closing.

I have signed an order that will fund an exodus fleet. A fleet of ships that will take us away from this threat once and for all, as we journey into uncharted space to search for a new home.

Again, I would like to reiterate that my decision has not come lightly, and will forever burden my dreams as I know we simply do not have room for every last survivor."

Commander Ortega stopped for a moment as the sound of cameras snapping throughout his conference room seemed to echo the fact that it was an historic moment.

"My advisory panel confirms that we will have room to house less than half of our survivors. I have personally overseen a lottery system in which we will select those who will accompany us into the stars.

One-third of the exodus from this plague will be comprised of those with extensive military experience. Their service and zeal will lend in the survival of our race. One-third of our exodus will be comprised of those who are deemed too important to leave behind. Among these people, doctors, scientists and teachers. Our race will not survive without the above mentioned. I truly believe that.

Finally, the remaining one-third will be randomly selected through an exodus lottery. This will provide everyone with a glimmer of hope for the future, and I assure you, the lottery will be random.

In fact," Ortega said, pausing as he carefully planned his next words. "I have personally decided to stay behind, as I could not live my life knowing I left a single person behind."

Pausing once more, the commander listened to the deafening sound of camera shutters.

"Any politician or military person who wishes to remain behind with me, may do so, and in turn free up a spot for a defenseless woman or child. That is a personal decision that I leave to each person listening.

As for myself, I will deem a commander for the exodus flight and then remain behind to coordinate one final stand against the enemies who approach our doorstep.

I would ask that everyone pray. Not only for your own fate, but for the fate of those around you. Live every single day for the moments contained within it, and prepare for the next chapter in the history of our race. Thank you, and may God find it within his heart to grant us mercy in such troubled times."

Rather than take questions, Commander Ortega quickly exited from the podium, obviously shaken by his own announcement.

"Sir, you must reconsider your decision to stay." one of Ortega's advisers pleaded, while the other quickly raced out to the group of reporters who seemed as though they were a mob. Readying himself to field questions and assure the people of hope.

"I've no intention of staying behind," Ortega replied, still visibly shaken. "I simply told the people what they needed to hear. They need hope at a time like this, and I gave it to them. When the plague arrives, none of us will be any wiser as to who is staying and who is leaving. I owe these people hope, but I also owe the exodus fleet stability in leadership." he replied.

"Yes sir, of course." his adviser replied.

Moments later, Ortega found himself inside the sanctity of his personal quarters. Deafening silence leading him into even deeper thought.

He wondered of Adam Michaels' progress, though he also wondered if their exodus flight was the solution to the plague of man, or a prolonging of their own deaths. Knowing such large numbers could easily lead to a lack of fuel, starvation or struggle for power.

Survivors? He thought, feeling pity for them as well. *Survivors for what?*

Ronica

As Adam walked slowly into the Hunters' castle, leather boots striking easily against the stone flooring, his eyes skimmed the immediate surroundings.

Call it a smuggler's intuition.

A large room, vaulted ceiling of multicolored glass, though most of it seemed to refract shades of dark red; surrounded by dozens of vampires.

Each of them wore attire of seemingly the utmost of importance. Most draped in a hooded coat of black, while a handful stood in the decorated armor of a warrior. Among them, Vladris.

He was the Hunters' champion; having survived hundreds of years while slaying hero after hero, as well as anyone else who opposed the rule of vampires.

A great-sword laced to his back with leather straps, its trunk as wide as a small tree, though its bite was far more deadly. A sword in which only the mightiest could wield; Vladris did so with a single hand, at times swinging it as though it were the weight of a feather. A testament to his brute strength.

"Speak clearly and choose your words wisely, as our elders have granted you the gift of an audience; one they do not normally grant." Vladris said with authority.

He was right. It was rare for a human to enter the chamber of elders, and unheard of while wearing the Benzan uniform. The mark of a clan of warriors which had waged slaughter against the vampires for centuries, and the vampires likewise slaughtered the Benzans.

Nevertheless, Adam Michaels was a Benzan, and having found the lost tribe of Benzans had given him something he was never in short supply of. Confidence.

Most importantly, he understood his job. He was there by the personal request of Commander Ortega. Ronica was the ideal planet to stage their exodus fleet, in fact, it was the only planet. Anything else was too close to the plague of man and would have been too quickly overrun.

As Adam entered the large chamber, reminding him of a very Gothic-styled judge's chamber, five vampires sat atop their own thrones, each one made of stone and trimmed in the sparkle of jewels.

He could tell from the look of them that each was hundreds, perhaps even thousands of years old, though he dared not question it.

Bowing low to the floor, a sight never before seen by someone bearing the mark of a Benzan, Adam stood slowly, preparing himself for such important negotiations.

"I thank you all for the opportunity to speak," Adam said, pausing for a moment. "And I have come before you to ask for help. To build a bridge between our people."

"Build a bridge? Your PEOPLE burned that bridge when they began genocide against our race!" Vladris yelled in response.

"You said I had been given the gift of an audience with elders, did you not?" Adam asked with confidence. "Then let me speak."

Though no reply followed, Vladris cut eyes onto the Benzan smuggler that would have intimidated most among mortals.

"The Benzan family in which I am allied; we have no quarrel with you. With any of you. Just as you do, these Benzans have lived on their own in peace." Adam said.

"Why is it that you would come here during one of our most ceremonious days, as an intruder, and expect help?" one of the elders asked.

"I had no idea I was arriving during such a time," Adam replied, turning to return a stare of dare onto Vladris. "For that I apologize," he added. "But I do so out of desperation. We face a new menace now. One that is much greater than any before this day."

"Let them wipe you out! What business is it of ours?" Vladris demanded to know.

"Vladris – let him speak!" one of the elders warned.

The Hunters' champion warrior simply bowed with obedience.

"The human race is only the beginning. Our new threat, the Priests, are after the entire system. Everything we know, everything we love. Including the precious rock we currently stand on; no matter how hidden you believe it to be." Adam said.

"We do not believe it hidden, because we do not hide. We do not cower from an enemy. Any enemy." one of the elders proudly stated.

"And I commend you for that. It is admirable. And though your hatred for the Benzans runs deep, we can all agree that they are a formidable opponent," Adam replied, watching the reactions of those in the room. One that spoke of the Benzans being a formidable adversary indeed. "I saw with my own eyes, hundreds of our best warriors fall within an hour to the Priests," Adam stated, doing his best to chide his tears. "Among them my wife."

It was an admission that struck home with Vladris, having lost the love of his life as well, though the wars were of a different manner. Loss of love feels one in the same.

"Now I'm asking you," Adam said, taking a moment to clear the emotional-cobwebs from his speech. "I'm begging you," he added, kneeling to the elders; something that had never been heard of prior to Adam's gesture, at least by a Benzan. "You have long been the mightiest warriors of the Skyla System; now I'm asking that you defend those who cannot defend themselves."

"I must admit Benzan, your gesture and statement seem true enough. How are we to know that you indeed speak the truth?" one of the elders asked, this time an elder of military background.

"He speaks the truth," Sarah Blaine replied, walking into the chamber, her mere presence instilling faith into everyone who lay witness. "I have known this man for a long time," she added, her voice turning to a softer tone. "Even loved him. He speaks from the heart. I can personally validate that."

It was a statement that struck Vladris by surprise – though it made sense. He had picked up on Adam and Sarah's uneasiness around him.

"Very well. Speak to us of your plans Benzan." one of the elders insisted.

"Have you all gone mad? Can you not see that this is a colonial trap?" Vladris yelled.

"Silence champion!" Sarah demanded, showing her status as queen for all to see. "Your caution as a warrior is welcome but your insubordination to your elders is not!"

"Apologies my queen." Vladris replied, kneeling a bit

though he did so reluctantly.

"The colonials plan an exodus voyage into the stars. This star system is lost," Adam said, thinking of a war they had no chance of winning. "Of the few remaining planets that are uninfected, Ronica is the only one large enough to use as a staging ground for our journey. We will need time to prep such massive ships and pull resources together."

"You are running away?" one of the elders asked, the entire chamber taken by surprise.

"We are beaten. Though it may be honorable to fight to the death, many of those who survive are simply women and children. There is no honor in that." Adam replied.

"Has it really come to this Adam?" Sarah asked, a concern for those in the Skyla System deeply embedded into her.

"Yes, it has," Adam replied. "We are overrun by a species that acts as though it is a virus. One for which we do not have the cure."

"And tell me Benzan. What would be the benefit of an alliance between us? What would my people have to gain?" an elder asked, impatiently waiting for an answer.

As he thought the coming moments through carefully, Adam reached around his neck slowly, removing his Benzan amulet and throwing it to the floor.

"The benefit of becoming a single people – rather than nations divided by race." the Benzan replied.

A gesture that sent even the eldest of vampires into deep thought for a moment.

"Please, I am asking you," Adam pleaded. "I'm asking you to view me as a person in need, not a Benzan. Not anymore. We are all simply people who have been overwhelmed with grief and loss for loved ones," he added. "It is my understanding that you protect the humans of Ronica because they could not protect themselves from war."

"We protect the humans on this planet because they

fought us with courage. Our champion was once theirs. His courage earned their freedom." one of the elders stated.

"Our soldiers have died by the thousands, each of them with courage. Though I'm no champion, I am willing to risk my life against your own champion, if need be. My own race at stake." Adam replied.

"It would be a foolish move human. For your own sake." Vladris commented with a grin.

"I know," Adam admitted, turning to the large vampire. "But I'm willing to sacrifice my own life to save those who cannot fight. Women...children. Are you? Are your warriors?" Adam asked.

"Silence," one of the elders demanded. "There is no need for our champion to prove himself. Vladris has done so before, countless times. Though we do respect your courage. Tell us of your intentions?"

"Our fleet will be comprised of as many ships as possible, but every world in our system will be represented by a capital ship. That ship will receive a vote in whatever our future holds, and if you extend help to us, I can promise your people a vote to call your own."

"Permission to speak?" Vladris asked, though he did so with great displeasure.

"Granted champion." and elder replied.

"We have seen threats like this before. When they arrive, we will cut them down, just as we always have." Vladris said.

"I guarantee you – you've seen no threats like this before." Adam stated.

"Speak to us of this threat." an elder insisted.

"The ability to infect a body, living or dead, by attaching to the spinal cord. Once they have infected, they can use the body just as the warrior was always of their race, bringing with it the battle-prowess of the warrior." Adam stated.

"In other words..." one of the elders began.

"In other words, every time a vampire falls, he will join the fight against you. Your own abilities in battle will be your undoing." Adam quickly replied.

"Can the enemy be killed?" Vladris asked.

"Yes," Adam replied. "But we've found that the only sure way is by burning the small creature. Or by finding enough luck to strike it in half with bullet or blade."

"Then the trunk of my blade will feast indeed." the Hunters' champion said with a smile.

"Any final words before we begin our own deliberations Benzan?" an elder asked.

"Yes," Adam replied. "I would ask that you not consider the history of our two races, but the future. For every warrior here that is willing to die with the honor of battle, there must be a group of people that love him. A family worth saving. I ask that you consider preserving the proud history of your race by becoming part of a larger society. One that is prepared to accept you with open arms. Thank you." Adam added, bowing a final time as he began to exit the chamber slowly.

"Benzan," one of the elders announced. "Your amulet."

"I've no further need for it," Adam replied, though his back remained turned. "I'm just a survivor now."

As his body began to hit the light of day, which draped down from the peaceful Ronican skies above, a group of nearly twenty soldiers awaited him.

"Did it go well?" a colonial soldier asked.

"I don't know," Adam replied. "I don't know."

Drift Planet – Sandila

"What do you make of it?" Cambria asked, easing herself down beside Dalton as his concentrated stare into the distant continued.

"I think if I would have bluffed a bit more I'd have won every hand." he replied, using the quick wit of a smuggler.

"I mean the lottery you meathead!" she said with a grin,

slapping him across the arm playfully.

"Honestly, hell, I don't know what to think," Dalton said as he took a pause for the cause; the swig of whiskey burning its way to his stomach. "Guess they are gonna do whatever they want to anyway. It's the political way. No sense in getting torn up over something you have no control over. I've never trusted the jack-jawed sumbitches and ain't about to start now."

"Dalton, I don't want you to hate me. I don't want that kind of awkwardness between us." Cambria said, her words falling as soft as drizzle.

"Hate you?" he asked. "We live in a world where the dead stalk the living and the living still can't be honest about their feelings. That's what I hate. Not you."

"I know there's something there. Something between us. I just don't know what, I guess I need time. That's all." she replied, her statement very candid and honest. "There, I said it. Aren't you proud?" she added with a soft smile.

"Oh. Good. I thought you were about to tell me I wasn't going to get paid or something." he remarked as they both began to laugh without hesitation.

"Well about that, it may be a little late. The whole zombie thing and all." Cambria added, causing them to laugh a bit louder.

"Darling, I hadn't been paid in so damn long that it doesn't even concern me anymore. I figure if I'm alive, got a pillow to lay my head on at night, a bottle of hootch in my hand and people around me that I care about," he said, pausing on that statement to glance to Cambria with strong intent. "I got everything I need."

A candid statement as well. One that led to Cambria leaning to the smuggler for a kiss.

She had thought he'd be completely happy with it, their lips finally having a chance to meet on good terms. However, as she leaned in, feeling a bit awkward, Cambria quickly pulled away and wondered what his hangup was.

"Dalton, I'm sorry. I shouldn't have." Cambria admitted as the smuggler sat there, eyes focused on a small window that was caked with the residue of cigar smoke aplenty.

"Dalton? Are you OK?"

"Zombies! Get outside, quick, otherwise they'll swarm us and trap us in this fucking rat shack!" he yelled, quickly turning to usher his love interest to the safest possible spot.

Robbing me of my kiss – 'ya undead fucks!

Gunshots began to snap out, dozens of survivors firing into a small group that sprinted toward their location.

They had banded together with others, nearly fifty total, and taken up residence in a very small village on the remote planet. It had been long-abandoned, which served the group just fine.

Each of them knew that eventually their hideaway would be found by the horde they feared, but each had secretly hoped that somehow, by some grand miracle, they would be left alone once and for all.

"Dalton, what are you doing?" Cambria yelled, slowing her run to watch the smuggler do a complete turnaround as he began heading into the direction of the vacated bar.

"Son of a bitches done took everything else from me," he responded with a yell of his own. "I'll be damned if they are getting my whiskey too!" he added, snatching up a half-empty bottle of rock whiskey before turning to sprint from the door once more.

Are you kidding me! She thought, ready to shoot him herself if he didn't realize the urgency of zombies approaching.

"He's got balls." one of the taunting bar patrons yelled, each of them slowing their sprint of desperation long enough to watch the slightly-tipsy smuggler risk his own neck for a bottle of bargain bin man-drink.

"Bunch of nasty bastards!" he yelled, sending two rounds from his magnum-style pistol before turning and beginning the quickest sprint of his life.

The survivors had dug into the small group of dwellings which was built within a thick nestle of countryside, though they knew that eventually it would come to this. Still, it had been their home for weeks. Each of them growing to appreciate it for what it was. Quiet.

Iron Grove – at least the name of it prior to the plague of man. Most of its citizens had long abandoned the sad excuse for a village, heading out on any available transport they could.

Some stayed. Choosing instead to defend their homes to the death, which looked to be beating down their door like an unwelcome salesman. One that peddled agonizing mortality.

What they didn't expect, however, was literally hundreds of Priest-controlled zombies that began filling the nearby hillside, as if it were certified death pouring into a tub of survivors.

Oh shit. Dalton thought, his mouth hanging down a bit as even he couldn't fathom an escape from such an ill-fate.

As quickly as his alcoholic buzz seemed to fade, Dalton realized that the survivors were backed into a corner. A bad thing considering their opponents. He understood the vile tendencies of a zombie, priest, or as he called them, nasty fucks.

Dalton understood the survivors were outnumbered ten to one, and had no strategic advantage. His military wisdom finally coming into play.

They had weapons, sure, but they were about to be swarmed and had the low ground. A snowball's chance in hell. Or, even worse, a rock whiskey bottle's chance in a Glimmerian bar. Zero.

"Keep running," Dalton yelled to Cambria. "Past our outpost. Get our boy and tell him to elbow to asshole up into the hillside as fast as he can!"

"But we would be safer indoors? Nightfall is coming. We don't even have supplies ready?" she replied.

"Cambria," he shouted, grabbing the woman firmly by both of her arms as gunshots rang throughout the encampment. "These people are already dead. In a couple of minutes, that horde will be here. A couple of minutes later, everything in this settlement will be dead. Just ain't no way these sad-ass wooden walls are going to hold them back. Get Skulls and head to that brushy part of the hill. Trust me."

"OK...I do." she replied with shock.

"Go." he added, the blue-haired bombshell turning to relay the message to their friend.

There are things in a man's life that he can never shake. Events that plague his dreams, night after night, for the remainder of his life – and this was one such moment.

As Dalton readied himself for the forced run ahead, his eyes were witness to survivors, many of them women and children, heading inside to escape the coming horde. He knew they would not last inside of a handful of minutes, and though he wanted to help them escape, it simply wasn't possible.

It was the first time in many years that Dalton James began to cry aloud. His tough image being overcome by his heartfelt sadness for those who would soon fall victim to the plague of man. The Priests.

"Dalton," Cambria yelled loudly, pausing her wording as she began to watch him, tears falling steady. "Dalton, we need to go. You said so yourself."

Skulls had joined her, the sniper also understanding the need for a quick escape. The settlement was beginning to flood with zombies and would soon be nothing but.

"Dalton please." Cambria said, grabbing his arm and captivating his thoughts for a single moment. Long enough to break him from sadness and throw him back into the military frame of mind.

"Yea," he admitted, quickly drying up his tears. "Haul ass, I'm right behind you."

The small group of three quickly slipped out through the side of Iron Grove which had not been slammed by zombies yet. Using the cover of a casting nightfall to mask their escape, though they would need to find cover only a few hundred yards from the deafening sound of painful murder.

"Are you alright?" Cambria whispered.

"Yea, I," Dalton began to reply, all three survivors nestled snugly into the thick of brush near enough by to witness the genocide unfold. "I'm sorry you had to see me like that. I don't know what came over me."

"I do." Cambria replied, easing her hand onto his, their fingers clasping together as she tried to comfort him.

"It's one thing when my own ass is on the line, or even soldiers around me," he admitted, trying to block the last remaining screams from his mind. "This is something different altogether. These people ain't equipped for this...they ain't soldiers." he added, thinking of the women and children he'd witnessed only minutes before. Each of them butchered by such a vile species.

"No," Cambria replied. "They don't deserve a fate like this."

"We just have to make sure they did not die in vain. Avenge each of them by the smooth grain of a bullet." Skulls added, his right eye pressed firm to the large scope which mounted onto his bolt-action rifle.

"You can bet your ass on that," Dalton responded, nodding his head with purpose. "Each one of these rank sumbitches are gonna pay."

For nearly an hour, Dalton, Cambria and Skulls had to remain patient. Hiding from plain sight as the walking dead scavenged over those freshly-slain. Eventually raising them from the dead and increasing their army's numbers.

Dalton had heard rumors of it, but never seen the turning with his own eyes. The Priests were a small creature, hard shell around it as though it were a sea crab, though it also had eight stringy legs and a rather long tail.

For the first time, the three survivors watched with horror – the way of the Priests.

They slowly attached to the back of a skull of the dead, wrapping clingy legs around to the victim's mouth. Then, as the creature gripped the mouth of the dead, it drove the long tail into the upper spine of the lifeless body, snaking the tale down. Finally covering the entire length of the spine from its inner most spot.

Then, seconds later, the fallen host began to stand. Becoming a soldier for their cause, completely under the control of the Priest which embedded into it.

The perfect army. The Priests would lose soldiers in battle, but as they fell the small creature would simply detach and then assume control of another body. The entire process taking less than sixty-seconds, depending on how close the body of a fallen host was.

From the perspective of a man who put in countless years of military experience, Dalton quickly understood why the populated worlds had fallen so swiftly. Why the colonials were getting their asses kicked. You could kill the Priests, but they would continue to come, using your own fallen soldiers against you.

"I've never seen anything like it." Cambria admitted, though she did so in a whisper as they watched.

"No," Dalton replied, pausing to swig deeply from his bottle of whiskey. "I've seen a lot of shit before, but I ain't never seen anything like that."

Ronica

"He looks just like you." Sarah admitted.

A true statement – the small child looking just as Adam

did at the age. The queen of vampires even began to, for a moment, imagine the infant with a duster to its back and a revolver on his hip. A smuggler in training.

"Thank you," Adam replied warmly. "Many nights, Avery has pushed me forward when I didn't think it was possible. My son has been a godsend when dealing with emotions."

"The loss of your lover?" Sarah asked.

"Yes, among other things." he admitted.

"Other things?" the queen asked.

"Guilt," Adam said, his tone of voice changing to one of true sorrow. "My group first discovered the Priests. They came back to the Skyla System by way of our ship."

"The Benzans?" she asked.

"Yes. Though we didn't realize it at the time."

"Does anyone else know this?"

"No," he replied. "And I would really appreciate if you kept it that way. I'm sure the blame of the lost lives would be thrown into my lap."

"Your secret is safe with me Adam."

"I've come to the point where I feel I should let them know. Let them throw the blame for all of this on me. I already harbor the guilt for it." Adam responded.

"Yes, but you did not mean to bring the Priests back? Correct?" Sarah asked.

"Of course not," he replied. "We set out in search of a Benzan colony. One that was logged into their history – its location secret to all but the highest-ranking."

"And you found them?"

"Yes," he replied. "Yes we did. It explains the ships and the weapons. The robe even. As we pleaded for their help, finally getting them to agree, we began stocking resources for the return trip."

"Their help in what?" she asked.

"Destroying the Hunters."

"You meant to destroy us?" Sarah asked, taken back a bit by the Benzan's confessions.

"Well to be fair, I had no idea you were here. When I last saw you Sarah, you were the pinnacle of hope for the colonials," he pleaded. "We were coming back to destroy a race that had taken so much from the Benzans. A race that has taken so much from you." he added.

"They've taken my father, this much is true," Sarah countered. "But they've given me so much more."

"What? What could they possibly have given you that could replace the loss of your father?"

"A true understanding of things around me. A true understanding of life." she replied.

"I'm not going to pretend to understand that. I'm just going to say that you seemed to have a good understanding of life before all of this. You had a big heart and a love for your people." Adam responded, patting his small son on the back a bit.

"I'm not the woman I once was Adam." she replied.

"Yea, I'm getting that," he responded, looking to her with a great deal of emotion. "And I harbor the blame for that as well."

"This is not your doing Adam, and it's certainly not a bad thing." the queen said with a smile.

"Yes it is. It is directly my fault. Had I just forgiven you, we would have walked away together and been married. I know that to the very pit of my soul." Adam replied.

"I can still remember you flying away. I remember watching your ship hit full-burn through the glass window of my colonial shuttle."

"Sarah, I'm sorry."

"Don't be. Vladris was too strong and remains so. Had you stayed behind he would have killed you and I would still be here as I am now." Sarah remarked.

"Perhaps. I guess we'll see," Adam replied. "Sarah, I will save you from all of this."

"Adam, it's alright. I'm content with my life now."

Cutting his eyes to her to reaffirm his statement, the Benzan smuggler told her once more.

"Sarah, I WILL save you."

Aboard Colonial Star Triumph

Commander Ortega remained standing, hands behind his back and clasped together while his eyes soaked in the view. The Drift planets seemed so peaceful from above. So relatively unscathed by the zombie plague, though only on the surface.

As his ship orbited the heavens above, coasting through the stars with a manner of technological beauty, the commander knew that the calm of dusty brown and pale red below was anything but unscathed.

He'd gotten reports for the past few months of zombies overrunning the planets. The local armies immediately falling to the mercy of such a threat while its citizens were no doubt in hiding and praying for a ship such as the colonial vessel Ortega stood aboard.

He had never quite understood their desire for such a primitive lifestyle. Blatantly shunning readily-available technology at every opportunity.

The Drifts had earned a reputation for being primitive, yet beautiful. Spaceships replaced with airships of glass and steel, crafted in a Victorian-style that had long been the signature of the planets below.

A vacation spot, if nothing else, for the people of the system that wished to escape the harsh work schedules which seemed to drag most down. Busy flight schedules by cramped shuttles, flying them to the surface of mundane planets and even worse, to unexciting routine jobs behind desks.

The Drift planets were of a different sort. They allowed only the essential technology, which meant two things. If you didn't work hard, you didn't eat. Their food came by way of farms across the lands of each planet, trading among themselves and priding themselves on being self-sufficient. The other, of course, is that it was the place to be rowdy. If you had it in you.

Throughout the Skyla System, fighting was heavily frowned upon and usually punishable with jail time. The more advanced society became, the more restrictions governments seemed to place on 'free' people.

The Drifts settled their arguments in the same manner. Fist to cuff. If a disagreement was had, fighting tended to ensue. Of course when the parties involved were done, they'd usually patch things up over a cold pitcher of beer.

Their shunning of technology, however, had placed them at a huge disadvantage when it came to the zombie outbreak. They received no warning, nor could they radio for help. Not that they would have regardless.

Commander Ortega knew the rules. He was forced under colonial code, even under such trying times, to make every attempt possible to contact their governments first.

The Drifts fell under colonial rule, but did not adhere to the same rules. That had been agreed upon many years before Ortega came to power, and though he did not agree with their primitive way of thinking, the commander did respect it.

"Ready and awaiting your orders sir." a high-ranking soldier said, firmly standing in the doorway of command center aboard the Colonial Star Triumph.

"You've attempted to hail the governments?" Commander Ortega asked.

"Yes sir," the soldier replied. "We've made several efforts to reach each of them. Our grid shows no airborne traffic and we cannot reach them through our com systems," the soldier added. "However, we have picked up droves of heat signatures on the surface. All of them consistent with what we've seen across the Skyla System. The Priests are indeed here."

"Very well. Begin taking the fight to them, and advise our soldiers to fire only if they can confirm their targets.

These people may live simple lives, but they are still people. Our people. Let's protect the innocent and exterminate the guilty." Ortega said.

"Yes sir, at once." the soldier replied, turning to execute his direct orders.

Commander Ortega glanced from a large window that looked across the stars once more. He had always been taught to think of the Drifts as a sanctuary, though he had never personally visited. Many times he'd found himself understanding what must drive people to live here, among the fringe planets of deep space. Family, love, a man's word and the benefit of hard work.

Things the rest of the Skyla System had long forgotten.

The commander had taken a personal interest in protecting the most innocent civilians he could think of, and though the colonials were losing a war on all fronts, he'd be damned if he would allow such a peaceful people to fall victim to the Priests.

His thoughts were backed with the remaining might of their fleet, evidenced by dozens of smaller ships, each full of soldiers who were armed to the teeth, descending to the planets below.

They would confirm their targets and then begin to string napalm in the areas affected. A second wave would provide colonial boots to the ground in an attempt to break the spine of such a large zombie force and finally, his diminishing fleet would deliver supplies to those who were in need. Providing hope to those who wished to remain with their homes, while offering to bring any survivors aboard his ship for protection.

Assuming they had arrived in time and his men were swift when taking the fight to the undead army.

Godspeed.

Ronica
"They must think us fools!" one of the largest Husk

stated firmly.

"Relax Rylak. We must bide our time and strike when it is meant to be." Troy responded.

"If we take out the head of the snake, the rest of it will fall with swiftness." Rylak replied.

"I agree," Troy stated. "But I have seen firsthand the abilities of the head of the snake. Vladris is not to be taken lightly. We must strike when it is least-expected. That is our only chance of winning."

"Then we will bide our time." Rylak agreed, each of the men bowing their heads slightly. A common sight among the might Orc-like Husk.

As Rylak and several of the muscle-heavy warriors walked away, each of them keeping their plans of deceit closely guarded, Troy began to think of a lot of times gone by.

A man who was like a father to him, not to mention the greatest warrior he'd ever known. Roman Raines. Cut down by Vladris following one of the most epic battles recorded.

Troy began to wonder if Roman would approve of his plan. If Roman would encourage the act of revenge or warn Troy off for his own safety. The young man had been trained in the arts of Husk war, and had excelled during each and every turn.

He had become one of the best warriors among his people, even if he was human at the core. What he lacked genetically, Troy made up for with speed and wit, becoming one of the most respected warriors in Husk armor.

Still, he knew of Vladris in battle. For many years the mighty Husk had tried to end the champion vampire. By all accounts, Vladris was responsible for hundreds of slain Husk, which provided extra incentive for the young man. Not that he needed an extra push.

Watching a man who had been like a father to him, a man that had first trained him with a combat blade –

watching him fall in battle was push enough.

Troy knew that their time for battle was coming. He planned to strike the lion by surprise and then earn his right among Husk royalty by ending the reign of terror that was Vladris.

-

As Vladris approached Adam and his escort which was comprised of colonial soldiers and Benzan warriors, the man stood to his feet.

A former ship's captain, colonial lieutenant and admitted smuggler, Adam had walked many paths in life. Though he understood the most important path was the one which lay beneath Vladris' feet as the vampiric warrior approached.

"Our elders place great faith in you Adam Michaels. They will allow your fleet to land on Ronica and use our far side as a staging ground under the terms that you proposed," the vampire said, his words firm. "However."

"I'm listening." Adam replied.

"Should I even suspect this is a ploy; a trap to overtake our fine planet," Vladris remarked, leaning in closely. "I won't hesitate to have my finest run you and your precious survivors down like fleeing cattle."

"That's not going to happen." Adam said clearly, though it remained unclear as to which part of Vladris' statement he was referring.

The champion vampire started at him for several moments, both of them unrelenting in eye contact; making it feel as though it were an eternity.

"Should I find out you're here for Sarah," the vampire warned. "You'll suffer a far-worse fate than death."

"I'm just here to help my people." Adam replied.

"We'll see." Vladris warned, turning to begin a long journey back into the castle.

"A bit of a prick, yes?" one of the colonial soldiers asked.

"Yea," Adam replied. "I would be too if this were my home." he added.

"Vladris!" Adam yelled aloud, jogging slowly as he caught back up to the seasoned warrior. "Thank you, truly."

As he finished his words, Adam extended his hand to the warrior of vampires, a gesture that was unheard of.

"Are you sure you want to shake the hand of the warrior who cut your friend Roman Raines to his grave?" Vladris taunted.

It was stunning news to Adam Michaels, a confession that mustered up a lot of hatred for Vladris as the smuggler considered drawing his revolver.

"Yes," he finally admitted, hand still extended. "The fighting has to stop somewhere for trust to begin."

"Interesting," Vladris replied, studying Adam a bit. "Prove your integrity to me Adam Michaels." the vampire added, shunning a handshake as he turned to head back into the castle, passing his queen on the way.

"My lady, you should be under guard at such times." Vladris said gently with a bow.

"I trust Adam and his group. Perhaps you would be wise to do the same?"

"My queen, I mean no disrespect," Vladris replied, biting a tongue that was growing ever-sharper for Adam Michaels. "It is in my nature to question the intentions of a race which has hunted us down for centuries."

"I understand your reservations," Sarah responded. "And you are a better champion for it. I have known Adam for a long time. I could easily see through his story if it were not indeed the truth." she added.

"Of course my queen."

"Gather some men and begin to clear enough area for what I understand to be a large grid of ships landing," she ordered. "And Vladris," she added, keening the champion's focus on their conversation a bit. "Keep our warriors posted within the staging area at all times. As a precaution."

"Of course my lady." Vladris replied with a grin, knowing Sarah's human side trusted Adam thoroughly, though her vampiric side trusted no one.

"May we speak Adam?" Sarah asked, approaching the embattled smuggler as he motioned his small group away.

There was a time when they communicated with the simplicity of a glance, the emotion of a kiss. But those times had become politically incorrect, which saddened the man throughout his heart.

"Of course."

He listened, though he wanted to talk. Scoop her up and take her away, just to talk for hours. His heart, his very soul, having missed her so badly that it physically hurt.

"I wanted to say I'm sorry," she admitted. "About Sasha I mean. I had no idea."

"I'm sorry, is that sarcasm?" he asked, truly questioning her display of emotions for a woman he'd left with.

"No, no. I am truly sorry. Becoming a Hunter has heightened my senses greatly and I can see the sadness in your heart. For that I am very sorry." Sarah responded.

Breaking down just a bit, Adam refrained from tears, though it seemed nearly impossible.

"Part of that is indeed for Sasha. Her loss has been unbearable. But much of the sadness you pick up on is for you. Seeing you here, knowing it's because of a choice I made."

"Don't be silly, I'm fine with being here. They have accepted me and their race is truly remarkable." Sarah replied.

"When I look at you, I don't see sadness. I just have the eyes of a smuggler." he said with a grin, bringing a grin to her face as well.

"You always had wit. I'll give you that much." Sarah replied, her face warming with an extended grin.

"I see a woman who I was ready to marry and call my

wife. I see war after war, each of them having pulled apart what was once my sole reason for living. I see what should have been."

His confession hit like a blindside of truth, stirring up many emotions that Sarah had dealt with as a human.

"Now if that complicates matters, I'm sorry. I thought the loss of Sasha was unbearable, and at times it seems that way. But looking at you and not admitting my continuing feelings for you, that's unbearable. I'd rather be cut down by Vladris' blade than pretend I don't still care for you." he added.

Sarah was shocked by his statement, turning to retreat from such truth into her castle, stopping long enough to ask one final question.

"Do you mind if I ask how Sasha died?"

It was a very blunt question, though such an attitude was not uncommon among the Hunters.

"She died protecting our son," Adam replied, choking back tears. "The Priests took our ship and there was a single lifeboat left. Two man vessel," he added. "I insisted on staying behind to provide them both time to escape, but Sasha pleaded with me, said I would be Avery's best chance of survival. That I would be able to protect him in the long run," Adam said, a single tear beginning to trickle from his eye. "Sarah, I have to protect my son."

To avoid tears on her own end, Sarah nodded her understanding before turning to enter the castle. Adam's confession of a child and his helplessness in defending the young boy leading her to a single conclusion.

Adam's son would be protected, even if it meant the death of every soul within the Hunter race.

Drift Planet – Sandilia

"I don't understand why we don't stay put now that they're gone. We have walls around us and a roof over our heads?" Cambria asked.

"Best I can tell, these things are like stray dogs. They

seem to move all over the place with no real direction, but I've learned enough about the son of a bitches to know that they do move with direction. They jump from place to place, each one a familiar spot," Dalton replied. "I just think it's best if we scavenge what we can from the village and then hike our asses back up a bit. Find some well-hidden high ground."

"I don't know if I can," Cambria admitted. "Not after getting to know these people."

"I understand," Dalton replied. "You stay put here and cover our asses. Besides, there's a good chance the fuckers dropped ailing bodies for fresh ones."

Cambria nodded, letting Dalton know she understood. Though she appeared shaken.

"We'll be done in fifteen, just keep your eyes open," Dalton said, comforting the woman with a meaningful hold of her upper-arm. "Come on worker bee, we got shit to do." he added, turning to Skulls with a smile.

"What if I don't want to be worker bee? What if I want to be something else?" the sniper replied with sarcasm.

"Carry your ass." Dalton replied, cutting through the chase as the two men walked slowly from the cover of brush. Entering a freshly-fallen camp under the cover of darkness.

"Looking for anything we might need for survival. Guns and grub, obviously, but anything that can make it more comfortable too. Blankets..." Dalton whispered, the two men having made it back to the deathly-quiet camp.

"Whiskey?" Skulls asked with a sarcastic eye roll.

"Well if the shoe fits."

"I figured as much." the sniper replied.

"Hey, don't knock my way of getting through things," Dalton scolded, though he continued to whisper in doing so. "We all deal with shit in different ways, and I've been through enough for the both of us."

"It's cool, I get it." Skulls admitted.

"How about you then? How do you deal with shit like this?" Dalton asked.

"Me? I just block it out. It plays out in front of my eyes, but I don't store it to memory." Skulls replied, rolling the body of a grown man over in search of weapons, instead finding a slain toddler in which the grown man had tried to protect from the horde of undead."

"Yea. Good luck blocking that shit out." Dalton said.

Aboard Colonial Star Triumph

"Sir," Doctor Arness said as he slowly entered the private quarters of Commander Ortega. "Preliminary reports show mostly wasteland down below. We've found a few pockets of survivors, but mostly just rolling hordes of Priests."

"Keep the search efforts going." Ortega replied.

"Sir, if I may," Arness replied. "These search choppers are using fuel that will eventually need. The tradeoff for only a handful of lives may not be worth it in the end. It may be in our own best interest to suspend the searches and focus on supplying our exodus fleet."

"I'm not in the business of doing what's in my own person interest. I'm in the business of doing what's best for my people. We don't know how many survivors are down there, but we know they are down there and in need. I won't leave them behind. You have my answer doctor. Continue the searches." Ortega said.

"As you wish sir." Doctor Arness replied with a nod.

Walking from the room, the doctor slowly closed the thick door of the commander's quarters.

"Well?" a second adviser asked as they both walked from the commander's quarters and into the bustling interior of the large colonial ship.

"Our commander has lost his way," Arness said without hesitation. "He puts the survival of our fleet in great danger by continuing this pointless search for survivors."

"Perhaps now is our time to strike?" the adviser asked. "I have the support of several, many within the commander's own military ranks."

"No," Arness replied. "At least not yet. Our move to power hinges on timing and execution," he added. "If we jump too soon, Ortega will look as though he is a victim, and will have the sympathy of the fleet. However, if we wait for opportunity, eventually one will present itself. At the first overstep of his power, we can strike and look as though we are heroes in removing him from power."

"I understand," the adviser replied with a smile. "It is a solid plan indeed."

"It hinges on your ability to gain support for our cause," Arness said, staring onto the slim man of fine clothing. "We must have a good portion of military with us, otherwise those who back our great commander will stall our efforts quickly."

"Understood," the adviser replied. "I'll get right on that."

"Cautiously," Arness warned, pausing his conspiracy partner's walk. "Be weary of including someone who may not share our vision of the fleet."

"Consider it done."

Drift Planet – Sandila

"Best be getting some sleep." Dalton remarked, turning to welcome Cambria, who eased into a sitting position beside him; both of them sponging in the serenity of a cold – but clear night.

"Hard for me to sleep, considering." she replied.

"Yea. I get that way with these stank-undead fucks roaming around here too." he said with a grin.

"Actually, I meant that," she replied with a smile of her own. "Stank-undead fucks aside; it's a beautiful night. A bit chilled with a slight breeze. Quiet. Almost seems like a normal moment. At least what I can remember of normality."

"Yea I," Dalton said with pause, eventually removing his brown duster and offering it to the welcoming hands of Cambria. "I can't get away from leaving those people behind. If there would have been any other way..."

"I know," the beautiful woman replied, snuggling into the oversized coat and feeling more secure than she had in a long time. "You didn't do anything wrong back there. If you hadn't of acted so quickly, Skulls and I wouldn't be here."

"I reckon." Dalton said, turning for a moment to watch the sniper rest, a deep sleep to be envied.

"I also have to admit," Cambria said, her smile turning a bit more serious. "There's something to this brown coat. When I first met you, I was skeptical, but now I get it. You're a complex man Dalton James."

"Not by choice, I'll guarantee you that," he replied with truth. "I've just been on the move so damn much I figure I'll bring the comforts of home with me. That usually means whiskey and a coat that doubles as a blanket."

"Sorry I've dragged you into all of this. Truly." she admitted.

"Ah, no need for that. I've been running with the undead at my heels for a long time now. Got nothing to do with you pretty lady." he responded.

"Also sorry for not seizing the moment. With you, I mean. I have this stupid way of not letting anyone get close to me. Even those I love." Cambria confessed. Her eyes seeming to gaze onto him with a sky-blue truth.

As Dalton began to lean in for a kiss, one that both had longed for; the smuggler froze. Staring into her eyes, though seemingly distracted.

"I'm sorry. I shouldn't have..." Cambria mumbled with regret.

"Shh." Dalton replied, holding the rough feel of his finger to her soft lips.

Though it seemed an awkward situation, Dalton

remained silent, his finger pressed to her lip. Partly because of his attention focused elsewhere, and partly because of her lip feeling so tender. So desirable.

At that moment, loud blasts streaked across the sky. Each of them trailing from colonial ships traveling at high speeds.

"Well I'll be a son of a bitch!" Dalton yelled, understanding their chances of survival had just increased drastically.

"Does this mean we're safe?" Cambria asked, turning to Skulls who had snapped immediately from his dream world, battle-hardened grasp onto rifle.

"Only if we figure out a way to flag 'em down." Dalton replied, scrambling around and thinking the situation through.

Finally, he began pouring what remained of his whiskey onto the ground. The dense soil soaking in both alcohol and curse words as Dalton felt bittersweet over the sacrifice. Striking his favorite cigar lighter, he then lit the alcohol and began grabbing any patch of desolate timber he could find.

"I knew I did the right thing by bringing you in. I knew your experience would eventually save our lives!" Cambria said with a yell, vibrantly smiling as she thanked the Gods above.

"Yea, well, you haven't paid me yet." Dalton replied, his joking a sure sign of relief as the sounds of thrusters neared their makeshift bonfire, while others streaked across the night sky and slapped burning napalm to the ground.

A moment later, Dalton was paid in full as her lips locked onto his; her statement one of truth. She was committed to the man who had earned her trust, and stolen her heart. Even if he reeked of cheap tobacco and tainted whiskey.

Ronica

It was a moment in which history would never forget. The colonials had begun staging their fleet on the surface of Ronica; large ships undergoing upgrades as they were stocked with supplies and munitions.

However, the historic moment before them was much more. As the Husk began to land, topped off eventually with a glimmer-green shuttle that was carrying their leaders, Hunters awaited.

For many years, thousands upon thousands, the Hunters and Husk had been at war. They had slain one another at every chance for as long as time could remember. The mighty Orc-like Husk clashing with the Hunters, a vampiric community which had remained shrouded in mystery.

As the shuttle began to open, however, their mightiest warrior was quick to walk onto Ronican soil. A sign that caution had been thrown into the wind during such perilous times.

Gore, the musclebound Husk, quickly approached the Hunters' welcoming party; which included several of vampiric society, among them Sarah and Vladris.

Such an historic event turned heads, and rightfully so, as everyone seemed to pause and watch the exchange. Both curiosity and caution to blame.

"My people appreciate your help. If I, or any of my kind can be of assistance, please let me know." Gore said, extending his arm for a handshake.

"What would our ancestors think if they saw their two finest shaking hands?" Vladris questioned, staring directly into the eyes of such a mighty Husk.

"They would know that we are at the end of times. Yes, I truly believe they would want their finest to band together and write history against such an unbeatable foe." Gore replied, his hand remaining extended.

"Perhaps," Vladris replied with authority. "And if you fight them with as much tenacity as you have fought us, together perhaps," Vladris added. "We can prove them beatable." the mighty vampire replied, finally offering his hand.

It was merely a handshake, though both warriors knew it would be talked about for centuries to come. Perhaps longer, if anyone survived to speak of it.

Though each warrior had fought for a different cause, they knew of the others ability in battle. Each becoming a legend to his own race while remaining a menace to the other. For them, the handshake symbolized a show of respect among warriors, nothing more.

Though it was a sight that most remained locked onto, Sarah quickly pulled her eyes away from the warriors.

Her attention fell to the shuttle as a familiar face exited, accompanied by one of the Hunter's own hellhounds.

"Troy?" the queen said in disbelief, walking from her own group's protection in order to greet the boy who had turned into a young man, wrapped tightly in the leather of a Husk warrior.

"Cookie!" the young man yelled, scolding the hell hound for baring its teeth as she approached.

"Cookie?" she asked with a grin.

"Couldn't come up with anything better at the time." he replied, still possessing a child-like innocence.

"I feel as though I owe you an apology." Sarah admitted, sincerity in her voice.

"You owe nothing. What is in the past, remains in the past. I just thank you for providing us safety as we try to save as many as we can." Troy replied, the large sword of a Husk tied to his back with leather strapping.

"Of course," Sarah replied, looking to him with so many memories. "You've grown into a strong young man, and, from the looks of it, a mighty warrior. This makes me proud."

"The Husk have shown me the path of a warrior. They have accepted me as one of their own, and for that I am truly grateful," Troy admitted. "Though I continue to wish the best for my old friends."

She answered his statement with a smile, though his mention of Adam sent her attention elsewhere; eyes scanning the background as they finally locked onto Adam Michaels.

One of the system's most notorious smugglers, not to mention a ranking member of the Benzan Mafia – at least what remained of it. Yet there he stood. Off to himself a bit and holding a child, no more than a year old, in an attempt to calm his son.

So many ships around, their massive cargo holds being filled, and colonials briefing others on the flight to come. Hulking vessels being welded for the trip to come. Firming their exterior for a trip that may indeed prove to be one way.

Others tested thrusters, short bursts of flame firing from engines as pilots gauged their controls; watching as swordfish fighters were loaded into the landing bays.

For all of the commotion, as though a small city had quickly formed by way of connected ships, there seemed to be a calmness in Adam Michaels. As if he held a son and thought nothing of the turmoil around him.

"You still love him, don't you?" Troy asked.

"Of course not, things are different now. Complicated." Sarah responded. Taken off-guard a bit by the young man's direct question.

"The world complicates things, but the heart doesn't," Troy said, nodding his head a bit. "Just some advice from a Husk-raised human with a dog I can't get rid of." he added with a smile.

Sarah laughed a bit, though her mind did begin to think of any possibility of a future with Adam.

"All joking aside, you should tell him. Especially now that all face the certainty of death. No telling how many days we have left to make things right." Troy remarked.

She began to wonder what he had meant about certain

death, knowing the exodus fleet was supposed to be their solution for survival.

Aboard Colonial Star Triumph

"I must admit Dalton James," Commander Ortega remarked. "Your ability to survive time after time amazes me."

The commander sat behind a large military-grade desk in his personal chamber, reviewing a file of the brown coat laden survivor who sat directly in front of him.

"Timing really. I can't take all of the credit." Dalton replied, feeling a bit out of place.

"Well, be that as it may, good timing seems to follow you," the commander said. "Two major wars on Glimmeria, skirmishes with the Hunters and now this? Some would consider you to be a beacon of good luck."

Dalton thought of that statement. All of the near death encounters with Hunters. The hordes of zombies giving chase. He couldn't understand being a beacon of good luck, having always considered himself the exact opposite.

"How would you feel about swearing in as a colonial soldier once more?" the commander asked.

It was a right hook to Dalton's expectations, stumbling through a list of responses. He had expected to be given a steak dinner, slapped on the ass and dumped off at the next available planet. Not even remotely considering the possibility of enlisting once more.

"Well sir, I haven't even given it thought to be honest. I haven't showered in a week, and just yesterday saw a lot of innocent people butchered by the undead. I just," he replied, taking a moment to emotionally collect himself. "I just need a few moments to wind down and get past what I've seen. What I've lived through."

"I understand, and your concern for the innocent is both obvious and admirable. The exodus fleet will need people just like you if it is to survive. So you think on it Dalton James. I've signed off on fast-tracking you into the fleet,"

Ortega said. "It's now a matter of paper that needs your signature."

"I don't understand?" Dalton asked.

"It means your record speaks for itself. I'm deeming you too important to leave behind," the commander said, grinning a bit. "And too lucky." he added. "Now, go get some rest and sort your priorities out a bit. Then come back and let me know what you decide on becoming a colonial officer."

"Thank you." Dalton replied.

Officer? Just yesterday I was drinking the cheapest of hand me down whiskey? The good-fortune patterned smuggler thought.

"May I ask you one question sir?" Dalton asked, standing to his feet.

"Of course." Ortega replied willingly.

"I saw you on the com stating you were staying behind when the exodus leaves. Just want to know why?" he asked.

"Well," the commander began to reply, softly laying the Dalton's folder onto his desk. "I believe that if humanity is going to survive, it will need faith in its government," he added. "It's in my own personal opinion that people will restore their faith in government if its leader sacrifices first."

"But there is no chance of survival if you stay behind. You must know that?" Dalton asked. "I've seen these things up close for far too long. There's no winning this one."

"Perhaps. But throughout history, people have fought against insurmountable odds a lot more willingly when doing so behind a leader who showed no fear. If I accompanied the exodus flight into the stars, those left behind would have no hope. Though it may be true that we have no chance of winning, if I remain here to lead a final stand, those who remain behind with me will at least have hope."

"Forgive me commander, but I don't understand the reasoning. It seems as though you would be of more service leaving and keeping the fleet in order." Dalton admitted.

"Think of those innocent faces you saw yesterday Dalton. Think of how they must have felt with no hope. Thinking of certain death before it came. By choosing to sacrifice my own life in staying behind, I save thousands of innocent faces that same fate. They may perish, but will do so with the hope of survival," the commander said. "The sacrifice of self for the better of those in need is the mark of a true leader. Remember those words Dalton James." Ortega added.

"Thank you sir." Dalton replied, nodding as he turned to exit the commander's quarters and return to the loving arms of a woman he was meant to be with.

Ronica

"I must admit Adam Michaels," Sarah remarked as she approached the man under a perfect Ronican nightfall. "I never thought I'd see the system's most notorious smuggler comforting a child.

"Yea," he replied with a smile, holding his son close and walking through a small area of tall grass in order to sooth the infant. "Honestly though, it's what I have always wanted."

"A child?" Sarah asked, seeming a bit taken back by his confession.

"A child. The calm a child brings. The innocence of the moment." he replied.

His words were true, and that was obvious to the queen of vampires. Many times she had looked into his eyes as a lover, but this moment was different. Sarah saw a spark of importance, as though he lived for a higher purpose.

"When nothing else in life seems to be going right, I just hold my son. It's a temporary fix, I know, but when I have him in my arms the world just feels right." Adam stated.

"May I hold him?" Sarah asked.

For anyone unfamiliar with their history, it would have seemed odd. Unheard of, even, for the queen of vampires to hold Adam's son.

However their history was deeply intertwined. They had loved one another, and thought of the each other as their sole reason for living. Each had made mistakes along the way, and each had harbored both guilt and anger toward the other.

But times were different. Adam had left Sarah standing alone, choosing another lover during a moment of extremes, and it had led her to the walk of a vampire. Likewise, Adam had suffered the loss of his lover, and both felt it was God's way of punishing him for his mistake.

Both Adam and Sarah had matured beyond resentment. They had agreed, though unspoken, that the heart-wrenching mistakes of their past would remain in the past, while the good memories would remain.

"Of course." Adam replied, easing the baby over to the shoulders of such a mighty queen.

Immediately, Sarah felt the calm. She understood how something as innocent and precious as a child could eliminate all else. The war, the hatred; all of it.

Though she was now queen of vampires, there was still a piece of her that remained human. A small part of her that remembered her love for Adam and their dream of having a child together. Though Sarah realized it was a life that was no longer possible to her, the Hunter DNA to blame, still she felt comfort in knowing that Adam had found his peace.

"He seems to take to you." Adam remarked, surprised at Avery's snuggling to the queen of vampires.

"And his father?" Sarah asked.

"Well," Adam began to reply, finding himself thrown into a very uneasy moment of conversation. "You must know I still have feelings for you Sarah?"

"I do." she replied with a smile.

"I have only two things in this world that push me from the bed each morning. The need to keep my son safe and the belief that I can save you from all of this. I know there must be a way, I just haven't thought it through hard enough. There has to be something I'm missing, because my mind and heart are in so many different places right now." Adam said.

"I'm sorry, I did not mean to overstep." she admitted.

"No, please don't be," Adam replied. "It's just," he added, seeming to prepare for the worst. "I'm still not over Sasha. I'm truly not. Her death has taken its toll on me."

"I understand." she replied.

"No, you truly don't," Adam said, his tone changing to one of desperation. "I love you."

His confession turned both lovers as quiet as the babe whom snuggled to her.

"Sarah, I love you. I always have. When I left with Sasha, I did it because I was pissed off. I held a grudge against you for holding us at gunpoint, and I just couldn't let that go. You have to understand, I thought a few weeks would pass and you and I would have another showdown. I didn't know this was going to happen. Sasha was a good woman, she truly was. But you and I were meant to be together. We were supposed to end up together, and because of my stupidity, my bad judgment...we're not."

"I," Sarah began to say, her emotions getting the best of her. "I'm not sure what to say?"

"There's nothing you can say. Every single night I lay down and think of three things Sarah, three. My son, the mother who died to protect him and the woman I should have married. I love you to the pit of my soul and feel guilty because of it. I hate myself for leaving you there, but I love my son. I live every day in a prison that I created. This, all of this, is on me."

"It's not all on you Adam. We've both had a hand in this. I cannot help but think that perhaps fate has crossed our paths once more for a reason." Sarah commented, handing the small child back to the arms that used to hold her so lovingly.

"If we somehow make it through this...if we somehow survive," Adam said. "I will make everything up to you. I will love you again."

Sarah responded to his promise with a warm smile, though no words were to follow. She walked away as silently as Vladris had stood, watching their conversation from a distance.

Though the champion vampire felt sudden anger, Vladris also felt the truth in Adam's confession. He too had once loved, only to lose his lover in times of war. Vladris wanted to hate Adam Michaels, but also found a bit of common ground with the smuggler as his stare of concentration continued.

Aboard Colonial Star Triumph

"What's wrong?" Cambria asked, walking from her rack.

"Just can't sleep, that's all." Dalton replied, sitting at a small table near the cabin door, though he did so in the dark.

"You should try. We land on Ronica within hours, you'll need your sleep," she commented softly, placing a hand on Dalton's back in comforting fashion. "Our government was unorganized before all of this. You can imagine the hell we'll have to go through now." she added, smiling wide.

"You know, under any other circumstances, I'd be trying to bed you down right about now." he said with a bit of a grin.

"Well you wouldn't have to try all that hard I'm afraid," Cambria replied, changing her voice to that of a pure-western girl. "It seems I've taken to this mysterious cowboy draped in brown and masked in whiskers." she added, holding her hand to her forehead.

As Dalton sat silently, Cambria's own demeanor changed to a more serious one.

"Well, if my damsel in distress routine didn't get you it must be serious. What's going on?" she asked.

"Been thinking a lot about those people we left behind yesterday. Their faces."

"Dalton, it is not your fault. Worlds full of people just like that have fallen all across the Skyla System. The Priests are to blame, not you. We had no choice."

"I was the one who had the experience among them. I should have stayed. Should have stayed behind to give those people hope – not left 'em to die with fear."

"You wouldn't have made it out alive. None of us would have." she replied.

"Maybe I wasn't supposed to." Dalton said.

"Don't talk like that. Not after I've fallen for you," Cambria said, pausing to look deep into his eyes. "I've fallen for you Dalton James."

With her statement came a kiss. Followed soon after by a bonding of souls' only feet from the door that separated them from their resident sniper. All without the use of whiskey, which, perhaps, was a first for the man known as Dalton James.

-

"Wake up my friend," Skulls pleaded, doing his best to usher the brown coated smuggler from a foggy world of dreams. "We're landing on Ronica."

"Damn," Dalton was slow to acknowledge. "My head is splitting. Feel like I've been hit by a train. Almost like a hangover?"

"Something like that." Cambria replied, covertly eluding to their session of lovemaking.

Of course, Skulls never caught on. He was quick to sway his eye to the scope and fetch a guaranteed kill, that much was a fact. However, his ability to catch onto an inside joke, or, in this case, an inside conversation – was lacking.

"Hadn't felt this rough since I got hold of some tainted rock whiskey back on Phinamore." Dalton said tauntingly.

"Oh really?" Cambria said, playing along. "You sort of have the look of a long night of binge-drinking alright. Just seems like you've been laid up with the finest of liquor."

"Liquor? You mean hootch?" Dalton asked, his question changing her facial complexion drastically.

"No, I mean liquor. As in fine wine. The kind that's been on the shelf for a mighty long time collecting dust. They say it gets better with age." Cambria insisted.

"Well, I'd say as a long time connoisseur...and I mean long...I'd have to admit that it seems like the wine that's been sitting so long is most likely the best I've ever had." Dalton replied.

"Most likely?" she asked.

"What about you? Walking a bit rough this morning?" Dalton asked.

"So am I, this space travel will do it." Skulls added.

"Wow, you too Skulls? I'm impressed. There are only so many hours in a single night?" Cambria asked playfully.

"Oh hell no," Dalton insisted. "There is a select list of consumable wines in my book. That's it, if you know what I'm saying?"

"I do," she replied, checking her pistol before snugging the oversized revolver into its hip-holster. "I just feel a little stiff, that's all. I need to get out and stretch my legs a bit. I need some exercise."

If Skulls wasn't here, I'd stretch your legs and give you some damn exercise. Dalton thought, though he did his best not to moisten his lips with the tip of his tongue. A habit he found hard to break.

As Skulls prepared his own rifle, Dalton and Cambria continued to stare onto each other. It had been a long time since she'd felt this way about someone. In fact, it had been years. She'd once planned to marry the most notorious gunslinger in the Drifts, but it simply wasn't meant to be.

Cambria had a thirst for the stars. A life filled with adventure beyond compare. Her then lover, Johnny, wanted a simple life. He'd always made the claim that he'd both live and die in the Drifts, and the gunslinger wasn't bluffing.

He had chosen to stay behind. Chosen to do his best in waiting out the plague of men from the rocky cliffs of his home planet, doing so with a small gang of friends and co-criminals.

Cambria was saddened by his decision, of course, but it was his to make. She would always have feelings for the man that remained behind, but love is what she had come to feel for Dalton. True love.

She'd greatly misjudged the smuggler during their first meeting. He seemed as though he was old and broken down. Cambria soon learned, however, that he was quite the opposite. He was alive, and full of the kind of life she thirsted for. Adventure.

He'd been a part of every major event during his lifetime. Every war, every skirmish. He'd ran with convicts, fought vampires, ran from zombies and even co-existed with the mighty Husk race for a short time.

Most importantly, however, he had a good heart. She could see the hurt in him, a sign of compassion. Her time in the adventurous line of work, smuggling, had been short. Still, she felt safe around the man who reeked of cheap whiskey and cigar smoke.

He was the closest to a cowboy as Cambria could have imagined. Tough, rugged, experienced, and behind closed doors, sensitive. There was a good man behind that rough patch of whiskers; an honorable man beneath that tattered brown coat.

"Fuck," the honorable man shouted, seeming to break

Cambria from her imaginative spell. "These fucking landings. Every single time, these landings." he added loudly, grabbing a steel shelf which was bolted to the ship's wall, as the large vessel descended on Ronica.

"Such language." Cambria replied with a smile, bracing herself as well.

"Hey, I got liquor or I got language. Right now, I'm fresh out of the good stuff."

As the ship began its harsh descent into the atmosphere of Ronica, forcing everyone aboard to brace themselves while hushing to a quiet calm, Dalton began to think.

He'd been in so many ships; so many descents. Still, he remembered every single one. His early days during the first Glimmerian War, the smuggler counted nineteen drops altogether. Most had come after a Legion ass-whipping and colonial retreat.

He also remembered the countless drops from space that he and his former crew had undergone. Most of them successful, while a few were...not so much.

Dalton had successfully survived two crash landings under such conditions, and remembered the day he walked away from his first. Promising himself on that very day that his boots would never again touch the inside of a spaceship.

Yet here he stood, leaned over and holding onto the frame of a door as if his life depended upon it.

Stupid! You are one stupid son of a bitch!

"Are you alright?" Cambria yelled with a smile, her lover having grown as quiet as a church mouse, though his thoughts would have scarred said church mouse for life.

"Fine," Dalton said, lying through his teeth in the process. "About to fall asleep actually."

As long as I live, my damn boots will never touch the inside of another ship. Not for this shit. He thought.

Roncia

Ships had been coming in for days on end, the sound of thrusters seemingly commonplace to those already assigned to Ronica. However, the larger colonial star ships were a different story. Earthquake loud and nearly large enough to blacken the sky, two traits that demanded everyone's full attention.

Especially Adam, who did his best to calm his son as the shiny armada of the sky slowly touched ground.

The Hunters called Ronica home. The Husk had arrived, as had the Benzans and every smaller, yet organized, force throughout the Skyla System. Finally the colonials had come. Their commander just moments away from unifying the people who had arrived under his direction.

"Now my queen," Vladris said with a sharp tongue. "Now we will see with our own eyes. Now we discover the truth of our place among this fleet."

"Indeed," she replied, her attention on the recently-landed ship. "Though I believe they will welcome us. I have a long history with Commander Ortega."

"Does your history include his eyes catching sight of you as a Hunter?" Vladris asked.

It was a legitimate question, at least from Sarah's perspective as they joined everyone in watching the large group of soldiers exit, escorting Ortega.

"People have a way of viewing our race negatively based on our looks. Though our intentions may be true." Vladris added.

Near the rear of the group, which consisted of hundreds of lives, Dalton, Skulls and Cambria exited the large ship. Their lungs welcoming the fresh air, though Dalton's craved the smoke of a cigar.

The fact was, Sarah first caught sight of the small group. Dalton's brown coat a beacon of smuggling among the colonial blue. That said, Dalton immediately caught sight of Adam Michaels a mere moment later.

"Well fuck me raw." Dalton exclaimed loudly.

"Here? In front of hundreds, even thousands? Well it sounds crazy, but we can try it." Cambria replied, motioning for her belt buckle as a gesture, though she had no intentions of going through with it.

Without an answer, Dalton blew off her advance, immediately walking toward a man who was like his own brother. A hasty strut quickly closing the gap of several hundred yards.

"Well who'd you go and knock up?" Dalton asked, the crisp of his voice immediately grabbing Adam's attention.

Turning, Adam's face told of relief. A welcomed reunion among old friends.

"Dalton James." Adam said, doing so after finding himself without words. Happiness in no short supply.

"Why is it every damn time I run from the undead, you show up? I'm starting to put two and two together." the smuggler replied, hugging his old friend firmly, their reunion conjuring up a lot of great memories.

"I wondered about you. Hoped you had made it out, but had started to worry." Adam admitted.

"Nearly didn't, bunch of half-dead fucks. Didn't know they was up against the old smuggler extraordinaire."

"And who are these good people?" Adam asked, both Cambria and Skulls approaching.

"This here is Skulls, the finest sniper around," Dalton said, turning to Cambria and quickly finding himself at a loss as to how he should introduce her. Cambria slowly locking her hand into his and squeezing tight. "This here is my girl. Cambria."

"Your girl?" Adam said with a grin. "I thought love was for suckers? What happened to the three women on..."

"Hey man." Dalton warned.

"I'm only kidding, glad to meet you," Adam said, shaking hands with both the sniper and Dalton's eye candy. "Any friend of Dalton's is a friend of mine."

"So man, you never gave me an answer. Who'd you knock up?" Dalton asked.

Hesitant to answer, Adam simply began to walk away as Sarah approached. Her champion by her side.

"What's his problem?" Dalton asked.

"Adam is still grieving with the loss of Sasha. His son reminds him of her very much, I think." Sarah replied.

Both Skulls and Cambria seemed intimidated by the idea of Hunters standing before them. Particularly Vladris, who was both hulking in appearance and scarred from battle.

"You need not fear us," Sarah admitted, extending her hand to the blue-haired beauty. "Dalton is an old friend of mine, and Vladris is a great warrior no doubt, but he fights for your cause. For the defense of the innocent."

Though she seemed to be shaken a bit, Cambria indeed shook hands with Sarah, a queen among the race of fear.

"Ah shit." Dalton said.

Saying nothing, Sarah turned to listen to the smuggler.

"Didn't know he had lost someone important. Put my foot in my mouth, as usual."

"I see," Sarah replied. "Should you need anything, any of you...don't hesitate to ask."

"Thanks Sarah. I appreciate you taking this old hound dog in." Dalton replied with a wily grin.

With hundreds of bodies bustling around in preparation for the exodus launch, Dalton's group watched the queen and her champion walk away. Heading back to the sanctuary of castle walls.

"She seems a little strange." Cambria confessed.

"The bitch has always been crazy, no doubt about it," Dalton replied. "But the good kind of crazy I guess."

"Wait, were you and her a thing?" Cambria asked, feeling a bit awkward.

"Oh hell no!" Dalton insisted. "Though I'm sure she's wanted to jump on my Glimmerian stick a time or two. Who hasn't?"

Smacking the man across his arm as a stern warning, their sniper finally began to make a clear picture of the situation.

"So you guys are together?" Skulls asked, the large bolt-action rifle hanging from his shoulder by a thick nylon strap.

"Um yea, hello?" Cambria replied.

"Oh dear God," Skulls admitted. "I thought I dreamed those noises last night. They were so vivid. Some things cannot be undone." the sniper confessed with shame, head hanging a bit in doing so.

"Just start worrying less about my sex life and more on keeping an eye on that hulking sumbitch," Dalton said, motioning to Vladris as the champion and his queen made their way through the settlement of survivors. "He's tried to kill me more than once."

"He didn't? Wow," Cambria replied. "I'm impressed. He's like twice your size."

"Fuck 'em," Dalton barked. "I guess I showed him that size doesn't matter. It's the amount of fight inside."

"Oh, he looks like he has plenty of fight inside of him." Cambria said, taunting her lover a bit.

"What the fuck?" Dalton questioned, turning to the woman who openly joked about wanting to bed the champion vampire.

"Oh Dalton James," Cambria said, portraying her damsel in distress act once more. "You know you're the only one for me." she added with a snicker.

"Yea, yea. I hear 'ya," Dalton replied, continuing to stare down the vampire's back. "Bet I could drink that sumbitch under the table."

"Sarah Blaine, it has been a long time. Too long," Commander Ortega remarked, surrounded by colonial soldiers as he approached the queen. "I humbly thank you and your people for providing us a safe haven."

"It was not an easy sell. My people agreed to it with the

belief that they will be treated equally." Sarah replied, shaking hands with the commander.

She was surrounded by a group of guards. Though numbering less, their armor spoke of true ability in battle.

"That will be the case, I assure you. Your people have my word."

"Thank you commander. We should talk in detail on this as soon as possible." Sarah pushed.

"Sooner than I had hoped, I'm afraid. My scouts have confirmed a large armada making course for Ronica. Presumably the Priests. We will need to call a meeting quickly to discuss the future of our people as one, and, unfortunately, devise a plan to defend the invaders long enough to stage our exodus into the stars." Ortega responded.

"We need no plan when it comes to defense. My people are masters when it comes to defending their homes against those who would take it from us." Vladris replied swiftly.

"I do not doubt your ability in combat warrior. For I have heard stories of your ability on the battlefield, you are truly a hero among your people," Ortega replied, soothing Vladris a bit. "But the threat which comes is too large. They have the bodies to simply overrun this planet, growing their numbers as they shorten ours."

"We understand your urgency commander." Sarah replied, while casting a stare of scold onto her champion.

"Sarah, I do think it best if your hero were to lead the defensive efforts. He knows the layout of Ronica as well as any. That is if he is willing?" Ortega asked.

"I am willing to go wherever my queen commands – defending her, along with my home, to the death."

"I agree commander. Vladris should lead our spearhead of defense." Sarah replied.

"Fine. Vladris, you will command your finest, as well as the finest of the colonials, Benzans and Husk. Place them strategically and stagger them in a way that makes it possible to fall back. Eventually, when your force falls back to the fleet ships, you'll board and we'll begin our flight into the stars." Ortega said.

"Understood. If the Benzans or Husk are unwilling to follow the lead of a vampire?" Vladris asked.

"Then they will be left behind as our fleet sails into the stars of night. I will brief them myself. You and your people are no longer the enemy," Ortega said, his eyes turning to the champion vampire. "You are a part of this fleet now, I am a man of my word, and you will be treated as such. I'll see to it personally."

"You are an honorable leader. Thank you." Vladris replied with a nod.

-

It was a scene for the archives of man. A large meeting hall nestled inside the stone of castle walls, heavily guarded by dozens of soldiers of all nations and creed.

"We must first decide the government that will continue as our exodus begins." Commander Ortega said.

He sat at a large table of polished wood, as did nineteen other leaders, all of them in agreement. So many powerful leaders confined to the meeting hall.

"I'm not exactly sure how we are supposed to do that during such times of chaos?" Cherlon, the Theron leader replied in question.

"We must remain a democracy. If the people have no voice, they have no hope." Gore added, proudly representing the Husk.

"I agree," Commander Ortega replied. "At final count we have forty-seven ships that can make such a voyage. Four of them colonial Stars. It is in my opinion that they should remain to the corners of our fleet. Military buffers against any and all would-be threats."

The room seemed to easily agree with his statement, essentially turning the colonial stars into the backbone of their military.

"The ships we assign for government should remain to the center and must remain a mixture of our races. Everyone is to be represented. It will make my job a lot easier up there."

"So you are not staying behind?" Sarah asked.

Indeed she was right, her question followed by an unnerving silence throughout the room.

"Of course not," he replied, chatter begin to spread throughout the room, even among the posted guards. "Though I do feel it important to have two leaders in place. A civilian leader and a military leader, both equal in terms of power over our future." he added.

"I disagree!" Gore said with conviction. "I feel as though a single leader of strong military background is needed if we are to survive."

Gore's statement caused the whispers to grow louder, finally pushing Commander Ortega to acknowledge them.

"I do not," Ortega confessed. "Our military should be strong enough to keep our people safe, but our ultimate goal is to find another home. To start over. Rebuild our civilization elsewhere. It is therefore important to retain a leader who will handle everything non-military."

With that, the whispers seemed to calm a bit. Sarah finding herself proud of Ortega, who she'd personally selected as her own successor once upon a time. When she was a Colonial leader, though it seemed so long ago.

"I think," Adam Michaels said, representing the Benzans at the meeting, though very few remained. "I think it is important to integrate those aboard our ships as well. Force them to respect others from the start so that we may put our past hatred behind us." he added.

"Absolutely not!" Gore refused. "My people will not allow Hunters to board their ships and consider them home."

"Yet your people run here to our home, only to be welcomed by the Hunters?" Sarah replied.

"Enough!" General Ortega demanded, silencing the bickering.

A very eerie quiet fell across the room, as if decades of fighting were about to resume.

"We are a single people now," Ortega said, this time a bit calmer. "The Hunters are to be treated the same as Husk or even my very own race," Ortega added. "I will oversee the exodus lottery in less than one hour. After which, I will personally see to it that each ship's manifest is integrated. Starting with yours," he said, looking directly to Gore. "You will captain a Hunter-built ship as the exodus pulls out, and a Hunter will captain your own. If you, or any among your people disagree, you are free to go your own way. Perhaps leave the luxury of your ships to journey into the nearby hills to defend us, as so many Hunters do this very moment."

Gore offered no reply, though he cutting stare could be counted as such.

"And of your mighty colonial star ships? Will they too be integrated, or are your people above your own laws?" the Theron representative lashed out.

"Every ship, including my own, will be staffed accordingly. Captains, their executive officers and even the soldiers aboard will be assigned based on their military experience. Fairly and equally." Ortega defended.

"Very well then. You have the blessing of the Therons on this, as well as everyone else I believe."

"Gore? Do the Husk agree to these terms?" Ortega asked with authority.

"Yes," the mighty Orc-like Husk replied. "Though I wish to personally see the manifests before they go into effect." adding suspicion to his arsenal.

"Very well." Commander Ortega responded, proving to the room he had nothing to hide.

"The exodus lottery seems to be all that remains?" A leader of the Drifts commented; his rough beard testament to a life lived simply.

"Indeed. Now it is time for our computers to decide who is allowed to join us on our exodus into the stars." Ortega replied. His statement effectively ending the meeting of leaders among what remained of the Skyla System.

"How will the moment of our launch play out?" a leader asked, representing the small moon of Novak, which neighbored Glimmeria.

"That is a very good question, I'm afraid," Commander Ortega replied. "I don't think anyone has the answer. I do know that those who are in the hills to defend us have been promised a spot on the fleet, should they make it back alive. As they become overwhelmed, I've instructed them to fall back. Several lines of soldiers lay in wait, though they do so in a staggered position." Ortega added.

"You mean to slow them down?" Gore asked.

"Precisely," Ortega replied. "Rather than having the horde land and begin a sprint to our fleet, they will be forced to attack the soldiers at each staggered position, which has been strategically placed as far apart as possible. It will force the horde to zig-zag to us, rather than giving them a straight line of advancement."

"That's a good plan." Adam commented.

"It's a good start," Ortega replied. "But I fear as they bear down on us, even the best of plans will begin to fall apart," he added. "Our people will begin to panic. We must do our best to maintain order and provide those who have earned their passage a way through, while keeping those who are to be left behind at bay."

"How do we do that? Begin shooting our own people?" the Theron representative demanded to know.

"Of course not," Ortega replied. "If it came to that, we'd be no better than the horde that approaches," he added, doing his best to calm the fears of other leaders who carried the same concern. "We will have to launch our fleet at a different time than announced."

"We are going to do what?" Adam Michaels asked.

"We need to give our people a set time in which we will

launch. Allow them to drill it into their minds. Then, when the time is right, launch before they have time to respond." Ortega replied.

"You mean lie to them?" Adam asked.

"I mean do what's necessary in order to give our people a chance to thrive once more. If that means lie to them, so be it." Ortega admitted.

Adam was a lot of things. Smuggler, solider...and even compassionate at times. At this moment, however, his skills at the card table came into play. An ability to read the faces.

He's bluffing.

Something told Adam that Commander Ortega was not being honest. At least not completely.

-

"Sarah, may we speak?" Adam asked, catching up to her and her escort team as they left the meeting chamber. As did the other leaders who survived.

"Of course." she replied, turning to face her former lover.

"My intuition," he said, pausing on those words as he carefully mulled his next. "Something is going on."

"I agree Adam Michaels," Sarah replied, having pulled the same feeling away from the meeting. "Though I'm not sure what."

"Sarah, you need to consider pulling your warriors back." Adam suggested.

"Pull them back?" Sarah asked.

"I can't put my finger on it, but I came away with bad vibes about our man in charge. I feel as though he may have suggested Vladris to lead the defenses in order to thin your ranks," Adam said, pausing for a moment. "I think he means to kill you."

As the words left Adam's lips, Sarah's guards firmed up; their muscles tightening as if they were preparing for battle.

"No," Sarah warned them. "Remain calm as if nothing is suspected. Wait for them to clear out, and then we will all decide on this in private."

"Sarah," Adam replied, turning to her with true concern. "Where is the safest place inside of these walls?"

"The keep, I suppose."

"Please," Adam replied, turning to her armed escort. "I need you to escort Sarah there and keep her there. Do not let anyone in, no matter their request."

The soldiers looked onto him for a moment, before turning to their queen.

"Sarah please." Adam said.

"Alright," Sarah replied. "Only if you agree to join us."

"Huh?" he asked.

"If something truly is going on, I want people around me that I can trust," she replied. "I trust you Adam."

Several moments of silence were strung together by a look of two past lovers.

"I need to get my son." Adam finally replied.

"Azan," Sarah commanded, turning to one of her six escort warriors. "Go with Adam and make sure he is able to do so unharmed. Protect him as though you were protecting your queen." she added.

"Yes my lady." Azan replied, bowing low to the ground.

"Someone please recall Vladris and his warriors. It would seem as though the enemy is not at the gates – but already among us." Sarah commanded.

"Please be careful." Sarah said.

"Scout's honor." Adam replied with a grin.

-

"Gonna be a bittersweet thing," Adam remarked, walking through the large hallway of the Colonial Star Destiny. One of hundreds which connected the most vital parts of the large ship. "Leaving the Skyla System I mean. So many memories."

"Yes sir, I'd have to agree," Dalton replied. "Been locked up on half of the colonized planets. Now we gotta leave 'em behind." he added with a chuckle.

"It's strange. I'm even going to miss that part of it. The shitty food, iron bars and hard labor." Adam said.

"Gonna be different up there. Months, maybe even years before we find something in need of colonization." Dalton hinted.

"Take plenty of booze." Adam replied as both men began to laugh aloud.

"Already covered," Dalton replied. "Didn't mean that earlier today. About knocking someone up," the smuggler added, both of the men watching Adam's son at peace in Cambria's arms. A large pane of shatterproof glass separating them as the blue-haired beauty stood outside. "I honestly didn't know."

"I know that," Adam replied with respect, patting his longtime friend on the arm. "Really hurt me to lose her," he added. "We've lost so many."

"Gonna lose more before this shit is over too." Dalton proclaimed.

"I'm afraid of that." Adam admitted.

"Sarah?" Dalton asked, though he did so in a casual manner to avoid prying.

"Seeing her again brought up a swirl of emotions. Things I thought were dead inside of me," Adam admitted, turning to his friend. "I think I still love her."

"Shit son, love is for idiots." Dalton boasted.

"And Cambria?"

"Well that's a little different. I mean, the girl is fine looking and has a good heart, but I don't know if we've made it to love just yet."

"Better work quickly my friend," Adam replied with a smile. "Because she is damn fine looking and appears to be real good with my son. I won't back-off forever."

"Like hell!" Dalton replied, both men laughing.

"In all seriousness though Dalton, if you feel for the girl at all, you should tell her. Don't wait on it too long. I think of all the time I wasted with Sarah. I let my stubbornness stand between my true feelings and what could have been." Adam remarked with seriousness.

"And the bitch held us at gunpoint. Don't forget that small detail." Dalton lashed out.

"You get what I'm saying?" Adam asked, staying the course of serious.

"Unfortunately, yes. It's killing my whiskey buzz actually." the smuggler replied.

As they both laughed aloud, Adam turned to his friend for a heartfelt nod.

"Dalton, we need to talk." Adam said.

"I thought that's what we were doing. You know, I open my mouth and words begin to come out?" Dalton replied.

"I don't think we're safe here." Adam suggested.

"What the fuck are you talking about? We're aboard a military ship." Dalton replied.

"I can't get into details, at least not yet," Adam replied. "I just need you to trust me."

"I do trust you Adam, you know that."

"I just have a really bad hunch that this arrangement between races is going to take a nosedive south very soon," Adam said, continuing to speak in a whisper. "Just be ready to move if that happens."

"Who are you talking to?" Dalton asked, boasting a bit. "I'm always ready to move."

Or drink. Or, well, you know. Dalton thought.

Adam answered his longtime friend with a firm pat on the shoulder.

"Well, gonna go collect my son from the hottest girl you've ever had a chance with."

"Shit son, I've been with the crème de la crème when it comes to women," Dalton boasted. "She's in my top five though."

"She's in MY top five," Adam replied, though he

continued a walk away from his friend. "Which definitely makes her your number one."

Yea, yea. You cheeky bastard. Dalton thought. Feeling at peace as he was surrounded by his friends once more. Though his mind began to wonder about the alliance of races.

-

As the day slowly turned to night, a shadow of moonlight crisping onto the shiny hulls of so many ships, a sense of urgency set in.

Urgency for a fleet which worked night and day in an attempt to stock their ships for a one-way flight into the tapestry of stars, and urgency for Dalton James. The word love having played heavily onto his mind since hearing it earlier.

"Tell her," he said, pouring a shot of rock whiskey and downing it with haste. "Tell her not." he added, pouring yet another.

As he sat alone, off from the bustling crowd of so many who remained hard at work, Dalton wrestled with the obvious. There was only enough for one more shot.

He would have to tell Cambria he loved her. The smuggler had feared nothing as much as he feared admitting that to her. Terrified of rejection.

Fuck it. He thought, though his mind remained locked onto every word of his coming confession. That he had truly fallen for the woman who was nothing like him. Yet made him complete.

So as the smuggler draped in his security blanket of brown leather marched on, as if he were marching into the teeth of an execution, he thought of those around him.

Women and children, who greatly resembled those he'd been forced to leave behind in the Drifts. He saw the faces of desperation and worry. Faces of survivors who seemed bewildered as they worried about their immediate futures.

Such a sight firmed Dalton up a bit. Realizing the admission of love wasn't the worst fate. Still he stopped in his tracks for a moment. Not for the thought of his admission of love that would soon follow; but for those around him. A group of survivors who had been collected from all parts of the Skyla System. A group that had lost so much, yet continued with hope. He thought of the sacrifice Commander Ortega had made for those very people, and it made him both sad, and proud as hell to be a colonial.

"Cambria Sims, I have something I..." Dalton announced proudly as he burst through the small door of their two-room shelter.

Stopping his statement however, Dalton saw a girl broken, her crying one of true sadness.

"What's wrong?" he asked, immediately grabbing her into his cowboy-strong arms and consoling her.

With her crying so heavy, no response would follow, just the gut-wrenching somber of a deep cry. Though he would soon discover the reason behind her sadness as he picked up an official colonial memo which lay near.

The colonial government regrets to inform you that you have been selected to remain behind. Our exodus launch is scheduled in forty-eight hours at the stroke of midnight. You have been assigned to the ground party, led by Commander Ortega. You will report tomorrow at sunrise to your assigned unit, led by Lieutenant James Locke of the colonial army.

Please know that your denial of flight does not ensure your fate. We are planning a very strategic defense against coming forces and remain confident that we will be victorious.

Thank you.

Benton Sanders.

As Dalton finished reading the death sentence of Cambria Sims, he crunched the official papers into a ball, as if it were designed for ass-wiping, his other arm still firmly wrapped around the woman of his dreams.

"Where are you going?" Cambria asked as Dalton pulled away, heading back to the door that had brought him to her.

"To fix this," he replied, angered by the development. "First though," he added, walking back to her arms. "I love you Cambria Sims."

His statement brought more tears, though it was a mixture of happiness and grief, the woman trembling as she had never trembled before.

"I love you too."

"I will fix this, I promise you." Dalton replied, leaving her grasp as he walked for the door once more.

"I made the flight!" Skulls announced, entering the small shelter as the sniper smiled wide.

"The fuck out of my way." Dalton demanded, shoving the sniper and good friend to the side, readying for a showdown with the horde of pencil-necks that would surely follow.

-

"Have you recalled our warriors?" Sarah asked.

The queen of vampires sat firmly on her throne, which shimmered with both jewels and gothic inscriptions formed into bronze plating.

"We have sent word, but it will take time," one of her soldiers replied. "Depending on their circumstances, I'm sure we can expect the return of Vladris soon enough."

"Very well," Sarah replied, looking onto the group which had gathered. Nearly thirty total. "We must begin to think of the survival of our own race, nothing more."

"Is it true? Do those who seek out protection plan to eliminate us?" one of the elders asked.

"We," Adam Michaels replied. "We don't know. Right now, we're just being cautious."

"You brought this onto us!" a second elder replied.

"I didn't know, I swear," Adam replied, raising his hand to face level in an attempt to reason with those who had gathered. "Even now, the commander lies to his own people. He's lost his way, and I fear that he lies to your people as well."

"Adam had no part in this," the queen warned. "In fact, he was the one who warned me."

"What proof do you have?" one of the elders asked.

"At the moment, none," Adam replied. "Just a gut feeling." he added with regret.

"A gut feeling?" the elder replied in mocking fashion. "You wish us to recall our soldiers and risk annihilation based on a gut feeling?"

"Send every soldier you have to face the coming horde, that's not my concern. Nor will it matter. They are coming, and nothing you have can stop that," Adam replied, this time with a bit of zeal on his words. "My only concern is for the queen. YOUR queen." he added.

"He believes they requested our champion lead the defense in order to separate us. Divide our ranks." Sarah added.

"If Commander Ortega has no intention of leaving as scheduled; no intention of remaining behind as promised, why would he send a defense in the first place? Would he not just raise the ships as soon as the horde got close?" Adam asked.

The room seemed to be in deep thought, each of them pondering the smuggler's questions.

"I've been a military man long enough to know that there is only one reason behind his decision," Adam said, pausing to look to Sarah. "He means to thin you out. Either to exterminate your race, or leave you behind to die."

"Was it not you that brought this to our doorstep?" one of the elders asked.

"I have no part in this. In fact, if I find out he is indeed trying to kill your queen," Adam said, pausing for just a moment. "I'll gun him down myself."

"He is with us!" Sarah yelled, commanding her elders back in line. "He fights with us and is committed to dying with us, if need be. We must begin a plan to counter such colonial treachery."

"Your plans my queen?" one of the higher ranking warriors asked.

"They believe they hold the advantage through surprise. Their downfall will be their arrogance and stupidity," Sarah replied, grinning a bit. "We will act as though we are none the wiser. All while slowly putting our own plan into place. When this fleet launches, we will be in control of it."

-

"A bit late to be out and around isn't it soldier?" a man asked, decked out in a colonial uniform as he sat behind the desk of an otherwise empty room.

"Ain't no solider. I'm here to see Commander Ortega." Dalton replied, already eying a single door which most-likely led to the commander.

"Who isn't? Had nearly a hundred of requests today. You'll have to wait your turn. Come back tomorrow and try your luck." the colonial soldier replied.

"I'm sorry, what was that?" Dalton asked politely, approaching the seated man.

"I said you'll have to..." he began to reply, stopping short as he was pulled from his seat by the front of his shirt; clean-jerked directly into a grasp which held him inches from the floor.

"Now you listen to me, you little puny sumbitch,"

Dalton scolded. "I was fighting wars and dodging bullets when you were still shitting baby green," he added. "And I've killed men twice your size over nothing more than sales rack whiskey. So believe me when I say it. You're gonna be on that com to inform Ortega that I'm here."

"They'll throw you in the brig for this!" the smaller man yelled, his only defense.

"Nowhere I haven't been before. Countless times. Now be smart about it." Dalton replied, turning his eyes back to a heavy revolver which hung by his side.

"Sir," the colonial soldier timidly said, "Hate to disturb you at such an hour," the man added, pressing a button on the com in front of him. "Someone here to see you. A Dalton?" he said, feeling a firming grip on the front of his shirt. "He's pretty persistent."

"Of course, send him in." Ortega replied through the digital com system.

"Yes sir, at once." the man said, finally removing his finger from the com.

"See there buddy, nobody even had to die." Dalton proclaimed, lowering the man to the ground and slapping his shoulder in good sport.

Immediately, the smaller man pulled away with anger.

"Of course, I do have to come back through here when I leave." Dalton reminded, taunting the man who cast a look of intimidation back.

"Dalton James," Commander Ortega said, welcoming the smuggler into his personal quarters. "I had hoped to see you again soon. Though I didn't think it would be after hours."

"Something came up." Dalton replied.

"Of course, of course," the commander said, motioning to his desk. "Have a seat."

"Been thinking a lot about what you said before. Most importantly, about the sacrifice you've made for your love of these people." Dalton said.

"You've decided to take up my offer on joining the fleet?" Ortega asked.

"No sir, as a matter of fact I'm going to have to respectfully decline," Dalton said, his reply shocking the man in charge. "Though I am going to ask for a favor."

"I see," Ortega replied with a hint of disappointment. "Go on." he added.

"You chose to stay behind and give hope to these people out of love. What I feel is the mark of a true leader; a true man. I also love someone. A girl that I couldn't imagine life without living. I refuse to leave into the stars and leave her behind, knowing it would be a death sentence."

"Perhaps not." Commander Ortega injected.

"Perhaps, but the odds of surviving are the slimmest imaginable," Dalton quickly replied, setting the tone of the meeting. "I wish to give her my spot on the exodus fleet, and I would like to remain behind with you, answering to your command."

"Dalton, I understand your passion. Truly I do. But you could serve these people best by remaining with them in the future. Your experience would be a great asset..."

"No," Dalton stated firmly. "My experience means nothing if I fight with an empty heart. I'm as good as dead if I know in my heart that the woman I love is doomed."

"Alright," Ortega replied. "I'll see that it's done."

"I also have one final request." Dalton stated.

"Yes?"

"The woman is very, very important to me. I simply ask that she be allowed onto the ship of my own choosing, surrounded by our friends." Dalton said.

"Very well. You have my word." Ortega replied.

"Sir, thank you,' Dalton replied with gratitude. "I feel at peace with this, and trust me, I'll give you everything I have when it comes time for slinging shells."

"I know you will son." Ortega replied, acknowledging the truth of his statement, though his own was riddled with lies.

"Well," Dalton said, standing to his feet and saluting his new superior. "I'll let you get back to it. Sorry for bothering you at such an hour."

"Dalton, I want you to know something," Ortega said, causing the sworn smuggler to pause his walk. "If our cause had more soldiers like you, we may just be winning this damn war."

"Not a big deal," Dalton replied calmly. "All of these years I've ran from death. But I've ran my course. Now I plan to run to it, guns a blazing."

"You're a model soldier Dalton James."

"Apparently you haven't read my file jacket hard enough." the smuggler replied with a grin as Ortega handed him a signed paper. One that would allow Cambria's future to exist on the exodus flight.

-

"I'm sorry for the breakdown earlier," Cambria admitted, approaching the man of her dreams as he entered their shelter once more.

"No worries," Dalton replied. "Told you I would fix it." he said, handing her the signed paper.

"What? How?" Cambria asked with a mountain of emotions running through her.

"I just did. Got a long history with the man in charge." he boasted, cut short by a clinging hug from the woman he loved to the bones inside of his body.

"This means we'll be together when the flight launches?" Cambria asked probingly.

"Of course," the smuggler replied, thinking himself a bastard for lying to a woman he loved. "Just focus on packing enough for the two of us."

As they held one another for several moments, Cambria's arms squeezing the man of her dreams tight, he felt sadness. Not for his coming death, but for the pain which he knew Cambria would eventually feel.

He also knew that a lie was necessary to get her aboard a ship. If she knew of his deal with Ortega, she'd never agree to it. He only hoped she would recover in time and live a long, happy life in the stars above.

"Skulls," Dalton said, his body still engulfed by the grasp of a love-struck woman. "Sorry about earlier, I wasn't thinking straight." he added.

"Think nothing of it brother," the sniper replied. "I understand what you must have been going through.

No, you don't. You truly don't.

-

When the first explosion rocked the surface of Ronica, everyone with a heartbeat knew what was to follow. An invasion. Panic set in throughout the large encampment as daybreak had only begun.

Sitting up as though he'd been awake for hours, Dalton immediately grabbed his revolver and readied for a fight.

"It's alright," Cambria said. "Far off, but it means we're on very limited time now."

Bolting to the door of their shelter, Dalton stood with revolver in hand and shirtless, watching the sprint of many colonial soldiers and civilians alike. Each of them expediting the process of their plans for the given day.

"I need to go find Adam. Have to talk to him before they get closer. You finish packing all of the essentials," Dalton said, throwing a green shirt on with haste and looking back to his lover. "Remember, it's a one-way flight."

"Be careful, please." Cambria replied, kissing Dalton passionately before turning to finish packing the needed supplies.

"Hey," Dalton insisted, staring at their sniper. "Keep her close and safe until I get back."

"You got it brother." Skulls replied.

As the smuggler began his own sprint from their

shelter, the ground seemed to tremble beneath him, nearly a dozen more explosions landing within a few miles of their basecamp.

The Priests had arrived.

Every time they launched an invasion, it began with explosions from warheads that rained down from the stars. Immediately followed by ships filled tight with soldiers of the undead. Infected. Zombies. Priests. Or, as Dalton usually called them, half-dead fuckers.

Either way, Dalton knew he was on borrowed time as he continued a sprint to the Benzan ship where Adam Michaels had been staying.

Just before arriving, his longtime friend exited the large ship, just as so many other Benzans had done only moments before.

"Adam, we need to talk!" Dalton yelled, doing what he could to become louder than the increasing explosions.

"What is it?" Adam replied, his voice also forced into a very loud tone.

"Cambria. I volunteered to give up my spot for her." Dalton said, though he did so with a heavy heart.

"What?" Adam asked, stunned by the admission. "You did what?"

"I'm staying behind so she can live through this. Ortega signed off on it. She's to be put on your ship, and I need your word that you will watch over her?" Dalton asked with near-desperation. "Please."

"Dalton, there has to be some other way?" Adam questioned.

At the moment he did so, a large explosion rocked through the settlement, destroying a large ship that had been assigned to Glimmerian survivors. One of two. Though it wasn't filled with bodies at the moment, he understood that many people who had been promised a ride into the stars would now be without one.

"There is no other way Adam, trust me. I don't want to die, I just don't want her to die a little more."

Adam was pressed into a tough spot, having been sworn to silence by the Hunters, though failure to speak may have cost his best friend his life.

"Dalton, listen," Adam said, smaller explosions tearing up the countryside around their basecamp. "The Hunters and colonials are about to come to a head. There's going to be war, and you need to be on this side of the fence."

"What?" Dalton asked.

"Commander Ortega is lying about a lot of things. He has no intention of staying behind, and he's lying to his people. I also suspect he plans to strike at the Hunters when the time is right." Adam replied.

"What the hell are you talking about? I just talked to Ortega hours ago, he assured me."

"Dalton, he is lying to you." Adam replied.

"Is he? Or have you lost your way?" Dalton questioned.

"What?" Adam asked, shock in his voice.

"You and Sarah are in love, you always have been, and I get it. I truly do. But she's not one of us anymore." Dalton stated.

"A lot has changed, sure..." Adam began to reply.

"A lot has changed, starting with the fact that she's a fucking vampire."

"Dalton, you said you trusted me. I need you to trust me." Adam replied.

"I need you to trust me when I say there's no way I'm putting my life into the hands of a race that's been trying to end it for years now!" Dalton yelled in response.

"The colonials will leave you behind the first chance they get Dalton."

"The Hunters won't? You'll be lucky to survive a month with those blood-sucking stiffs!" Dalton replied.

"Well," Adam replied, nodding his head. "The answer to your question is yes. Sasha has a place on my ship, as do you. So long as you know it's going to be a Hunter ship."

"Pass." Dalton replied with spite.

"Well, that's your choice to make. Either way old friend,

I hope you make it off this rock in one piece." Adam replied, turning to walk away from a man he once considered a brother.

-

"Hold your positions!" Vladris yelled. "The cowards fight with explosives for now, but soon they will test us on the battlefield. A test in which we will pass with the edge of blades!"

The champion vampire sat tall, a solid black steed beneath him as nearly two-hundred soldiers looked on. Many of them on horseback as well, though most would fight the good fight. On foot with a single weapon.

"Those of you who I consider brothers know of our ability on the battlefield," Vladris yelled, the thunder of explosions crackling around him as he looked onto the crowd of warriors. Many vampiric, though the sleek armor of Benzan, solid blue of colonials and green tint of Husk were in no short supply. "The rest of you will learn of it with your own eyes on this day, after which we will become immortal brothers, be it through life or death."

Though they awaited the worst enemy the system had ever known, preparing to face odds that were landslide in the favor of their invaders, the warriors cheered loudly. Readying themselves to follow the most-notorious warrior in recorded history into battle.

Though Troy readied for a different battle altogether.

The colonials and Husk had indeed been conspiring from day one. A plan to rid their departing fleet of anyone deemed a threat to future survival. Which included the Hunters.

Troy could still remember the day Roman was cut down by Vladris' blade. The man, who for so long had been like a father-figure to him, butchered before his very eyes.

At the time, Troy was too young of a man to strike back. Though he had begun the path of a warrior, he was weak.

That was long ago.

After escaping into the welcoming embrace of the Husk, Troy had learned the art of combat. He had perfected the art, in fact, as though he was meant to swing a sword.

His own sword not nearly as massive as those of his Husk family, but he had countered the absence of Husk-might with cunning. Troy had learned that timing was just as important as ability when it came to battle. And as the timing became right; Troy would have his revenge.

-

Adam Michaels glanced throughout the colonial star, standing on a large catwalk above the landing bay as he watched machines load several more Swordfish fighters inside.

He knew in the pit of his heart that it could be his last look inside of a colonial star, or any colonial ship for that matter.

The soldier turned smuggler began to think of so many many battles before. Many of which, he wore the colonial patch on his chest.

Adam seemed a million miles away, grabbing hold of several large tubes that would be responsible for pushing steam throughout the ship once it began flight. The primary heating system.

The former soldier tugged a bit, as if he were testing the integrity of such a mighty ship. Though he broke away to stare to those around him, Adam began looking to their background, focusing his attention to the ship's setting behind them.

He understood it would be the people's home for the foreseeable future, if not for the remainder of their lives. Their entire lives spent between the beautiful landscapes of planets, each with their own rich history and scenery. Traded now, for an eternity of looking to steel draping around them.

What choice did they have? Adam understood that no victory could be had in a war that had become a fight for their own survival. Their only chance of continuing the walk of humanity would be to do so by launching into uncharted space. Planets that had never before been explored.

He also knew in his heart that no peace would be had until either Commander Ortega and those who sided with him were taken from power, or the Hunters were wiped clean from their massive exodus fleet.

Adam Michaels understood that before their voyage was over, be it by natural death or the discovery of inhabitable soil, these people would come to know every nook, every cranny, of this massive armada of the stars. Perhaps even their children.

A fleet that was near fifty ships, though many of the larger ships included an array of small ones. Each in search of a new home, though politics would play as heavily as before. Every ship with its own agenda.

Each had its own responsibility in the grand scheme of things. The Florentine was responsible for keeping their food in storage, which could prove to be the most important asset to all, depending on how long their journey played out.

The fleet's mechanics were scattered throughout, though their resources were aboard the Iron Maiden. For lack of better terms, an airborne tugboat full of spare parts, along with every tool imaginable.

Four military ships were assigned, including the one Adam currently stood aboard. All colonial star vessels. The Triumph, God of War, Silver Hammer and Stalwart; though the God of War was designated as a troop ship and housed no smaller aircraft outside of dropships. The remaining three were to be used in protection of the fleet while in flight, relying on the skills of their pilots and housing many ship-to-ship fighters. Glimmerian designed Swordfish, though their design had been altered a bit to better fit deep space.

They were massive in comparison to the remaining ships of the fleet, even to their former models of colonial star ships. While the original ships stretched for thousands of yards and contained plenty of the Goliath model soldiers within its hull, the newly-designed colonial stars were much larger.

They were in a sense, small cities with thick armor around them and thrusters to their back. Capable of quartering tens of thousands, though supplies to furnish them would be limited.

The current model of colonial star ships were also stocked with hundreds of Goliath model soldiers, which was fancy talk for ass-kicking robots. The Goliath model aboard, however, were the recently upgraded V2 versions, which lent them a tougher exoskeleton of steel, along with the standard chain guns and anti-aircraft missiles.

The colonials had no idea what may lay waiting for them once the fleet made deep space. Be it fruitful planets that were ripe for the picking, or militarized civilizations that would swing at them with might; the colonials had to be prepared for anything.

Which they were.

After catching sight of a four-man colonial marine team, Adam began to think of their job among the fleet. Protecting those in need, while keeping order and carrying out the instructions of the politicians who would lead them. A tall order considering the Magellan.

It was their political ship, not to mention the one ship that was sure to be the highest priority. Every important political figure surviving, every recognized planet, was to be housed aboard the Magellan. That included the Husk, among others; which was sure to include trouble.

The decisions that would affect everyone in the fleet would have to be made aboard the Magellan – a ship that mixed shatterproof glass and steel as if it were a work of art. Several protruding spheres of glass giving it the look of importance.

The Magellan also had the distinct honor of being the only ship in the fleet, outside of military cruisers, to remain under constant escort. Two Glimmerian-designed swordfish fighters, though more could be scrambled within minutes if needed be.

The Glimmerians had originally designed the swordfish fighter as a ship-to-ship fighter, which had the ability to hug low to the ground and fly at incredible speeds. In working with the colonial design teams, a newer model was eventually released, making it deep space worthy while retaining all of its original signatures of perfection.

All of the military marvel housed within the mighty ships of the fleet. It was impressive. Still, Adam found his mind wrapped around a single thought.

So many races under the same roof. Races that had been slaughtering one another for as long as time could remember, now expected to shake hands and play nice.

Adam wondered how long such a mighty race would bow to the commands of a human leader. He knew it would only be a matter of time before the Orc-like race began its own plans to assume control of the fleet, if it had not already done so.

Of course, the Hunters were now in the mix as well. Vampires in every sense of the word, though they were unhindered by daylight, garlic or religious symbols. That's just a silly assumption to begin with. They are, however, hindered by the burst of a gun and the blade of a sword, when in capable hands. That much had been proven throughout the years. A very important fact that shouldn't soon be forgotten.

Adam wondered if the vampires could be trusted.

The fleet would make its important decisions aboard the Magellan, shaping humanity's future in the process. That said, their leaders would eventually disagree, and that could be disastrous considering the bloody past between their races.

Adam Michaels realized as he stood firm, watching the bustle of soldiers around him prepping their ship, the most vital part of their fleet. Those around him. Adam promised himself at that very moment that he would never forget that fact. Watching such a wounded people push forward, finding courage in the face of the inevitable loss of their homes. It made Adam feel honored to be a part of such a special group, though his allegiance to the vampires meant his time among the colonials was limited at best.

"It's amazing to see people continue on. To survive during such times." Sarah remarked, approaching Adam slowly.

"I agree," Adam replied, turning to the woman he once loved. "I was just thinking the same thing. Not to mention how daunting of a task it is going to be when it comes to keeping the peace between such storied races. What are you doing here? You should be in the keep under guard."

"I now know it is our race that will be persecuted at some point. If the others among us have any common ground, it is the hate for my people." Sarah replied.

"Yea, I know," Adam replied, turning to the bustle of his ship for a moment and noticing several among his crew staring to a Sarah a bit roughly. "It isn't going to make my job any easier. You know I'm with you until the end Sarah, as long as my son is safe."

"He shall be." Sarah replied, also picking up on the animosity of the crew's glances.

Moments later, several gunshots rang throughout the ship, causing an immediate reaction of panic from everyone. Including Adam.

"Remain calm Adam. Those are our shots." Sarah replied.

Before questioning her, Adam saw dozens of highly-armed Hunters entering the colonial star.

"What is this?" he asked.

"These people have taken from our race for so long. You didn't expect us to just shake hands and play nice, did you?"

"Actually..." he began to respond as the gunfire intensified.

"Adam," the queen said, pausing to stare onto him. "You have also taken from us," she added with a glare. "From me."

"Sarah, that's not fair. You know I feel guilt for this." Adam replied.

"As well you should," the queen replied with a snap. "But it does nothing to ease my pain."

"Sarah, I had no idea they would do this to you." he replied with a bit of zest on his own part.

"You left me standing alone Adam, what difference did it make to you where I ended up!" Sarah shouted.

"It makes a lot of difference. We've all made mistakes here." Adam admitted.

"Your biggest mistake was trusting our people with your safety," she replied. "The safety of your son."

"Sarah, you better not harm..." Adam began to reply with desperation, though his words cut short by the end of a rifle. Its stock held by one of several Hunter Elites who arrived to protect their queen.

"He's safe and will remain that way Adam, as long as you cooperate."

"Cooperate? With what?" the smuggler demanded to know.

"My men will escort you to our ship, at which time I will explain your punishment in further detail."

My punishment? You bitch! He thought, doing everything in his power not to strike at the woman – thinking for the safety of his son.

"I don't understand?" Adam admitted.

"Adam, when you first showed up here my heart exploded," Sarah replied. "I wanted to relive our love together," she added. "But as I continued to think about it, I remembered the moment you left me for dead."

"I didn't know, Sarah."

"SILENCE! I've had enough of your excuses! I see the love you still have for Sasha on your face. I know that you left me behind because you loved her, and your love cost me everything."

Adam didn't reply. Simply offering a look of disappointment and regret.

"Soon enough you will know my pain." the queen sternly promised, turning to walk away under heavy escort. Adam following slowly behind as well, surrounded by armed soldiers among the vampire race.

-

"The explosions seem to be getting closer," Skulls claimed. "A good sign we are losing the fight."

"And you're surprised?" Dalton asked, pausing to drink a healthy swig from an even healthier bottle of whiskey. "Been getting our asses kicked up one side and down another for the better part of a year now."

"I just meant we should consider readying ourselves quicker than we had planned." Skulls admitted.

"I was born ready son," Dalton confessed. "I once had a watch with no hands."

"Huh?" Skulls asked, confused by the smuggler's statement.

"In other words, it's always go time."

"I don't get it?" Skulls confessed.

"Ah fuck, this is killing my buzz," Dalton replied as his lover entered the shelter. "A watch, no hands...always go time. I'm always ready, no matter what time it is."

"That's hilarious." Cambria admitted, laughing aloud as Dalton explained himself as though he were on trial.

"Thank you. I worked hard on that." the smuggler replied with a grin.

"I still don't get it?" Skulls replied.

"Fuck sakes man, you need to get out more often."
Dalton scolded, the taint of whiskey on his breath.

"Now that, friend, I get." Skulls replied, openly
acknowledging the truth of Dalton's statement.

It was at that moment, words rolling from his tongue,
that a large explosion took place merely feet from their
shelter; slamming into the thick crust of ground near the
center of the fleet staging ground.

"Holy shit!" Dalton yelled, rushing to the window as
alarms sounded only dozens of feet from their shelter's
door.

"Told you they were getting closer," Skulls said, turning
to make sure both of his friends were unharmed. "Now
what's that watch saying?"

"Saying we need to get the hell out of here." Dalton
replied, forcing their door open as the scramble of
desperation had already led hundreds of people outdoors.

It was the sound of small arms fire, however, that drew
Dalton's attention.

"That's gunfire within the camp!"

"You mean the horde has made it in?" Cambria asked
with panic.

"Not unless the dead sumbitches dyed their hair white
and took a liking to leather trench coats." he replied.

"I don't understand?" Skulls replied.

"Ah shit man." Dalton nodded, preparing himself to
explain in detail.

"He means the Hunters are firing on colonials,"
Cambria interjected, as if to bust up the smuggler's
punchline. "Question is, which side are we on?"

"The side that ain't notorious for feasting on human
flesh," Dalton replied. "Not to mention being a thorn in
my fucking side." he added, pushing his brown coat back a
bit as his hand slowly pulled the heavy revolver to the
ready.

"I cannot believe this shit," Skulls complained. "I get a
winning lottery ticket and now I have to try and find a

ship that's safe. People are falling dead all over a camp that's now overrun with vampires – and zombies are on the way. I do not feel like a fucking winner!"

"Winners don't whine," Dalton said with a grin, glancing back to the sniper. "They win."

"How are we supposed to do that?" Cambria asked, all three of them looking from the shelter door which remained cracked.

"Just stay close," Dalton responded, turning to smile at his lover. "In case I get the urge for some fine wine."

"I don't get it?" Skulls admitted.

-

"I can still remember seeing you burn away – your ship screaming into the ocean of stars. I felt helpless. I've lived with the loss every single night, knowing you'd never know my pain," the queen said. "Now you will."

"Sarah, I don't know what you intend to do here, but Avery has nothing to do with this. You need to let him go and deal with me how you see fit."

"I am!" the queen shouted.

The group had boarded a large hunter carrier, one of several that was being stocked for the fleet's voyage. At least that's what had been thought, though Adam knew immediately upon entering that it was being stocked for another reason altogether.

War.

"You've no intention of joining the fleet." Adam stated.

"We'll join them in the sky, if that's what you mean," she replied as their group walked deeper into the heart of the large battleship. "Of course when we arrive my people will rip the colonial ships to shreds."

"Sarah, these people have done nothing to you!" Adam argued.

"Nothing? These people have done nothing to me? For centuries the colonials have hunted my people down and systematically slaughtered them!"

"The soldiers, maybe, but the people aboard those ships include a lot of innocent faces. Women and children that have no part in that!" Adam replied.

""Victims of war," she replied without emotion. "Just as my father was."

"Your father was a good man," Adam stated. "He would not have any part in this," he added. "You're lost to him. To the world that matters. Do what you will to me, I'm done playing games. The Sarah I fell in love with is obviously gone and the, thing, that stands in front of me – I have no use for."

His words stung her to the bone. Sarah had promised to forget the pain he'd caused her once upon a time, and now he had gashed the wound back open completely.

"You will remain in this room until I return. If you try to escape, my soldiers will gun you down. If I decide to take your words to heart, my soldiers will gun you down," she replied. "If you value the sight of your son EVER again – you should pray I continue to feel for you long enough."

Adam gave no words; no plea. He simply walked into a small room by gunpoint – its door slamming shut and bolting from the outside.

The walls seamless, the sheen of aluminum glaring around him with only a single chair inside. No windows. Nothing. Though it was evident that the ship's thrusters had begun to fire up to a burn.

-

"Dalton, we must keep moving." Cambria pleaded, helping the distraught smuggler from the colonial star.

"I cannot keep going. These people need help," Dalton responded, his eyes having dried but his heart still gaping wide. "I can't live with leaving more innocent people behind to die."

"I understand," Cambria agreed. "But one of those innocent people is Adam's son. We need to go get Avery and get him to safety."

"I know that," Dalton admitted. "I just don't know if I can." he added.

"Dalton James, listen to me," Cambria shouted, grabbing the man by his coat as gunfire rang out throughout their encampment. "I need you!"

His soldiering began to kick in a bit, knowing deep down that if he could push such great loss aside, at least for the moment, it could save the lives of many. Including Sasha and Avery.

"Alright," he finally responded. "You've got Skulls' ticket. Now we have to get Adam's son and get to that ship before it leaves us on this damn rock. The rest we can figure out from the sky."

"And you?" she asked.

"I've been a soldier most of my natural life. I know a lot of these guys, and they respect what I've done for the old colonial blue. I'll be fine."

"Alright, well, we need to get this done quickly. The horde will be at our front door in only minutes, and that's if our own don't kill us first." Cambria said.

It was a scene of total chaos. Soldiers clad in blue gunning down the vampire nation, and vice versa. Brother against brother, race against race, as everyone seemed to be staking their claim for a spot in the exodus fleet.

-

"Samuel. Dirsin. Twylan. All great great warriors who have fallen by your sword." Troy said,

"What is this you speak of human?" Vladris asked with a demanding voice, though his answer came swiftly.

The thrust of sword, its tip biting into the lower half of

Vladris' torso and sending the mighty champion to a knee.

"All of them great friends of mine," Troy said with a grin, their small group of surviving soldiers feeling as though the end was approaching by way of chaos in their leadership "But none of them respected by me as was Roman Raines."

The remaining Hunters immediately went for their blades, though the firepower of colonial rifles soon tipped the scales. The humans and Orc-like warriors executing a plan of deception, and a well-executed plan at that.

"They say you fight as though you are a wounded lion. So wounded lion, what do you think of your chances now?" Troy mocked.

Reaching down with a grimace of pain across his face, lips curling from hurt around jagged teeth, Vladris slowly wrapped a hand around the gushing wound as it drained him of blood.

"I would say you will fall just as your pathetic army did but moments ago." Vladris replied, squeezing pale flesh together in an attempt to slow the bleeding. Extreme duration of pain his biggest hurdle.

"Then you would be wrong," Troy said with a chuckle. "Do you not see only a handful of vampires, each of them surrounded by Husk steel and colonial weaponry?"

"I see only the coward spines of sheep. Such is the way of a lion." Vladris replied, looking onto the Husk-raised man with eyes fueled of revenge.

"Of course Vladris," Troy said, snatching an ax from the air, tossed to him by a Husk ally and awaiting the wounded champion to pull his own sword. "I am up for the task of ending your legend. I will be the one who strikes you down."

"Perhaps," Vladris replied, his face speaking of pain as he reached overhead to unsheathe his large sword, pulling flesh away from such a deep wound all the while. "Or perhaps you will fall just like the list of cowards you so easily name. All who thought they too were up to the task."

The Hunters had never seen their champion injured as badly, blood gushing from wound as though he were a stuck pig. Yet he circled a waiting human as though he were stalking.

"Your overconfidence will be your demise champion." Troy taunted, beginning a circle as well, readying himself for combat against the most legendary of foes.

"My confidence is earned through battle, while yours is earned through the shouting of retreat." Vladris stated, his words striking a nerve with the young man.

With a commanding leap, Troy slammed down to the ground, his ax biting into the crust of planet only inches from Vladris. Though a bit slower than normal, the champion Hunter arced a glancing shot of sword toward the skilled warrior, who easily parried it away with the thick armor plating of his forearm.

"Even wounded I expected better." Troy said, chuckling a bit as he recovered his ax and readied it.

"Yet you thrust steel into me from behind. Walking the path of a coward." Vladris replied, beginning to feel the effects of a sword shot which would spell his demise.

Wasting no additional time, Troy began hammering away by way of his ax, releasing swipe after swipe with the weapon which aimed for the Hunter champion with unrelenting power. At least by human standards.

Vladris felt himself weakening, as he continued to parry the ax with defensive blade strikes, finally dropping to a knee once more. His only defense becoming one of desperation as the mighty champion held his blade above him in an attempt to absorb the striking ax.

He had seen it before. Countless times. When he had an opponent beaten, their last defense before falling was the same.

Vladris had no intentions of dying like a wailing pup, opting instead to throw his sword to the ground and let his body absorb the next swing of ax. Something that was worthy of his legend on the battlefield.

For even the mightiest fall.

"A final word before I end you?" Troy asked with a smile pasted to his face.

"Yes," Vladris nodded with defeat. "Almost."

Almost? Troy thought.

Within the instant, Vladris had pulled a large dagger from his belt, carving into the boy's chest as the entire length of the foot-sized blade dug in. Troy immediately dropping his ax.

"You almost ended the reign of Vladris," the vampire said, slowly rising to his feet. "But not quite. That feat will one day be reserved for a true hero."

"Are you sure you can make the shot?" one of the colonials asked. Their ride bumpy to say the least.

Dalton James didn't offer a verbal reply. Just a single shot from his revolver which hummed through the thick-air of several hundred feet before striking directly to the forehead of Vladris, shattering the contents inside.

That's for Roman you son of a bitch.

"That was one hell of a shot!" one of the soldiers announced, several more agreeing.

"I have my days." Dalton boasted proudly, though his revolver remained in-hand.

He knew the very moment he fired his shot, which would become legendary by many eye-witness accounts; the love of his life was boarding a colonial star with Adam's babe in-hand, or so he thought.

Dalton also knew that his shot, the single bullet which had turned the tide of civil war, had cemented his seat on the exodus fleet.

He had Adam Michaels to thank. So many times before, Adam had forced him into practicing with a heavy revolver. Dalton could remember fighting it; even bitching about it more times than not. Still, he remembered Adam lecturing him on a man's sidearm being the most powerful piece of weaponry.

Elegance among smugglers.

All of these years he'd bitched. Growled about his shotguns and coveted the grenades. Yet his best friend, a man who had taught the smuggler so many things over the years, had preached the art of the revolver as if it were a religion.

Dalton knew with certainty that Adam had played a big part in slaying the Hunter. A thought which brought a large smile to the brushy-faced man.

-

"We'll be there shortly, but it's going to be a bumpy ride from here on out." the pilot warned, turning to deliver the warning to Dalton and crew.

Bumpy?

Before he could ask, however, Dalton began to see the horde. So many dead that they literally blacked out the ground below the shuttle with their bodies.

"Holy shit." Dalton admitted, laying witness to tens of thousands of warriors turned from the dead. All of them sprinting toward the colonial encampment.

The shuttle rocked heavily – caused by one of many mortar strikes. The colonials were leaning on the explosive rounds; their attempt to thin out the coming horde as the exodus fleet began to launch.

Just as the ground was blackened by the bodies of infected, the sky began to blacken with the shadows of ships lifting into the heavens.

It had become a non-stop ride of turbulence, with mortar being strung together with desperation. Yet Dalton could gather his bearings well enough to see nearly a dozen colonial ships yet to launch.

"The Legend of Stars is reporting engine malfunction!" the pilot yelled, taking a moment to point to the craft.

It was mid-sized and reserved as the home for survivors

of Alowin. A large planet of peaceful, yet tech dependent citizens.

"At least four-thousand souls aboard that rig!" one of the soldiers yelled in response.

"What of the God of War?" Dalton asked.

"The rest of 'em are reporting in with green lights. They're good to go. Just waiting for their shuttles to reel back in." the pilot replied.

Literally hundreds of shuttles, small choppers and merchant freighters made their way toward the large craft that were grounded and laying in wait.

The Legend of Stars seemed the focal point, however, as dozens of engineers worked on its exterior. Each checking the guts of the ship in an attempt to fix it.

"God of War this is Red Hound Fourteen, requesting landing grid position." the pilot said, speaking into his helmet's mic.

"We have you Red Hound 14, proceed to landing bay Seventy-One."

"Copy that."

-

Upon landing, Dalton's first reaction was to head to the observation deck. He knew his lover was aboard, and that she no doubt cared for Adam's son. His concern was for those innocent lives aboard the Legend of Stars.

It would seem the case for many others as well, Dalton discovered, as nearly a hundred had gathered on the observation deck to watch colonial engineers race against the coming horde.

"Dalton," Cambria said, her eyes filled with the truth of pain. "Dalton, they took Adam's son."

"Who?" he questioned, growling with anger. "What the fuck?" he demanded to know.

"Sarah."

"I don't understand?" he questioned.

"Sarah showed up with a group of armed soldiers. Took Avery right from my arms at gunpoint."

Standing for a moment – fighting the numbness that shivered through his extremities, Dalton searched for the reasoning. Searched for the motive.

Oh hell no.

"Someone get me on the damn horn with the commander – right now!" he yelled.

With several of the survivors turning to stare at him with question, Dalton grabbed a nearby soldier by the front of his blue uniform.

"I said get me on the horn with the commander. Otherwise, I'm gonna start cracking skulls." he growled.

"I can get him," a soldier shouted across the large room filled with people. "What should I tell him?"

"Tell him the vampires fucked us. You tell him to be ready for war by the time we top the clouds."

Sensing the urgency, the soldier began fumbling with his com system – finally reaching one of the soldiers who answered directly to Ortega.

"Launch squadron A." a voice announced over the com system, each person taking note.

Moments later, the onlookers could see dozens of Swordfish fighters launching from their own ship. Each blazing for the coming horde.

Though it looked impressive, Dalton knew it would not be enough. He had seen the horde with his own eyes. There was simply no stopping it.

Even as the Swordfish began to stream down napalm, bringing death to anything it fell onto, there were just too many Priests coming. Having busted their way through the mighty colonial staggered defenses in the process.

"Legend of Stars is operational." the com announced, bringing cheers to everyone on the observation deck. As their ships began to lift into the heavens, however, their excitement turned to horror as several engineering boxes on the Legend of Stars began sparking with fury.

Moments later, it had lost its altitude of just a dozen feet. Falling back to the surface in the process.

The survivors on the observation deck watched in horror as the horde began to overrun the fallen ship. Ripping metal sheeting from its hull while others smashed their way through otherwise-shatterproof windows.

Dalton just stood in place, watching the horror of mass murder as the colonial star finally broke into the clouds and welcomed its survivors to the black of space.

"Do not cry for them," Dalton scolded, several people having broken down from such a horrific sight. "Unless you also grieve for the millions we've lost up till now. Their death was no less tragic."

With his words, the smuggler began descending the catwalk steps which led back to C level, thrown a bit to the side as the massive ship shifted its bearing.

Always with these fucking ships!

-

Final Act

Dalton's gut had been right, just as it had been so many times before. The colonial stars had made the correct move by lifting to the sky – guns blazing.

The vampires awaited them in orbit doing the same.

Dalton clinched his lover tightly as she cried aloud, grieving both the young man gone missing and her fear of demise. The brown coated smuggler did what he could to console her, though he had also began to wonder the outcome.

He was military trained enough to know their ship was being hammered with gunfire. Dalton could hear explosions throughout the lower decks of his ship, which was consistent with approaching the end of the line. At least in a gunfight between sky galleons.

"You see Adam Michaels," Sarah gestured, having led him to the bridge of a vampire-loyal ship under escort. "The mighty fleet is falling. So many innocent lives."

"What do you want Sarah?" Adam demanded.

"For you to make a choice," she grinned, waving her soldiers to the ready. Moments later, a woman of Sarah's race carried Adam's son out to him – sound asleep. "Tens of thousands of lives aboard the dying fleet. Many children just like this, you said so yourself."

"What Sarah, what?" he angrily questioned.

"Either you leave with us as a vampire as you watch the fleet destroyed – or you watch your son leave with us, from the observation deck of a colonial ship which you helped save. Your choice."

"Sarah, I can't." he admitted.

"Either you make your choice, or I WILL have my soldiers execute you – at which time I will destroy the fleet anyway, keeping your son to boot." she replied.

A broken mess, Adam began crying heavily – his lips trembling too hard to reply.

"Your friends are on those ships Adam Michaels. All of them. Are you ready to show your forgiveness to me by joining the nation of vampires and caring for your son? Or are you as committed as you claim to save the innocent? What will it be Adam Michaels, self or selfless?"

Yet the smuggler continued to cry heavily, offering no response to his former lover.

With the incentive of a gun barrel pressing to his forehead, Adam continued to cry, though holding his hands up and slowing enough to eventually speak.

"How do I know you'll keep your word? How do I know you'll look after my son – allow the fleet to go safely?"

"Adam Michaels, I hate you," she replied, edging closer to him. "Even so, I loved you once. Because of that I promise you. You have my word as a former lover. As a queen to my people."

"Alright," he replied, calming his tears just a bit. "I'll go."

"Very well," she said, ordering her guards to remove Avery from his broken father's sight. "Now you will watch as your entire world pulls away in full-burn from the thick of glass windows." she replied without emotion.

Leading Adam onto a small shuttle, the queen turned to those operating her capital ship.

"Hail the colonial fleet and let them know we intend to stand down. Tell them we are sending a colonial package to them by way of shuttle," the queen said. "A broken one." Sarah added, turning to look onto Adam with disgust.

"Sarah Blaine," Adam said, doing his best to block the loss of his son from memory. "I will be back for my son," he added with truth. "When I do. I will end you."

Offering no reply aside from a look of annoyance, Sarah pressed a sequence of buttons which ejected a thick slate of shatterproof glass, jolting between them.

As his shuttle began to depart from the vampire's largest battleship, Adam stared at his former lover, signaling her death as he used hand motions to aim at her as if it were a gun.

"Jump our people to the designated coordinates." the queen demanded.

"Right away." a vampire clad in solid black replied, beginning to enter information into their computer systems.

Adam Michaels had never cried as hard as he did the moment the vampires began to fire their thrusters, leaving him helpless as his eyes watched them take his son away – breaking his heart in the process.

-

Accepting the lone shuttle, though they suspected a trap, the soldiers aboard the badly-damaged colonial star approached the shuttle with caution.

As they opened the door, each of the trained protectors of peace expected the worst. Instead, they found Adam laying in the corner – sobbing without reserve.

"Everybody out of the way," Dalton growled. "I know this man."

"Who is it?" a soldier asked, gun still locked onto the broken man.

"My brother." Dalton replied, kneeling down to scoop his longtime friend from the shuttle.

Fitting, as Adam had did the same for him during the first Glimmerian war many years before.

"Cambria, we need to get him to the rack and let him rest for a bit."

"Absolutely." she replied.

Standing to his feet moments later, Adam felt weak – as if his body was just learning to function as an adult.

"Adam," Cambria said, tearing up a bit." I'm so, so sorry." she added, feeling guilty of the entire event.

Staring at her for a moment, Adam wrapped his arms around her and began crying once more.

"Nothing you could have done. Nothing I could have done." he responded.

"Alright, alright – damn. Break it up. My playground brother." Dalton yelled with sarcasm.

Causing the broken man to grin just slightly, Adam finally turned to face his longtime friend, offering him the same embrace of a thick hug.

"Well this is uncomfortable." Cambria jested.

"Yea, no kidding," Dalton added. "Don't start dry-humping my leg or anything."

Laughing through the pain, Adam finally broke away and smiled. Though everyone knew what was on his mind. Avery. Revenge.

-

Twenty-Three

As the primitive alarm sounded, waking Dalton from a world of dreams, he quietly cursed the Gods for not allowing a longer sleep.

"Already?" Cambria asked, turning to her lover as they both lay in bed.

"Fuck yea." Dalton replied, his words loaded with regret.

"Speaking of." she replied with a smile.

"If I had time," Dalton said, grinning ear to ear. "I'd certainly do the crime."

"Crime? Really?"

"Well, you know," Dalton replied. "One of those upscale crimes. You know...high class."

"Well in that case Dalton James," Cambria replied, her best damsel in distress now in full swing. "I suppose I'll save myself for the next time."

He chuckled a bit, but seemed to be distant from the conversation.

"What is it? Adam?" she asked.

"Well it is now!" he replied with a bark.

"Oh, yea, it's day twenty-three. Big day, huh?" Cambria said.

"Just another day," Dalton replied as he stood from their bed and began to drape himself in colonial blue. "Except I'm without a bottle of scratch."

"I think you can function without it." Cambria said with a large grin.

He simply replied with a tough stare. The one-thousand yard variety.

"At least I guess you can."

"We'll know soon enough me suppose." he replied, though he did so with a bitching tone.

Taking a moment to brush his hands through his whiskers, Dalton stared at himself for what seemed like an eternity. Glaring into the mirror which hung above the steel sink of their quarters.

"You look nice." Cambria remarked.

"That sucks," he replied. "I was going for mean."

"Well you're one mean hunk of cowboy. That work?" she playfully replied. Her body nude under the sheets of the large, overstuffed bed.

"You be sure you have your ass here when I get back. We have some things to," he said, glancing to her lower body. "Work out." he added.

"Oh Dalton James, you simply take my breath away." Cambria replied in distress.

Punching several numbers into a keypad by the door, reinforced steel quickly opened to expose a large hallway, well-lit with the white of halogen.

"Commander." one of the two stationed marines said, both men saluting.

"At ease boys, I ain't officially the commander until this afternoon," Dalton replied. "As of now, I'm still just a guy they suckered into the job," he added. "Take care of my girl."

"Yes sir." the marine replied, both men standing guard once more.

Just another sucker. He thought as everyone seemed to turn to him, his walk throughout the busy ship one of history. *And a sober one at that.*

During the final assault between the Hunters and colonials,

Ortega had been gunned down.

Something that did not fade, however, was his commander's log. Mandatory entries, though the last was anything but. He has spoken of both the grit and compassion of Dalton James; even going far enough to name him the man in charge should he ever perish.

His entry was logged less than twenty-minutes before the Hunters began their final push, and those who survived looked to Ortega as an honorable man. His wishes for succession to go unchallenged.

As with colonial law, when a commander departed by resignation or death, the government would swear in a successor exactly twenty-three days following. Each day representing a major civilization under the colonial banner.

Though Dalton secretly admitted he knew nothing about leading such a proud people, he also believed that many commanders before him knew less than that, and they were able to pull it off. In fact, he was guilty of slugging one and bedding down the daughter of a second, though her looks fell way-short of her political standing.

Blame the whiskey.

Either way, he was about to lead the colonial people. At least from a military perspective. A civilian was to be sworn in as well, the wishes of Commander Ortega, and they would share power while working together.

So it was to be.

Dalton expected a pretty big ceremony – though he knew there would be a shortage of man-drink, but he was not prepared for the coming inauguration.

At least two-thousand people, all seated and awaiting the ceremony. A large podium, with several ranking officers sitting close by, both civilian and military. Everyone awaiting a man who was minutes late for his own swearing in.

Ah shit. He thought, knowing it wasn't possible to slip in unseen to the witness of thousands who sat quietly.

The sound of his boots seemed to echo throughout the landing bay as they clicked to the cement floor. He would have cursed the floor and the people for listening so damn hard, if the military branch of their government hadn't stood up in salute.

It brought a smile to the man's face, continuing his walk proudly. Though he noticed something odd. A harsh look from the politician in which he would share power. Even a whisper by the man to another high-ranking politician.

"Doctor Arness has delivered his speech," a man said, his role of organizing the event pretty obvious. "Everyone awaits yours."

Speech? You've got to be shitting me! Nobody mentioned a speech!

Stepping to the podium, Dalton cleared his throat a bit, looking onto the crowd and trying to imagine them naked. Quickly realizing a majority of them were male, however, he began to think of his lover naked instead.

"The truth is," Dalton said, adjusting the microphone a bit as the crowd remained silent. "I don't have a prepared speech." he admitted.

The crowd began to whisper a bit, in disbelief of his statement.

"Anyone who knows me, knows it wouldn't be my style," he said. "I speak from the heart unless cheap whiskey is involved."

His statement brought laughs and cheers from most of the military branch, while the civilian branch seemed mixed in their reaction.

"Please, I appreciate it, but don't cheer me. I'm just a man. No different than the millions who perished during this war," Dalton said, hushing the crowd in an instant. "I'm being honest when I say I've worked beneath a variety of men in power. Some that I respected, some that I scratched my head in wondering how they even got into power to begin with," he added. "What I've learned is that I want, more than anything else, the respect of those who work for me. I plan to do anything I ask someone else to do and lead by example."

Heavy cheers began to roll in from the crowd, bringing the new commander a moment unlike any he'd ever experienced.

"So with that, let me just say this," Dalton said, giving the crowd a moment to settle down. "I'm not a commander that believes in delegating my job. You ever have a problem, any of you," he added, speaking to them with truth. "You come and see me personally."

The entire group began to erupt with cheering, although his

political equals wanted none of it.

"Just because you were Ortega's lapdog, doesn't mean you belong here. Just play your part and stay out of my way." Doctor Arness whispered as the roar of cheers continued.

As Dalton looked onto the man, fresh-cut hair of solid black and the face of a young buck, Dalton raised his hand to acknowledge the crowd's growing cheer.

Lead by example. Fuck it. Commander James thought.

Moments later, he decked Doctor Arness in front of thousands of eyes which turned cheers into shock. With it, the military began to scuffle with the political – on stage and in front of those who represented the entire fleet.

"In fact," Dalton said loudly into the microphone. "As you can see, anyone who speaks for his own benefit and not that of the innocent voices of this fleet," he added. "Really pisses me off."

Knowing someone would most likely be killed if he didn't, Dalton exited the podium area and began a walk from the ceremony. This time under guard for his own protection.

"Sir, that was one hell of a shot." one of the marines boasted.

"Think so?" Dalton asked. "I think I knocked two of the son of a bitch's teeth out."

"He has plenty more." the marine replied.

"Hated to put you guys in this position son, I just..." Dalton began to explain.

"It's alright sir, several of us heard his words toward you. I've been wanting to deck the bastard for nearly a year now."

"Either way, it will most-likely cause tension within the fleet." Dalton admitted.

"Within the ranks of the political parties' maybe, but not to those who matter. I think that shot to his chin earned you the respect of a lot of civilians, sir."

"I'm hoping with the military as well. If it comes down to a battle of books and guns, I'd love to know you guys have my back." Dalton said with a grin.

"Sir, you had that before you decked him. You've proven yourself time and time again on the battlefield."

At that moment, Dalton James – in this case Commander James, realized that the marine's statement rang true. All of the shit he'd been through as a military grunt; a glorified fetch boy, had finally paid off.

As Commander James entered the ship's CIC for the very first time, its staff stood to their feet, clapping loudly and even whistling. They had heard his speech over the com system, as well as the report of him loosening the teeth of a certain politician. Making him a hero in their eyes.

"Thank you, thank you," Dalton said with a grin, calming the CIC crowd down a bit. "Now, can someone please walk me through what the hell I'm supposed to be doing exactly?"

His words erupted laughter as most went back to their workstations.

"I can help you with that, if you promise not to slug me?" a well-dressed soldier replied.

"Alright son, you have my word." Dalton said with a grin.

"Com Officer Paul Anthony, sir," the man stated. "A privilege to have someone like you leading our CIC."

Dalton nodded his appreciation to the man, who was clean shaven and not a day over twenty-five years of age. Several medals pinned snugly to his chest.

"Sir, we've mapped out several locations that our fleet may able to survive a journey. I've marked a couple of routes into deep space that our scouts have confirmed may be rich in resources." the com officer said.

"Don't need a map. I know where we're going." Dalton replied.

"Um," Anthony replied with confusion. "Alright sir. Where would that be?"

"To get my best friend's son back."

"Sir, with all due respect, we don't even know where the Hunters are?"

"No resource ships in their fleet. Means they have to be somewhere in the Skyla System, and I can promise you," Dalton said with stern truth. "There's not a rock in this entire system that the bastards are going to be able to hide under when I'm finished." he promised.

"Alright sir." Anthony replied, though he seemed reluctant to do so.

"So you send our scout ships back out and you have 'em comb the system. When they find the Hunters' fleet, you have 'em float over a message in a bottle," Dalton said, choosing his words proudly. "That we're coming – and I'm bringing motherfucking revenge with me."

"Will do sir."

"Who in here served on Glimmeria the first time around?" Dalton asked loudly.

Three hands were raised. Two of them deck officers, while a third was a colonial soldier stationed on the door of the CIC.

"How many friends did each of you lose?" Dalton asked.

A strange question, though each respected his command enough to offer their answer. Seven. Four. Eighteen.

"Congratulations, you're my new XO. Now get your ass up here." Dalton demanded of the soldier stationed on the door.

"Sir?" the soldier asked.

"Commander, you should consider this decision wisely." Anthony pleaded in a soft voice.

"Who's a better candidate to lead a group of people that have lost so much - then a man who has also lost, and done so while fighting for the right side since day one?"

"Sir, I just think..." Anthony began to plead.

"I don't want you to think," Dalton replied sharply, staring the man down. "I want you to execute my damn order. Every minute the vampires are out there is a minute that filthy bitch has her hands on my godson."

"Yes sir."

"Come on private, carry your ass up here." Dalton insisted of the guard by the door.

"Yes sir, I'm just taken back by the promotion. I think very highly of you and appreciate you thinking so much of me. Hope I don't let you down when I admit I know nothing about these computer systems?" the soldier asked.

"Well," Dalton replied, reaching over to read the soldier's name tag. "Sergeant Cohen, it can't be too damn hard," he added, leaning over to whisper into his new XO's ear. "Everyone in here has soft hands. How hard can it be?"

Smiling to his new XO, Cohen eventually smiled back – understanding that he and Dalton were cut from the same cloth. Hell-raisers for the same cause. Defense of the defenseless.

-

"Maybe you're thinking on it a little too much." Cambria suggested.

"Maybe," Dalton replied, sitting at a large desk of polished wood as he studied the papers carefully.

"You should rest," she said with concern. "Particularly your slugging hand." Cambria added with a chuckle.

"That sumbitch had it coming." Dalton replied in his own defense.

"Alright, if you say so," Cambria replied, placing her hands in the air. "Just don't hit me." she added with a grin.

"Oh, you're a wise-ass." he commented, offering her a wide grin in return.

"Speaking of," Cambria said, placing her palm to her head as though she were suffering. "You owe me cowboy."

"I reckon I do." Dalton replied, cutting his full-attention to the woman who awaited his embrace.

"I would hate to think that our mighty leader was no good on his word." she said playfully.

"I'm good for my word alright," he answered, standing to his feet as Cambria now lay there, half-nude and teasing him. "Or, as so many women have called it," he added, drawing a disapproving look from his lover. "Just plain good."

"Really?" she asked.

"Just get over here and love on this old hound dog. That's an order." Dalton said – technically his first command as the man in charge.

"What?" one of the two stationed guards asked as the other stared to him.

Answering his question with a continued stare, it was evident that the thickened-steel walls weren't thick enough.

"Block it out." the guard added, Cambria and Dalton growing louder – as if wild animals were mating on the other side of the door.

A smug look came across the face of the quiet marine. His way of saying impossible.

"Try." the first marine added, escaping into deep thought for a moment.

It's gonna be a long damn night.

-

Commander's Log

The first of many, I suspect, as life seems to have thrown a curveball right into my lap. Still, as commander of this fleet, I'm tasked with providing hope. A task I welcome.

Seeing the pain in the eyes of my best friend has been indescribably hard. He is a brother. The closest thing to family I've known since I was a child. So, as I look into the eyes of those around me among the fleet, I understand their loss.

The good news is that we've confirmed across the fleet that no infected made the exodus. The bad news, of course, is that we have no real idea of direction. We simply do not know what perils or wealth of resources await us beyond the line we consider uncharted space.

We've deployed probes that have relayed information back to us, but only the basics. We've no idea if life exists out there. No real number of days we can actually survive based on our food storage and fuel counts.

We have literally become a race that is chained to our ships. Bringing with us only what we could stock in rush, which doesn't amount to much in terms of comfort.

Some among the fleet think we need to revisit the planets throughout the Skyla System once more. Perhaps salvage more of what we need before setting sail into the stars beyond.

Not revisiting the planets among our former system seems to be the only thing Doctor Arness and myself agree on. The sumbitch. I can already see that he plans to be a constant thorn in my side, though he will do so with a few teeth missing.

They say that assuming power changes a man. I don't know about that. I've changed, that's for sure, but I do not credit my new position of power for it. I credit loss.

As I look back on all of the memories gone by. The bars. The bar-fights. The jail time. The bedding of women. Well, to be frank, this list could go on for quite some time. Being an official entry and all, I'll cut to the chase.

The loss of so many who I cared for has changed me. Many of my good friends. My crew...hell, even my dog. They've all been taken from me, each one taking a piece of me with them to the grave.

The moment I held true love in my arms - I became a man. So I accept the challenge of leading these people to a new home. I'm ready.

I'll lead these people as the man they need me to be. The man that life has molded me to be.

The whiskey though, I'm not giving that up. I've grown into a man, but I ain't dead.

-Commander Dalton James

Follow John M. Davis on Twitter (@johndavisbooks) for news on future works!

CPSIA information can be obtained
at www.ICGtesting.com
Printed in the USA
LVHW052256170222
711450LV00014B/786